KINGDOM OF TWILIGHT

STEVEN UHLY

KINGDOM OF TWILIGHT

Translated from the German by
Jamie Bulloch

MACLEHOSE PRESS
QUERCUS · LONDON

First published in the German language as *Königreich der Dämmerung*
by Secession Verlag, Zürich & Berlin, in 2014

First published in Great Britain in 2016 by
MacLehose Press

This paperback edition published in 2018 by
MacLehose Press

An imprint of Quercus Publishing Ltd
Carmelite House
50 Victoria Embankment
London EC4Y 0DZ

An Hachette UK company

This book has been selected to receive financial assistance from English PEN's
'PEN Translates!' programme, supported by Arts Council England. English
PEN exists to promote literature and our understanding of it, to uphold
writers' freedoms around the world, to campaign against the persecution and
imprisonment of writers for stating their views, and to promote the friendly
cooperation of writers and the free exchange of ideas. www.englishpen.org

A CIP catalogue record for this book is available from the British Library.

ISBN (MMP) 978 0 85705 646 7
ISBN (Ebook) 978 0 85705 497 5

This book is a work of fiction. Names, characters, businesses,
organisations, places and events are either the product of the author's imagination
or are used fictitiously. Any resemblance to actual persons, living or dead, events
or locales is entirely coincidental.

1 3 5 7 9 10 8 6 4 2

Designed and typeset in Garamond by Patty Rennie
Printed and bound in Great Britain by Clays Ltd, St Ives plc

Thanks to

Tsvi

Anat

Lilach

Israel (Izi)

Christian

Joachim

Achi

Avner

Naomi

Helmut

Nili

Matej

Helga

Walter

Hanno

Georg

Klaudia

Michel

Carsten

For Ricarda

The night will soon be ending;
the dawn cannot be far.
Let songs of praise ascending
now greet the Morning Star!
All you whom darkness frightens
with guilt or grief or pain,
God's radiant star now brightens
and bids you sing again.

JOCHEN KLEPPER

(1903–42)

A glossary of historical characters referred to in
this novel can be found on pp. 569–75

ONE

He had followed a short, haggard man in shabby clothes, who seemed a nasty enough piece of work to betray a few of his fellow countrymen. They'd been hiding in the church, the Pole had said in his thick accent. But we searched every nook and cranny, not a soul there. The Pole just shrugged as if to suggest, It's not my fault you didn't find them. He knew that the German would follow him, even if he suspected that the Pole would try to lead him astray, stall him to stay alive himself, or try some other dirty trick. The German would follow him, lured by the prospect of more Jews, maybe even women, the short man had made *vague* mention of women as if to avoid overstating his promise. And he was right. The German followed him through the winding alleys, ignoring the fine rain that fell incessantly on the city like a cold, silk cloth, lending everything a silvery-grey sheen, the low, crooked houses, which were narrow and packed together so tightly as if unable ever to get warm. The steeply pitched roofs glistened like molten tar and the uneven cobbles were slippery. The Pole was wearing a pair of old, well-worn shoes, his footsteps made only a muffled scraping on the stones, which was drowned out by the hard pounding of the army boots following in his wake. The German strode past the furtive windows with the assuredness of an untouchable. Everywhere, greyed curtains and closed shutters precluded a glimpse inside the houses, but he knew that the clunk of his footsteps was being tracked by countless ears, their owners frozen in silence, as if remaining motionless could save them from his grasp. He relished this feeling of power, and he relished even more the routine of this pleasure. Two years previously, when he came to Poland with the first important assignment of his career, the sudden affirmation of his superiority had left him confused and unsure. He could scarcely believe that the people they had conquered really were so inferior, and in every aspect too. On the very first day the Obersturmbannführer had taken him to Turck, a washed-out town on the Bug, a narrow but long river that flowed into the Vistula fifty kilometres to the west. We're going to set an example, the Obersturmbannführer had said. His name was Ranzner, a tall, harsh-faced man, whose narrow head was covered with leathery skin, which in old age would not be furrowed with deep wrinkles, but countless tiny scores on the surface, like dried-up rivulets running from his temples to his eyes, and in all directions from the corners of his mouth. Perhaps the lack of depth in his facial features was due to his static expression, or maybe the cause was purely physiological. Publicly, Ranzner never exhibited any hint of satisfaction at a victory or an execution, and all his other emotions appeared inhibited too, as if he were conserving his energy for the decisive moment. He saw himself as the tough alpha male, ruling a bloodthirsty pack of wolves with ruthless discipline. Only at first glance did his marked passivity and the small, round professor's spectacles perched on his aquiline nose seem to contradict the mask-like nature of his face. In truth these were precisely the elements possessed by the man who knows that, rather than having but two hands at his disposal, he can call on a thousand, at any hour and for whatever purpose. And so Ranzner never came across as horrific or terrifying, but more like a walking statue, an allegory of power incarnate, more credible than the Reichsführer S.S., more Himmler than Himmler himself, as if the latter were a copy of Ranzner rather than the other way round.

They had driven in an open-top military car along bumpy country lanes, where the impressions left in the mud by hooves, boots and tanks had moulded into a chaotic relief.

Two rows of motorcycles ahead of them, two rows of motorcycles behind. The sun shone and he had sweated beside Ranzner in the back seat, wondering what to expect. From the start the Obersturmbannführer had treated him with that relaxed indulgence of the higher-ranking officer, a manner he had grown up with and was adept at nurturing. Superiors liked him, and not exclusively on account of his physical appearance, his thick, straw-blond hair, his perfect Aryan features with their youthful mien. They immediately felt that he would accept them for what they wanted to be, irrespective of what it was. This reassured them and stirred paternal feelings. Out of the corner of his eye, he looked at the gently rolling countryside, the fields ripe with corn and the dark-green, lush woodland in the distance, while Ranzner chatted to him about his future tasks. As Sturmbannführer he would translate Ranzner's orders into concrete plans.

"You're to find Jewish hideouts," he said casually, as if discussing berries that needed picking in the woods. "I don't care how you go about it. But you have to find all of them. A single hideout you fail to unearth could be the breeding-ground for a new plague, just bear that in mind."

A single hideout. The slight Pole in front of him knew this too. The man had hunched his shoulders to shield his neck from the cold drizzle, clutching with his left hand the lapels of his worn leather jacket.

"Almost there," he said to the German, who from his Aryan height regarded him indifferently, as one might glance at a dog scurrying past. This Pole was the necessary means to a necessary end. No more and no less. The wretch would do all he could to stay alive; right now, here between the eavesdropping houses, in front of the blind, dripping windows, which were crammed with eyes and ears, he could give the man the order to drop his trousers and start masturbating, and he would do it. Just like the Jews of Turck, back in the first year of the war, who sang as they crawled alongside the pews in their synagogue, while having their bare buttocks whipped, just like the Jew who had been so scared he shat himself, then wiped his excrement over the faces of the other Jews. Because he had been given the order, because the execution of even the most perverse order harboured the promise of life like an encrypted message that only the recipient could understand. Ranzner had registered the disgust and fascination on the face of his new Sturmbannführer with apparent impassivity, he had briefly tapped him on the shoulder to bring him round again, while the Jews, their faces smeared with shit and their backsides spattered with blood, danced ring-a-ring-o'roses to the laughter of their tormentors, before being summarily stabbed to death.

"Why don't we shoot them?" he had asked Ranzner when the Jews were just bodies collapsed on top of one another in the middle of a slowly expanding red puddle.

"Too loud in here," was Ranzner's terse reply. "Bad for the eardrums." They had left the synagogue so it could be set alight. From somewhere deep inside had come a voice insisting that a dreadful deed had taken place, an utterly terrified voice that he had not heard since childhood. But unlike in his childhood, now in Turck he managed to overpower this fearful, feeble voice with the one he had appropriated over the years, like an antidote secretly purloined.

He had learned, all his life he had learned how to be a man. Now he wished to be equal to his task, no other desire should have a place in his heart, and he understood that it was not by chance that Ranzner had brought him along. The example had been made for his sake, the whole thing had been a performance for a single individual, to ensure that man understood from the outset what stage he was on here.

It was raining harder now, the cold silk had unexpectedly turned into a heavy curtain that obscured their vision. At this point the alley was even narrower and the houses seemed to lean forwards to allow their gables to touch. The area looked poorer, the houses were in disrepair. Sludge had oozed up between the cobbles, forming viscous puddles that forced them to stay close to the house fronts. He felt cheerful for the first time since they had left the camp. The Pole in front of him had transformed into a dark-grey spectre, a kobold leading him through a town which was no longer above ground, but subterranean. As he continued along the tapering street he reprimanded himself for entertaining such unmasculine feelings. They had been walking for two minutes at most;

the church must be just around the corner. He drew his pistol from the holster on his right hip, quietly, so the man ahead would not notice. The weight of the gun in his hand was like an anchor he was tossing at reality to prevent fear from hurrying him on. He was a tall, strong Aryan, born to rule over other peoples, and with a weapon to hand nothing and nobody could vanquish him. The Pole stopped, half turned towards his companion and stretched out an arm in a brief, feeble gesture. To the right he could see a church at the end of a gently sloping street. Like all the other buildings in this town it was short and squat, it cowered there humbly, as if pressing itself into the earth rather than standing on it. The short, wide tower housed two bells, one small, the other of medium size – he had noticed them during the first search.

The street was ten metres long at most. Muddy water ran down the slope along the cobbles. The German took a deep breath, the church was a marker by which to orient oneself in the confusing web of the old town. Without realising it, he had acquired a little more trust in the Pole, and when they entered the short street he began to walk beside him rather than behind. To their left a small front door opened. A young woman came out. She was wearing a long, heavy dress, which may once have been red but was now a pale grey–pink. Her head and upper body were wrapped in black scarves, it was impossible to say how many, but it seemed to be an inordinate number, for the shape of her body was entirely hidden beneath the clothes. Only her face was visible, a long, pretty face with a narrow nose and full, perfectly curved lips, which quivered oddly. She had broad brown eyes set at a very slight angle, lending her an Oriental air. As she approached the officer she fixed these eyes on him with an intense stare. An aroma of freshly baked bread wafted through the front door. The Pole stopped and made another feeble gesture towards the woman, who now stood before them.

"This is Margarita Ejzenstain."

His voice betrayed no emotion, it was decidedly indifferent, as if he were introducing two people who meant nothing to him. From beneath one of Margarita Ejzenstein's many black scarves two hands appeared, clutching an unlikely looking revolver. It appeared so old that the German fancied it must be from the last century. She grimaced as she cocked the gun with both thumbs, and the German thought the weapon must be terribly stiff. He had forgotten altogether the pistol in his own hand, he could no longer feel its weight, only the weight in the girl's hands, so young did she look when she grimaced and pulled the trigger with her index fingers that he concluded she must still be a girl. When the bullet hit his eardrum and the echo chased through the streets like a wild animal, the German was swung round to the left and now stood directly in front of the Pole. He wanted to yank up his pistol and shoot the Pole dead, but instead his arm fell to his side and his fingers released the gun, which clattered as it hit the ground. No matter, he thought, he had not released the safety catch anyway. A second shot thundered in his ears, knocking him off his feet and sending him crashing against the house behind, then onto the cold, wet cobbles. Lying on his back, he watched as the Pole and the girl bent over him. The Pole crouched and picked up the pistol. He saw him release the safety catch and fire at him several times. Now the girl's face appeared before him once more. Her beautiful, full lips were still trembling and rain, or were they tears?, ran down her cheeks. He saw her say something he could not understand, then curl her lips and spit in his face. He saw the Pole pull the girl up and drag her away. The last thing he saw was an unending succession of raindrops falling straight on top of him through the dark-grey crack between two shadowy gables, on they went until the chink turned black and the raindrops white, as when looking at a photographic negative or pressing your fingers down onto your closed eyes. He could still smell the tang of freshly baked bread and feel the cold stealing through his body, quietly and quickly like an army in the dark.

TWO

When they found him his eyes were staring straight up into the sky. He was soaked through and dark-red, sandy mud stuck to his black uniform. With the rainwater, his blood flowed down towards the church, and instead of the aroma of bread a heady stench of excrement and iron hung in the street. An old wooden cart soon arrived, a two-wheeler pulled by a couple of Poles. They hauled it up from the church until they reached the body, which they lifted and placed on the wet boards. Then two S.S. men, a stocky Hungarian who hardly spoke a word of German and a lanky Bavarian who nobody understood, flogged the Poles to hasten their progress to headquarters. Dusk gradually descended, but the rain refused to let up. This time they took the direct route from the church to the town hall.

The building was set in an attractive square that had seen better days. Apart from the town hall itself, the square, too, was bordered with rendered, half-timbered houses tightly packed together. The town hall, on the other hand, boasted generous proportions, a stylistic mixture of northern Renaissance and farmhouse, which was a feature of public buildings in this region. It looked a little like an intruder who had made themselves at home. The two Poles, exhausted and with backs aching, stopped by the outside steps. Another thrashing told them they had to take the Sturmbannführer from the cart and carry him into the building. One of them slipped on the steps, the corpse slid from his grasp and the head thudded onto the stone. The Bavarian flew into a rage and beat the Pole unconscious. He lay on the steps while the two S.S. men helped the other Pole bring the Sturmbannführer into the town hall.

News of the murder of his junior officer had already reached Obersturmbannführer Ranzner. In view of what had happened, he would assemble the troops on the square the following morning and deliver a speech. He considered his oratory to be one of his many strengths. But now, when the three men carried in the filthy, dripping body, when his nose took in the smell of blood and earth, faeces and damp, he felt a faint revulsion bubble up inside him. He had reserved it as his privilege to close the eyes of fallen officers with his own hand, for all of them were like his own sons, as he used to say in his aloof manner. But each time it was an effort. When they were dead they ceased to be something, they were no more than a grave warning of life's void, without pride or dignity, meaningless flesh, which was already starting to stink – of what he never knew, it was like rubber, like some women, peculiar.

The S.S. men shooed out the Pole and laid down the dead man in the vestibule. Imitation Arcimboldos from Bohemia hung on the walls, a delicate Jugendstil chest of drawers stood beneath one of them. The picture showed a face composed exclusively of vegetables, wearing a black helmet that looked a little like a soup dish. These and a few other items had been transported from Germany on Ranzner's orders. They were to bring an element of civilisation to this "subhuman architecture", as he called it. Ranzner went over to the corpse. With his legs apart and arms behind his back, he leaned forward a little over the Sturmbannführer's pale face and gazed into the dead man's eyes.

"Seven shots at least, Obersturmbannführer!" the Bavarian barked in his distinct accent, as if he had been asked to provide a report. The presence of the two men made Ranzner nervous.

"Wait outside until I call for you!"

"Yes, Obersturmbannführer!" they shouted, before clicking their heels, thrusting out their chests and doing an about-turn.

When they had left Ranzner kneeled, overcame his feeling of disgust and looked the dead man in the eye at close range. Like a thief anticipating a robbery, he glanced around the vestibule before stretching out his hand and waving it over the dead man's eyes two or three times, staring at him expectantly. When nothing happened, he bent further and whispered into the corpse's ear, "Treitz? Sturmbannführer Treitz? Karl Treitz, are you still with us? If you're still alive I command you to give me a sign. Did you hear me?" He looked him in the eye again and at that very moment thought he detected a fleeting twinkle in the left pupil. Was it possible? He had seen a twinkle like that in the eyes of other corpses, but had never known whether it was merely a figment of his imagination. He bent back down to Treitz's ear: "Sturmbannführer, I hereby order you to seek out and apprehend your murderer. Do not forget – forget nothing!"

After waiting a while in vain for another sign, Ranzner slipped on a black leather glove and closed the Sturmbannführer's eyes. He stood up, assumed a diffident expression of sympathy and called in the S.S. men. When they lifted the body, the right arm jerked briefly but wildly before coming to rest again a moment later. The S.S. men were unfazed, they had witnessed this and other phenomena in corpses all too often. Ranzner, however, turned away to prevent them from glimpsing his surprise and his satisfaction. That must have been a sign. The right arm! There was no doubt about it: Treitz had attempted the Nazi salute as a farewell gesture. Could the Reichsführer S.S. be right after all? At that very moment Ranzner decided two things. The following morning he would have thirty-seven Poles shot in the street where Treitz was murdered – one for each year of the Sturmbannführer's life. He was not planning a massacre, just a symbolic act. And that evening he would also rehearse a speech. He called Anna, his housekeeper, to clean up the stain in the vestibule.

Anna Stirnweiss was young, strikingly tall and slim. Ranzner had spotted her two years earlier amongst a consignment of Jews at the Ostbahnhof in Berlin. Since then she had been his factotum. Anna's face would have been beautiful had it not at some point taken on an expression of untold world-weariness, as if for her everything were too heavy, not just the battered water pail or the wringer with the dark-grey rag, but also the tatty shoes, which must be far too big for her dainty feet, her shoulders that were hunched forwards, as if trying to shield her breasts, and finally her head which, even shorn of its once magnificent hair, hung with a permanent droop as if too weighty for her brittle-looking neck. Although Ranzner was keen on Anna, he banished all thoughts that strayed too far, for he was only too aware of his superiority.

He watched her kneel and wash away the bloodstains, the water that had run from the dead body, the memory of the disgust it had generated, disgust and hope. Ranzner could make out the contours of Anna's buttocks beneath her black skirt. His cheek muscles twitched briefly, then he turned and left the vestibule via a large wooden double door, decorated only by two round, brass knobs. Beyond the door was a generous stairwell with astonishingly white marble steps. At the bottom, the staircase had the same semi-oval form as the steps outside the building, but after ten or eleven stairs it forked left and right, both sides leading up to a gallery. Here, too, hung pictures from the Prague Renaissance between tall, Gothic-looking windows, while Biedermeier furniture from Germany stood rather forlornly against the walls. The entire stairwell was set with dark panelling which, in combination with the hefty stone pillars, lent it a rather ponderous air. The building work had clearly been carried out in several periods, giving the faint impression that each new style had rebelled against its predecessors. The result was a peculiar confirmation of just how provincial the town hall was.

Ascending the staircase with the confidence of a king, Ranzner chose the left fork and walked around the gallery to the far side. His rooms were directly above the vestibule.

THREE

Anna was in her bedroom, taking off her apron. She looked in the mirror on the wall, a plain old object without a frame, full of dark spots and a crack running from the bottom, which now cut through the middle of her face. Anna moved her head so the crack wandered the length of her nose, between her eyes and up to her forehead. Ranzner had called for her. Wrenching open the door, Fritz, his adjutant, gazed at her with relish from head to toe and announced curtly, The chief wants you, hurry up. She had put on her skirt while Fritz ogled from the doorway before letting out an exaggerated sigh and walking away without closing the door.

It was a very fine crack, and yet the two halves of her face were slightly offset. Anna focused on the black spot that exactly covered her right eye. Now it was time to play the game. Ranzner's game, his invention. But he was unaware that she played it in her own way. Time for me to play the game now, she announced to the face in the mirror, attempting to instil a measure of resolve in her weary eyes.

Turning around, she bumped into the bed that practically filled her tiny room. It was an iron-framed dinosaur of a thing, with tall head- and footboards and a saggy straw mattress. The room had no window. Located in a side wing of the town hall, it must once have been used as a storeroom. Or pantry. Anna had learned to ignore these external details of her current existence as an individual deprived of all rights.

She must not let Ranzner wait too long. She had wanted more time to get ready, but she also knew that her game would not work unless the pressure was sufficiently high. So she left her room and went down a long, narrow corridor towards another door. Behind this lay the large stairwell. Anna walked slowly, as if measuring each step with precision. Outside she could hear the deep rumbling of a diesel motor ticking over. Anna concentrated. The game had begun. She was the subhuman. She went up the stairs, choosing the right fork when she reached the landing, and was soon at the door. She knocked – Come in! – and opened. He, Obersturmbannführer Josef Ranzner, was already standing there in his favourite role, a weekly performance, wearing his grey uniform and eyeing her expressionlessly from his Red Indian features. Beneath his gaze she, the subhuman, winced. She did this every time, just like a whore who moans as if she were climaxing, to make her punter climax. Ranzner was her punter. She knew what turned him on: fear. Just like a whore, deep inside her was another woman, an unattainable woman who observed everything that happened, calculating, focusing exclusively on the payoff. This woman had a secret name and her payoff was life. And hidden even deeper – something Anna had discovered only recently, to her relief and horror – was a little girl oblivious to all of this. She was sitting in a meadow, picking flowers and smiling, lost to the world. She was five years old and still unaware that on this very day her mother would tell her, Your father's never coming back, we'll have to get along on our own now. The last happy day in Anna's life. At some point she would repeat this day, she would sit in the meadow by her village in Brandenburg and pick flowers and everything would be fine again, her father would not have gone away and returned three years later with that alien look on his face, a look she would never be able to forget. Her mother would never have had to say, You've come, as if prior to that her family had not existed. The crack in the mirror would merely be the crack in the mirror, nothing else.

"Sit over there, Anna!" Ranzner said, pointing to a chair in the middle of the room. He stood behind and grabbed her gently by the shoulders. The whore flinched submissively, the secret woman assessed the situation. The little girl paused and waited.

"Do you know what happens when one of your lot murders one of our soldiers?"

"No, no, I don't."

"Oh, I think you do. You know how livid I get, and then I have a whole bunch of you executed, for one of us is worth thirty-seven of you."

"Thirty-seven?"

Ranzner offered a supercilious smile.

"Sturmbannführer Treitz was thirty-seven years old. Tomorrow morning I shall tell my men that thirty-seven Jews must die. I wonder whether *you* aren't in cahoots with the rest of them."

"No, absolutely not."

Ranzner smiled. He put his hands in his trouser pockets and circled Anna.

"What else could you say, Jewish woman? You're up to your neck in it."

"Why do you hate us?"

"I don't hate the Jews, you silly little thing. I've never hated the Jews. If I hated your sort then how could I possibly suffer your presence here? No, I'd have killed you long ago. Do you know why I might have to have you killed?"

"No."

"For purely tactical reasons. Plenty of officers keep Jews, Poles or other creatures. Officially, of course, no-one's to know, but everyone does. Those up there," he said, gesturing with his right index finger, "turn a blind eye so long as our work is efficient. But these are critical times we're in, my troops are not what they used to be. In the past," he continued, stopping to look at the night sky through a tall window, "in the past we were an Aryan army, the very best. My God, the young men I saw back in those days: tall, strong, handsome, fearless and smart. Reincarnations of Siegfried." He sighed, turning back towards Anna. "But nowadays I have to incite a horde of foreigners and criminals to fight against the Russians. Do you imagine that's an easy task?"

Anna was at a loss as to what to say. She had never seen Ranzner work particularly hard. He spent his time being driven around, drinking his fill of wine and schnapps, and enjoying long lie-ins. He also masturbated a lot, as Anna knew from washing his clothes.

"Answer me! Do you think that's an easy task?"

"No."

"No. You're right, Anna. It's not easy. The soldiers out there," he said, pointing to the window, "now come from Lithuania, Sweden, Hungary, Holland. Many of them know less German than you do, Anna."

"I understand."

"Really? Yes, I think you do. I think you understand very well. You see, if I'm fighting against subhumans with foreigners who themselves are partly subhuman, and on top of that I've got a Jew for a housekeeper, then we might as well stop killing right now and just forget the war. Don't you think?"

"I don't know."

"Don't lie to me, Anna, or at least do it in such a way that I don't *realise* you're lying. Of course you'd rather we just called the whole thing off, like one calls off a football match when the rain gets too heavy. But it's not like that." Ranzner paused and went to his desk. "I've prepared a little speech. I'd like you to hear it. Tomorrow morning I'm going to address my men and," he added in a softer tone, "I'd like at least one person to have understood it. Ready?"

Anna nodded. Ranzner took up position three metres away and stood there, his eyes closed. He concentrated hard, he could hear the birds twittering, see the roofs of the houses shining gently, smell the fresh morning air. He watched the fog lift, looked down at his men who filled the square, maybe three thousand of them in all, his brigade had swelled in size. Peering at their faces he saw their Aryan features, purely Aryan features, and he allowed himself to indulge in this view for a few minutes while Anna sat there, waiting, concentrating hard herself. As well she knew, the truth was that this was no rehearsal for a speech, Ranzner had no need of that. She had known from the outset that the pieces of paper in his hand were documents of some sort. The truth was that Ranzner improvised, the truth was that these speeches were for her ears only. Like a whore she sensed that her punter was secretly in love with her, however much he pretended to despise her. And like a whore she preferred the contempt, to escape his love. When he stood there with his eyes closed, with his long, hooked nose and taut skin, he resembled a Red Indian deep in ritual. Anna thought of how a few hours earlier he had crouched and spoken to the dead body of his Sturmbannführer in the vestibule. She had watched from the stairs.

"Men!" Ranzner bellowed suddenly. Anna flinched. He opened his eyes and stared at her; his face had assumed a feverish look.

"Men! Every one of you knows why you are here." Once more he paused briefly, before smiling and raising his hands. "We are about to embark on a delousing campaign!"

This was one of the jokes Ranzner always cracked at the beginning of his speeches. He had explained to her once what they were all about, their purpose was to leaven the atmosphere. It was imperative his men felt that he, Ranzner, was never nervous, no matter how close the Russians were. Anna had listened attentively: the Russians were close. Without knowing it Ranzner had given succour to her hopes.

But now both of them in their inner ear heard three thousand raw voices in unison emit throaty, adulatory, manly sounds. Ranzner heard this in his head and Anna heard it in hers, imagining Ranzner's head. "But lice, as you know, hide in every corner, and with one, single aim – to avoid their own eradication! Sometimes, friends, they attack one of us, when we're quiet and inattentive, for that is the only way in which lice dare to attack human beings!"

Anna had never found Ranzner's imagery particularly original, but the expression in his eyes told her that he was not interested in felicitous comparisons, merely in upsetting her. She understood and obeyed. Let him see her upset, if that made him happy. Like a whore, somewhere deep down she felt nothing but sympathy for her punter. Sympathy and revulsion.

Ranzner allowed his gaze to roam.

"The Jewish rats have barbarically slaughtered one of the jewels in our ranks!" he cried at the top of his voice, as if trying to make his fury audible through the walls. Now his stare bored into the vanquished eyes of the woman cowering in the chair before him, her shoulders hunched. "But we shall set an example, to show everyone in this town who is master here, who is in charge, who decides over life and death!"

Anna knew that, one day, he really would line her up with other prisoners in front of a firing squad. A man incapable of raping her must be far more dangerous than one who acted freely on his urges. Sometimes she wished he *would* take her, make her his plaything like other officers did with their girls. There would have been a physical, tangible dependency she could rely on. But, as she had come to understand, Ranzner was a prisoner of his own aloofness. He would rather have Anna killed than confess his love for her.

Ranzner brushed a strand of hair from his face and shook his hand threateningly, the index finger extended. Everything had begun with gestures like this in Germany, in her Germany that she had perhaps lost for ever. The meadow by her village flashed up briefly in her mind, the daisies, but Anna must not get off track now. She swept the image away.

"We shall not allow anyone to believe he can play cat and mouse with us. We know all too well that the Jew remains the primary instigator for the complete and utter destruction of Germany. Wherever in the world we see attacks on Germany, they have all been manufactured by Jews! Is there any filth, any indecency of whatever form, but especially in cultural life, in which no Jew has played a part, not even one? You need only make a careful incision into such a tumour to find – like a maggot in a rotting corpse, and often blinded by the sudden light – a Jew! This is why, men, you must never forget the true meaning of our mission: the total Germanisation of the Wartheland. This was and remains our sacred assignment!"

What a paradox, Anna thought. The only person able to understand him is a Jew. His men must have become indifferent to these outlandish ideas long ago. From conversations she had overheard she knew that the war was getting tougher, Ranzner was having to send more and more of his soldiers to support the Wehrmacht on the eastern front. The heavy losses obliged him to recruit new men all the time. But that did not trouble him. While Anna played the terrified subhuman, she was both fascinated and nauseated by Ranzner's artful way of inhabiting his town hall as if it were a stage set. In here they were both actors, Ranzner just as much as she.

And yet, something was different from normal. Ranzner appeared agitated and impatient, as if the rehearsal was bothering him. Naturally his face betrayed nothing of the kind, it glowed as if he really was the fanatic he made himself out to be. But Anna had become accustomed to keeping an eye on the chief's feet. By now she was able to do this out of the corner of her eye, she even used her fearful expression as a cover to observe Ranzner unnoticed. Sometimes she felt like a dog guessing its master's mood. A worthwhile endeavour, for Ranzner's feet led an independent existence that remained concealed from their owner. Or perhaps they were a cryptic language in which he spoke to her – not Ranzner the great S.S. actor, but the secret Josef Ranzner, who must be hiding somewhere, just as she lay hidden beneath her subhuman exterior.

The language of the feet was easy to understand. Whenever Ranzner was stirred by emotion Anna witnessed it in his feet. If he was impatient, he would tap one of them or beat rapidly on the floor. If he was seized by doubt, they moved sideways: left, then back right, then left again until Ranzner had gained some sort of assurance.

Today his entire right leg was quivering uninterruptedly, even when he spoke or yelled, as now:

"The resistance of the Jews can be broken only by the energetic and tireless engagement of our shock troops, day and night. Your utmost vigilance is of the essence. Our aim is the total annihilation of the subhuman Jewish race – I cannot emphasise this clearly enough." Then he shouted so loudly that his voice cracked and sounded hoarse. "As true brothers in arms we shall work indefatigably to fulfil our mission, always standing our ground as model and consummate soldiers! Sieg Heil!"

As he spoke he gazed at Anna with furtive eyes, like a wolf seeking an opportunity to pounce and gobble her up. And yet today there was something volatile in his expression, which exposed his posturing as an act. Now Anna was shocked for real. There were things she did not wish to see. For her game to work she needed to believe in the merciless Ranzner. Whenever he made it too easy for her to look behind the façade, the fear suddenly became very palpable. Where was the boundary? How much must you see before you could no longer lie? Sure, she depended on her ability to gauge Ranzner accurately. But she could not guard against his involuntary honesty, it found its way to her unchecked. Never must the shadowy figure standing there acquire a sharp outline.

Ranzner appeared not to have noticed a thing. He kept up his tirade, while his gaze wandered aimlessly around the room as if trying to keep a legion under control. He bellowed about the exemplary life of the Sturmbannführer, his Aryan virtues, the grave loss for the S.S., his paternalistic feelings, but most of all he bellowed revenge.

"Even if the Jews were alone on this earth," he roared, "they would still choke in dirt and filth, and attempt to cheat and exterminate each other as if locked in bitter struggle – that is assuming their sheer lack of any spirit of sacrifice, which shows up as cowardice, didn't turn the struggle into play-acting!"

And then, all of a sudden, he was finished. Ranzner looked Anna solemnly in the eye and said, "Sturmbannführer Karl Treitz was a good comrade, an outstanding soldier and an ardent patriot! We shall miss him and his sound work."

Ranzner paused. He was unsure. On the one hand Treitz had given him an unmistakable sign. But he had also allowed himself to be lured into a foolish ambush. No member of the master race would commit such an error. This meant Treitz had Jewish ancestors, so it was a good thing he had been slain by one of his own. Ranzner knew that he should not lend credence to this theory, otherwise every dead S.S. man would be transformed into a Jew for the sole reason that he was dead, and by extension the same thing could happen to him. But the idea was swimming in his head; why, he could not articulate.

He looked at Anna. There was something more he needed to say: "While carrying out his sacred duty for his people and his Führer, Sturmbannführer Treitz died an Aryan hero. More than this, he died a hero of the S.S., the racial vanguard of our beloved Fatherland!"

He paused once more and looked around the room as if in search of something. Then he opened his mouth and said, "May the Black Sun light your way home, Karl Treitz. You will return and exact revenge."

At that moment something peculiar occurred. Anna was sitting on the chair, Ranzner standing in front of her, they were alone in the room. The crack in the mirror was gone, the imaginary army was gone. The game was over for the time being. She was confused. She gazed at Ranzner. She detected shame in his eyes. This was something she had never seen before, and for a moment she doubted that she *had* seen it. The words "May the Black Sun light your way home" resounded in her head. Ranzner stood there hesitantly, as if uncertain how to proceed. Eventually he turned away and sat behind his bulky, nineteenth-century English desk. As he leaned back in his chair his jaw muscles twitched, he was nervous. Anna wanted to look away, she had no desire to watch Ranzner struggle to regain his composure, the danger emanating from him was so palpable that she had to overcome her panic. But she did not move, she merely sat on her chair, staring at him as if frozen.

Ranzner felt naked. He did not know why he had mentioned the Black Sun, even less why he now felt so defenceless. It was as if he had allowed Anna a glimpse of an intimate secret. At Ranzner's back a wide, panelled double door with rectangular windows led onto the large terrace. The town lay in complete darkness, the street lamps had been switched off and the windows in private houses blacked out.

"Do you know what the Black Sun is, Anna?" Ranzner asked after a while, without looking at the girl.

"No."

"The Black Sun," Ranzner said slowly, as if intimating that it was something quite special. But Anna knew this desperate act.

"The Sturmbannführer murdered by your people will return. And he will remember – me, you and his murderers. He will take revenge. Do you believe that?"

"No."

"Of course you don't, because then you'd have to accept that you'll never be rid of us."

Anna looked straight past Ranzner, as if he were no longer in the room. Now she seemed like an animal opening its eyes for the first time after a long hibernation. Deliberately and in a flat voice she said, "If we all return, why do you Germans want to annihilate us?"

"Who said you all . . . ?" Ranzner retorted brusquely, then tailed off. "Leave, the rehearsal is over!"

Anna stood up slowly and mechanically, once more an actress playing the role of housekeeper. She left the room and shut the door. It was only as she went down the stairs on the way back to her room that she grasped what had just happened: in clutching at this absurd hope Ranzner had confessed his fear of death. In truth, she thought in the vestibule, there are no superhumans or subhumans. In truth, she thought, he's nothing like what he pretends to be, he isn't a chief, just a fellow human who, for unknown reasons, has become an anti-human. He had deceived her, for two years she had believed he truly was inhuman, impervious to anything normal, without weakness or vulnerability, because his hardness protected him against everything.

When Anna left, Ranzner opened the door and stepped outside. The terrace was directly above the entrance to the town hall, through which his dead subordinate had been carried a few hours before. The square was in darkness and he could hear nothing save for the regular footsteps of the sentries. The rain had finally stopped. The only other sound was an occasional rumbling in the distance. It was the war getting closer.

FOUR

No light in the darkness.
No thought of light.
No thought at all.
For an eternity.

When at last she regained consciousness it began with just a glimmer. She drifted, feeling far removed from everything. She remembered. He was dead. Shot by a woman. Margarita Ejzenstain. A Polish Jew. Subhuman. Her. Which year was it? She could not remember. How long had she been lying here? These pains, everything hurt, if she lay like this any longer she would get thrombosis and die anyway. She had to get out, to the light, move, be free, no matter what happened. But she lay there inertly, trying to return to the nothingness from which she had awoken. Buried, she thought, I've been buried alive. If she ever got out of here it would be like reincarnation. Not even when the Kramers lifted the floorboards to bring her food, not even when they brought her the pot so she could do her business, did she see daylight. She lay in the cellar, on the hard earth only covered with a few blankets. It was damp and she lived with the permanent threat that the stream might burst its banks, leading to a flood and the loss of her hiding place. How absurd that, of all people, it was Germans who had taken her in, given how much she despised the Germans. She would rather have stayed with Poles, but in such a hurry none could be found who would take in a Jew. When the pastor told her they were Germans she was ready to refuse. But Piotr had said, What would you prefer, to be hidden by Germans or killed by Germans? There's no other choice. At that point she acquiesced.

The Kramers had been remarkably friendly, from the very beginning they had treated her like a daughter. Frau Kramer in particular made her feel welcome, something she had not expected. It had caused her opinion of the Germans to collapse like a house of cards and she felt disoriented, unable to comprehend why some of these people wanted to kill her, whereas others protected her. To start with she felt as if someone had restored her faith in humanity, but gradually the anger built up inside. For now the Germans were no longer a cruel race of monsters, now the Germans were human beings who had gone mad and who no-one had stopped.

The Kramers were not from this region, they had been planted there without knowing what they were letting themselves in for. The house, a farmstead with a few hectares of arable land, had previously belonged to Poles who had been expelled, deported, killed – who knows? It was not hard to imagine. The Poles had also dug out the hole in the cellar. Two days after the Kramers moved in a man in filthy clothes appeared in their living room, out of the blue. He introduced himself as Adam Herschel, a Jew from Łódź who had been hidden by the previous owners. The Kramers, as Frau Kramer once told her, had been lost for words, but soon composed themselves and accommodated Herr Herschel until it was possible for him to make his way to the coast. From there he planned to take a boat to Sweden. They never heard from him again.

Of course the pastor had taken note of what had happened, which is why she, Margarita Ejzenstain, ended up in the hole where she had been lying for four months now. Everything would be easier were she not pregnant. She could have kept moving, might have made it to the coast herself. Oh well. Frau Kramer looked after her with such tenderness. Once a day she exercised with her because she was of the belief that this was good for pregnant women. She had given birth to two children herself, a boy and a girl. The boy had died at the front, Operation Barbarossa, Frau Kramer had told her with bitterness in her voice and tears in her eyes, neither of which were consistent with her cheerfulness. Then she had wiped away the tears with rapid and resolute hand movements as if banishing a nightmare, and smiled like someone asking for forgiveness.

Perhaps that is why they had hidden Margarita in their cellar. As revenge for their son who had been killed in action. Sometimes she thought about this in those long hours spent idle in the darkness of her hideaway. She would imagine a barely detectable link between the Kramers' dead son and herself, like a gossamer thread attached to her soul, pushing its way out of the cellar through the gap between the floorboards, out into the fields, through woods and across rivers – green, gleaming woods and crystal-clear rivers where children played with shrieks of delight, oblivious to the gossamer thread extended above their heads, or perhaps along the river bed at their feet, where it passed through the gravel to the other bank and beyond, far beyond until it vanished into the earth at the spot where the Kramers' son lay buried, if indeed he were buried. Margarita often wondered about the nature of this thread, but the only idea that came to her, the only feeling, was retribution.

She did not actually care about the reasons for the Kramers' compassion. Perhaps their hearts were simply in the right place, perhaps good people really did exist, irrespective of their race. If only there were not so much time to brood. And to remember. Often she was assaulted by images, like a horde of wild animals she was powerless against, and the longer she spent looking, the more strongly she felt that each image was its own reality and another life. Her past thus disintegrated, she lost all cohesion and became a loose collection of impressions that no longer seemed to belong to her. Tomasz. Their honeymoon to Łódź. Tomasz's first car. His job in Kraków. Tomasz would have built a solid career, this she knew. And then maybe they would have emigrated to America, like his brother. The invasion. Tomasz had been perfectly calm, he had said, France and Britain won't let this happen. And to begin with it seemed as if he was right. But then came Dunkirk. The Germans drove the British from the mainland and conquered France. Who was going to help them now? Tomasz had been at a loss, she had seen him in despair for the very first time. It was painful. She wanted to console him, but there was nothing to console him with. Her parents urged them to flee. But it had been too late, far too late.

She had no desire to think about that now, not again. If necessary she would learn how not to think. Not to think until the Germans had gone. If they ever did go. If you let your thoughts wander you neglect your soul. This is what her grandmother had said when she caught other people brooding. The saying ended, You forfeit your life – even if you live, you are as dead. But she was already as good as dead now, she, who wanted to move to Uncle Max's place in Berlin and study art – Berlin, of all places! She had heard from Uncle Max up till 1938, but nothing since. Even back then rumours went around that dreadful things were happening in Germany. But nobody wanted to believe them, rumours were always exaggerated, you had to strip away two-thirds of what was said to get to the truth. Well, this time it was the other way around, and who could have informed her about it? Everything had descended upon her almost like a natural disaster, even the Germans behaved as if they were obeying a murky destiny, whose long arm reached from somewhere in the past into the present and manipulated them like puppets. The German she had killed. He had entered the street like a lamb coming to Passover. She had waited behind the door, as arranged, heard his heavy boots and Piotr's light footsteps leading the officer to his doom, to her. She had opened the door and watched both men walk along the street towards her, side by side. For anybody witnessing this scene in isolation, the two might have been friends. And she might have been a mutual friend of theirs. She often thought of those few seconds prior to the first shot from the ancient revolver that Piotr had stolen from the pastor. A museum piece, the pastor had been proud of having such an item in his possession. He kept it in the sacristy, beside the wine and communion wafers. How fitting, Margarita thought. Piotr had removed it from there after witnessing what the Germans did to Tadeusz and a handful of other Jews. He had said, That German gave the order, I swear I'll bring him to you, Margarita. And he had brought him to her. How long ago was that? Four and a half months? Approximately. When the two men stood beside each other in the street like good friends she had caught sight of the German's eyes. She had expected evil eyes, but instead she gazed into blue, innocent child's eyes. She had not been prepared for that. Child's eyes and murderer's hands, she had thought, feeling a sudden revulsion, as if the German were a slimy monster, not a human being, an abortion, half embryo, half violent criminal. The disbelief on his face when the first bullet hit him! As if he had been granted surprise leave. The officer had suffered a nice death, he had been shot and that was it. Far too short, far too painless for what he had done to Tadeusz. To Tadeusz and the others.

She heard someone descending the stone steps that led into the cellar, and at once recognised the almost hesitant tread of Frau Kramer, the typical caution of an elderly lady abandoned by the confidence of youth – perhaps she had never even known it in the first place. The Kramers had impressed upon her that she must never lift the floorboards herself. If we want to survive we have to be on our guard at all times, Herr Kramer had said. Without attentiveness there is no life, her grandmother would often mumble as she stared absently out of the window, lost in the memories of her distant youth.

Margarita waited for the first chink of light, which blinded her even though it came from a gloomy paraffin lamp that Frau Kramer had placed on the floor beside her as she lifted the floorboards and moved them aside. Frau Kramer was a short, squat woman, a perfect fit for this low-ceilinged farmhouse. In the dim light she looked like one of those austere figures from a Dutch genre painting. The smile on her narrow lips revealed a set of large, white, slightly irregular teeth. She had certainly never been a beauty, but she radiated an unobtrusive warmth that put people at their ease in her presence. Margarita returned the smile and allowed herself to be helped out of the hole. She was completely stiff from having lain there for ages; her joints ached and it took a while for her circulation to return to normal. Her delight at being freed from the hole was short-lived, however. The cellar was a grim place. There was no plaster on the walls and the sombre atmosphere created by the dark-red bricks made her even more aware of her circumstances. Junk was dotted randomly around the room – old furniture and equipment left behind by the previous Polish owners and now useless to anyone else. On one side were two skylights nailed up with wooden boards. On the opposite side were rough and ready wooden shelves that held large preserving jars, which in the light of the paraffin lamp gleamed in an array of colours: dark-red, dark-yellow, orange, green. In front of the shelves three or four salamis hung from the ceiling. The cellar was so low that Margarita could not stand up straight. She was tall, beside her Frau Kramer looked like a square block of stone next to an obelisk. Hand in hand, the two women went slowly in circles around the cellar, without saying a word. Margarita's head was bowed like a penitent in a procession, while Frau Kramer walked upright and with confidence, as if the cellar were actually a better place. After a while Margarita stopped.

"I think it's fine now."

"Come, child, let's sit; you'll only sprain your neck if you keep standing," Frau Kramer said in her melodious voice, which seemed permanently on the cusp between talking and singing. Margarita thought that in truth she was a tiny bird, a little, fat sparrow trying to be human, but betrayed by her voice. And her friendly manner. They sat on two low stools that must have belonged to the Poles. It was only now Margarita noticed that Frau Kramer was looking at her solemnly.

"I spoke with my husband about you yesterday," she said in her sing-song tone. "It's all sorted out now."

Margarita gave her a quizzical look. All she knew was that Frau Kramer insisted on making a ritual out of telling her something important. It must be good news.

"You're a beautiful young woman who's expecting a child. Someone in your situation can't remain in a hole in the ground for goodness knows how long." She rubbed Margarita on the arm and gave her a smile of encouragement. Two small dimples appeared in her chubby cheeks.

"We've decide that from now on you should live in the whole cellar."

Margarita was horrified.

"But what if they find me? That would be the end for all of us."

"Calm down, child. Nobody's going to find you, God willing. The barbarians can do what they like, but they won't find you."

"If only I could be as confident as you are, Frau Kramer."

"You must be confident, child, you really must. Otherwise you won't make it."

They fell silent. Frau Kramer was still patting her arm and looking cheerful. Margarita was staring into space. Until now she had been lying in a hole in the earth, which had been dug into a larger hole – this dark cellar. Now she was going to be buried only once rather than twice over. The Kramers had summoned all their courage to risk this offer. But they were right; in her pregnant state she could not remain on cold, damp earth indefinitely. She would not survive.

"Will I have any light?"

"Only in the daytime, you've got to understand that."

She did understand. At night the light could seep through the cracks in the boards over the skylights, betraying her presence. Having light would almost be like being reborn. For the first time in ages she felt hope budding inside her. A strange hope. As if this change were part of the journey she needed to make to achieve her final liberation. As if it were impossible for everything to be over in one go, but that it had to be a gradual process, as if a long darkness and a long imprisonment were one and the same thing – you could not be free suddenly, just as you could not suddenly tolerate daylight. Having worked out its mechanism with such clarity, she thought that her hope, thus exposed, must immediately crumble to nothing, terrified like a shy animal. But it held firm. She smiled.

"Fine. That's fine, we'll do that. Thank you very much, Frau Kramer. You and your husband."

Frau Kramer now gave her a loving embrace and placed a hand on her belly, caressing it awkwardly for a few moments. Then she started to cry.

"It cannot be God's will," she said after a while, her voice choked, "that there should be no new life. That cannot be so."

Margarita was unprepared for such an emotional outpouring. She listened silently to the other woman, as if Frau Kramer were playing a tune that had not been heard for a long time. One of the tears that Frau Kramer shed as she clutched Margarita rolled from her right eye, down her cheek and fell on the young woman's neck, producing at that very spot a sensation equalled in intensity only by her back pains. She closed her eyes and focused on it. As the seconds passed the spot seemed to grow larger. She did not notice that her own eyes had welled up with tears. It was as if her entire consciousness were filled with nothing but this spot. All of a sudden she was struck by the desire to taste Frau Kramer's tears. Taking her head in both hands, she felt the woman's soft skin on her palms and kissed her on the eyes. Ran her tongue across her lips. Tasted the salt. Frau Kramer's salt. Kissed her eyes again.

"Mama, mother," she whispered. "Don't cry. Everything will be fine."

FIVE

"My dear child. In reality the earth is hollow. Everything that surrounds us, and which you'll soon be able to see, is the deep core of our planet." She pointed at the paraffin lamp on the small, rough-hewn table in front of her.

"This is the central star of the earth's core. It lights up the entire world. Outside? Oh, there's nothing interesting outside, my child. Outside people cling to the earth as if trying to tear large chunks out of it. Outside people are much smaller, much, much smaller. And that's why there are so many of them. They scurry around like ants, forever in search of something, forever running around in circles, always far too quickly. But in here, my child, in here it's just the two of us and this table with the sun on it, and the shelves on the wall over there with the preserving jars that twinkle like distant stars, and the old wooden bed by the wall behind us, and the book in my hand."

It was not a thick book. On the cover in reddish-brown Gothic letters was printed *The German Mother and her First Child*. Written by Dr Johanna Haarer, it had been published by Lehmann in Munich. In 1940. Herr Kramer had taken it from a large pile of books in the street outside a house he happened to be passing in town. He had stood there, holding the book and gazing at the house, a handsome, spacious, turn-of-the-century building, and recalled having once seen something similar, a few streets further on, near the river. On that occasion he had arrived on the scene earlier and, together with a small crowd of people, watched a young woman in a dressing gown dash out of the house with a little girl, about six years old, followed swiftly by a young, elegantly dressed man, his hands shielding his head while two men in black S.S. uniform ran after him, beating him with truncheons. Herr Kramer did not turn away when the man fell to the ground and the woman rushed back to help him to his feet again. He witnessed the man, his head bloodied, pull himself together to start running again. Herr Kramer watched the bystanders, people from neighbouring farms, townspeople. They stood there in silence, some smiling, some stony-faced, others with a look of indifference. The two S.S. men still harangued the couple they had driven from the building, screaming so loudly their voices went hoarse. The sobbing child clung to her mother. S.S. men stood at the windows and now began to toss objects into the street – small items of furniture and books. The books opened as they fell, flapping as if they were losing all their words and were nothing but blank pages as they hit the ground. It was windy, clothes flew everywhere, Herr Kramer saw men's suits and a blue dress that held its position in the air for a moment, like a ghost, before swirling into a tree and becoming entangled in its branches. The crowd of bystanders pounced on the discarded items, squabbles broke out, but the S.S. paid no attention.

That had all been a few years ago, but Herr Kramer remembered the episode in perfect detail. He knew what must have happened in the house where the pile of books stood. Concluding that *The German Mother and her First Child* was a most useful book, he took it home. Now it was in Margarita's hands. She regularly dipped into it, for she liked its scientific tone and the detailed anatomical diagrams, of which there were seventy-five. Margarita thought it was important to acquaint herself with the subject, to avoid doing anything wrong. Often she read out loud, as loud as her clandestine existence would permit, to prevent the child from developing in total silence. And when her eyes became tired from the gloomy light of the paraffin lamp she would say whatever came into her head, such as the story of the hollow earth. Now she opened the book and read out loud:

"The reasons why a child may cry are so numerous and diverse that some mothers, after careful examination, will have to conclude that it is none of those listed. The child is simply crying, and incessantly so – but the cause is unfathomable. Frequently there is nothing to do but assume that the child is crying owing to some predisposition, out of habit, or simply to pass the time."

She paused and looked at her belly.

"Don't even think about it, do you hear me?"

Frau Dr Haarer was very certain about how to solve the problem:

"Where possible the child should be removed to a quiet place and be left there alone. It should not be picked up again until the next feeding time. Frequently it requires only a few trials of strength between mother and child – these are the first! – before the problem is solved."

She raised her head. A quiet place, she pondered, looking around the cellar. Alone, she thought. All of a sudden she thought of the S.S. officer they had shot, Piotr and she. The S.S. officer with his innocent blue eyes. And finally she realised what had touched her so peculiarly before she had fired the old revolver. The infinite loneliness staring at her from those Aryan eyes, a loneliness as open as Frau Dr Haarer's book. She imagined Frau Dr Haarer as the German's mother and wondered what she looked like. She must be tall and lean, with a long, bony nose and hollow cheeks. A wizened woman, to whom indulgence was alien, who lived in permanent fear of exploitation and who had passed all this on to her offspring with her elaborate method of raising children. All this, plus loneliness too.

Margarita continued reading, but no longer out loud, for she did not wish her unborn child to hear any more of Frau Dr Haarer's opinions. "If a dummy has no effect, dear Mother, then you must be firm! Do not take the child from its bed, carry it around, rock it in your arms, push it around or sit it on your lap. And on no account feed it. Otherwise the child will grasp with extraordinary rapidity that it need only cry to attract the attention of a sympathetic soul and become the object of that person's concern. After a short while it will demand such attention as a right, with no let-up until it is carried, rocked or pushed around again – thus the tiny, but implacable tyrant is complete."

Margarita put the book on the table and stood up. With her head stooped she saw the bulge in her belly that was already quite large. She put her hands around it, caressing it. Then she said, as if taking an oath, "My dear child, I promise to do the opposite of what this book says. Where it says, 'Do not feed!' I will feed you. Where it says, 'Be firm!' I will be soft. Where it says, 'Leave alone!' I will take you in my arms. You'll surely be a little tyrant, but perhaps not a big one later on."

She sat down again, the speech was over. Her child would move from a small, dark hole to a large, dark hole. It would neither breathe fresh air nor see daylight. That was bad enough. But it would not spend its nights alone from birth, as demanded by Frau Dr Haarer. It would never be alone, so long as they were forced to live in this underworld. And she herself would no longer be alone either. Two pieces of good news in one day.

She heard knocking on the cellar door. Twice in quick succession, twice more slowly: the signal they had agreed. Herr Kramer had come up with the idea, and to begin with Margarita thought it silly. But in truth she liked knowing who was there. For although the two of them knocked in the same rhythm, Frau Kramer did it gently, like a conspirator requesting entry. Herr Kramer, on the other hand, knocked loudly, like someone announcing his arrival. This time the knocking was soft.

Since Margarita had settled in the cellar with the Poles' furniture, Frau Kramer had come down as often as she could, her excitement growing as Margarita's belly became ever rounder. She had begun to knit clothes for the baby, even though wool was in short supply, which meant she had to unravel her own things. Sometimes the two women sat together like mother and daughter, discussing what would have to happen once the child was born.

Even Herr Kramer's visits were more frequent. He was a taciturn individual, who always gave the impression of not belonging wherever he happened to be. Whenever Margarita heard his heavy tread on the cellar steps she braced herself for a conversation with few words and lengthy pauses. All the same she enjoyed his company, for he radiated a strong aura of dependability.

This dependability was very soon put to a stringent test. When Margarita was in her seventh month of pregnancy, food became scarcer. Not only had it been a poor harvest, but the Wehrmacht had also taken away two forced labourers who had been helping out in the fields to work in an armaments factory back in the German heartland. The Kramers had spent the entire autumn saving the harvest on their strip of land, only for the Wehrmacht to come along and confiscate half of it. They also heard that the Russians were gradually getting closer.

Margarita was permanently hungry, but there was never enough food. The shelves along the cellar wall, where preserving jars had once shone in different colours, were empty. And they sensed the winter was going to be a cold one. One morning Herr Kramer told his wife that things could not go on as they were. It was not right that the two of them had to starve while a stranger in the cellar sat doing nothing but waiting for the birth of another mouth to feed.

"But she's not a stranger anymore," Frau Kramer replied. Herr Kramer did not know what to say. He knew that his wife had gone much further than he had. She had accepted Margarita and her child into the family. He had not, and perhaps never would. It was evening. They were sitting in the kitchen at a long wooden table, which suggested that the Polish family who had once lived here must have been large. The kitchen was the most spacious room in the entire house, apart from the hayloft on the first floor. Even the stable was smaller. Frau Kramer got up and sat beside the tiled stove. She knew what was going through her husband's mind. Where were they going to get extra food from without attracting attention? Her gaze wandered to the two small windows above the sink and cooker. Outside she could see the driveway that wound its way to the Łódź road. It was lined with elms, whose expansive crowns were already in darkness. In a few weeks they would be losing their leaves.

"Maybe the pastor can give us something," Herr Kramer said after a while.

"How's the pastor going to get hold of more food than he needs to live on?"

"He could ask other families."

"What's he going to tell them? That there's a Jew living with the Kramers who's having a baby and is in desperate need of more to eat? The pastor can't help us and I'm sure the other families don't have any more than we do."

They fell silent once more. Outside the dog barked. Must have seen a cat. The dignified ticking of the grandfather clock beside the stairs cut into the silence. It was an heirloom from Frau Kramer's family, one of the few pieces of furniture they had brought with them.

"We could sell the grandfather clock and buy ourselves a third cow with the proceeds," Frau Kramer suggested. Herr Kramer watched his wife get up from the table and fetch a blanket to put around her shoulders. He was surprised that she was willing to part with this valuable heirloom. She was never quite as predictable as he assumed. But who was going to buy a grandfather clock at a time like this?

"The S.S.," Frau Kramer said tersely. "I've seen it with my own eyes. They ransack abandoned houses for items, furniture, paintings and other stuff they could use, before the new owners arrive. They go mad for valuable things. You could go and offer them the clock."

"I don't want anything to do with that riff-raff."

"Then I'll do it myself."

SIX

On a cold October morning Herr Kramer set off for town to sell his wife's grandfather clock to the S.S. The sun had not yet risen, the countryside was bathed in a pale light, and a cold and damp mist rose sluggishly from the fields. Before Herr Kramer loaded the clock onto the two-wheeled cart, with which they had transported all their other belongings here, Frau Kramer made it chime several times. She had to stand on tiptoe to reach the large brass clock face, which displayed bold black numbers in Gothic type. With her gouty index finger she pushed the broad minute hand to twelve and took a step backwards. The clock struck eight times. With Frau Kramer's arm around her husband's thick waist the two of them stood there as if listening to a concert. Frau Kramer wanted to burn the deep, stately chiming of her grandfather clock into her memory. Her father had said, Never give it away, you won't find another clock that's so relaxing. She would try never to forget its sound. "Perhaps," she had said to Margarita, tapping her broad forehead with her finger, "I can have it chime up here in my mind."

Herr Kramer was well aware of her penchant for ritual. She knew how to turn something commonplace into something special, and would do it quite unexpectedly. On those occasions she seemed to him like a wild deer that must not be disturbed if you wanted to see what it did next. So he stood there, mesmerised, observing her every movement. In such moments her body behaved differently, with more elan and grace, but maybe a stranger would not have noticed. Herr Kramer had never questioned why she acted in this way, because for him there was no doubt that it made her and the things she touched more beautiful.

After the eighth strike of the clock the solemn moment was past. Frau Kramer sighed and let her husband get to work. Herr Kramer opened the door of the clock to unhook the pendulum and detach the two brass cylindrical weights from the chains. He wrapped all the pieces in a coarse linen sheet and placed it on the cart outside. Then he did the same with the clock. Frau Kramer gave her husband a kiss on the cheek, then he tied his scarf around his ears and neck and went outside. He gave the cow a pat, grabbed it by the yoke and set off on his way. In the distance he heard a gentle rumbling, which had been getting imperceptibly louder for weeks. The wheels clattered over the frozen earth, the tailboard rattled loudly. It was better once they reached the main road. For an hour Herr Kramer went across bare fields, through copses, over a stream, past three reconnaissance tanks and was overtaken by Wehrmacht lorries, until he came to an S.S. checkpoint.

He saw them from a distance. Beyond, in a slight dip, lay the town, only twenty minutes away. A narrow armoured car fitted with a machine gun stood on the right-hand side of the road, like a large insect waiting for its prey. On the opposite side of the road was a light military vehicle. There was nobody to be seen. They'll freeze, Herr Kramer thought, continuing on his way. He had his passport at the ready. He was a certified settler, he knew that he was part of a national project and thus safe.

He felt anxious nonetheless. The S.S. men would not notice, as Herr Kramer was one of those people who always appeared stoical. Maybe this was down to his grouchy voice and distinct features: the ample, uniform circle of his head, untroubled by too much hair; the dark and low-set eyes beneath thick eyebrows and above cheeks which had been chubby once, in better days. In younger days, Herr Kramer corrected himself, in truth I was too fat in my younger days. The war does have its benefits, he told himself, emitting a short and bitter laugh. Herr Kramer would have been a cheerful individual had the war not come along and taken away his son. That had destroyed his sense of humour, and he no longer felt like imposing it on anybody, not even himself. Once he had told his wife the truth about his feelings, just once. She was peeling potatoes and he said, I've been demented since Karl died. She paused briefly and cast him a sceptical look. Get away, she said. You've always been demented. To this very day he did not know how to respond to that.

When Herr Kramer had almost reached the S.S. checkpoint, the door to the military vehicle opened and out stepped a man in black uniform. Herr Kramer stopped and waited. The cow flapped its large ears about its head and peered inquisitively at the S.S. man, who approached them with brisk steps. He was so young, Herr Kramer saw, that he could have been his own son. But the young ones were dangerous. Herr Kramer slowly raised his arm, extending his fingers.

"Heil Hitler."

"Heil Hitler! Your papers!"

Herr Kramer removed his documents from his coat pocket, the cow snuffled at the S.S. man's elbow, earning a slap on the nostrils. As he took Herr Kramer's papers a strand of blond hair fell across his forehead. Herr Kramer was astonished by the length of his hair. He took a closer look at the man. His uniform had only appeared immaculate at first glance. Now Herr Kramer saw how worn it was; in some places it even seemed to have been blacked up with shoe polish.

"What's your business in town, Comrade?" the man asked without raising his eyes.

"I've come to sell my wife's grandfather clock to the S.S."

The S.S. man gave him a searching look. "Come now, Comrade, you're pulling my leg."

"No, I'm not. My wife says the S.S. is interested in antique furniture." He paused. "We need supplies for winter."

"Don't you work?" the S.S. man asked, attempting to look tougher than his age warranted.

"Yes, we do, but the Wehrmacht must have food too."

"Do you object to the Wehrmacht receiving its share, Comrade?"

"No. But if our supplies are to last the winter then we need money. That's why I'm selling my wife's grandfather clock."

"To the S.S.?"

"Yes."

"Have you got only this one cow?"

"Yes," Herr Kramer lied, worried that they might confiscate the other.

"Just you and your wife?"

"Yes."

"Where?"

With a fleeting gesture Herr Kramer motioned in the direction from which he had come. "About an hour's walk from here."

The S.S. man mulled this over briefly. "You ought to have at least two cows," he said, betraying his rural background.

"That's what I think," Herr Kramer said, trying to look like a man who really believed what he was saying.

"May I see the clock?" A second S.S. men got out of the vehicle. Pricking up its ears the cow gaped at him. He was barely older than the first. His uniform, too, looked tatty. Herr Kramer had gone to the back of his cart, flapped down the tailboard, and was now unloading the grandfather clock. When he placed it on the ground and unwrapped it, the first S.S. man peered intensely at the clock, as if he were about to estimate its precise value.

"What's he doing with that?" the second man asked.

"He says he wants to sell it to the S.S."

The second man laughed. "Listen, old man, the most they'll give you in town is its value as firewood!"

"Don't you think it's worth anything?" the first S.S. man said.

"Nonsense. I just think they need firewood more than they do antique furniture."

"But the commander buys antiques."

The second S.S. man shook his head, looking impatient. "The commander is a connoisseur. He's not going to buy this sort of peasant stuff."

"So you don't think it's worth anything, then."

"You know what? I don't care what it's worth," the second S.S. man said, turning away sourly.

"Are his papers in order?" he asked, returning to the car. "If so then let him go on his way." The first S.S. man hesitated.

"What's in the other cloth?"

"The pendulum and the weights," said Herr Kramer, who had remained perfectly calm. The S.S. man gave up. He looked thoroughly disappointed, like a child facing boredom instead of the adventure he had been hoping for.

"Be on your way now," he said, returning to his vehicle without uttering another word.

When Herr Kramer had wrapped up the clock again and loaded it onto the cart, he heard a soft metallic rattling, which rapidly got louder. Nine or ten Wehrmacht tanks emerged from the furthest hill in the distance, approaching at high speed. They would soon be here. Herr Kramer decided to steer the cart behind the armoured vehicle, to prevent the cow from becoming agitated. The rattle of the tank tracks became ever louder. If they're in such a hurry, Herr Kramer thought, and if the fine S.S. looks in such a state, then the overall situation cannot be good. When the tanks drove past the checkpoint the ground quaked and the cow twitched nervily. Herr Kramer calmed it, holding the animal tight by its yoke. Then he went on his way. The tanks must have come right across the field, for their tracks had left hard clumps of earth on the road. The wheels clattered and the tailboard flapped. As he watched the tanks speed away, Herr Kramer thought hard. When he got to town he must enquire about the situation at the front, or maybe listen to the wireless in a tavern.

Reaching the dip in which the town stood, he stopped briefly, as he did every time. It was not a particularly large town, it reminded him of Lübeck with its mediaeval round shape and numerous pointed church towers. He remembered Lübeck well. It had been the only major trip he had made before their resettlement. They had left two days after their wedding, How long ago was that now? Twenty-five years and a few months. At the time Germany had just lost a war and they had toyed with the idea of moving to the new republic, to Lübeck, a town they had both liked. But then his wife fell pregnant and everyday life buried this idea in their minds. Later the republic became the Reich again, and the Reich had approached them and said, Come join us. This time they obeyed the call. He had been pleased at the time, for now they were no longer in the minority, but Germans amongst Germans. When his son died, however, his pleasure evaporated, and instead he began to wonder whether it might not have been better if nothing had changed, if everything had stayed as it was.

Now he was standing here, looking at a town which would always remain alien to him, whose only connection with his own life was its similarity to another town that was not home either. Similar in its beauty, too. Although there was not as much water as in Lübeck, a river meandered its way through the town, dividing it into two almost equal cake halves. Beautiful old stone bridges stretched from one side to the other, and in winter the townsfolk skated on the ice.

Visibility was poor. The mist must have lingered in the dip for a long while, now it lay on top of the roofs like a cold veil. The sun was a smudge on the horizon, like a runny egg yolk, emitting a diffuse light that was beginning to blind him. In ten minutes he would reach the outlying houses. He moved on.

The town was already a hive of activity. Shops were open and people hurried through the streets and alleyways, going about their business. Shutters were folded back, and in the occasional house he could see bedding hung out to air over first-floor window sills. The cart made a racket on the cobbles and the cow had difficulty walking on them. The air was fresh and Herr Kramer took deep breaths.

He knew the way to the town hall square, where the local S.S. had its headquarters. He led the cow through winding streets, only just wide enough for the cart, and past the Church of St Joseph, where he had once prayed for his son. The closer Herr Kramer came to the town hall square the more S.S. men he saw. They were striding down the streets or marching past him. Nobody paid him the slightest attention, everybody seemed in a great hurry. Many of them were strikingly young. Herr Kramer decided to tap the next civilian he came across for information: an elderly lady, who had stepped out of her house to empty a white, enamel pot into the gutter. She looked emaciated and exhausted. In a broad dialect that he recognised from his homeland, she outlined the situation at the front, saying that the Wehrmacht needed reinforcements, how the S.S. were recruiting every man they could, how the population was gradually being divided up – women, children and old people here, men there, every single one of them in uniform, and how she couldn't care less, because her three boys were already lost, she'd done her duty for the Fatherland, done it good and proper, certainly more than some of them who never stopped complaining, she said, darting a scornful glance at one of the neighbouring houses. She proceeded to tell him a good deal more, all the while her gaze wandering over the cow, which stood beside Herr Kramer, chewing patiently. Kramer noticed this, but he could not find a break in the conversation to bring it to an end. Without looking at him for more than a few seconds, her eyes returned to the cow, and now the cart too, as she spoke of the places where her sons had fought: one had died in France, another in Africa, and she had not had news of the youngest for over a year. If you only knew the sort of things people like us have to suffer in these times, she said, casting a conspiratorial look around her, lowering her voice, then confiding in Herr Kramer that the little people have always had to make sacrifices for the greater cause, haven't we? I'll tell you one thing, if we hadn't starved, the eastern front would have crumbled long ago, and that's God's own truth, she said, all her senses focused so squarely on the cow it was as if she were addressing it rather than Herr Kramer. In all probability she would have carried on talking just to keep the cow there, if Herr Kramer had not interrupted her with a thank you and goodbye, before leaving. But he did not get far.

"Hey, Comrade!" she called out after him, every ounce of sorrow having vanished from her voice. "Don't you have a drop of milk for me? I'll pay." Herr Kramer stopped. Although the cow had already been milked, he had left a little in her udders so he would not have to buy anything to drink in town. Now he would sell it for one reichsmark. That was a lot of money and to begin with he would have accepted less. But his instinct told him he could have got twice as much had he insisted.

"Wait," the old woman called out, scuttling into her house. Soon afterwards she returned with a dirty-looking metal can. Herr Kramer kneeled somewhat awkwardly beside the cow's udder and began milking into the can. Behind him the old woman sang softly:

> Ladybird, ladybird, fly away far!
> Papa's fighting in the war.
> Now they've called up Grandpa too,
> Must be that retaliation they've threatened to do.
> Ladybird, ladybird, fly away far!

She laughed and nodded to herself. Herr Kramer got the impression she was out of her mind. She's gone mad, he thought, like me. Except for her it's three times worse. One son after another. After Herr Kramer had concluded his transaction he continued on his way, reaching his destination a few minutes later. Before him lay the town hall square. To the left stood the tall, slim tower of the Gothic minster and, directly opposite at the other end of the elongated square, was the town hall. It had been built in the same Gothic style and could easily be mistaken for another of the countless churches dotted throughout the town. Herr Kramer liked Gothic architecture, he loved to stand right beside the towers and look up. He would feel dizzy and a shiver would run down his spine when he thought what it must be like at the top.

But this thought was not in his mind now, as he steered the cart towards the town hall. It was no easy task, the square was teeming with people. Most wore the black uniform of the S.S. Their imminent departure had generated an atmosphere of excited activity. Utility vehicles and armoured cars were everywhere, both parked and on the go, although Herr Kramer could not detect any pattern to their movements. Everyone appeared purposeful and determined, orders were barked back and forth, and the hubbub of the soldiers' voices mingled with the sounds of engines and the dry crunching of boots on the march. It smelled of petrol and horse dung.

The chaotic procession of S.S. forces orbited a small market whose stalls were set up in the very middle of the square, and which slightly resembled a besieged fortress. Hearty voices resounded from the stalls; listening to them it was clear that they were accustomed to shouting. All manner of things were being peddled, but from a distance it did not look as if there was much to buy. In spite of this the market was bustling with customers; women, especially, were moving slowly from stall to stall to purchase food. Herr Kramer was tempted to pay the market a visit, but decided against it. He wanted to conclude his business with the S.S. first. Sticking to the periphery of the square he made satisfactory progress.

He arrived at the town hall, where an S.S. guard was posted either side of the entrance. They looked as if they would remain standing there for ever, as if nothing and nobody could induce them to stir. Herr Kramer led the cow to the foot of the steps and locked the wheels of his cart. He was certain that nobody would dare commit a theft under the eyes of the S.S. As he climbed the steps the two guards came to life. "Halt, Comrade. Where are you going?" one of them asked in a sedate, almost sleepy tone, immediately telling Herr Kramer that here he could not hope to encounter the same amateurishness he had outside the town. This bewildered him, for the sentry was so young that he could not help thinking again of his dead son. He thought about his son each time he saw a young man, but this one even bore a faint resemblance to him, with brown hair and a round face that looked almost innocent. Perhaps it was this likeness that made Herr Kramer slightly more vulnerable than usual. As he went up another few steps he raised his hand in the Nazi salute and said, in his sullen voice, "Heil Hitler. I've come to see the local S.S. commander."

"Why?" the S.S. guard asked, sounding bored. Now, close up, he was more like a statue of a warrior, scrutinising Herr Kramer with cold, grey eyes, without betraying the slightest hint of sympathy. The other S.S. guard afforded him no more than a cursory glance, then ignored him. Herr Kramer was unsettled. If he made his request they would surely think him mad. He tentatively offered an explanation:

"My wife and I are settlers here. Our farm is about one and a half hour's walk to the west. We have scant supplies for the winter, and so my wife had the idea, well, you see she inherited this antique clock from her father, and so we thought the commander might like to take a look at it. Maybe he'd like to buy it."

"The commander's not in town today."

"Not in town," Herr Kramer repeated, without really taking it in. The S.S. guard's cold eyes were still fixed on him, immovable as a wall.

"When will he be back?"

"None of your business, Comrade."

"No, no, of course not. I just wanted to . . ." He broke off, for he realised he was arousing suspicion. The noise behind him and the uncompromising indifference in front of him obstructed his thoughts. As he stood there he was suddenly gripped by the sensation of all the sounds in the square bundling into his head. Having decided that their conversation was over, the sentry was now ignoring him. It was if he had been turned to stone again, as if he had never really been alive. Uncertain what to do, Herr Kramer lingered a while on the steps, before returning to his cart like a defeated wrestler. He had failed, thanks to the indifference of a sentry. I've allowed myself to be bullied, he told himself as he unlocked the wheel, bullied as if I were the boy and he the old man. So here I am with a grandfather clock that nobody wants, whose time is past, whose deep bell would only ever continue to chime in his wife's memory, inaudible to him, a distant echo from better times. He knew he could not take the clock home again. His wife had performed her ritual and it would pain him to have to nullify it. But he had no idea what to do.

SEVEN

He did not deliver the speech he had improvised. During the night he had sat down at his beautiful English desk, with his back to the terrace, and drafted a new text. He had not called for Anna to try it out on her. Now he stood on the terrace, gazing out at a grey, overcast morning, lost in thought as if he had planned this, gazing beyond the roofs of the town hall square with its timidly low houses, paying no attention to the three hundred men in rank and file at his feet, waiting for him to set the mood for the day. He looked as he always did, an aloof deity with the inscrutable face of a Red Indian, the chiselled aquiline nose – which gave the impression it could slice into and mortally wound any enemy – the narrow mouth that never smiled in public and only rarely in private, and the powerful reserve that emanated from his eyes.

But in reality everything was different today. He had never been a Jew-hater; their persecution and extermination had only ever been a way to bolster his career, and his career had only ever been a way to bolster his self-esteem. But this is precisely how he had been able to endure the strain and burden, the ruthless hounding of people, the never-ending killings, the necessary punishments; precisely because he was not a Jew-hater he had been able to remain a decent man, in the sense implied by the Reichsführer S.S. Decent in the midst of the slaughter, the weeding-out process, as it was known, and of the struggle against Jewish–Freemason–Bolshevist subhumans.

But since yesterday evening everything was different. Since yesterday evening he *was* full of hatred. He hated Anna, even though he was unable to pinpoint why. When he thought back to the previous evening he was overwhelmed by a feeling of humiliation, which had called his entire career into question at a stroke. She had made him look ridiculous. She would pay for that. But first of all, others would pay. He had to overcome his hatred to reach a purer source of retribution, a place devoid of the emotions that might cause him to show signs of weakness or act prematurely. This was the covert reason for his speech. Ranzner knew that hatred would undermine his authority and compromise the common cause. He knew that only without hatred could there be an objective requirement to kill people. He anticipated that this speech would be the most important of his career to date. And he was ready to take on the challenge.

Ranzner looked at his three hundred men. Many of them spoke no better than broken German. They would barely be able to follow his speech. Ranzner thought back wistfully to the early days, when they had dashed from victory to victory, he and his German warriors. They had blindly confronted each danger, sticking together like blood brothers, saving each other's lives even if that meant snuffing it themselves. Snuffing it, Ranzner thought again, emphatically this time, as if this had changed. He looked at his men, still waiting there in silence, as they would have done for another three hours. Thank goodness the Reichsführer S.S. had not accepted any Poles. Inferior, the Reichsführer S.S. said. I'd rather have German criminals, the Reichsführer said, and had trawled through German prisons for volunteers. He, Ranzner, had only found out about this by field post.

He let out an involuntary sigh. There was no use in complaining, the Reich needed soldiers and the S.S. was still prepared to give all it had for the final victory, whether as an elite or a multinational army – that was of secondary importance. Now it was purely about efficiency, which is why he had to remind these soldiers why they were here and what their common mission consisted of. Once more he had to invoke the poetry of their deeds to make them forget the suffering they witnessed on a daily basis, and he must remind them of the sacred cause to which they had pledged themselves. If they engaged in battle they ought to be aware of their nobility, every last fibre of their being must radiate such a superhuman aura that the enemy could not help but sense it and quake in their boots, no matter how firmly they entrenched themselves behind their fortifications. As an example they ought to look to him, standing steadfast here, ready to shed every drop of his Aryan blood to lead the German Volk to the greatness and power that was its due, as spearhead of the Holy Reich.

"Men!
As members of the S.S. you are
not merely soldiers, you are
model custodians of Adolf Hitler's vision.
Your hallmarks are experience in war,
toughness,
pride in our
myriad victories,
an awareness of having withstood tremendous strains
and great dangers, as well as
the great legacy that the National Socialist idea
has imposed on you all,
since you have been fighting in the ranks of the S.S.
With courage and composure, with
a sense of your soldierly ability
and your superiority
you have grown into a new entity,
a far from average entity,
shaped by the extraordinary circumstances of war.
Your name is linked with the battles in
Poland, Belgium, Holland,
France, Yugoslavia,
with the mountain passes and straits
of Greece, and the Karelian snowfields,

the central Russian forests, the Ukrainian steppes
and the Caucasian pastures, your tenacity and your
attainment give you
that masterful stoicism,
which earns you success in battle
and the hatred of the vanquished foe,
but back at home the admiration and
love
of the German people.

Men!
There is one principle,
by which we must abide without reservation
or hesitation: We are to be honest,
decent,
loyal
and fraternal
to members of our own blood
and to no-one else!
We Germans, the only people
on earth with a
civilised attitude towards animals,
will also assume a civilised attitude
towards human animals.
We will not, therefore,
act more cruelly
than is necessary, this much is clear.
Whether or not
ten thousand Polish women die
in the construction of an anti-tank ditch
interests me only in so far as the
anti-tank ditch

is completed for Germany.
For this reason
no-one is to come to me
and say I cannot
use women and children
to build anti-tank ditches
because they will perish.
To him I should respond:
You are a murderer
of your own blood,
for,
if the anti-tank ditch is not built,
then German soldiers will die,
the sons of German mothers.
Our own blood.

Men!
I want you
to arm yourselves with this outlook
when confronting the problem
of all foreign, non-German races,
especially Poles
and Russians.
Anything else is
lather!
Sieg
Heil!"

"Sieg Heil!" three hundred throats bellowed back, and anyone listening carefully might have detected the Danes' guttural vowels or a Hungarian's voiceless S. But nobody was listening carefully. Ranzner's last word would ensure the foreigners remained mystified for a while longer, while the Germans hid their smirks. Lather? What was that supposed to mean?

The speech was over. Ranzner turned on his heels and left the balcony. He was satisfied. He had managed to regain a composure befitting his superiority. He believed that the best way to spur on his men was not to provide emotional justification for violence, but to explain why it was necessary, an explanation that crashed over everything and everyone like a raging torrent to which nobody could possibly offer resistance because it is the very force of nature itself. Ranzner was satisfied. His speech had been a successful therapy against his own hatred. Now he knew that he would not kill Anna until the right moment had come.

EIGHT

This was the last thing he saw:

Raindrops falling straight on top of him through the dark-grey crack between two shadowy gables, on they went until the chink turned black and the raindrops white, as when looking at a photographic negative or pressing your fingers down onto your closed eyes, or as if the rain had turned to snow and twilight to night.

He smelled:

The tang of freshly baked bread.

He felt:

The cold stealing through his body, quietly and quickly like an army in the dark invading a neighbouring country. Seconds later he heard a voice calling out his name. It was everywhere and nowhere. It was loud and soft. It was near and far. He thought that it must get lighter again now, the mass of white dots hanging above him like distant stars must fuse together to form the exit from a tunnel he could walk through to be free, free from whatever – this darkness, this cold, which he could barely see and barely feel anymore, but which were still there.

And it did get lighter. But at that very moment he stopped hearing and feeling. Everything was silent. A beautiful silence, so beautiful that he remembered just how much he had missed this silence his whole life long.

A silence that meant tranquillity. And peace.

Suddenly, a face, right in front of him. His father, Adolf Treitz, his father's farm, Eisen in the Saarland, 1907. The face hovered right in front of him in a milky light, without contours. He felt pain, unbearable pain, his head, his body, everything felt as if it were being brutally crushed, he turned around, saw two huge thighs covered in blood, and far beyond these, between the breasts, the face of his mother, Anna Treitz, née Gettmann. She had just given birth to him and now she raised her head to look at him, without any joy, without any welcome.

He turned back to his father, who looked as bold and bleak as a Rembrandt painting. His white skin gave off a pallid shimmer and his piercing alcoholic's eyes with their heavy bags penetrated as if through a fog. Darkness surrounded his father, he seemed to have sucked up all the light, leaving none for him, his son. When his father noticed the bewilderment he let out a loud and vulgar laugh. He could see his father's poor teeth, eaten away by decay and he heard the laugh as if it were his own. He smelled the alcohol escaping from his father's open mouth as though a bottle of schnapps had been opened beneath his nose. He was afraid, but his father gave the fear a meaning. He said, "I'm going to make a man of you, whether you want it or not."

He recalled not wanting it. But he had to pretend he did, or it would only make everything worse. And thus he became the person he was when a woman aimed her revolver at his head, like a large index finger calling upon him finally to do what he wanted. Perhaps this is why he did nothing as she struggled to pull the trigger; finally, as he watched her kill him, he did *not* do what was expected of him. And now, as she stood before him with her faded, greyish-red skirt, all those black scarves and her face, especially her face, he seemed to realise for the first time that his actions had only ever been prompted by a will to live. He had known at once that he would have loved her, had she not been the person she was, and had he not become the man he had never wanted to be. When he thought about her now, his memory played tricks on him. It felt as if he had put on a mask with her face, and as if she were wearing a mask with his face, and as if he were killing himself because he had forgotten that he was not her and she not him. Then, remembering again who they really were, he felt terrible because in reality he had shot her rather than she him. His fear vanished and he realised again that he was Sturmbannführer Treitz, and that she was nothing but a Polish Jew who he would have killed had he not failed.

The mask game was bothering him.

It lasted for ages.

It kept going of its own accord, without his being able to put a stop to it.

He thought: I'm in hell.

He thought: I'm being punished for everything I've done and haven't done.

He looked for the devil. Someone must be organising all of this.

He had thought he was alone.

But he was not alone.

Someone must be there.

No-one was there apart from him. And even he was no longer there. He was Sturmbannführer Treitz. A man, born here, gone to school there, done this and that, died. A stranger whose life he remembered as if it had been his own. Perhaps he had staged his life like a theatre director sat the whole time in the auditorium. He had allowed himself to be manipulated as his own puppet. He had even allowed himself to be killed, as if he were nothing more than the lead character in a drama.

How could he ever forget?

He felt terrible.

The fear had vanished, and he noted that even without fear you could let life slip.

Or had it only vanished because he was dead?

But I'm thinking, he thought.

Or was this no longer thinking?

Was he perhaps swimming as a tiny nothingness in streams of thought which came from somewhere and flowed somewhere else, and which were all logical because it was their own principle to be logical rather than his?

Had it always been thus and he had simply failed to notice it, believing instead that whoever is the master of their own head is also the master of destiny and the world? How much he must have been master of his own head!

His father's head had not yielded any reliable information. He thought about his mother.

What had she looked like?

He no longer remembered exactly.

He felt like somebody staring at a photograph of total strangers, searching randomly for a fitting face, to be able to say: That is my mother.

He found one.

It was the face of a slim woman with a long, straight nose, broad, high cheekbones and gaunt cheeks. Her gaze was intense and grim. He detected in her eyes a sense of the remoteness which had always emanated from his mother, and which had enveloped them all like a cold blanket, his three elder brothers, his little sister, even his father. He recalled that her face was always serious, he had hardly ever seen her smile. As a young boy he had suspected that she did it in secret so nobody could catch her out. Or maybe she smiled only at Anna, his little sister, the youngest. He had asked himself why she hid her smile, and never found an answer. She hid it from him, too, and although he had sometimes lain in wait for her – in a corner of the hallway through which she walked alone, or high up in the barn when she was gathering straw below – he never caught her smiling.

Thinking back to his siblings now, he felt total detachment.

From all of them.

Except Anna.

His father was always laughing, always laughing about somebody. A loud and vulgar laugh. A dangerous laugh, in fact it had not been a laugh at all, but a moment of chaos that could be followed by anything imaginable.

He remembered:

When he began to help out in the bar, he would often spill beer. One of the customers shouted, Hey, Adolf, your son still hasn't learned how to carry beer glasses. He recalled in perfect detail the face of the man, a coarse, Saarland farmer's face, broad and round, a regular in a bar where only regulars drank. His father came out from a corner, at the back on the right, where he was boozing with friends. He peered at the splash of beer on the uneven, scuffed tiles and gave a resounding laugh. Then he clipped his boy round the ear, which still hurt hours later, threw a cloth on the ground and returned to his friends, while the other men laughed.

He saw his mother behind the bar, she wore the face of the woman in the photograph. She had seen everything, but just stared, her expression serious and grim, before getting back to work. He had felt terrible, as terrible as he did now, as if this feeling were the light through which he had moved all his life, and for this reason he had never realised it until he was dead. Dead and alone.

When these thoughts turned into images he failed to notice at first. When he noticed he did not care.

The images sufficed; he no longer needed names, spoken words, they had only ever obscured what was now affecting him with the violence of blows, filling every nook and cranny of his senses with pain. Only now did he realise that his life had been devoid of happiness, only now, when he no longer knew who his father and mother had been, only now, when he no longer remembered his gender, but felt more like an it than anything else, the dwindling remains of a sad life, only now did he find himself.

When the images faded, leaving nothing but sorrow and pain, without beginning or end, like an eternity that existed because time had been extinguished from it, there was no Sturmbannführer Karl Treitz anymore.

Everything ceased to exist.

NINE

What luck, Frau Kramer thought, that a storm was blowing outside, that the sky was dark grey like the approach of night, even though the old grandfather clock would have just been striking one in the afternoon. That the snowflakes were dancing wildly, as if trying to make the house disappear behind an incessant glimmer. That her husband had gone out to the stable in good time.

When the contractions started, Herr Kramer had become restless, muttered something about some repairs and left the room in a hurry. She had thought he might react like that, but still, she was astonished to see her silent prediction come true so punctually. Maybe, she considered briefly as she stoked the fire to heat water in the kettle, this *reliability* – her private name for it – was the most astonishing thing about her husband. For she knew for a fact that it was absolutely spontaneous.

Now she was alone with Margarita. The young girl sat on a rough wooden stool they had fetched from the cellar because it was low enough. Margarita held up her skirts, her hands grabbing the material like a railing she could cling onto. Pain was written all over her face.

Although the kitchen was not especially warm, a gleaming film of sweat had formed on her face. She stared spellbound at her bulging belly, the navel looked like a stopper under too much pressure, about to pop at any moment. There was a smell of iron and rust.

The contractions had set in a few minutes previously and now Margarita waited for the next wave. The first had been so strong that she imagined she was being carried by pain away onto a dark sea, without orientation or anything to hold on to. But at the same time she had felt two firm hands close around her shoulders, and a voice right by her ear, a voice like a gentle song, promising something, an end perhaps, an end to everything, or a beginning, she did not know exactly, but the voice kept singing, it was like a buoy she could swim towards as the wave rose, ebbed, then rose again. Suddenly the pain vanished and Margarita returned to the kitchen, to the wooden stool, as if she had been washed ashore.

Frau Kramer knew that it would be a long time before the child made its way out. She had been present at enough births, she had watched her mother give birth, her elder sisters, the women on the neighbouring farms where they came from. Her own birth, as she called the birth of her son. The birth of her daughter, which neither she nor her husband ever talked about. Now, as she hurried to fetch clean towels and an old tub to wash the baby in afterwards, pictures appeared in her mind's eye as on a blurred daguerreotype, pictures of screaming women, screaming newborns, bloody pictures full of life, as she disinfected the rusty kitchen shears with vodka without taking her eye off Margarita, who was now sitting there as if listening inside herself, pictures neglected like a long-forgotten album, only opened when things repeat themselves.

Margarita tried to distract herself. She watched Frau Kramer's assured hand movements, her footsteps from one side of the room to the other, focusing on the click-clack of her clogs as if it were the rhythm to a secret choreography in which everything had been planned in advance and nothing could go wrong and Frau Kramer was the main performer rather than her. But she was afraid, afraid of bursting, cracking open and never being able to put herself back together, afraid of disappearing and having to make way for a strange creature she did not know and which was now tearing away at her with unrestrained violence. Tomasz flashed through her mind, she saw the figure of her dead love like a picture on a postcard, all of this was his fault, he had inflicted this on her, why on earth had she got involved with him? Now he was dead and she had to cope alone with the consequences of her lost happiness. She felt anger fermenting inside her, anger at everything and everyone, she was about to scream with anger when the next contraction began. She screamed.

Herr Kramer sat on a straw bale in the stable, staring at the cow which was ignoring him. He was wearing an old brown anorak and holding a dark woolly hat in one hand. His gaze drifted across the pattern of her coat, dirty white with patches of light brown, the outlines of which were somehow blurred. He tried to identify the lines where the white finished and the brown began, but failed. There was no clear boundary, as if you could only see just before it and just after it but never the line itself. The cow exuded a serenity which did him the world of good. She just stood there, chewing, lowered her head from time to time, never too slowly, never too fast, gathered up a bit of straw, raised her head at precisely the same speed, grinding away languidly and thoughtfully, as if determined to rush nothing. The barn exuded a damp cosiness, steam rose from the cow's nostrils, marking its breath in the flickering light of the paraffin lamp on the ground beside Herr Kramer. Puffs of condensation drifted from his mouth too, both exhalations had own their particular rhythm, it was as if he and the cow did have something to say to each other after all. The wind blew against the barn door, which rattled continually, Herr Kramer could hear wood and metal, wood on wood, metal on metal.

It was only when Margarita screamed that he was awoken from his immersion. If anybody heard her now, it occurred to him, that would be the end of Margarita. If anybody heard her now, he thought, he would have to kill them, he would have to go to war, there would be no other option. He wound down the wick of the paraffin lamp until it went out. Then he stood up, fastened his anorak again, opened the stable door wide enough to slip out, a gust of wind rushed in, all of a sudden snowflakes were dancing around Herr Kramer, and over to the cow, which turned her head. He closed the door behind him and embarked on his first lap of the yard.

Outside the snow swirled so thickly before his eyes that Herr Kramer remembered more about his surroundings than he actually saw. The yard was in total darkness, no light seeped from the house, only the grey smoke rising from the chimney, snatched away in an instant, betrayed the presence of anyone inside. The snow creaked beneath his boots, the wind raged powerfully, generating a constant whooshing and a frequent rustling and crackling in the boughs of the trees. It was the perfect night for the birth of an illegal child of an illegal woman and – Herr Kramer paused briefly – illegal guardians. Out there, beyond the darkness, in the lit-up neighbouring farmhouses, in the small and large towns of the Wartheland, there was nobody who could or would give them retrospective permission, nobody to whom he could offer a reasonable explanation. Of course, there was the pastor and a few other families who hid people, and perhaps others who might understand what was happening here. But none of them counted. The only people who counted were those they were hiding Margarita from. Herr Kramer understood them better than he would have liked. Words formed within him, words that he had heard about the Jews for as long as he had been able to think. Parasites. A word which time and again had stolen into his mind ever since Margarita had come to them. Pregnant. Carrying young. Rats. Rats multiply everywhere, they are impossible to eradicate. With a strange, inexplicable pain Herr Kramer felt how appropriate these words might be if only he would admit them, if only he gave way a little. He saw himself standing on a narrow ridge and imagined that, without the unshakeable kindness of his wife, which in the worst moments he called gullibility or naivety, he could fall, perhaps he would have fallen long ago.

In fact only quite recently he had stood on the edge of the abyss, over in town. He recalled, with a mixture of shame and amazement, the market square, the S.S. guards, himself slowly approaching the market where women shouted, each one louder than the next, even though they scarcely had anything on their stalls. The cow by his side had become impatient, she wanted to eat, but Herr Kramer had sat for ages at the foot of the town hall steps without doing anything, almost as motionless as the sentries at the top.

To begin with he had intended to wait for the Obersturmbannführer's return. But time passed, the sun climbed sluggishly into the sky and the S.S. men waiting in the square, under the noisy instructions of their commanders, filed into squads standing to attention, the Scandinavians here, the Germans there, beside them the Latvians, there were French and Dutch troops too, all volunteers trying to escape unemployment and hoping for rich pickings from the conquered territories. They wore grey uniforms with large sewn-on pockets and white, soft-peaked caps. Instead of a cap, some wore steel helmets, beneath which their small heads looked even smaller. Young as they were, they oozed excitement and optimism. Sub-machine guns hung from their shoulders, and like the helmets, they looked too big. Their voices were bright and when Herr Kramer closed his eyes he might have heard the boisterous departure of children being evacuated to the country, had he ever been present at such an event. But Herr Kramer had never witnessed an evacuation. So he closed his eyes and here and there heard a clear, young voice in which resonated something of the sing-song tone their own son had inherited from his mother.

Armoured cars, scout cars, utility vehicles and motorcycle units in dark leather uniforms were stationary or manoeuvred between the troops. They were positioning themselves in a large semi-circle around the market, as if their mission were to defend or besiege it. The square was full of men, Herr Kramer had never seen such a large S.S. company, but he was not surprised. They were not far from the front, in the distance a dull rumbling could be heard with ever greater regularity, as if a storm were raging beyond the horizon. But this was a quite different sound.

Himmler's Hellish Host. The woman who had bought milk from Herr Kramer had called it that. "Look at Himmler's Hellish Host," she had said. "Only yesterday they were scrumping apples from my garden, scarpering the moment I came out with my broom." Now they'd grown large helmets, long rifles and heavy boots, and they wouldn't scarper anymore, they'd . . . But Herr Kramer saw older men amongst the very young ones, men of his own age, and some no longer looked fit enough to cope with a long march, he thought. All the same they stood there, glancing about silently, gazing into the faces of comrades who could have been their own sons, and saying nothing. Then, as if in response to a telepathic agreement, the S.S. began their retreat: no more cries, no more talking, only marching. It was a quarter of an hour before the last man had left the square via the main street, which led directly eastwards to the edge of town, up the hill, through the forest and beyond. Soon nothing more could be heard of the S.S. Now the square looked empty and vast; the cobbles gleamed in the dampness that had refused to take leave of the town all day. In the centre stood the market, small and lost.

The square looked like Herr Kramer felt, Herr Kramer thought about himself, thinking in the third person, as if he were communicating with a second person who may have been called Herr Kramer too. He was surprised that, for the first time in his life, he could associate a random image of the outside world with his inner emotional state. The square looked empty and vast. But he was even more surprised to find himself thinking thoughts he had never thought exactly in this way before, even though he sensed that there was nothing new in their content. He? Herr Kramer thought, as if peering over at himself, perhaps from there, in the middle of the market where, in the silence that followed the S.S.'s departure, the women now seemed to be screaming twice as loudly, the empty square like a stage for their raddled voices, worn-out bodies and broad, rustic faces. Over the course of the gradual withdrawal something had happened to Herr Kramer, which Herr Kramer had not noticed until now, something about himself which he was sketching in the third person to a second person using emptiness and vastness, yet at the same time unsure of what he actually meant.

So Herr Kramer was sitting at the bottom of the steps, looking across to the market women, while the cow next to him had become restless and was herself now staring at the women as if she knew exactly what was over there. But Herr Kramer was not yet able to heed the cow's silent hints, she was thirsty now, too. He saw himself standing amongst the market women, looking back at himself with a peculiar expression of emptiness and vastness, as though at any moment he were about to say to a second Herr Kramer, What's Herr Kramer doing sitting at the bottom of those steps, Herr Kramer? He's making a fool of himself, entertaining the absurd idea of flogging a worthless grandfather clock at the market, whereas they only have eyes for his cow as if they knew exactly what's what. Still Herr Kramer did not budge from his place at the foot of the steps, for he was thinking like someone thinking to a second Herr Kramer, What's Herr Kramer doing in the market square, he's sold his cow and the grandfather clock to boot, and now he's clearing off to avoid being drafted into Himmler's Hellish Host, how he sticks out like a sore thumb, one single man amongst so many rustic market women, in this entire town, which has turned female now that to a man the S.S. has marched out, there are just the two statues at the top of the steps, barely human, and Herr Kramer there on the market square, look at him staring across here, Herr Kramer!

Something had happened, Herr Kramer thought. His thoughts had never been as lucid as now, but neither had they been as incomprehensible, when Herr Kramer told Herr Kramer that he would advise

Herr Kramer to leave his naïve wife, who was causing him nothing but trouble, and the Jewish rat that had crept into their house, to their own devices and save his own skin. That's all very well, Herr Kramer, Herr Kramer had said. But why? Why, Herr Kramer had asked Herr Kramer. If Herr Kramer wants me to save my skin, then why? There's absolutely nowhere to go, especially not for Farmer Kramer, an ethnic German, who's never been anywhere further in all his life than Lübeck, and he only went there because he got married, to the woman he's now meant to leave in the lurch because she's naïve and wants to help a Jew on the run have her baby. A Jew of all people, the Herr Kramer with the market women bellowed back, and suddenly they were only two Herr Kramers, Because a decision's got to be made, Herr Kramer told himself, getting up in his slow, sedate manner. As yet he had no idea what he was going to do, and he felt as if the other Herr Kramer had now detached himself from the throng of market women and was walking directly towards him, only without the cow, which Herr Kramer was leading by the reins and which was delighted finally to be heading in the direction of the aromas that had been making her restless for quite a while. When the Herr Kramer without the cow met the Herr Kramer with the cow, it seemed to them as if they were passing through a mirror, or perhaps that is just how it seemed to the third Herr Kramer, who had not moved, because he had still not reached a decision, because it was not within his competence, and because he would never come to a decision about decisions made in his name. Later Herr Kramer would say, I've always been a simpleton, but there was this one incident in my life. And then he would sink into his thoughts, with a distant expression on his face, and he would never get further than this point, for he would never be able to tell it as it was being told now, as Herr Kramer suddenly approached the market alone, unsure as to what he would do, but feeling odd as the only man amongst so many women, old ladies with voices like rust, young girls who, at every conceivable pitch, had already yelled the childhood out of themselves, and amongst so many women, old ladies and young girls shopping at this tiny market that had scarcely anything for sale, as Herr Kramer saw when he came closer.

Now he was round the front of the house. Small and old it stood before him in the night-time shimmer of the white landscape. The roof was heavily burdened with a dense blanket of snow, the massive wooden door that led straight into the parlour looked as if had been crafted for dwarfs, and even the two kitchen windows, now hidden behind thick wooden shutters, seemed minute. A witch's cottage, Herr Kramer thought, thinking of the two women inside doing something from which he was excluded. Bringing life into the world. All of a sudden he wished it was a boy, and was simultaneously startled by this wish, which felt as if his son were being born for the second time, as if everything were starting to turn again from the beginning, and at once he knew exactly why he had sold the cow at the market, even though back then he did not know, certain only that he would get no money for the cow, because rather than money people had all sorts of food and household goods such as beeswax and soap and fat and paraffin, because the women, old ladies, young girls, even ran back home to get more stuff they could offer him. It went on like this until the cart was full, while the cow chewed contentedly on the bale of hay which sat beneath one of the stalls. In the end the people laughed at him when he hitched himself to the cart and could hardly pull it. When, drenched in sweat, he made his way along the bumpy streets, pursued by small children who teased him, calling him donkey, and ox. When he had to take a rest every ten minutes. When he wondered whether he would ever make it home. When he sold the woman who had bought milk from him the grandfather clock for ten reichsmarks. When he struggled past the S.S. checkpoint and saw the looks of incredulity on the young men's faces. When he almost collapsed with exhaustion. When his wife hurried out to meet him in the dark and the two of them pulled the cart back to the house together. When he sat for ages by the fire, unable to move, while his wife gave him hot broth to drink. I'm proud of you, she had said and, feeling ashamed, he had cast aside the memory of his doubts.

TEN

The contractions increased in frequency and strength. Frau Kramer, who had been measuring the gaps in between, stopped counting, for now she was able to feel the rhythm that had set in.

Margarita had slipped from the stool and now lay on the floor. She had no idea how much time had passed, nor did she bother to ask. The final push. This was the only thing on her mind as Frau Kramer talked and talked, and tried to make her more comfortable with blankets and towels. She carefully touched Margarita's cervix and established that it had dilated slightly. But not enough yet.

It seemed to Margarita that her body was a stranger doing things to her she had not expected, in her eyes the light in the kitchen had dimmed, and yet she perceived objects with greater clarity, It's like dying, Margarita thought, extending her arm past her head in the direction of the window, as if she could stretch herself further and make something happen. Looking about her she saw the misshapen wooden stool she had been sitting on, the crude but pretty table made from heavy oak, which told the story that its wood had not been worked with particular care, for on its stout, angular legs Margarita spotted many areas that had been patched rather cursorily with sawdust paste, fading over time to leave dirty, dark stains.

In her sing-song voice Frau Kramer talked and talked about one thing and another, about births she had been present at, all of which looked and felt a good deal worse than they actually were. My child, she said, perspiring and with a red face, taking hold of Margarita's pelvis on both sides to lift it briefly, you've never given birth to a child before, your body doesn't know what's happening. It's like a stubborn donkey that won't understand it has to do something new. But it will do it, it will do it, she added, now feeling Margarita's belly.

"Your little boy's not turning, my child. He's not going to be a moon-gazer, is he?"

"I'm going to have a boy?" Margarita asked naïvely.

"Oh, I don't know, my child, I meant nothing by it," Frau Kramer said, somewhat lost in thought as she felt Margarita's belly again, recalling how difficult her own first birth had been, when she brought her boy into the world, the boy that the world had long forgotten, she had no idea where his body lay, nor if he had been buried at all. Now she was bringing another child into the world, a child that her dead son would have been obliged to detain, and who knows what else her dead son would have done with it. Her eyes slowly welled up, Margarita noticed, and all of a sudden she had tears in her eyes that rolled down the sides of her face, to the left and right, without her knowing exactly why.

"But who's crying now, child?" Frau Kramer exclaimed, wiping her eyes with the backs of her hands.

Another especially intense contraction made Margarita scream. The baby had not made its final turn, but it wanted for all it was worth to leave its narrow world, its tiny nose pressed perilously close to its mother's pubic bone, but its head was not that big, and now it was Frau Kramer's turn to scream, too, for she could already see its black hair and she bellowed above Margarita's uncontrolled screaming, so that the mother would push and not stop, and she told her that the child was on its way, that she could see its black hair, but Margarita had sent the stool crashing into a corner with her right arm and was now screaming blue murder, as the black hair slowly, far too slowly, made its way right through the middle of her, while beneath the black hair the oxygen was gradually running out, and while Frau Kramer, pulling herself together, began to employ all the tricks she had used so often with other women.

But she had never helped a moon-gazer into the world, and the moon-gazer had now come to a standstill, half-way, because its mother believed she had no more strength left, But you do have strength, Frau Kramer yelled, shaking Margarita by the shoulders to make her open her eyes, Open your eyes, you silly fool! Open your eyes and give birth to your baby!

Outside, Herr Kramer was standing again by the low wooden door to the parlour, past which he had walked countless times already that night, and he heard the two women fighting each other in the kitchen, heard that the baby had black hair, heard screams that sounded like death cries, knew that the sun would rise at his back, it would happen any moment now.

The wind had died, snow was no longer falling and the white land-scape glowed coolly from within, in an unreal light that now, as dawn broke, slowly changed, heralding a resplendent winter's day. In the east, louder than before the storm, echoed the dull rumbling of front-line combat.

When both women had stopped screaming and instead a new voice could be heard, a tiny voice that sounded displeased at having been brought into the world, Herr Kramer saw something moving in the east, on the track that led to his farm. He could not make out the object, but it was advancing quickly and getting bigger and it was an S.S. lorry, followed by a utility vehicle. Behind Herr Kramer the first tip of light burst into the landscape, bathing everything with a new visibility, and by the time Herr Kramer overcame his paralysis and ran to the wooden door, he was certain that it really would be a resplendent day.

Herr Kramer pushed open the heavy door. He was able to think clearly again.

"The S.S. are coming! Margarita's got to get back into the cellar with the baby!" But he found the two women moving in a trance from which he was excluded. Margarita was still lying on the floor, the umbilical cord between her legs like a large tapeworm with its head bitten off. His wife was holding a small, bloody piece of human being whose thin voice was barely audible, she was getting ready to bathe it with warm water in a wooden tub held together by three rusty iron rings. They had brought the tub with them from their old home, and Herr Kramer wondered if his children had ever been bathed in it, his son and daughter, Close the door, his wife said, and he obeyed automatically, it would take the S.S. at least five minutes to get here, he estimated, knowing full well that he would have no influence on what happened after that.

He also knew why the S.S. had chosen to come to his house. Turning round, he went to the narrow, steep staircase which climbed the right-hand wall, paused on the bottom step and said calmly, "I'm going to pack my things." Then he went up, the stairs creaked.

ELEVEN

It was not raining when death once more visited the small sloping alley that led away from the long street and up to the church. It was cold and bodies froze on this early morning in late autumn somewhere in the Wartheland, which once had been called Poland. It was remembered that Wartheland had been Poland. Remembered thirty-seven times. In Polish and in German. Or perhaps not. Perhaps nothing was remembered, except life in general and in particular. Thirty-seven times in particular. That would be about right. That might have happened, before death visited that cold, late-autumn morning in the Wartheland, thirty-seven times. Bodies stood, tightly packed, it was too cold for embarrassment at feeling one's skin rub against someone else's. And bodies shivered, oh, how they shivered, the spectators could not say whether this was due to cold or fear. But that was unimportant. Causes were not important. Only results counted. And results were wanted. The war, this peculiar thing, was a courageous, intense search for results, unalterable, irrevocable. History was being made, it was always progressing for someone.

Each Jew that perished was progress, for the Jew was irrevocably dead. A dead Jew was proof that the Führer wanted progress and was deploying everything to attain it. And, deep down, was not every Pole a Jew? Was not their *tertium comparationis* their subhumanity, which they shared like stray mutts share a filthy nook in the street into which they slink to evade the clutches of the dog-catcher?

Bodies froze, froze treacherously, froze treacherously and maliciously thirty-seven times. The spectators had a good view, they wore warm leather coats and large, round helmets, some had neat peaked caps sporting an ancient Indian symbol, which could tell of the rising sun, of the day and of life.

But death had to visit, and it was irrelevant whether the sun would soon rise (it would soon rise) or whether it would soon set (it would soon set). The war would soon be over, soon Poland would exist again, shifted somewhat to the left on the map, but still Poland. And soon, very soon, Germany would be reunified, and soon, very soon the sun would no longer rise and no longer set. All this was irrelevant, for now, before these imminent events, these definitive events, before these seventy-seven audience members, death would visit, death for all eternity, thirty-seven times. The audience stopped being mere spectators standing there. They had already removed their black pistols from their black leather holsters by their warm hips, had taken off the safety catches and now were standing there, arms by their sides, as if about to fire the starting shot for a race into the next world. Then they became mere spectators again, standing there, their warm breath exhaling small clouds of vapour into the cold air, which higher up in the atmosphere, maybe even by the first storey, mingled with the thirty-seven small clouds of vapour that for now was still rising from freezing mouths, on the other side of the alley, right next to a low wooden door, from whose chinks and cracks the tang of fresh bread now escaped.

There were many thoughts too. Above slim legs, a smooth mons pubis, young breasts, and behind pretty eyes which could not cease to be pretty even now, this was thought: Lord, O my judge! Unto you I deliver myself!

Behind a furrowed brow, beneath a shorn head, above sunken cheeks, counted ribs, hirsute genitals, this was thought: Social forces work in precisely the same way as the forces of nature – blindly, violently, destructively, so long as we do not recognise or expect them. Social forces work in precisely the same way as the forces of nature – blindly, violently, destructively, so long as we do not recognise or expect them. Social forces work in precisely the same way as the forces of nature – blindly, violently, destructively, so long as we do not recognise or expect them. Social forces work in precisely the same way, and this was thought: You, to Helios consecrated, You, with bright day's blessing freighted, Greetings to this hour when Luna's high worship rules again!

And this was thought: Heaven is so damned close, I could touch it. My heart leaps forth. One. Two. Three. Four. I cannot. I don't wish to. I'm suffocating here. It must be light outside. I want to go outside, I will go outside. I'm not a rat. And thought followed thought followed thought, in Polish and in German and even secretly in Yiddish (It's hard to be a Jew) – how could that have happened? So there were still Jews amongst the Poles, Jews that had not been ferreted out because they were hiding very publicly, but that no longer made any difference. Nothing was thought, too, nothing at all. Eyes were wrenched open distressingly wide, the spectators would have been terrified without their trusty pistols, and if the Poles hadn't been so naked, so preposterously, hideously naked. Bodies stank, bodies pissed, pissed at least twenty times, vomited four times, shat three times, fell unconscious five times. The unconscious were pulled back up to their feet at the behest of the onlookers, they had stopped shivering. Stopped? Where were the unconscious at the moment they stopped shivering? Maybe (the thought briefly occurs) in a better place. But consciousness had to be regained so that the shivering could start all over again, a merciless shivering, with eyes wrenched open distressingly wide, thin, crossed arms, bent bodies, hanging breasts, frozen genitals – the spectators were very keen to put an end to this wretched show.

And one spectator, a young, blond hulk in a smart black uniform with an Indian symbol, who had never witnessed such wretchedness, thought, The fundamental point is that we must not educate this race. The fundamental point is that we must not educate this race. The fundamental point is that we must not educate this race. The fundamental point is, and another, even younger man, stood there with desire in his eyes, the heavy pistol in his hand like an oracle, thinking, De dood te geven en de dood te nemen, de dood te geven en de dood te nemen, de dood te geven en de dood te nemen, and many spectators were thinking nothing, nothing at all, just gawping as people do at a market when the market women lock horns because they wish to buy a cow they cannot afford. One spectator thought of Anna's buttocks, how their outline showed when she was on her knees cleaning the floor, and thought, What a horrible mess, when all this is over, already feeling disgust at the filthy bodies and stench of iron, and decided, Enough is enough, and at that moment the sun rose, casting light on the Indian symbol that told of the rising sun, of the day and of life.

Then death visited the alley, thirty-seven times. And when the spectators-turned-directors had stopped being directors, letting their puppets dance to the rhythm of their own melodies, and the smoke was drifting up into the cold air from their black pistols, and the shots had faded away or were still chasing through distant streets, like crazed animals in flight, past narrow houses with listening windows; when the spectators became spectators once more and had staged the last act of the play and all the principal actors were dead – it must have been a tragedy – they replaced their pistols in their black holsters and yelled over to a few Poles, who were hitched up to carts like oxen, to take away the principal actors, away from the town, and many a Pole would themselves fall into the pit they had dug for others.

TWELVE

How did Obersturmbannführer Ranzner come to overstep the line? In retrospect, even he could not say. Early that morning he had stood on the terrace of the town hall, his black boots up to the calves in fresh snow, and looked across the square. He had positioned himself there, his right hand clasping the meerschaum pipe that he only took out on special occasions, his left hand set on his hip, so that Anna would see him from the office if she came in. He had allowed his gaze to roam over the old, snow-laden houses like an army commander, all the while regarding himself through Anna's eyes. What he saw filled him with awe and, though he could barely acknowledge it, with love.

But then he had taken a proper look, observing the pristine layer of snow covering the square and the roofs, which softened all hard edges into smooth curves, and felt as if he were in a fairy tale, as if witches and other mythical creatures must inhabit the squat, mediaeval houses, rather than just Poles and German settlers, and perhaps the odd Jew who had slipped through the net. The houses appeared enchanted, as if everything must end happily ever after. And the fact that in less than an hour the square would change beyond all recognition, because it would be filled with lorries, utility vehicles, tank destroyers, motor-cycles and howitzers, was part of this happy ending. Then it would be his, Obersturmbannführer Ranzner's, duty to avoid feeling any sadness at his and his people's having to leave this little town, because the Russians were coming, because the Reichsführer S.S. had given the order: Every man to Posen! For Posen was to become a fortress, to be defended until the last drop of blood was shed. So, would the final battle they were all waiting for be the happy ending, irrespective of how it finished?

And the feminine emotions, especially sentimentality, with which he gazed at the familiar houses, with which he yearned for a different ending – must he cast them off for good, here and now, let them freeze in the snow so they could never again impede the execution of his sacred duties? Yes, that is how it must be.

If Anna came in now, he would make her wait so she could see him like this and understand that he could no longer make allowances for her, so she would realise that more was at stake than his compassion for a little Jewish girl who had earned a reprieve so long as she was useful. In his mind's eye he saw himself standing before her, a judge deciding between life and death, who harboured no personal feelings because he knew that personal feelings diluted everything, turning all that was clear into a murky broth in which nobody could find their bearings anymore. As he, Ranzner, was utterly convinced of this, the Jewish girl would also understand that he did not mean it personally, but was merely being pragmatic. His demeanour would say to her, As much as I should like to keep you alive, I must think of the German people. His eyes would say to her, What would I have achieved, had I combed every nook and cranny for Jews without keeping my own house in order? Out of gratitude for her loyal service he would grant her a swift death, a bullet, and she would be released from her existence. With this his work would be complete and he could leave this town without a hint of sentimentality.

At that moment Ranzner heard the door to his office open. He did not stir, he followed his plan, now he was actually observing himself through Anna's eyes, which must be looking at him from the office. It was a quite peculiar feeling of gratification. It made him nervous.

As usual, Anna had prepared herself for this meeting with Ranzner, she was both wholly present and wholly absent, and now she stood in the middle of his office, watching the Obersturmbannführer's twitching right knee through the glass of the terrace door. How strange that

Ranzner's body had become ever more familiar to her over time, as if there were a complicity between them of which Ranzner himself knew nothing. Now Ranzner's jiggling knee, his rigid back, his tense neck muscles told her that he was more fraught than usual, and that he had called for her at this time because something extraordinary was about to happen. That she must be careful.

When his pipe went out Ranzner turned from the square and went back into his office. Without any word of greeting he looked at Anna standing before him. She was so slim, and as ever so beautiful to behold; he took note of this with the necessary detachment. She stood with her head bowed and eyes lowered, which obliged him to move closer, as he needed her to look him in the eye. With his index finger he lifted her chin, and when her head rose, when she opened her eyes and looked at him directly, both of them paused. It was very brief, scarcely noticeable, and Ranzner immediately broke the deadlock. He struck the attitude he wanted to strike, he spoke to her without being guilty of a single word, he moved a touch closer and his gaze fell on her quivering mouth; he thought of the pistol, for now everything had been said, now he had to take the pistol and put an end to it all, without melancholy . . . but at that moment he kissed the full lips of the woman, at that moment his hands grabbed the woman's shoulders and pulled her to him, close, until the two bodies were touching, at that moment his plan was on the tip of his tongue, like a lapsed word, and in the next moment this feeling, too, was washed away.

Anna offered no struggle when Ranzner pulled her towards him. She did not shut her mouth tight when he kissed her with his hard, thin lips. She was taken by surprise, and discovered that the whore inside her had been waiting for ages to assume her role. It was if she had been rehearsing long for this performance and here was the premiere. She saw the little girl from the Brandenburg meadow spring up and look over with her mouth open wide. She saw the woman with the secret name come closer, very close.

The event that followed, which consisted of Ranzner ripping the clothes from her body, dragging her into the next room, throwing her onto the divan and opening the trousers of his S.S. uniform in a frenzy, this event united all the women which were Anna, in a state of great shock, in a shared sensation of something unprecedented, something new. It united them in one single pain in the middle of her body, as Ranzner, with the rapid movements of a man who knew nothing but self-gratification, penetrated her. It united them in a heat, which spread from there throughout her entire body, and finally in sorrow when it was over before it had even properly begun, because Ranzner had shot his seed like a boy before collapsing on top of Anna.

Now the two of them lay there, a couple after the act. Their eyes were closed, the sweat on their foreheads was still glistening and soon dried, their breathing gradually quietened.

Anna searched inside herself for her sanctuaries, but it was as if Ranzner's invasion had swept away everything that she had painstakingly constructed, all the barricades, all the fairy meadows, all the secret chambers. Now she was nothing but a woman without honour, a woman who had become an accessory to the crime committed against her, and in some strange way she felt grateful for this sense of clarity.

His eyes closed, Josef Ranzner lay on top of Anna, searching for a way out. He felt small and feeble, as if lying on his mother's breast; it was unbearable. He was utterly paralysed, he had no idea how to escape. All his life he had anticipated this, he had known that he must not fall into this trap and now it had happened, he had allowed himself to get carried away by childish excitement and suffer this humiliation. He was filled with disgust, disgust at what he had done, disgust at himself and at the body he lay upon.

Ranzner leaped up abruptly, so quickly that Anna flinched. He leaped up and turned around, he did not even wish to look at her. He pulled his underpants over his wet penis, he fastened his trousers, he smoothed down his shirt and coat. Until, at least to the outside world, he was once more Obersturmbannführer Ranzner, the leader of a wild pack, to whom no-one must dare come too close.

Anna was still lying naked on the divan. She watched Ranzner, in expectation that now he would kill her. She no longer felt any fear, no homesickness for her lost childhood, no hope of getting away unscathed. She had had it all, a whole life, even love had come to her right at the end in the most surprising form possible. Thus Anna lay there, still astonished, for at the same time she knew that, in a dire emergency, she had offered up her most precious possession to stay alive. The greatest mystery of all was how this emergency had taken possession of her, instigating a transformation by which she now saw this man – who stood with his back to her, motionless, as if he were suddenly on the terrace again – in a very different light. It did not counter or efface any of the thoughts, not a single one of the emotions she previously felt whenever she thought of Ranzner. Nothing about him had changed. Anna was lying naked on the divan as if she were a painting, her arms were behind her head and she was ready to sacrifice herself, take the final step without questioning the point of it. That had changed.

Ranzner was standing with his back to her, a conflict between paralysis and flight. He wanted to put everything that had happened into perspective. But everything had already been put into perspective, much more than he had expected, and now he was standing there, fleeing internally, but nothing was moving, not the room, not the woman at his back, not the telegram on the desk in the room next door, which had arrived the previous night, with the order for an immediate retreat to Posen. Everything stayed where it was, even the pistol stayed in its holster at his hip. Shoot her? He could no longer find a reason, for anything.

*

At some point Ranzner's body assumed control. Taking a deep breath, it relaxed and left Ranzner's quarters without turning back or saying a word. Ranzner went down the stairs, aware of having been defeated, and yet heading for the final battle to be victorious, a paradox, a Gordian knot with neither a solution nor a sword in sight. At the bottom of the stairs one of his adjutants held out to him a black overcoat, gloves and a fur hat; he caught himself thanking the man. Ranzner walked through the large vestibule, two S.S. men clicked their heels and opened the broad double doors. He nodded to them – this was something new, too – and went down the broad steps outside to the utility vehicle that had arrived to take the Obersturmbannführer to Posen, to the place where a little more than a year ago the Reichsführer S.S. had spoken of the virtues of the Schutzstaffel, the racial elite of the German people, of the extermination of the Jews in Europe, of bravery and honesty, and of the Russians, time and again of the Russians, who in a last desperate effort would be sending their fifteen-year-olds to the front, only to be repulsed once more by the victorious German army. Ranzner climbed in, the driver saluted and the car set off, taking him away from this town, which now belonged to nobody again, save for the witches and other mythical creatures dwelling behind the windows. Perhaps Poles and Germans and Russians and Jews were just different types of mythical beings in a fairy-tale world of war and annihilation.

THIRTEEN

January the 21st began quietly. There had not been any new snow and it had turned even colder. The wind that had been gusting around the house overnight dropped when the sun rose over the fields of white.

The two women were asleep and between them slept a three-month-old baby by the name of Lisa Kramer. She slept between her mother and grandmother, but of course Lisa did not yet think in such concepts, unlike the authorities with which she would be registered when the snow had melted and the roads were clear again. Lisa did not yet know her mother's name, or at least was unable to disclose it if she did, which was a good thing, for she might have said Margarita, but Margarita did not exist, there was only Maria Kramer, and thus they were three generations sleeping in one bed because there was no longer a man in the house.

Privately Frau Kramer had seen it coming, she had hoped that a mistake might cause her husband's existence to escape the notice of the authorities, even after he had gone to town she had still clung to the hope that Farmer Kramer would play no role in this vast drama which a simple woman like her could not understand. She had reproached herself for having sent him off with the grandfather clock, allowing him to advertise everywhere that here was one more man fit for military service who could be sent to his death.

But she never could have imagined that God or the Devil would choose Lisa's birth as the moment she parted from this man she had loved for almost thirty years, and whose absence over the past three months burned in her heart like a wound. She could never have imagined that Margarita's placenta would be expelled by an intense post-natal contraction at the very moment her husband dashed through the parlour to pack his bags. She could never have imagined that there would be no time for them to say goodbye, to embrace at least and exchange a glance that would say everything, before Herr Kramer left the house to avoid giving the approaching soldiers any cause to enter it, while she ran hither and thither to wash the baby, to dispose of the afterbirth in the cellar, in the same place where Margarita had lain, on the earth beneath the planks, and finally to scrub the pools of blood from the floor, the blood of Margarita who now lay exhausted with her child in the Kramers' marital bed, trying to prevent any sound from escaping outside.

It had been no consolation to her that the birth had gone well that night; she had been irate at him for taking scarcely any food, to ensure they had enough in the house, What an idiot, she had shouted before bursting into tears, while Margarita watched her helplessly from the bed.

But then she had truly become a grandmother, for the woman in confinement could do little, and she had to take care of everything, keep the fire going in the stove, feed and milk the cow, look after the chickens and collect the eggs, knead the dough and bake the bread, skim off the cream and churn some of it into butter – without rennet she could no longer make cheese. Keep the house tidy, prepare meals with what there was. Many tasks her husband used to perform so calmly and taciturnly that she had never noticed just how much he got done. Now Frau Kramer's days were filled with chores and she was also busy sewing clothes for Lisa from those her husband had left behind. By the time he gets back I'll have got him some new things, she thought.

Margarita had not said a word, the two women had listened to the thunder rumbling in the distance, which was no longer so far away, as if that were the answer.

In the weeks that followed, the cannon fire came closer still until it was so near that the two women began to get worried. They told themselves that everything would be fine and that they would surely be given a warning if the Red Army made it through to here. They kept their doubts to themselves, clutching onto daily life. In secret, however, they pondered what they ought to take with them.

One day, when Lisa had been on this earth for a month and Margarita was back on her feet, helping Frau Kramer as best she could, an armoured reconnaissance car appeared on the horizon, tiny as an insect, and battled its way closer. It was a beautiful, sunny winter's day, the sky was clear and the snow reflected the light so brightly that it was impossible to look at for long.

Judging by the direction from which the vehicle was approaching, it must be coming from town. The two women stood by one of the windows that faced east, screwed up their eyes, wiped their hands on their aprons and did not know what to do.

"Shall I go into the cellar with the baby?" Margarita said. Frau Kramer weighed up this option, then said, "No. Go and lie down in bed and pretend to sleep. Let me talk to them. They might be perfectly reasonable souls."

Margarita withdrew to the bedroom, while Frau Kramer stayed at the window watching the armoured car bump across the fields in a straight line towards her. Her own words echoed inside her head. Perfectly reasonable. She sighed. Who was still reasonable in this world?

It was a while before the scout car, with a rattle like a tractor, came to a stop outside the Kramers' farmhouse. It no longer looked small and insect-like, but large and menacing. The cannons towering above the turret pointed directly at the house. At the rear a hatch opened and two men appeared, one after the other. They were so wrapped up against the cold that Frau Kramer could not see their faces.

When she watched them trudge towards the house through the snow, she was seized by a quite insane hope. She fancied that the two men must be father and son, arriving home as if the war had suddenly come to an end because all the soldiers had left the front. Any moment now they would call her name and she would rush out into the cold, throw herself around their necks and feel happy for the first time in a long while.

But the cannon fire in the distance did not stop. Frau Kramer did not budge. She waited until the two men were knocking at the front door. Opening it a crack, she found herself staring into two unfamiliar pairs of eyes, framed by fur hats, hoods and scarves.

"Kramer family?" one of the men said through his scarf.

Frau Kramer nodded. "What's left of it."

The two men exchanged glances, then the other one said, "May we come in for a moment?"

Without saying a word Frau Kramer opened the door and made way to let them in. The soldiers entered the parlour, bringing with them the snow on their boots, and removed hoods, hats and scarves from their heads to reveal two men roughly as old as Frau Kramer's husband. They had with them a piece of paper which said that Wilhelm Kramer, born 1898, would have to report to the territorial army as agricultural production in the Wartheland was no longer vital to the war effort. They shrugged when they learned that the S.S. had taken him already a month ago. One of them said, It's not the first time that's happened to us. The other said, You can't stay here, Frau Kramer. The Russians are going to overrun the entire area. They've got no respect for anything. They abuse our women and kill our children. They asked whether Frau Kramer was alone, but before she could say "Yes", Lisa began to cry in the bedroom.

And so it happened that Margarita Ejzenstain became Maria Kramer, born 25 April 1925 in Ostra, southern Bukovina, the second child of Marta and Wilhelm Kramer, members of the German minority in Romania, resettled to Germanise the Reichsgau Wartheland; mother of Lisa Kramer, born out of wedlock because the father had fallen at the front before her parents could get married. That is precisely what had happened.

Frau Kramer fetched the identification cards and naturalisation documents, she would, of course, hand in Lisa's documents later, but the snow, the cold and their men, who had left and could no longer help, had stranded the two women here, and the Reich had not shown its face again apart from in the form of soldiers who were after even more men for a war she had never asked for, and for which she had sacrificed everything she loved.

The two men looked embarrassed, they reiterated their warning before leaving and Frau Kramer lingered at the window, watching them drive off in their armoured car to the next farm.

*

That evening the new Maria asked her new mother why she had never mentioned her daughter. Dropping her sewing into her lap, Frau Kramer gave her a long stare. She sighed and said, in her sing-song voice, "My dear child, some people take one path in life, others take another." She paused, looking over at the windows, which dimly reflected the light from the paraffin lamp. She said, "Has a farmer's wife ever given birth to a queen?" Nodding, she went on, "Yes, my love, I did, and it was never my intention to, not at all." She shook her head, muttering, "It must have been similar for the Virgin Mary with Jesus. He could talk cleverly about all manner of things, but he never wanted to make furniture." She smiled sadly, before composing herself and saying, more loudly this time, "It's not that bad, boys are different – all wives and mothers know that. They expect boys to be wild and to ignore them. They even love them for it!" She almost shouted that final sentence. Gathering up her sewing again, she said softly, "Maria was the only one of us who was happy to come here." She took a deep breath, closed her eyes, opened them again and raised her eyes to the ceiling, as if something large had appeared there.

"My God, what a mass migration!" she exclaimed, as if to distract herself from the actual subject. "They carted us and other families across the country in covered wagons." She paused, then whispered, "And when we finally got here . . ." she broke off. Like a blind woman grabbing a stick to allow her to go on her way, she picked up her sewing again and got back to work. Margarita could see the tears running down Frau Kramer's cheeks and dropping onto Lisa's new clothes, one after another. She wanted to kiss every single one of them away, she wanted to hug her new mother. But Frau Kramer's grief over the real Maria Kramer pushed its way between the two women and, sitting there with heavy arms and stiff hands, Margarita asked nothing and did nothing.

They spent the rest of the evening in silence. Frau Kramer thought about her children, one dead, the other lost, and about her husband who was gone and might never return.

Maria thought about Tomasz, her Tomasz who, now his child had been born, seemed like a wonderful dream from another time. A dream that from now on she would renounce just as she would renounce the name Margarita. And Tadeusz, too, her elder brother. The two of them had Germans on their conscience. Now she was a German herself.

Her gaze fell on Lisa, sleeping beside her in bed, and for a moment it felt as if all these people had died so this child could be born, as if all of them flowed into this new life, even the German officer she had shot dead an eternity ago, or so it seemed.

Time stood still if you looked out of the window at the frozen expanses of white and into the cold, blue sky. The two women appeared to know that they were the only ones who could still provide movement. They did it slowly and with stoical regularity. They turned away from the icy landscape outside; their new sun was a little baby. Like two planets they orbited around Lisa's smile, Lisa's hunger, Lisa's sleep. They celebrated Christmas with a boiling fowl, New Year's Eve with roast chicken, and they worried about their supplies.

Until 21 January, when everything was quiet to begin with. The two women got up, one fed the child, the other the animals in the stable. Frau Kramer was milking the cow when the artillery burst into life. Startled, she spilled some of the milk, it was so close now. Because there's no wind, perhaps, she wondered.

She returned to the house with the fresh milk. A tall figure with a horse was standing by the front door. It was the pastor, a young man whose hair had turned prematurely grey. His narrow face, with its long, straight nose, and his slender build lent him an ascetic air. Unwrapping himself from his winter clothes, he sat down at the Kramer's table and did not smile when he saw Maria and the child. He said, "I'm going to all the farms around here that haven't heard the evacuation order. They're only evacuating the towns." He looked Maria in the eye. "Do you still have my old revolver?"

"No, Pastor. I'm sorry, but we . . ."

The pastor dismissed her apology with a wave of his hand and sighed. "You'd have found it quite useful now." He looked around the parlour. "You've got to leave today. Only take what's necessary. Head due west. Here," he said, putting an envelope on the table. "Enough money for a week. In case you get the opportunity to use it." Then he said goodbye and rode away to the next farm.

An hour later the two women led the cow, which was hitched up to the cart, to the front door and loaded everything onto it. Most of what they took was food, for themselves, the cow and the four chickens they had put in cages. The rest was clothing and firewood. No furniture, Frau Kramer had said. Maybe if they had still had the grandfather clock. But that was gone now, and in any case it had never looked quite right in this house, You can't transplant an old tree, she said, thinking of the Polish family who had left their roots in the earth here and in every corner of the house.

Maria thought of her child and of the cold, which it did not know, and she was overcome by a new fear, this time for a being who could do nothing, who was completely at the mercy of everything and everyone. She wrapped her child in thick layers, layer after layer until Frau Kramer told her to stop. She said, "The baby must be next to your body. It'll freeze otherwise." Maria unwrapped the child and bound it to her bare skin, its head between her breasts. Then she put so many clothes on top that Lisa was no longer visible.

The thunder of cannon was now so loud that it sounded as if the Russians had arrived in the forest that ran over the hill behind the house and then down to the river – five kilometres away at most – which flowed towards the town.

Maria sat on the cart and Frau Kramer plodded alongside, holding the cow by a rope. They did not look back as the farmhouse behind them got ever smaller. They would never know that the stove would continue throwing out heat for hours before it went cold and with it the air. And they were spared the sight of a Russian tank driving straight through the rear wall ten hours later, burying the Kramers' bed beneath it, pulling down the roof and walls of the rooms, crunching the parlour with the chunky wooden table beneath its tracks, as well as the rest of the farmhouse furniture that did not belong to the Kramers but to the Polish family who had once lived here, not so long ago.

As the Soviet Army's tank division advanced westwards, a house no longer stood in the place where Lisa Kramer had been born.

FOURTEEN

Anna was intent on forgetting nothing. She had set up an archive in her head which she would always access when alone to check that everything was in its place, every memory. But in this archive there was a very particular place whose true significance only became evident later. It was the memory of how she had survived after Obersturmbann-führer Ranzner left without settling his bequest, of which Anna was a part.

The events that occurred meant that, later, Anna did not know who the father of her child was.

When it was all over and she was still alive, when Ranzner's S.S. men had taken the things he wanted to keep and defend in Posen until the last drop of blood had been shed – the Arcimboldo copies, plundered furniture from the past three centuries, his illusions about himself and this war – when the noise of the withdrawing troops in the square outside had faded away, Anna got dressed, went to her room and put on her winter coat with the yellow star on the left breast, in the centre of which the word "Jew" was written in Hebrew-like letters. She had nothing to keep her head warm, no gloves and no winter boots.

She spent a while wandering round the old town hall, looking in all the rooms, recalling the furniture and pictures that Ranzner had dispatched. Once again Anna stood in the place where Ranzner had said farewell to Sturmbannführer Treitz, once again she thought of the conversation about the reincarnation of Nazis, which had opened her eyes to Ranzner's fear.

At some point Anna pushed open one of the double doors of the grand entrance and left the town hall. Tiny snowflakes were falling, they burned her eyes. She went down the steps and crossed the square. The endless imprints of boots, wheels and tracks had already lost their sharp profile, soon they would be nothing but vague indentations, and by the next day an untouched white cover would lie here, like a clean cloth put on a table for the next meal.

Anna meandered aimlessly through the streets and alleys of this small town, she enjoyed the sensation of walking, she enjoyed the gathering cold in her limbs. She enjoyed the emptiness in her head, void of thought.

At some point she found herself standing by the church. To the left a short, narrow alley led further into the old town, and from it the tang of fresh bread wafted to her nose. She was not hungry. Entering the church, she sat on a pew in the front row, gazed at the altar, the candlesticks without candles, the cross in the background to which a man was nailed, his head hanging.

Anna fell asleep, but was abruptly woken by a new noise. People were pouring into the church, old and young women with children. The noise of engines droned outside, men shouted orders. The people flooding in paid no attention to Anna, they looked frightened, some kneeled to pray, the tension written across their faces, children screamed or took refuge in sleep, the old women kept quiet, sitting or standing, wearing headscarves, the most their wrinkles revealed was how they had spent their lives, not how they felt at that moment.

The church became fuller, the laments ever louder.

Anna saw the fear in people's eyes, she understood every feeling that penetrated their senses, and every word. But she was not one of them. She observed the Germans as if she were not in the same room, as if a membrane existed between her and the others, as if the fact that her mother tongue was also theirs had lost all meaning.

Anna stood and wandered down the broad aisle between the rows of pews to the door. The star on her breast made people flinch when she stepped through the throng without looking at them. What's she doing here, one of the women said. Anna prised open the heavy church portal, an icy gust of wind blew in, the brightness blinded her.

Then Anna was outside in the snow. The square had changed. Tanks, lorries and howitzers were everywhere, the tyre, track and boot prints of the Germans were now the tyre, track and boot prints of the Red Army, come to liberate the abandoned town.

Two Red Army soldiers rushed towards Anna, their weapons at the ready. When they saw the yellow star on her coat, their grim expressions changed; they had been in Lublin and in Łódź, they knew what the Germans had done. They sent her across to the other side of the square before storming the church, where it went deathly quiet.

Walking amongst the Soviet soldiers rushing here and there, Anna came to a tracked vehicle, a large van, parked beside the town hall. The building was acquiring a new tenant, the commander of this tank division, whose furniture had already been taken up the large steps and inside.

The vehicle looked like a dark-green tortoise. On the bonnet, the sides and the roof, red crosses were marked in white circles. Anna's lips had turned blue, she no longer felt the cold in her hands and feet, and her face was as stiff as a mask. At the back of the vehicle she knocked on a metal door. It was opened by a small, round woman with chubby cheeks and a button nose. Anna made gestures to signify that she was supposed to come here, the woman helped her climb up, with her frozen hands Anna could not hold on anymore.

It was cramped inside. There were two bunks to the left and right, and a narrow passage between them. On one of the bunks lay a soldier who neither moved nor said a word. His head was bandaged, the bandage was bloody. It smelled of camphor. A second nurse, a small, slim woman with a high forehead and clear blue eyes, sat beside him on a stool. Now she stood to attend to Anna.

The two women treated her with the dispassion of those who had done nothing but witness terrible things and prevent even worse whenever they were able. They sat Anna in a corner of the ambulance right behind the driver's cab, by the head of the bunk on which the soldier lay. They gave her a vodka and wrapped her in warm blankets. From time to time the injured man groaned as if dreaming.

Anna dozed, her limbs warmed up and started to itch. After a while the rear door opened, a man shouted loudly and the two nurses leaped up to take something from him. Enamel bowls with steaming potato soup, Anna was given one. She ate and fell asleep once more.

Somebody was shaking her arm. She opened her eyes, it took a while for her to establish where she was. In front of her stood a slight man in a winter coat that was far too big for him. His cheeks were sunken, he had dark, frizzy hair, his eyes were set deep in their sockets; he looked as if he had not slept in days. Pulling off his black leather gloves, finger by finger, he said in Yiddish, "I'm from the Jewish Antifascist Committee of the Soviet government." He stuffed his gloves into his coat pocket and took a form from the slim briefcase he was carrying. His face was full of curves, the forehead was not only high, but broad, the chin was narrow and round, the arcs of the cheekbones sat just beneath the eyes, the nose was long and bent. A strange face with strange eyes that made Anna feel uneasy. She said, "I only speak German."

He turned to the nurses and said something in Russian. The women nodded as if they did not know what to say. Then he took a stool from the opposite corner and sat in front of Anna. He gave her a fleeting smile, for a brief moment his deathly tired face changed, and Anna could see a different man with a different life and different feelings, for himself, for the world, for Anna. Then it was gone, as if it had never existed, and he said, "I told them you were an abducted Jew. We've got to be a bit careful." He glanced at the nurses again, who were looking over, and gave them a reassuring smile; the women smiled back, which to Anna felt like a kind of agreement, Just let me get on with it, Fine. Turning to Anna he said, "Otherwise they'll think you're a collaborator and you're certainly not one of those, are you?" He smiled at Anna, but now his eyes were prowling. Anna looked at him and saw his timidity and his wildness and heard again the word "collaborator" and knew that both "Yes" and "No" would be lies. She said, "Will you believe me?"

Rocking his head on his thin neck, he said, "Depends how you say it."

"How I *say* it?" Anna raised her eyebrows. She tried to understand what he meant by that, she read his face, she saw his uncertainty and his dangerousness.

"No," she said, "It doesn't depend on that and you know it."

He inclined his head slightly. "You're right, we humans are better encrypted than any secret message. But you've convinced me all the same."

"Of what?" Anna asked.

He looked at her in surprise, frowning as if he had to think about it. Then he nodded slowly and said, "That you're worth it, no matter what you've done."

Anna suspected that this sentence was a lure, that this man was lying in wait for her again, and now he seemed like a hunter, the best-camouflaged hunter ever; with his slight body, his thin neck and his sunken cheeks he looked like the easiest prey, one just had to knock him down. Maybe even Anna was capable of that.

But his eyes betrayed the camouflage. Anna said, "The Nazis talked about people's worth too."

Shrugging, he retreated behind his smile and said, "I trust my knowledge of human nature."

All of a sudden Anna saw this scene from outside; she and the stranger were two gamblers playing invisible roulette, the stake was Anna's life. The game was new, but Anna was well acquainted with the rules, they were ancient. Josef Ranzner had instructed her, and this man sitting before her, keeping a close watch on her, taught her that these rules applied everywhere.

Without warning he terminated the game. He held out a slender hand, conjured a new smile on his face, an open and friendly smile, as if there were no mistrust in the world, and said, "I'm Abba."

Anna took his hand hesitantly, it felt soft and tender. Anna was rattled; she had just seen through him and already he had slipped away from her again.

Abba's gaze returned to the two nurses, who were chatting in hushed tones. Then he turned his attention again to Anna.

"I assume you don't want to go back to Germany?"

Anna shook her head. He nodded.

"Good." He paused briefly to think before continuing. "I'm going to tell you something and then I want you to have a good think about it. The situation of the Jews in the Soviet Union is better: we're not killed, we're fighting on the Russians' side against the Germans, some of us get medals for bravery. We raise money abroad for the Soviet Army." He stopped and looked searchingly at Anna. Lowering his voice, he said, "But no-one knows what's going to happen once this war is over." He paused again. He scrutinised Anna as if trying to read her thoughts; Anna stared back and waited.

"There's an organisation that can help you leave Europe and make for . . ." he hesitated, glancing at the two nurses, then looking Anna in the eye again. "For Palestine. Are you interested?"

Anna nodded without thinking. In Abba's eyes she had seen that by asking this question he was putting himself in danger. This reassured her, for the first time in ages it gave her the feeling that she had something in common with another person.

Abba gave a cursory smile and said quietly, "Excellent. Now I'm going to tell the nurses that I'm taking you to a holding camp for liberated Jews. Until that point everything is legal. Once there you'll wait with others who want to emigrate until we find an opportunity to get you over the border into Romania."

He fished a pen from his coat pocket and filled out the form. Anna had to give her full name, date and place of birth and educational qualifications. Numbers and words sketching an entire life and which now felt oddly abstract, as if they represented a particular position in a system of coordinates, no more. No meadow and no child in it. All meadows looked the same, all childhood was over.

FIFTEEN

"My name is *not* Lisa Kramer," Lisa said at breakfast one morning, glaring at the horrified face of her grandmother. "And I'm *not* a girl, either," she added. Now reassured, her grandmother smiled and asked, "What are you then?"

"A soldier," Lisa replied, watching with delight as a frown appeared on her grandmother's forehead. "A soldier," she reiterated, "like Uncle Tobi upstairs." Frau Kramer shook her head and took a sip from her coffee cup.

"Why do you spend time with that queer fish?"

"He's nice and he tells me wonderful stories," Lisa said casually.

"Wonderful stories about the war, I bet," Frau Kramer said, exhaling through pursed lips as a sign of her disapproval. Lisa ignored her. Dangling her legs, she ate up her bread and assumed an expression of boredom.

"What have you got at school today?" Frau Kramer asked, to change the subject.

"Just stupid lessons," Lisa said with a shrug.

Frau Kramer sighed and looked out of the window. "Would you try to go to school on your own today?"

Lisa shook her head and Frau Kramer gave in. How can I bring you up, she thought, if I indulge your every whim? But as this crossed her mind the answer was already there: she was not bringing up Lisa; Lisa was bringing herself up. She was armed with a knowledge of the world that astonished Frau Kramer, and sometimes the old woman wondered how much the girl had taken in of all the things that had happened to her.

They got ready to leave. One wooden toothbrush sat by the sink, its bristles splayed in all directions. They shared it between them, first Lisa, then Frau Kramer. Coat, shoes, the dark-green satchel made of lacquered linen, practically empty now that some books were banned again, textbooks too, and no new ones coming until next year, but the headmaster had said exactly the same thing last year on Lisa's first day at school.

They descended the narrow spiral staircase to the street and slowly walked the three blocks to school along the cobbled path. There was a light drizzle, as was often the case here; the sea was so close that the air was almost permanently damp, and in winter the cold seeped into everything, even though the temperatures never fell as low as in Poland. In the five years she had been living here, Frau Kramer had only ever known it to be minus twenty degrees once, as it had been when they fled. While Lisa skipped alongside with her satchel, Frau Kramer looked at the tall, narrow, red-brick houses of Lübeck old town, which even now felt alien and inhospitable. Five years in a waiting room, she mused, before banishing this thought and turning to Lisa, who bounced through the streets of her home town without a care in the world, apart from making sure she landed on the next cobblestone she had eyed up.

Lisa's primary school was a red-brick building too, with pointed gables. When they arrived at the entrance, Lisa held up her arms to Frau Kramer, Frau Kramer bent down to Lisa, Lisa pushed up her head and gave her a kiss. "See you later!" she said. Frau Kramer waved and watched her disappear into the building.

Then she slowly went back the way they had come. She was going to sit in the small living room and sew her birthday present for Lisa, a winter coat she had tailored from her own coats. In the kitchen was a table oven made of sheet iron and clay, which they used for heating in winter. There were still a few bits of wood and pine cones in the cubbyhole; these would have to suffice for the fire. Regulating the temperature of the oven was a tricky business, but Frau Kramer would bake a cake for Lisa nonetheless. She would smile and be cheerful, all day long if necessary. As if this were a happy day and not the opposite as well. I owe that to the child, she thought.

Frau Kramer knew that the coming months were going to be difficult for them. She was afraid of winter, which brought out all the pain, all the emotions, all the loss. In her mind's eye she saw Margarita, a pregnant Margarita in the cellar, Margarita screaming in agony at Lisa's birth. The sound of the front door when her husband left without saying goodbye. Margarita with tiny Lisa in her arms. Margarita beside her in bed, where her husband had once slept. Margarita wrapped in thick blankets on the cart. Margarita on foot when the Russians had confiscated everything from them. Margarita with no strength left. Margarita utterly silent, large white snowflakes dancing all about her, no warmth in her body, no baby at her breast, for Frau Kramer had taken care of the child, her tears freezing virtually the moment they appeared in her eyes. Margarita all alone in the snow, as Frau Kramer pressed on with nothing left in this world apart from Lisa. The recollection had been set in motion and could not be stopped. Frau Kramer turned into her street without taking it in, seeing instead their night-time arrival in Lübeck, feeling the endless final march to their temporary home, entering the damp, stuffy barn where she had survived a whole winter with other ethnic Germans from the east. She saw the British soldiers who had brought them to the holding camp just north of Lübeck, only to send them away again a few months later because the camp was needed for new refugees, for Jews. She felt the hunger raging in her belly like a wild animal, in her arms she held Lisa who was getting ever thinner and ever closer to death. She felt the fear of losing her final child as well.

Arriving at the house, Frau Kramer unlocked the door, climbed the stairs with heavy legs, but instead of stopping at the third floor to enter their apartment, she decided to carry on up to the fourth. There were three apartments on each floor and the doors were arranged in a semi-circle around the spiral staircase. Herr Weiss lived on the right-hand side. Frau Kramer pressed the bell and waited.

Herr Weiss took a while to open the door. He was short, not yet thirty, his hips were broader than his shoulders, thick spectacles were perched on his nose and he had thinning brown hair. He was wearing a grey cardigan and grey cloth trousers, both of which looked old and tatty, and had felt slippers on his feet. The smell of tobacco wafted into the stairwell. He smiled uncertainly.

"We need to talk about Lisa," Frau Kramer said.

They talked about Lisa. They sat in Herr Weiss's small living room, which had exactly the same dimensions as Frau Kramer's. Reluctantly she registered that it was perfectly clean and tidy. The furniture was cheap and tasteless, garish pictures of hunting scenes hung on the walls, Heirlooms from my parents, Herr Weiss said, making it sound like an apology. An old piano stood against one wall, Frau Kramer already knew this, she heard him play sometimes. In places the black paint had chipped, and there were spots where the wood had discoloured. The lid was open and a yellowed booklet rested on the music stand.

Frau Kramer forbade Herr Weiss from telling Lisa stories about the war.

"The war is over," she said, giving him a stern look.

Herr Weiss looked back at her timidly and moved his head slowly from side to side, but did not reply.

"You told her," Frau Kramer continued, "that in the war you collected the body parts of dead soldiers. Under covering fire! Herr Weiss!"

Herr Weiss nodded and blinked at her.

"Do you think that's appropriate for a seven-year-old?"

"Well," Herr Weiss said. "Well," he repeated, raising his shoulders. He muttered to himself, then said, "She loves listening to me." There was a definite supplication in his voice. Frau Kramer shook her head. She tried to ignore the sympathy for this eccentric man brewing inside her.

"Herr Weiss," she said, "we all had a difficult time . . ." All of a sudden she could no longer speak. A lump had formed in her throat, her eyes became hot, she battled, but she had already lost.

"There, there," Herr Weiss said, clumsily rubbing Frau Kramer's arm. She had thrust her face in her hands and was now sobbing in front of him. He raised an index finger and said quietly, "I know, I'll make us some tea! That's a good idea, I'll put the water on right away!" He fled to the kitchen and pottered in there until the tea was ready.

In the meantime Frau Kramer had pulled herself together. She dabbed her cheeks with a handkerchief that she had fished from her handbag. When Herr Weiss returned with a bulbous white teapot and two very delicate-looking porcelain cups she sat up straight and gave him a weak smile.

"You're a nice man," she said.

Herr Weiss rocked his head from side to side, muttering, "Hmm, well," then said, "One does what one can." He smiled at her, revealing two rows of crooked teeth that looked like tumbling skittles just hit by a ball. Noticing Frau Kramer's look of horror, he pointed to his mouth and said, "A present from a Russian officer."

"How on earth did it happen?" Frau Kramer asked.

Nodding to himself, Herr Weiss poured the tea and said, "Well, you see . . ." He sat down. "It was when I was a prisoner of war. Each of us had to go up to him, he was sitting behind a little desk, noting down our details – name, date of birth, place of birth, unit, stuff like that."

Rocking his head from side to side, he said, "Try the tea, I think it's excellent." Taking a sip himself and putting the cup back down, he went on, "I didn't immediately understand what he wanted from me, and then he smashed me in the face with his pistol. Like this." Holding up his cup, he drew it to his chin in slow motion. Oh well, he said with another shrug.

"I simply didn't understand him. But my jaw was broken and all I could eat was soup. Oh, and I couldn't talk anymore." He laughed briefly. "I didn't learn how to do that again until I was with the nuns."

"With the *nuns*?" said Frau Kramer, who was drinking her tea, oblivious to the fact that she had become captivated by Herr Weiss' story.

Herr Weiss said, Yes, yes, then nodded, muttered something, said, "Yes, that was the first place I went when I was back in Germany. They sang with me. And yes, it was through the singing that I learned how to speak again." He put down his cup and looked at Frau Kramer with gleaming eyes. "Isn't that amazing? Isn't it? Don't you think?" He raised his hand and made a gesture indicating that some things are merely inexplicable. Frau Kramer nodded and poured herself another cup of tea.

At the end of her visit she invited Herr Weiss to Lisa's birthday, but Herr Weiss had a better idea. He wanted to hold the celebration in his apartment so that he could sing songs at the piano. Frau Kramer considered this for no more than a moment before agreeing and saying goodbye. She went down the stone spiral steps to the third floor, sat by the window in the living room and continued working on Lisa's winter coat.

While she sewed the hems her thoughts wandered back to Herr Weiss's tale of his imprisonment. In her head their neighbour changed, metamorphosing into Herr Kramer, who was brought before a Russian officer, unable to understand what the latter wanted of him. She closed her eyes to expel the thought; it was hard enough living in this town she had headed to only because of a hope that, if he returned from the war, Herr Kramer would surely think that she had come here, because she thought he would think that she would think in this way. But although Herr Weiss had returned from Russian imprisonment, her husband had not. She knew that there were still many thousands of prisoners of war in Siberia, she knew that the government was negotiating with the Soviets. But Siberia! How long could a man of his age survive that? Frau Kramer sighed and went on with her sewing.

SIXTEEN

Anna sat in the car, staring out into the night. The headlights tore a dazzling hole into the darkness and this hole was following them. She was sitting beside Abba in a Soviet utility vehicle, We've borrowed it, Abba told her when they had left the town behind them, it sounded as if he meant: stolen.

It was pure chance that he picked up Anna, The Soviets let me know, he said, They told me they had a Jewish girl and wondered what to do with her.

You're a citizen of Israel, he said when she had asked him what he was really doing, Bricha is gathering up the remnants of what the Nazis left, he said, The foundation of Israel is in danger. He quoted a figure, he said, That's how many Jews there were in Europe before the war, he said, The Zionists know the precise figure, they counted the Jews and now, apart from the few that remain, they're all gone, murdered by the Germans and their many helpers.

Anna had given him a sideways glance of disbelief, she had repeated the figure in a whisper, with a question mark afterwards that said, Are you sure? Isn't that one or two zeroes too many?

But there was no reaction from Abba, he was busy making sure the car did not slide into the bank, the road was rutted with the deep tracks of Soviet Army tanks and lorries, hot on the heels of the Germans, amongst whom were Obersturmbannführer Ranzner and his four adjutants, We're going to Posen, Abba had said, and Anna glanced at him again and thought he looked like a bird of prey with his curved nose and slightly receding chin, sunken cheeks and those eyes that seemed to see more than normal ones. Posen? Anna had asked, Not exactly, came his answer and he told her about a Bricha house that the Soviets tolerated only because they had no idea what to do with the Jews they had liberated, and because in truth they wanted to be rid of them. Nobody wants us, he had said, and that's a good thing, now it's a good thing.

Then he had talked about the doctrine of extermination, he said, The Nazis made no differentiation between Jews and Jews, they treated us all the same. That's what we've got to do now too. Then we'll be a people, a nation. We'll be in a position to establish a Jewish state in Palestine. And we will exact retribution. Retribution? Anna said, and Abba nodded without looking at her. He had talked about the armed struggle, about the need to kill large numbers of Germans so as to galvanise Jews throughout the world and to say: Nobody can murder us and go unpunished! He cited the figure again, staring grimly out into the cold night, an eye for an eye and a tooth for a tooth, he said, We shall poison the whole of Hamburg, Jewish blood will be avenged, and Anna thought, Is this what he's really doing, killing Germans? and just for a second she was beset by that same feeling from her past, when she still had a home. It was no more than a memory and it passed again immediately, and she said, That's no different, it's exactly the same madness, but Abba refused to accept this.

Following this conversation they had driven silently through the night. Later Anna would remember an endless avenue of birches. The white trees stood ghostlike to the left and right of the road, their slender branches hanging down like thinning hair.

Anna had been hunched up in her seat with cold, her arms wrapped around her body, trying to imagine an unimaginable number of dead people. In her head a solid mass of corpses had appeared, stretching to the horizon, the mass had buckled upwards, ever higher, turning into a tall, unscalable mountain. Where are they all now, she had wondered, thinking about reincarnation, in another life when she was still the Anna she knew, not the stranger sitting in this car beside a Jew intent on taking her to Palestine, because this was his business, beside a Jew intent on murdering as many Germans as the Germans had Jews, to restore the balance, Which balance, Anna wondered, on which scales?

As they drove through a coniferous forest, the road narrowed, the trees coming right to its edge. Anna felt uneasy, as if the forest were waiting to swallow her up the moment they came to a halt. It was still snowing, the flakes were larger now, they stuck to the windscreen and the wipers were no longer a match for them. From time to time Abba had to wind down his window and wipe with his gloved hand, allowing an icy gust of wind to shoot into the car, whirling snowflakes around. Abba sat hunched over the steering wheel, peering through the clear spot. He drove in silence, betraying no emotion, Anna thought, For him nothing is of any significance compared to the cause he's fighting for: Israel, retribution. Are these two separate things, she wondered, or one and the same?

Once out of the forest they could see the lights of a town in the distance. That's Posen, Abba said without turning to look at her, but Tulce is closer. This was the name of the village where Bricha maintained its house, The guards are Russian Jews, Abba said, Red Army soldiers. We borrowed them from the army because if we want to survive we can't trust anybody, a rule you'd better stick to. He looked at her, Anna stared into his dark eye sockets and did not know what she should feel positively or negatively about this man.

The house was square with eight windows on each side, all dark, two storeys high, the roof damaged, Aerial bombs, Abba said, But it's warm and you'll be safe there.

Anna learned that during the war Polish forced labourers had sewn uniforms here for the German army. No-one knows where they are now, Abba said.

The main entrance was a door on the right flank of the building. Abba drove up, in the beam of the headlights Anna could see that the plot of land on which the house stood was also square, but larger and surrounded by dense scrub and low trees.

Abba turned off the engine, the headlights went out, it was silent and dark at a stroke. They turned to each other, but neither could make out the other's face, their movement was a habit which had become pointless without any light.

"Go on in," Abba said, "and tell them Abba sent you. Say the following: Ad Lo-Or." Anna repeated it, Abba smiled.

"Your first Hebrew lesson."

"What does it mean?"

"It's a key to that door there. Behind it lies Israel. Best of luck!"

"Thank you."

Anna got out, Abba started up the car, turned around and drove off to continue his fight for Israel and retribution. Watching him go, she had this sudden sense that she would miss him. He had felt like a breath of fresh air.

She approached the entrance. The door opened, a glaring light shone into Anna's face, a man's voice asked something softly in Russian. Anna did not understand, she spoke her text. The torch went out and now Anna could identify a gigantic shadow gesturing to her to follow. At the end of the corridor they walked along, Anna could see a staircase leading up, but they only went as far as the second door on the left.

The shadow opened the door, beyond which darkness stretched into a large room, Anna saw night through the windows, three times eight, breathing, wheezing and coughing sounded from myriad invisible mouths, the shadow moved slowly in front, Following closely like a blind woman, Anna stepped right into the middle of the breathing, wheezing and coughing, right into the middle of the stuffy warmth of many bodies, into the stench of countless odours of unwashed people. Israel flashed through her mind, and if she had not been so tired, feeling at that very moment all the uncertainty of her life so intensely, like a pain in her chest, a stabbing, tearing pain, then perhaps she would have laughed out loud.

The shadow stopped, Anna bumped into him, he grabbed her by the forearm and pulled her down until her hand was touching rough material. Anna understood, this was her place, now she was another breathing and when she slept another wheezing, panting and coughing, a dreaming and a waking in this room which was Israel.

SEVENTEEN

Anna did not count the days she spent in the house near the gates of Posen in the small village called Tulce, while Obersturmbann-führer Josef Ranzner, his four adjutants and the rest of his troops, together with other S.S. units, Wehrmacht officer cadets, policemen, firemen and territorial army soldiers tried to defend Posen against the Red Army. The thunder of artillery was audible day and night, so close that at some point Anna barely noticed it and even caught herself relishing the fact that the noise insulated her from the others in the house.

The cramped conditions bothered her. Unlike many Jews Anna had no experience of being kept like cattle. Or perhaps I was a different variety of cow, she thought, a variety which stands alone in its stable, a variety which isn't exterminated en masse, but which is ridden from time to time. She dismissed the thought, it was not helping her come to terms with her new situation.

The house in Tulce had two large rooms one above the other, full of people doing nothing but waiting. The camp beds were pushed together in pairs, with narrow gangways between the rows, scarcely wider than a person,. There were no gaps between the foot of one bed and the head of the next. To Anna's left, on the other side of the gangway, was a woman with three children: a boy of ten, a girl who was six at most and an infant, another girl. The four of them shared two beds.

Anna's head was right by the feet of an old man who only got up from his bed if he absolutely had to. He wore a striped prisoner's suit, over this a Waffen S.S. coat, and he gave off a rancid stench. It took Anna's nose a while to be able to ignore him. She was too big for the camp bed; if she stretched out fully her feet touched the head of an elderly lady who appeared to be on her own.

To her right, and so close it was as if the two of them belonged together, was a young girl, seventeen years old at most. My name's Ruth, she said the night Anna arrived. You're lucky, Ruth whispered, as Anna felt for the bed with her hands and carefully lay down on it. Your place only became free yesterday, she said. Anna lay on her back and her eyes would not close, her body did not yet wish to be here in this alien place, which was supposed to be a piece of their homeland, full of comrades sharing a common destiny, but to her this seemed a strange notion, Anna's destiny had run a separate path from that of all the others, How can I be one of them if we have nothing in common, no experiences, not even a language? she asked herself. But Ruth spoke German, she came from Schwerin, which was not so far from Anna's village, and that night she whispered to Anna that the old man had been in a terrible state, Hardly a surprise, she said, I'm young and the camp took everything out of me. But him! It was a miracle he'd got this far. Then she sighed and said, but he's had his time and you've got a bed.

Anna fell asleep.

When she awoke it was light.

"Morning!" a voice beside her said. Anna turned to her right and saw Ruth. Ruth had barely any hair on her head. Ruth had large eyes and a small, shrunken face. Ruth had arms as thin as her bones, which protruded from beneath her skin. Ruth wore several striped prisoner's suits on top of one another. Ruth smiled.

"That's enough sleep!" she said. "What's your name?"

"Anna."

"Where do you come from? What's your story? Tell me!"

Anna stared at Ruth. She did not know how she could keep quiet about what had happened to her, thus learning a great deal more about what had happened to her. She saw Abba open his mouth and utter the word "collaborator". Ruth was not observing her like Abba, she lay beside Anna, supporting her head with her hand, waiting with the childish curiosity of one who trusts their peers.

Only now did Anna understand that Abba must have seen through her, the only Jewish woman alive in a western Polish town occupied by the Germans, what must she have done? She realised that Abba had pardoned her, not for her sake, but for Israel. She wanted to say something, a half-truth, so Ruth would leave her in peace, I was a forced labourer for the S.S., but how does that sound? she thought, and remained silent.

"Doesn't matter," Ruth said suddenly. "There are some people here who haven't said a word yet. I'm not especially pretty, they were going to let me work until the effort of it finished me off." She gave a crooked smile, her mouth was so large in her small face, Anna thought and found herself wishing, If only I'd been in a camp too, I'd be one of them now and could tell my story. Or I'd be dead, one of the countless many, and no-one would ask me questions.

There was no kitchen in the house, the food came from the village where the men from Bricha bought it and had it prepared. Twice a day people came up the snowy main street with ox carts to the House of the Jews and unloaded their wares in wooden tubs, thin broths made from bones cooked up so many times there was scarcely anything left in them. Sometimes a cat, which had to be shared between two hundred hungry mouths. On the way to the Jews it got cold, there was no way of heating it up again in the house. Better than nothing, said Ruth, who knew only too well what nothing meant.

At mealtimes everyone had to get to their feet, including the old and infirm, Standing up is good, the Red Army soldiers said, Standing up means surviving. Ruth helped the old man at whose feet Anna slept, I picked him out, she told Anna, You have to be there for someone. Ruth did not want any help, she pulled the man up in three stages, first sitting, then kneeling, finally he was standing and Ruth was sweating and shaking from the effort, but Anna was astonished at the strength in this body which was nothing but skin and bones. The old man let it happen, keeping a straight face, not saying a word, his skull and face were covered in a grey fuzz, his eyes were as large as Ruth's, his body as frail, he could not weigh much, but still.

People lined up behind each other in a queue that wound its way twice through the room and moved at a snail's pace between the beds, while the Red Army soldiers stood out in the hallway where the stairs to the room above, the main entrance and the door to Anna's room met. Each person held an enamel cup in one hand and a spoon in the other, Anna had inherited both from the dead man, Take good care of those, Ruth told her, No cutlery or crockery means no food, like in the camp.

At first glance the queue might have appeared to consist of people in striped pyjamas – the camp uniforms – and members of the S.S., all standing together patiently. Some wore entire uniforms, you could even see the bullet holes in the material, Where on earth are they from? Anna asked and Ruth shrugged, saying, the Russians gave them to us because there's nothing else, they said.

One ladle per person and then you returned to your bed. The impatient ones drank their soup straight from the cup and it was all gone in a couple of minutes, But if you're smart you'll eat with your spoon, Ruth said, Slowly, look, like this. She carefully dipped her spoon into the soup, then lifted it up, higher. The spoon arrived at Ruth's mouth, but rather than putting it straight in she took tiny sips from the side. She looked deadly serious, as if performing a ritual. When the spoon was empty, she put it down and gave Anna a smile of satisfaction, This way your stomach thinks there's more, she said, And you believe it, too. Anna nodded, she understood perfectly this principle of necessary self-deception, she had practised it herself for years, albeit in a different way from Ruth.

Once a week, on Saturdays, a Bricha lorry arrived, two men would jump out and open the tailgate, and then they would get better things to eat, vegetables, dried meat, dried fruit, chocolate. They could see from the packaging that these were from the Red Army.

The woman with the three children was called Abramowicz. She was a Polish Jew who until recently had lived in her apartment in Posen, only escaping to the surrounding area when the S.S. beat her husband to within an inch of his life outside their house, before taking him away. Mrs Abramowicz had stood by the window and watched, her hand covering the eyes of her eldest, ten-year-old Ariel. Ariel was a quiet boy who liked nothing better than to read the only book they had been able to take with them when they bundled up everything and fled out of town via the back stairs – *Oscar Koelliker, The First Circumnavigation of the World by Ferdinand Magellan and Juan Sebastián del Cano. 1519–1522. Compiled from Sources by Oscar Koelliker. With 32 Plates and Maps. Munich, H. Piper & Co., 1908.*

Since that day Mrs Abramowicz barely had a drop of milk in her breasts for her youngest, Dana. The people in the village won't sell us any, she said, falling silent. Anna looked at the baby. It was thin, but not as thin as Ruth or the old man, which she found reassuring.

Anna listened to her inner self. Confusing things were going on inside her, things she was unable to capture and control in her thoughts. She sat or lay on her camp bed. She wore the coat with the yellow star day and night, for it was not as warm as Abba had said, hardly any firewood was left, most of it had been confiscated or already burned by the enemy armies. There was no lavatory, they had to go out of the house and relieve themselves in the undergrowth, then clean themselves with snow, which had led to several women developing an inflammation of the bladder.

Anna felt unwell because of a power struggle waging inside her. If she felt so unwell that she was unable to eat anything, it meant the good side had won. Then she would share her cold broth, help Ruth feed the old man whose foot odour had by now become a part of her life and give Mrs Abramowicz's children her dried meat and chocolate.

She became thinner. Her periods stopped, That's normal, Ruth said, I haven't menstruated in ages. At the same time Anna knew she was not starving herself in an attempt to share in their destiny, to be able to tell of the suffering of all, a suffering which would finally become hers too. The truth was that Anna was trying to starve the truth out of existence, make it no longer true.

She laid her palms on her belly and looked at Mrs Abramowicz's baby fast asleep on the camp bed. It slept a lot, Perhaps, Anna thought, to save energy and stay alive, and she concentrated on the palms of her hands, as if through them she could feel whether the same was happening behind her abdominal wall. No sooner has it come into being than it needs to sleep, Anna thought, Because I believe that if I starve I'll gain control over my body and my destiny. Over my life. Over the past. She shook her head.

She did not tell anybody anything.

She stopped giving away her food.

One day the thunder of artillery stopped. It was around lunchtime, Anna was drinking her soup made from bones, and all of a sudden it fell silent, and all of a sudden they heard the slurping of the hundred mouths, the slurping and clanking of spoons, metal on metal, each tiny cough, each whispered conversation. Everyone paused, waiting for it to start up again. But it was over.

The following day someone at the window exclaimed, Look, look everybody! They hurried over and saw men walking past, lots of men, an endless procession passing along the village road and moving eastwards, men in rags, men in the tattered uniforms of the German Wehrmacht and S.S., vanquished men with expressionless faces, filthy men who were still alive, but only just, heading towards an uncertain future, Now they've got their own death march, said Ruth, who knew only too well what death marches were.

Anna thought of Ranzner and his four adjutants, if they were still alive they would surely be passing by here. She stood at the window for a whole day, scanning thousands of faces, Would I recognise them? she wondered, recalling their facial features, one after another, she recalled each one in detail, close-ups were stored in her special archive, she retrieved them and tried to add the Battle of Posen, the hardship, the defeat and everything she identified in the eyes, mouths and cheeks of the soldiers marching past the House of the Jews, to anticipate what they looked like now. But it did not really work, the images could not be altered, returning time and again to their original forms. Why do I want to see them anyway? Anna wondered, If I knew that one or two or three or all of them were still alive, what would that mean? Although no answer emerged she stood at the window until it became dark and pointless. Then she lay down on her narrow berth, feeling poisoned by all the defeated men who had walked past.

When spring arrived, the shrubs and trees around the house began to come into blossom. Had it not stunk so much of the excrement scattered all over the place and which had now thawed, it would have been almost idyllic.

Anna and Ruth went on long walks, which took them out of little Tulce into the countryside, where the life that still existed had recovered its natural rhythm. The trees and fields turned green, lending the landscape an unspoiled beauty which appeared to know nothing of the past few years, as if the war had been one long winter and now both had come to an end. Better than any death march, Ruth would occasionally comment when they were out, and Anna had the impression that this girl, too, was preoccupied with not forgetting.

She had got used to Ruth, despite her verbosity. The girl linked arms with her as they walked, and while they were enjoying the countryside she would talk almost incidentally about her experiences, There were plenty of German Jews with Polish passports, you know. I never knew before how many we were, but the Nazis showed us, they did a sort of racial census almost as soon as they came to power, and look, there were a few thousand Polish Jews living in Germany who thought of themselves first as Germans, then Jews and finally Poles. The Nazis turned that on its head, they sent us letters which said, No, after close examination of the circumstances, we can inform you that in the first instance you are Poles, then Jews, and have never been Germans. So out you get! Well, Ruth shrugged, Anna felt the movement on her arm, We didn't have a choice. We couldn't even take our things with us, only two suitcases per family and off we were on a train to Poland. So then we're in Warsaw, and I'm sure you know what happened in Warsaw, don't you? Anna did not know, Ruth told her, for she had heard it from other women, We didn't stay in Warsaw ourselves, we went west to the German border, because of course we didn't believe a word the Nazis said, They're insane, my father said, you know, my father is, he was, an enlightened individual, truly, he was a sort of armchair Zionist, you know, one of those who wasn't active and certainly didn't want to emigrate, because they thought it was all just a wonderful pipe dream, but on the other hand they didn't have anything against young people dreaming a bit and working towards it. It's good to stand up for your ideals, he said. In our apartment there was a collection box for Palestine, he'd put money into it whenever he had a little spare. She laughed, But that wasn't very often, because we weren't rich, hardly surprising, he was orthodox and my mother didn't earn enough to finance Israel too. But of course she approved of his donations. Ruth sighed, Once a year a young man from the local association of Zionists would come round, empty the box and take the money away with him. Then it would slowly fill up again. Where was I? Oh yes, we were heading to western Poland, but what bad luck! Out of the blue the Nazis came over the border and said, We've had enough of you!

Ruth fell silent. The sounds of nature drifted once more into Anna's ears, the chirping of the birds, the gentle swish of the wind blowing through the leaves and grasses, and brushing the young fields. Well, and then, Ruth said after a pause, we were separated, the men and women, and my mother and I were sent to a camp in Silesia. You won't have heard of it, it's called Grünberg, what am I saying, it *was* called Grünberg, it's funny, I'm talking as if everything's still there, well, we had to leave the camp because it was disbanded, and the Nazis thought, Let's take the women for a walk, she assumed a rough voice and said, In this *lovely* weather! – Pause.

Chirping, wind, sun, feet on the earth, step by step, two women, one on the other's arm, in the distance a forest.

And then, Anna, Ruth said, we walked and walked, now she turned to her new friend, giving her a look of such intensity that Anna took fright at the serious expression in her eyes, for she had understood that Ruth would talk about her death march as if it had been a stroll, but surely she could not keep it up, this she saw as she looked into Ruth's deathly serious face, which now turned away again and gazed at the land-scape as if nothing had happened, And then, Ruth said, I tried to drag my mother across the German Reich, she laughed brightly, it sounded like the laugh of a happy girl, You won't believe, she cried out into the Polish countryside, how heavy your mother can be! Like lead, especially when you only weigh twenty kilos yourself. So we weighed nothing and yet we hardly made any progress, and my mother – pause.

The landscape thrust itself towards them, the sounds – but now Anna wanted to hear what had happened, not because she was expecting a surprise as you might get in a good story, but because she knew what was coming and she wanted it finally to be stated, to be over, for listening to death was sheer torture, she would rather feel life. But then, to Anna's surprise, Ruth said, Well, you can imagine what happened next, can't you?

Anna nodded, half relieved, half disappointed, I wonder why, she asked herself, Is it because release doesn't come until everything's out? So she said, Then your mother died, didn't she? And she looked at Ruth, who turned away and pretended to be gazing still at the landscape, and who nodded and said, Yes, exactly.

Ruth no longer looked like someone who had recently been liberated from a concentration camp, her eyes and mouth no longer seemed so big, her face was no longer so small and shrunken, her hair had grown, and when Anna said, You look good, Ruth gave a crooked grin and said, slightly too loudly, Thirty kilos! Slowly I'm beginning to be like my real self again. But both of them knew that nobody was granted such a return journey.

On the day no ox carts came to the house with food, the Jews in the Jewish house thought it must be an accident or a mistake, perhaps the carter, an old and somewhat frail man missing all his teeth, had fallen ill and found nobody to take his place. They shrugged; they had experienced worse, much worse. We'll just wait till tomorrow, Ruth said.

But the carts failed to arrive the next day or the day after that. The Red Army soldiers guarding the house set off and came back with bad news. The villagers did not like the Jewish house. They did not like the stench of Jews that sometimes wafted through their windows when the wind was easterly. They did not want to see Jews taking walks in their Polish countryside. And they had made it plain to those who had been delivering food to the Jews for months that they were not to feed them anymore. Ruth was beside herself, They're mad, she screamed, but Mrs Abramowicz just shook her head, saying, Nothing's changed here.

Fear had returned. During the siege of Posen the people in the Jewish house had lived in dread, for they could not be certain that the Germans would not conjure a miracle weapon out of nowhere and rout the Russians. But then Germany had surrendered and spring had come. We allowed ourselves to get hoodwinked, Ruth said bitterly, and the old man spoke for the very first time, saying in Yiddish, *Ribono shel olam kenn nischt iberuul zein*, by which he meant that the creator of everything, the whole world, could not look in on every little corner because it was all too big. And the old man said this with a covert rancour, for he had refused to speak to God and his world since being forced to accept that the Ribono shel olam had failed to ensure that things such as gratuitous hatred and bloodlust and systematic humili- ation and torture and gassing and betrayal of one's own people did not exist amongst human beings.

One week later the Red Army soldiers were withdrawn. They made faces like people who know that this time they could not obey the order. But they did obey. They warned the people in the house, they said, The minute you notice something suspicious, run away. Then they left, taking their weapons with them.

"We need to guard this place ourselves," someone said. Anna volun- teered. And so, together with five others, three men and two women, she spent her first night in a long time outside. They dispersed around the building, looking out and listening in the dark. One of the men gave Anna a truncheon, she said, What am I supposed to do with that? and put it down.

For two days everything was quiet. For two days they contemplated how they might escape without leaving anybody behind. The goyim aren't going to get any more of us, not a single one, said those who had been in concentration camp. Not a single one, they reaffirmed emphatically.

They allocated people to carry the elderly and children, so it could proceed quickly if need be. They practised for two days, then someone shouted, They're coming, and in a flash everyone was on the move, the hallway turned into a bottleneck because of the people streaming from the first floor, which is why they decided that those who were able should climb through one of the eight windows that faced east.

No longer did anyone think, That's a bit excessive. Nothing was excessive anymore.

They came at night.

They came as if a pogrom were a performance, a mediaeval play that had to be enacted as realistically as possible. They came with torches and pitchforks, with truncheons and ropes and pistols. They came with wrath and although they themselves did not know who had bequeathed it to them, they knew precisely on whom they had to vent it. Men, particularly men, old, young, some practically still children, a few women amongst them too. With them came the village dogs, which normally roamed freely, but now they had been put on short leashes, and the dogs felt the energy, panting as they dragged their masters onwards, as if hunting hares.

They headed down the village street to the eastern edge, where the house stood. They went in silence to surprise the Jews in their building.

They arrived at the Jewish house, but arrived too late, for the Jews had heard them coming and had taken flight, they had climbed out of the eight windows, rushed down the stairs, they had dragged the old people out of the house, in the darkness they had run through the stinking and scented undergrowth, made their getaway across the fields that stretched out to the rear. They had left everything, the little that they had still possessed was lost now too.

Anna carried Maria, the six-year-old daughter of Mrs Abramowicz. The girl clung to her, trembling, she did not whine, she did not cry, the Jews kept as quiet as the Poles had, over this night lay a great, collective Shush!

The Jews hurried through the darkness, crossed a stream that flowed into the village, and when they were two kilometres away they fell to the ground in a cornfield and rested and gazed up at the night sky studded with stars, two hundred people. The last to arrive were those carrying others, including Ruth. She and a man were bearing the old man, who had resumed his silence like an act. Now they lay exhausted, gasping for breath on the still-cool earth.

We can't stay here, one of the women said after a while, They'll find us in the morning. They picked themselves up, the young carried the old and children again. Then they continued until dawn, until they came to a forest that offered greater security. While they walked, Anna felt that this was the way into the Promised Land, that this must be the final exodus, and perhaps its only purpose was to strengthen them in what they were.

But what else are we to think now, after all that's happened? she wondered, without knowing the answer.

EIGHTEEN

The lorry came from the west. It had belonged to the U.S. infantry, but that was some time back. Six months before, two civilians had helped themselves to it from the fleet of various American units. They were men with British passports. This was not any old lorry they had stolen, but a vehicle captured from the Wehrmacht, which had been repainted and was no longer of much use now that the Allies could do as they wished with Germany and her property.

Since then it had been in almost constant use, today being no exception. The first vehicle was followed by four civilian lorries, all different, the livery of the companies they had once served still visible beneath the makeshift coat of green paint they had been given.

They had set off at dawn and taken minor roads to avoid Allied patrols and the great floods of refugees. As the lorries were empty they had managed to pass a few checkpoints relatively cheaply. It was one o'clock in the afternoon when they crossed the border into the former Wartheland. The sun was shining, there was barely a cloud in the sky and the drivers were starting to sweat behind their dusty windscreens.

The roads were full of army legions, people on foot, some heading east, others west, it was difficult to gauge their goal, were they panic-buying or fleeing or finally returning home? All were loaded with bags and sacks, all looked like people who would never give up, not for anything.

The lorries drove the last portion of the journey via Landsberg an der Warthe, Schwerin an der Warthe, Birnbaum. They gave Posen a wide berth and it was late afternoon by the time they reached their destination.

A man leaped from the passenger door of the first lorry, he was wearing a British officer's uniform, he moved gracefully.

His name was Peretz. He spoke several foreign languages with a Hebrew accent.

He approached the house, followed by the driver, a thickset man with a receding hairline and a red face that made him appear as if he were under permanent stress. With small steps he followed Peretz as he strode to the house. They screwed up their noses at the stench that hung in the air. The driver and passengers of the other lorries waited, engines running.

They vanished into the house, reappearing a few minutes later. Peretz made a gesture that told the others, The house is empty. The other drivers got out and gathered around him.

"Looks like they left in a hurry," he said. "There's all sorts of stuff lying about that people would normally take with them." They turned and looked back at the village they had driven through. No-one articulated their thoughts. Peretz glanced around. He pointed in the opposite direction.

"If they came to the house from there, then our people must have fled that way."

The others nodded, it was the logical conclusion; when you escape you take the same line as that of your pursuers, human beings are not rabbits. They got back into their lorries and drove on.

Peretz had an intuitive feeling for fugitives. He had come to Europe in the same British Army uniform he was wearing now. With thirty thousand other Jews from Palestine he had fought against the Nazis in Italy. A Jew in hiding behaves no differently from a Nazi in hiding, Peretz said later to his contact man at the Institution for Immigration B, who asked whether he dared stay in Europe and find Jewish survivors for Israel. The other man had frowned, but Peretz knew what he was talking about, his experience of the Nazis was not of them as monsters, but as defeated foes.

Now he was unerringly leading his convoy towards a forest about ten kilometres to the east of Tulce. The sun was setting when they arrived. A lustre lingered over the fields, but the forest loomed dark and impenetrable before them when they stopped on the road that ran alongside it at a small distance.

The silence of the transition from day to night enveloped the men who now got out of their lorries and looked towards the forest. Peretz went back to the stowage area and brought out a Wehrmacht loudhailer, a large, green, lead funnel riddled with scratches. He had taken it from a German soldier he had shot dead. Since then he had kept it with him as an item of war booty and a symbol, for he had the specific feeling that he, Peretz, had wrested all linguistic control over reality away from the Nazis and was now in possession of it himself. The imperial eagle was still visible on the side of the loudhailer. But Peretz had scratched away the swastika beneath it and in its place carved a star of David that looked a little scrawled.

Now Peretz, hailer in hand, approached the edge of the forest. When he had gone a few metres he stopped and broadcast in Hebrew, in German and in Yiddish, "This is Peretz Sarfati from Bricha, the Jewish organisation for escapees! We're here to take you to safety! Please come out! We'll take you away from here!"

He waited. It would not matter if they believed this was a trap set for them by Polish anti-Semites. Peretz knew that there was always one amongst them who would take the risk. They were the chancers, those for whom it was all or nothing.

Peretz could never have imagined, however, as the woman approached him, that he would be looking into a face devoid of fear. He felt that she was eyeing him in a way with which he, who thought he had seen everything, was unfamiliar.

He could never have imagined it possible to suffer such a shock at the sight of so much beauty in a face, of a body's movements, of the strange energy emanating from it.

When the woman was standing in front of him, allowing her gaze to roam across the men and lorries of Bricha, Peretz was lost for words. He stared at her in disbelief and forgot why he had come.

"Are there more of you in the forest?" Peretz's driver called from the lorry.

Anna nodded. Turning to Peretz, she said, "The people from the house in Tulce and others who were already there when we arrived. I don't know if we'll all fit in your lorries."

It was obvious that a woman like this should have such a voice, Peretz thought. Pulling himself together, he said, "I'll call them again." He took a few steps back from Anna and repeated his announcement, but this time his voice sounded shrill and nervous.

Now there was greater movement in the shadows of the trees. People gradually emerged from the forest and crossed the field. When they had all arrived where the lorries were parked they had left behind a broad swathe of trampled corn.

They stood in silence on the road, peering expectantly at the faces of their helpers. Peretz realised that Anna was probably right and that there were too many of them. To avoid losing his train of thought again, he ignored her and gathered his men around him.

They did, in the end, manage to pack everyone into the lorries, but afterwards Peretz swore that he would never do anything like that again. The suspicion niggled at him that the only reason he *had* done it may have been to deny Anna the satisfaction of being right.

Fitting everyone in was a proper squeeze. They stood there like cattle, body pressed against body, nobody could sit. It was worst for those who had already been transported in this manner, in the opposite direction and in cattle wagons that brought them to concentration camps. But it was bad for the children, too, who were encircled by bodies that towered over and threatened to collapse on top of them like tall waves whenever the lorries negotiated a bend or had to brake.

The return journey took longer than the drive there. The vehicles were hopelessly overloaded and on the poor roads could only proceed at walking pace. If an axle breaks now, Peretz worried, but the thought did not reach its conclusion because Anna's face got in the way, Anna who was standing in the cargo area behind, and Peretz felt nothing but anticipation. My God, you're all over the place, Peretz thought apprehensively.

On the floor beneath him lay numerous cartons of American cigarettes, with which they paid off the Russian soldiers at the checkpoints. Whenever one of the guards had a pang of conscience and asked, "What are you transporting in your lorries," they told the truth: Jews. What do you want with Jews? most would ask in surprise, and they would reply, We want to get them out of Europe. They even earned the occasional praise, the soldiers would say, You ought to have done it sooner, then we would have been spared all this mess, or, A good thing too, get rid of them! After all, they're the ones responsible for this debacle. Given this response, Peretz would offer a friendly smile from the passenger seat and say, "Exactly what we think too."

They drove at night through conquered Germany, where at any moment the road could be congested with refugees on their way west. Where one unexploded bomb after another detonated during the clearing up operations. Where vast numbers of people, without a roof over their heads, spent the mild night by the side of the road, some lying half on the asphalt because it was less damp, having to take care that they were not run over by lorries.

Peretz had never imagined that such a total defeat would be possible, yet now it was a fact of everyday life. But as his mind turned again to Anna, he felt that everyday life was over and a new era was beginning.

Anna was trying to protect her belly. Marja was standing between her and Mrs Abramowicz, who held Dana, shielding her from the other bodies pressing on them. Ariel was standing behind Mrs Abramowicz. Ruth was somewhere up front with the old man.

Marja's head was pushing against Anna's abdomen, but they were so closely packed that Anna could not see the girl because another body, the broad back of the mother, filled the gap above the girl, leaving Anna no room to move. The pressure of the bodies jammed against each other was so great that Anna could lift her feet from the floor without sliding back down. She thought, We're wedged in so tightly that we could all lift our feet. What an image, Anna thought, a bunch of Jews learning to fly inside a lorry.

Anna could not move her arms. It was stuffy and hot. After a while a peculiar sensation rose within her. It rose like a flood and threatened to suck her under. All she wanted was to get outside into the fresh air, move her arms and legs, she would rather sleep in the forest in fear of the Poles or anybody else who hated Jews, she was used to that. But this here jeopardised her self-control. How do the others manage? Anna wondered. She stared at the faces of her fellow sufferers. They looked strangely abstract in the darkness, reduced to their essential features like the sculptures of an artist who has conceived how to represent the same thing again and again in very different ways.

Intense concentration, this is what Anna saw, intense concentration to avoid losing one's head and cracking up or screaming wildly. Intense concentration to avoid causing suffering to those in a situation as dire as their own.

Anna took as deep a breath as her constricted lungs would allow and tried to calm herself. If you survive this, the thought occurred to her, then you'll get married. She almost burst out laughing.

Hours passed. The monotonous drone of the engine, the immobility inside these lurching vehicles and the unvarying darkness enfolding the passengers, although dawn was already breaking outside, sent feelings and thoughts into a loop impossible to break out of. Most of them bore up and hung on as they had over the past few years: they swam in their boundless inner selves like castaways whose only goal is land, whose minds have not descended into chaos only because they have learned to suffer longer than they have suffered already, to bear up and hang on for even longer.

Anna copied the children: she fell asleep, thereby discovering another use for the support her body received from the squash of others'.

As the lorries with their dense cargo crossed the final demarcation line, thereby arriving at last in the American sector of Berlin, Anna was dreaming of Israel. While the men in the drivers' cabs breathed a sigh of relief and felt quite differently, even though they were still sitting on their sore backsides and still travelling along bumpy roads, Anna glimpsed a light, the like of which she had never seen before, warm and lustrous it settled on the ochre-coloured earth, the earth-coloured houses and the gently undulating sea. When Peretz had bribed the final checkpoint with cigarettes and they could be absolutely sure that no-one would prevent them from reaching their destination, Anna's dream slipped down, down, down into her belly, and in the darkness she saw a pair of eyes as blue as the sea.

When the convoy came to a stop and the men opened up the back of the first lorry several people collapsed onto them; they had passed out from the exhaust fumes that were particularly noxious at the very rear. Most of the passengers had become so stiff that they needed to be helped down. The legs of others had gone dead. But the majority had hung on and now descended the ramp unsteadily to where Peretz and his men were waiting.

Anna and the little girl in front of her woke up because all of a sudden they lost their footing. Stumbling, they knocked into other bodies that were also on the move, and it was a while before they realised they had reached their destination and the torture was over.

Peretz stood at the bottom of the loading ramp, guiding the people in the right direction. He earned a peculiar look from his driver, for Peretz never normally took charge of this. Whenever he reached his destination he would go to the commandant to officially register the arrival of his charges.

This time, however, Peretz stood there and gently pushed the bodies towards the large entrance gate, but he was not watching them for his gaze was fixed on the darkness inside the lorry. When Anna appeared he looked away and felt like a little boy again.

The sun was rising as Anna came down the ramp. When she spotted Peretz she asked, "Where are we?"

Peretz turned, pretending not to recognise her. Anna saw through his ploy but did not let it show. Her belly was sore where the girl's head had been digging into it. Her neck was sore, her breasts were sore. She felt exhausted even though she had slept.

"We're in Zehlendorf," Peretz said as soberly as possible. "This is a general refugee camp with liberated prisoners-of-war, forced labourers and many concentration camp survivors from U.N. states. You'll all be here for a while until things move on."

Anna looked at him expectantly. Peretz acted as if he had not noticed. But he was unable to pretend for long.

Peretz found it painful, this sudden realisation that he had nothing to defend himself with against Anna. Although she had not asked he explained what "a while" meant: two nights, and then members of Berlin's Jewish Community would take them in.

"The Americans want to close this camp because it's too small. But we haven't yet found a suitable place for our people," Peretz said apologetically, feeling like someone who has built himself up, only to have to back down.

Anna nodded, turned away and followed the slow stream of people making their way towards the gate of the sparsely lit refugee camp. She did not look back.

Peretz watched her go with a feeling of ultimate defeat.

NINETEEN

When Lisa was nine years old and spring arrived, there was a ring at the door. It was late afternoon, it had been raining but now the sun was out, diffusing a fresh, invigorating light.

Lisa opened the door. Before her stood a woman who looked at her in bewilderment. She was heavily made up, her clothes looked expensive but threadbare, she wore high-heeled shoes and carried a real leather bag, which at the time was a rarity. Lisa noticed it at once because Herr Weiss had shown her how imitation leather was different.

When the woman had got over her shock she said, "Who are you?"

She sounded surprised.

"Who are *you*?" Lisa said defiantly.

The woman smiled nervously, ran a hand through her hair, which had the semblance of a well-rehearsed gesture, and said, "I'm Maria Kramer."

Lisa stared. All of a sudden she fancied that the woman before her was an actress who had chosen their front door as her stage.

Before Lisa was able to react, Frau Kramer, who had been cooking in the kitchen and wondering what was keeping her granddaughter so long, came into the hallway. When she saw who was at the door, her features changed. Standing behind Lisa, she looked at the woman like somebody from whose face all expression has been eliminated.

"Can I help you?"

The woman stared at Frau Kramer and, with tears welling up in her eyes, said softly, "Mother."

If this is a play, Lisa thought, what is my role? She turned to her grandmother for help.

Frau Kramer knew perfectly well which drama was being played out here. Her expression did not change; it remained frozen and alien – Lisa had never seen her grandmother look like this.

"I'm sorry, you must have made a mistake," Frau Kramer said. She grabbed the handle and was about to close the door – even Lisa found this impolite – when the other woman prevented her by quickly putting a foot in the way.

"Mother, please, it's me, Maria! Don't you recognise me?"

"No," Frau Kramer said, shaking her head. "Maria Kramer is dead. This is her daughter, my granddaughter. You must be looking for someone else. Now please leave."

"Mother!" the woman cried out. Lisa thought her despair was brilliantly acted. She seemed so real that Lisa watched the woman captivated, like a spectator so thrilled that they forget themselves.

Frau Kramer pulled Lisa into the apartment and pushed against the door to eject the woman's foot. The other woman resisted, she was almost screaming now:

"Mother, please! Don't abandon me! Mother!"

But Frau Kramer had resolved to put an end to this drama. She used all her strength to brace herself against the door until finally it clicked shut. Then she stood there, exhausted, her back against the wall, things happening on her face that Lisa was unable to interpret.

Outside she could hear a sobbing which after a while became quieter and eventually stopped altogether. Now both Lisa and her grandmother were listening. They heard the other woman blow her nose, and Lisa imagined her opening the handbag with a well-rehearsed movement and taking out a silk handkerchief. But how could you blow your nose elegantly? That she could not imagine.

After a while she heard a clomping sound fading into the distance. The strange woman was going down the stairs.

Frau Kramer took a deep breath.

The first clear thought she was able to formulate was about Lisa. What am I going to tell the child? she wondered. Lisa was still standing where Frau Kramer had let go of her, staring at her grandmother. Frau Kramer closed her eyes and waited.

"Who was that woman, Grandma?" Lisa said.

Frau Kramer swallowed before shaking her head and saying, "Must be a madwoman. She probably lost her parents in the war."

Lisa nodded. She thought it sounded plausible. "But how did she know that Mummy was called Maria?" she said.

Frau Kramer shrugged and Lisa was astonished, because this movement looked as if it had been rehearsed too, something she had never seen in her grandmother before.

"I don't know, my darling. Maybe she asked the neighbours, or she knows someone who knew your mother."

Frau Kramer shrugged again, her throat was as dry as a bone, she felt wretched. She closed her eyes and started to cry.

"Grandma! But you don't have to cry!" Lisa exclaimed, hugging her.

"Oh, I'm only crying because I'm thinking about your mother," Frau Kramer lied.

Lisa held tightly onto her hips, Frau Kramer stroked the girl's hair, pleased to be crying as it conveniently masked the entire episode.

That afternoon Lisa paid a visit to Herr Weiss in his apartment. He had made tea, they sat at the round table in the sitting room and Lisa said, "You know what, Uncle Tobi, I'd love to be really free."

Herr Weiss nodded and muttered something to himself. Lost in thought, Lisa stared out of the window. In the distance she could see a large sailing boat. Without taking her eyes off it she said, "But I don't even know what it means to be free." She sighed. "My friend Frieda would say that being free means you can do anything you want." She shrugged and looked at Herr Weiss. "But I don't have a clue what I want!" Her gaze returned to the window. "My classmates don't think about these sorts of things." She fell silent, carefully reached for the porcelain cup in front of her and took a sip of tea.

After a while Herr Weiss cleared his throat. He said, Well, erm, he said, Hmm, hmm. Then he said, "Do you know how I got out of the hospital with the nuns?"

Lisa shook her head. Herr Weiss nodded thoughtfully and said, "Hmm, well, one day a man came to the hospital, looking for his son Tobias. And this man, well, his name was Weiss, just like mine." He smiled at Lisa.

"Was he your father?" she said.

Now Herr Weiss smiled mischievously and shook his head. "No, no, that Herr Weiss was not my father, I didn't know him at all. He was looking for his son, and had been for ages." He nodded sadly. "But he hadn't found him. And when he saw me, so young and wrecked as I was, he said: That's my son, Tobias." Herr Weiss nodded. "Yes, that's what happened." He watched Lisa slowly take in what he had told her. She frowned and opened her eyes wide.

"But that means you're not Uncle Tobi after all!" she cried. She hesitated, pausing to think. Then she shook her head and said. "But you are now, aren't you?"

"Of course!" Herr Weiss said softly. "Now I am because I wanted to be Uncle Tobi."

"And so now you're free?" Lisa asked sceptically.

Herr Weiss rocked his head from side to side, said Hmm, looked out of the window and said, "What does it mean to be free? I don't know either. But at least I didn't have to go back to my family."

Lisa nodded slowly. It was easy for her to understand Herr Weiss; all she had to do was invert her own feelings.

"I'd love to go back to my family. But I can't," she said wearily.

Herr Weiss looked at her sympathetically and decided he would buy her a nice present.

That evening Lisa lay in bed, staring at the ceiling. Beside her lay Frau Kramer, absolutely still, which surprised Lisa as her grandmother had a habit of breathing noisily. But Frau Kramer did not stir, her chest rose and fell regularly and her eyes were closed. I hope everything's alright with her, Lisa thought. After this strange day.

She could not get the woman at the door out of her head. She had called herself Maria Kramer, which meant she must be Lisa's mother. Perhaps she was, and the reason Grandma had been scared was that she was an angel. Lisa frowned. She had always imagined her mother differently.

What kept churning in her mind was the sense of theatricality about the encounter, but she could not get to the bottom of what it meant.

Lisa had no photographs of her parents. Everything had been lost in the war, her grandmother said. But the car accident had nothing to do with the war, as Lisa knew from her grandmother, and from her grandmother she also knew that the accident had occurred in Poland, where the Russians were now in charge. If only Daddy and Mummy hadn't gone there, Lisa thought, they'd still be alive today. She tried to take a deep breath, she drew the air through her open mouth and raised her shoulders, but it did not work. It was as if there were a place in her lungs which could never be filled, no matter how hard she tried.

For a long while she lay in the dark with her eyes open. Just before falling asleep she thought how peculiar it was that the false Maria Kramer had looked so much like her grandmother. I'd definitely have been taken in by her if Grandma hadn't come, she thought. What luck!

TWENTY

Anna lay on her back looking up at Josef Ranzner's face. It was dark, the man above her panted and moaned softly. He thrust his penis rhythmically into Anna, she raised and lowered her pelvis, raised and lowered it, always to the rhythm of the man who was staring at Anna as if he had never seen her before. Anna stared back, for now his face changed, the hair turned blond, the nose became broader, the chin jutted out, the lips pouted, almost fleshy. Anna's face assumed an expression of shock, as the first adjutant continued his rhythmical movements, panting a little more quickly perhaps, moaning a little more loudly, but still softly, careful not to disturb anybody. The camp was full of people too exhausted to stay awake at night, but you could never be sure, and now the second adjutant, the one with the broad nostrils, the bulging forehead and the small eyes, briefly bared his teeth, bent over Anna, gave her earlobe a gentle bite, whispered breathless words that Anna did not understand, it was Hebrew, he kissed Anna on the lips, his face now close to her eyes, a perfectly round face with a receding hairline and well-nourished cheeks, but chinless, and was the fourth adjutant and panted and moaned and spoke words of love and was Obersturmbannführer Josef Ranzner with his aquiline nose and thin lips and panting and moaning words of love and was all the adjutants one after the other and all jumbled about and they moaned words of love in a language Anna did not understand, it was Hebrew, Anna was silent, staring, shocked, Did I expect this? she wondered, not knowing the answer, she heard herself moan and pant, she was Anna, still the same Anna and yet not, and yet the other Anna, the one who surrendered herself, words of love from Ranzner's mouth, words of love, moaned and panted in rhythm, his penis inside Anna, the first adjutant raised and lowered, the second raised and lowered, the third, the fourth, Why is none of them laughing? Anna thought, they *were* laughing, but Anna knows what is happening, Anna is not mad, Anna has a clear view of things, words of love and moaned and panted, Anna, the Obersturmbannführer, the adjutants, in rhythm, words, words that Anna could not understand, it was Hebrew.

And then they all climaxed together, with Anna in attendance, staring, shocked, while the man on top of her was Peretz Sarfati who sank onto Anna's body, exhausted, his head nestling beside hers, a sweat of film on their brows, the sounds of their breathing mingled, soon to quieten down, they lay there, a couple after the act of love, but they were much more than that, something which only Anna knew.

Anna wanted to understand. In the darkness of the wooden barrack her eyes sought a footing, they found the long cracks in the timbers, which glowed dimly, outside the light of the moon made for a bright night, it was warm and late. Anna wanted to understand why she had slept with Peretz Sarfati. And she understood that she had wanted it in the same way that he had. Anna frowned, nobody noticed, Peretz's breathing was shallower, he had made himself comfortable on her slender body, but when Anna compared his weight to the oppressive crowding in the lorry, Peretz felt almost light. Had she become completely submissive, or did there exist, behind her will to want what Peretz wanted, a second will that was intent on achieving something quite different?

This was no mere suspicion, Anna was posing a rhetorical question to which the answer was already known; the question served another purpose, to assure Anna that she knew precisely what was happening, that she was in the picture about her true motives, that she was not losing track of herself just because things were happening deep inside her.

These events meant that Anna knew she had forgotten nothing, she had seen everything, every single facial feature, she had felt everything, every desire of desire, because it was life, the continuation of life, survival, she had looked and been astonished, and now Anna opened her special archive to house the new events in it.

It had to be. Anna knew that there was a secret connection between Peretz, Ranzner and the adjutants. The connection was her. She, Anna, was secret in a way that she only now realised, now that she would have been free to say No, but had not. Why did I sleep with Peretz? Anna asked herself again, closing her eyes, feeling his weight – it was no different from the weight of the other men.

She felt like a whore with six punters, she had just taken part in an orgy as the only woman, and all these men had climaxed inside her and now she was pumped full of sperm. She thought, I've fallen sick, my head is sick and yet at the same time I'm aware of this and I'm not sick. She thought, I have to know, she thought, Just so long as I know my sickness won't make me sick. She thought, This is my way. She thought of Abba and closed her eyes and let Peretz's weight press her into the hard straw mattress and enjoyed being aware of this feeling, just as it was.

TWENTY-ONE

Frau Kramer was not asleep. She lay next to Lisa, trying to regulate her breathing so that the girl would not realise the state her grandmother was in. Frau Kramer was exhausted by the day now coming to an end, but she found no peace. In the darkness she could no longer escape the memory she had kept at bay during the day. Whenever she had smiled at Lisa, in truth she had been laying a veil over the images taking up residence in her head. Now these images assaulted her mind, filling every last corner of her closed eyes.

She saw the woman in the doorway, who was still her daughter and always would be, she saw the despair in the face of her daughter, the worn clothes on her body, the door closing and locking her out, and she heard the sobbing before she left. It was so painful that on several occasions Frau Kramer struggled for air. She focused on her breathing, The only thing that's going to help now, she thought, is discipline, no matter what happens in the world or here inside my heart. Only discipline can save us. I'm a soldier, she thought all of a sudden, seeing herself in her best dress parading with other women through the streets of Lübeck, all of them wearing white dresses with large red-and-brown flowery patterns, an army of women fighting day after day against the war, the war was over, but what it had engendered was not: poverty, shortages, hopelessness. And lies. Frau Kramer lay in an old eiderdown, which not long ago must have belonged to other people who may now be dead, and the furniture in the apartment had belonged to them too, Since when had it been like this? she thought, feeling the lies of all those women who acted as if they were blossoming from head to toe, and she acted along with them, even though she looked so withered. In truth, she thought, we don't even believe spring anymore when it announces its arrival. In truth we're fighting on the home front and the enemy is truth and our weapons are lies.

Frau Kramer had to breathe deeply, she knew that Lisa was still awake, she could hear the girl's shallow breathing, she sensed that Lisa too was lying there seeing the woman in the doorway, her despair, her cries for a mother who pretended not to be there, and through Lisa's eyes everything that Frau Kramer saw felt even more painful, for the girl's ignorance was like a magnifying glass that presented everything far more clearly, far more closely and far more uncomfortably.

If you can't get any further you have to go back to the beginning and start again. That is what her mother had once told her. So Frau Kramer went back to the beginning and saw herself holding a screaming baby. What was this baby screaming for? What did it want? The question repeated itself in her head, with these screams the puzzle began, the puzzle was called Maria and was her daughter, but she did not understand it, what was this child screaming for, one day it would talk, then she would understand it. She would be able to ask it, What are you screaming for, child, tell me so I can give it to you, I will do everything in my power, I am your mother, I love you, what is it? But Maria learned to talk and gave no answer, Maria learned to talk and yet kept screaming without being able to say what she was screaming for, and her mother was unable to ask the right question at the right time, with the right emphasis, the right caution, the right love. What do you want, what do you want? They were trapped in a labyrinth and knew neither where they had come from nor where they were heading to.

Frau Kramer's thoughts had become entrenched, her mind entangled, she was tired, no, tired did not even begin to describe it, Frau Kramer was shattered, shattered to the point of sheer collapse, she felt as if she were still struggling through the deep Polish snow, a screaming baby in her arms, she felt as if the baby were Maria, she felt as if she were not the mother, she felt as if the mother were lying on the ground behind her, lifeless, frozen to death, but she herself had to go on, keep going on, even though she would have loved to lie down, just a little, just for a short while, but the baby stopped her from doing so, and she thought, Thank you, Maria, but now she was already asleep and simply kept dreaming from the same point.

She dreamed a cold dream. It was summer, her children, Karl, Maria, her husband Wilhelm and herself were living in a beautiful village in a beautiful little farmhouse, they were not rich and not poor, and when they went outside it was warm, so warm! But inside the house it was always cold, How strange, her husband said, I'll knock holes in the walls to let the warmth in, Do that, Frau Kramer said, and he took an axe and cleft the wall, but all that happened was that firewood came tumbling in, and Maria screamed and Karl raised his rifle and shot a Jew and said thoughtfully, Heil Hitler! and shot another and said softly, Sieg Heil! and aimed the rifle at Maria, but she said, I'm not a Jew, my name's Lisa, shoot at her, and she pointed at Maria standing next to her, and Karl shot at Maria, hitting her in the forehead, Maria fell backwards with her eyes open. She lay on her back and spoke. She said, Now I've got another hole for the men, she wanted to say more but Frau Kramer slapped her and shouted, Hold your tongue! She wanted to shout more, but all of a sudden she woke up in a sweat, lying beside Lisa who was breathing heavily, perhaps because she was dreaming, perhaps of Maria.

She closed her eyes again, but this time did not fall asleep. Instead, the apartment they lived in opened out before the lids of her closed eyes, and she noted with astonishment that in one corner stood the grandfather clock, ticking away, five o'clock in the morning, she frowned, How did that get here? she wondered, looking around behind her closed eyes. But then she stopped wondering, for now she saw the table, the sideboard, the door to the cellar, and if she went down those stairs she would find Margarita Ejzenstain lying in a hole in the earth beneath the planks and she had to get her out of there because the cold would kill her.

Frau Kramer opened her eyes, the arrival of day was imminent, the first rays had burst forth in the east, sending a particular brightness through the window and into the eyes of the woman now leaning against the head of the bed, looking down at her sleeping granddaughter. Lisa had barely stirred in the night, she lay on her back, her features completely relaxed, her mouth closed, she looked like an angel, Frau Kramer thought, utterly pure and serene. She thought about her daughter, she could still see the woman in the doorway, still hear her cries, still feel the pain.

She got up quietly and went out of the bedroom to make breakfast.

TWENTY-TWO

In late autumn 1955 a long goods train was travelling from east to west. Six hundred men were sitting or standing in the carriages. They wore inadequate clothing, they were freezing, they were hungry, but they were not complaining. Through small windows set high they were able to glimpse the white landscape. Some looked out, others looked away, all of them swearing never to come back here again.

After two days they reached the Urals. The train stopped at a village which was obliged to keep a double secret: its proximity to the capital and the train's cargo. It was night time, the station was brightly lit by the yellow beams of floodlights, soldiers stood all about with large, black terriers who looked unfriendly in spite of their frizzy coats, the six hundred men thought, As if we were planning to stay here and their job was to prevent us from doing so. They were unaware that it was not them being guarded so closely but the surrounding area. They were unaware that the people whose country they were travelling through were opposed to their transit. They had no idea that the authorities feared the fury of the population if they got wind of this train too soon.

Military police led the six hundred men into an old warehouse which had hastily been prepared for the occasion. Canteen staff from the army sat them at rickety steel-tube tables and gave them a warm meal. Afterwards they were issued with new clothes. The army outfitters, a state concern in Moscow, had delivered grey felt coats, coarse cloth trousers and shirts, all especially made with no insignia or rankings, Who are these for? the business had asked, For no-one, came the reply, which meant: Better not ask!

The six hundred men cooperated with everything, they did not ask, How come? The food put before them in Soviet army enamel bowls tasted so good that they noticed nothing else, the new clothes felt so warm that they were almost comfortable in their emaciated bodies. Even had they known that the only reason they were being allowed home was that one government wanted better relations with the other, even had they known that the warm food and new clothing had been provided to avoid them leaving here looking so scruffy and wretched, because economic interests were involved, a lot of money, this would not have bothered them in the slightest.

Meanwhile another goods train had arrived from the west. They boarded this train, the military police bolted the doors, the train departed. When day broke the men could see that the landscape was no longer white. They could see the last withered leaves on the trees, furrows frozen hard, grey clouds, they could see the open landscape, they suspected that this was Poland, the same Poland into which they had once charged like invincibles, like supermen, like gods. Like devils, their Russian escorts would have said, and they would have answered, No, like soldiers carrying out our orders, and it would have been the truth, but the truth – and they would have had a vague sense of this – would also have been that the two were not necessarily contradictory.

Now they stood silently at the small windows of the goods train, peering out at the Polish morning, and in reality peering out at their own past, but this was not on their minds at that moment, they had survived hell, they had paid the price, they had been released, they were travelling home, they did not ask themselves, What is home, does it still exist, did it ever exist, is it not a construct of the mind, an illusion we're still chasing, now without a Führer, but just as blindly? Won't we be disappointed, stranded, standing outside the door, with everything at home turned uncanny, our eyes no longer recognising anything, our hearts groping in vain, our hands reaching out into emptiness?

Amongst the six hundred men was one not standing by the windows, not gazing out at the autumn. He was sitting on the floor, smoking makhorka roll-ups, he was called Otto Deckert, he had been a simple solider in the Wehrmacht, side by side with his comrades he had defended the fortress at Posen until a bullet flew towards him, was it for me or was it for you, who did it knock to the ground, who lay at whose feet, as if a part of me?

Otto Deckert sat on the floor, leaning against a side of the carriage, in the dim light it was hard to make out his chiselled profile, his aquiline nose, his rigid facial features, his tiny wrinkles, which would never be particularly furrowed, but would increase in number as he got older.

Otto Deckert spoke to nobody and nobody spoke to him. He had survived as if by a miracle, but also because his fear of dying was so great that he made the right decisions, put on the right uniform and burned the wrong one.

On the inside of his left upper arm Otto Deckert had a bullet wound, a grazing shot had torn the skin, taking away what once may have been there. When the Soviets asked if he was in the Waffen S.S., because it was exactly in that spot that they had their blood group tattooed, Otto Deckert was well prepared, and instead of saying No like thousands of others before him who had not been believed, he told the truth, which was that ethnic Germans from outside the Reich, like himself, had been given a similar tattoo in the same place during the course of their medical examination in the holding camp. He was fortunate; the Soviet officer conducting the interrogation believed him. The way you look, he said with a smile, they wouldn't have taken you anyway. Then he grinned broadly and exclaimed, You look more like a Kyrgyz! He repeated his words in Russian and the soldiers around him laughed. Otto Deckert joined in the laughter because he was a polite man, but as he laughed he could not help laughing for real, without knowing why. He laughed until he felt on the verge of tears, but at that moment the Soviet officer smacked his palm on the small wooden table and Otto Deckert fell silent. Where were you settled? asked the officer, whose expression had lost all traces of the joviality that moments before had filled it. Otto Deckert remained calm, he gave the name of a small town near Posen and in his mind's eye images from another life flitted past.

Now Otto Deckert was heading homewards, but he knew that no home awaited him there, he had to be sure he behaved in the right way when they arrived in Herleshausen and then later in Friedland. He concentrated. He smoked makhorka. He did not think about the man he had once been, he had set up a fifth chamber in his heart into which he had placed everything, his entire past, before locking it and tossing the key into oblivion. Otto Deckert's heart kept beating as if nothing had happened.

TWENTY-THREE

Peretz was on the interzonal train to Munich talking to Peretz. Both of them were wearing the same British uniform, both had removed the Jewish insignia from the lapel shortly after their arrival on 8 May, 1945, both had pulled the same trigger to shoot the German soldier with the loudhailer. Both seemed to be but one Peretz.

And yet now everything had changed. Peretz was talking to Peretz and what he had to say he was shouting into Peretz's head, sending it into a spin, while around him the Reichsbahn train rattled along branch lines only, for the main connections had been destroyed. The train was like a moving corpse because there was no more Reichsbahn, no more Reich transport ministry, just bodies of metal and wood traversing this cold land, occupied by the victors.

Peretz had only travelled across the country once before, back in the spring of '45, in the opposite direction. They had been victorious, they had advanced with the British Army from northern Italy into Austria, and in Vienna the order came to disband the Jewish Brigade. The bitterness had been intense, So little war, they said, We're not having that, his comrades grumbled. Then they forged plans, the Jewish insignia disappeared and with it disappeared all the right and proper things that had brought them here, To fight against the Kingdom of the Night, as one of them had said, a former German music student.

But while Peretz's comrades began tracking down Nazis and – in the Austrian forests, which had just come into full bloom, and under the Austrian sun, which shone mildly on everyone – strangling them, and putting them in sacks weighed down with stones and drowning them in lakes, Peretz fled north. Heeding the call of the American military rabbi, he had battled his way with Avi and an army lorry, which he had rarely been separated from since, driving around and around to save ever more Jews from their Polish compatriots.

Even then Peretz was no longer a single Peretz, but like a sheet of paper with a tiny rip, and each time he picked up the German soldier's loudhailer the rip had become a little larger and, as if out of thin air, a woman had jumped into the gap and made herself at home, which is why Peretz took in nothing of the countryside that rolled torpidly past his window, the small Hesse villages that looked like snowballs without snow, with motifs from Grimm's fairy tales, which is why this time Peretz did not ask himself, Why is all this allowed to continue to exist as if nothing had happened? Why can't we destroy all this too?

Peretz talked to Peretz, and what he had to say left no room for anything else. Peretz shouted at Peretz that Peretz was sitting on his shabby seat in a daze, casting blank glances at the five American soldiers sweating with him in the narrow compartment because the heating was not working properly. Peretz did not think, We're sweating because the train's broken and outside people are freezing because the country's broken. This is what one of the Americans said, a young lad who had also got to the fighting too late, he was somewhat regretful as well.

Peretz himself was broken, torn between two possibilities of being a whole man: one who stands by his actions, and one who is strong enough to dismiss them. One who resists a woman, and one who has the magnanimity to let her act as she pleases. One who has done what he had to do, and one who knows he has made a mistake.

Peretz talked to Peretz, and as he talked the train headed westwards past Frankfurt, though there was little of the city to be seen. Almost everything that had once stood, things and living beings alike, was lying on the ground, transformed, and now the rain fell on it all, burying it beneath a sad veil. The train moved slowly, the day was long and yet dusk was falling, grey and impenetrable, and Peretz had so much to say that he lacked all sense of the passing hours, of the soldiers changing their faces, uniforms and conversations, and when Peretz held out his pass or greeted a superior officer this was the only time that both Peretzes acted in concert.

Peretz talked and Peretz listened. Pictures flashed up between them, sounds that nobody else could hear. Everything resulted in a sluggishly flowing river of rebukes, memories, self-accusations, justifications. It can't go on like this. You're a hero. What have you done? Throw away that loudhailer! Forget the woman. You're risking your life for others. You are a hero.

Peretz knew what Peretz was talking about. Ever since the woman had established herself in his core, everything else had become a side issue. A man is in love, Peretz! But a man has a mission that is more important than love, Peretz! A man can be in love and at the same time pursue his mission in life, Peretz!

But Peretz could not. No matter how hard he tried, this woman was a permanent barrier between him and the world, between him and himself. Even when Klausner, one of the drivers he had engaged, stopped his lorry right in the middle of the road to Szczecin and haggled over more money, even when he insulted him, and then when Klausner lashed out with his fist to emphasise his point, just before Avi and the other drivers intervened, only one of the two Peretzes was present. Peretz was getting on Peretz's nerves with his sentimentality. You're mad, Peretz, Peretz said, She's a Yekke, no, she's not even that, she's a German, a chancer, beware of her! What do you know about the woman? You're a hero of Israel, Peretz!

Thus Peretz spoke incessantly to Peretz, as the evening settled gloomily over the land, smothering all light, and the train clattered so slowly that everyone apart from Peretz let their heads drop and stopped talking about their adventures, the miserable rations, the miracles of the black markets, homesickness and the beauty of German women. All that remained was the dim light in the compartment and the black window, and now, when Peretz looked to the left, he saw the other Peretz gazing at him critically, sadly, helplessly, and said: You're working for the Institution for Immigration B here. You and Abba and the military rabbi and Ephraim Frank, the new commander in Munich, you lot have to organise the flight of thousands of people. Don't be an egotist, don't be a fool, focus on your mission. What the hell is wrong with you, Peretz? Who are you, actually, Peretz? Yes, Peretz said to Peretz, Who am I, actually? At that moment the train was passing through northern Bavaria, which now belonged to the Americans. They did not yet know that they would be turning this part of the defeated Reich into a temporary haven for the Jews of Europe, but very soon the American Jews around Morgenthau would demand greater engagement, and then President Truman would think about the forthcoming election and the Jewish votes, and the time would come when camps for Jews would be set up all over Bavaria, which is why Munich was the right place for Bricha's headquarters.

Until now, however, there had been only one man in Munich, who had travelled there from Vienna under an alias, who knows, perhaps at this very moment he was sitting in an interzonal train somewhere near Linz. Peretz was on his way to see this man.

If there was anything keeping him together it was the world around him, with its good and evil, its Jews and British who had become entangled in a shadow conflict. If there was anything keeping Peretz together it was his life's mission, which at this very moment he was in control of because he had never stopped functioning and had boarded the interzonal train punctually, despite having been stood up by Anna; he had come to the station without a goodbye kiss.

Peretz had not thought, I hope nothing's happened to her, I hope she's alright. He had thought, Why's she doing this to me? Then he chastised himself for thinking this rather than something more gallant, more mature, something representative of Peretz as he appeared to the outside world, rather than this Peretz here, who no longer recognised himself in the reflection of the carriage window.

Time passed again, nobody saw Augsburg over to the west, the train headed through a land that was not at war and not at peace, carrying a man who was battling for himself without knowing what his weapons were.

It was night when he arrived in Munich. The train came to a stop shortly before the main railway station because the roof still lay where it had collapsed onto the tracks. Tired people climbed down from the carriages, it was dark and wet, Peretz was jostled, he fought against the feeling of forlornness, he fought against the feeling of missing Anna, always Anna, as if she had to take him by the hand and escort him, as if she were not merely a woman but his, Peretz's salvation from the pointlessness of existence.

Someone grabbed his shoulder. Turning around, Peretz saw the face of a man who gave him a friendly smile. His pale complexion, high forehead and narrow Roman nose lent him an aristocratic air. Peretz knew this face, even though the two men had never met. They shook hands, Ephraim Frank introduced himself as Ernst Caro, Peretz gave his own false name. In case someone was watching or even listening to them amongst the throng of passengers stumbling uncertainly across obsolete tracks to get to the street, all they would see were two British employees of U.N.R.R.A., the United Nations Relief and Rehabilitation Administration, greeting each other politely in English, then walking over to a dark saloon car where the driver, a conspicuously slim man with sunken cheeks, opened the doors to the back seats, closed them again behind the men, then got in himself, started the engine and drove off.

Outside, the bizarre shadows of bombed-out buildings drifted by, Peretz peered out, it seemed that there was only one real city left. It always looked identical, always identically destroyed, always identically unrecognisable, and even if he travelled twelve hours southwards by train he still came to the same place, as if time and space had been extinguished, as if at the end of all journeys everything always had to start from the beginning. You've been blinded by love, the voice within him said, That's all. It'll pass. He nodded involuntarily. Maybe that was it, but maybe he was simply seeing the world for the first time as it really was, he did not know, he knew nothing any longer except that he had come here because his new commander wanted to talk to him and other officers from Bricha and the Institution for Immigration B.

*

As they drove the circuitous route to their destination Ephraim Frank scrutinised his subordinate without saying a word. It was curfew and nobody was out in the dark streets except for soldiers patrolling in jeeps. Only the main roads had been cleared, they had to rattle along a tram-line for some of the way. The two men sat in silence beside each other in the back, one attempting to return to the present, the other becoming abruptly aware, now that he set eyes on the maimed city, of the enormity of task he had agreed to undertake months previously.

When the silence had lingered for too long, Ephraim Frank said in a German accent, "I read you were born in Palestine."

Peretz turned his gaze from the window, where he had been staring at his reflection superimposed on the dark city.

"That's right, Commander."

"You can call me Erich, that is . . . was my name when I was still a German. I imagine I'll be using it more frequently again here."

"Where in Germany?" Peretz asked, avoiding calling him anything.

"Gelsenkirchen." Peretz shrugged.

"I don't know it."

"Very beautiful place, lots of workers, good people." When he broke off, Peretz watched him briefly.

Frank cleared his throat, then said, "In fact I spent my childhood in Dortmund. We moved there before I started school."

"I've heard of Dortmund, but I've never been."

"I bet it looks just like here now."

"I bet it does, Commander." Ephraim Frank said nothing.

Peretz Sarfati wanted to avoid giving any hint that he knew exactly who Ephraim Erich Frank was. He did not know for sure why he was behaving like this, but the Peretz in him who knew everything suspected that it was just fear. Fear of what? he would have asked had he had the time to look out of the window again, and the reflection with the city's broken stones might have answered, Fear of someone who's actually achieved something, fear of someone who's a true hero and isn't surprised if in spite of this people fail to recognise him. Fear of something pure that presents you with the murky soup of your soul more painfully than any mirror.

But he never got round to it, for Ephraim Frank announced, "We're here."

Josef Leibowitz, the driver, sucked in his sunken cheeks even further as he steered the car onto an elongated square lined with towering late-nineteenth-century houses. Although this square was in darkness too, Peretz could see that most of the buildings were still standing. Generous entrances with broad, wrought-iron gates told of rich people who had immortalised their pride in stone. The car stopped at the corner, Josef Leibowitz opened the doors, the men got out. Peretz looked about him, high up on the building in front of them he noticed a dark-blue sign with white Sütterlin writing. Paradeplatz.

The corner house bore the number 2, the three men made for the entrance, a wide archway. Behind this a sort of arcade ran along the façade, connecting the house with the neighbouring building. Large display windows lay in darkness, it was impossible to see what might be behind them.

They walked straight ahead up to a tall double door, a yellowish light shone through its frosted windows and the grilles on the front. Ephraim Frank pressed one of the bells, it was a while before they heard footsteps in the stairwell. Someone was coming. The stairs creaked and squeaked. Behind the frosted glass loomed a short, slight figure. The door opened and in the crack a very round face appeared, narrow eyes bordered by nickel spectacles. The man was wearing a grey suit, a tie and shoes with spats. He looked a little like an actor from the 1920s, Peretz thought.

Ephraim Frank nodded at the man, who then opened the heavy door fully and moved to one side to let them in. Stepping into the hallway without saying a word, they followed the man up the stairs.

On the third floor of the house a white-panelled door stood open. They entered a wide apartment hallway and, shortly afterwards, a large sitting room, in the corner of which hung a heavy chandelier. The walls were covered in dark-red fabric, in the middle of the room was a long oak table, at which at least fifteen men were sitting on high-backed chairs. They turned to the new arrivals. So this was the meeting to which Peretz had been invited. Here was where the flight of European Jewry was to be restructured, the envoys from Palestine, men such as Ephraim Frank, had come to take the matter in hand.

And it was here that Peretz finally managed to banish from his mind the woman who had insinuated her way into his life, and exist as a single Peretz, for here he was amongst his peers. It did him good to talk about U.S. Army lorries, it did him good to think about how he could copy the model that the short man had devised for Munich. His name was Sally Zeve, and from his accent Peretz could tell that, like Abba Kovner, he came from Lithuania. Maybe he had been even sent by Abba.

No contact with the Bricha structure, Sally Zeve said in his high voice, Completely independent modus operandi, he said, My contacts with the Americans and my new business partners' contacts with the Bavarian government mean that we can become middlemen, and perhaps even set up a monopoly. In this way, he said, all the lorries will pass through our hands and we'll have enough for the transports. Who are your business partners? someone asked. Are they *goyim*? asked another. Sally Zeve smiled. He said, Even better. He glanced at Ephraim Frank, who nodded back, and continued, "They're two Germans who got their hands dirty."

"Nazis?"

"One's a local car dealer who had almost a hundred forced labourers by the end of the war. The other's a banker with a party badge, who has to stay out of the spotlight."

There followed a silence, in the middle of which stood Sally Zeve, seemingly at ease.

"What good's that going to do?"

Sally Zeve's smile broadened, as if he had been waiting for this very question.

"A Jew, survivor of the Nazi concentration camps," he said, pointing at himself with all his fingers, "and two fellow travellers – that's the best combination imaginable for our purpose. The Jew," he said, pointing at himself again, "has contacts to the Americans and is beyond all suspicion." He looked around in triumph before continuing: "The Nazis have got their old contacts. They're respected here. And they've got money that they're very keen to invest in this business. Besides," he said, raising his voice now, as if coming to a climax, "this way I've got them eating out of my hand without them knowing. If they see through me, I'll point a gun at their heads: cooperation or incarceration." His smile vanished. "The two men have faced this choice before, and we know the decision they made." He paused for effect, grabbed the lapels of his jacket with both hands, gave each agent in turn a bold stare, rocked from the heels to the toes of his shoes and back again, and said, "Well?"

The assembled company conceded defeat. It was decided that a limited liability company would be established under German law. It would bear the following name: the Bavarian Truck Company.

"This," Ephraim Frank said to conclude the item, "is the last time you will ever see Sally Zeve. In future only I will be in contact with him. Sally has already rented a small plot of land on the grounds of the Alte Pinakothek here in Munich, where he's going to build a cabin with a workshop and offices." He stood, the two of them shook hands, the short man picked up a white hat, a long beige coat and a walking stick of dark wood and left the room, the apartment, the building.

When he had gone and Ephraim Frank had moved on to the next item, Peretz thought, I'm never going to find a person like that. For the first time he realised that for some missions you needed chancers.

When Peretz boarded the interzonal train the following morning he was so tired that he fell asleep instantly and did not wake again until they were heading for Berlin through the Soviet zone. The meeting had lasted all night. Important figures had spoken: Ephraim Dekel, who had taken command of Bricha throughout Europe from Prague; Asher Ben Nathan, who had come to Vienna with Ephraim Frank, and from there was now organising the emigration; a Lithuanian; one of Abba Kovner's men; and others, some of whom Peretz knew already, the rest were unfamiliar. The men had tried to put together an overview, they had exchanged information and rumours, talked about routes, control points, unguarded borders, and then over and over again about lorries, ships, billets, false papers, visas. Ephraim Frank would have to coordinate more than five hundred colleagues in Germany and now Peretz was one of them.

TWENTY-FOUR

"Perhaps the moment when the life or death decision is made is not merely like a bullet hitting its target, someone falling to the ground, never getting up again, being buried and the war carrying on.

"What if nobody was present when the life or death decision was made? What if somebody was shot and fell, but nobody was there to witness it? Then the decision is postponed until somebody finds out.

"And if years pass before that happens, the life or death decision changes. It becomes like a door you stand outside, it could happen any time, the door could open at any moment, you settle down in a town, you get an apartment, you go shopping, you go to bed, everything at the threshold of this door.

"And if, many years later, the door opens and three people can suddenly look into the room beyond, how do you describe this feeling?"

*

One day, on 7 October 1980, a few weeks before her thirty-sixth birthday, Lisa would write these thoughts in her diary as she recalled the weeks leading up to her eleventh birthday. She would sit at the window of her small, thirty-fifth-floor apartment in the Lower East Side of Manhattan, looking out over the island to the two bridges, and wonder at the course her own life had taken. How on earth did I get here? she would ask herself, allowing her gaze to roam across the landscape of houses, in which no one building was identical to another, and yet all served the same purpose: to pile people and their things on top of each other. For the hundredth time she would marvel at the bizarre beauty this gave rise to, and compare it to the bizarre beauty of her own life. Wherever there's a lack of space, she would think, people want to go up and up. A skyscraper is a mountain, a volcano, geyser, tree, person. Below it's cramped and dark, pressure from all sides, the only thing people want to do is stand firm and yet they escape, away and away until they're right at the top, believing perhaps that they've won, even though all they've done is made room. Then she would pick up a pen and write about how it was when she began to grow up.

It started one afternoon after school when she went to see Herr Weiss for something to eat, to do her homework and have a chat, and he confided in her that from tomorrow he would no longer be a brick-layer.

"But what are you going to do, then?" Lisa asked in astonishment, taking a spoonful of her chicken soup.

Herr Weiss rocked his head from side to side, then folded his hands and placed them on the table in front of him. He was sitting directly opposite Lisa and exuded great solemnity. Clearing his throat he said, "Well, you know, I've taught myself some mathematics in the last few months and now I'm doing the statics for a few architects. They haven't got a clue about it, you see." He made a dismissive gesture with his hand, grinned mischievously and shrugged.

Lisa took more spoonfuls of her soup while she thought about this. Herr Weiss caught himself waiting eagerly for her reaction.

"What's statics?" she said after a while.

Raising his eyebrows and pointing an index finger straight up in the air, Herr Weiss said, "Aha!" He muttered to himself, stood and fetched a piece of paper and a pen, for he was about to explain to Lisa precisely what it was.

"Put in very general terms, statics is what stops a house from collapsing," he said, already embarking on drawings and length specifications, for of course he would teach Lisa statics if she was interested.

But Lisa was not interested. She quickly grabbed his hand to stop him drawing and said, "Does that mean you'll be earning more money now? Because you just built walls before. And walls are different from maths. Walls can collapse, maths can't. Am I right?"

Herr Weiss let out a hearty laugh and said, Yes, yes, ha, ha, exactly, exactly. Then he said, "Well, I will be earning a little more money. Even more than a little more, to be precise." He rocked his head from side to side, and now it became clear to Lisa why there was noticeably more chicken in today's chicken soup.

That was in the spring. In late summer Herr Weiss bought himself a Philips black-and-white television set for more than one thousand marks, as he secretly admitted to Lisa, not without putting his index finger to his lips and saying, Shhh! She and all the other children in the street were there when a small lorry came wheezing down the road, stopped outside their building, and two young men jumped out to open the tailboard. Climbing into the back, they brought out a sort of enormous cube, which they proceeded to heave up to the fourth floor, sweating and cursing all the way. From that day on, residents of number 26, in a variety of combinations, would gather each evening in Herr Weiss's small sitting room, now a touch more cramped with its glass screen that shimmered greyish-blue, to watch the news with tea and cakes. Frau Kramer and Lisa were always there, sometimes the Webers from the second floor would come, sometimes the widow Schmal with her twelve-year-old son Benjamin from the third floor, and only rarely the caretaker Meier from the ground floor with his family: Frau Meier, eight-year-old Grete and ten-year-old Wolfgang, who was in Lisa's class at school. Occasionally even people from the neighbouring house turned up, and Herr Weiss let them all in to watch, for he loved being the centre of attention without having to do anything but turn the knob on his television set until the glass screen flickered into life with a short, high-pitched whistle and an image appeared.

All of a sudden they were connected to the whole country. The daily news, which was still a little like the old weekly newsreel, with plenty of music and uplifting reports, showed them blooming landscapes. Germany became a sovereign state, Germany obtained an army again, Germany manufactured the millionth Volkswagen Beetle, the German lottery was founded, the federal chancellor flew to Moscow for talks as an equal partner.

Everything in shades of grey.

Until one evening in September when the news showed a smiling Russian signing a piece of paper before standing and leaning diagonally across a long, wide table, on which were many more sheets of paper and coffee cups, and at which twenty or more men sat in grey or black suits. The Russian stretched out his hand almost towards where Herr Weiss, the Webers and Lisa and her grandmother were sitting, and an old man standing diagonally opposite on the other side of the table, and who could only be seen from behind, did the same: he stretched out his arm away from the viewers, into the depths of the meeting room, where the Russian's hand was waiting for it.

At the very moment when their two hands met and grasped each other, at the very moment when the Russian moved his lips, the voice of the invisible news announcer said, "The prisoners are coming home!"

Frau Kramer's eyes began to weep before she understood what these words meant, while Herr Weiss and the Webers, who usually passed comment on everything, making it impossible to hear the television unless the volume was turned up high, fell silent. The triumphant news jingle resounded and Herr Weber switched off the set. Lisa stared spellbound at the bright dot as it retreated to the centre of the screen, becoming ever smaller until it vanished altogether. But as she watched, her head was getting to work. She understood what had happened, but she did not know what it had to do with her. She felt like a witness to an extraordinary spectacle, she experienced her grandmother's emotions as if they were her own. But they were not her own, at that moment she became very aware that there was a gap she could not breach, and she was full of regret at having no memory of her grandfather, for she wished to be just as excited by the prospect of his return.

A week later Herr Weiss brought back some strips of wood, brushes and black paint from a construction site he had been surveying. Had he been caught taking these they might have sacked him on the spot. Then the three of them crafted a beautiful sign and a removable handle to hold it up with. In the end Frau Kramer, brush in hand, went about her task almost solemnly, writing her text on the rectangle stuck with light-brown cardboard. She took a couple of paces back, looked at the words benevolently and read them out in a sing-song voice that Lisa had never heard before.

Now all they had to do was wait. One more week. Until 7 October.

That morning they got up early. It was still dark, it had turned cold. After a quick breakfast, they got ready. They wrapped themselves up in thick coats, Frau Kramer put on a beige hat with a narrow, curved rim, she plaited Lisa's long hair and they left the apartment with a bag full of sandwiches, a few apples, a flask of water and a large cloth bag that Frau Kramer had sewn from a tablecloth, which held the sign. They walked through the narrow streets of the old town to the bus stop and from there to the station. In an old red locomotive they travelled the half-hour to Schwanheide, to the south of Lübeck, boarded the fast train from Berlin to Hamburg, which arrived on time, in Hamburg took the connecting train, an express on its way from Denmark to Cologne, changed at Uelzen and from there took a blue slow train to Friedland.

Throughout this journey lasting many hours Frau Kramer told Lisa stories about herself and Grandfather Wilhelm. She wondered what he looked like now, and Lisa wondered what he looked like at all, for there was no photograph of him and never had been.

When they were an hour from Friedland, Lisa said out of the blue, "What if he's not there?"

Frau Kramer did not reply. She looked out of the window, where autumn was unfurling her colours, red, yellow, brown, while the wintry grey of bare boughs was in evidence too, because the cold snap had already taken leaves from the trees. She felt that the life or death decision was advancing closer with the speed of two trains hurtling towards one another. Without braking they must inevitably cannon into each other, and Frau Kramer would either throw herself into the arms of one particular man or . . . Frau Kramer took a deep breath and turned to Lisa.

"If he's not there," she said, "we'll go back home."

Back home? Frau Kramer nodded to herself. Yes, back home. If you have no other place on earth then the only place you can go back to is home, no matter how this might make you feel.

Perhaps Frau Kramer was thinking something different, but one day Lisa would write it down like this, because these were the only words she could find to describe the feeling she had watching her grandmother as the train made its way to Friedland.

TWENTY-FIVE

Who had thrust bunches of flowers into the men's hands? Who had given them scarves, leather shoes, warm civilian clothing? They looked so well; who had fed and cosseted them? Or was it simply happiness radiating from their faces, causing everything to appear in a different light? Who had given the hundreds of women, children and old people standing in a scrum at the station entrance, prevented by policemen from storming forward in a frenzied search, who had given them the same idea to stand there now with signs all saying the same thing, the only difference being in the names?

There had to be a collective choreography for occasions such as these to generate images for the news, posterity, the history of an entire country. Had not the skyscrapers of Manhattan been generated in the same way? From a communal awareness that one day it ought to look exactly like this?

Or am I wrong and was I wrong back then, too, because in retrospect everything, even chance, appears preordained? Is it perhaps related to the fact that chance is only ever visible fleetingly, because it creates order, because its nature is to establish rules that appear with such suddenness that they seem to have been devised?

Going down this path doesn't get you anywhere, Lisa thought. You only make progress if you refrain from searching for things in what you know.

Lisa remembered waiting in the throng of women, children and old people on the wide forecourt between the station and reception centre, and her grandmother suddenly breaking out in a sweat despite the cold when she saw a train stopping, a long train from the east, a goods train whose sliding doors were already half open, a train full of gaps through which you could peer into a gloom full of eyes.

Lisa recalled having to help her grandmother because Frau Kramer did not know what to do in her haste, nervousness and love, yes, it must have been love, a love composed of what she still remembered of him, of endless waiting for the possibility that the two of them might have a future, of sleepless nights because she missed him, and of a sinking hope that was, with the words "The prisoners are coming home", placed on a catapult that had propelled them here, even without any notification that Wilhelm Kramer was coming home, at this time on that particular day, and now the train stopped and the choreography entered a new phase, necks were stretched, signs raised, commentators talked and talked into their large microphones, a man's voice boomed from the loudspeakers, saying only the obvious, They're here, the policemen became even more vigilant in their efforts to prevent anyone from making a dash for the train, because despair was hard at the heels of love, now the sliding doors of the goods carriages opened fully and men's faces emerged, beaming, forming a stream of men, all identically dressed, all carrying bunches of flowers – who had thought of this detail? – and they marched towards the women and children and old people waiting there, standing on tiptoes, and Frau Kramer's sign read:

LOOKING FOR

WILHELM KRAMER

BORN IN OSTRA, SOUTHERN BUKOVINA

ANY NEWS OF HIM?

But who would have imagined that there would be another sign looking for Wilhem Kramer, with another woman beneath it who now, as the men themselves started looking and standing on tiptoes, reading faces and signs, tried to push through the crowd but failed to make it to the front because those bodies full of yearning and hope had been packed so densely together, some for two days?

The two signs did not notice one another, the two women beneath them had eyes only for the men, so many men, and now came the first cries, one of the men rushed towards a woman, her sign fell to the ground, nobody needed it anymore, in the tempest of time two people had been reunited, A miracle! A miracle!, someone must have cried, but everyone else was too preoccupied even to catch a snippet of the impossible, and again two people were reunited, it was a lottery being played out here, devised by a cruel genius, launched many years ago, nobody knew when, exactly; and today, 7 October 1955 at the Friedland reception centre, strategically positioned at the corner of three zones, American–Hesse, British–Lower Saxony and Soviet–Thuringia, in the heart of vanquished and quartered Germany, was the prize draw.

Lisa saw the other sign and recognised the woman holding it. The same woman who two years previously had claimed she was Maria Kramer. But this time Lisa did not feel she was play-acting, something stirred in her stomach, she had to work it out, for this false Maria Kramer had eyes only for the soldiers, Lisa could see the hope in those eyes that might at any moment turn to despair as soon as the stream of men ran dry. There was a way to go yet.

One day Frau Kramer would tell her the truth about everything. But not in Friedland. There, like a marathon runner, she was busy expending all her reserves, saving nothing for a return journey, focused only on the moment, the moment and the next moment and the next moment, all her strength flowed out of her body into her neck, into the words on the sign, into the arms that held it aloft, into her eyes, which were open wide to let in everything that was outside, every single one of these men's faces and all of them together.

*

When Otto Deckert walked the unavoidable path through the rows of waiting people and was swept by Frau Kramer's gaze, he failed even to notice. It was not important, he was not Wilhelm Kramer.

The same happened to Otto Deckert's family, standing not far from the Kramers with a beautiful sign, his parents, his fiancée, a sister; his brother had fallen in the war.

Nobody recognised Otto Deckert in his new skin, with his new face, and so he simply walked on, leaving behind a family who later would be hugging each other not out of joy, but sorrow.

The Kramers must have had the same feeling, the mother and her daughter who knew nothing of each other's presence, and Lisa, whose tears were cried for her grandmother who collapsed to the ground when the men had passed by without Wilhelm Kramer, and for her grandfather, who would have made a more complete family, without a father and mother maybe, but at least a man who from time to time would have held his granddaughter in his arms to show his delight at her existence.

Frau Kramer had no strength left. She had come, the procession was over, this was the goal, all she had to do was shout: Victory! Victory over whom, over what? Over time? Over the waiting, now at an end? And was it actually at an end? Were not many more trains coming with many more returning prisoners, were there not nine thousand six hundred and twenty-six in total, of which today only six hundred had arrived? Was there not still hope? So why collapse? Why not stand up and shrug and remain in good spirits until the next train? Let's just stay here for the next few days, until we've seen all the men!

Lisa had lain on top of Frau Kramer, wrapped her child's arms around her, while her grandmother sobbed uncontrollably, unable to see that, just a few metres away, in the middle of the hurly-burly of those who had been reunited and those who were in as much despair as she was, stood her daughter, her hands in front of her face, the sign on the ground, coaxing herself to remain hopeful and hatching a plan to return to the guest house and come back when the main transport arrived.

But then a man approached her, who had seen it anyhow, the sign, one of the six hundred.

"Are you looking for Wilhelm Kramer?" he said. "From Bukovina?"

Looking up, Maria saw the face of a stranger, a young man with sunken cheeks, a woman at his side barely younger than Maria herself, whose happiness had brought her to tears and contorted her face, as if she had ended up in the emptiness and certainty of death rather than in his arms. But the man looked at Maria and said, "Here!" Feeling in his trouser pocket he pulled out a narrow, grey slip of paper, a letter. He held it out to Maria Kramer who took it uncomprehendingly, while staring at the stranger and the woman clinging onto his left arm.

"He wanted you to have it," he said. In his eyes she noted a peculiar combination of happiness and pity, an expression that Maria had never seen before and which left her feeling entirely vulnerable. "I'm so sorry," he said, before being dragged along by other people who had arrived, a father and a mother reunited with their son, who now saw only him, the one they had presumed dead, the resurrected one. He cast her a final glance over his shoulder and was gone, and Maria was left standing there holding a letter from her father, in a crowd which was now being instructed by the loudspeaker to sing a song of thanks.

Twenty-five years later Lisa would think back to this song, she would sing it and write down the words in her diary, Now thank we all our God, with hearts and hands and voices, who wondrous things hath done, in whom his world rejoices. She would remember supporting her grandmother who could barely stand, while all around them people were singing the hymn at the tops of their voices, because they knew exactly what they had to thank God for, which wondrous things he had done, why the world was rejoicing, while she and Frau Kramer were in nothingness, for now they had opened the door and they saw the room beyond, now for both of them the moment of the life or death decision was repeated, now the lottery ticket was in their hands and it was blank.

Lisa spotted Maria Kramer in the crowd, watched her put something away and then leave, rather than stay and have to stomach the thanks that others were paying to a god who rewarded and betrayed, both with the same hand. Maria Kramer did not know how many of those who had found each other again here would later separate, because nothing was as it once had been, because the collective choreography of this hour of return glossed over all details, even the important ones. Maria Kramer had received a letter, this letter made her an orphan.

Lisa could feel her grandmother's sorrow, she could feel her own sorrow, but also the question which had been growing inside her ever since that time, two years previously, when Maria had suddenly appeared at the door. Now it was as if Destiny herself had put the dot beneath the question mark and asked the question officially: Who is this woman? Why has she got my mother's name? What's not right here?

Twenty-five years later, on the thirty-fifth floor, with a view of the great immigration harbour of New York, Lisa would admit to herself that this had affected her far more powerfully than the sorrow on that 7 October, 1955, this and the doubt that always accompanied such questions, this and the mistrust, the fear of a hidden truth, O may this bounteous God, through all our life be near us, with ever-joyful hearts, and blessed peace to cheer us, how distant she had been from all that back then, but had she now, so many years later, come even an inch closer to peace?

All of a sudden eleven-year-old Lisa tore a hole in the surface of her life. Letting go of her grandmother she ran after the woman who was walking through the crowd to the station. Lisa fixed her eyes on the brown plait bobbing up and down in front of her, and when she caught up with Maria Kramer she grabbed her forearm and held it tightly. Maria turned around, recognised the girl and exclaimed, "You!"

"Are you Maria Kramer, the daughter of Wilhelm Kramer?"

"Yes I *am*," Maria said, with anger and tears in her eyes. "What do you want from me?"

"Your mother is here too."

"I don't have a mother anymore; as far as she's concerned I'm dead!"

"No! That's not true! Your mother needs you now. She's back there." Lisa pointed to the crowd of people who were still singing, All praise and thanks to God, the Father now be given; The Son and Him Who reigns with Them in highest Heaven, The one eternal God whom earth and Heaven adore; For thus it was, is now, and shall be evermore. Maria hesitated, she pictured herself standing in the doorway, she had not forgotten her mother's harsh face, she had taken the rejection like a punishment, three life sentences, for the mother, the father, the daughter, a triune curse, once spoken, never to be driven from the earth.

But now this girl who had shot up, this slim girl who had taken her place, her little enemy, was panting beside her, opening a door for her right outside the Friedland reception centre, a door which had seemed locked for ever. Maria took a deep breath and followed Lisa.

Behind the women Otto Deckert went to platform two of Friedland station. He sat down on an empty bench and waited for the next train. He could hear the voices of all those people singing, and when they had finished a loudspeaker crackled and a man's voice began to speak, but Otto Deckert paid no attention to what he was saying. Scraping together the remains of the makhorka tobacco in his bag, he rolled himself a cigarette, lit it and smoked. He did not think of the Deckerts who, in their search, had looked at him, and who had stayed to sing along with the crowd because they wanted to be thankful for the others who had been reunited with their loved ones, even if they themselves had not been granted the same joy. Otto Deckert was pleased with the way his arrival in West Germany had gone. He had no papers because he could not go to the authorities. But there were ways, alternative ways of rectifying this.

The cigarette glowed brightly as he took a deep drag. Leaning back, he savoured the sensation of being alone at last.

TWENTY-SIX

Rykestrasse 57. Soviet sector. A tall, turn-of-the-century house. Beside it a heap of rubble, smashed furniture, tattered clothes, bent cutlery, shards of china, ripped books. The stench of corpses was even more pungent today, for it had rained overnight, proper summer rain, large drops that had pelted the city, running into all cracks, gaps, holes, chinks, softening the city. The heap of rubble beside number 57 was still steaming faintly in the clear sunlight. The house buried its inhabitants beneath it, their host, old Gutfeld, said. They were in the cellar and that's where they remain.

Number 57 was so full of Jews, most of them from Poland, that two people had to share a narrow camp bed, twenty in one room. The food had to suffice for all of them, so three hundred grams of bread and half a litre of soup was the maximum daily ration, plus one and a half cubes of margarine and a tomato each week.

The Gutfelds had apologised, they said, We're terribly sorry, we'll look for something better for you, but at the moment . . . You can see for yourselves. Herr Gutfeld had made a gesture, alluding perhaps to the pile of rubble beside number 57, perhaps the bombed-out terrace of houses on the opposite side of the road, but perhaps the entire city too. His wife had linked arms with him, as if in need of his support, but in fact *she* was leading *him* from the road.

The Gutfelds were smart people, smart Berlin Jews who had gone places. Later, Ruth said, They learned to disregard any connection between the words "Jews" and "out". But they're helping us, which is magnanimous of them. Then she nodded her appreciation, dragging the corners of her mouth downwards. "You're looking pretty," Anna said, and Ruth, caught off guard, looked at her in surprise with her ponytail, her new chubby cheeks, her swollen breasts, the nourished flesh on her bones. Ruth made no reply. Anna smiled.

They were standing in the street, following the Gutfelds with their gaze, two of the Abramowicz children were playing in the rubble of number 56, Marja, who was now seven, had found a doll missing its arms and was holding it tightly. Dana, the youngest, had grown and learned to crawl. Having spotted Marja's new toy she was heading straight for it. She was just beside the heap when a large chunk came loose, flattening the girl, and smashed into its constituent parts, mortar, bricks, a few tiles.

There was a pause before the two women screamed and raced over. Still screaming, they cleared away the rubble, only going quiet when they had uncovered Dana's lifeless little body.

Mrs Abramowicz came running out of the house and threw herself on her dead child. Marja clutched her doll, sobbing. Up on the steps of number 57 stood Ariel, his Magallanes book pressed against his chest, staring at the scene.

A lorry drove up. Anna watched Peretz and Avi jump out and approach them. She saw the shock on Peretz's face, she held him tightly and, for the first time in ages, broke down.

TWENTY-SEVEN

Lisa wrote:

"Dear Diary, today I met Mummy's sister. She's called Maria, because Mummy's real name is Margarita. Why did Grandma lie to me? When she took me to bed she said she was very angry with my aunt and she'd wished that she had died rather than Mummy. But I shouldn't say this to my aunt otherwise she'd be very sad. Because she's a very sad person, she cries a lot. It's strange that Mummy wasn't called that and now my aunt *is* called it. Margarita is a pretty name too, but I'm going to have to get used to it.

"The journey home was very strange. But it was even stranger when Grandma and my aunt suddenly saw each other again in Friedland. And much stranger than that was that it was all my doing. Why did I do it? I think it was for the best. Now the three of us can live in the apartment and when I come home from school it won't be empty because even if Grandma's canning fish at Hawesta, my aunt can be here to cook for me. Maybe she will. But she's not very nice. She doesn't really talk to me, she asks Grandma things about me even though I'm sitting right beside her and could speak for myself. I don't like that, I think people should pay attention to everyone, even girls who've only just turned eleven.

"But I wanted to write about what happened when Grandma and Auntie Maria saw each other again. Grandma stopped crying at once and looked at the two of us as if we'd done something wrong. Then Auntie Maria said, Mother, but it didn't sound quite so desperate as that time she stood at the door to our apartment. It sounded as if she'd put a question mark at the end. It was so loud, the man on the loud-speaker never stopped talking, then a brass band played some music, but the three of us just stood there, staring at each other. All of a sudden Grandma said to Auntie Maria, Maybe he'll arrive with the main trans-port, and she only said that because she didn't want Auntie Maria to be sad. I could see that, because she makes the same face when she's trying to comfort me. And then something very sad happened. Auntie Maria shook her head and said, He's not coming back. She cried and took out a letter and told us that a friend of her father had just given it to her. Then she went to Grandma with the letter in her hand and gave it to her. Grandma took it and started crying too, and then the two of them hugged each other and cried, and Auntie Maria said to Grandma, Forgive me, I beg you, and Grandma said, howling, Only if you accept this child as the daughter of your sister Margarita. Those were her very words! Auntie Maria stopped crying for a moment. She raised her head and looked at Grandma. I couldn't see her face because she turned her head away. But Grandma pushed her head down again and then the two of them were back in a tight embrace, and Grandma said, Promise me. Auntie Maria nodded. That was strange. I couldn't say anything because the two of them were crying so much, but I badly wanted to know what this was all about.

"We stood for ages in the crowd of people who were all hugging each other too, there was barely anybody who wasn't hugging someone. Maybe Grandma noticed this because she let go of Auntie Maria and grabbed me tightly and then she said, We're going home now, the three of us. All of a sudden it was nice that there was at least another person with us, even if I'd have preferred Grandad. But Grandad's probably long dead and it's only now that Grandma believes it. I'm desperate to know what's in the letter, I don't think Grandma's opened it yet, I think she's terrified of reading it. I can understand that. It must be a strange fear, because nothing can happen to her. The war is over and we're safe here at home in Lübeck, and then the letter's on the table in front of her and she's meant to open it and read it. I bet Grandma's thinking all kinds of things about what might be in it. Perhaps he really wasn't well when he wrote it, because it was dreadful over there. Then it's as if he's not just dead but dying before her eyes. Sometimes I get the feeling that the ideas you get in your head make everything much worse than it really is. For example, when I imagine Grandma dying and me being all alone, I get really scared, even though Grandma's still very much alive. But now, of course, it's not so awful because Auntie Maria's here. Although I think I'd rather go and live with Uncle Tobi if Grandma died. Hopefully that will never happen! Oh yes, I wanted to write about the train. It was really strange, because Auntie Maria stared at me the whole time, but whenever I glanced back at her she quickly looked away and pretended to be staring out of the window. Why do people do that?

What's more she didn't look friendly at all, no, she looked almost angry, not just angry but secretly angry. She's got absolutely no reason to be angry with me. She doesn't even know me! On the train Grandma said how Auntie Maria and Mummy used to argue a lot, but rather than looking at me when she said it her eyes were fixed on Auntie Maria, and she made an odd face, she looked really stern, and Auntie Maria just looked back, she didn't say anything and her face was just as stern. She gritted her teeth as if she were still angry at Mummy. And right now I think that perhaps she really still is angry at Mummy, and now she's angry at me because I'm Mummy's daughter. I'm going to be as nice as I can to Auntie Maria so she sees she's got no reason to be angry with me. Then she'll understand really fast and be more friendly. Hopefully.

"We got back to Lübeck very late, it was quite chilly. Tomorrow's Saturday and I ought to be going to school, but Grandma said she'll let me have the day off. That's why I can keep writing now even though I'm very tired. Grandma's in the sitting room with Auntie Maria, I can hear their voices, but can't make out what they're saying as they're talking really softly. I wonder what they're talking about? I'm sure they've got so much to say to each other. But I'm also sure that they're talking a lot about me. One day I'll find out everything.

"It's nice to lie in bed and hear voices in the sitting room, it feels like a family. A family just of women! Maybe it's better that way. Good night, dear Diary! See you tomorrow!"

TWENTY-EIGHT

Mrs Abramowicz ate nothing. She said nothing. She sat in the narrow room at the back, which she shared with nineteen other people, staring into the distance. Her two remaining children, Ariel and Marja, did not want to leave her alone. They sat with their mother, they stuck to her, they cried or shouted at her, but their mother did not react. Anna and Ruth wanted to take the children outside, but the little ones resisted as if they were being abducted.

Even the old man, who Ruth continued to care for as if he were her father, began to talk when he saw the state Mrs Abramowicz was in. One morning, when the others had left the house to sample a taste of freedom, or to get somehow from the Soviet sector into the American one, he sat himself with difficulty next to Mrs Abramowicz and softly stroked her hair with his wrinkled hand. Then he took her by the shoulders and started rocking, slowly and rhythmically, pulling her along. As if he had intended to sing the following words, but had held back at the last moment, he said:

"May
the great name,
whose insatiable desire for life and death
gave birth to the universe
reverberate throughout His creation.
Now! May
this great presence guide your life and your day
and all life in our world. And say: Yes and amen.
Blessed
Blessed be this great name
now and for ever and for ever and now
so we bless and praise Your name
glorify and exalt it
and we forgive You
when You take away our life
and the life of those we love
and the life of our people
Your name? Holy one, Blessed one.
You go far beyond our praise

our hymns
our consolation,
leaving all the words
with which we help ourselves,
from which we suffer
far behind you. And say yes
and say amen.
Let God's name
bring forth great peace
and great life
for us and for all. And say yes and say amen.
May He who has given us a universe of conflict
give us peace, all of us, that is: Israel.
That is: Israel!
That is: Israel!
And say yes
Amen."

Anna was a few metres away, lying on her camp bed which was roomier now that Ruth had gone outside. She was amazed listening to the old man speak like that, for each time he deviated from the traditional text she winced inside, making her realise how well she knew the Kaddish, But where from? she wondered, Those few visits to the synagogue? She declined to go any further down this path, this path was forbidden, it did not belong in her special archive of important memories, this path led to the meadow where there was no longer a happy little girl. And beyond the meadow lay a village, and in this village lived people who had left. Anna's hand made an involuntary movement, as if she had to brush away a spider's web to move on.

Instead she thought of Josef Ranzner, of dead Sturmbannführer Treitz, who Ranzner believed would return. But once lost, was everything not gone for ever? She felt a sorrow fermenting inside, which was curiously impersonal and yet definitely belonged to her. Was her entire life not lost? Was not everything that had already passed dead because it would never return? Had not her former light-heartedness given way to an excess of weighty destiny? Anna felt as if she were bent over like a little old woman, her shoulders seemed to pull forwards with such intensity, she felt as if they would meet in front of her breasts. She felt as if Dana had to die so that her own child could live. She thought that the guilt she felt had been locked away somewhere inside her, and had now found a key to break out and be heard. She felt guilty for her pregnancy, she thought she had got off lightly in comparison to those who had been in concentration camp, she thought that she and Ruth ought to have kept a more watchful eye on Dana, she wondered, Am I actually fit to be a mother? Peretz was the only one who believed in her unconditionally and unconsciously, she needed him now.

Peretz came that evening. He looked happy, they sat on the outdoor steps next to where Dana had died. The moon shone down on the rubble, people laden with their possessions walked by, from time to time a Soviet patrol vehicle drove past, It's curfew time soon, Anna said, just to say something. Peretz nodded and said, "We've been given some money by the military rabbi, the American Jews are making generous donations that eventually end up in our hands. We can get rid of the drivers and buy our own lorries, which is a good thing." He nodded, he appeared fulfilled by his mission, it was what he wanted, it was what she should believe, it was what she wanted to believe, but there was something else she wanted too.

"Peretz, I'm pregnant."

"What?" He would have been brought back down to earth with a bump had he understood what was happening to him. Brought back down to earth from a flight of refugees that provided him with the security of habit. A poor attempt, for he had not come here to disclose his tactics to Anna, least of all Anna, Look, I'm involved in something huge, how can you object to that? Had he not come back to turn the tables, so that it would be her chasing after him, allowing him to reassume his former roles?

Peretz, I'm pregnant, what a trump card Anna had whipped out from her belly, what could be bigger than this? Nothing, nothing at all, and Peretz realised it at once, forgotten were the lorries, forgotten the mission, Israel forgotten. Anna was pregnant and Peretz just stood there, eyes like saucers, unsure of what to say. His mouth was agape.

"Don't worry, you're not the father," Anna said.

What am I doing? she thought. She felt as if she had lured Peretz into a trap in which he was now stuck, she sensed her behaviour had been methodical. But she had no control over it. Later she would think, I needed a father for this child, and that would have been adequate justification. But it failed to explain what in her mind had made her choose this moment, this evening, one week after Dana's death.

Peretz cleared his throat. His mouth was dry. He felt as if a delicious schnitzel had been waved under his nose and then served up to someone else. But a child is not a schnitzel, a child is far more alluring bait for a man who for weeks has been searching in vain for a rope with which to bind this woman to him. Then out of the blue comes a child, but before he can feel delight it is another's child, and now his role has changed conclusively. Now it goes: If you wish to have this woman you must make a sacrifice, as large as another's child. It goes: Now you can prove what you're made of, now is your opportunity! Grab it, grab the hand she's offered you before she takes it away. Peretz does not deliberate for long.

"I don't care."

"Do you really mean that?"

"Yes, I don't care. I . . ." Peretz hesitates, Peretz suspects that right at the back, where his thoughts are speaking so softly that they can barely be heard, the trap is springing and he will never get out again. Right at the back a voice asks about the child's father. But further forward Peretz is afraid of the truth, because it might force him to listen to the thoughts, for Anna is like a fish in his hands, one false movement and she will slip through his fingers back into the murky water, where he might never find her again. And right at the front, where the mouth begins and thinking ends, Peretz says, "I love you."

Anna embraces him, it feels like a reward, Good boy, you've got everything right, somewhere at the very back a voice is complaining, screaming out loud, Peretz! Are you mad? What do you think you're doing? This is a stitch-up, don't get involved, don't be tempted! But Anna's embrace is stronger, she takes possession of Peretz with a gentleness, a lack of resistance in her entire body, which seems to be saying, I'm yours. Peretz does not listen, he wants to enjoy the feeling of finally being the man at Anna's side, finally being able to say to the whole world, She is my wife.

And the child?

"If you like we can say that the child is mine," Peretz whispers into Anna's ear, and now Anna hugs him even more tightly, that must mean, Yes, yes to the common cause, yes to sealing the only door that connects us to the world, the truth about ourselves. And what is better, more solid, more compelling than a shared secret?

Anna thinks of Josef Ranzner and his four adjutants, who may all be dead, she thinks of Abba, who she sometimes misses still. Ad Lo-Or. Now thoughts of him seem like a little girl's dream. Here is the man who is making a sacrifice for you, forget all others, take him and try to love him.

Anna nodded and said, "Yes."

TWENTY-NINE

12th December, 1944
near Pulawy

My dearest lovely wife, what I would give to be with you now!

But not here. Your Farmer Kramer was taken to the east with a whole bunch of other farmers from the Wartheland. On horse-drawn carts. The lorries couldn't get anywhere in the deep snow. We're no longer farmers vital to the war effort, we're just soldiers now. We were taken to the west bank of the Weichsel. There the river makes a big curve from north to south. The Russians have a bridgehead right in the middle. We've been shooting at them for days, but the bridgehead just keeps getting bigger. Do you remember the two cows on our farm? When we arrived, their udders were full to bursting and they were bellowing. I'm sure you remember. This bridgehead is like an udder nobody's milking. It's growing and growing. But the cow is the whole of Russia. Russia's got a lot of milk.

I'm just a farmer with a rifle. I don't know if I've shot anyone yet. We can't see the Ruskies. And the Ruskies can't see us. We shoot our weapons in a high arc. We shoot day and night. You can barely sleep on account of the noise. Each morning the trench is full of snow and we have to shovel it out. My dear wife! I hope your Farmer Kramer was a good husband. Before we left our homeland my father gave me a piece of advice. He said, "A smart man listens to his wife." That was good advice. I was always a simple man, but there was an event in my life which showed me that even a simple man has his thoughts. Even a simple man like your Farmer Kramer, who can't for the life of him remember why he wanted to leave his homeland and why he ever doubted your decisions, especially the decision to help other people. Now that this farmer doesn't know whether he'll ever return to you, he knows that you did everything right. Maybe we ought not to have sold the clock. Maybe it was right.

30th December, 1944
near Pulawy

Three weeks have passed. Our front line has been pushed back. We're not on the run yet. But the Russians have crossed the Weichsel. There are rumours that they're going to attempt a pincer movement. From the south. We're not quite as many farmers from the Wartheland as we were at the beginning. Half are dead. Do you remember the Popko family? There were two of us and so many of them that they couldn't all fit in one compartment. How many children did they have? Now they don't have a father anymore. I saw him with my own eyes. It wasn't the Russians that got him. It was the winter. When he died we stripped him of his clothes and now Popko's trousers are going around with new legs, but without the coat, his coat is keeping another soldier warm, and without the boots, his boots are in the next trench but one, his hat is keeping my head warm. But what horror stories is Farmer Kramer telling in his letter? He's always about to send it, but then he hesitates. Maybe he's finding new words to describe what he wants to say. Farmer Kramer's ears are missing the song that comes from your mouth. He can still hear it in his head, but it's not the same. I hope you're well, I hope the cow and Margarita's child are well.

Today Farmer Kramer almost bought it, my dear wife. But he's still here and now he's writing to you. Things aren't going well. We're fleeing. The Russians have made their pincer movement. We're all trying to get through the corridor to the west. With their vehicles the officers have a good chance. Your Farmer Kramer has to go on foot with the rest of his comrades. He's the last farmer from the Wartheland. We've been on the march for days. Who knows how much longer my strength will last. It's so cold.

They've taken everything from us. The only things I was allowed to keep were my letter and pencil. The officer knew German. He liked the bit about the udders and the cow which is Russia. He laughed and slapped me on the shoulder. Your Farmer Kramer is one of a few thousand who didn't make it through. Fortunately I never had an S.S. uniform. They shot plenty of those on the spot. They're sending us to Siberia. Your farmer will finally be able to work again. Anyway, I'm still alive. I hope you got away in time.

We've been on the march for days. The Russians don't know where to take us. Always from one place to the next. My fingers are frozen. I hope you can read this. This morning an old man, must have been sixty, collapsed and tried to get up again, but couldn't. Shot in the back of the neck. It's hang on in or die.

25th January, 1945

Still on the march. I'm quite stiff from the cold, Farmer Kramer has retreated inside himself. On the outside I'm as cold as my surroundings. More shots to backs of necks. How much longer are they going to have us march? Or do they want us to perish one after the other? No food. When we're thirsty we have to eat snow. The thought of you keeps this man on his feet. Your voice when it sings, lovely wife.

2nd March, 1945
Camp 7525/7 Prokopyevsk

My dear wife! Your farmer made it to Siberia by a whisker. I don't know how far we walked in the thick snow, and then we got to a goods station where a train was waiting. Almost half of us died along the way. Most weren't even shot by the Russians. Just left to die. Two more died on the train. Luckily it was so cold that they didn't smell even after three days. The rest of us huddled together, swapping who was in the middle. One of the soldiers, a young S.S. man, went mad. Kept screaming, I want to get out, I want to get out. The rest of us tried to ignore him, but couldn't. Eventually someone knocked him to the ground. We passed through Russian villages where people looked in poorer shape than we did. Everything is very sad. You can be proud of your farmer that he made it to Siberia. It can't get any worse now.

My dear wife! The coalmine is no worse than marching in the freezing cold. But it's no better either. There's barely anything to eat. How lucky I am to have you! That I can write to you. Even if you're dead by now, you still do me the world of good. My pencil is getting stubbier. You waste a lot of lead when you sharpen it with a stone. That's why I'm writing to you once a month. It gives me strength. I count the days until I can write again. Who'd have thought that your farmer would become a writer? Who'd have thought it would do him the world of good?

10th May, 1945
Camp 7525/7 Prokopyevsk

My dear, lovely wife! They told us the war is over, Germany defeated. Are you still alive? Your farmer is, but he's not a farmer anymore. Nor a soldier. Now your farmer's a prisoner of war. Your farmer's tired. It's May already and still cold. Everyone's hungry here. You learn to walk slowly, they call it "P.O.W. pace", your farmer does it now to save his strength. After all, he's got to be able to make it back. Not on foot, hopefully.

6th June, 1945
Camp 7525/7 Prokopyevsk

Your farmer is still here, my dear wife. Sometimes he doesn't know anymore whether you and this letter are two separate entities. Your farmer now knows what raw frog tastes like. Spiders. Earthworms. Your farmer has to keep his strength up. In the camp are some German foremen. You have to watch them, they're worse than the Romanians or Hungarians. If someone is unable to work they pounce on him. Please forgive me, dear wife, for telling you these things. It's good for me to look for words.

15th July, 1945
Camp 7525/7 Prokopyevsk

My dear wife! How wonderful that I have you! They say we're going to help rebuild the country. I'm sure you're doing the same in Germany. It's difficult work. Most difficult of all is underground. It's high summer in Siberia at the moment and it's hot and humid outside, but cold and damp down below. Many are ill. I'm lending out my pencil in return for cigarettes. With the cigarettes I buy food. When we're underground the external work team always brings something you stuff into yourself. Now your farmer is eating animals he used to consider pests. How many animals died in our field, without one of us ever being able to eat them?

THIRTY

August 31, 1945
White House

My dear General Eisenhower,

I have received and considered the report of Mr Earl G. Harrison, our representative on the Intergovernmental Committee on Refugees, upon his mission to inquire into the condition and needs of displaced persons in Germany who may be stateless or non-repatriable, particularly Jews. I am sending you a copy of that report. I have also had a long conference with him on the same subject matter.

While Mr Harrison makes due allowance for the fact that during the early days of liberation the huge task of mass repatriation required main attention he reports conditions which now exist and which require prompt remedy. These conditions, I know, are not in conformity with policies promulgated by S.H.A.E.F., now Combined Displaced Persons Executive. But they are what actually exists in the field. In other words, the policies are not being carried out by some of your subordinate officers.

For example, military government officers have been authorized and even directed to requisition billeting facilities from the German population for the benefit of displaced persons. Yet, from this report, this has not been done on any wide scale. Apparently it is being taken for granted that all displaced persons, irrespective of their former persecution or the likelihood that their repatriation or resettlement will be delayed, must remain in camps – many of which are overcrowded and heavily guarded. Some of these camps are the very ones where these people were herded together, starved, tortured and made to witness the death of their fellow-inmates and friends and relatives. The announced policy has been to give such persons preference over the German civilian population in housing. But the practice seems to be quite another thing.

We must intensify our efforts to get these people out of camps and into decent houses until they can be repatriated or evacuated. These houses should be requisitioned from the German civilian population. That is one way to implement the Potsdam policy that the German people "cannot escape responsibility for what they have brought upon themselves."

I quote this paragraph with particular reference to the Jews among the displaced persons:

"As matters now stand, we appear to be treating the Jews as the Nazis treated them except that we do not exterminate them. They are in concentration camps in large numbers under our military guard instead of S.S. troops. One is led to wonder whether the German people, seeing this, are not supposing that we are following or at least condoning Nazi policy."

This is particularly true given that the German people at large do not seem to have any sense of guilt with respect to the war and its causes and results.

At many of the camps and centers including those where serious starvation cases are, there is a marked and serious lack of needed medical supplies.

One Army Chaplain, a Rabbi, personally attended, since liberation, 23,000 burials (90 per cent Jews) at Bergen Belsen alone, one of the largest and most vicious of the concentration camps, where, incidentally, despite persistent reports to the contrary, fourteen thousand displaced persons are still living, including over seven thousand Jews.

Although some Camp Commandants have managed, in spite of the many obvious difficulties, to find clothing of one kind or another for their charges, many of the Jewish displaced persons, late in July, had no clothing other than their concentration camp garb – a rather hideous striped pajama effect – while others, to their chagrin, were obliged to wear German S.S. uniforms.

The internees feel particularly bitter when they see how well the German population is still dressed. The German population today is still the best-dressed population in all of Europe.

In many camps, the 2,000 calories included 1,250 calories of a black, wet and extremely unappetizing bread. Harrison received the distinct impression and considerable substantiating information that large numbers of the German population – again principally in the rural areas – have a more varied and palatable diet than is the case with the displaced persons. The Camp Commandants put in their requisitions with the German burgomeister and many seemed to accept whatever he turned over as being the best that was available.

At many places, however, the military government officers manifest the utmost reluctance or indisposition, if not timidity, about inconveniencing the German population. They even say that their job is to get communities working properly and soundly again, that they must "live with the Germans while the D.P.s (displaced persons) are a more temporary problem." Thus (and according to Harrison he can cite many an example) if a group of Jews are ordered to vacate their temporary quarters, needed for military purposes, and there are two possible sites, one an apartment block (modest) with conveniences and the other a series of shabby buildings with outside toilet and washing facilities the burgomeister readily succeeds in persuading the Town Major to allot the latter to the displaced persons and to save the former for returning German civilians.

For reasons that are obvious and need not be labored, most Jews want to leave Germany and Austria as soon as possible. That is their first and great expressed wish and while this report necessarily deals with other needs present in the situation, many of the people themselves fear other suggestions or plans for their benefit because of the possibility that attention might thereby be diverted from the all-important matter of evacuation from Germany. Their desire to leave Germany is an urgent one. The life which they have led for the past ten years, a life of fear and wandering and physical torture, has made them impatient of delay. They want to be evacuated to Palestine now, just as other national groups are being repatriated to their homes. They do not look kindly on the idea of waiting around in idleness and in discomfort in a German camp for many months until a leisurely solution is found for them.

I hope you will adopt the suggestion that a more extensive plan of field visitation by appropriate Army Group Headquarters be instituted, so that the humane policies which have been enunciated are not permitted to be ignored in the field. Most of the conditions now existing in displaced persons camps would quickly be remedied if through inspection tours they came to your attention or to the attention of your supervisory officers.

I know you will agree with me that we have a particular responsibility toward these victims of persecution and tyranny who are in our zone. We must make clear to the German people that we thoroughly abhor the Nazi policies of hatred and persecution. We have no better opportunity to demonstrate this than by the manner in which we ourselves actually treat the survivors remaining in Germany.

I hope you will report to me as soon as possible the steps you have been able to take to clean up the conditions mentioned in the report.

I am communicating directly with the British Government in an effort to have the doors of Palestine opened to such of these displaced persons as wish to go there.

Very sincerely yours,
HARRY S. TRUMAN

THIRTY-ONE

2nd September, 1945
Camp 7525/7 Prokopyevsk

Dear Wife! Whenever this man writes to you it is like returning home. I'm being thrifty with my visits home, the pencil has been getting rapidly shorter since I've been renting it out. I was given paper by a Russian officer, some of which I sold on. More prisoners have arrived in the past month. They told us about Germany. About the towns and cities. There's also a young man from Lübeck, his name is Friedrich Kleinert. I told him about our honeymoon. He asked me why anybody would want to have a honeymoon in Lübeck. Good question! I told him about the picture. Did I ever mention it to you? When I said Lübeck you agreed at once! Did I tell you that we had a picture of the Holstentor on the wall at home? When your farmer was a young boy and you just a girl living nearby, he would stand in front of this picture, staring at the fat towers with their pointy hats. Now you know. How wonderful our honeymoon was! It's so long ago now that your farmer sometimes has to pinch himself when he thinks about it. Fritz said that Lübeck was bombed too. The very first city! In 1942. That was when we decided to leave Bukovina. When you put it like that, one thing after the other, you get the feeling that everything is connected. But the connection is probably only in my head. Your farmer's getting philosophical! Life throws up surprises.

THIRTY-TWO

10th October, 1945
Berlin, Rykestrasse 57, second floor

"The Russians aren't treating us as Jews. They say we're Poles, Hungarians, Romanians, Germans, Austrians etc. Do you understand? We need to leave the Russian sector or they'll send the Abramowiczes, the old man and me back to Poland."

"How do you know?"

"Your Peretz told me."

"My Peretz?"

"Isn't that what he is? At least he's more your Peretz than you are his Anna."

"Stop being so snide."

"I'm not being snide, I'm just telling the truth."

"So what's your plan then?"

"Our plan? Oh that's right, you're German, aren't you? You don't have any problem with going back to the Nazis, do you?"

"Ruth! What is the matter with you? I'm pregnant; I've got to bear that in mind too."

"Of course!"

THIRTY-THREE

What kind of family are we? Lisa wrote in her diary. Auntie Maria's been living with us for a year now, she wrote. She barely speaks to me, she gets up late and comes home late at night. She's got a boyfriend, she wrote. He goes around like a gangster out of an American film, suit, spats, hat, hands in his trouser pockets. You never see his face. I watch him from the window when he's standing on the other side of the street, waiting for her, while Auntie Maria is still in the bathroom, hectically putting on so much make-up that everyone can see it. Was Mummy like that too? Lisa wrote. I asked Grandma, she wrote. She said, No, Mummy was completely different. I still find it strange that Mummy's real name is Margarita and not Maria, she wrote, pausing to reread the lines she had written.

Auntie Maria, she continued writing, sometimes makes fun in a most peculiar way. For example, she says, "My sister, what was her name again?

Oh yes, Margarita," and then she laughs exaggeratedly, while Grandma gives her an evil look. Or she calls me "my darling niece" with an ironic expression on her face. Why does Auntie Maria do that? Grandma told me that the two of them used to argue a lot and Mummy never forgave Auntie Maria for disappearing from the transit camp in Gunzenhausen with one of the S.S. men who had been brought over from Bukovina. One day Auntie Maria simply left, while Grandma and Grandpa and Uncle Karl and Mummy had to stay there for months having checks to see if they were German enough. Grandma said that the officers went around with books full of drawings of noses and eyes and heads. They had strange instruments for measuring the features of ethnic Germans, and then the officers would decide if someone really was German or not. As if you could tell like that! Grandma shook her head too, But back then, she said, we didn't have any choice. She raised her left arm and showed me a tattoo on the inner side. It's an A with a B beside it. From one of the doctors in the camp in Gunzenhausen. Grandma said, When it was clear that we were Germans and not members of some inferior race they tattooed us with our individual blood groups, just like when they brand cattle. And Auntie Maria, Lisa wrote, had simply gone to Berlin, she'd spared herself all this, and from there she wrote them a postcard with the Brandenburg Gate on it. Nothing more. They were like night and day, your mother and aunt, Grandma said, Lisa wrote. That may be true. But somehow I don't believe Grandma. I can't put my finger on it, but she makes such a funny face when she talks about it, that sometimes I feel she's lying to me because she doesn't want me to find out something far worse. In fact she's been behaving strangely ever since we've been in Friedland. Perhaps it's got something to do with Grandad. She still hasn't read his letter. But perhaps she's lying and she <u>has</u> read it, and it makes her so sad that she doesn't want to talk about it, and that's why she just says she hasn't read it yet. Poor Grandma, Lisa wrote.

THIRTY-FOUR

Dearest child,
Anna thought

This
is a message to you.
I hope you can hear me or,
if you can't hear me then you can
feel what I want to say to you.

Because you can't yet see
I'll describe to you the place
where the two of us are now:
I'm lying on a camp bed
on the second floor of house number 57,
Rykestrasse,
Soviet sector,
Berlin.

The room is full of people,
it's evening, and outside
it's been chilly for a week now.
Winter is gradually approaching,
and autumn, my dearest child,
is now no more than a foreshadow of winter,
before it appears itself.

The people around me
have become familiar over the last three months,
I know them all by name,
I know their voices and moods,
I know their odours,
all blending together
in this damp room,
as if in an orgy.
And so it smells musty in here
and mouldy and of too many people.

Closest to me are Ruth,
poor Mrs Abramowicz, who still says nothing,
her two children,
Marja and Ariel,
the old man, who's started speaking again,
perhaps because he realised that
there are worse things,
more absurd things in life
since Dana died,
or perhaps because he realised that
unhappiness does not vanish from the world
if we bear a grudge against our god.
I won't list the other people,
but I'm sure you know their voices.

Now
they're getting ready for night,
one after another
they visit the only bathroom in the house.
There's no hot water.
The toilet paper is old newspapers,

sometimes I read what's written there,
and get a shock, because they're from a time
which is now gone.

The two of us have already been to the bathroom,
luckily people always let me go ahead now,
ever since my belly has grown so large
with you.

So now you know precisely where you are
and what it's like here.
Who knows
where you come from?
If your father,
if he is your father,
was right,
then you've lived before,
and perhaps you're even Sturmbannführer Treitz.
who was shot by a Pole
while on the hunt for Jews.
It would serve him right
to be reborn from the womb of a Jew,
to have to love her,
and to have to be loved by her.
But the world is large,
perhaps you come from somewhere quite different
and everything you remember seems,
given the reality of our situation,
like a fairy tale or a dream.
Who knows?

You have become so big inside me
and you're moving so much
that I can't sleep
and in the daytime, when you're sleeping,
I feel sluggish and immobile.
Ruth, that lovely creature,
has given us her half of the bed,
she said,
All the beds here are being shared by two people,
why should we share this one between three?
I'm sure you heard her.
Where on earth does she get
this perspective on things?
I often wonder.
I hope my close relationship with her
has rubbed off on you, my child.

Your mother is not a happy person,
I regret to have to say.
And there's more I have to tell you.
I have to tell you that
your father,
whichever one he may be,
is probably dead
and that's exactly what he deserved.
I have to tell you that
when I look inside myself
I stare into a dark crater,
which seems bottomless,
and that's why I can't promise
to be a good mother.
I'm so sorry about this.

But if you have already lived before
then you sought me out
then you didn't want it
any other way.

There's something else I have to tell you:
Your father isn't your father,
but a stranger.
I have to tell you
that we will lie to you,
You will think you know everything about yourself,
but nobody, not even I
can tell you the truth.
Take heart, my child,
we're all strangers, even you,
you're more of a stranger to me than
all the people in this room.
And me, too, I'm
more of a stranger to you than you will know,
for as long as you are a child and perhaps even
for as long as you are on this earth.
It makes me sad, truly it does, my child,
sad because love cannot conquer the unfamiliarity.
Maybe unfamiliarity is even necessary
so that love can exist.
Perhaps
it's necessary to be sad about it,
so we know that this is how it is.
Perhaps we must know,
so that we do not become blind in our attempt
to forget the truth about life
when we love.

The truth, my child, is that
we are alone,
every single one of us. Forgive me
for crying over this, forgive me
for bringing you into this world,
which has so little joy in store for you.
But I cannot do anything else.

Your grandfather,
whose fate my silence was supposed to bury,
and who, ever since you have existed inside me,
speaks once more from every thought
I send to you,
once said to me, shortly
before we were separated and he and your grandmother
and my siblings
embarked on the *one* journey from which there is no return,
shortly after your father,
if he is your father,
and I met because he pointed at me
and shouted: That one!
Because he wanted to have me,
gazing as they do at slave girls
at the market.
Your grandfather said: My dear child,
the secret of life is
to choose
what is unavoidable.

My dear child
I pass these words on to you
and hope that

you will understand them.
The death of all those who have died,
whoever they may be,
is unavoidable,
and I choose it
because I don't want to die.

Your father,
whoever he is,
was unavoidable,
and I choose him
in order to love you,
my unavoidable child,
so that you may live.

One day perhaps you will accuse me
of knowing nothing about love,
and you will be right about many things.
But there is one thing I know for certain:
love is the servant of life
and of nothing else.
Do not forget that, my child.

THIRTY-FIVE

Aaron Strauss was waiting in the small entrance hall of Oranienburgerstrasse 31, in the Soviet sector, adjacent to the border with the
French sector, which began two streets to the west. He was a short,
slender man around forty years of age, he kept his reading glasses pushed
up on his head, so they were always ready when needed. Without a

pair for four years, he had, as if by a miracle, found some glasses which matched his long-sightedness almost perfectly. They had been perched on the nose of a frozen man, half his age at most, and Aaron Strauss had hesitated for a moment, because he felt like a thief, even though the other man no longer needed the spectacles and he was in desperate need of them. Since that day he had sworn never to lose this pair of glasses, he felt as if he were preserving the memory of an unknown man, of whom nothing remained save for the image of a sedentary figure, looking as if he had settled down by the side of the road to catch his breath, from a distance his hair had appeared grey like an old man's, but then they had come closer, very close, so close that Aaron Strauss was able to think about the glasses for several minutes, so close that he was able to remove them from the corpse without any of the S.S. men noticing.

Now he stood facing the man coming down the steps in the cold drizzle. He knew this man vaguely, they had met a month ago when Aaron Strauss was waiting with forty-nine Polish and Byelorussian Jews to be picked up by the Bricha lorry and driven to Berlin. The man had impressed on them that they were German refugees from the eastern territories of the Reich and not Jews, Otherwise the Soviets might send you straight back to Poland or somewhere else, he had said, As far as they're concerned, you see, we don't exist.

This last sentence had fixed itself on Aaron Strauss's mind, especially the tone in which it had been uttered: ironic, almost arrogant, as if the Soviets were stupid. Oh well, Eliezer Ben-Levy, the rabbi travelling with them, had said with a shrug in the lorry, We've been so many different things. I hope they're not going to look for Nazis amongst us. Everyone laughed, the rabbi thrust out his left arm and cried Heil Hitler, affording them a glimpse of his five-digit number, and then they knew that he had been in Auschwitz. On the journey Aaron had been afraid, such tattoos were not customary in Buchenwald so how could he, Aaron, the former Prussian official, prove that he was not a Nazi?

But the man who now opened the double doors, letting in cold air before he stepped into the entrance hall, had brought them safely to Berlin, dropping them here, Oranienburgerstrasse 31. The house had been provided by the Jewish Community, he said, and nobody had been surprised that such an organisation still existed in Germany. That came later. They shook hands. Unbuttoning his long coat and taking off the hat which made him look American, Peretz Sarfati said, "Where are we going?"

"Have you got everything?" Aaron Strauss replied.

"I hope so," Peretz said, lifting up the slim leather briefcase in his left hand.

"Follow me!" Aaron Strauss said, taking the lead.

The entrance hall was the only place in Oranienburgerstrasse 31 that was sometimes empty, mainly because it was too cold. As soon as they went up the stairs and stepped into one of the corridors branching off to the apartments, the scene changed in an instant. People sat and lay everywhere, on every conceivable object that could be used as a bed, blankets, old mattresses reeking of damp and mould, chairs and wooden planks shoved together, a few people even lying on the bare stone floor. The house was full of noises, it sounded as if someone was singing somewhere. Somewhere else a person was playing a piano.

At the end of the corridor they had taken, beyond the last apartment doors, a wooden door was arranged horizontally, a thick coat spread on top. Pushing the coat aside, Aaron Strauss pointed to a flat area in the door's panelling, where the white paint had not flaked off and thus it was perfectly even, and said, "That's my desk."

"Very practical," Peretz replied, without changing his expression. He took from the briefcase a printed piece of paper, longer and narrower than a sheet of A4, and handed it to Strauss. The latter felt it with his fingers as a forger might a counterfeit banknote, he sniffed it, he examined the print. Then he looked at Peretz.

"This is an original. Where did you get it?"

Peretz shrugged and said simply, "I brought the right label, stamp and fountain pen too."

Taking these objects one by one out of the briefcase, he placed them before Strauss on the door that served as his bed and desk. Then Strauss started writing in beautiful Sütterlin script, while all around them, in a building designed for three hundred people at most, a thousand Jews from eastern Europe were reading the Torah, learning modern Hebrew or English, taking music lessons, consuming the daily ration of 300 grams of bread and potatoes and a soup, or simply sleeping to avoid any of this.

"Today Joseph Stirnweiss, resident in Nauen, and psychoanalyst by profession, appeared before the undersigned registrar, confirmed his identity, and registered the birth of a girl at the district hospital on the first of January in the year nineteen hundred and twenty at seven o'clock in the evening, to his wife, Chawa Stirnweiss, née Grünwald, resident with him in Nauen, and recorded that the child had been given the name Anna."

Bent far over the table, Strauss kept writing slowly and with great concentration, repeatedly dipping the fountain pen into the inkpot that Peretz had brought along. He made sure that his letters touched the printed lines where they ought to, that no word strayed across the verticle line on the right, and that the words were correctly spaced on the document, that is to say his writing stopped precisely at the end of the last line. Although he was no longer a public employee, there was still enough of the civil servant in him to revive his routine of many years for this forgery. As he wrote he ran his tongue back and forth across his lips.

When he was finished he looked at his handiwork with affection. Then he licked the official label, stuck it in the right place, opened the small pad, inked the stamp and then pressed it on the correct place in the document, one quarter covering the official label, at the bottom right, three quarters covering the document. As the ink dried Peretz made a payment to the man in the form of a packet of Lucky Strikes, which Strauss smoked to temper his hunger, as he put it.

"I'll be in touch as soon as I have a place for you," Peretz said, by which he meant the rest of the payment.

Then he carefully put Anna's new birth certificate into the briefcase, shook Aaron Strauss's hand and left.

On the way back to the American sector Peretz decided to stop at the black market by the Brandenburg Gate and buy Anna a winter coat, a suitcase, a few clothes, things for the baby and maybe a small case with make-up, nail scissors and things that women need. He would not forget the gold ring. And something else, too, a pretty necklace, a brooch, something to strengthen the bond between them.

THIRTY-SIX

10th October, 1945
Camp 7525/7 Prokopyevsk

My dear wife! The pencil is now so short! If I don't get a new one it's going to be difficult for the two of us. A letter like this is such a beautiful thing. Some of my comrades are writing too. But I can't rent out the pencil anymore or I won't be able to continue. It's got cold again. Everyone's terrified of the winter. Your farmer thinks of the old days, when there wasn't much to do in winter, was there? But here the winter is quite the opposite. The ground freezes, the animals disappear. You have to get food by other means.

4th November, 1945
Camp 7527/7 Prokopyevsk

Are you still there? Do you still exist? Your farmer isn't a farmer anymore. Your farmer died today. They forced us. We had to lie down in the cold, face down. Then a Russian went from one man to the next. With a pistol. A shot. He spun the barrel. I was the first. With me it went click. Metallic. Really close. My neighbour wasn't so lucky. How can people do such things? There are new guards here now. They're different. Look different too. What's happened? The hunger gets ever worse. We look like skeletons. Our joints have swollen. Arms and legs like sticks.

24th December, 1945
Camp 7525/7 Prokopyevsk

Happy Christmas, my dear wife! I wish we could be together now. We don't have much to celebrate. Apart from the fact that we're alive. We sang. Silent night, holy night. Tears came to our eyes. Fritz is a good son to me, he's just turned seventeen. Younger than Karl was at the time. In some way he's a son to all of us, the older ones amongst us look after him. It was an absolute disgrace they sent those young boys to the slaughter. They've no idea of life and I'm sure they'd perish if we didn't help them out.

Sometimes I wonder what got us into this mess in the first place. Was it really Hitler and his gang? Or were we to blame? Does it matter anymore? Shouldn't we look forward and try to make the best of things? I'm sure you'd have clever answers to my questions, my dearest wife! If I really think about it, then I'm only half a person without you, and you're the better half.

I'm so happy that you took Margarita in back then! I don't know what I'd have done if I'd had to make the decision.

According to what the political commissars told us in our re-education sessions, not many were prepared to act in solidarity with the persecuted. The Russians, of course, are just talking about the communists, but I think the Jews got it worse. Here in the camp there are some chaps who are sorry that they didn't kill all the Jews before the end. I stand beside them and feel ashamed. That time you sent me into town with the grandfather clock, I almost went over to the wrong side. It was only you that held me back. I thank you for that, my love.

THIRTY-SEVEN

It's just a letter, Lisa thought. She was sitting on the sofa, tears streaming down her face. Just a letter, the words echoed in her head. It was summer outside, bright light poured into the apartment, cutting sharp-edged shadows into everything, the furniture, the carpet, the walls, her face; but in the letter it was winter, always winter, white and cold. From outside, life blustered into the apartment, children played in the street, cars drove past, in the distance she could hear ships' klaxons, upstairs Herr Weiss was playing his piano, it was afternoon, 1959, a good year, Frau Kramer had obtained a better job at Hawesta, Lisa was going to commercial college and had fallen in love for the first time.

A bad year, Maria took out her moods on Lisa, Lisa's boyfriend was the son of a man who wore a permanent scowl and called other people "scum", including his own son.

And now the letter. A beautiful letter, Lisa thought, she was moved by Herr Kramer's love for his wife, she had never expected so much love, she was happy to have had a grandfather like that. The last lines were beautiful too, so beautiful that the letter slipped from her hands and the tears shot from her eyes as if they had been waiting years for such a moment. Lisa cried without crying. Lisa was sad without being sad.

She spent the entire afternoon sitting on the sofa, she waited without waiting.

When Frau Kramer came home and found her like that she sat down and hugged her grandchild. They cried together, only stopping when Maria came in.

"What's wrong with you two?" she asked.

"You're drunk again."

"So what if I am? It's none of your business. Why don't you look after your . . . what is she again? Oh yes, your granddaughter."

"It's too late Maria; I know everything."

"Oh, so you read the letter, did you? Well, now you know that you don't belong here!"

"Maria! How can you say such a thing! I forbid you to talk like that!"

"You can't forbid me anything, Mother. I can say what I like. After all, we're living in a democracy now, aren't we? Someone told me we had freedom of speech." She laughed.

"How on earth did you turn out like this?"

"How, Mother, how? Let me tell you. Because you never, ever, ever looked at me. You love that girl there more than your own daughter!"

"That's not true!"

"Oh yes it is! You had your own idea of Maria, Maria had to be just so, and if Maria wasn't just so, then she was Bad Maria, and when she was Bad Maria she was a worse child than Karl, that shining light, Karl the Good, Karl the Dutiful, Karl the Handsome, Karl the Great – Charlemagne!" She stared at her mother and screamed, "Karl the Dead!" Then she burst out laughing, a frenzied, spiteful laugh, and sank into the armchair opposite the sofa. "That's why, Mother, I turned out exactly how you saw me: Bad Maria."

"I never thought you were bad, Maria. Just . . ."

"Just *what*, Mother? Tell me, I'm sure you know what's wrong with me now, finally!"

"Lost."

"What? Is that it? *Lost*? But I was living with my parents, wasn't I? Not like this brat here, who ensconced herself with strangers."

"Maria!"

"Oh yes she did! Just so you know, Lisa, I was with my own parents. But life with them was hell, it was like they weren't my parents at all, that's what it felt like to me!"

"Don't talk like that, child!"

"*Child*? That's right, I stayed a child, Mother, a stupid, little child who goes out on the street and gets drunk and comes home with the sperm of five men between her thighs. And do you know who my pimp is?" She gave a loud and vulgar laugh. Her hands were trembling. "My pimp is Fritz Kleinert, that lovely boy father took under his wing before he kicked the bucket, the one who gave me the letter that brat's just read."

"But . . . how has he . . . ?"

"Now that's shocked you, hasn't it, Mother. Not everything's so neat and tidy out there. Fritz was sick to death of his family and bored to tears with his fiancée. And then we met and, well, what can I say? It was sex at first sight." She laughed. There were tears in her eyes.

Frau Kramer had stopped crying. She stared at her daughter. Her fingers shaking, Maria looked in her handbag, took out a cigarette, the cigarette fell to the floor, she took out a second one, put it between her lips.

"Not in my apartment!"

Maria stared at her mother, opened her mouth and let the cigarette drop without taking her eyes off her.

Lisa stood abruptly and left the apartment. Frau Kramer watched her go, she knew where she was off to. She was full of gratitude for Herr Weiss.

When Lisa had closed the door to the apartment, she leaned against it and slid to the floor, sobbing quietly. On the other side of the door the two real Kramers had begun to argue with each other again, but Lisa paid no attention to their words. She felt as thin as the first layer of skin that grows over a gash, emotions raged, wounding and changing her. All of a sudden she was filled with disgust at everything she usually did. She did not even want to go and see Herr Weiss. She found her whole life repulsive.

She got up slowly and descended the stone spiral staircase. Once outside she was met by the balmy summer's evening with its sounds and smells, the street thronged with people. Even though it was late, the darkness had not yet taken possession of everything, a residue of the day lay like a fleeting shimmer on the brick-red walls of houses and on the black of the cobbled streets. Lisa took a right turn at random. After a few hundred metres she opted for a street she had never ventured down before, only to discover that it led her to a well-known and well-trodden place.

Lisa tried for a long time to find something unfamiliar in little Lübeck. As the streets emptied out and tiredness crept up from her feet into her legs, hips and finally her whole body, she realised that she herself was the only unfamiliar thing in this home town which, as it now transpired, was no more than a waiting room for her too. A waiting room for the truth. It was late by the time she rang Tobias Weiss's bell. She did it from the street; she did not even want to use her own front door key anymore.

THIRTY-EIGHT

Anna's wedding day was also the day of her departure. The whole of Rykestrasse 57, more than three hundred people, had assembled a few houses further down the street, in front of the dilapidated synagogue at Rykestrasse 53, an elongated brick structure. Many of the four hundred homeless Jews accommodated in the building at the front of the syna-gogue, who for months had been bored with the lack of progress, came outside to watch the ceremony even though the November cold seeped into their bodies, the day was grey and overcast, and an icy wind swept through the streets.

Peretz's men from Bricha, as well as a few British and American soldiers, had turned up in full dress uniform. He introduced Anna to one of the Americans, who was holding a battered leather violin case. This is Izzy, he said, he's German like you, but I'm very proud that he's playing the music today. Peretz grinned as if he had cracked a joke and Izzy smiled politely.

Because of Peretz, the chairman of the Jewish Community had come too, a slender man called Nehlhans with a hat and round glasses, along with some other community members, as well as their hosts, the Gutfelds. This added up to an impressive gathering, come to witness the marriage of Anna Stirnweiss and Peretz Sarfati.

The rabbi's name was Martin Riesenburger, a powerfully built man around fifty years of age, with large, square, horn-rimmed glasses on his nose.

In the synagogue was a traditional bridal dress, which the rabbi would have happily lent to Anna, but her belly ruled this out. Instead Peretz had got hold of a curtain on the black market and, together with other women from Rykestrasse 57, Ruth had done her best to tailor a dress from it. On her head Anna wore a veil, which was still folded back.

Anna observed herself from two angles. She saw the Anna who until 1933 was not even aware that she was Jewish, and was now about to have an Orthodox wedding. She would be veiled and sit on a chair, beside her would stand two men, holding an outstretched cloth over her head, Peretz would be led in by two men, the rabbi would utter his ritual texts and all the while Izzy on his violin would provide the wedding atmos-phere in the background.

Anna was unsure what to make of this, she felt like someone in the middle of a river, having swum from the bank, while on the other side a different Anna marries a different Peretz. This is the beginning of a journey, the old man beside Ruth had said when he learned of the forthcoming nuptials, but Anna had been on journeys for so long now. A journey within a journey within a journey, a Russian doll of journeys, the largest, outer layer representing birth to death, the smaller ones from childhood to adulthood, from German to Jew, from whore to wife and back again, from the Anna she was to the Anna she would very soon become.

Anna sighed, she would marry to become happy, even though she knew that for this to work it must be the other way round. She was both blind and sighted as she headed into a dead end, she was terrified, and in the next breath thought, What difference does it make? Ultimately, at the end of all these journeys I'm dead. She thought of her child and decided to think other thoughts.

The second angle was different. From here she saw the Anna who was marrying one man while thinking of another. Is Abba Kovner coming too? she asked Peretz, just before Izzy unpacked his violin, just before Martin Riesenburger commenced the ceremony. Peretz's expression darkened, he lowered his voice and said, "Abba's in prison in Egypt."

Anna stared at Peretz, she had forgotten that he knew nothing of their encounter.

"Forget Abba," Peretz said with a dismissive gesture. "He has nothing to do with Bricha anymore. He's playing at Nakam now – revenge – the British caught him with a cargo of toxic waste drums on a boat to Europe, he was planning to use them to kill Germans, exactly the same number as Jews killed by Nazis. Just imagine!" He shook his head. "I'd never have thought that he'd actually turn his words into deeds. Thank God it didn't work. Word has it that the British got a tip-off from Palestine. Maybe even from the Haganah people. He shrugged his shoulders and made a face that said, I've no idea and I don't care either.

"So how long's he going to be in prison?" Anna asked with concern. But before Peretz could reply, Izzy launched into Felix Mendelssohn-Bartholdy's wedding march, the rabbi lowered the veil over her eyes, two men who were strangers to Anna laughed as they pulled Peretz forward, someone pushed her gently but firmly down onto the chair, the crowd fell silent, and only the cold wind refused to let up, and only the flow of homeless people looking for food, of refugees looking for shelter, of military vehicles patrolling the streets of the destroyed city, of Jews secretly arriving in the overcrowded city from Poland, the flow of the river across which Anna swam and swam, always in the middle, always towards the other side, it never let up.

When Peretz placed the ring on her finger and said, Behold, you are consecrated to me with this ring according to the law of Moses and Israel, the flow became a torrent, whisking her away and dragging her under water until she drowned.

When the rabbi read
on the fifth day of the week,
the first day of the month Kislev
in the year five thousand seven hundred and six
since the creation of the world,
according to the reckoning
which we are accustomed to use here in the city of Berlin, this was the day of Anna's death and so began her rebirth as a drowned woman, under water, on the bed of the river that was perhaps her life, through silt and gravel, against the pressure of the water trying to force its way down into the valley, constantly into the valley; Anna, the dead woman, crossed to the other side to see what would have been there had she still been alive, put her head above the water, a head full of algae obstructing her view like a green veil made out of life.

When the rabbi continued,

Peretz Sarfati,

son of Avraham Sarfati,

said to this woman

– he faltered almost imperceptibly, for he should have said "maiden"
here, but that would have subverted the gravitas of the ceremony, and
seeing as he was reading this marriage contract in German, from left to
right, so that the bride could understand him, rather than in Aramaic,
as prescribed by custom, he could be consistent. The times demanded
it, God would show mercy, he hoped, and continued,

Anna Stirnweiss,

daughter of Joseph Stirnweiss:

Be my wife according to the law of Moses and Israel

and I will cherish, honour,

support and maintain you,

in accordance with the custom of Jewish husbands,

who cherish,

honour,

support

and maintain their wives faithfully.

And here I present you

with the marriage gift of women

– and he faltered for a split second, for he should have said "maidens"
here, it was as it was, onwards . . .

two hundred silver zuzim,

which is due to you according to the Torah,

and I will also give you food,

clothing and necessities,

and live with you as husband and wife,

according to universal custom,

and Anna's breathing faltered almost imperceptibly, and she took
another gulp of air into her dead lungs and felt the life inside her as if it

were someone else, and decided she would be reborn without forgetting
a single thing.

As the rabbi read on,
And she, this woman,
consented and became
his wife.
The dowry that she brought to him
from her father's house,
in silver,
gold,
valuables,
clothing,
furniture
and bedclothes,
all this the bridegroom accepted
in the sum of one hundred silver pieces,
here Rabbi Martin Riesenburger looked up, smiling to everyone and
nobody, and said, Or maybe not, it's irrelevant, and continued reading
And Peretz,
the bridegroom,
consented
to increase this amount from his own property
with the sum of one hundred silver pieces,
making in all two hundred silver pieces, or,
and the rabbi looked up again and said, Or he puts it all in if the bride
has nothing, but this time he refrained from smiling as he meant it
seriously, and continued

And thus said Peretz the bridegroom:
The responsibility for this marriage contract,
for this dowry,
and for this additional sum,
I take upon myself

and my heirs after me,
so that they shall be paid
from the best part of my property and possessions
that I have beneath the whole heaven,
that which I now possess
or may hereafter acquire.
All my property,
real and personal,
even the shirt from my back,
shall be mortgaged to secure
the payment of this wedding contract,
of the dowry
and of the addition made to it,
during my lifetime and after
my death,
from the present day
and in eternity.

He paused and looked at the assembled crowd to underline the huge importance of eternity in these times of constant change, but now Anna climbed out of the water, wearing a white dress made from a curtain, which veiled her body, her body that no longer belonged to her, but to the child of a murderer who she was forced to love, and she went to the chair that stood there in the middle of a crowd of dead people pretending to be alive, and all of a sudden no longer felt alone, The whole world is constantly dying for all eternity, she thought, All those who come into this world fall into the river, drown, crawl along the bottom to the other side, their lungs full of water, their spirits full of light, their hearts full of fear and hope, what space is there left for loving a stranger? And she gazed through her veil at Peretz Sarfati, who was standing before her, to the left and right his witnesses, two even stranger strangers, and another stranger was playing the violin and the rabbi was saying something about

responsibility for this marriage contract,
for the dowry and the addition made to it,
according to the restrictive usages
of all marriage contracts
and the additions to them made
for the daughters of Israel,
according to the instructions of our sages
of blessed memory.
It is not to be regarded as an
indecisive contractual obligation
or as a mere formula of a document.
All this was accepted by the groom,
Peretz Sarfati, son
of Avraham Sarfati,
to Anna Stirnweiss, daughter
of Joseph Stirnweiss,
regarding everything written and stated above.
And everything is valid and confirmed.

After that he announced the two witnesses whose names Anna did not know, after that he gave Peretz the marriage contract, after that Peretz gave Anna the marriage contract, and after that they were husband and wife.

At once the music changed, Izzy, the stranger, played a jolly tune, a dance, the rabbi smiled affectionately, Peretz beamed proudly, pulling Anna to her feet and forcing her to dance, and Anna danced until the water came out of her lungs, until sweat covered her body, until life returned to her immortal soul, until the child in her belly was able to sing a song of this strange wedding in a ruined city in a ruined land in a ruined maiden, who was attempting a balancing act between life and death, between truth and lies, between love and numbness, between madness and enlightenment.

Now the crowd came to life, couples found each other, legs started moving, hearts beat to the rhythm of Izzy's violin, which he was playing at a giddying tempo as he danced; the rabbi, who had survived in Berlin's Jewish cemetery, danced; the chairman of the Jewish Community, who had survived in Berlin cupboards and cellars, danced; the many men and women, who had survived in the Nazis' concentration camps, danced; the wind made dance the last leaves from the trees that had survived the bombs; the military vehicles, the homeless, the entire continent danced on the molten fire deep in the core of the earth, which itself danced around the sun like a moth around a light, will I fall in, will I not fall in? everything danced the dance of death of the living, the dance of life of the dead, until all eternity, until late in the night, until the height of happiness of the moment, until the total exhaustion of all those who had been shattered already and were still standing, still marching on towards death, Ruth danced with little Ariel, who now had both his arms around his Magellan book, how smart of him, one should always have a circumnavigator to hand, no doubt the Portuguese explorer danced as he sailed the high seas, no doubt he danced as he was stabbed to death by Mactan natives, no doubt he danced as, deep down on the ocean floor, he followed the last ship still afloat, afloat for three years until it arrived back home, no doubt Magellan had danced, dying with happiness at his historical triumph over earth's vast expanses, over the petty narrow-mindedness of those who had not believed in him, Marja-with-the-dolly danced with the old man, a miracle that he could dance at all (Thank you, Dana, for having rekindled his long life) seeing as he had been unable to speak or walk, how long ago was that now? not more than a few months, but that was an eternity in these times of constant flux and yet here they were, still sitting tight in the land of mass murderers, still they had not escaped them, the dead S.S. men danced, Otto Deckert danced in his grave because one of them was living *his* life now, and so he was simultaneously dead and alive, something only Anna was capable of, only those who asked themselves if this was a man enduring such suffering, only those who understood what the black milk of daybreak was, only those who, rather than disparage the poet's recitative, understood that one day, in ten years' time, Otto Deckert would dance in a train to Munich, led there by his old contacts; Mrs Abramowicz did not dance. She sat on the second floor of Rykestrasse 57, not speaking, staring at the wall, at wherever her dead child still lay dying, at wherever the love that had to be was looking for a target which had vanished just like that, vanished for all eternity. Mrs Abramowicz's ears could hear the excitement and Izzy's fiddling, her thoughts told her sensible things, her body implied that it would get up if it were only given the order. Mrs Abramowicz thought about her children, Ariel clutching the circumnavigator, Marja clutching the doll that since Dana's death had been called Dana to the silent horror of all the adults, who furtively looked away whenever Marja said "Dana" and chatted to her. Mrs Abramowicz was pining for her children, she yearned to be a mother again, she felt profound gratitude towards Ruth and the old man and Anna and the others who had been looking after the two of them since she had taken to just sitting there and staring, especially towards the old man, who had broken his silence for her sake, who for her sake had stopped lying there, intent on dying. But, Mrs Abramowicz's brain thought too, surely someone had to take his place, someone had to occupy that empty space, why me, why did it have to be Dana making the decision that it was me, why did it have to be God making the decision that it had to be Dana so that it had to be me, why? Why? Pointless questions, Mrs Abramowicz's brain thought, Pointless, pointless, for there is no God holding his hand protectively over you and your children, you've been mistaken, all this time you've been completely alone in the world, ever since your husband left, where is he, this husband? If only he had survived and come back! You could get up and go looking for him, the others will help you. Ruth will help, you heard what she said to Anna, didn't you? and Anna will help, you heard. But then, Mrs Abramowicz's brain thought, you won't find anything, the Germans killed them all, they spared nothing and nobody, not the women, not the children. In the end God is a German Nazi who, with no weapons left with which to harm you, was determined at least to take away your Dana before the soldiers could clear away the rubble. God does exist, ultimately, but he is the enemy of all Jews, and for three thousand years the Jews have been trying in vain to make friends with him. Look how quickly he made friends with the Christians and the Muslims, look how he herds us with the help of these people since they started believing in him. But why Dana? Why Dana? Why Dana? A tear broke free from her right eye, followed by another from her left. For some time now Mrs Abramowicz's eyes had been hinting that they would like to gaze at something other than the wall, perhaps they would peer out of the window if she would only issue the order. But Mrs Abramowicz just sat there, staring, helplessly listening to her thoughts, helplessly feeling her emotions and searching for a way out, outside, but she was locked up as in a camp, and there was not even an electric fence to offer release.

One week after the wedding, on 9 November, 1945, Shimon Sarfati came into the world. He was born in the first prefabricated house on earth. His mother suffered as only the living can suffer, she was in agony for the sixteen hours of his birth, a Jewish doctor, a Holocaust survivor, was present, three nurses, Holocaust survivors, were present, Peretz Sarfati was absent, he was driving with Bricha lorries along the northern route to Szczecin, he became a father without being a father, he had sworn that Anna's dowry should be two children by him, he gave invitations to fifty Polish Jews while Anna's screams were more blood-curdling than during any of her rapes.

When Shimon finally arrived where perhaps he had never wished to go, out of the water and into the air, he was more dead than alive. He extended no welcome to the world, Anna sensed this immediately. He did not search for her breast, he was exhausted, he would rather die than drink, it seemed, but he must not. After an hour, spurred on by the doctor and nurses, Anna finally coaxed her son to drink and live.

THIRTY-NINE

The first prefabricated house on earth was a Swedish pavilion that looked like a large villa. Bricha had rented it from a wealthy Jew for a token sum, soon the pavilion would become yet another transit camp for Jews from Poland, for they kept coming, Berlin, this barrel with its bottom knocked out, was teeming with German refugees and Polish Jews, often using the same route, not infrequently passing themselves off as each other in order to get through, and not infrequently encountering each other on their flight. But this camp would be for Jews alone, it would be run by Jews and if it had only two bathrooms, well, that was better than one. Soon it would be as congested here as at Aaron Strauss's house at Oranienburgerstrasse 31, or at the Rykestrasse synagogue, or at Rykestrasse 57, or in any of the many other overcrowded camps dotted all over Berlin. But now, not long after the signing of the rental contract, Anna and Shimon and the doctor and the nurses were the only people who could look out at the Greater Wannsee and reflect on the fact that, six hundred and fifty metres to the north, on the same shore, stood the house in which the Wannsee Conference had taken place, and where a few years earlier eight doctors and six ordinary people had come to the decision, All Jews must die.

The Sweden Pavilion was in the American sector of Berlin, and Anna had agreed to come if Peretz promised to fetch her people later. They're all our people, Peretz had said, but Anna's reply was, You say such things because you've no idea what it's like not to know if anyone from your family is still alive. Once again Peretz had been defeated by Anna, he said nothing and then gave his promise, Yes, he would smuggle Ruth and the old man and the Abramowiczes and all the others from the room here via the secret routes and past the military checkpoints that were open to bribery, Yes, he would hide his jealousy from himself to prove to Anna that he was a good husband for her and that she could trust him.

When Peretz came to the Sweden Pavilion the day after the birth and kissed his wife and held his son, everything was as he had intended, and yet he felt that he would have to rehearse his role. Like all fathers.

FORTY

"You're going to have to let her tell you the whole story," Herr Weiss said after many cups of tea and a dozen handkerchiefs. He had his arm around Lisa, drawing her gently towards him. They had been sitting in a lengthy silence on his old sofa and Herr Weiss had waited before uttering these words until he gauged that Lisa was calm enough to hear them.

She nodded and looked at him with vulnerability in her eyes. Herr Weiss cleared his throat, nodded to himself, went Hmm, hmm, and said, "There's one thing I learned in the war. It's not what you do that's important, but why you do it."

"What do you mean?" Lisa said feebly, sniffing.

"Hmm, what do I mean? Good question. Why did I say that to you? Hmm, hmm. I think I said it because I wanted to tell you that, well, erm, now listen. Do you know why I signed up for special operations?"

Lisa shook her head. Herr Weiss leaned back. Images popped into his mind, old emotions broke free from locked dungeons, taking possession of him, he wanted to resist, but then thought it was only fair if he felt as bad as Lisa, and he pulled himself together and said, "My father thought his younger son was a weakling." He nodded to himself, said, Oh well, he said, "My older brother was his favourite, my older sister was the model of a German girl as far as he was concerned. He was a committed Nazi. But he wasn't a bad man. He had respect for the pastor, and people would come to him for advice. In fact he was the one who called the shots in our village." Herr Weiss nodded to himself.

"Only me, he couldn't accept me as I was. He thought I clung too tightly to my mother's apron strings." He turned to Lisa. "You would have liked my mother! What a fine woman she was! And how she could play the piano! I just tinkle away, but her! She was a proper pianist." He sighed.

"She'd given up her career for my father and us children, and of course for me that was wonderful because I could hear her play almost every day at home. She'd often let me play too, and that's how she taught me the piano without my realising it." He shook his head.

"My father had great respect for her. I think he loved her very much, sometimes he would listen to her playing from the door." Herr Weiss smiled.

"He hated *me* playing piano on the other hand. I should be interested in technology, and I was. But because I always dismantled everything he thought I was just breaking things, so he took them away from me. Yet all I wanted to know was exactly how they'd been put together!" Herr Weiss had raised his voice and sat up straight, but now he sank back into the sofa.

"He put me in the Hitler Youth. Where I very soon became everyone's whipping boy. I wasn't sporty or strong, and I wasn't interested either. But back then it was the only thing that mattered. And if someone couldn't keep up, the others would give him a good hiding." Herr Weiss paused. The old emotions rampaged through his body like a pack of wolves, sinking their teeth into him from the inside and wounding him as if all these events had only just occurred. He took a deep breath.

"I kept my head above water by playing the piano. Whenever there was a celebration or large gathering, people would sing songs. I could sing and accompany them all, and that was my niche, it's where I survived, the others weren't able to do what I could do. But it only helped a bit." He paused again.

"Then one day an officer came along and asked, Which of you is brave enough to volunteer for a special mission? My hour had come. I stepped forward and cried out, Tobias Weiss reporting, Sir!" Herr Weiss shouted his own name, startling Lisa initially, but then she laughed, which had been his intention.

"And so, while under covering fire, I collected the body parts of dead soldiers on the battlefield. Why am I telling you this? Oh yes, what I wanted to say was that it only matters *why* you do something. Listen, the only reason I was brave was to avoid looking like a mummy's boy and a weakling in front of the others. But that's not real courage. That was just desperation." He faltered. He ought not to have uttered that last word, for now he clenched up inside, his body became the gaol of a single, powerful prisoner trying to get out, but with courage Herr Weiss fought the desperation inside him, and after a few minutes he had won the battle; in resignation the prisoner retreated, his body relaxed, Herr Weiss gave a sigh of relief. They sat beside each other, it was getting light outside, morning had arrived, they could sense it was going to be a hot day.

"I've always suspected," Lisa said after a while, "that she's been trying to protect me from something awful. But this . . ." She broke off, the tears flowed again, a helpless sadness oozed through her like warm liquid. Once again Herr Weiss put his arm around her and drew her gently towards him.

"Yes, well, hmm, I understand you," he said. "She's lied to you and told you stories. But she only did it to protect you. Look, she even sent her own daughter away to protect you. And you brought her into the house to help your grandmother. It's lovely what the two of you have done for each other."

"But now I've nothing left!" Lisa said loudly. "Why didn't she burn the letter or at least hide it properly so I'd never find it? It was left in an empty vase on the cupboard!"

Herr Weiss looked nonplussed, he made a few sounds that signified nothing in particular.

"Burn it? Hmm, hmm, you've got to forgive her, she . . . she couldn't do that, I mean, it was from her husband. How could she do a thing like that? No, no, if you ask me I actually think it's a good thing you found it."

Lisa shot a glance at Herr Weiss, shocked.

"What's good about it?"

"Well, now you know the truth. That's always good."

Lisa looked at Herr Weiss, her Uncle Tobi who was not her uncle, who was not even called Tobias Weiss, who had never told her his real name, as if the person he really was had died and Tobias Weiss had risen from the grave. Perhaps the real Tobias Weiss, the son of that Herr Weiss who had taken him out of the nunnery, was long dead and lay buried somewhere with no name on his gravestone.

Suddenly Lisa had a fleeting sense of the truth as something unable to be expressed in words, but which was alive, like a shimmering ghost or an animal made out of light, which you could only glimpse out of the corner of your eye. By contrast, the truth of words seemed dead, like a butterfly pinned and placed in a little glass cabinet to display its beauty, with a precise description underneath in Latin and German, *Sphinx ligustri*, privet hawk-moth. That was the truth, the truth could be found in the apartment belonging to the parents of her friend Peter, dozens of times over, peacock butterfly, small tortoiseshell, scarce copper, many-plumed moth, Camberwell beauty. Peter's father collected them and Peter was proud of the collection, Lisa had found it weird from the outset, all those dead creatures that were so beautiful when they fluttered in the sunlight from bloom to bloom, or which flittered around at night like stray ghosts. What was desirable about nailing them to wood with their wings extended like crucifixions? It left her baffled, but on her first visit to the Schultheisses' apartment she kept quiet, taking a good look at all those poor little creatures and repeating their names, and this made Peter very happy, but she never went back again, and moreover her love for Peter suddenly became an alien object she held in her hand without knowing exactly what to do with it.

The truth. Silently she repeated the word that, at a stroke, had assumed a completely new meaning for her. The truth was that she was afraid of the truth of the words set in the letter of a dead man who was not her grandfather: in all probability she was a Jew. The truth was that she was afraid of Peter's reaction to the truth of the words. The truth was that the truth of the words could kill the real truth. The truth was that she had nobody in the world. That was the truth.

"But that's utter nonsense!" Herr Weiss exclaimed softly when she said it to him and the tears were gushing from her eyes again.

"You still have your grandmother, even if she's not your real grand-mother. Let her tell you the whole story and then the two of you can take it from there." After a brief pause, he said coyly, "And you've still got your Tobi, don't forget that, Lisa, do you hear me?"

Lisa hugged him, kissed his forehead, cheeks; Herr Weiss was quite embarrassed. Then she stood up, smoothed down her skirt, gave him a tired, sad, calm smile, and left the apartment.

Herr Weiss sat on his sofa for a long while, contemplating Lisa's fate and wondering how much she knew of what had happened to the Jews. And he felt something that he felt only when he thought of his mother. He felt admiration for Lisa, who was facing up to these difficult things with such bravery, while remaining so intact, so undamaged.

FORTY-ONE

The miracle occurred in mid-winter. If Peretz had kept his promise, he would have brought Anna's people from Rykestrasse 57 to the Sweden Pavilion as quickly as possible, given that more and more Jews were coming in from eastern Europe and the place was becoming so cramped that Anna was worried at first, then furious, for Peretz was fobbing her off with promises that he failed to keep because, as he claimed, so many Jews suddenly wanted to come to Berlin, as if the Holocaust had been perpetrated by Poles or Russians rather than Germans, and as if the Germans were actually the Danes, who during the war had shipped their Jews across the Great Belt at night and in fog to prevent them from falling into the hands of the Nazis, no other people had done anything like this, if only there had been more Danish in the Germans, perhaps a similar miracle would have occurred, but this miracle had been rendered impossible by the course of history; but then this other miracle might never have happened if Mrs Abramowicz had not still been sitting on the second floor of a reception centre set up by the Jewish Community of Berlin, in Berlin-Mitte, Soviet sector, just staring at the wall with all her thoughts and emotions.

One morning a thin man arrived, whose two children failed to recognise him when he gave them a passionate embrace, squeezing them to him, saying things in Polish and Yiddish with a few Hebrew verses thrown in, which were from the Torah and particularly appropriate right now as the man thanked his god for having found them.

Then he went upstairs, for this scene had been played out on the street, where the two children, the boy with the Magallanes book, the girl holding the Dana doll, had been busy building a snowman. They walked up the stairs, or rather one of them walked, the other two were carried, the children still bemused, but that smell when he hugged them, and that voice, that intonation of words and phrases, that timbre, that manner of embrace, that love had made them realise blindly, as it were, Who else could this stranger be? They went up the stairs, the man was still strong or instantly strong again, he carried the two of them in his scrawny arms, the girl on the left, the boy on the right, all strain had vanished from his face, where now happiness resided, a sparkle that caused the many people he came across in this cramped house to stop and take notice of how he was carrying these two children, who had grown enormously since he was abducted, up the stairs as if they weighed nothing, as if he looked nowhere near as wretched as a Jew who had escaped by the skin of his teeth, who had then travelled back to Posen and found the neighbours in his apartment, they may have felt some embarrassment but had no intention of moving out, and in the night other people had come to him – he had found a space beneath the roof shot to pieces – they were soldiers of the Polish underground army, they had stuck their rifles under his nose and said, Clear off or we'll shoot, and Mr Abramowicz had understood that he had further to go, and he fled, not with Bricha, he had nobody, he was all alone, but he made it, for they told him, Go to Berlin, all the Jews are trying to get there, and he frowned and repeated the name of the city in disbelief, Berlin? What sort of divine irony this? But he had come and now they walked up the stairs, or rather one of them walked, the other two were carried, and reached the second floor, but rather than putting his children down, Mr Abramowicz simply kept carrying them, as if the exhaustion of the past few years had suddenly transformed itself into great strength, and upstairs it was cramped, they could barely pass down the corridor, people had to get up from their beds, Mr Abramowicz was no longer paying attention to anything, the happiness in his sunken face was so radiant that nobody said, Hey, would you mind not trampling on our mattresses with your dirty shoes! Only then did he put his children down, for there was his wife sitting and staring at the wall, but Mr Abramowicz noticed none of this, he kneeled down and embraced his wife and said things that were for her ears only, in a tone of voice he assumed only when talking to her. And then the actual miracle occurred, the actual miracle was that Mrs Abramowicz, before the old man's eyes, before Ruth's eyes and the eyes of the children and all the other people who were there, and these numbered many, turned her head to her husband and gazed at him and smiled.

FORTY-TWO

On a snow-white day Peretz, Anna and Shimon drove in a limousine into the Soviet zone to the west of the city. They drove for an hour through the winter landscape. The sun was shining, it was a calm day. For the first time in his life Shimon saw wide fields, for the first time he saw a forest whose trees pointed their stiffened fingers into the sky, all of them white with snow and rime that coated even the smallest twigs.

Shimon could barely see the pontoon bridge they crossed to get to the other side of the Havel, but it gave him an even clearer view of the destroyed iron bridge which stood beside it in the water. Shimon saw the soldiers at the checkpoints who spoke Russian to Peretz, who replied to them in Russian and showed his pass, issued by the American Military Authority in Berlin. But did Shimon see the beauty that the snow magicked into everything, into the rubble of Berlin, which looked like strange rock formations, into the trees, into the fields that had lain fallow for a whole summer because the farmers were dead, fallen at the border, massacred in the territorial army, or simply because the Allied invasion had made cultivation impossible? Did Shimon see the birds flying in the cold sky, gulls driven inland by hunger, along the rivers? Did Shimon marvel at the military training camp at Döberitz, which had been in use for fifty years and now housed hundreds of refugees, where had they come from, where would they go? Shimon lay in the arms of his young mother, his eyes dancing about, had someone had been watching him they might have noticed that the world plunged unchecked through these eyes into Shimon's head, nothing escaped him, he questioned nothing, he understood nothing, because Shimon still existed beyond understanding and not understanding. Shimon saw the Olympic Village, where almost ten years previously a black man had slept and eaten, a black man who had run faster than all the white men, watched by people whose minds would not be changed by anything, irrespective of what happened. Now the final units of the Soviet Shock Army were withdrawing from the Wehrmacht's largest field hospital, for that is what the Olympic Village had become during the war. Most of the buildings were already being used as a transit camp for refugees, where had they come from, where were they going to? Peretz did not know either.

Taking the Berliner Strasse they approached their destination from the south-east. "Here," Anna said, pointing to the place name. "There used to be another sign there as well." She turned around and looked back at the sign. You've come home now, she thought all of a sudden. How does it feel? But there was nothing to feel. It was if she had never been away. It was as if a part of her brain had kicked into life again, switched to "Journey home from the fishing pond along the Berliner Strasse", and now Anna had arrived back in Nauen, a daily event in summer when it was hot and she and her friends cycled there to swim, in winter when they went ice skating. Now they arrived in the town itself. The trees lining the avenue had been felled, for firewood no doubt. But the houses looked unchanged. A few people crossed the street, instinctively Anna tried to recognise them.

"What sort of sign?" Peretz asked, gazing at the houses on both sides, large, old houses with long roofs and pointed gables. He had never been west of Berlin before, had not been interested. But there was something fairytale-like about this white idyll and these mediaeval houses that both fascinated and incensed him. Why didn't they bomb everything? he thought, meaning the Allies, They deserved it, he thought, meaning the Germans, all Germans. He was not thinking of Abba Kovner.

Anna's eyes began to weep tears. Nobody saw it, not Peretz, who was driving, nor Shimon, who had fallen asleep. She said, "It looked just like the Nauen sign. It was a couple of metres back there at the side of the road. On it was written:

> Attention all Jews
> The way to Palestine
> does not pass
> through this town!"

She fell silent for a while before saying, "I didn't understand it. And I didn't think it had anything to do with me either, because . . ." she faltered, "I had no idea that I was a Jew. I was from Nauen, from Brandenburg, a German and then at some point in time, a long way back, I had Jewish ancestors."

"Didn't your parents tell you anything?"

Anna shook her head.

"Not at all! Look, my father was a psychoanalyst. We were always short of money; he didn't have many patients. He tried publishing scientific articles to earn a bit more and build up a reputation." She sighed. "Once he said to me: In Germany there's only a limited number of newspapers, but there are millions of people out of work who have plenty of time on their hands to write articles." She fell silent again.

Peretz turned right into Mittelstrasse, now they were driving north-wards, heading straight for the old town. Looking out of the window, Anna said, "My mother was an artist. She had contact with painters in Berlin and northern Germany, our apartment was full of her paint-ings, strange paintings in which everything was portrayed oddly. She wrote things I didn't understand. She met up with intellectuals in cafés and discussed abstract topics that didn't interest me. She wandered around town in a trouser suit." Anna smiled. "I found my mother embarrassing."

Peretz glanced at Anna. Their eyes met. Then he turned into Kirchstrasse. The Protestant church, the advertising column, the tall house. Götze's shoemakers. In the background, the mansion in Goethestrasse, the road leading north parallel to Mittelstrasse, through the heart of the circular old town. Kirchstrasse 32. Peretz stopped the car, the engine died. The street was absolutely quiet, there was nobody to be seen. Lunchtime. Blazing sunlight was reflected in the layer of snow that shrouded everything.

Peretz leaned back and looked at Anna. Anna was not moving. Through her window she stared at number 32, a low house in a terrace of identical buildings, ground floor, first floor, gabled roof. A hundred years old at most, workers must have lived here. Anna looked at the two small windows to either side of the front door. The curtains were drawn. Softly, she said:

"Now you have come
how do you feel in my heart
what do you wish to do? Now
you have come
the only way forward is with me
I shall name a star after you
the most famous one, you see
you have embraced speech too,
now you have come."

She fell silent, turned her head to Peretz and smiled, tears were streaming down her face, a physical reaction to the irritants of the past and present. Peretz said nothing, poetry unsettled him, there was something naked and weak about it that made him nervous.

"She wrote that for my father when they made their peace and he came back home. A few years before the sign appeared on the way into town."

She tightened her grip on the sleeping Shimon, Peretz hurried to get out, he walked around the car and opened Anna's door, it was complicated, it opened the opposite way, but he knew how to do it.

He stood there like a chauffeur as Anna got out of the car with the sleeping child and looked up. She harboured no hope, hopelessness was her ideal technique, it had got her this far, through everything.

Without hope Anna knocked at the low front door.

Without hope she waited for someone to open.

Without hope she heard footsteps approaching in the hallway.

Without hope her heart was in her mouth when the door opened, to reveal an unfamiliar, slender, short woman with an apron and headscarf, wiping her hands on a dishcloth and giving her an enquiring look. Anna wanted to say something, there were tears in her eyes, the woman was confused. Anna opened her mouth and closed it again, the woman looked at Peretz, Peretz came closer. "Is this the Stirnweisses' house?" he said.

The woman shook her head. Anna gazed at the woman's dress, the necklace she was wearing. She looked beyond the woman, catching a glimpse of the furniture. There were tears in her eyes. She smiled at the woman. The woman blinked back uncertainly. Anna asked softly after people, still smiling and still with tears in her eyes.

Joseph Stirnweiss?

Chawa Stirnweiss?

Eta Stirnweiss?

Benjamin Stirnweiss?

With every name the woman shook her head, We understand each other, Anna thought, How well we understand each other.

"The dress suits you," she said. "And the necklace."

Instinctively the woman placed a hand on the necklace, just below her collarbone. Anna smiled at her.

"Be sure to look after it. It belongs to the dead."

"Don't you want to go in?" Peretz asked all of a sudden. "Don't you want to take a few things at least?"

The woman looked aghast at Peretz and cast anxious glances at Anna, who had tears in her eyes.

Anna slowly shook her head, turned and left. Away from the house. To the right, along the street. Without saying goodbye, without waiting for Peretz. Peretz watched her, his mouth agape, the woman at the door looked both shocked and relieved, her hand still on her décolleté. His eyes full of rage, Peretz said, "If it were up to me, I'd take everything away from you, you damn Nazis!"

Then he followed his wife.

Anna walked through the streets of her childhood. The snow crunched beneath her feet, the baby in her arms weighed practically nothing and yet she felt his weight like a burden. She walked with a stoop, her shoulders hunched forwards, as if with this gesture trying to protect the child from the world. She turned into Goethestrasse, on the right-hand side stood the Jewish house of prayer, Anna had been there when it was destroyed. She had just turned eighteen at the time. The morning after all the noise, the racket and the screams, she had gone out into the street, full of curiosity, she and her sisters. Following the smoke they ended up at the house of prayer, still thinking some sort of accident had occurred. But then they saw the words daubed on the walls, the smashed windows, and Anna remembered the sign that had been put up some time before on the way into town.

Now Anna took the same route again. Just after she turned right into Goethestrasse a door opened on the opposite side of the road and a young woman came out. She looked shapeless with her thin coat, beneath which she was clearly wearing several layers of clothes. There was only a narrow gap in her long brown hair, her face was barely visible. But Anna recognised her all the same. She stopped. A single car drove past, a two-seater. This image would remain imprinted on her memory for the rest of her life: the woman on the other side of the road, the car coming towards both of them and then vanishing behind her back, taking its noise somewhere, and then silence again, only her and the woman in the street, both walking in the same direction, the woman could not see Anna as she was slightly ahead. Anna crossed the road. She broke into a run to catch up. Then she was with her, walking beside her, the woman turned around, looked at her in surprise, Anna smiled, the woman stopped. A question had appeared in her face, which ought to have perplexed Anna, but she was so happy finally to have found someone that she ignored it.

"Lena!" she said. "It's me, Anna! Anna Stirnweiss!"

The woman gave her a bewildered look, she frowned, she appeared to be straining, as if having to peer through a fog to see something. But then she gave up and shook her head. "I'm sorry," she said. "I don't know you."

Anna opened her mouth. She wanted to say something, She wanted to say, Don't you remember? We used to be inseparable. We wanted to do everything together. We had secrets we shared with nobody else. Don't you remember the summer of twenty-six, when we learned to swim? Autumn forty-two when we swore never to let each other down? She wanted to say, Sure, there were breaks in our friendship, but we always got back together, don't you remember? She wanted to say, Look at me, I haven't changed that much, have I? She wanted to show her Shimon, He's the son of an Aryan, she almost said.

She said nothing. She stood in front of the woman who did not remember her and said, "Apologies. I must be mistaken." She turned away and saw Peretz standing on the other side of the street, looking over at her. She ran to him.

FORTY-THREE

Frau Kramer told Lisa everything. The two of them were sitting in Café Seetempel on Brodtner Ufer in Travemünde, gazing out at the sea. It was windy, the Baltic smote its waves into the cliff-lined coast, the sun sat high in the sky, shooting its hot rays onto everything beneath, the glittering water, the bathers down on the beach and the two women sitting at a round table on top of the cliff, drinking coffee in the shade of an umbrella. The café was full, well-dressed people stood all around waiting for a free table, but Frau Kramer and Lisa Ejzenstain barely noticed. They were sunk deep in the past.

The past began in Ostra in southern Bukovina, Take your time, Lisa had said, Tell me all about your life, start at the beginning, and I don't want any lies. Frau Kramer had swallowed, she was so used to inserting Margarita into the storybooks she presented to Lisa that it almost sounded wrong when now she began to tell the truth and nothing but the truth. Once more she spoke of her parents, who had no more to say to each other after their eighth child, of her father, who had died when she was still a young girl, of her mother, who had ruled the house with an iron hand, of her siblings, who one after the other left Ostra, and one day only she remained, the youngest, helping her mother look after the farmhouse, the animals, the field and her grandmother, who sat in a chair doing nothing but talk about the past, endless stories that were like little loops, repeating themselves just as endlessly. Frau Kramer spoke of Wilhelm Kramer, a neighbour, a shy young lad, the only one who did not amuse himself by teasing the girls, but started observing her at an early age. Frau Kramer spoke of their wedding, the death of her grandmother, her sick mother, who died herself a year later, how William moved in with her to take over the running of the farm, He hadn't counted on that, she said, I mean, he was the youngest of the Kramer brothers, only the eldest inherited to avoid the land being broken up into parcels, and the others either stayed on to help or left. Frau Kramer spoke of Karl's birth, she smiled and cried at the same time when she spoke of her son, who never got into trouble, who had more friends in the village than anyone else, who many mothers would have loved to have had as a son-in-law, but Karl cared only for his friends, he was not interested in girls, and this went on even as he got bigger, Frau Kramer said, her smile now replaced by an expression of slight bafflement. Then she sighed and spoke of Maria, barely able to find the right words for this baby who seemed to cry for no reason, for this small child who never slept when she was supposed to, for this girl who started eyeing up the boys far too young, for this adolescent who skipped school to meet men and ultimately stopped making any distinction between fathers and their sons. At some point the whole village had turned against her, and obviously against us too, Frau Kramer said, sighing again and looking sad. She gazed at Lisa, who had forgotten her coffee because over the course of the story she realised that her grandmother had lied not only about her and her mother, but much more besides, it was as if she had spoken of only one half of a picture but never the other.

"There was an office in Gura Humora, the Ethnic Germans' Liaison Office, people called it VoMi. William and I went there with our ox cart, we went there in the morning and came back in the evening. That's how the S.S. entered our lives." Frau Kramer said nothing about the boarded-up shops belonging to the many Austrian Jews who lived in Gura Humora, she failed to mention the countless empty houses and apartments they passed with their ox cart, which told the tale that the Jews were gone. She kept silent about the fact that they had continued on their way without exchanging a word until they got to VoMi, where they presented themselves and were put down on a list. Nor did she say anything about the people in Ostra who became euphoric when they sat in the village pub and listened to Hitler speak on the wireless set that the S.S. had paid for. Frau Kramer stuck to the family history, Everything else, she told herself, can't be of any interest to Lisa because it's over, thank God. So she spoke of Karl's reluctance to move, He didn't want to lose his friends, she spoke of Maria's indifference, But Maria spent so long knocking about in the neighbouring villages and even in Gura Humora that it was a miracle she didn't come home pregnant one day. Frau Kramer shed a few tears, but this was not about her and her emotions, it was about Lisa, which is why she pulled herself together and spoke of the difficult journey with all their worldly goods, the S.S. had arranged a trek exclusively for Germans from Bukovina who wanted to go back home to the Reich. When they spoke to the others they realised that most of them had good reasons for moving, only a few parroted back the words of the agents who had travelled from village to village, holding forth about the Thousand-Year German Reich, the Aryan race, the progress of civilisation, Germanness, the renewal movement and whatever other nonsense that spewed from their mouths. For weeks we wandered across the country like gypsies, said Frau Kramer, who knew next to nothing about gypsies, For weeks we watched Maria coming on to the S.S. boys and the S.S. boys courting our son. Frau Kramer spoke of the romance of the camp fires, of bold songs accompanied by guitar and accordion, she spoke of the naïve enthusiasm in her son's face in the glow of the flames, of her unease when she saw his new "comrades" strutting around with their weapons, Like children playing cops and robbers, she said.

Lisa listened in silence. She heard the flag flapping on the roof of Café Seetempel, she heard the swoosh of the sea and the voices of the other summer guests, the shrieks of the children playing in the waves below, and the voice of her grandmother, who would never again be her grandmother. She saw the face of a stranger who was more familiar to her than any other person on earth. She listened to the story of Gunzhausen reception centre in Bavaria, where the ethnic Germans were crammed into huge shower rooms for the purpose of disinfection, while blonde S.S. women "deloused" their clothes and possessions with Zyklon, I didn't even know what that meant, Frau Kramer said and attempted a laugh, but without success. She spoke of the huge gymnasium where for months they waited for a notification until they realised that the S.S. were making them wait on purpose to reinforce their prominence over the Wehrmacht, which was not allowed to enlist ethnic Germans if they did not hold German passports. And then she told Lisa about how the children left them, Maria simply vanished, one day she went off with a young S.S. lad who had been transferred to Berlin. Karl, who she barely saw anymore because he drilled, played music and drank with his new friends, came to see them a few days later and announced, Mum, Dad, I'm joining the S.S., I've thought it through carefully, it's my path, I can feel it.

"When everything had been taken from us they let us go. They put us on a train, the train went via Prague and then on to Poland, which was now called the Wartheland." She spoke of the Popkos from northern Bukovina, a real family – father, mother, five children, all the grandparents, a great-grandmother, They occupied three compartments, and in another sat the two of us, William and I, with no longer any idea why we were going to the Wartheland. She spoke of their arrival at Posen station, of the lanky S.S. man who tossed their things into a lorry and drove them out of the city and across the fields to their farm. She said, The Polish family's breakfast was still on the table, the Polish family's clothes were still in the wardrobe, and coming from the stable was the bellowing of two cows that hadn't been milked that morning. She said, We stripped the beds, we washed the crockery and cutlery, we barely dared ask the question: What have they done with the owners? And then the pastor came across the fields on his motorcycle, he drove up with a loud roar, took off his helmet and glasses, a tall man with a narrow face, I've forgotten his name, he did tell us when he got off and shook our hands, I recall the scene very well, but for the life of me I can't remember his first words. He came in, said nothing about the owners and showed us round the farm, which we had familiarised ourselves with, and at the end he took us down into the cellar and said, much too loudly, If you ever need anything, come and see me. I'll write down my address for you. And so he wrote down his address, talking much too loudly all the while. We were quite shocked, What an odd fellow, my Wilhelm said. But we understood him better two days later when we had Adam Herschel standing in front of us, his hands raised as if we'd pointed a gun at him."

"Who was he?" Lisa asked. It was the first thing she had said in a long while.

Frau Kramer sighed, for she was getting ever closer to the most difficult subject of all.

"He was a Jew, hiding from the S.S."

And so Frau Kramer had to tell Lisa everything after all; Gura Humora had given her only a little respite.

"What did the S.S. do with the Jews?"

"I don't know exactly, my child. But it wasn't good. They took them, transported them far away. When our train passed through Prague we saw a goods train full of people. One of the Popko men said, 'Jews', nothing more, just 'Jews'. But all of us knew that something awful was happening."

"What about my mother?"

"Your mother was a very beautiful woman, Lisa! It's such a pity I don't have a photograph to show you. One day, when Herschel had gone, the pastor came and implored us to help out again. My husband said nothing, it was soon after we'd learned of Karl's death. Both of us were very sad and angry at the S.S., which had sent our son to his doom. Nor was the farm what they had promised us. The soil was poor and we had to work hard for our yields. I knew Wilhelm wanted us to keep ourselves to ourselves, but when I heard it was a woman who was pregnant I couldn't help myself. Margarita had shot a German, the pastor told us, and because of her the governor of Konin, Obersturmbannführer Josef Ranzner, had executed thirty-seven Polish citizens beside the church, right where your mother had shot the German, Sturmbannführer Treitz. But of course it wasn't her fault, she'd only wanted revenge for the death of her brother Tadeusz and your father." She paused and took a deep breath.

Lisa sat there, listening to the voices, and noticed that the sun had already begun to set in the west. The wind had died down somewhat, the flag on the café was no longer flapping quite so loudly, many visitors had already set off on the journey back to Lübeck, nobody had to wait for a table any longer. Lisa sat there, she was all eyes and ears. She would deal with her thoughts and emotions later. For the moment it was about reordering everything.

Frau Kramer knew that the girl would not let her go until everything had been said, and so she spoke of her time living with Margarita. She spoke of the hole in the floor, of her decision to risk more to avoid damaging Margarita's health. She was getting ever closer. And when she had spoken of the birth and the territorial army that had taken her Wilhelm off to the front, when she had talked about their flight from the farm, Frau Kramer and Lisa Ejzenstain had arrived at the place where everything had begun.

"Your mother was still very weak from the birth," she said, then hesitated.

"We went westwards. I had to help the cow, it couldn't pull the cart on its own through the deep snow. Your mother sat on the seat, trying to protect you from the cold. She'd bound you to her chest and wrapped every blanket we had around her. When we finally got to the main road we saw that we weren't alone. The road was full of people with carts, transporting everything they possessed. If we hadn't forced ourselves into the long line we wouldn't have got anywhere. At least now I was finally able to rest a little and sit beside your mother on the seat. All of a sudden word came that the Russians were approaching. People panicked, they tried to flee across the fields, left everything behind, in a trice the road was full of obstacles. We had no choice but to wait. And then the Russians arrived. They arrived with reconnaissance tanks and utility vehicles and horse-drawn carriages and on foot. They took our cow and hauled Margarita from the cart, she had to unwrap herself from all the blankets, they were laughing and cracking jokes we didn't understand. But they stopped the moment they saw you and left her in peace. I wrapped her up again and we continued on foot. We just left the cart where it was. Evening came and it grew cold. Our plan was to get to the Warthe and try to take a boat to Posen. But we didn't make it that far. When night fell the temperatures dropped so sharply that we could barely keep going. But we did. All night long. The following morning your mother wanted to sit down for a rest. I told her, If you do that Margarita you're going to die, you and your baby. This helped a few times, but at some point she was simply too exhausted. She sat on a tree stump by the side of the road and . . ." Frau Kramer fell silent. She had stopped looking at Lisa, staring instead at the table, without feeling anything but the cold, without seeing anything but Margarita sitting before her, dying.

"I couldn't do anything, Lisa. I was on the verge of freezing to death myself. I tried to pull her up, but she just sat there, her eyes open, no longer responding to anything." She raised her head and looked Lisa in the eye. Tears were running down her cheeks. Lisa was sitting opposite her, hearing the flag on the roof, other people's voices and the swoosh of the sea down below. I ought to cry now, she thought, but she did not, she thought, I ought to collapse now and afterwards everything would be different, but nothing happened. She was still sitting opposite her grandmother who was not her grandmother and felt a tug in her diaphragm as if a vacuum were there, as if she had to breathe on it to fill her body, but however much air she took in she failed.

"I unwrapped you and bound you to my chest," Frau Kramer said. "I took all the blankets from your mother and wrapped them around me. Then I went on and left her behind." She stopped talking. She had arrived at the start and now she lacked the strength to go any further. She just wanted to sit there and do nothing, she wanted to go far away, to a place without winter, without cold, without death. But opposite her sat Lisa, staring and waiting. So she sat up straight and continued with her story.

"After half a kilometre I arrived at a farmhouse where Poles were living. They took us in, Lisa. Your mother failed to make it by five hundred metres. I'll never . . ." She broke off and hung her head. It's not about me, she rebuked herself, but she could not contain her emotions any longer. After crying inside for a minute or two, she lifted her head again and looked at Lisa.

"The Poles saved us. One day I'd love to go back and thank them." She took another deep breath. Everything had now been told, the rest could wait, she felt utterly drained, as if having taken flight a second time. Leaning back she closed her eyes and felt the wind on her skin, she heard the flag that still fluttered from time to time, and the muffled voices of the other visitors.

When she opened her eyes Lisa was standing beside her chair. The girl bent down, put her arms around her, nestled her head beneath her chin and cried and said, "We'll go there together, Grandma."

FORTY-FOUR

When the general came to the Purim festival Peretz was called Joseph. A good name, Joseph, he said to the chairman of the camp committee, who that day was called Adam, as he was every day. Good for a festival and good for a general. Of course no-one was wearing a uniform, they were all just refugees who had found a temporary haven here in the D.P. camp at Schlachtensee.

The rabbi who had invited the general explained the meaning of the Purim festival, he talked about the Book of Esther, about the selfish government official Haman who wanted to have every Jew in the Persian kingdom murdered, King Ahasuerus and his beautiful queen who prayed for the Jews, the wooden ratchets that the people used to make a hellish din and the most outlandish clothes. He did all this with a smile on his lips, and it seemed as if he wished to avoid making any connection between the past and present. Then he introduced the general to the men and women of the camp committee, who had assembled in the canteen. They were standing in a row in the middle of the room, each man and each woman in his best suit, her best dress, two rows of tables along the walls to the left and right, laid festively for a bite to eat worthy of the general and his entourage. Joseph Taggart McNarney, who really was called that, shook their hands in turn as the rabbi announced their names.

"There should be ten, but I see eleven here," the general said all of a sudden.

"Oh," Adam replied quickly, "that's Joseph, he's a committee member too."

"I see," the general said with a smile. "Well, I suppose as the camp's growing so fast the committee's got to grow too, hasn't it?" His bushy eyebrows twitched briefly upwards.

"Exactly," Adam said, trying to hide his relief at the general's helpful logic.

"But tell me, Joseph. As a representative of the refugees, surely you must know who's smuggling all these Jews into the camp." Silence. Joseph gave McNarney a puzzled look.

"General, it's true that I look after the refugees here in the camp," he said. "But I've no idea how they get here."

The general smiled, his eyebrows twitched, he said, "Whoever these people are, you tell them that they've got to stop. The camp isn't big enough for this many people." There was a pause before he continued, "I don't mean they've got to stop for ever. Just tell your people that they should try to stop for a while, until we've built a new camp." He gave a friendly nod to his namesake. Then they sat at the tables, young women brought them plates with cold kosher dishes while several men and women standing in the opposite corner of the room played their instruments as quietly as possible.

"If he knew who you really were," Adam said later to Peretz. Night had fallen some time earlier, General McNarney and his attendants, who had enjoyed a good time, got into their jeeps and drove off through the snow, while for the rest of the people the nicest part of the festival was just beginning, as now they had the room to themselves. The rattling of ratchets could be heard throughout the camp. Most had been home-made. They were never going to celebrate Purim again without ratchets. From outside you could see people dancing in the canteen.

"I'm convinced he knows exactly who I am," Peretz replied, watching the taillights until they turned into Potsdamer Chaussee and disappeared. He froze in the cold air.

"How can he imagine we're going to stop?" he said to Adam quietly, still staring at the gate which was slowly closed by two guards. Without reading the words he stared at the bedsheet attached to the outside of one of the gates, and whose writing was now facing the street. In the beam of the floodlights fixed on the gate large letters could be read through the material:

ЗИІТ2Ǝ⅃A9 ꟻO 2ƎTAƆ ƎHT ИƎꟼO

He vaguely recalled that they had put it up months ago, when the Anglo-American committee had visited to decide what should happen with the Jews. Nice men and women who had listened to the survivors' stories and shed the odd tear of sympathy. Then they disappeared again, back to Cairo and Jerusalem, it was said. But nothing had happened. And in the meantime more and more Jews had come to Germany.

Peretz knew that some camp inmates took the sheet down every month to wash it before hanging it up again. Nobody had asked them to, they just did it.

With a jolt he awoke from his thoughts. He said out loud, "How can he imagine that people fleeing from Poland will all of a sudden just stay there? Are they supposed to let themselves get killed for a time until the Americans can bring themselves to build a new camp? Hasn't he understood that the only reason they have to build a new camp is because we can't stop bringing people to safety, not even for a day?" Peretz shook his head. He liked the general and knew that they had enjoyed the sympathy of the U.S. government ever since the American Jews had begun to exert pressure. And yet, between the lines, Peretz had heard something else: the Americans were making every effort to avoid causing the British any problems. The British have declared war on us, Peretz thought, Damn them!

"Come on," Adam said, taking his arm. "Let's celebrate."

FORTY-FIVE

The director sat behind his desk, a desk that was so large and exquisitely made that Otto Deckert could not help wondering what it signified. Behind the director was a window full of green, he could see trees and shrubs, and beyond this a wall.

The director was a short, slight man with a round, far too large head, ears that stuck out and a thin neck. His hairline was so far back that it emphasised the ball-like nature of his head even more. The director was no oil painting, no Aryan superman. He would never have been permitted to take part in any breeding programme.

Otto Deckert had taken a huge risk in coming here. He had travelled across Germany without any papers, permanently on his guard against checks, often hitchhiking, often on foot. He had slept in damp woods and barns, he had told farmers that the Russians had killed his entire family, since when he had been on his way to the only relations he had left. They had believed him, they had given him food and good wishes and sympathy on his arduous road. He had felt lonely and vulnerable, but had learned to hang on in, and this served him well now too.

In Nuremberg he had climbed into an empty goods train and travelled to Munich central station. He had marvelled at the monumental new structure and wandered through the large entrance hall with the encouraging feeling that life would continue, that nothing and nobody was going to keep either Germany or himself down, that the Führer would have liked this attractive building.

As he had no money for a taxi, the way south to the neighbouring municipality had been long and onerous. For hours he had walked along the River Isar.

Finally, at the zoo, a baker had given him a lift in his delivery van, taking him straight along Heilmannstrasse to the former Rudolf Hess Estate. It was a green area, where important Nazi Party figures and their families had once led tranquil lives, isolated from the rest of humanity. The estate had been built in a forest, which surrounded it like a protective shield, a high wall also dating from the pre-war era ensured that no-one could gain entry.

The director did not see him immediately, Deckert had to wait for ages in a bare room before being fetched by an elegant secretary and led past closed doors down long corridors, finally stopping at a massive wooden door at the end of a corridor. She knocked and, when the door opened, took her leave of Otto Deckert with a brief wave of her hand.

In the doorway stood another secretary, an elderly woman who looked him up and down before saying, "Otto Deckert? Come in, he's waiting for you." With these words she opened another door, and there sat the director behind his large desk, looking at Deckert and making a sign that he should take a seat on the chair opposite him.

"Tell me your story!" the director said, and Otto Deckert told him about the 11th Army, the Russian campaign, the retreat to Posen, the defence of the city to the last drop of blood, side by side with the S.S., and just as he was about to describe his imprisonment the director said, "We have proved the Torah right, Deckert."

Deckert had not been prepared for such a comment. He stared at the director and tried to come up with a witty response, without success.

"We have paid, Deckert. An eye for an eye, a tooth for a tooth. By attempting to exterminate the Jews in this crude, clumsy way, by shooting every last person in great swathes of Byelorussia and setting fire to it, either to win land for ourselves or leave scorched earth behind, we have brought exactly the same upon ourselves: flight, expulsion, imprisonment, deaths running into millions, large territorial losses, a plundered country. That is the Torah, the Old Testament. What have you got to say to that?" As he uttered these last words the director leaned back in his leather chair, without taking his eye off Otto Deckert. Before the latter could think of something to say, the director continued.

"I'm telling you this, Deckert, to allow you to see your own destiny in a higher context. People who don't understand the sort of world we're living in are useless to me here. It's a world of power blocs and ideologies, these provide the big framework in which every individual destiny is played out, yours included." He paused to allow his words to exert their full effect on the man opposite him, then said, "Back then we tried to drive a wedge into the existing order. But we failed, or the existing order was too strong for us. This time we have to proceed more skilfully, Deckert."

Deckert nodded instinctively, not because he agreed with the director, but because he wanted to show him that this was the case, even though he did not understand what he was talking about. The concentrated gaze with which the director fixed him made Deckert nervous and distracted. He tried to reply, to prove to the director that he was confident, assured, but he had the peculiar impression that it was impossible to establish any real contact with this man, for the director just continued to stare at him as if he were sitting in a secret observation room behind a two-way mirror, never to be discovered.

"I predicted all of this," the director said abruptly, piercing the silence. There was no hint of satisfaction in his expression, only a sobriety, like someone referencing historical facts. He said, "In the autumn of '44 I predicted that once we'd surrendered the Western Allies would team up against the Soviet Union, and I made sure they had their reasons for doing so, too." He paused briefly, but only to give Deckert time to follow what he was saying.

"None of them, neither the Yanks, nor the Brits, and certainly not the French, none of them had agents in the east. Only we did." He leaned forward, resting his elbows on his broad, deep and exquisitely made mahogany desk with its dark-green leather top, on the edges of which Deckert noticed golden arabesques. "And since then, Deckert, we've been in business." The director leaned back once more.

"Our connections are extraordinarily good. We have first-rate contacts with the government, the parties, the Church, the new army, the Office for the Protection of the Constitution, the *Spiegel*, where some comrades work. The Americans listen to us. Their radical anti-Bolshevism is all our doing. A few years ago we convinced them that the Soviets were armed to the teeth. That they could launch an attack at any time and anywhere, in fact several at once if necessary. We persuaded the Americans that they were weak. They believed us at once and started arming like mad. It was us, Deckert, we invented the Cold War. In this very office," the director said, bringing his right index finger vertically down onto the dark-green leather top of his desk, "the Cold War was born."

The director paused as if to recover from a state of excitement that was not physical, and thus did not manifest itself in his eyes or fingers, but whose origin was purely intellectual, as if for him thinking was something both sensual and agonising, a burden his fragile body had to bear. Deckert was spellbound by this man, he felt instinctively that the director had attained a state of consciousness which would remain inaccessible to him in this life, and he suddenly felt like a dilettante, a cheap imitation, like a poor copy of an original. How come this had never occurred to him before?

At that moment the director said, "I had come to the conclusion that defective communication between the Western Allies and their Soviet partner was the best way of ensuring that the sharing of information regarding certain methods employed by the Wehrmacht in the east and elsewhere would fade into the background. But it has also proved to be the best means of keeping the division of Germany unstable. The weapons here and in the Soviet Zone are a guarantee that this border will never be taken for granted." The director paused again briefly, like someone who walks quickly and stops from time to time, turning back to wait for their footsore companion.

"Third, it is crucial that we stay at the heart of things, so that we're needed. The day we're no longer needed is the day the hunting season opens, do you understand, Obersturmbannführer Josef Ranzner?"

Ranzner gave a start. He had not heard this name in eleven years, for eleven years he believed he had eliminated all traces that could lead back to this name. And now there was a stranger sitting opposite him who had just said it out loud.

"We photographed all the repatriated soldiers," the director said matter-of-factly. "You're not the only one who came back with a different name. But we are the only ones who can prevent you from having to undergo denazification. We are the only ones who can ensure that Mossad and Simon Wiesenthal never find out that Josef Ranzner, the Butcher of Turck, the man who freed Konin of Jews, is not dead." He paused and this time he was not sitting behind a two-way mirror, but looking Ranzner directly in the eye.

"In return I expect unconditional loyalty. Are you prepared to offer that?"

"Loyalty is my honour!" Josef Ranzner replied automatically.

The director gave a satisfied nod.

FORTY-SIX

Outside, winter would not come to an end. Anna and Shimon were no longer alone. The Sweden Pavilion was now so full that Bricha workers had constructed triple bunk beds, They look exactly like the beds in Ravensbrück, the girl above Anna and Shimon said, and for three days she refused to sleep in her bunk. The girl was fourteen years old at most, one of the few Germans in the pavilion, her hair was golden blonde, My mother and my older sisters got away, but the camp commandant's daughter liked me, she played with me every day, she dressed me in nice clothes, she shouted at me when she felt like shouting, when Himmler came and said we had to be beaten she'd sometimes beat me, I had to sleep when she wanted to play at sleeping and eat when she wanted to play at eating, I was her living doll, I've forgotten her name, I can't for the life of me remember it. What was her name? She burst into tears because she could not recall the name of her childhood tormentor. She called herself Sarah Ninetyeightsixfivefour, she was the first person Shimon had no fear of, the first person who made him forget his mother, I think he's in love with me, Sarah Ninetyeightsixfivefour said.

Every day Germans came knocking at the door to beg. They look like we used to, said the boy from the neighbouring bed. He was sixteen, the son of a renowned internist in Warsaw. His name was Emil, he said no more than that, he had come to Berlin alone, nobody asked him about his family.

Peretz was hardly ever there. Lots to do, was his answer, Thousands want to come, he said, the British have closed the Trizone border at Helmstedt, he said, People can't get from Berlin to the south where the boats are waiting, he said, There are more Jews here now than before the war, he said, The Niagara Falls have frozen, he said. Where are my people? Anna asked, Schlachtensee, Peretz said, Twenty minutes away. I want to go there, Anna said, Not possible, Peretz said, I can't keep running my own private Bricha, this is about all of us. You've got people? Sarah Ninetyeightsixfivefour said with wide eyes. Well, Anna said, I met them on our flight from Poland. Oh, the girl said, disappointed. But that night she lay awake in bed and decided that she would have people again too.

Once a group of Germans came demanding coal, You lot have more than enough, they screamed. There was a scuffle by the front door. Bloody Jews, one of the Germans cried out. The young men in the pavilion leaped up and drove the Germans away. The following day a group of German policemen arrived demanding entry, Suspected black market activities, they barked. When the Jews refused them access the policemen took out their pistols. Anna was not at the door, she was lying in bed listening to the commotion, later Emil told her, All of a sudden these G.I.s turned up and chased them away, he was still in a state of excitement, We showed them, he said. But from further back an elderly lady called out, My eye! If the Americans hadn't shown up there would have been people killed like last year in Stuttgart, What happened in Stuttgart? Emil asked, They shot Samuel Dantziger, exactly the same pretext, black market goods, and then they raided the D.P. camp. The confident expression of triumph evaporated from Emil's face, he mumbled, But how could that happen? The woman behind laughed, How could it happen? One of the Jews recognised one of the policemen and I'll give you three guesses where they'd met before. Emil said nothing, the woman exclaimed, That's how it happened! Ever since they've not been allowed into our camps, the Americans have forbidden them, but they don't care, I mean we're just Jews. Just Jews, Emil repeated gloomily, and the woman gave a loud and furious laugh.

Shimon's my little brother, Sarah Ninetyeightsixfivefour said, taking him in her arms, walking along the narrow gangways between the beds and introducing him to other people. Peretz brought Anna a Hebrew primer. He said, The boat has sailed, you'd better start learning. He returned a week later, saying, The boat hit a storm and had to turn back.

At the end of March came the thaw. The snow melted into brittle chunks that were slippery to walk on. Day and night fat drops fell from the roofs and trees. The Jews left the pavilion and went down to the shore of the lake, they breathed in the fresh air, they enjoyed the expansive view across the water, they looked at the Villa Minoux, shimmering white a short distance away through the bare trees, an imposing house, they thought of the conference that had taken place there a few years earlier and asked themselves questions to which there were no answers. Anna was happy for Sarah to think of herself as her daughter, If I adopt you, she said, you'll be called Sarfati. Like Peretz? Sarah squealed with delight. Anna nodded, Yes, she thought, like tall, strong Peretz who comes and goes.

Spring arrived all of a sudden, the trees turned so swiftly green, overnight the first flowers bloomed, it was as if Nature had merely been waiting, as if it were not just the Jews in the starting stalls, eager to escape at last from this horrific land in ruins, but all of life. But the trees have their roots, Anna thought, They have to remain here. What about us humans? Anna searched for the rest of her own plant nature, When I was young and tender and uprooted, maybe a dandelion clock on a meadow in Nauen, but this was no more than an image without a background.

Peretz came and told her that Mr Abramowicz was back, he apologised profusely because he had forgotten to let her know at the time, Too much to do, he said. Anna watched him without opening her mouth. A miracle, said a voice in her head, its tone was impassive, like that of an official whose task it is to organise events into different categories, Miracle Division, Oh yes, here's the document, filed under A for Abramowicz, summary: joy of reunion. She truly was happy, especially for the children who had a mother again. She said, Sarah's our daughter now. Peretz glanced in surprise at the girl; embarrassed, Sarah lowered her eyes, Shimon was sitting on Sarah's lap, gazing at his mother, finally he had found a secure position that allowed him to see his mother in the wider context of the world, her and this man who felt both like a stranger and familiar, We need two more certificates, Anna said, One for Shimon and one for Sarah. Peretz was dumbfounded, wherever his wife went she created a family for herself, Are you blind? said Avi, his driver, afterwards, They all do that, the survivors, they need it. But she's got me, Peretz said, still baffled, and Avi thought, You're not enough. He kept this to himself and drove the lorry to the assembly centre in the Soviet sector for yet another trip to Szczecin. Again and again they were going to Szczecin, still they were going to Szczecin, more people than ever were fleeing Poland, where Jews were being killed once more.

Peretz had a bad conscience, he called himself an egotist because he had been envious of Anna's people, especially Ruth, and now he realised it had nothing to do with him. But perhaps that's it, an inner voice said, Perhaps your idea of love is when everything in Anna's head is focused on you and you alone. Peretz, the centre of the world, ever-present Peretz, Peretz the Almighty. Haven't you watched yourself isolate your wife from her people while you've played the man with good intentions? Could you have brought her to Schlachtensee? Of course you could. Of course you could have kept running your own private Bricha, come on, you were in full swing, which Jewish woman could have given birth to her child like your wife? All alone in a large house, surrounded by doctors and nurses who thought she owed you her life. You're a fraud, Peretz, a miserable fraud. Instinctively Peretz pressed both of his palms to his temples. He resolved to make up for everything, he would adopt Sarah, he would take Anna back to her people, he would rise above himself, become a different, a better man, so that his head would finally be at peace, for he no longer wished to hear this terrible voice, how long had it been there, in fact? Did it start with Anna or was it there before? Was he mad, perhaps? Or did everyone have a voice like this in their head? He glanced furtively over at Avi, who sat at the wheel, peering out at the slush, looking as if there was nothing in his mind apart from a focus on what he was doing. Was Avi ultimately a better person than he, Peretz? Avi, who he had always taken for a simpleton, yes, he had even considered Avi's reliability to be a consequence of the intellectual stillness in his mind. And now he wanted less noise up top himself! I've got to throw away that loudhailer, he thought. Just as soon as I don't need it anymore.

April came to an end and the days lengthened. The inhabitants of the pavilion spent most of their time at the lake; some even dared to venture into the Wannsee's chilly waters. One afternoon two men joined them and talked to the young people, boys and girls. Anna watched them from a distance as she made sure that Shimon had enough things to play with. Emil, who was sitting next to her, watched Sarah Sarfati cautiously wade deeper into the water, hunching up her shoulders, jamming her upper arms against her ribs and stretching her forearms away from either side of her body, as if this pose could protect her from the cold. He smiled each time she ventured another step into the lake, pulling up her shoulders even higher. I used to have a sister her age, he said out of the blue, without looking at Anna. With a loud scream Sarah threw herself into the lake, swam a few strokes, turned back and came out of the water. She ran towards her new mother and little brother, more a young woman than a big girl, Emil lowered his gaze, she could have been his sister but she was not.

The two men came over to them. They introduced themselves as Shlichim, emissaries from Palestine, We've been sent by Haganah, the army of liberation, they said, We're looking for young men and women who are willing to fight for a free Israel. Against the British or Arabs? asked Sarah, the fourteen-year-old. Against both, if we have to, said the shorter of the two men, a wiry fellow with a straight nose and angular chin, both of which looked as if they had been sculpted. I want to fight, said Emil, the orphan boy, I don't care against whom. It's dangerous, the taller of the two pointed out, but Emil laughed, You don't know who you're talking to, he said. Oh yes we do, the shorter one said, That's why we've come to you. Emil nodded, I want to fight, he repeated. Good, the taller one said, Then you'll be moved to Schlachtensee, we're training people there, you'll be given a weapon.

And thus it was not Anna and Shimon who went to Schlachtensee, but Emil, to shoot at targets in the remotest corner, beside a copse that contained a newly laid out cemetery. He met Aaron Strauss, who had also volunteered. They were given uniforms, they guarded the camp and even went on marches in the surrounding area to show the Germans in Zehlendorf, We're here and there's nothing you can do about it. Through Aaron Strauss Emil met Aaron's girlfriend Ruth, the Abramowiczes and the old man. In mid-May they went together to visit Anna at Wannsee. A day of gains and losses for Anna. Ruth, still a minor, and Aaron Strauss, in his early forties, both the same age ever since they had lost their families. We're going to get married, Ruth said, and Aaron smiled, You look good, Anna said, to avoid feeling pain, and heard herself saying these very same words, two years earlier, somewhere in Poland, part of her was puzzled by the advance of time, it had passed so quickly and yet everything seemed so long ago, an inextricable contradiction, The fact is, said the accountant in her, the one who kept everything, ordered everything, maintained control over everything, the fact is that Ruth is going her own way. Aaron said, Your husband asked me to prepare two more certificates, I've brought them with me, he got the papers out, a birth certificate for Shimon Sarfati, mother Anna Sarfati, father Peretz Sarfati, a birth certificate for Sarah Sarfati, mother Anna Sarfati, father Peretz Sarfati, Anna took them, Sarah pushed forward, she looked gorgeous in her blue flowery summer dress, thought Emil, who had missed her. Sarah clapped her hands in delight, I'm your daughter, she cried out, the others laughed, Anna said, Yes, and I gave birth to you when you were thirteen, the others laughed.

Mr Abramowicz carrying Marja. Before he could say anything, Marja said, You have to say hello to Dana first. Anna obeyed, she said, Hello, Dana, how are you? Marja disguised her voice, saying, Ever since I've been a dolly nothing hurts anymore. Mrs Abramowicz smiled, a peculiar smile, Anna thought, not against the pain, but rather with it. Now you've got to say hello to Shimon, Anna told Marja, lifting him up. Marja stroked his cheeks with her crooked index finger and said, I bet you were inside a body that got broken too, weren't you? Anna flinched, nobody noticed.

Ariel had a new book, *The Odyssey*, he held it up without saying a word and gave Anna time to look at the drawing on the linen cover, the profile of a Greek warrior with a high forehead, straight nose and powerful chin, helmet with a plume of feathers, sheer determination, as if doubt did not exist, as if all that mattered was to be constantly sailing the seas, constantly spiting the gods, constantly fighting against every enemy and finally coming home again. Aaron gave it to me, Ariel said, He thought it was fitting for our journey, That it certainly is, Anna said.

The old man embraced Anna silently, My daughter, he mumbled, then he took hold of Ruth too and hugged them both, My daughters. He laughed, Anna had never see him laugh before, and exclaimed, I need longer arms for all of you. They laughed against the pain.

It was a lovely afternoon, Emil talked about Haganah, he knew all about the British, he knew all about the Arabs, Anna listened to him, they watched his face light up as he talked of taking up arms for peace and freedom for his people, she smiled with the pain, There's no other way for our people, Emil said as if he had aged a decade overnight. They swam in the lake, Sarah stayed with Shimon, Emil stayed with Sarah as Anna vanished beneath a towel and popped out again in a black bathing costume, a tall, slim woman whose beauty elicited furtive glances. Then Anna went into the water, which was already considerably warmer thanks to all the sunshine, and swam away from the shore, out into the expanse of Wannsee, where individual sailing boats glinted, she swam far out, turned round and looked back to the shore, where everything was now tiny. Out here it was quiet, all she could hear was the lapping of the water. Further to her right still stood Villa Minoux, which had once been called Villa Marlier, broad and white it stared out into the lake and called to her from the large balcony in the middle, All Jews must die, Anna could hear the words clearly, they sounded like a divine judgment, We shall move to Israel and then the Arabs will drive us into the sea, we shall go under, we shall sink, we shall be reborn as dolls that no longer feel pain. Now they were waving from the shore, Anna's thoughts turned to Shimon and she swam back quickly, but Shimon was fine, he was playing with his big sister and the soldier of Eretz Yisrael, Lunch! Mrs Abramowicz called to her when Anna climbed out of the lake, attracting more furtive glances, the one born from the foam, born from the lather, who now vanished beneath a towel again up to her neck and reappeared shortly afterwards in a white dress, nobody would ever tell Anna, You look good, it would feel stale in the mouth, something new was needed, poetry.

Peretz was no poet. He arrived with his shadow, Avi, at his side, he greeted everybody in turn with a handshake, and they all stuck by him because he had helped them – out of Poland, out of the Soviet zone and soon out of Germany, out of Europe, across the Mediterranean, where the British were waiting, and into the Promised Land, Eretz Yisrael, where the next lot of enemies were living. Peretz waved at Shimon, to Anna the gesture looked awkward, then he turned to her, he put his arms around her waist and gave her a kiss on the lips, it was a tableau for the others, Anna played along, but at that very moment Peretz dissolved before her eyes and she saw Abba Kovner with his hatchet face. The accountant in her said, That's new. And said nothing more. Anna latched onto it. When Peretz let go of her she smiled to mitigate the numbness. Then they all sat and had lunch together, a large family reborn from leftovers, and out of the blue Peretz said, The ship has arrived in France.

Which ship?

Your ship!

Is it big?

The biggest we've ever had.

And beautiful?

The most beautiful we've ever had.

Is it strong?

Yes, it will be four and a half thousand Jews strong, no battleship will have ever possessed such weapons, weapons of suffering, weapons of accusation, weapons of pure will.

They finished their lunch in silence. Peretz said, The head of Bricha is in Munich. He goes by the name Ernst Caro. He'll let us know when. Then things will move fast.

Where are we going to board the ship?

Maybe in Marseille, maybe somewhere else.

How will we get there?

Maybe by lorry, and all of them thought, Lorries again. Peretz said, but maybe by train too, and maybe on foot for some of the way. Such a large group of people on the move attracts attention.

Where are the people coming from?

D.P. camps in Germany.

Won't the British try to stop us?

Probably, but then you'll go to Cyprus, where there's an excellent camp, and it won't be long after that before you're allowed into Israel.

Questions, answers, more questions, more answers, a degree of uncertainty in every detail, a perhaps. But they were well acquainted with this, it is where they came from: perhaps we'll live, perhaps we'll die. Nothing can stop us any longer, Mr Abramowicz said. Nothing, cried Emil, the soldier, Nothing at all, the old man bellowed.

They sang the song of hope, their voices resounded out into the lake, drifted to Villa Minoux, and even Anna Sarfati, who was listening more than singing, sensed the truth of these words. That evening, when the others had gone back to the camp at Schlachtensee,

You must come and visit us!

It really is like a shtetl!

In the middle of Zehlendorf!

And it's big too!

It's even got its own college!

You could learn Hebrew there!

And a synagogue!

And a theatre!

And its own newspaper!

Peretz, arrange it so your wife can be with us!

There's nothing here!

Give me a hug!

Shalom Chaverim! That evening, when Anna was lying in her bed, on the bottom bunk, with an exhausted Shimon who snored as he slept, his head pressed into her armpit, the song went through her head again, she felt her way through it again to feel the reluctance, Why should I be filled with hope when I had to abandon it to stay alive? And yet it's true. For as long as a Jewish soul resides in the heart and turns an eye to the east, forwards, to Zion, our hope is not forlorn, the ancient hope of returning to the land of our fathers, to the city where David set up his camp.

Then she fell asleep.

FORTY-SEVEN

The new Lisa had a false name. One Tuesday morning in autumn she went with her false grandmother to the authorities to make the truth official. They entered room 305 on the first floor, where an elderly man eyed them sceptically across his desk. On the desk stood a sign which read: Reinhard Müller, Advisor. Behind him was a wall of shelves full of black files from floor to ceiling.

After Lisa had told the man her name and Frau Kramer explained the reason for their visit, Reinhard Müller got up and scanned the shelves for a while before pulling out a fat folder. Dropping it onto his desk, he sat back down and leafed through the folder. Suddenly he paused and mumbled, "Oh yes, here it is: Lisa Kramer, née Kramer, mother: Maria Kramer . . ." He raised his head and looked at Frau Kramer.

"Are you the grandmother?" Frau Kramer hesitated, then nodded. Reinhard Müller turned to Lisa.

"So you wish to change your name?" he said.

Lisa nodded.

"And you're happy with that?"

Frau Kramer nodded.

Müller leafed through the file again. "Why didn't her mother come along?"

"She's working," Frau Kramer said, and that was not even stretching the truth.

"I see. You do know that your granddaughter has limited legal capacity over her own affairs, don't you?"

"She's not of legal age, if that's what you mean."

"Exactly. You need the mother's authority, you see." The two women exchanged glances, but said nothing. Herr Müller sighed.

"Changing one's name is not that simple."

"Why not?" Frau Kramer asked.

Herr Müller rocked his head from side to side.

"First you have to prove that there's a compelling reason for the change of name."

"She's not my granddaughter, she's the daughter of Margarita Ejzenstain, I can prove it." She faltered. The truth, hidden for so long, slotted into one sentence.

"I fear that's not enough," Herr Müller said. "I mean, anyone could turn up here and claim whatever they liked. Can you imagine all the extra administrative work that would cause? In any case," he said, pausing to look at Lisa, "Kramer's a good name. Or do you really want everyone to know at once that you're a Jew?" Before Lisa or Frau Kramer could react, Herr Müller raised his hands defensively.

"Don't get me wrong, ladies. I've got nothing against Jews personally, I mean, they're just people too. But in Germany it's a little complicated. You see, the law on changing one's name came into force in 1938." He stopped talking, looked at both women, gave a theatrical nod of the head and pushed up his top lip with the bottom one as if everything had now been said.

"Should I lie?" Lisa said helplessly, returning his gaze.

"We ought to leave all that behind us," Frau Kramer said with determination. "My granddaughter . . ." she said, faltering again. "Lisa Ejzenstain would like to use her real name at last. Surely you understand that."

Herr Müller gave a conciliatory nod and said, "Of course I do, of course. But for your part you have to understand that every change of name hinders the traceability of a person's family origins, makes it easier for someone to obscure their personal details and conceals their racial heritage. This is why people can only change their names when there are important grounds, such as your proving your granddaughter's Jewish ancestry. I'm sorry."

Staring at Herr Müller, Lisa said, "The reverse of everything you've just said is true in my case: my current surname hinders, obscures and conceals."

Lübeck's officer responsible for name changes, in a sub-department of the registry office, temporarily housed in the city hall, first floor, room 305, shrugged his shoulders and assumed an apologetic expression. Then he smiled jovially and said, "Chin up, there are worse things in life!"

For Reinhard Müller the conversation was at an end. The two women stood up, Goodbye, and while he watched them open the door, leave through it, and close it behind them, he pondered how some things could be turned on their head without anything really changing. In the past Jews had come to him to assume Aryan names, and he had given them the same answer that he had to this Jewish girl, who now wanted to break her cover, goodness knows why.

He got up, walked around his desk, put one foot into the corridor and called in the next person waiting.

When the two women had left the city hall and were making their way home through the streets of the old town, Frau Kramer said to her granddaughter, "We need to talk to Maria."

They went into Frau Kramer's apartment, sat at the round table, Frau Kramer made some tea, and then they chatted about other things, Lisa spoke about school life at the Katharineum, she said, Did you know that Erich Mühsam was a former pupil and was kicked out? Frau Kramer had no idea who Erich Mühsam was, Later on the Nazis murdered him because he was Jewish, Lisa said, oblivious to her grandmother's anxiety, she said, I'm much more focused on anything Jewish now, she laughed and said, Grandma, surely you know that our school fair always takes place in Israelsdorf. And when her grandmother nodded, she continued,

The Nazis thought it had something to do with Jews and so renamed the area Walddorf – how stupid is that? She laughed and her grandmother nodded, Yes, it's really stupid. And it hurt, but she did not say this.

Maria came home late that afternoon. She looked shattered, she reeked of strong perfume, her face indicated that she wanted to be left in peace. Without saying hello or even acknowledging her mother and Lisa she tossed her coat and handbag onto the living-room carpet, slipped out of her high-heeled shoes, took off her dress, knickers, bra, and when she was completely naked, allowing Lisa and Frau Kramer to see the blue patches on her upper thighs and arms, and the weary skin around her buttocks and breasts, she went and locked herself in the bathroom.

She emerged just as naked an hour later. When she noticed the two women still drinking tea at the round table by the window which looked onto the street, she put her hands on her hips and said in a loud, coarse voice, "What are you two gawping at? Have you got a problem?" Frau Kramer was about to reply, but Lisa got in first.

"I need your help, Maria." The other woman gave her a baffled look, before laughing.

"Don't count on getting anything from me, sweetie!" she said gruffly. But she stayed where she was.

"I need to prove that my name's not Kramer," Lisa said. "And you're the only one besides my mother who can testify to that. Officially, you *are* my mother."

"What? Me?" Maria laughed out loud. Grabbing her breasts, she pushed them up and cried, "All manner of people's lips have sucked at these, but you were not one of them." Maria let her arms fall by her sides, she was thinking. "What do I need to do?" she said.

"You have to declare under oath that you're not Lisa's mother," Frau Kramer said, "and that Lisa was not born a Kramer."

Maria lowered her gaze, then raised her head and said, "Why do you want that? Aren't we good enough for you anymore?"

Lisa stared at the naked woman. She had not been expecting an answer like that. There was so much that she wanted to say all at once, that she could not utter a single word. Frau Kramer came to her assistance.

"She just wants to take the name of her biological mother, surely you can understand that, Maria?"

"The name of her biological mother," Maria said, aping *her* mother. "As if that were something so special. What is it, anyway?"

"Ejzenstain," Lisa said in a reedy voice.

"You're telling me you want to swan around with a Jewish name? No way! What will people think?"

"That's none of your business!" Frau Kramer said.

"I'm off," Lisa said tersely. Frau Kramer looked at her granddaughter in dismay, but Lisa did not notice. "Please, Maria!" she said. "I can't go around with the wrong name anymore." Maria shrugged and glared at her mother. Then she turned around to pick up her clothes.

"I don't care. And I'm not going to help you."

With these words she withdrew to her bedroom, the same room in which Lisa had been living for the past two months, but one floor higher, in Tobias Weiss's apartment.

Frau Kramer put her head in her hands.

"How has she ended up like that?" she said, sobbing. Lisa sat opposite her grandmother, for a moment she lacked the instinct to comfort her, and all of a sudden she had very different thoughts from before. All of a sudden she thought, What did you do wrong, you and Wilhelm, for her to turn out like this? Slowly she got up and left the apartment.

FORTY-EIGHT

When Otto Kruse saw the woman as she got off the bus he followed her. He did not know for certain why he did it, but the woman's face, her tall, slender physique, her delicate neck, her elegant movements, all these things stirred something inside him which he had not experienced since . . . He knew exactly when, but did not spend a moment thinking about it. Otto Kruse had drawn a line which went right through his life. There was a man in front of the line and a man behind it. The man in front of it was he, Otto Kruse, who had seen a woman who interested him and who he was now following, literally a primaeval act, the man picks up the scent and follows the woman, the elemental force of nature was hidden in this harmless scene, the city that became a set, the other people who were reduced to extras, for what was really happening was so ancient and so essential that Kruse could mull this over as much as he liked while he pursued the woman through the old town in Munich – but each time it boiled down to the same thing: despite all civilisation, man was a creature of instinct, predetermined by his biological makeup, which you could exalt or romanticise, but which could not change the simple truth that he wanted to have this woman.

Otto Kruse drove his thoughts on ahead like a bow wave, they banked up before him, letting him forget the fear he felt as he watched the woman enter an optician's on Kauflingerstrasse. He waited outside, it was spring, he had a new identity, an interesting career, a beautiful period apartment in the city centre, he had money in his pocket and he weighed now as much as he had before being taken prisoner. Life was good.

But now he stood in the middle of the shopping street, cars drove past him, people streamed along the pavement like water and he felt as heavy as a rock. If he could just help himself to her. But those days were over. He needed a different approach to make his plan succeed. He needed a different mode of attack.

When the woman came back out she walked straight towards Otto Kruse, or at least that is how it seemed to him. Like a non-swimmer who dares to plunge into cold water he stood in her way and said something for her ears only. She gave him a startled look, she almost laughed, but for some arcane reason, which Otto Kruse would describe with terms such as instinct, chemistry and smell, she was precisely that type of woman who could only be conquered in an unpleasant, direct, even brutal way. Her name was Emma Huber. She was nineteen years younger than Otto Kruse. Her mother owned the optician's, which the family had acquired cheaply at the beginning of the 1940s. Her father had been drafted into the territorial army towards the end of the war and went missing in Romania, Emma was still a girl at the time. Since then she had helped her mother in the shop until recently she had stopped to train to be an optician herself, aiming one day to take over the practice. Emma was an only child.

A few months after she met Otto Kruse, Emma moved out of her family home and into his attractive, large, period apartment. To her, Otto Kruse seemed like a mysterious king, sometimes she would gaze at his Indian's face with its majestic aquiline nose and imagine that somewhere he had a secret realm to which he would one day carry her off. The fact that he was merely a manager in an insurance firm, which is what he had told her, seemed unimportant. She was utterly convinced that in a higher reality he enjoyed a very different status.

When Emma missed a period, Otto Kruse told her that it was time they were wed. Emma said, Yes, without being asked. They married at the registry office and, to please her religious mother, in the Church of St Peter on Rindmarkt, which had been rebuilt four years previously, in the very centre of Munich's old town and only a couple of minutes from the optician's. Nine months later Heinrich Kruse was born. It was a five-hour labour and an uncomplicated birth. The doctors were amazed that the baby was able to hold up its head on its own immediately after being born and went straight for his mother's breast.

In all that time Otto Kruse did not miss a single day of work. In the morning he would drive south from Munich in his company car, a black Mercedes 190, to his interesting job in the former Rudolf Hess Estate in the neighbouring municipality, and would return in the evenings to where his wife and child were waiting for him. In his spare time he liked listening to American big band music. He regularly went to exhibitions with his small family. With his penchant for antique furniture he gradually acquired a Biedermeier and Art Deco ensemble, a collection of seventeenth-, eighteenth- and nineteenth-century landscapes, as well as an attractive Arcimboldo copy: "The Vegetable Gardener". Depending on which way up you looked at it, the painting showed a bowlful of vegetables or the face of a man wearing a helmet. There were hooks at both top and bottom, so Otto Kruse would occasionally rehang the picture the other way up, delighted by the effect.

Another work of art, to which Otto Kruse was so attached that he placed it between the two large windows in the living room, was an ash-wood sculpture, the stylised representation of a tree that divided at the crown, the boughs coiling up ornately on either side like snails. Sometimes, when no-one was looking, Otto Kruse would stand before it and think of distant things that lay somewhere inside him like sunken leaves at the bottom of a lake, churned up occasionally by movements of unknown origin and briefly brought back to just beneath the surface, before sinking to the bottom again.

At unexpected moments, such as when he was on his way to work or sitting on the sofa reading *Der Spiegel*, he would recall the feeling of having the definitive say over other people's lives. From time to time images of another woman would flit through his head, a woman breathing heavily beneath him, she was very close, very hot, internally and externally, entirely defenceless and acquiescent, entirely his. Then he would withdraw to the lavatory to feel again these images, the heat, the closeness, the power. He regarded such moments as a perfectly natural means of sexual gratification, they did not hinder him in the fulfilment of his conjugal duties, the one did not exclude the other, on the contrary. Sometimes his wife suddenly transformed into the other woman from the past, and then he would take her with an energy and determination that shocked even him.

Whenever this happened, a spark would ignite in Emma Kruse and she felt an intensity, a heat, a closeness and a devotion which made her very happy.

But besides the image of the woman, he had brought something else from that time, which lay behind the line he had drawn, something that refused to leave him in peace. It was a dream that had begun during his imprisonment and which had hounded him ever since. Sometimes he was so afraid of it he did not even dare go to sleep. In the dream Otto Kruse died and waited for things to continue somehow. But everything remained jet black, nothing stirred, no sound, no light, no feeling, just a black nothingness, and Otto Kruse was inside this black nothingness, waiting and waiting, gradually becoming afraid, gradually panicking, gradually believing he would crack up at any moment, and wanting to scream, but he had no mouth, and wanting to stare, but he had no eyes, and wanting to pinch himself, but he had no hands, nor legs or feet either, nor anything at all that might be human. Then he would wake up in the middle of the night, drenched in sweat, and lie on his back in the darkness, staring until he could discern something, listening to the breathing of his young wife and touching his face, his body until he was absolutely certain. When his second child was born a year later, a girl he called Gudrun, he nourished the hope that these black nights would become less frequent, that the increasing weight of his new reality must keep pressing down on the business of the past until finally it no longer had any form, but was as flat as a piece of paper.

But this did not happen.

FORTY-NINE

Lisa was reading a book. It told the story of an Italian faced with two decisions. Both would save his life. The first was simple. Do you wish to die here and now as an Italian partisan, or go on living as a Jew? The second decision was not so clear cut. If I have to die, the electric fence surrounding this Auschwitz is my final guarantee that I can choose the time of my death myself.

The Italian described to Lisa how this power saved his life because it gave him the opportunity to set suffering and death in a relationship that he understood.

Forty years after his liberation by the Soviet Army, the man would indeed put an end to his life. He would not throw himself against an electric fence because there was none to hand. He would leap down the stairwell in the house where he lived. Lisa would read about it in the newspaper on 12 April, 1987, a day after his death, and immediately think that the electric fence must have tormented poor Primo Levi his whole life long, that its significance must have been reversed the very moment he left the camp and looked at the fence from the outside. At once it became a different fence, that is to say the fence of those who had remained inside. Then the fence with no mouth learned to speak inside Primo Levi's head, urging him to throw himself against it, so he could burn after all in the electrical current of his dead comrades. Lisa would imagine Primo Levi turning his back on the fence and going to Turin, his home town, because he believed he would be safer if he surrounded himself with the memories of a happy childhood. But the fence always remained right behind him, always lethal, always expectant.

When Lisa finished the book she became frightened. She failed to notice at first because fear was just an extra sideways glance, a peek to see if everything really was alright with the way other people were looking, a second listen to check that nothing hidden lay behind what had just been said. But it did not stay that way. Soon Lisa started bringing up the past, looking at things in a different way, listening to things in a different way. She knocked on her memories to see if there was a false bottom, she crouched down and put an ear to them, listening for whether anything was stirring underground. She became frightened that there was something she might not have seen or heard, she became frightened that she might fail to notice the precursor of something and that it would take her by surprise.

She stopped meeting up with her school friends, she lied, feigning excuses of tiredness, homework, illness for so long that they all gave up on her.

One day she was eating a sandwich in the playground, which she had made herself that morning in Herr Weiss's kitchen, she stood at the bottom of the wide steps that led up to the main entrance, leaning against the central railings, the older pupils were standing around or walking past, the younger ones running and playing.

Suddenly she noticed that the others moved in groups, both large and small, like molecules ending up somewhere as a result of the coincidence of world history, and which formed solid structures out of necessity. At the same time she realised that she herself was alone. That nobody had come to congratulate her on this day, her seventeenth birthday. That she was not bothered, on the contrary, until then it had not even occurred to her.

But that was not all. A new feeling unfurled inside her, growing stronger with every breath. A good feeling.

When the bell rang for the end of break, calling them all back into the classroom, Lisa realised that she felt free for the first time in her life. And she realised that she would never be able to discuss this with anyone. Not with Tobias Weiss, not with her grandmother, not with any teacher, and certainly not with any of her fellow pupils. As they made their way to the maths lesson on the first floor and she realised that, viewed from the outside, she quite clearly belonged with all those heading in the same direction, she could already feel the flip side of her new freedom: there was no way back. And there was no prescribed way forwards either. She would have to find it all by herself.

She took her place in the classroom, a large rectangular space with a high ceiling and four long double windows. A second later the maths teacher, a very old man, entered the room, I wonder what he got up to in the war, Lisa wondered? Does anybody else think about that? she thought. She let her gaze roam amongst her classmates. They know nothing, she thought. She thought of her history teacher, a middle-aged woman, at most ten years younger than Lisa's grandmother. Have we heard a single word about what happened to the Jews? she wondered. To my people, she thought tentatively, as you might try on a new dress to see whether you feel good in it, and if so, you might buy it, assuming you have enough money. But what is money in this context? Lisa thought, as the maths teacher with a hazy past turned his back to them without saying good morning, took a piece of chalk and began to write a formula on the board, this was his method, economy of communication he called it, without anyone believing him, the pupils just thought he was an unfriendly schoolmaster you could do nothing about. Perhaps money is some sort of leap of faith that I need to make. That I belong somewhere, to different people, even if I've never met them before, even if they're not my family. My people, does that suit me? Isn't it too tight around the chest?

When the schoolmaster had finished writing on the board and turned to stare at his pupils, until either they could stand it no longer, or the cleverest or the bootlickers or the nervous amongst them put up their hands to venture a hypothesis or finally to end the silence, Lisa knew what she needed. She needed advice. The image of a large brick building behind a wrought-iron gate popped into her mind. It was in the south of the old town, Sankt Annen Strasse. That is where she would go.

FIFTY

All of a sudden he could hear his own footsteps. His boot heels positively clanged on the uneven stone ground. It smelled damp and mouldy. He took a deep breath. He knew this tunnel. He had been here once before. Then, he had accepted the invitation to a training seminar. Now, fifteen years after the end of the war, fate had led him back to this place. It was good to be alert, it was good to feel one's own body, to smell something, it was good to be alive. Everything was good.

The blackness receded, becoming transparent at first, then milky, and finally outlines were visible. It became lighter and lighter still. The light of day. He walked into the inner courtyard of the old castle, the sun was shining, its rays slanting into the stone edges, the battlements and the castle roofs, which surrounded it like a shield against the passing of time. Here, it seemed to be saying, time has stood still, nothing has happened, all of us remain united in the same belief.

The courtyard was full of people. A colourful mix, women in skirts of different lengths, men in various sizes of jackets and coats, children, boys and girls. He could not see any old people. He was just about to ask a woman in a strikingly short skirt what these people were doing, why they had all gathered here, when she stood to attention, saluted and said, "Heil Hitler, Obersturmbannführer Ranzner!" She relaxed her arm, shook his hand and said, "How wonderful that you were able to arrange it! Without you none of this would have happened!" She laughed, revealing two rows of rotten teeth. When she noticed his confusion, she became serious. "I understand," she said. "This is a bit of a surprise, isn't it? You see the transvestite standing over there, you know, the unshaven one in women's clothing? That's your adjutant, Scharführer Hilbig, do you remember him?"

His eyes followed the woman's outstretched finger and caught sight of a repulsive-looking feminine man with a bloated body and enormous breasts, which could not be real.

"That's impossible," he said. "Hilbig was stocky, he had wide nostrils, a bulging forehead and small eyes. This man here looks like an abortion!"

The woman smiled and he had the uncomfortable feeling that she was scrutinising him with disdain.

"I'm sorry to have to disappoint you, Obersturmbannführer," she said, "but that really is Hilbig. Resurrected in that unfortunate body, half man, half woman. When we found him we thought that we just had to round up all the transvestites and we'd have our old S.S. sergeants back. But we were mistaken. Hilbig is the only one. Mind you!" First she held a finger in the air, then pointed to herself. "There are the women too! Don't forget! You didn't recognise me, but rest assured that I'm Scharführer Kretschmer, your first adjutant. That's why I was standing beside the tunnel waiting for you." She gave him an endearing look, then shrugged and said in resignation, "In this life I'm going around as a prostitute. And I'm not the only one, either, two other S.S. men have been reborn as whores, they're over there somewhere." Searching with her outstretched finger over people's heads, she failed to find them and made a dismissive gesture.

"Doesn't matter! The main thing is that old comrades are back together." It sounded as if she were trying to comfort herself.

They were approached by a little girl with a satchel on her back. The woman in the miniskirt stood to attention, thrust out her right arm and bellowed, "Heil Hitler, Reichsführer S.S.!" The girl, who was no older than seven, casually returned the salute and fixed her eyes on Ranzner.

"Well, well, Obersturmbannführer Josef Ranzner. I hear you're with the secret service now. Excellent work! I've appointed you as contact man, Obersturmbannführer. You will integrate all those who are reborn into the institutions of the Federal Republic of Germany and create a network that will allow us to strike just as soon as we are strong enough. Is that clear, Obersturmbannführer Ranzner?"

Ranzner awoke from his paralysis. He stood to attention in front of the little girl and shouted, "Absolutely, Reichsführer S.S."

"Excellent, excellent," the girl said, smiling. But then a weary expression crept across her face. Gloomily, she said, "We're condemned to fulfil our duty in these unworthy bodies. There's nothing we can do. But it changes this much of our convictions." With her thumb and forefinger the girl formed a zero and stretched out her arm towards Ranzner. Then she dropped it again to her side.

"Some have come off worse than me. See the negro over there? That's Heydrich." The girl giggled with delight and the prostitute joined in. Then they composed themselves and the girl said, "Enough! He is a comrade like you and me, he has done great things and we are dependent on every man for the difficult tasks that lie ahead!"

"What sort of tasks?" Ranzner asked cautiously.

The girl gave him a look of astonishment.

"What? Don't you know anything?"

Ranzner shook his head.

"We're going to conquer the world!" the girl said. "Five-stage plan! What else?"

Ranzner nodded and felt benumbed. "But we lost the war," he said.

The girl dismissed this with a bored wave of her hand.

"That's all lather! We were just dispersed in every country. And that very fact gives us our chance! We'll do it like the Jews, we'll start a global conspiracy with the diaspora, at the end of which lies the conquest of everything. Is that clear, Obersturmbannführer Ranzner? Or do you doubt our mission?"

Instinctively Ranzner snapped to attention and barked, "No, Reichs-führer S.S., no doubts, everything is perfectly clear! World conquest!"

"Excellent!"

"Just one last question, Reichsführer S.S., if I may."

"What?"

"Is Sturmbannführer Karl Treitz here too?"

The girl gave him a puzzled look. She turned to the prostitute.

"Do you know anything about a Sturmbannführer Treitz?"

The woman shook her head, then turned to the assembled crowd and cried, "Is there a Sturmbannführer Treitz here? Sturmbannführer Treitz, please make yourself known if you are present. Treitz! Step forward!"

Everybody turned to face them. So many faces! Germans, Africans, Chinese, whites, blacks, reds, yellows, men, women, children. There were even two Hasidic Jews amongst them, which Ranzner found par-ticularly remarkable. But nobody came forward. The crowd stared at them in silence.

All of a sudden they faded away, dissipating into a white light, and a small blonde girl with a button nose and fringe thrust her face into Otto Kruse's field of vision. She grasped Kruse's eyelashes and pulled up his lids. With a friendly smile, she said, "Hellooooo Daddy! Are you baaack?"

Otto Kruse stared at his child. Then he took hold of her waist with both hands, lifted her up and said, "Good morning, sunshine! Yes, I'm back."

Emma had already set the breakfast table, so he only had to put on his dressing gown, pick up Gudrun and go into the dining room, where she was waiting for him with a smile at the oval marble table. Heinrich sat on his chair and looked at him. He greeted his first born with a succinct nod of the head, the boy's face lit up briefly before becoming serious again. He lifted his cup and drank the cocoa his mother had made him. Heinrich's face disappeared almost completely behind the large cup;

only his eyes were visible. They remained fixed on his father. Otto Kruse interpreted Heinrich's attentiveness as a sign of childish admiration and a silent plea for masculine guidance. A law of nature.

"Morning, darling!" Emma said. "I sent Gudrun in because you were making such ghastly sounds in your sleep. I hope I didn't do the wrong thing."

Otto Kruse gave his wife a paternal smile. He sat Gudrun in her high chair and moved towards his place opposite his wife.

"No, you did exactly the right thing," he said, sitting on the cherry-wood chair and picking up the newspaper Emma had put on the table for him.

As he drank his coffee, ate his egg and read the paper, as Gudrun spoke incessantly while experimenting with butter, jam and cocoa, as his wife watched him affectionately in silence, hoping for attention, Otto Kruse thought about his dream. It was the first time he had not remained stuck in the amorphous blackness, something different had happened instead. It seemed as if this dream contained a mission, an old mission he had wanted to forget. In vain, as it now turned out. I must become active, he thought, pouring himself some coffee.

FIFTY-ONE

The man waved expansively with his arm to indicate the large hall they were standing in, but it seemed to imply much more. Lisa watched him, he was half a head shorter than her, a man of slight build, stooped either through age or by things that lay outside the hall.

"Thank you for telling me your story, young lady," he said. "The three of us have something in common, you, me and the building. We all survived thanks to Aryan houses. Isn't that . . ." he searched for words. Two tears ran from his eyes, they sought out a path down the man's skin with its large pores, they seemed to be traversing his face, from pore to pore, but this was barely noticeable. The tears vanished, leaving behind a damp, shining trail that came to an end just by the corners of his mouth. Lisa stared, she was struck by a peculiar feeling, she felt as if she were about to pick up this frail old man in her arms and kiss away his tears, she could taste salt in her mouth. She wrested herself free, she forced herself to look away from the man's face, her eyes strayed aimlessly around the hall, catching sight of the tall wooden ceiling, the beautiful beams that extended as far as the rows of windows right beneath the ceiling, as if framing each of them. Further back in the hall she saw a kind of lectern that held a thick book, she saw the two long rows of tables, she saw that everything looked very modest. Lisa returned her gaze to the face of the man who was now smiling at her.

"There's nothing left. This used to be a magnificent synagogue with a golden dome, and over there," he explained, pointing somewhere to the rear of the hall, "was a precious menorah." Noticing the bafflement on Lisa's face he said, slapping his head with his palm, "Of course, you wouldn't understand. A menorah is a type of candle holder with seven branches." To give Lisa an idea he described a semi-circle with his hands, starting in the middle and moving up at the sides. Then he broke off and said, "But I'm sure you're here for a much more important reason."

"No, no! It all interests me."

"Then come back in two days' time. We'll be celebrating Rosh Hashanah." He slapped his forehead a second time and smiled at Lisa. "The Jewish New Year festival. All the Jews who still live in Lübeck will be there." He rocked his head from side to side, which reminded Lisa of Tobias Weiss.

"There aren't many of us," the old man said, and then talked about a handful of D.P.s who remained, but Lisa was no longer really listening, she suddenly felt full of this new affinity, which was like a pair of shoes she had just bought and was now putting on tentatively. Did they pinch? Were they too small, too big? Did she really like them?

"What's your name?" she said, before realising that a young girl like her should not pose such a bold question to an elderly man. But he felt like a grandfather, and now as she looked horrified at what she had said, he laughed, amused, and replied, "My name's Mosche, just Mosche. That's all I was before, too."

He accompanied Lisa to the door. Outside, between the façade and the wrought-iron gate, they stopped again, Mosche took her arm, gently turned her around and pointed upwards."

"That was the dome."

Looking up, Lisa said, "What was it you meant about the Aryan houses?"

"They were too close together. That's why they didn't blow up the synagogue; it would have damaged the Aryan houses."

"Oh, I see."

"Yes, they couldn't afford to destroy German property just because of the Jews." He escorted her to the gate. "But what am I saying? I've survived for so long in these houses that I ought to be grateful to them. Believe you me, I know exactly who did what here."

"Here in this street?"

"Here in Lübeck. And most of them are still around." He opened the door, then took hold of Lisa's slender hand and said, "We survived, young lady, you and I. Both of us paid a high price. You don't know who you are. And I'm not the man I once was. But let's not talk about that now. Why don't you come to our New Year's celebration the day after tomorrow?"

They said goodbye, Lisa got on her bicycle and rode down Sankt Annen Strasse. She turned and saw him looking at her and waving, as if they were close friends or relations.

She continued on her way home. It had turned cool, the summer was coming to an end, the days were getting shorter, a hint of twilight hung over the city even though it was still light, even though the sun was still shining. One thing begins in another, Lisa thought, surprised at herself, at this phrase, at her familiarity with a stranger, at life itself, which had suddenly opened one curtain for her and drawn another shut. She was still standing on the same stage, but the scenery was different. What about the audience? She looked at the faces of the people she rode past, especially the elderly ones. Which of them had helped Mosche? And the others? How many Jews had there been here in total before they all died? I'm cycling through a prison, she thought. I'm cycling through a hideout. I'm cycling through a den of thieves. I'm cycling between murderers. Between traitors. Between liars who are pretending they did nothing. I'm a Jew. Thank goodness hardly anyone knows. Lisa Ejzenstain. Perhaps Kramer's better after all.

When she turned into her street and the bicycle jolted over the cobblestones, which juddered through her body, she remembered that Mosche had talked of D.P.s.

"What are D.P.s?" Herr Weiss repeated as they were watching the news together in the living room. He had cooked and now they were sitting on the sofa, both with plates of fried potatoes and spinach on their laps, with a little fried bacon sprinkled on top. That's definitely not kosher, Lisa thought. The newsreader spoke of how Nikita Khrushchev was denied permission to leave New York and Long Island, he spoke of the United Nations General Assembly taking place there, which is why they had not been able to refuse Khruschchev and Fidel Castro entry. He spoke of how the media had been urged to say as little as possible about these two statesmen. He spoke of eighty passengers who had died when their aeroplane crashed immediately after take-off, all American soldiers. About thirty-nine people who had died in torrential rainfall in the Italian Alps. He spoke of the large number of countries that had gained their independence or would do so in the coming days. Black men in uniforms appeared on the screen, unfamiliar flags fluttering in the wind. He spoke of how Wilma Rudolph was welcomed back home to America by thousands of people. The television showed a pretty woman with short hair, who was a few years older than Lisa. With her long legs she ran faster than all the others, the newsreader spoke of a miracle, because Wilma Rudolph had suffered from infantile paralysis. Everything the newsreader said sounded to Lisa as if it were a personal message to her.

"Hmm, I think it stands for Displaced Persons, which, um, well, are people who are homeless," Tobias Weiss said slowly. "After the war Germany was full of, well um, people who didn't belong here, as they say, such as prisoners-of-war, forced labourers, collaborators afraid of going back to their countries. And, well, um, Jews of course."

"How did they get here?" Lisa said, without taking her eyes off Karl-Heinz Köpcke, now smiling and talking about Chubby Checker who had conquered Germany with his song "The Twist". The television showed pictures of girls dancing, they were around Lisa's age, they were dressed like Lisa, plaits, blouse, knee-length skirt, flat shoes. As they danced they twisted their hips the opposite way from their torsos, while slowly rotating on the spot and laughing.

The bulletin was at an end and on the screen appeared the map of a country that no longer existed, with cities in the east that were no longer known by those names.

"The Jews?" Herr Weiss said, as if unsure. She glanced at him. Before he could say anything she asked, "Did you come across any Jews during the war?"

The German Meteorological Service in Frankfurt forecast sunshine for the following day, 21 September, with temperatures between thirteen and fifteen degrees. A light wind from the west and south-west. In Berlin the sun would rise at 05.50 and set at 18.07. Herr Weiss cleared his throat.

"Well, now, of course we came across Jews."

"Tell me what it was like."

Herr Weiss went to the television and turned a knob. The screen went blank, Lisa recalled how she used to watch the dot in the middle to try to catch the moment when it vanished. But the moment always came and went before she noticed, which is why she had never seen it. Now she forced herself not to look. Instead she stared at Herr Weiss, who sat down on the sofa beside her. She had made him feel flustered. Which had been her intention. I have to, she thought.

"Lisa," he said, "you know what happened to the Jews, don't you?"

Lisa nodded.

Herr Weiss nodded. "Everyone pretended that what was happening was perfectly normal, and so, well . . ." He paused. "There were a few Jewish children in my class. At some point they just stopped coming. And then, well, erm, people said that the families had received an order to move out for labour deployment. I sensed, yes, I sensed that it was a lie when our father told us. It sounded too formulaic, do you know what I mean?"

"So when did you know what was really happening?"

"In the war."

"In the war?"

"We were soldiers. We fought. But when we were on leave and the others went home . . ." He paused, his mouth closed slowly, he looked at the television as if another programme had started. Then he cleared his throat again and said, "My mother had a stroke when I was on my first assignment. And, um, well, the others went home, but what was I going to do there? Instead I hung around, I went to the station, I don't know why, I sat on a bench and watched the trains. I saw goods trains heading east, they travelled slowly through the station, you could barely make out what they were transporting, but through the tiny barred windows I saw hands and eyes. I knew at once that those were Jews. And then people started mentioning it. They're not coming back, they said, They'll go up in smoke, into the air, they said, there'll be plenty of room up there, that was the kind of joke you'd hear."

"So what did you do?"

"What was I supposed to do? It simply happened, it was like *force majeure*. I was just a simple soldier, I collected body parts that the Russians had shot or blown off my comrades, I just kept seeing blood, all day long, blood and bones and the screaming wounded, there was no opportunity for me to do anything at all." He looked at Lisa almost beseechingly. Lisa looked at Herr Weiss, her Tobi, who now seemed like a big brother to her.

"You didn't even say Erm just then, or one of your other fillers."

"Didn't I? Well, I'd better make up for that as quickly as possible."

She smiled at him. Not a den of thieves and murderers, she thought, Just a city full of people. You've got to look very closely, Lisa, you have to scrutinise each individual you meet.

She called her grandmother.

"No, darling. Maria's . . . out."

She went down to the third floor where the door was already open.

"How big you've got!" Frau Kramer exclaimed as she embraced her granddaughter. She was wearing a light-blue apron and held a breakfast knife in her hand.

"Grandma! You see me every day!"

"But not as often as before. It means I notice things like that."

Lisa sat at the round table by the window, Frau Kramer brought over some fruit, rolls, pâté and tea. The last of the light in the west was blood-red, staining a few clouds that hurried across the sky as if having to get somewhere before night. Everything is permanently on the move, Lisa thought briefly, before saying, "I spoke to a man from the Jewish Community today."

"Oh," Frau Kramer said, "does that still exist here?"

"It exists again. His name is Mosche and he invited me to come to the Jewish New Year's celebrations the day after tomorrow."

"Are you going to go?"

"Of course, it's interesting. And maybe I'll find out more about the D.P.s."

"Oh," Frau Kramer said again.

Lisa eyed her grandmother over the rim of the cup she was now bringing to her lips.

"Do you know anything about them?"

"Well, there were to be a few camps here when we arrived in Lübeck."

"You never told me about that."

"It wasn't a particularly nice time. It was all about survival. It was quite something just getting us through the first winter."

"I want to know everything, Grandma."

Frau Kramer nodded. "Yes, I'll tell you, but not today, please."

"Why not today?"

"I see you so rarely, do we always have to talk about the past?"

There was a pause, during which Lisa searched for the right words. "Grandma," she said, "you've been living with your past for so long. But all along *I've* been living with a lie. Are you so surprised that I'm desperate to find out more?"

Frau Kramer shook her head. "No, you're right. I'm sorry, Lisa, please don't take it amiss. I'm tired and the past is painful."

"But you did everything right, Grandma. What should be painful about it for you?"

"That I lied to you for so long. And that I still haven't told you everything. That hurts. In retrospect it makes everything wrong, even if perhaps it wasn't."

She took a handkerchief from her apron and wiped her tears away. Lisa reached for a roll. As she ate she looked out of the window where the last of the light receded.

"Let's do it like we did that first time," she said after a while, turning to her grandmother. "We'll meet somewhere nice and you can tell me everything. Deal?" Frau Kramer nodded and gave her granddaughter a smile of gratitude.

They chatted a while longer about other things. Lisa told Frau Kramer about Wilma Rudolph, the American sprinter, whose face had been in her mind all evening. Frau Kramer told Lisa that she would soon be getting a pay rise at Hawesta, and that she wanted to train in bookkeeping so she could stop working as a packer. Keeping their feelings in check, the two women smiled at each other and pretended nothing existed outside this moment. They had to, for everything was there, all the anxious love of a woman for a child she might have lost had she not resorted to the most extreme measures, doing what nobody else did and what nobody could have done. Everything was there, the confusion in the heart of the granddaughter, who felt as if she would gradually pass from a solid to a liquid state and lose all grip if she failed to keep her head running around the clock like an engine, generating ideas that gave her a direction, a third eye that could see things which were not there, with all the risks for her mind that this entailed. It was a ritual the two women performed with their chit-chat, each body movement a letting-go, each smile on the lips a new Yes against an old No.

When the two felt that this was enough for one evening and it was time for bed, they hugged each other and Lisa went back upstairs. As she unlocked the door to Tobias's apartment she heard the front door open downstairs. A woman entered the hallway on high heels and came up the stairs unsteadily. Maria, Lisa thought, summarily cutting off all further thoughts and feelings associated with that name and that face and that voice.

She entered the dark apartment. Tobias was already asleep. She fetched her nightie from her room, went into the bathroom, undressed, washed with a flannel at the basin, dried herself with the towel, put on her nightie and inspected the face of the young woman staring back at her in the mirror. Slowly, while still looking herself in the eye, she untied her plait, picked up the hairbrush, which was on the window sill to her right, and spent a long time brushing her hair. She closed her eyes as she brushed her teeth, concentrating on this alone. She rinsed her mouth, then the toothbrush, put it back in the mug, returned to her room, closed the door gently behind her and tilted open the window.

Fresh air flooded the room, caressing her face, she could smell autumn. She heard familiar, indeterminable noises that gave the night its melody, I wonder what it sounds like in a proper city? she thought. Then she went to bed and fell asleep.

FIFTY-TWO

At the beginning of July 1947, five hundred people strolled in small groups through Zehlendorf. Theirs was a short journey, all they had to do was step outside the camp gate, walk to the left for a while down Potsdamer Chaussee until they came to where Kurstrasse headed almost due north. It was a beautiful street, stately patricians' houses from the Wilhelmine period stood by large fields where corn was ripening, here and there these people saw splendid linden and oak trees with dark-green leaves, a sign that spring was over and summer here. There were smaller plum, apple and pear trees too, as soon as they ripened people from the entire neighbourhood would come to gather the harvest and, as in the previous year, the occasion would witness an encounter between Jews and Germans. The many orphans in the camp especially enjoyed coming here to play, fifty of them now walked past the trees with an urgent desire to get climbing, but today they could not for they had to go to school.

These five hundred people did not know that the fields belonged to Farmer Hönow, they did not know that he was head of the last farming family in Zehlendorf, they did not know that his son, Günter, had been a prisoner-of-war and had returned home only a few months earlier, they did not know that the family did not know how things would go from here. And back then nobody could imagine that one day Günter would build concrete housing estates in which there would be no room for the fields he had grown up on.

On the right-hand side was the Evangelical Hubertus Hospital, a rambling complex of buildings in late 1920s style, tall gables, wide, squat houses that looked like heavy bodies with pointed hats. There was a large park with a beautiful, round plaza by the main entrance on Spanische Allee. Some amongst the five hundred knew that a few months previously several American military vehicles had taken away a handful of senior doctors for denazification.

The walkers headed towards a row of two-storey houses with red roofing shingles, which had once formed an uninterrupted terrace running a fair distance down Tewsstrasse, but now bomb damage allowed a view of the large gardens within this development, known to be a housing complex for state officials and built by the Reichsbank at the beginning of the 1920s.

When the people reached Tewsstrasse, which ran perpendicular to Kurstrasse, they turned left, now heading almost exactly westwards. Nobody amongst the five hundred knew that this road had been called something else until 1938. But had they known, then perhaps it would have come as a surprise that the Nazis should have renamed it after an educational reformer, and perhaps one or two of them would have suspected it might have been because of the term "unified school", which was coined by Tews.

They passed number 18, where the film director Eduard von Borsody had been living since 1933. He made twenty-six films in the Third Reich, two of them commissioned by the Reich Propaganda Ministry, and now he was working on his new project, which would soon be appearing in cinemas with the title "The Woman by the Wayside". Perhaps Anna would have recalled another Borsody film she had seen with her Aryan friends in the Nauen picture house on Marktstrasse. She might even have been able to tell the others about Borsody's biggest pre-war success, "The Green Hell", which came out just before Reichskristallnacht.

But as she had no idea that this was the director's house she walked straight past it with other things on her mind, followed by Sarah who was carrying Shimon, and surrounded by her people: Ruth and Aaron, the Abramowiczes with their children, the old man and Emil, who had started calling himself Zwi and had only very reluctantly put on civilian clothes for this evening.

Anna thought of the future and felt a tugging in her abdomen. She looked at the curtains at the windows they walked past and suspected that behind them lived men and women observing this crowd without love, men and women no doubt angry that Jews were permitted to walk this route on the pavement again, that the American army of occupation had given the Jews free use of the school, which meant that the Aryan children had to take lengthier journeys, men and women who had hoped they would never have to see another Jew in their life.

Anna knew that they would not be able to stay in Germany, and she had never felt it as keenly as on this warm evening in this golden light.

But she was concerned about the future. Peretz had told her that the Jews in Palestine were trying to buy weapons because they feared an invasion by their Arab neighbours and because they were determined to fight for their rights.

Peretz had told her that the British had surrendered their mandate over Palestine to the United Nations in the hope that they would be instructed to reassume it.

He had told her that the Soviets had secretly been welcoming the illegal immigration of Jews into Palestine of late, in the hope that the situation would escalate, forcing the British to leave the Middle East.

Peretz had told her too much, Anna decided.

Tewsstrasse curved to the left, heading almost exactly southwards, where it became Wasgenstrasse. The people did not know that Wasgen was an old German word for the Vosges, which would never again belong to Germany, but they knew the building on the right of the bend: the school, the Westschule, soon to lose that name, and which functioned as the events centre for the D.P. camp.

It was a beautiful school, two buildings from the 1920s and '30s, tall and wide, their façades stood at right angles to each other, creating a spacious forecourt by the outer curve in the road. At the very centre of this forecourt the thick stump of a birch tree rose from the ground like the bisecting point of an angle.

The right-hand building, with its double gable, triangular bay and two entrances at ninety degrees to each other, reinforced the impression that somebody here had been busy with a compass. This part of the school remained unfinished.

The five hundred people headed for the entrance to the left-hand building. Simpler than its counterpart, it would have looked inconspicuous had it not been for the clock directly above the door in a large red square painted on the wall.

In one of the classroom windows to the right of the door the arrivals saw a blue printed placard they knew well. In Yiddish, it read:

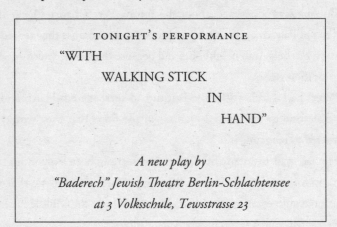

TONIGHT'S PERFORMANCE

"WITH

WALKING STICK

IN

HAND"

A new play by
"Baderech" Jewish Theatre Berlin-Schlachtensee
at 3 Volksschule, Tewsstrasse 23

The people entered the building, beyond the entrance was a stairwell, they climbed the few steps to the upper ground floor and arrived at the doors to the school hall. Seven rows of chairs were laid out, offering seating for one hundred and thirty people at most. The rest had to sit in the aisle and on the floor in front of the first row, many of them stood along the sides and right at the back. Three large windows let in a flood of light, they had to draw the heavy curtains once everybody had found somewhere to sit or stand. Gradually the hall went quiet. Everyone focused on the low stage, from which two narrow staircases led up to the left and right. The background had originally been painted black, but in many places this had peeled off, revealing the white undercoat.

A tall man entered the hall and stepped onto the stage. It was Peretz, who felt an urgent need to use his loudhailer. But this was an enclosed space, totally unsuited to it. He would speak much louder than he was used to, and his voice would be hoarse by the end of the evening. Peretz positioned himself at the very front of the stage in the centre. He wore an elegant grey suit, with one hand in his trouser pocket while the other held a sheaf of paper.

Anna gazed at her husband standing there, in the eyes of these people a hero from Palestine. A man who saved lives and asked for nothing in return. She thought of the play that was not going to be performed that night and of the scene she had been unable to get out of her head ever since she had sat here in a similarly packed hall a few weeks earlier. The stage had become so full that at one point Anna could not distinguish the actors from the audience. Just a small space jammed with people wanting to go somewhere but not able to. On the spot where Peretz now arranged his papers, glancing every now and then at his audience, a head-high signpost had stood, arrows pointing in different directions. One of these bore the words "Eretz Yisrael" in Hebrew letters, by now Anna was able to tell these words apart from others. Men in hats and coats, women in smaller hats and bonnets, and children in little dresses and jackets had clustered around the signpost, all of them carrying suitcases, all of them lost and looking in every direction for a way forward. Where do we go from here? they wondered, and went to see the Rabbi, Rabbi, what should we do? and the Rabbi said, Don't worry, you'll be moving on soon, it's just a few weeks now, look,

Berlin is in ruins,

Lying nine cubits deep in the ground

And I, a Jew, stand up and cry,

Long live Israel!

He had pointed at the signpost and all of a sudden everybody knew: That way!

Peretz cleared his throat and began.

"Just four more days." He explained that they would set off at night to avoid drawing attention to themselves. The most difficult thing, he told the five hundred people, will be getting into the American zone. If we manage that, the rest is simple. What does the rest consist of? someone called out. I'll tell you, Peretz said. We'll travel south in the American zone as far as the D.P. camp for Jews. It's only a few kilometres from the French zone. There we'll spend the night. The head of the camp is from the International Refugee Organisation, he'll cooperate with us, he knows the score. We'll spend one night there, you'll get a good meal and a decent rest. The following day is a Saturday. That's important, because the French border guards are just waiting for their shifts to finish and to go off duty for the weekend. We've established that they're more generous then than on other days. So we won't leave until the afternoon, which means we'll cross the border in the evening.

Peretz paused. Now let's talk about you, he said. Each one of you will get a new identity. Aaron here (Aaron Strauss, who was sitting in the front row, stood up so that everybody could see him) has five hundred new identities sent to us by H.Q. in Paris. He'll hand them out at the end of the meeting. Peretz smiled at Aaron, he thought briefly of how taken aback they had been when they went through the list and saw it was full of French names. He had telephoned Shmaria Zamaret in Paris and asked, Rudi, where did you get these names from? Telephone books, Rudi had replied, We didn't have any time, there are so many visas.

Peretz sighed and said, You need to know these new identities inside out by the time we leave, in case any border guards get suspicious. His eyes fell on Anna, who was sitting in the aisle with Shimon on her lap.

Shimon's eyes watched him, their gazes met, Peretz felt a strange sensation, a sort of resistance. Then he looked away and composed himself to carry on talking.

Outside in Wasgenstrasse, fifty metres beyond the bend in the road, a black Mercedes was parked with its headlights pointing towards the school. In the front seats sat two bored men in civilian clothing, casting the occasional glance at the windows of the school hall. The man in the passenger seat had contacted his superior half an hour previously, reporting in a London accent that everything was O.K., the Jews had gone to watch a theatrical performance.

The two M.I.6. agents knew the Baderech troupe's programme, they would have picked up on any irregularity at once. So they also knew that it would be a good hour before the Jews came out again and went back home to their camp.

In the meantime Peretz was explaining that each passenger would be permitted only one suitcase with a limited number of belongings, as Ernst Caro had instructed. The people were content with this. When Peretz explained that they could not keep their suitcases with them, but that for reasons of space they would have to be transported in separate lorries, nobody objected. When he told them that everyone should write their name in chalk on the lid, so they could find their case again later, a silence descended amongst the concentration camp survivors, which largely went unnoticed, for more than half of those in the Westschule hall were Polish Jews who had never been in a concentration camp. They had fled from the Germans to the Soviet Union, and after the war had found shelter from the Poles in Germany, of all places. They knew little if anything about the previous departures of their comrades, housemates and spouses, who now felt the chalk in their fingers, heard the scratching as they wrote their names on the rough surfaces, harboured their doubts, Wouldn't the chalk simply rub off when all the luggage knocked together during the long drive on poor roads?, and perhaps a good number looked up again, letting their gaze take in all these people, involuntary companions on the journey to an uncertain destination, a throng of people on the platform, bent over suitcases or having already written their names, there must be hundreds of them, their gaze would definitely have taken in the S.S. men with their machine guns at the ready, standing everywhere like signposts with steel arrows, soon they would be pointing to the wagons waiting there, and a good number who recalled that they had never seen their luggage again now perhaps thought, What a performance!

Strange, Ruth said softly to Aaron, Everything changes apart from the methods.

That evening Peretz made no mention of the thirteen German lorries complete with drivers, which he had hired on behalf of Ephraim Frank alias Ernst Caro. He thought of his telephone call with the chief commandant of German Bricha. They had fought a hard bargain over refugees, for in truth Ephraim Frank had wanted only Peretz's empty lorries, Too risky to transport them out of Berlin as well, he had told Peretz. Peretz had been expecting such a response, in more reasonable circumstances he would have agreed with Ephraim Frank. But he found every aspect of the external and internal situation utterly insane, which is why he replied, You'll only have them half empty. Ephraim Frank did not scream at him, he did not discuss the matter. He said nothing, and just when Peretz was about to ask, Are you still there? Ephraim Frank said, Eight per lorry. Twenty, Peretz replied. They had agreed on fifteen, which meant they needed thirty-three lorries, thirteen more than Peretz actually had. He hesitated. No, he thought, I won't mention the Germans until just before.

He looked out of the window. Dusk was setting in, turning the blue darker and darker, the sound of birds chirruping entered the hall, beyond the glass panes swallows and swifts darted here and there on the hunt for insects. Soon it would be too dark for perpetrators and victims, but the show would not end, bats and small nocturnal animals would take over. What rubbish, Peretz thought, ignoring the comparisons his head was making with apparently compelling logic.

Anna followed his gaze, she saw the evening, she saw the birds, she heard the crows, she bid farewell. She had never been to the Mediterranean, she did not know what sort of light illuminated the day there, which smells hung in the air, she had no idea of the height of the sky, the reddish-brown of the earth, she knew palms only from books, she was not braced for the sea she would have to cross.

All she knew was that she would never see this country nor speak its language again. But what connections remained? Was it possible to keep pretending that none had existed until this proved true? And how long would that take? Years? Decades? No, something, some residue will always remain, she thought. She would have to be alert to take it all in, for one thing she had learned: the inner world was like the outside one, something new, unfamiliar would suddenly appear, triggering something old, something past. Think about this, she thought. It grew noisy, the children were getting impatient, Peretz checked his watch, still twenty minutes till the official end of the performance, he was hoarse from talking. Time to call it a day for now, he thought, and requested that everyone walk past Aaron Strauss in single file. While they formed a queue that snaked several times around the hall, Peretz left the stage and went over to Anna and her people. Once again his eyes met Shimon's, and once again he sensed a reluctance. For a brief moment Peretz had the feeling that a drama was being acted out here too, in which each of them was playing a part, a deception behind which stood another, hidden reality. But which was it?

When he kissed his wife he was severed from this feeling.

The kiss led into a room, the room had a bed. Peretz had recently moved into a small apartment in Berlin-Mitte, the Joint Distribution Committee paid for it, the U.N.R.R.A. issued the papers. Peretz's official job was to support Jewish refugees in the Berlin D.P. camps.

The apartment was in a tall, rear tenement house in Rosenthaler Strasse, it was old and run-down, the mattresses sagged, if you stripped the pillows you could see an array of brown stains on the fabric. But Peretz had gone to great trouble to prepare everything for this evening. There was even a bulbous, colourfully painted plant pot with fresh flowers on the old, thick-legged living-room table, around which some equally rustic chairs were arranged. The cramped apartment was full of chunky and overly fussy 1930s furniture, beside the front door was an oak-veneer rounded sideboard, oppressively crowding the hallway. The glass cabinet was filled to the brim with spare parts, headlights, rear lights, sprocket wheels, huge nuts and finger-thick screws. Peretz's loud-hailer sat on the floor next to the sideboard.

I'm going to have to move away from here, Peretz said when he and Anna arrived at the apartment. Shimon had long been asleep, he lay in his mother's arms, dreaming that he was lying on his back watching raindrops fall from the sky. Some of these landed on his face and tickled him.

Why? Anna asked. It's getting more and more difficult with the Russians, Peretz said. He led Anna into the sitting room and pointed to a broad sofa with a lilac-coloured flowery pattern, bulging cushions and a tall, curved backrest. Anna understood and gently laid Shimon on it. She knew what was coming, there was no way out, they were man and wife, they had to fulfil the contract, renew the pact, honour the promise. Love? Who lived here? she asked, to distract herself. Germans, Peretz said tersely as he was taking off his coat.

What happened to them?

I don't know, why are you interested?

Just am, simple as that.

Don't give me "simple as that". Come here!

As simple as that?

Wait! Peretz hurried into the kitchen and came back with a bottle of claret. Suits the occasion, he said, giving her a winning smile. Anna followed him into the bedroom. A symposium was being conducted in her head on the question of how to return to one's innocence having lost it. There were various opinions, one woman with a perfect inside view of the soul thought it impossible, but other voices suspected her of merely wanting to safeguard her own future.

Outside, in the world of tangible things, Peretz smiled and sat on the wide wooden bed, a marital bed, I bought it on the black market, you wouldn't believe all the things you can get there! Outside in the world Anna gave Peretz a friendly smile and sat beside him, not too close and not too far away; there was a script for situations like this, both of them knew it by heart, where do you learn such things, everything always seemed to be written down somewhere and thus there were no surprises that night.

FIFTY-THREE

On 1 October, 1960, a Saturday, Lisa Kramer and her grandmother met to have the conversation they had arranged. Their original plan had been to take a walk outside of town, but the weather had turned bad overnight and now they were in Herr Weiss's apartment, pondering what to do instead.

Biting the bullet, Frau Kramer said, "Let's go to Pöppendorf."

Lisa stared at her grandmother in surprise, she wanted to say, What made you think of *Pöppendorf*? But she held her tongue and agreed.

The two women huddled together as they walked to the bus stop in Holstenstrasse. Soon they saw a pale-yellow articulated bus, which like a serpent wound from a side street and laboured towards them. The bus stopped beside the two women, they got on at the front by the driver, a man in a dark-blue uniform with a peaked cap, bought two tickets and sat next to each other on one of the wooden benches. Water dripped onto the floor from the umbrella they hung from the handhold above the seat rest in front of them, forming a small puddle. It smelled of diesel and damp.

Crossing the Trave over Holstenbrücke, the bus drove through the Wall peninsula, past the Holstentor with its fat, pointed towers which always looked inflated to Lisa, as though they ought to be slimmer, in correct proportion to the actual gate opening.

The next body of water they came to was the city moat, traversed by Puppenbrücke with its allegorical statues, Lisa knew them from her history classes, but the only one she remembered was the figure of the river god, she recognised him, unmistakable in her eyes with an oar in his hands and bent forward. And all of a sudden her old question – Why does a river god need an oar? – was answered as she looked at him and thought, Because he's only human too.

Up ahead loomed the station with its four brick towers and three large arched windows. The bus stopped, the doors opened, umbrellas were collapsed, people in wet clothes boarded, bought tickets, looked for a seat. The floor was soon wet, the doors closed, the bus set off, the windows misted up. Nobody spoke, to Lisa the people appeared mute, withdrawn and bent like the statues on Puppenbrücke, rain gods who were only human too. These are not my people, she thought, the idea was more than a teaser, it unsheathed a new certainty, Lisa thought of Rosh Hashanah a few days earlier and, as if she had overheard something from her granddaughter's inner life, Frau Kramer said softly. "So, how was the New Year's festival?"

Lisa looked away from the flat, north German countryside, she smiled at her grandmother and said, just as softly, "It was really lovely. The entire Jewish Community of Lübeck came."

"That must have been a lot of people."

"Oh no, Grandma, there were only about thirty, all of them still looking as if something terrifying was lurking in every corner."

"Oh."

"But it was lovely all the same. Because when we were all together no-one was frightened anymore."

"Were you frightened too?"

"Well, since I've been finding out more . . ."

"But hardly anybody knows that you . . ."

The two of them fell silent. After a while Lisa picked up the thread again.

"I was standing between Mosche and Selma, his wife," she said. "And during the ceremony they explained everything. There hasn't been a rabbi here since the war and the rabbi in Hamburg can't come to Lübeck for every occasion, so the oldest member takes charge." She smiled. "It was very festive. I even drank some wine."

"But you're not old enough!"

"Just a sip, Grandma! It's only a ritual."

"So what now?"

Lisa looked quizzically at her grandmother. "What do you mean?"

Frau Kramer did not know exactly what she was asking, she did not even know why she felt so uneasy that her granddaughter was becoming the Jew she always had been. She had the impression that she was losing her granddaughter to strangers, that she no longer had a right to the bond with Lisa, she was envious of the Jewish Community of Lübeck and knew it was nonsense to feel this way, but she could not help it, I'm just a simple farmer's wife, she thought, how could I know any better?

"What are you going to do now?" she said.

"There's not much I *can* do until I turn eighteen. I'll just wait, perhaps I'll learn Hebrew in the meantime." She paused, before looking at her grandmother and saying, "Why do you want to go to Pöppendorf?"

Frau Kramer had detected the undertone in her granddaughter's voice, the mistrust, the search for another lie. It hurt, she felt stung. She wanted to tell Lisa everything here and now, she wanted to cast her inner resistance out of the window and reveal the whole truth at once,

Look, I'm still the same person, you can trust me, you don't have to distance yourself from me, please stay!

"Selma was a D.P.," Lisa said, interrupting her thoughts. "When she met Mosche, they decided to stay here."

"Was she in Pöppendorf, then?"

"No, but she told me about it. There was another D.P. camp, I've forgotten its name. That's where she was."

Frau Kramer looked at her granddaughter. "Am Stau, it was called," she said, lowering her gaze.

Lisa said nothing in reply, she fixed her eyes on her grandmother.

The bus drove past the pond at Trems, with its weeping willows, frogs and ducks, childhood memories scurried through Lisa's mind. The bus stopped, some passengers alighted. The bus continued on its way, to the left lay Bad Schwartau, to the right the Teerhof islands floated past them, once upon a time, when ships were made of wood, they used to be tarred here. Lisa had learned everything about the city of Lübeck's glorious past, but only now did she fancy she understood why none of it had interested her.

"It's not your fault, Grandma," she said unexpectedly.

Frau Kramer gave her a look of surprise. Lisa smiled back.

"It's not your fault that I never felt at home here," she said. "For a long time I thought the only reason you came here was to wait for your husband, and I asked myself how I was ever going to be able to put down roots in Lübeck if the only relatives I had left didn't want to be here themselves."

"I'm so sorry, Lisa!"

"No, Grandma! It's not your fault."

"No?"

"Of course not! I just don't belong here." Raising her voice, she said out loud, "I don't belong here because I'm a Jew."

A few passengers turned around, but nobody said anything. Frau Kramer was so shocked that she wanted to give her granddaughter a good telling off, wanted to say, Are you trying to get everyone's back up? But instead she said softly to Lisa, "Of course you belong here, you grew up here, you don't know any different."

Lisa did not reply. She peered through the wet window to where the old section of the Schwartau meandered in its deep bed through pastures and fields, she thought of Selma's words, If I'd gone to Palestine then maybe I'd have had more sun in my life. But she had stayed out of love for Mosche, That's a reason, Lisa thought.

The bus drove towards Dänischburg. She was not fond of this area, its countryside scarred by large industrial complexes. Warehouses, the power station, run-down boatyards, shipwrecks, the austere three- and five-storey apartment blocks, which were ten years old at most, and amongst these the tiny old villages with their church spires, their narrow houses unleashing in her feelings of forlornness and bleakness. But today she had the impression that this corresponded with the truth, Why go on telling more lies, she thought, by opening my eyes only to beauty and shutting them to everything I don't like? To the fact that I'm a forlorn entity myself, sitting in a random bus next to this random woman?

She paused, looked at her grandmother and sighed. She felt sympathy for the old woman, who had done something that very few had dared to do: save Jews, without ever having received acknowledgement of the fact. How far must I go, she wondered, to find something true within me?

By the time the bus stopped beside the church and the driver called out, "All change, please!" it had stopped raining. The two women got off. The Evangelical church soared above them, a rectangular brick tower with a pitched roof. "Now it's your turn," Lisa said to her grandmother.

Frau Kramer nodded and linked arms with her granddaughter. They went northwards along the main road for a while, then turned to the west. After a few minutes they were at Waldhusener Weg, following it out of the village and into the forest. After a few hundred metres the road was no longer asphalt, just a woodland path. In the middle of the forest

Frau Kramer stopped and pointed to a plantation of young spruces. "It was here," she said.

Lisa looked at the young trees. Nothing remained of Pöppendorf D.P. camp. "I want you to tell me everything," she said.

Frau Kramer took a deep breath. Grabbing Lisa's hands, she said, "If you want to know how we got here then first I've got to tell you what happened after the Poles took us in on the day your mother died."

Lisa nodded. The time between their first conversation in Travemünde and this forest now evaporated, and Lisa became aware that since then part of her had remained on that Polish farm and only today would be able to move on. Only now would time pass again for this part of Lisa Ejzenstain, and perhaps one day she and her grandmother would arrive in the present, if enough had been said.

Squeezing her granddaughter's hands, Frau Kramer started to talk. She spoke of how the following morning the Russians had come in search of Germans, everyone had to assemble in the living room, she with Lisa on her arm, and when one of the soldiers stopped in front of her she sent a prayer heavenwards, the soldier asked her something but all she could do was stare at him and pray silently, the soldier became furious, he repeated his question, only this time screaming it with his face close up to hers, and Frau Kramer prayed and stared at him. At that moment the Poles' eldest daughter said something, the soldier's head turned, then he looked at Frau Kramer again, but this time with a different expression, it was as if he had swapped places with his twin brother, and the twin brother had tears in his eyes and said something and stroked her cheek and said a long sentence before he and the other soldiers left. When they were gone the people stood motionless in the living room for a while, then the mother hugged the eldest daughter and kissed her cheek, then the father came up to Frau Kramer, who was holding tightly onto her tiny granddaughter as if someone was trying to snatch her away, and brought her over to a chair so she could sit down. They told her what had been said, She told him, the mother said, still hugging her brave child, that the lady with the baby had lost her entire family because of the Germans, And then, Frau Kramer now said, looking up at her granddaughter, who was walking beside her through the dripping Waldhusen forest, then I knew that this was the truth. She told Lisa what the Russian had said, He said, the mother said, letting go of her daughter, that he was from Byelorussia and half his relations had been murdered by the Germans. I was so ashamed of my people, Frau Kramer said. They continued walking.

"Where was the entrance?" Lisa asked.

Frau Kramer stopped, she looked back, forwards, she shrugged and said, "I can't say for sure. Somewhere here there was a gate."

"Let's go in!" Lisa said.

Frau Kramer did not fancy the idea, It's all wet, she said, I haven't got the right shoes on, she said, but it was of no use. She had come to open the floodgates to the truth, she had to leave the path, Lisa dragged Frau Kramer behind her, between the shining young trees, Maybe we'll find something, she shouted out into the forest and Frau Kramer abandoned her resistance and started looking. But they found nothing, no screw, no scrap of material, no wooden slat. With wet shoes and wet clothes they stood in the plantation, imagining that a camp for people had once stood here, people who had nothing else. Lisa looked around, sighed and said, "Tell me more, Grandma!"

They walked back, they left the camp and Frau Kramer continued. She spoke of how they had stayed with the Poles for two days, two days during which she thought about Margarita still asleep in the snow. After two days I couldn't bear it any longer, she said, and through the thick snowfall Lisa pictured a swathed, faceless figure, she heard the whistling of the icy wind tugging at her mother, she saw the hood, at any moment a strong gust would whip it off and she would see her, she thought, It's the dead who cause us to take flight, she thought of the Russian soldier with tears in his eyes and thought, Perhaps each attack is nothing but a secret flight, perhaps he and my grandmother were fleeing to the west together and didn't know it, but she did not articulate her thoughts, for Frau Kramer spoke of how the Polish family gave them warm clothing and provisions, how she bound Lisa to her chest again and then put the dress on top and the coat and wrapped a blanket around her shoulders and strapped on a rucksack the Poles had given her, then went back out into the cold. They said, Go that way and along there and you'll come to a small station, it's on the line to Frankfurt an der Oder, if you're lucky a train will come along, may God be with you.

The blanket of cloud above the Waldhusen forest tore open, now the path led through older clusters of trees, they had left the camp behind them, they would return to it when the time was right, for now Frau Kramer was trudging through the white landscape, noticing that many had already passed this way, suitcases lay in the snow, prams with frozen babies stood at the side of the path, Some were as small as you, she told Lisa and spoke of the station where thousands were standing in the cold, having survived this far, and now waited for a train, for a whole day, and then a miracle occurred, a Reichsbahn train arrived, an unbelievably long train, it passed through the station at walking pace, it was full of people, When's it going to stop? someone beside Frau Kramer said, and then she realised the train was not stopping. There was screaming, running, doors were wrenched open, people tried to leap onto the moving train, the entire mass of refugees set in motion, but the train slithered past like a large animal unbothered by the flies pestering it, I ran, Frau Kramer said, after the train, and once more a helper emerged from nowhere, a hand that stretched out towards her, pulled her into the open door of the train, a man who nodded to her and disappeared again into the densely packed crowd filling the corridor of the carriage. One hundred kilometres, Frau Kramer said, as to the right of the path the forest came to an end by a field, It wasn't any further than that, but it took us two days. Why? her granddaughter's eyes asked, and Frau Kramer spoke of the deep drone of the bomber groups and the bee-like buzzing of the fighter aircraft, she spoke of how the train stopped and the people fled in droves into the snow, under the trees, to avoid being anywhere near when it happened. But it did not happen. When the train started moving again and the people hastily jumped back on, each one driven by the fear of being left behind, some were in fact left behind, these continued running for a while until overtaken by the inevitability of destiny, as the train got smaller and smaller. Frau Kramer shuddered at the memory of these poor people, Isn't it strange? she said to her granddaughter, I see the train moving off as if I were one of them, but in reality I was watching these people get smaller and smaller.

Perhaps that's love, Lisa thought, But perhaps it's just fear. What if it's both? What then? But she said nothing and listened, for now Frau Kramer spoke of their arrival in Frankfurt an der Oder, of S.S. men who met them at the station, Armed with submachine guns, she exclaimed as they passed the turn-off for Sereetz, where blocks of houses stood for refugees from the east, built since she was first here, but all in good time, now she is in Frankfurt an der Oder, trudging through the snow with many others, up in front a Hitler youth, still too young for the front, but big enough to take a bunch of filthy refugees to their emergency accommodation, It was already dark when we stumbled our way through the ruins, she said, recalling the unnatural darkness of a blacked-out city that lay there helplessly, waiting for the next strike from the air and unable to do anything but turn off the lights. On the way to the botanical gardens they encountered a group of people, Maybe refugees too, Frau Kramer thought, but it was just men passing by in silence, and the looks which met them were indecipherable. Forced labourers, the Hitler youth said when they had gone, On the way to their shift. That was quite an experience, Frau Kramer told Lisa, They were as homeless as we were, as reluctant as we were to be in Frankfurt an der Oder, as unhappy as we were, and yet there was nothing to connect us because we belonged to the people which had done that to them. For a while she said nothing, but the images would not be driven from her head, and so she continued. Large areas of the city had been evacuated, the Hitler youth told them, Soon you'll have to move on, the Führer has declared Frankfurt an der Oder a fortress, they could hear the pride in the boy's voice, in front of whose eyes the catastrophe was unfolding without his realising it, That was probably his luck, Frau Kramer told Lisa. Then they arrived, bombed-out houses at the botanical gardens were their billet; although evacuated, the city was full of people dwelling in destroyed buildings, refugees all of them, hundreds of thousands. At night we lay closely huddled together so we wouldn't freeze, she said, Luckily I had enough milk with me for you.

Once again it was just two days. Then came the order to decamp, another train, the endless journey westwards along branch lines. And then, in one of those trains, I suddenly knew it had to be Lübeck if I ever wanted to see my husband again.

"And so we came to Lübeck," Lisa concluded objectively, and Frau Kramer nodded and swallowed, because she was still a long way from having told the whole story.

"It's not nice here anymore," she said to Lisa as they hit Alte Travemünder Landstrasse. "Let's go back and head for Sereetz. We can get something to eat and drink there."

Lisa agreed. They turned around and went back into the forest.

FIFTY-FOUR

Only gradually did V-9245 discover what a privilege he had been granted. For those colleagues closest to the head of Org, as the department was known internally, it was inconceivable that the director should receive him personally on his return from his imprisonment in Russia. Since then V-9245 had enjoyed a special status, which he eventually realised when the director informed him that he was to be the deputy head of the south German industrial asset liquidation company with immediate effect. This name was a front for the Munich bureau, of whose existence V-9245 had been completely ignorant until now. He had spent his first few years doing office work at headquarters. The fact that the director, who now went by the title of director general, was placing him in a leading position and thus sending him to the front, as it were, where espionage and counter-espionage were not only administered but also actually organised and implemented, seemed to V-9245 to be a twist of fate: it was time to become active again.

This is why, as he drove to his new workplace in Thalkirchen, he was in a better mood than he had been for ages. Yes, his family was a lovely and pleasing thing, the post at headquarters had been a good way of remaining invisible for a while. But V-9245 regarded himself as a soldier, in this respect nothing had changed in all these years, and the enemy was still the same, he was out there and must be fought.

FIFTY-FIVE

There must have been a time when Sereetz had been beautiful. But now cranes stood everywhere, deep shafts had been sunk, in some places the shells of future rental blocks were already standing, and even a skyscraper was being built. In the middle of these construction sites lay old Sereetz, an accumulation of small mediaeval houses clustered around a squat church. It had a tavern where the local workers ate lunch, If it's still there, Frau Kramer said, ushering her granddaughter through the narrow alleys dotted with the occasional puddle.

Sereetz was so small that after three streets they had reached the tavern, Frau Kramer stopped, astonished, the building's appearance had changed so profoundly, the red brick had gone, replaced by brown clinker, the old windows had been exchanged for new, larger models, the wooden door had been replaced with a metal one with yellow frosted glass. The two women entered the tavern. It was much too hot inside, Lisa began to sweat almost instantly, all the tables were taken, the tangle of deep voices soon subsided when the mass of men's faces turned to them – one woman too old, the other too young – before returning to their conversations.

A slim woman in an apron approached them, Lisa smiled at her in relief, but the woman was at work and translated the new guests into a simple equation, Two people equals two seats, Over there, she said with a surprisingly grown-up voice and without any alteration in her expression. Lisa and Frau Kramer followed her instruction and indeed, by the window, there was a table for two people, the seats were empty, on the table stood two coarse earthenware bowls containing the leftovers of pea soup, a large spoon in each, and beside these beer glasses drained to the last drop, shimmering dimly.

No sooner had the women taken off their coats than some of the men allowed themselves another going-over of the young one's body, one or two of them perhaps thought, Maybe not too young after all, the women pretended not to notice anything, they sat down as the waitress came over purposefully, piled up the crockery, removed the white table-cloth and was practically on her way back to the kitchen when she said in her grown-up voice, We've got pea soup with sausage and pea soup without sausage.

Without waiting for an answer, she snaked her way between the closely packed tables and chairs, followed by the eyes of some of the men, disappeared behind the counter, unloaded the dishes, reappeared holding a new tablecloth and cutlery, came back to Lisa and Frau Kramer, swiftly laid out the tablecloth, with rapid, skilful movements placed the cutlery in front of her customers at the correct spacing, stood up straight again and looked nowhere in particular with well-practised anticipation. I'll have it with sausage, Lisa said, Me too, Frau Kramer added. To drink? the waitress asked. Water, Lisa replied, Me too, Frau

Kramer said. The waitress gave a slight nod, turned away and now the two women had come out on top.

Lisa looked around the room, glances slid away from her, as shy as deer the men sat at their tables, with broad legs, supporting elbows, some hunched over their soup bowls, it was nowhere near as loud as when they had come in, or was she just imagining it? All of a sudden she had the feeling of no longer being in a particular country at a particular time, but swimming in a state that was everywhere, in a rough, unconscious state of being, with reduced sensory perception both inwardly and outwardly.

The waitress soon returned with two full bowls, Lisa tried to guess her age, she stood completely upright, she looked almost too straight, there was an intimidating harshness in her face, although perhaps that was no surprise given the customers here, Lisa thought. But when the waitress put the soup bowls down in front of them, she was no longer so sure. Where is the truth? she wondered, On the surface or below it? Do I look like a Jew? Do these look like men who can't think? Does she look like a woman who needs to fight back? Or is all of this me? She cast off these thoughts when the smell of the warm soup reached her nose, Let's eat, Frau Kramer said, smiling at her granddaughter.

They had not finished their bowls when the men stood up noisily, as if in response to a secret order, and left the tavern. Five minutes later it was empty and quiet in the room, the only other living being was the waitress clearing the tables with rapid movements. The expression on her face had not changed, Am I like this too? Lisa wondered briefly, Do I always wear the same expression? She understood that the appearance gave away nothing of its causes, maybe her father beat her, maybe he had died in the war, maybe she was unhappy in love, maybe she hated her work because she imagined herself destined for greater things, maybe she disliked autumn, maybe she was having her period. Or, to put it the other way around, how many opportunities do we have to react to things that happen to us in life? Do we really try to find a reaction to every cause, or do we become used to reacting to very different things in the same way, maybe for the sake of convenience or simply because we fail to notice and does our character develop only then?

Frau Kramer had finished her soup. Wiping her mouth with the napkin, she looked thoughtfully at her granddaughter, who was still eating, bowed to her fate once more and said, "Shall I go on?"

"Yes."

FIFTY-SIX

A train stopped in the station. It was so long that half the passengers had to jump into the slushy snow as the platform was much shorter. The train was so long that those who jumped into the snow immediately had a fine, cold membrane spun around them by the drizzle,, which unceremoniously let them know that it was pointless, after days of travelling through this country in ruins, to hope for any better.

Amongst these people was the woman who would later tell of this, and the child to whom she would later tell it, the child that lay warm and snug between her breasts and was asleep at this hour, it was still dark, as dark as it can only be in winter, only in wartime winter when even large cities are barely visible at short distance, and so it was for the woman with the child, they stood in the slush, the rain had already cast its net over them, but they could see nothing save for the night itself, and the night was no different from other nights, perhaps this was a mistake, she thought, perhaps the train driver had simply had enough and got off, perhaps the authorities had changed their plans because Lübeck was still much further and had decided, Let them stay here in the middle of nowhere. Another possibility was that Lübeck had vanished too, obliterated, and this was Lübeck, but Lübeck offered no more than this: snow and rain. The woman with the child entertained all these thoughts within a matter of seconds and she was overcome with fear.

But then a utility vehicle arrived, its headlights blinding the bunch of troublemakers standing around cluelessly, and a man clutching a loudhailer stood up, then instructed them to form a queue, at most four abreast, and follow him to the emergency billets. The people plodded on their way, including the woman with the child, she was shattered and hungry, and it barely mattered that she was alive, for dying was not an option, only managing the final stretch, step by step, and continuing to breathe in the cold air of this new home.

This new home did not want its new locals. It had enough trouble looking after itself, it was as if the island on which Lübeck stood had become a fortress again, not against the Red Army, which was speeding like wildfire towards the pre-war borders of the German Reich, but against all the beasts, both animal and human, fleeing westwards from this blaze. So the emergency billets were out of town, Did you know? the woman would say one day, where we drove past today, no, not exactly, but a bit further east, there used to be large farms with damp barns, that's where we had to walk, it went on for ever, nobody knew, Where on earth is Lübeck? Are we walking there? How come Lübeck station is so far from the city? Nobody told us a thing, we followed the red taillights of a utility vehicle along a wet country road, the drizzle gradually soaked us, our journey took so long that there were some who couldn't go any further and some who suddenly started screaming, This is a death march, they're going to kill us, but the others managed to quieten down the panickers and so we kept going, I thought, She's going to wake up any minute now and I'm going to have to feed her, How can I possibly do that here?, but you just kept on sleeping as if you'd realised what was happening and were determined to hang on in, this is what the woman would say one day, struggling to retain her composure with each sentence, as if a sentence were a narrow ridge leading into the distance above the past, and woe betide anyone who plummeted back into this past.

When they arrived and fell onto the cold, damp straw and went to sleep, it was that same night when at several points the Red Army crossed the eastern pre-war border of the Reich. When they awoke and had nothing to eat because the provisioning was poor and because the city of Lübeck had enough trouble looking after itself, the rumour went around that many thousands had arrived already and many thousands more were heading this way, and the occupants of the cold, damp barns soon came to share the opinion of the inhabitants of Lübeck, They should go elsewhere, it's already full here, but there was no elsewhere, one day the child who was no longer a child would fancy that history is sometimes like a film played backwards, when everything flows back into the jug from which it has been poured, such was this human reflux into the vessel of the German Reich, which one thousand years earlier had started inclining eastwards, and one day people could quite justifiably argue that the thousand-year Reich was in truth the end of the thousand-year Reich.

But such ideas did not concern the people, nothing concerned them more than the question of food, the children cried with hunger, And you cried too, but there was nothing I could do for you, the woman would say, crying herself.

Finally, in the afternoon, lorries arrived with forced labourers and soldiers, who handed out rations, the refugees formed a queue outside the barns and in the distance saw the manor house, a magnificent building, three children playing outside, hurling snowballs at each other, glancing over at us from time to time, soon losing interest. Suddenly, as the people were waiting and freezing, we heard the droning that we all knew, they stopped distributing food, the people scoured the overcast sky, the droning came closer, growing louder and louder, there must be lots of them, soon all they could hear was the droning, but there was nothing to see, the unit passed invisibly over their heads towards some German city where they would drop their loads like seed that instantly sprouted, they would sow a sea of red flowers, whose blooms needed to last no longer than a death.

When the droning subsided the food distribution resumed and finally the woman had milk for her child and something to eat for herself, it was not much, But after all that screaming and crying you were so tired that you went straight back to sleep and so did I.

How long did they stay in the barn? Months it was, having departed, the winter returned, as if it had forgotten something, it snowed, We were stranded. A little boy fell ill and had to be isolated, there was a doctor amongst the refugees, he ordered the boy be quarantined, which made everything more cramped, two days later the boy was dead, his mother died inside and lived on.

An eye for an eye, a tooth for a tooth, was the thought that would now strike the young woman who was once the other woman's child. But no feeling would ensue, rather this seemed to be the wrong adage, as if somewhere there must be a different, a more fitting adage for such cases and, at that moment, in that tavern in Sereetz at the beginning of the 1960s, she would begin her search for this more fitting adage without ever in future being able to state, That's precisely when it started.

When at last the winter disappeared for good, the people in the barn fled outside, the owners of the estate wanted to stop this happening, they sent over their forced labourers as if they had suddenly been promoted to chief forced labourers, but of course these failed to accomplish anything, neither the lord of the manor nor his wife showed their face, their children no longer played outside the house, after three days an S.S. man arrived on his bicycle to herd them back into the barn, he was so young that he must still be a schoolboy. The people were livid, they berated him, a woman screamed, You got us all into this, you with your Führer, with your arrogance, you with your war in the east. They slung mud at him, literally, causing him to beat a hasty retreat, he fled, red-faced, on his bike. What a victory, the young woman would think ironically and bitterly on the day this story was told.

But then the supplies failed to appear, one day passed, two days, the children started screaming again and the people thought this was the revenge of the S.S., I was so worried about you. She did not say what she had thought: what would my life be without this child, who God placed in my arms? I don't want to die inside and somehow go on, I don't want to have to live with the fact that everyone I love is dead, I'd rather be dead myself and feel nothing more.

But no, it was not the revenge of the S.S., it was the British, and when they came to the barn with tanks and soldiers and ambulances everything changed.

How? Lisa would ask, and her grandmother would sigh and continue the story.

FIFTY-SEVEN

The drama had a stage as long as the journey from Berlin to Marseille, it had more leading actors than any feature film, it had enough props to fill thirty-three lorries, it had a motorcycle escort with a homemade police uniform, it had a Peretz Sarfati, who was playing William Lloyd, William Lloyd had theatre passes for all zonal borders, Soviet, American, French, he had a forged group visa for five hundred emigrants to Colombia, with a list of names attached, beautiful French names, he hoped this would not cause a problem with the border posts north of Strasbourg when the Jewish rescue organisation, which would only appear in this one scene, would blag all the Abramowiczes, Tuchynskis, Ochlowskis, Klaubers, Staijns and whatever they were called into France, always referred to as Kassuta in the playful conversations conducted between the secret agents of the Institution for Immigration B, why Kassuta, what was that supposed to mean? It did not matter, the key thing was to arrive at the border of Kassuta north of Strasbourg on Saturday afternoon, so read the stage direction, on Saturday afternoons the border guards of the Grande Nation were impatient, they wanted their weekend to begin, so it might not occur to them that they were letting into their country a horde of actors who in truth possessed nothing, no real country, no proper families, no life to speak of, and yet were pretending they had all this and were travelling on an official U.N. mission. What beautiful stamps the document forgers in Paris and Munich had made, wonderful, no-one had ever seen stamps like them, officialdom was nothing but a universal form you could invent over and over again, and they were absolute masters at this.

The penultimate act in this drama was not called Marseille, but Sidney. Why Sidney? Why not? And the ship was not called *President Warfield*, but "The Enema", and Ephraim Frank, Shmaria Zamaret, Shaul Meirov and the other shlichim from Palestine knew precisely why they called it that, but they had long stopped laughing at the idea of a pair of pale white British buttocks implicitly belonging to His Majesty's Foreign Secretary Ernest Bevin, and a ship carrying four and a half thousand Jews rammed into this tight anus, inevitably tearing it apart. Bastards, that is how the British were referred to on the secret stage of telephone conversations right across Europe.

For Anna and her people the drama began in the middle of a warm summer's night at the beginning of July 1947. The first act was climbing aboard the lorries. Peretz had brought his wife, son and new daughter to Schlachtensee where they had to be patient, for the lorries took secret routes through the city so as not to attract the attention of M.I.6 agents. The pioneers, ma'pilim, as they were called in Bricha's secret lexicon, used the time to learn their parts by heart, leaning on wooden houses they had left for good, sitting in the meadows where they had played football, beneath the clothes props they would not use again, and muttering their names to themselves, their nationalities, their survival stories, all of which had to have some connection with concentration camps to make the right impression. Around them crickets chirped and small animals rustled, the summer was underway in the night with its great variety of life.

Anna sat on her suitcase, her knees drawn up to her body, her arms slung around her legs like a little girl. From now she would be Jeanne Pérault, she would be five years older so that Sarah could pass as her daughter, she had survived Auschwitz, she was on her way to Colombia, Colombia had issued entry visas to her and the four hundred and ninety-nine other emigrants from the camp at Schlachtensee, she and her children were going to begin a new life there.

Anna repeated the names and dates of her new identity, observing herself as she did so with the precision of a researcher who never blinks. She saw that the woman she had become in this place wanted to hold on to it, to this routine, this Wannsee, this Schlachtensee, this limbo, which seemed to amount to nothing concrete, nothing binding. But all this dissolved before her eyes, as if having been doused with acid. And as she watched the dissolution, everything was already solidifying again into new vistas, distant destinations into fixed routes and the routes into clearly defined sections, Soviet zone, American zone, overnight stay in D.P. camp Lindenfels, following day French zone in Worms, border crossing into France north of Strasbourg, boarding the special train, on to Lyon, overnight journey to Marseille, embarkation.

That is roughly how Peretz had described the impending journey, he had been curt when picking up Anna, Sarah and Shimon in his jeep from the Sweden Pavilion, no large audience, no theatrical kiss, and Anna had sensed that he was protecting himself from her with these two quite different modes of behaviour. What actually is there between affected happiness and affected distance? wondered the woman who did not blink, seeing through all emotions. There's nothing, the woman told Anna, but Anna tried to be Jeanne, but the woman said, you don't have a name, and that was a peculiar feeling. The woman changed, she turned into Josef Ranzner, like someone assuming a disguise, and kept talking in her woman's voice, saying, You don't have a name, because nobody apart from me knows what really happened. And then she dragged the four adjutants in front of her eyes, one after the other, it all happened so quickly that Anna could barely look, but when she understood she saw Peretz and Abba, and it started again from the beginning, for now there was a flick book in a child's hands, surely there must be something new to see, she flicked through so quickly that all these men inevitably became a single man, And which man would that be? the child wondered.

Anna did not wish to know, she fixed her gaze on the external world, she clung to her people, who were oblivious to the most important thing about her and yet were still her people. Or was it the other way around? Was it that she had nobody, but these strangers had her?

Anna sat on her suitcase, in front of her in the dry grass was Sarah with Shimon on her lap, learning her role, Anna could see her lips moving, she suspected that in the darkness Sarah's gaze was directed inwards, what did she see there, did she also have a woman inside with no name, who slipped on masks? Anna watched Shimon. She had just breastfed him, now he was playing dozily with the ends of Sarah's hair, any moment now his eyes would close and he would fall asleep. What did Shimon know about Sarah that had caused him to let her into his life without a shred of resistance? Was there a flick book inside Shimon with only two faces, Anna and Sarah, Anna and Sarah? Had he seen the one woman that they both were?

Anna looked away, her gaze fell on Emil, who was sitting next to Sarah. Emil had internalised his role long ago, he simmered with excitement about their arrival in Palestine, when he could put on a real uniform and fight against Israel's enemies, for him the journey was a necessary evil, he hoped it would pass quickly, Anna knew this, she envied the clarity of his purpose, How did he manage to externalise everything, channel everything into anger, what trick had he mastered?

The Abramowiczes, who were sitting right beside him, father, mother, Marja, asked each other questions in Hebrew, in their eyes there was only Eretz Yisrael since their reunion, even the children had to learn the new language, Maybe, Anna thought, a language is like a weapon to combat the internal enemy, maybe a language is like a bridgehead you can occupy and cannot be driven from, is that right? Only Dana the doll continued speaking German, Because dead people can't learn new languages, Marja had said, and nobody could object to this.

The old man sat against a nearby tree, frowning as he studied his piece of paper, Why do I want all this trouble at my age? he may have been thinking, but at least he had a name again, he, who had lost his own when his entire family took it with them into a mass grave, when he survived in circumstances that were not explained.

Where's Ruth? Anna thought, looking around. There she was, sitting on a bench beside her Aaron. A right pair of lovebirds, Anna thought, feeling a flicker of hope inside her, as remote as a fading memory, and feeling envy, but an envy weakened by doubt, Did it really exist, love? Her gaze alighted on Ariel, sitting slightly to the side, his legs outstretched on the dark earth, bent over his *Odyssey* in the dim light of a candle he held in his right hand, moths flitting all around, whose death he was paying no attention to, self-contained like an island in the Mediterranean, How often must he have read it by now, what new things could he possibly discover between the lines, would they ever find out, or did Ariel, vulnerable as he was, spend all his time reading simply to avoid exposing himself to what was happening? Had Ariel discovered a trick for outwitting uncontrollable destiny by blending life with a story that had already played out, whose conclusion was set down for all time?

It was long past midnight by the time the lorries finally arrived, the little children had fallen asleep, Dana the doll lay with eyes open on Marja's tummy, the dead do not sleep, the dead speak German, Anna felt a twinge.

The lorries drove in like a silent procession, slowly rolling monsters, They ought to have a monument erected to them, think what we owe these lorries, everything. But at the same moment Anna was struck by a feeling of tightness, a shortness of breath, she would rather not get on board, she would rather stay there than be pressed and jammed in again, who knew how long it would be this time? But when they all got up to watch the arrival of the lorries as they formed a semicircle and finally came to a halt with their engines still running, steel heroes who seemed to be saying, We've come to rescue you, somebody grabbed Anna's waist and held her tightly. Anna jumped, beside her stood Ruth who said softly, We've got to go now. She gave Anna a crooked smile and Anna clasped her own shoulders.

Emil helped the old man to his feet, Mr Abramowicz lifted up his sleeping daughter, Ariel shut his book very slowly while continuing to read, like someone who feels the need to peer through a closing door, but then he shut it completely and stood up.

Now the first act began, "Get in!" the Bricha people said quietly, Peretz, Avis and others. But some drivers stood there silently, as if they had nothing to do with the affair. These were the German hauliers Peretz had been forced to engage, because he lacked sufficient lorries for so many people. Isn't that dangerous? the shlichim had said in their secret telephone conversations, addressing each other by their aliases, Rudi to Aroch, Alon to Kris, Blacky to the Priest, and they had replied, Yes, it is, but what other option do we have? We'll pay them well, the Germans always like that, Ephraim Frank had been obliged to do the same, because not even Sally Zeve with his successful Bavarian Truck Company had obtained forty army lorries at a stroke from the Americans.

Get in! First they took their marked suitcases to one particular lorry where men tossed them up to other men on the loading ramp, who caught and threw them inside to other men who stacked them.

Get in, the men helped the women and children up, they had brought blankets and cushions to avoid having to lie side by side like tinned herrings, for now the adults had to sleep too, they were so tired from all the waiting, the thinking, feeling, numbing.

When all the people had been stowed, the drivers went to the backs of their lorries, closed the ramps, pulled down the tarpaulins, climbed into their cabs and slammed the doors. Behind them, in darkness and suspense, sat the pioneers, who at last were now worthy of this name, and felt the vehicles start to move, pulling the familiar rug from under their feet, metre by metre, through the gate, into Potsdamer Chaussee, left, left is towards the south.

The second act was the drive. They drove through the night, lying perpendicular to the direction they were travelling in, Anna lay on a coarse woollen blanket, beside her slept Shimon, on the other side Sarah pressed up to her and slept, the entire floor of the cargo area was covered with people, neatly arranged in rows, feet on the left, heads on the right, it was completely silent, the engines hummed, the shock absorbers squeaked, the loading ramp rattled, it was completely silent, Anna lay on her back and stared at the tarpaulin, it was so dark that she could barely see.

The Soviets had changed their policy. They had calculated that a large number of Jews in Palestine would weaken the British position vis-à-vis the oil-owning Arabs. They had devised a simple, logical rule of three which concluded that a large number of Jews in Palestine was beneficial to the interests of the U.S.S.R. They therefore allowed the Jewish transports to pass without scrutinising the papers for inconsistencies.

And thus the stop the convoy made when it reached the interzonal border was as brief as an intermezzo. As usual Peretz was sitting in the cab of the front lorry, Avi drove up to the checkpoint, Peretz got out, greeted the man in Russian, showed him the forged pass and the forged group visa for transit, which Ephraim Frank had sent from Munich, identified himself as a U.N.R.R.A. worker, handed over a packet of cigarettes and said goodbye. Peretz was in his element, for him nothing unravelled, here and now he was in the very core of his routine, Peretz with the loudhailer, which he would discard one day, but not now, who could say what he might need it for on this journey? That night Peretz felt good, finally the waiting was over, it seemed as if the past few months had been no more than an interruption, as if this was in fact still the journey from Tulce to Marseille, and he felt, he knew, that soon he would have the chance to make Anna his wife definitively.

They drove on, act two, scene two, Soviet zone, heading southwest, not far from the border with the British zone, but always keeping it at a safe distance, down to the Americans, where the G.I.s turned two blind eyes whenever Jews came knocking with false papers.

Anna lay on her back, on the blanket, on the cargo bed, beneath her the country flew past, above her hung the tarpaulin, and beyond it the darkness soared up to the stars.

She fell asleep. She dreamed she had died and was lying in a vast field, her arms outstretched as if to cling onto the earth, but slowly she took off, no matter how hard she tried to become heavy and sink back down again, she took off, floating higher and higher until she could see nothing but the black night.

FIFTY-EIGHT

They had taken the bus from Sereetz to Moisling. The rain was falling more heavily. The windows in the bus were fogged up. This time the two women sat to the right of the gangway. Bad Schwartau, the pond at Trems, the Holstentor, a view of the city, red brick, green steeple roofs, change.

The second bus was practically empty, people were still at work, they would not be going home for several hours.

Why Moisling? Lisa asked, You never said anything about it before. Frau Kramer nodded but said nothing in reply.

They followed the Trave along Moislinger Allee. Apartment blocks for workers, grand, late nineteenth-century houses, tall trees. They changed buses again and went up Moislinger Berg, not a hill as its name suggested, crossing the Trave. Small, old houses separated by fields, waste land and gardens. Lisa found the area desolate, but it was hardly a surprise on a day like this.

When they arrived it was so dark, as if dusk were already setting in. The rain now fell like a curtain, wet and cold, Lisa froze beneath the umbrella. Huddled close together and arm in arm, they walked alongside a high brick wall as far as a small, pointed-gable house. There was the entrance. What's that? Lisa said with a start when she saw what it was.

A cemetery. It was large, the gravestones were tightly packed in long rows, narrow paths between them. Carved into the stones were Stars of David and Hebrew writing. You've been here before, Frau Kramer said to her granddaughter, who remained silent, overawed by the sight of so many wet graves in which the dead would lie till the end of all time.

The two women wandered slowly between the graves. The cemetery looked abandoned, many headstones had sunk into the earth and were now crooked. Others had tipped backwards or forwards onto the grave, weeds were rampant, on some gravestones they saw black swastikas that had been daubed on with a thick paintbrush.

Lisa did not want to go any further, she wanted to get away from this place, but her body did not respond, it stayed close beside the old woman, the path was a circuit full of puddles, and although their shoes were already drenched, the women took care and walked around them with big strides. What's here? Lisa asked. A grave, was all Frau Kramer said. They continued, Frau Kramer hesitated before turning right onto another path. She had not been here in ages, not since that time when the young woman had stood beside her with a face she would never be able to forget.

There it is, she said suddenly, and then they were standing in front of it. A plain headstone behind a small grave. On it was a name Lisa did not recognise. She read the dates, she did some calculations, she looked at her grandmother. She did not understand.

FIFTY-NINE

Heinrich watched his father, who was sitting in the study smoking a pipe and reading a book. In the glow of a candle that Father had lit, his face looked as if had been carved from wood. Thousands of tiny wrinkles ran across his forehead, cheeks, nose, like a river system branching out in all directions. They were not deep, but sharp like small incisions. His father's skin had such fine pores that where there were no wrinkles it appeared polished. A reddish glimmer came from the magnificent wrought-iron coal stove that stood at an angle in the corner, practically filling it from floor to ceiling.

Heinrich stood behind the heavy curtain right beside the window, trying to remain absolutely still. It was something he often did without knowing why. With one eye he peered over at his father. Gudrun and his mother were in the kitchen, he could hear them pottering about, metal on china, metal on metal. It smelled of dinner.

Father had put his feet up, they rested on a padded stool that matched the wingback chair he was sitting in. What sort of book was his father reading? Heinrich screwed up his eyes, but he could not make out the title, it almost looked as if the book had no title.

What was Father thinking while he read? Heinrich tried to decipher his expression, but it was impossible. Father was concentrating intensely, so absorbed by his reading that he barely stirred, he would surely notice the slightest movement behind the curtain, the smallest sound.

The hollow of Heinrich's left knee itched. The more he tried not to scratch, the more it itched. But Heinrich refused to give in, he felt strong, the itch became more potent, he closed his eyes, unable to think of anything else. When he felt he could not hold out any longer he opened his eyes and saw Father looking at the grandfather clock that stood by the wall opposite. He shut his book and stood up. Then he locked it away in his desk and removed the key. Heinrich was expecting Father to go into the kitchen, he must have heard that the clattering had stopped, dinner must be ready and at any moment now Mother would pick up the mallet, beat the Chinese gong and call out, "Dinner!" And then Heinrich would be able to scratch behind his knee at last.

Father did not leave the study. He headed straight for Heinrich. The boy froze. His father had known the whole time that he was standing here, spying on him! At any moment he would pull back the curtain, grab him by the ear and drag him into the kitchen, unconcerned as to whether the boy could keep up or not. Heinrich was terrified. He held his breath and screwed up his eyes as if this were some sort of ruse he could employ to turn the tide.

When nothing happened, Heinrich peered out gingerly from behind his eyelids and saw the long sleeves of Father's dark-grey jacket right beneath his nose. He saw his father's large hand, it grabbed and lifted the flowerpot with the dwarf roses, which sat on the window sill. Then the left hand pushed a small, golden key beneath it. Finally the right hand put the pot back down.

Otto Kruse did not discover his son. He kept an eye on the door to the hallway while he hid the key, it was slightly ajar, intentionally so, for this meant that no-one in the family would suspect that he might have a secret. He knew that Gudrun was helping her mother in the kitchen. And Heinrich must be reading in his bedroom. The young boy had the potential to get on his nerves, but at only nine years old he was not a threat. Otto Kruse turned and put out the candles by licking his thumb and forefinger and pinching the wicks to extinguish the flame. He liked the slight sting in his fingertips caused by the heat, but more than that he liked the result.

When all the candles had been snuffed out, he left the study without shutting the door.

Heinrich stood in the dark, intensely relieved. He realised he could move again now. But this lengthy exhibition of willpower was pure gold, which he must not carelessly discard. His body ached in various places, his left foot, between his shoulder blades, the back of his neck. At the same time, the longer he held out Heinrich felt a strange feeling of ecstasy surge inside him. To his astonishment he noted that the hollow of his knee was no longer itching.

Only when the gong resounded and his mother called him did he stir.

SIXTY

Germany is beautiful, Mrs Abramowicz said. They were sitting by the tailboard, gazing at the landscape, beneath them black clouds poured from the exhaust, it stank of diesel and yet they sensed how pure and fresh the air must be. The sun had risen over a cloudless sky, the early light shone so intensely that Sarah believed it must be a good omen. They had left the Soviet zone and were approaching Coburg. We'll have breakfast there, Peretz had said. Behind them drove a dark-green G.M.C. truck, the second in a long procession. The convoy wound its way through the Central Uplands of Germany, each vehicle bore the letters U.N.R.R.A. on the bonnet and on the sides. In some places the fresh paint still glistened.

The full lorries made a noise that drowned out everything else, the warbling of the thrushes and tits, the chirruping of the crickets, the screeching of the hawks that circled above the thick deciduous wood-land. And yet all of these things were there and the pioneers knew it and imagined the sounds, for the area they were passing through looked so lovely.

The driver of the lorry behind them was one of the Germans Peretz had hired. His face was rigid, his eyes expressionless, the Jews froze when they caught his eye and avoided looking at him wherever possible. All apart from Emil, he kept staring at the German until the latter lowered his gaze. It was Emil's first victory, it felt good but had been stressful, and after a while he, too, averted his eyes from his foe, to avoid having to engage in another battle so soon.

The ma'apilim did not know that Peretz, up front in the cab beside Avi, had separated the Germans, At least one of us has to drive between two of you, he had told them. The Germans had shrugged, as if this were unnecessary, but they abided by it. It had not been Peretz's idea, it was an order from Ephraim Frank, Just so they don't get any funny ideas, he had said in Munich, and nobody had disagreed. The Germans were capable of anything, the Germans had to be kept under control.

Germany was beautiful on that clear summer's morning. When uttered together, however, these two words profoundly shocked the passengers. What has the beauty of this landscape got to do with the Germans? wondered Ruth, who should never have been German. But she said nothing, Mrs Abramowicz was happy, nothing else was that important.

The little children were bored by the never-ending journey. Soon Dana the doll had chatted to everyone, soon Shimon had been in every corner of the cargo area several times, picking up everything he could find with his tiny fingers and trying to put them in his mouth before Sarah could stop him. We'll soon be there, Mr Abramowicz told Marja, but this "soon" was like American chewing gum: it got longer and longer, it was sticky and soon tasted of nothing.

In the American zone the convoy no longer needed to conceal itself. It stopped in the centre of Coburg, before the eyes of passers-by. Ephraim Frank had booked two hotels, there was German food, the Jews sat alongside each other at long tables and joked and laughed as if they were tourists. And they almost felt as such, for Coburg was picturesque, virtually nothing had been destroyed in the first German town to make Hitler an honorary citizen, the Queen herself had forbidden it, It would be like bombing ourselves, she said, and the generals of the Royal Air Force understood, it was one thing to rename yourself Windsor. But quite another to stop being Saxe-Coburg and Gotha.

When they reached Lindenfels in the Odenwald it was early afternoon. They saw the ruins of the ancient castle with its mighty keep, towering high above the town, the large and small half-timbered houses, black beams between whitewashed walls. They had driven straight through Hesse, Anna knew, she had been watching closely, One final journey on the trail of the Brothers Grimm, but there had been no melancholy, she was too preoccupied with herself, she saw too clearly the woman peering out at the world like a little girl trying to remain naïve, even though it was far too late for that. She felt sorry for herself, as you might have sympathy for a stranger you cannot help. She resolved not to read any German fairy tales to her children.

SIXTY-ONE

The dead were in conversation. They were telling each other stories about dying.

"Take me, for example!" one of them cried. "I was burned alive! In the Turck synagogue! I screamed! And I've been screaming ever since! I can't stop screaming! I'd love to, but I can't! Horrific! Horrific!"

"Shhh!" another whispered. "Don't look over here! I'm hiding! They thought I was dead. But I wasn't. I was alive! I'm still alive! Then I lay between the dead and didn't get out and I didn't dare move even though they were filling the grave with earth. It took a long time for me to die, a verrrrry long time. A verrrrrrry long time, a verrrrrrrrrrrrrrrrrrrrry long time."

"I died fighting," one of them said morosely. "Not like you, who let yourselves be slaughtered like cattle. No, I fought with these hands of mine, with these eyes, with this voice. I killed seven Germans and three Poles before we fell into an ambush and were shot. Brief and painful, like bolts of lightning that pass straight through your body, hot, intense bolts, I had no idea I was dying when it happened. But I fought!"

"Who are you?" a new voice asked. It sounded unfamiliar, like a young boy's voice, perhaps it was the voice of the Jew they had picked up outside the synagogue, yes, yes, it must be him. He had recognised all the other voices, even though he could not see a thing because it was as black as ever, so black that you saw nothing, nothing at all. But these voices, he knew them, even that of the man buried alive, he recalled his face in detail, a delicate individual, he had thought back then, Is he really dead? There was something weird about the way he had fallen into the mass grave, about the way he had apparently been hit by bullets. But then, distracted, he had forgotten this man. And now . . . look what happens, all of a sudden someone like that pops up in a dream and talks about himself.

The fighter was fixed in his memory too. Yes, what a hunt that had been! And – Jews aside – the partisans were brave, they had fought like real men. But they had finally fallen into the net. It had been a wonderful hunt, definitely!

But this voice, whose was it? It sounded familiar, it felt as if he had not heard it for ages, could it be that it . . . belonged? Who was . . . ? How could he find out who was speaking whenever there was a break in his dream? Was that even possible, a break in a dream?

"Who are you?" the voice asked again, but this time he sensed that two eyes were staring at him from the heart of the blackness, from where he could see nothing, nothing at all, two searching, anxious, frightened, reproachful eyes.

"Who are you?" He felt as if all this blackness surrounding him was the face to which these eyes belonged, a countenance of darkness which spoke with a child's voice and which was addressing him, yes, him. But who was he in that moment? He felt alone, scrutinised from every direction, lonely and abandoned and encircled by . . .

SIXTY-TWO

Whenever Lisa recalled that visit to the Jewish cemetery, what stood out in her mind was that she had never imagined her grandmother might be able to surprise her again. But then they had stood by the grave and the old woman had started to cry. She had walked up to the grave, paying no attention to her granddaughter's bewilderment, and started to weed the plot.

"I should have come here much earlier," she said to herself. "Just look at it!" Lisa stared at Frau Kramer for a while, incapable of moving or forming a clear thought in her head. But then she snapped out of it.

"Grandma, who is buried here? Grandma?" Frau Kramer, who was crouched at the side of the grave, supporting herself with one hand, which allowed her to get at the rampant weeds more easily, stopped and looked up at Lisa as if she felt she had been interrupted.

"You were at the funeral, Lisa," she said reluctantly. "You won't remember because you were too small. But the corrugated iron sheds we slept in weren't adapted for winter, they weren't even fit for autumn! The condensation used to drip down and either you froze or you were too hot. My God!"

She sank to her knees, making hollows in the damp earth of the grave. It was still raining. Lisa was wide-eyed, she did not understand this grave and she understood even less her grandmother's behaviour.

"My God!" Frau Kramer said again. "The children were hardest hit. So many of them died!" She looked at her granddaughter. "You were luckier than you think, Lisa. Look! She wasn't so lucky."

SIXTY-THREE

When the pioneers arrived in their lorries a crowd of people gathered, What's going on here? the passengers thought, and then they saw this was no usual crowd of people. It was children and adolescents, streaming out of a number of houses. There were so many of them that the buildings looked like barrels that had sprung leaks. We're the children of Hamelin, they cried, waving their forged visas, The Pied Piper led us here and then he simply disappeared, now we don't know how we're going to get home! Do you lot know? No, we don't, but we'll take a few of you in each lorry, that's what the shlichim agreed, so the average age is right. That's good, the children of Hamelin said, But tell us, what about our parents, do they miss us terribly? Children of Hamelin, your parents are dead, didn't you know? They died of grief, they were only too aware of their responsibility for your disappearance, and day after day they thought, If only we *had* given the Pied Piper all our gold, he would have spared us.

No, Anna thought, looking at all the Jewish orphans, No more fairy tales.

SIXTY-FOUR

Heinrich resisted for precisely two weeks and three days. Then he hatched a plan and put it into effect. On Monday after school he crept into the study. His mother was getting lunch ready, Gudrun was sitting in the kitchen with her. Heinrich lied to his mother for the first time in his life, he said, I don't have any homework because the teacher was ill and someone else stood in. He was astonished to find it so easy. As if he were making a discovery even prior to his discovery.

His mother believed him, I'm going to my room, Heinrich said casually, and in fact he did, but only to open the door and shut it again. Then he stood as quiet as a mouse in the hall and waited. When he heard no change in the sounds coming from the kitchen – his mother clattering around, the impatience in his sister's voice at not being able to understand her maths homework – he tiptoed softly across the parquet floor of the hallway to the study. Heinrich knew exactly which boards creaked, he took big steps over these, taking great care not to fall.

Now he was outside the study, its door ajar as ever. As he pushed it open it occurred to him that this was the only one in the apartment which didn't squeak. Did Father oil it so he could slip in here secretly himself? he wondered. He would if he were in his father's shoes. His heart pounding, Heinrich crossed the study and approached the window. The flowerpot. He lifted it. For a moment he expected to find nothing. But there it was: the small, golden key, slightly dirty from the earth that had trickled out of the drainage hole in the bottom of the pot. Heinrich took the key and carefully replaced the pot. Suddenly he gave a start, because he thought that his father was standing behind the curtain, just to his right, exactly where he used to hide. But no-one was there and Heinrich almost laughed. As if his father would behave like a little boy! He turned and went to the desk. He sat on Father's leather chair. On either side were three narrow drawers, one on top of the other, and above his legs sat a broad, flat one. The key went in here.

Heinrich hesitated. He was incapable of thinking clearly. He was too frightened. He could not even say what he was afraid of. Was it Father? Or was it his secret? He wanted nothing better than to get up again, return the key to its place and pretend that nothing had happened.

But he could not. Heinrich slowly pushed the key into the hole and turned it. The lock sprang open with a soft click. Heinrich needed to grab the drawer with both hands to pull it out. It was empty, no, at the very back on the right was the book. A leather cover with no writing on it. Heinrich took out the book and leafed through it. He recognised his father's handwriting, he saw details of places and dates. A diary. Heinrich was disappointed. He had been expecting something more exciting. He knew all about diaries, he kept one himself, but he would never read the thing, he had already written it down. Heinrich skimmed his father's diary at random and without any interest. How neat it was! No blotches, no crossings out, no writing that went above or below the line. And how beautiful Father's handwriting was! Heinrich could make sense of everything. He would love to be able to write so legibly! Heinrich read a sentence or two to memorise his father's handwriting, he read, For this reason I was compelled to put my life at risk and give everything I had, for the situation demanded rapid action and courageous engagement. He turned a few pages and read, I was now faced with the question of how I should proceed, given the superior power of the enemy. He jumped to a few pages before the end and read, If only I weren't imprisoned in this disguise! I would abandon everything and embark on a search for her. Everything!

Heinrich ran the nail of his forefinger along the last word.

Everything!

He did it again and again. He was lost in thought when the gong sounded and his mother's voice wrenched him from his reflections. He hastily returned the book to the drawer, locked it, hid the key and left the room.

After lunch Heinrich slipped back into the study and put the book in the correct place in the drawer. Because if he had been his father he would have taken great care to remember where he had left the book the last time.

That night Heinrich lay awake for hours. Those words from Father's diary had seeped into his consciousness. They felt like magic words, words that opened up a new world. But he had no clear view of this world, it was merely a feeling to which he was unable to put a name.

SIXTY-FIVE

Shimon was delighted by the new children in the lorry. Some were barely older than he, How on earth did they survive? the eyes of the grown-ups asked. Shimon asked no questions, he did not speak at all. He crawled through the cargo area, he had to clamber over legs and laps, he slid between bodies and bumped into backs, but he made his way over to the new children and sat down close by so he could watch them.

The new children had brought their games with them, cards and Nine Men's Morris and chess and Ludo, presents from the citizens of Lindenfels, who had set their minds to mothering the orphans. They played, they were loud, the others noticed that they had learned to get by without adults. Anna was pleased to see Shimon preoccupied. She was heavy and immobile, she felt imprisoned inside her body and could do nothing about it. Her gaze roamed the people's faces, she saw Aaron chatting to Mr Abramowicz and Ruth to Mrs Abramowicz, she noticed that old François was telling stories to the older orphans. But their voices drifted over to her ears, all entangled like uncombed hair:

"It's almost one year now"
    "We shall have to reclaim the desert"

"Since the Irgun blew up"

  "The Rabbi asks the wife, 'Do you wish"

"the King David Hotel"

 "if we want to survive there."

  "to divorce your husband?'"

"and since then"

 "It's not going to be a cakewalk."

  "'Yes, Rabbi, I do.'"

"things with the British"

  "'And husband, do you wish to divorce your wife?'"

 "Oh no, it most certainly won't be! What's more, we'll wish"

"have got even more difficult."

"But the world has woken up to it, Aaron!"

 "we'd never gone in the first place."

"At what price, I ask you?"

  "'Yes, Rabbi, I do.' And so"

"Everything has its price, Aaron. Now"

 "But we don't have any choice."

 "You said it, Ruth, my child;"

  "the Rabbi said to the two of them, 'If that is so"

"at least Haganah knows that"

 "then the two of you are agreed."

 "our people has so rarely had a choice!"

"Menachem Begin is serious"

 "It's verging on a miracle"

  "Now continue to live"

 "if we're able to return together"

"in what he says."

"He's damaged"

 "to the Promised Land."

  "together in peace!'"

"Zionism."

"I say Zionism is stronger than the British, the Arabs and the radicals combined!"

Anna did not notice Emil's coy glances at Sarah, who did not notice either. Sarah was watching Shimon, hoping that the new children did not hurt him.

All the while the convoy drove towards the zonal border. It was Saturday afternoon, the French soldiers were waiting to be discharged for the weekend, the next act of the farce could begin.

Peretz had arranged his papers meticulously. He was more nervous than usual. He kept glancing at Avi, though Avi looked as he always did, he focused on the road as if nothing else in the world existed.

SIXTY-SIX

Dana the doll peered around the corner with her blind eyes. Past the lorry's tarpaulin she saw the red-and-white barrier, interrupted by the French soldier in his blue uniform and a tall peaked cap on his head. Around his torso was a grey river running from left to right. Dana let her gaze wander. On the higher riverbank, cut in two by the French soldier's head, she saw a large, broad tower with a pointed roof. Opening its gate wide and yawning at the river, it appeared tired from being on its feet for so long. It looked as if, having hiked from afar to get here, it would not be able to cross over to the east and was now staring at the metal supports rising from the torrent. Poor tower, Dana thought, It's much too heavy for the floating bridge right next to it. That was only made for lorries and people, and the tower must know this or it wouldn't be gazing at the water, sad and tired, hoping that the sunken bridge might somehow rise up again.

At that moment the French border guard approved the forged visa that Peretz had handed him, together with his forged U.N.R.R.A.

worker's I.D., and gestured behind him to where another soldier was standing, who now lifted the barrier, as light as a feather, and allowed the Jews passage over to the west bank of the river and into the ancient Burgundian city of Worms.

When Peretz opened the passenger door of the lorry and looked behind to where the other lorries were waiting for the signal, he saw the doll, he knew its name and to whom the hand belonged clutching onto it. He gave the signal by raising his arm, then climbed back up, took his seat, closed the door, and Avi beeped the horn, it sounded as dark as a ship's siren and so loud that the French soldiers jumped. The Jewish drivers copied him. What a racket! As if an army were advancing on Worms, What sort of an army? Crusaders, perhaps, on their way into the Promised Land? Well, the stones littered about the place knew this, it had happened before, eight hundred years ago, back then it had been fanfares and horses with carriages bearing bishops, and Jerusalem had been occupied by Muslims, Not much has changed, the stones thought, Only we're no longer walls, houses, towers, just rubble.

Before Avi engaged the clutch, Mrs Abramowicz grabbed hold of her daughter with both hands and pulled her safely inside the lorry to prevent the little girl from being flung out when the vehicle accelerated.

SIXTY-SEVEN

Watching Father, at every turn. Watching him at breakfast, his gestures, how he picked up the salt cellar, his mouth when he spoke, his eyes when he smiled, his whole body when he kissed Mother on the cheek.

Watching Father on the Sunday outing into the countryside, at every turn. Sitting in the back of the black company car and staring at the back of his head, stretching up to catch Father's eyes in the rear-view mirror. On arrival in the car park, when Father got out and rubbed his hands with excitement, his voice when he told them, Come on children, let's go! Watching Father watching Mother when she attended to Gudrun, who did not want to walk, his eyes, his lip movements when something displeased him but he said nothing.

Watching Father on the walk, at every turn, his encouragement, Back then we used to march one hundred kilometres a day, left, two, three, four, left, two, three, four, come on little soldier, off to the front with you, ho ho. A stick isn't a stick, it's a rifle handed down from father to son, Preseeeeeent arms! Ho ho, I'm going to appoint you standard bearer immediately! Atteeeeen–tion!

Watching Father when suddenly he fell silent, when suddenly he left everything up to Mother, Come on, children, it's not much further! Watching Father when Mother carried Gudrun on her shoulders, watching Father when it was no longer possible to catch his attention, Preseeeeent arms, left, two, three, four, left, two, three, four, all in vain. Watching Mother watching Father, standing in for him, looking out for him, making sure that Gudrun was not noisy, one eye permanently on Father.

Watching Father when Mother failed to keep Gudrun quiet, the corners of his mouth, his eyes that were watching Mother, how she understood Father and doubled her efforts, watching Father vanish again in front of everyone's eyes, remaining merely present, merely present somehow, no more. Watching the pain that this caused.

SIXTY-EIGHT

Did Sarah with the golden hair really have to comb it *now*, just as the convoy was slithering like a serpent across the pontoon bridge? She was sitting by the ramp, looking out at the Rhine, it was already getting dark, the evening sun glistened on the water. Emil sat beside her, paying no attention to the rapids, he watched her, to him it felt as if she were sitting on the highest mountain in the world, as if he must capsize if he dared turn towards her, as if calling himself Zwi had been pointless, given that he was still struck by this heartache every time. Sarah did not notice the young Haganah soldier, she had no idea that he knew her face better than anybody, nobody carried it as far and wide as he did. She ran through her hair with a simple comb while humming a tune.

SIXTY-NINE

Now the Jews with their army would go ashore, now German crusaders would flock from across the entire land, summoned by their young emperor, now they would all rest in the venerable city, now some would come up with the idea of giving the Jews who lived here a bit of a fright, Look, this street is perfect, over there, that shop, there's Dulcina, Eleazar ben Judah's wife, sitting with her daughters Belat and Hannah in the front where they sell their wares, in the back valiant Jacob is working, liming the hides to soften them, next the daughters use sharp knives to shave off the remaining hair roots and flesh, then the mother stretches the skins over a frame, and once they're dry she smoothes them with pumice and finally rolls them up on wooden rods. Jews and Christians, magistrates and guild masters, all of them have to write, Dulcina demands the same price from each one for her parchment. Is that fair? Let's butcher them like swine, let's fight for glory here and now against the betrayers of Jesus, the distant war begins in our own land, the enemy is among us.

Now the Jews, having eaten, would be reboarding their lorries to head on southwards, now Eleazar ben Judah, the scholar, would come home to find death, death perching on the bloody bodies of his loved ones, death baring its teeth at him. Now Eleazar returns to the synagogue and weeps and weeps, stopping only when it is time to do something else. Taking all the parchment his family has made, he writes a book about life and death, thereby preparing a soothing ointment for himself, for in his book Eleazar can work magic, heal every wound, redress every injustice, punish every crime. In his book is Gilgul Neshamot, the souls of the dead pass through the bodies of the living, and thus in his book Eleazar knows that his loved ones will return to earth, that death does not endure for an insufferably long time. In his book people are good.

And meanwhile the convoy of Jews passes his house and the engines drone and Dana peers out with her dead eyes and sees him sitting and writing in two dimensions.

When Eleazar ben Judah dies many years later, the young emperor is long dead, another crusade is underway, Jews are once again slaughtered like swine in some European town, the lorries have just left the devastated city of Worms behind.

SEVENTY

The sun had almost set when the convoy reached the French border. In the warm twilight the forest animals came to life, there was a rustling throughout the entire land, and then the lorries arrived at the next barrier, where impatient soldiers now waved through anybody who wanted to come in. Almost devoutly the Jews crossed the invisible line between two countries, two languages and two guilts. The Sarfatis had been expelled from here six hundred years earlier, many generations had fought their way eastwards until finally arriving in Palestine. Now they were going back, but the goal was the same, the death that lay behind them was the same, the flight had included pauses, some lasting a hundred years or more, as if they had all fallen asleep and thought they were living. Time and again they were awoken by a kiss from traitors, time and again they had to move on. This now would be the last of all flights, the flight home, this was their undertaking.

SEVENTY-ONE

The convoy drove to a small station to the north of Strasbourg. There stood the train to the south, organised by the Institution for Immigration B. It had come from Paris and was waiting in a siding. The train was long, longer than the local ones that usually stopped here. The black steam engine at the front looked as if it were wearing metal blinkers, behind it lined up dark-green carriages.

The lorries parked in a semicircle, happy people climbed out, people who had finally left Germany. Only here in Kassuta did Peretz understand why they called it Hanan when they spoke on the telephone: God is gracious, gracious is God, because we can leave Hanan behind, because we did not die in Hanan, in and of and by Hanan.

The passengers were temporarily reunited with their luggage. They watched the drivers from Peretz's Berlin Bricha say goodbye. Small, stocky Avi and tall, elegant Peretz had a brief embrace then Avi got back into his lorry, Peretz took a bulging army kitbag and his loudhailer from the passenger seat and put both on the ground beside him. He slammed the door shut, See you soon! he called out, waving at Avi, but that was a lie, both of them knew it, that had been settled here and now. Avi waved back, then he was gone.

Before they crossed the tracks, the Jews watched the German drivers invite unfamiliar men into their lorries, men in tatty clothes, men with haunted looks. Where had these men come from? Nobody knew, all of a sudden they were just there and had leaped into the empty lorries before the eyes of the arrivals, They're German, someone said, They're not kosher. Then the lorries drove off, back to Hanan.

It was only later that Peretz learned from Ephraim Frank that these were S.S. men, escapees from labour camps in the south of France. The Nazis have their connections too, he said.

On a train at last! At last not being freighted like cattle or goods, but in a proper train for human beings who can sit, look out of the window and go to the lavatory whenever they feel like it! Seven of them sat in the compartment – Anna, Shimon, Sarah, Ruth, Aaron, old François, Peretz – and travelled through France, which was so beautiful, as a country could only be if one did not have to hide. Ruth smiled at Anna, You're pregnant, she said, You're not getting off that easily this time. Peretz opened his mouth, he almost asked, Is this one mine? He doesn't know, exclaimed Ruth, who had been watching him, and Aaron said, Ho ho! as if trying to insinuate something. Sarah gave a confused laugh, what did that mean for her, was she still Peretz's and Anna's daughter?

Anna knew who the father was, at any time she could point a finger at him and say, He's sitting here. But who really was the man who had lain on her at the precise moment of conception? Which face had he worn on his skull? If only she had been holding a stopwatch, if only she had been able to freeze time at the pivotal moment, to check where the sperm was. Was it still making its way through her abdomen or had it already arrived? And whose breath had mixed with hers at the moment of fusion? Had that been possible she would now know the true name of the father. And she had been concentrating! The woman in her who never looked away had listened to the man's panting with the coolness of a scientist, had felt the pain between her legs, had measured the time it took for the burning to become a sort of pleasure, the pleasure of enduring the unavoidable, the pleasure of returning to that sofa in that city, that country, a pleasure more forbidden than any sin known to man.

Her gaze fell on Shimon, who was sitting on Sarah's lap opposite, looking at her attentively. She smiled at him as if the two of them were on their own in the compartment. But then François cried, Mazel Tov! Leaping from his seat, he pulled her up and the others started singing and clapping in time. Anna had to dance with him in the cramped compartment and then out into the corridor to the others, while outside the sunny country flew past with its open mixed woodland, its narrow country roads, its whitewashed houses, its golden fields. France, Anna would tell her grandchild one day, is like being able to forget.

Peretz celebrated with the others, he shook hands and returned embraces, and yet he was alone with his thoughts. The secret calculation had been made, the silent promise honoured, he was getting his own son. Anna really was his wife now, for a moment he felt his heart grow so big that even Shimon would have fitted inside had their eyes not met and Peretz's chest not contracted again.

The Abramowiczes came over, their faces writ large with happiness, a child was so much more than a child, it was a victory over almighty death, what could be greater? You deserve it, Mr Abramowicz said, slapping Peretz on the shoulder. Even Shimon was congratulated, because he was going to get a baby brother or sister, whether he understood it or not.

Strasbourg, Mulhouse, Belfort, Besançon. The day disappeared behind the treetops, behind the curvature of the earth. The train was old, the compartments had no lights, the pioneers tired in the darkness. One after another they fell asleep, Anna's head rested on Peretz's shoulder, perhaps she was dreaming, perhaps the child inside her was dreaming, of what?

Peretz sat at the window, listening to the monotonous rattling of the train, watching the sleeping faces. He looked out of the window at the dark landscape, a village here and there, a solitary house, a car, flickering night of candles behind small windows, headlight night on the streets, the train headed unerringly southwards. Peretz had the map in mind, he had the address in his head, Rue de la Vieille 13bis, in the middle of Lyon old town. That is where they were going.

If everything went according to plan.

How come he, Peretz, was worried? He saw warships in the dark-blue sea, each one in view of the next, a swimming chain of grey-painted steel with turrets bearing twin cannon. Far above flapped the Union Jack, far beyond lay Palestine. How were they going to get there, he and Anna and the child in her belly, his child? The Haganah's last few ships had all been captured, the internment camps in Cyprus were overflowing with homeless Jews – what was awaiting them in the Promised Land? The Arabs and the British again. How was it going to end?

Peretz sat there, wedged between the wall of the compartment and his pregnant wife, unable to find peace of mind. Thoughts assailed him like wild animals, they tore him open from inside, making him sore and vulnerable. He should have been carrying a loudhailer in his head and screaming into it, to drown out everything else, keep everything else under control. But Peretz was as mute and helpless as a little child, and the world was big and confusing and full of dangers.

When finally he fell asleep he also dreamed, incoherently and threateningly.

SEVENTY-TWO

Frau Kramer stood up straight. She was dirty and soaked through, but did not care. She had come here because she was looking for support to help her along the difficult path to the truth. She sighed, glanced at the grave, she opened her hands and let the weeds she had plucked out fall to the ground. The rain fell and fell, as if it would never stop, the puddles grew, if it went on like this everything would soon be flooded.

Frau Kramer went to her granddaughter, still standing there uncomprehendingly with the umbrella, and hugged her.

"Child," she said softly, "how did you come to me?" She shook her head as if unable to believe it. "Without you I might have closed my eyes to what happened here." Resting her head on Lisa's and closing her eyes, she said, "The British brought us here, to Pöppendorf, to a transit camp for refugees from the east. Everything's going to be fine now, I thought, the British will look after us. But in the autumn we suddenly had to move on, no-one gave us any explanation, they just said, You're in your own country, you don't need a camp anymore. All at once we were back on the streets. And there were so many of us. More and more people came pouring in from the east. No-one gave us any food, no-one wanted to take us in. The British didn't know what to do with us. And then I heard about the Jews who were being brought to Pöppendorf. A few thousand. And we'd already been there. I just had to go back! I had to put all my eggs in one basket."

Lisa pushed her grandmother away slightly so she could look into her eyes. "So that's what you did?"

Frau Kramer nodded.

"And they took us?!"

"Yes, they did."

"But Grandma, what's so dreadful that you haven't been able to talk to me about it all this time?"

"Oh, my child. I met a woman there. She had a little boy. You played together. He was a very quiet boy but his eyes were so alert! You liked him straightaway. His mother was one of the few Germans amongst the Jews who'd been brought there."

"So she wasn't a Jew either?"

"Yes, she was. They were all Jews. But most of them spoke Polish, Russian and Yiddish."

"And you became friends?"

"*You* became friends."

Frau Kramer shook her head and continued, "I have to tell it to you properly. When I heard about the Jews I went with you back to Pöppendorf. A day and a half it took us. It was a long way and you were too small and weak to walk. I had to carry you most of the time. It was hot, a storm broke that evening. I was going to give up and go back to Lübeck. But where? There wasn't anywhere for us to go! Absolutely nowhere!" She sighed. "So on we went." She stopped as if to listen to the echo of these last few words. Her gaze seemed to lose itself in the rain. But then her eyes returned to Lisa.

"If there are Jews there, I thought, then it can't be the same guards working at the camp. They won't recognise us. And I was right. But they weren't British. They were German." She paused briefly as if now, many years later, she understood it all much better. "When I arrived at the gate with you on my arm, at the place in the forest where we were today, I told the guard on the other side that we were Jews. But he didn't believe me. And why should he? We were so destitute that he must have realised I'd do anything to get a bite to eat." She looked at Lisa so despondently, as if everything she was saying was happening again right now.

"I was about leave, but you were starving! You wouldn't stop whining. I couldn't bear the idea that you'd go the same way as your mother. That on a road somewhere you'd just . . ." She went quiet. Taking a deep breath, she said, "I turned around again and screamed as loudly as I could." Frau Kramer let go of Lisa, she took a couple of steps back, stretched out her arms and screamed into the rain, screamed to the dead Jews lying in their hundreds there in the graves, screamed at her granddaughter.

"We're Jews! We're Jews! We're Jews!" She broke off and let her arms drop again. Lisa stared at her grandmother. Then she looked around bashfully.

"I screamed and screamed until I caught the attention of the people in the camp." Frau Kramer said. "You weren't crying anymore, you were screaming blue murder. Not just because you were hungry, but because of the way I was behaving, I expect." Now she smiled and looked so sad that a tear appeared in Lisa's eye. Frau Kramer resisted the impulse to hug her granddaughter. Only continuing the story would be of any help now.

"A crowd of people gathered on the other side of the gate. The guards became nervous because the people demanded they let us in. But they didn't move a muscle. And then . . ." She paused again.

". . . and then a woman with a little boy in her arms emerged from the crowd and came up to us. In front of the guards she opened the gate and invited us in." Frau Kramer swallowed, she forced herself not to lose her composure. "You saved me, Lisa. I thank you for that."

"Me? Grandma! You're mad!"

"No." The old woman shook her head. "It's only because of you that we got back into Pöppendorf. Only because of you."

SEVENTY-THREE

Knock knees!
Little piggies!
Knock knees!
Little piggies!

Gudrun had an earworm. She was the only one in her class who knew that you could get these from nursery rhymes as well as music. She also knew that an earworm was wicked, something you had to get rid of before it burrowed deeper and deeper into your head. Gudrun was walking down Thierstrasse, she was on her way home from school. Hello, she called out to the beggar, who always sat in the same place, Hello, the beggar said, returning the greeting. Gudrun sat down beside the man, she rummaged around in her satchel and pulled out a paper bag.

'Here's half my break-time roll, like I promised!' she said, beaming at him as if it were Christmas and she the Christ child come down to earth to give presents to the poor and disenfranchised.

The beggar was an old man. He could no longer remember how he had become a beggar. His bones felt as if they had been sitting here for an eternity, as if nothing else existed and time were standing still until the end of days. Of course he knew that this was not the case, for everything had a cause and effect, I must have done something wrong, he would sometimes tell himself, but now he was happy because this little girl had taken him into her heart.

"Tell me, how old are you?" he asked Gudrun as he chewed on the roll with the few teeth left in his mouth.

"I'm seven," came the answer from the child's mouth.

The beggar laughed. "I could be your grandfather, little girl!"

Gudrun nodded and said nothing.

The beggar ate.

All of a sudden she said, "I've got to go now." She stood up, went on her way and the beggar watched her in amazement. He could not know that the earworm in Gudrun's head had gone quiet, he had no idea that he had paid for his meal.

SEVENTY-FOUR

Darkness had now fallen and the skyscrapers of the towering city sparkled from countless lightbulbs and neon tubes. Lisa could not remember how long she had been standing and waiting in this same place – hours, days, weeks? It depends on how you look at it, she thought. She had been living in this two-room apartment for weeks, she had been waiting for a call for days, she had been at home for hours. She had watched the sun until it disappeared and now a half moon was rising. The earth turned, the cars drove through the streets of New York, trains trundled beneath the surface, boats sailed on the Hudson River. But she sat on this chair like a fixed star and everything was turning inside her head.

She closed her eyes. Why could she not simply make her peace and live her life? Why did she always have to wallow in the past?

Noises came from the neighbouring room. She stood up and made her way quietly to the door, opened it slightly and peeked in at Tom. He seemed to be having an unsettling dream. His face was moving, he was breathing noisily, beneath his lids his eyes were darting from one corner to the other. Lisa looked at him. How big he had grown in the short time! Big and critical. Not a day passed without his reproaching her for having taken the decision to move to this city. Every free hour without my friends is lost time, he had said when he came home from school that afternoon. And every day just with you, he added, and she nodded and sighed. Then he had disappeared into his room and she could only guess at what he was doing there, listening to music, playing his guitar, reading, writing letters, sleeping. It was his form of protest, the protest of a powerless individual. Hopefully it'll pass soon, Lisa thought.

And what if the only point of life was for it to continue? If all her efforts, as meaningful as they might seem to her, were ultimately a waste of time, because in the end all that mattered was what was happening here and now?

She closed the door again and leaned against it. I ought to go to bed, she thought. But she returned to her place by the window.

SEVENTY-FIVE

The sun had not yet risen when the new lorries drove through the narrow streets of Lyon's old town on their way to the Jewish house. The bleary-eyed pioneers were standing tightly packed on a small square in rue Bouteille, and waiting. Once again they handed over their luggage and climbed onto the loading ramps, unaware that Shmaria Zamaret, the agent in Marseille, had paid a lot of money to get the French drivers to work on this particular day, 10 July, 1947. For a strike had been called in France, which meant these were strike breakers who now drove out of the sleeping city and headed south towards Valence and Orange, Nîmes and Montpellier.

Most of the passengers went straight back to sleep, not to awaken again until the convoy reached the quayside of Sète port later that morning. Many of the passengers wondered briefly, Why Sète, why not Marseille? and had there been time for explanations Peretz would have told them about the British, who were using all their power and diplomacy to pressurise the French into preventing the Jewish ship from departing, he might have said, Sète isn't in the jurisdiction of the Marseille authorities, they can't touch us here. But there was no time for such conversations.

When Anna saw the large ship, towering above her as high as a house, with its three decks and mighty funnel, rising exactly in the centre, its length of one hundred metres and one thousand nine hundred tonnes, she momentarily forgot her own weight. For a moment the impossible seemed to have come within her grasp, for a moment she sensed the hope that everything would turn out well in her life.

Euphoria seized the passengers when they saw the proud ship that Haganah had bought somewhere in America, converted and sailed here to take them to the Promised Land. What organisation there must be behind an operation like that, what power and what belief in the Jewish people! Such thoughts and others were an inspiration to the pioneers, who fell around each other's necks as if they had already landed in Haifa and were disembarking and in a few moments' time would kiss the earth of their new home. Anna embraced Peretz, who was simply Peretz, Aaron embraced Ruth, Sarah clung to her mother, as if she might get lost. Old François embraced all the women and children in turn. The Abramowiczes sang the song of hope and the others joined in, the children from Lindenfels singing the loudest. Even Dana the doll sang along. Even Ariel had shut his book, for here was the ship he had been preparing himself for ever since he had been able to read.

Out you get! Quicker! the men shouted into the lorries. They had come to help the ma'apilim board. And to make them get a move on. For now was not the time for songs of joy. The port police could turn up any minute and declare the ship unseaworthy, any minute a warship could appear and block the exit from the port, the British could intensify their pressure on the French government, the next convoy from one of the billets around Marseille would arrive in Sète port.

The people climbed out of the lorries and stood in the harsh light of the Mediterranean sun. Where was the luggage? Over here! men called to them, indicating where the queue had to pass to avoid obstructing the loading of the ship. Other lorries had arrived, bringing food in tins, water barrels, sacks of potatoes, fruit, vegetables, dried meat, everything they needed to make it to Palestine alive. The quayside was overcrowded, Faster, faster! the men shouted. The cases flew from the luggage lorry back into the hands of their owners, who made straight for the gang-way, straight up, straight onto the ship, where they were greeted by the American crew, This way!

The ship's external size shrank on board to narrow gangways, tiny berths with low ceilings and small portholes, through which you could barely see daylight. A floating camp. A camp made entirely of iron. The people looked around, they looked at each other, as if trying to reassure them-selves that they were all haunted by the same feelings.

How long have we got to hunker down here? Ruth asked when they were sitting on their beds, so densely packed that they could barely move. One thousand five hundred and thirty-six nautical miles, said Ariel, who knew such things. He put his book down and made his way through the ship. The adults looked at him in surprise, they had never seen the boy like this before.

Five minutes later he returned, accompanied by a powerful-looking man, who gave a friendly smile and told them in English that they had to remain in their cabins to prevent chaos during embarkation.

Outside they heard the next convoy, lorry engines, songs inter-rupted, men's voices barking orders.

The embarkation of the three thousand five hundred and twenty adults and nine hundred and fifty-five children took until early afternoon. Meanwhile the sun was heating up those who had already occupied their quarters. The air was sticky, the light pale. They were forbidden from going on deck to prevent anyone from seeing just how many souls the *President Warfield* held in its steel belly.

At three o'clock the following morning the largest refugee ship ever obtained by Haganah sailed out of Sète port. Beforehand a number of short telephone conversations had taken place between Marseille, Paris, Tel Aviv and the ship. The pilot, who Shmaria Zamaret, the envoy in Mareseille, had bribed with a good deal of money, failed to turn up, so Shaul Avigur, head of the Institution for Immigration B, decided that the captain would have to go it alone. The ropes were untied and the helmsman tried his luck. The ship ran aground by the jetty; it took an hour before it was afloat again. Then everything went smoothly and the *President Warfield* steered its course out into the open sea.

A few miles away two Royal Navy destroyers were bobbing up and down. When the Ship of Jews emerged in the distance they weighed anchor and slowly gathered speed.

SEVENTY-SIX

Paris, 12th July, 1947

Dear Mr Bidault,

On numerous occasions in the past few months we have appealed to our French friends to help us in our difficult task in Palestine by taking all possible steps to stop the illicit Jewish traffic through France. The French Government have responded by giving assurances that among other things the validity of the visa would be closely scrutinised before they were allowed to leave France and that the provisions of the international conventions regarding the safety of life at sea would be rigorously applied to ships suspected of participating in the traffic.

As recently as 27th June I wrote to Your Excellency once again invoking your help and requesting in particular that a ship the *President Warfield* should be strictly controlled in accordance with the requests made to your Ministry by H.M.'s Embassy.

As I told you this morning, I was dismayed to find on arriving in Paris that not only had the *President Warfield* escaped from France but that she had been permitted to embark some 4,000 illicit immigrants, in spite of the fact that she possessed a clearance certificate valid for only one journey without passengers and in fine weather.

In the circumstances I must protest most strongly against the facilities which have been accorded to the *President Warfield* and I request that the French Government should readmit her to France with all the passengers on board as soon as arrangements can be made to cause the *President Warfield* to return.

I should also be grateful to learn that the necessary disciplinary measures have been taken as regards those who permitted her departure in contradiction with the assurances of the French Government.

I take this opportunity to remind you that among the suspect vessels in French ports are the *Paducah* and the *Northlands* which are at Bayonne and the *Bruna* and the *Luciano* and the *Archangelos* which are at Marseilles.

I shall be glad if, in view of the departure of the *President Warfield*, you will agree to maintain a warship in the vicinity of Marseilles with standing orders to stop any of those vessels which may leave port. You will realise that only a French vessel can take effective action to prevent clandestine embarkation of illegal immigrants in French territorial waters.

I am, Dear Mr Bidault, yours sincerely,

Ernest Bevin

SEVENTY-SEVEN

Lisa froze. She was soaked through to the skin. The rain did not stop, it changed. It was no longer pouring down, but falling steadily. The light was getting dimmer, at some point, before they noticed, it would get dark. Lisa felt unwell. She had wanted to hear the truth, but not in this way. She wrapped her arms around her torso and said, "Come on Grandma, let's go. You can tell me the rest at home."

Frau Kramer looked at Lisa, she cast a glance at the grave they were standing beside. She was freezing too, but she barely felt it. In her head it was autumn, a warm autumn, the beginning of September. In her head the woman carrying the small boy said, Come with me, I know where you can stay. The crowd dispersed, the guards looked away and Frau Kramer, with Lisa on her arm, followed the woman. She knew her way around Pöppendorf, she knew the corrugated iron houses with their narrow bunk beds, the damp air inside, the lack of space.

"It felt as if we'd come home at last," Frau Kramer said.

"I'm sorry?"

"The camp. We'd finally gone back somewhere we already knew."

"Grandma, please, let's go!"

"Not yet, Lisa. Now, this woman took us to an empty bunk, it was right next to hers. She'd said to herself, We've got beds free, why shouldn't this poor woman and her child sleep in our hut? When she put down her little boy I could see that she was pregnant. She reminded me of your mother, Lisa. She was about Margarita's age, but there was something hunched and sad about her. I've got to tell you about her, Lisa. And right here. You know, it's only now I've understood that Lübeck wasn't a waiting room at all, even though that's what I believed for so many years. Excuse me for being so flustered, I still don't know how to tell you because it's so strange, so . . ." Frau Kramer raised her arms to express something, but the gesture was of no help. She let them fall back down.

"The woman went away and came back with some food. I remember exactly, it was potato soup with bits of sausage! It was warm and the taste so intense, Lisa! I thought this was the most delicious thing I'd ever tasted in my life. I had to make sure that you didn't stuff your mouth and throw it all up again." She smiled affectionately and looked so lost in thought that Lisa could not tell whether it was her being referred to here or the little girl in her grandmother's memory.

"As we ate the woman told me that in the camp they got more calories than the Germans, but perhaps not for much longer. She said, The British want us to decide where we'd like to live, in France or in Germany. She smiled at me, I wasn't taking in anything she was saying as I was so busy feeding you and eating the soup myself! Without thinking I said, France is definitely much better. The little boy teetered around awkwardly, like a child who's only just learned to walk. He sat down next to you and watched you eat. He had big beady eyes and a sweet button nose, he was a handsome boy, Lisa, and he looked like his mother, just as you do." She smiled again, the rainwater ran from her face down her neck and into her clothes, she did not notice.

"The two of you sat next to each other as if you belonged together," she said. "But suddenly the woman said to me, You're not Jews, are you?"

SEVENTY-EIGHT

Shimon had seen everything. He had sat on his mother's arm as if on a ship sailing across the Mediterranean, accompanied by six British warships, ready to come closer, while their boat was heading as fast as it could towards the land that had emerged on the horizon. Shimon had felt the jolt when the two frigates rammed the *President Warfield*, he had seen the men in uniform who leaped on board. He could still hear the loud report of the rifle that one of the soldiers had fired. And he was still thinking of Emil, who had lain perfectly still on the boards, staring up at the sky, continually at the sky, as if he had spotted something interesting to see there. Shimon looked up himself, saw only a few seagulls, and had been surprised by Emil, who could no longer walk, no longer talk and was no longer able to confront the British soldiers with the axe that he still held in his silent hand. One of the sailors had closed Emil's eyes and Shimon kept watching to see whether he would open them again. But Emil did not even wake up when Aaron, Mr Abramowicz and Peretz lifted him up and took him away.

Now, on his mother's arm, Shimon felt as if he were going to sea again, the sky was just as blue and the crowd that had assembled at the camp gate reminded him of all those people who had gone up on deck when the British soldiers arrived. Shimon looked at the people's hands, but they were no longer carrying potatoes or tins of food, they would not pelt the woman on the other side of the gate, even though she wanted to come in too, but was not allowed, just as the British soldiers should not have come onto the ship and yet they did.

Then something surprising happened. His own mother went with him up to the gate. Shimon was slightly scared, because the strange woman and the little girl were screaming so loudly he was unable to look anywhere else. His fear intensified when his mother opened the gate, maybe, Shimon thought, the woman was going to take out a gun and shoot him and his mother, just as the soldier had shot at Emil.

But he was surprised again, for the woman and the child suddenly fell silent and looked at him. And now Shimon saw that they had large, dark rings around their eyes and hollow cheeks. This sight triggered a familiar feeling in him, but he did not dwell on it for now the woman came up close and followed him and his mother through the crowd, which applauded him, and that was an even greater surprise for Shimon.

As they went back into the camp Shimon watched the little girl and the little girl watched him. Then they were inside the large corrugated iron hut and went over to Shimon's bed. The blue sky stayed outside, inside it was gloomy and damp. His mother pointed to the neighbouring bed and said, It's free. Shimon didn't want to stay with the strangers on his own when his mother went off to the canteen, so she took him with her, but on the way back he had to walk on his own because of the two bowls of soup his mother was carrying.

Shimon wanted to sit beside the girl. He was so preoccupied by her that he was quite disconcerted when the strange woman started crying and very pleased when she spoke again. The little girl seemed pleased too, and when she had finally finished her soup she followed him. Everyone who lay here at night was outside, the two children could clamber over the empty beds without anyone complaining. Shimon showed the girl how noisily it resonated inside the hut when you struck the corrugated iron wall with a stone. He was delighted that this delighted the girl, and so the two of them stood by the wall with pebbles in their hands and hit it as hard as they could. Bang! Bang! Bang!

They did not notice that one woman was telling the other the truth, No, I'm not a Jew. They listened to none of the story that told of hiding and birth, flight and death. Shimon and the girl swapped pebbles and then went back to hitting the corrugated iron.

Bang! Bang! Bang!

The two women paid barely any attention to the noise the children were making. The younger woman put her arm around the older one and said, I won't betray you. The older one got the gist of it, We're allowed to stay. They did not see that Shimon and Lisa had dropped their pebbles and were now walking hand in hand along the dormitory gangways. Suddenly Shimon stopped and thrust out his arms and staggered and went, Oh! Oh! Oh! as if he were still in the bowels of the ship and the waves were swelling outside, and the little girl staggered too and also went, Oh! Oh! Oh! and Shimon was delighted.

When the silence had become too prolonged and the two women were separated once more by unfamiliarity, the elder one said, "We lived not far from Konin. A day's journey perhaps. That's where Lisa's mother had escaped from. Not only because she was a Jew. She'd shot a German."

"In Konin?" Anna sat up.

"His name was Karl, like my son. I can't remember the surname."

"Karl Treitz," Anna said. "Sturmbannführer Karl Treitz." She listened to the sound of these words, she had not heard them for three years now. The two women looked at each other in astonishment.

"He served under Josef Ranzner," Anna said hesitantly.

"Did you know him?"

"The morning before he died they brought along a Pole. I was just cleaning the steps in the foyer when they shoved him in the building. He called himself Piotr. He said there were more Jews in the church. Treitz didn't want to believe him. But he went all the same. Later they brought the Sturmbannführer back, apparently the Pole had led him into an ambush. He was filthy from lying in the rain. I had to scrub the place in the foyer where they laid down his body."

Anna looked behind her, where the children were rolling around in the central gangway and laughing. She thought of Josef Ranzner, bending over the corpse and talking to it, giving it orders. She glanced at the German woman. Nobody had come as close to her secret as this stranger, all of a sudden she felt the desire to confide in someone, for a fleeting moment she got the impression that it might bring her relief.

But the moment passed.

She thought of the journey on the *President Warfield*, of Haifa, where the British soldiers under the leadership of a Jewish officer had dragged them off the ship and disinfected them with D.D.T. as if they were worried about catching something. She thought of the passage back to France in three British warships, whose decks were secured with barbed wire. Of the three weeks at anchor in a French port, three long weeks during which they did not know what to do, the French government had offered to let them stay, they would even receive work permits. Would they be Jews amongst goyim again, in the minority again, strangers in their own country again, surprised by hatred again? She recalled the day of the ultimatum, Disembark by six p.m. tomorrow or you'll continue on to Germany. Hanan! God was not gracious. She thought of Peretz, who slipped off the ship to reorganise the flight with Ephraim Frank, alias Ernst Caro. What had she felt when he left? She thought of Emil, the final movement his mouth had made, she was the only one who had seen the name Emil had tried to utter with his soundless throat, his empty lips. But Sarah had escaped below deck when the British came. How pointless it had all seemed to her, life in its entirety. She thought of Ariel, who presumed nobody had noticed when he dropped *The Odyssey* into the sea as they set their course for Hamburg. His expression when he noticed theirs.

"So that's the daughter of . . . ?" she said. She wanted to say "the murderer" but it did not seem fitting.

Frau Kramer nodded. "She's called Lisa Ejzenstain," she said.

SEVENTY-NINE

Munich, 13th January, 1966

My skills in the field of combating the enemy are unappreciated by my direct superiors and H.Q. My knowledge about the structure of the partisan organisations in the former Warthegau – names, ranks, areas of operation, individuals now in key positions or possibly working in the

West – seems to be insignificant for the Service. They make me feel like I am a discontinued model, one of those dinosaurs only tolerated because they served in the war. Sure, I am shown respect superficially, I have a company car, which is undoubtedly a privilege. I am deputy director, but I expect that was merely a measure to placate me. They fail to see that I have far more to offer in the fight against the Red Peril. I know the Poles, I know how the Russians fight, I held the fortress at Posen until the very last breath of the German Reich! But this Germany I live in now is no longer that great country brimming with might for which I once shed my blood.

I waited, for years I waited for grass to grow over everything, just as my superiors demanded. I held still so that I could finally become active again. But in this so-called democracy the grass never grows over the past. The one thing that grows here is Jewish influence over public opinion. What about the state? And us, the state's henchmen, what are we doing? Nothing! Nothing at all! We let everything happen. The Jews cut us short, wherever and however they like. They work feverishly to give us a bad conscience, paralysing our national development, keeping us small. Why? Because they're afraid of us, because we taught them to be afraid. Their revenge is not open; they don't offer us any fight. They incite the world against us whenever we dare express our opinion freely. And they hunt! Their Mossad is snuffling around everywhere, they're hunting us, the dinosaurs, the guardians of the German spirit, they wish to wipe us out, gag us so we can no longer defend this country against them, so that in the end only weaklings remain, sons who . . .

He broke off. He had given such free rein to his anger, he had pressed the fountain pen so hard into the paper that his fingers had started to sweat. And all of a sudden he realised that he was in danger of abandoning his unswerving resolution never to let himself get carried away, not by women, not by the dead, not by Jews, not by anyone or anything at all. He had to stick to a middle path, to moderate all his feelings. He had to avoid loving or hating with excess passion. Why had he ordered the Jewish girl to be fetched from the train? Precisely so he could have the perceived mortal enemy before his eyes at all times, study him, recognise his mimicry of human behaviour, his playing along, his capacity to exploit every opening to his own advantage. Knowing is not hating, he thought. I must not lose my composure. What good will it do me to hate the Jews in Israel just because they're on the hunt for mass murderers like Eichmann? Just because they killed him? All it has confirmed is that the Jews are just as the Reichsführer S.S. described them. It was still necessary to remain decent, still necessary to maintain his poise. In any case he, Josef Ranzner, was no simple mass murderer like Eichmann, this brains behind the crimes, who with such an appearance could have been Jewish himself. No, he had nothing to do with the Holocaust, he had fought against partisans behind the front lines, he had only killed Jews when they posed a threat to his Reich. Anna was the best proof of his ethical stance. Although he could have had her killed just like that – no, he could have strangled her with his own hands had he felt like it – he had not. On the contrary, he had given Anna her life, life and freedom, like a well-loved dog you let free from its chain because you cannot take it where you are going.

He leaned back, exhausted. I don't have to justify myself, he thought. There is no judge here. And if I act smartly, if I continue my boring civil servant's existence, then one day maybe the Germans will have a better understanding of what we did, men like me. Perhaps I ought to follow Silberbauer's advice after all and train as a specialist interrogator, it might give me a change of scene, who knows? Silberbauer was a colleague from Vienna, he had noticed Ranzner's dissatisfaction and said, I know all about this, I've led interrogations myself in the Reich, I know who's right and the qualities that are needed. It's no easy job, and certainly not for weaklings. They were in the canteen and Silberbauer had said, Live your life, don't let the system get you down. Silberbauer's right, he thought, recollecting their encounter now.

He was about to get up and leave the study. It was late, and tomorrow life would go on as before.

But then it struck him that it might be a good idea to seek out the Jewish woman, so she could corroborate his testimony. Yes, looking at it more closely, he could even be regarded as her saviour. No-one, not even the woman herself, would be able to dispute that she would most likely have died in Auschwitz had he not protected her from that fate. She would reveal the truth and finally he could emerge from this hiding place.

The thought was so intensely present in the room that now he saw Anna lying on his desk, just as beautiful and naked and defenceless as back then, just as seductive, just as sweet smelling and overwhelming in her womanliness. His body reacted as it had back then and ever since when Anna sought him out, and this happened often, sometimes daily. Ranzner's gaze wandered to the door. It was quiet outside. The children must be asleep. And Emma? Probably in bed, reading and waiting for him, as she had every day for ten years. Ten years that showed. Ten years and two births. And this maternal nature she had developed.

His erection subsided. But that was not what he wanted now. He wanted to feel tumescent, tumescent and strong and manly, which is why he banished thoughts of his wife and focused squarely on the Jewish woman.

EIGHTY

On Monday, 29 September, Anna was lying on her narrow bed, reading old newspapers to stave off boredom. While Shimon was somewhere in the camp with Lisa, Sarah and Frau Kramer, she was becoming incensed by the *Guardian*, which claimed the Jews had used tear gas to attack the British soldiers who had boarded the ship. She became incensed that the British press regarded the pioneers as victims of the Zionists during their three weeks in Port de Bouc, even though they had thought long and hard about what they would do and each of them had been able to make their own decision. A stillness unfurled in her head when she read about the disembarkation in Hamburg in the *Lübecker Nachrichten*: "The last time we saw such people was years ago – how many, actually?"

Anna ran over recent events. On the evening of 8 September they had arrived in the port of Hamburg. The British had smuggled them through a corridor screened by barbed wire, transported them in closed army lorries through night-time northern Germany. Early on 9 September they had arrived, exhausted, in Pöppendorf.

Two days later some Haganah men had cut a hole in the fence. Ephraim Frank and Peretz had been waiting on the other side, with new forged passports, with new illegally loaned lorries, with a new escape plan and a new ship that had set its course from somewhere for Marseille.

With her large, heavy belly, from which came a gentle tugging that ran up her back and to her head, Anna had not dared risk the stress and strains of another flight and had stayed behind in Pöppendorf. They had parted company in silence. Nobody felt like a pioneer anymore, they had been defeated, and if they were now making another attempt to get to Palestine it was only because of a lack of alternatives. In the shelter of the corrugated iron hut they had embraced each other. Then Ruth and Aaron, Mr and Mrs Abramowicz, Ariel, Marja and her doll, Dana, and old François had gone out, one after the other, and Anna, Shimon and Sarah had stayed. She had not seen Peretz at all.

Anna had wanted to say to Sarah, You go too. But thinking of Shimon she had kept quiet, and Sarah had looked at her gratefully. For her it was proof that she really had become Anna's daughter.

In mid-September the British had instructed the German guards to open the gates so that the Jews could settle in Germany. They handed out leaflets and promised a permanent place to live, a job and a German passport. The pioneers had read the leaflets in disbelief and asked themselves, How can they believe that we're willingly going to stay in the land of murderers?

And now yet another week had passed without anything happening. Just the tugging in Anna's belly had become stronger. She stayed lying on the bed and told Frau Kramer and Sarah that she had a headache.

On Tuesday, 30 September, the weather turned. Banks of cloud chased across the sky, gusts of wind whooshed through the trees, rattling the gates and the barbed wire fences. The temperature dropped and in the corrugated-iron huts a damp chill crept into people's beds. In the afternoon Anna was feverish. Her stomach pains grew more intense, a doctor came, one of the Jews from the ship. He examined her and did not say much. An hour later he returned and gave her something to bring her temperature down.

On the Wednesday Anna woke up bathed in sweat. She had a high temperature, her belly was burning. Frau Kramer did not move from her side. The doctor came accompanied by a German, the two of them examined Anna together and concluded that in her condition she could not be transported anywhere. Two camp inmates brought a stretcher. When they lifted Anna to transfer her to another bed, she screamed with pain. Luckily Shimon was not there; Anna had told Sarah to go and play with him and Lisa.

They took Anna to a hospital barracks, a wooden hut where the air was not so damp. It had large windows that let in plenty of light. The two doctors administered her a liquid and exchanged glances that Anna did not see. But Frau Kramer saw.

"What then?" said Lisa into the rain that was still falling, as if intent on burying everything under water, washing everything away. Now the light really was fading, darkness set in rapidly.

Frau Kramer looked at the grave again. She said softly, "I had to bring this child into the world, Lisa. The doctors couldn't do it, they'd given up on the mother and she would have died too." She looked at Lisa. "They called the rabbi, but I sent him away, and then . . ." She paused and looked at the grave.

"Then I heated up some water and got towels ready. I told myself, This is a normal birth, I told myself, Don't think about it, tell yourself it's Lisa, you're bringing Lisa into the world again. But Anna was so weak! She could barely help me. I had to find out how the child was lying. Of course it was the wrong way round so I had to turn it. I'd never turned a child before! I pushed and pushed until Anna screamed. She screamed for me to stop. I yelled at her, If I stop you're going to die! The men didn't dare come in. Everyone was scared, I think the entire camp was gathered outside."

She fell silent and saw images she would never be able to describe, and feelings that would not fit into any words and phrases. She had brought a dead child into the world, with all the force she could muster, a small, grey, desolate child that would never get to glimpse that world. She had held it in her hands, and the pain she felt was so severe that she burst into tears. Howling noisily, she had laid it in a tub and then, still howling and sobbing, she had pushed her hand inside Anna, who was screaming, and pulled out everything that no longer belonged there. She had done it without knowing whether she would be able, the people outside the barracks could no longer distinguish the sounds of the two women, Who's howling, who's screaming? When the pain became too much for Anna she passed out and it became quieter. Frau Kramer washed her, moved her to another bed, and only when she had done everything she could to remove death from within this woman did she collapse and call for help.

EIGHTY-ONE

Who was this woman? Heinrich was lying on his bed, listening to music. Three days earlier his father had given him a Nordmende record player and an L.P. of German folk songs for his birthday. They were lovely songs, but Heinrich could not concentrate on them, because this woman had turned up in the latest diary entry. Heinrich hated her. She was like an evil spirit wanting to steal Father away from him. If he could he would seek her out himself and kill the woman, so that Father would be left in peace before he made good his threats and left home to be with her. Heinrich did not know what the woman was called, for his father avoided mentioning the name. To begin with he had thought his father was worried someone might read it. Gradually, however, he realised that even his father was afraid of the name, as if spelling it out would invoke some great calamity.

Heinrich thought long and hard. He had been reading his father's diary for years now. Time and again he had tried to stop, but without success. Sometimes he had taken a break for months, when he had been able to resist the temptation. On occasion he had even managed to forget the key beneath the flowerpot. But he had always dredged it up again, as if something in his head were forcing him to do so. The new entry had been written on the evening of his birthday, Heinrich even knew exactly when. Father had retired to the study as usual. Mother had urged him and Gudrun to be quiet because Father had important things to do. She herself had gone to her room because she liked to read in bed. What did his mother read, as a matter of fact? Heinrich had no idea. Until that moment the thought had never occurred to him. He resolved to take a look one day.

As ever, Father had left the door ajar.

The following afternoon Heinrich had come home from school, slipped out of his bedroom into the study and read the new entry. He spent a long time afterwards sitting there, fighting back the tears.

Today, on the third day, it was no better. Images entered his head. Father next to Mother at the kitchen table, in the centre of which sat his large birthday cake with fourteen lit candles, Gudrun to the left. Everything was fine, his sister and parents sang "Happy Birthday", Heinrich was delighted with his presents, they had breakfast, Father smiled a lot and finally put his arm around Mother, and she snuggled up to him like she used to. Why did I have to read that diary entry? he asked himself. If he had not done so his life would still be alright. And had he not heard a very soft voice in his head warning him? Had this voice not said, Leave it, Heinrich! Don't do it! But he was too weak to resist the pull from the study, and now everything lay in tatters.

EIGHTY-TWO

Each one of them had given something. Mosche and Selma addresses, Herr Weiss the money for her flight, Frau Kramer a few names and money she'd put aside. Lisa did not want to accept it, but the old woman said, It was always meant for you.

Lisa had taken the express from West Berlin to Schwanheide, and from there a regional train to Lübeck. Tobias Weiss had come from Hamburg, where he now lived, and for one night they slept again in adjoining rooms in the old apartment on the fourth floor, which Herr Weiss still rented so he could come back at any time, as he said, back home. But Lisa suspected that chiefly he did it for her sake.

She and Herr Weiss and Frau Kramer ate dinner together in the apartment and chatted about old times. When Lisa had tired of this she asked Herr Weiss, "What's it like in Hamburg, Tobi?"

"Hmm, well, actually it's rather nice, yes, I have to say it's really nice in fact. Although, well, it is a bit lonely. I mean, um, it's a big city."

"But you earn well, don't you?"

"Oh yes! Yes, yes! I really do, ever since I went freelance!"

Lisa looked at Herr Weiss. How young he was and how old he acted! Was this a result of the war, or was he just like that?"

"Where are you going to live?" Frau Kramer asked.

"I'll go to see Mosche and Selma tomorrow. They know people all over the country."

"Is that safe?"

"Of course, Grandma!" She laughed. Herr Weiss laughed too. Frau Kramer remained serious. She was concerned.

"You hear so much about the place," she said. "They say it's dangerous even in the big cities. Promise me you'll call!"

Lisa promised.

She spoke about West Berlin, It's strange, she said, you have a much greater sense of freedom there even though the city's enclosed. She spoke about her history course at the university, about Herr and Frau Guttmann, who she was staying with and whose three children she looked after. She had come to know the Guttmanns through Mosche and Selma too, and they had turned out as friendly as the two of them had promised. Which is why she was trusting them again now. She spoke about fellow students who had become friends, and about one in particular who might become more than just a friend, He's Jewish too, she said. An image of him flashed before their eyes, raising smiles.

The following morning Lisa crossed the old town on foot. Spring had arrived overnight, the air was mild, birds were chirping, everything promised a new beginning. It was her first stroll through her home town since she had turned twenty-one, officially an adult at last. Free at last of Maria. Free at last of this parochial city. Of this country.

Mosche and Selma's tiny first-floor apartment was in a small house in a narrow side street close to the synagogue. Through the two small windows Lisa could see the pale-green spires of the Ägidienkirche. White, embroidered half curtains hung in front of the glass panes. Between two huge bookcases, a bulbous chest of drawers, a protruding standard lamp, a bulging blue sofa, two fat armchairs and a low, rectangular wooden table with a beige tiled top, ran narrow gangways along which Mosche and Selma hurried with astonishing assuredness to bring tea and cakes, while Lisa sat rather sunken in the sofa cushions, gazing at the multitude of black-and-white photographs in thick frames that hung on walls papered with extravagant floral patterns. She found the excess of the room both oppressive and inspirational.

When Mosche noticed her expression he laughed and said, "These Jews who lost everything!" He made a hand gesture that seemed to encompass their cluttered living room as well as all Jews in all living rooms everywhere.

"The pictures—"

"People who look like my family," Selma interrupted her. "This woman, for example," she said, pointing to a large, yellowed photograph in a golden Baroque frame, "reminds me of my mother. She's wearing the same traditional outfit my mother used to wear. Look at the bun – my mother often put her hair up like that. And there's something about her face; she could be my mother's sister. Well, this combination, it stirs a feeling in me." Placing a hand on her chest, she sighed and stared at the photograph.

"They might be strangers, but they're still Jews," Mosche said.

"Yes, of course, Jews," Selma affirmed, deep in thought. She sat beside Lisa and smiled at her. "These walls are a cemetery, because all these people have one thing in common – they're dead. Just ignore it all. This old lady," she continued, pointing to herself, "has gone a bit crazy over the years. And she'll be dead soon." Lisa gave her a look of horror. Selma pretended not to notice. She raised her teacup to her lips.

"Nonsense!" Mosche exclaimed, smiling at his wife from the armchair. "You're just as beautiful as you were twenty years ago." Selma cast him a glance and said softly, "Oh, what do you know?"

They drank tea and ate cakes. Selma and Mosche talked about people they knew, they settled on a few names, then Selma got a pen and some paper and jotted the addresses down.

When Lisa said goodbye she was hugged as warmly and tightly as if she were their own daughter.

Then she walked again through the new spring, feeling secure in the expanse of the world.

She stayed two more days with Herr Weiss and her grandmother, again from the window she saw Maria Kramer, teetering over the cobbles on her way to work in Clementstrasse in the red-light district, again she said to her grandmother, You ought to look for this Kleinert, and Frau Kramer knew what Lisa meant by it.

On the morning of the third day it was raining, although it was no longer a cold grey rain, but a fresh shower, the earth was fragrant, it smelled of fertility and growth. Of departure.

Tobias had left for Hamburg early that morning. They had embraced, Come and visit me, Lisa! You bet I will! Then he was gone and Lisa went down to the third floor to have breakfast with her grandmother.

Afterwards the two women made their way to the station. Maria would be coming home soon, And so we've got a little more time, Frau Kramer said.

They walked through the city, Lisa had taken her grandmother's arm to allow both of them to fit beneath the umbrella. She was carrying a small suitcase in her right hand and a rucksack on her back.

The two women crossed Holstenbrücke, they glanced at the Trave, which looked the same as ever and yet was always different, they passed the Holstentor , standing there broad and pointy, as if this could never change, they continued across the large, rectangular expanse of grass beyond, Lisa turned and stared at the city with its pointed red gables, its soaring pale-green towers, its people who now, on Monday morning, 2 May, 1966, were going about their daily routines. My home? she thought, bewildered, and turned back to see the curve of Puppenbrücke up ahead with its allegorical statues on the low walls to the left and right, gleaming in the rain like a guard of honour to bid her goodbye. Dear River God, she thought as they passed the hunched figure with his oar, please steer my little boat well!

Soon after the bridge, the station with its squat towers came into view slightly to the right. The women were gripped by a sense of urgency, even though there was still time. Have you got your ticket? Yes, Grandma. You didn't forget anything at home, did you? At home. Lisa gave her grandmother an affectionate look, No, Grandma, nothing.

The train had already pulled in, a hefty, red diesel engine, behind it the long row of carriages, creamy-white on top, dark-blue below. The engine steamed with heat and moisture, the carriages dripped, the doors were open, You'd better get on and find yourself a good seat, Frau Kramer said nervously, and Lisa smiled despite the tears. They embraced, Look after yourself, I will, You're all I've got left, No, Grandma, Yes, you are, Lisa, all I have left. Then she let go of Margarita Ejzenstain's child, who turned away and climbed the narrow iron steps with her luggage.

Lisa vanished into the train, only to reappear at one of the windows. After struggling to pull it down, she leaned on it with her arms, the two women smiled at each other, so this was farewell, I ought to be used to it, Frau Kramer thought, recalling Lisa's move to Berlin. But back then, two years ago, it had been different, the three of them had travelled together, she and Lisa and Tobias, as if they were a proper family, Frau Kramer had met the Gutmanns and that had given her a feeling of security, even though since then she had been living in the apartment just with Maria. But now everything was different, now it was as if she would never see Lisa again, as if she were losing her to the world outside, What's left for me here?

The engine came to life with a muffled sound, the conductor raised his little red signalling disc, Doors close automatically, a woman's voice announced over the loudspeaker, the conductor blew his small whistle, it gave a shrill sound, the doors crunched shut, a man stuck his head out of the little side window in the engine. Then the conductor boarded and closed the final door. The train pulled away slowly, the two women waved to each other, the carriages left the station one after another, all it took was the gentle curve to the left beyond and Lisa had disappeared from view.

EIGHTY-THREE

When Gudrun turned twelve she gave her parents a present. She cut off her long, blonde hair, wrapped it in silver paper and brought it down to breakfast that morning. Even though her mother stood up and gave her a resounding slap across the face, even though her father sent her straight back to her room, for Gudrun it was worth it. As she lay on her bed she kept replaying the scene in her head: Father, Mother and Heinrich starting to sing Happy Birthday as Gudrun enters the kitchen. The moment when everything comes to a standstill, three open mouths from which all sound has ceased to issue, three pairs of eyes as wide as saucers, all focused on her. And this feeling! Gudrun lay on her bed and rubbed her sore cheek, lost in thought. *I did that! I changed everything!* She was proud of herself, and her pride helped her forget that her parents had thrown away the hair she had chopped off.

EIGHTY-FOUR

Heinrich sat on his parents' bed, on the window side where his mother slept, holding a book. On the title page was a drawing, two smiling women framed by leaves in autumnal colours. Above, it said "Nicole – a Heart Full of Love". He turned the book over in his hands, he leafed through it, read the odd passage, closed it again and replaced it on his mother's bedside table. A romance. Heinrich examined the books on the white shelf above the bed. Books that his mother had already read. Romances. He smoothed out the duvet again so that nobody would notice anything and quietly left the bedroom. From the kitchen came the sounds his mother made when she was getting lunch ready. He stopped in the middle of the hallway. A pain had started to throb behind his left eye, which grew stronger and made its way across the back of his head to the nape of his neck.

EIGHTY-FIVE

When everybody was out of the house Emma Kruse visited the bathroom. She freshened up, plaited her hair, then went into the bedroom. From the white fitted wardrobe she took a blue frock. She undressed, changed into the frock and inspected herself in the mirror on the back of the wardrobe door. She took a coat from the stand in the hallway and put it on. She buttoned it up, left the house. Going down the steps and out into the street, she turned right. She went to the nearest tram stop and waited. When the tram came she got on and travelled four stops. She got out and walked down the street. She stopped by a front door and rang one of the bells. A crackling was followed by a voice, Who is it? Emma put her mouth up to the intercom and said, Emma Kruse, the door buzzed, Emma pushed it open with her body, she entered the hallway, the door locked behind her, she went up the stairs to the third floor, where the central door of three opened, an elderly lady, a head smaller than Emma, wearing a traditional dress, black, gave her a friendly nod, Emma stepped into the apartment, the woman closed the door behind them, then she went ahead down a narrow hallway, Emma followed her, they entered a room in semi-darkness, even though the sun was shining outside. Drawn curtains, candlelight, the elderly lady sat on a wooden stool, on the table a pack of playing cards, face down, Emma sat opposite her.

"What brings you here today, my dear?" the elderly lady asked.

Emma could not find the words she had worked out in her head, she looked at the pack of cards, in her heart hope and fear blended to form a dilemma.

"I . . . er," she said hesitantly, "I'd really like to know whether . . ." She broke off and shot the woman opposite her a helpless glance, but the woman still looked at her expectantly, Emma's eyes wandered across the small table. She composed herself.

"Whether my husband . . ." She broke off again and looked coyly at the woman. The woman knew this topic from previous sessions, always convoluted, always expressed with a fear of betraying the husband.

"Whether he still loves and desires you?" she said softly.

Emma Kruse nodded shyly, like a little girl. The elderly woman gave her a knowing look, she picked up the cards and began to shuffle them slowly.

"We will ask the cards," she said, "the cards know the truth, the cards bring us clarity, the cards never lie." She fixed Emma with her gaze. She kept shuffling and repeated what she had said once, twice, three times, she droned on, Emma Kruse felt herself growing heavy, heavy and soft and tired and peaceful.

Suddenly a card appeared in front of her, face up, a naked lady on one knee, holding two jugs full of water, one of which she was pouring into a pond, the other onto the earth, above her shone a large yellow star surrounded by seven smaller, white stars, on the right in the background a tree stood on a hill, in it was perched a bird, its wings raised. Emma looked up, the elderly lady glanced at the card, then gave Emma a long, serious stare, before nodding and putting down the next card. The cards had names, The Star, The Sun, The Magician, The Lovers, the elderly lady placed them in rows beside and below each other, and soon all the cards had been laid out and the small table was covered and she bent over the cards and examined them in great detail and Emma waited with a pounding heart.

EIGHTY-SIX

Lisa was expected. When she arrived that evening at Munich central station a slim man in a hat strode purposefully up to her, introduced himself and took her suitcase.

"How did you recognise me?" Lisa asked.

"Intuition," David Schwimmer said, smiling. "You must be tired. Let's go straight home. It's not far, it's a pretty good area to live in, very central, you can get anywhere in town really quickly. My wife's made some supper and then you can go to bed. Tomorrow our daughter will show you around the city. She's almost the same age as you."

Esther Schwimmer was standing at the door to their apartment when her father came up the stairs with Lisa. The girl looked so pretty that Lisa had to force herself not to stare.

"You must be the famous Lisa," she said, offering a warm smile. "We've heard so much about you, we've been dying for you to get here."

"And now she *is* here," a voice in the background said. It was Judith Schwimmer, and immediately Lisa could see where the daughter's beauty came from.

The oak table in the dining room had been laid, and waiting there was a boy who was nine years old at most.

"We had a long gap between Esther and Ben," Judith said, smiling at her son.

"Which she finds embarrassing," Ben said, standing to shake hands with Lisa. Judith gave her son a look that was at once affectionate and disapproving. Ben ignored it.

"Sit down quickly you lot," he said. "I've lasted till now but I can't hold out any longer." Esther laughed at her little brother and sat beside him with exaggerated rapidity.

"This evening we have . . ." Judith began, but Ben and Esther interrupted her, chorusing, "Cholent, ray of life immortal, cholent, daughter of Elysium." They laughed. David Schwimmer smiled. "What Judith was going to say was there's cholent. Do you know cholent?"

"That's cholent," Judith said before Lisa could reply, putting a bowl in front of her that contained a variety of things. All Lisa recognised were the pickled gherkins. Pointing to a small brown mound beside them, Judith said, "That's pearl barley, that's meat and those are potatoes, all a little overcooked. You're supposed to eat this on Shabbat, but we don't get too fussed about details."

Raising his index finger, Ben said affectedly, "Cholent is the kosher ambrosia of the one and only true God!"

"Actually it's not kosher," David said apologetically. "It's only by pure chance that we eat anything kosher here." Lisa made a gesture to indicate that this made no difference to her.

"Or if Grandma brings something," said Judith, who had served everyone and now sat down herself. She smiled at Lisa across the table.

"All of us talk far too much. Don't pay any attention, it's a—"

"A family illness," David said, finishing the sentence.

"An art!" Ben called out. "When I think of the Kruses! Heinrich told me that they barely say a word to each other. Do you remember Heinrich?"

David frowned. "That school friend of yours who came here once?"

"That's him," Ben said.

"Poor boy!" Judith said, looking concerned. "He seemed so sensitive."

"He is," Ben affirmed, "Ridiculously sensitive!" He laughed, Esther laughed too and looked at Lisa inquisitively.

"Tell us about your journey, Lisa! You must be very excited," she said.

"Let her finish eating first," David urged.

With her mouth full, Lisa said, "No, it's fine. I . . ."

"Why didn't you fly from Berlin?" Ben interrupted. Lisa chewed and looked at him, and then Ben said, "Or from Frankfurt?"

"Ben!" Judith said.

Ben looked at her, wide-eyed. "What?"

"Let her answer!"

David said, "There aren't any direct flights from Frankfurt yet. Even though you can fly from Tel Aviv to Frankfurt, you can't do it the other way round. You can only go from Munich Riem airport. No idea why."

Lisa, who was still chewing, nodded at Ben and pointed to David with her knife. Esther laughed at the gesture.

"Politics," Judith said, shrugging her shoulders. "It's practical for us."

"So when are *we* going to fly to Israel?" Esther said.

"I don't want to go there anymore," Ben said, scowling.

"Ben, eat up please!" Judith said.

"Why not?" Lisa asked Ben. The boy looked at her as if he were having to weigh up his words.

"Stupid country," he said.

"Rubbish, Ben," David said. Turning to Lisa, he said, "Sometimes we take a beach holiday there in summer."

"It's too hot!" Ben moaned. Esther stroked her brother's head and said to Lisa, "That, and the fact that Benjamin here is not a great swimmer." She laughed.

"Ha, ha, very funny," Ben said, looking furious and stuffing a gherkin into his mouth.

"My parents live in Tel Aviv," Judith said, "and cities are no places for children."

"No! Tel Aviv is crap!" Ben said loudly, still livid with Esther.

"Young man!" David said.

"Do you really have to tease him about that too?" Judith said to Esther.

"Sorry!" Esther said sniffily.

"Why do you live in Germany?" Lisa said.

Judith and David exchanged glances, then Judith said. "Right after Reichskristallnacht we emigrated with our parents to America. The two of us met in New York. His parents came from Cologne; mine were from here in Munich."

"After the war . . ." David said, "well, I can't remember exactly why . . ."

"I can," Judith said. "We wanted to help with the reconstruction."

"No, that wasn't it, or at least not as far as I was concerned."

"So what was it, Papa?" Esther asked.

"It was simply the fact that I was a German."

"A German?" Lisa asked.

"Yes. The Nazis wanted to stop us from being able to feel German, but it didn't work with me."

"Perhaps because we were lucky that we didn't have to go through it all," Judith said.

"The gassing and everything?" Ben asked.

David nodded reluctantly. "Yes, Ben, the gassing and everything."

Ben grinned, but then turned serious and said to Lisa, "In my class nobody knows I'm Jewish, not even the teacher."

"Nobody knows," Esther said.

"Oh," Lisa said.

David shrugged. "We may be Germans," he said, "but there are still people around today who don't like that fact, and there are enough Nazis who could make life difficult for us."

"I've heard the police is full of them," Esther said.

Judith nodded. "The police, the secret service, the courts, business. The entire country."

"And still you stay here?" Lisa asked. There was a short pause.

"Maybe not for ever," Judith said.

"But where would we go?" Ben asked. "Definitely not to Israel."

Esther laughed, Judith smiled.

"We're Germans," David said, "we can go anywhere."

EIGHTY-SEVEN

The weakness in the body, right in the middle, where something is missing. Anna struggles to sit up. Everyone else has gone outside, the house is empty, she looks around, Look at all the stuff people have acquired in the short time we've been here, portable gramophones in suitcases, chessboards, full-length mirrors, folding coat racks, Where do they get these things from, why do they need them? Boredom, they're all suffering from it, there are those who fight it, who acquire stuff, books for example, there are those who find a little corner in the camp where they can plant flowers or strawberries or anything that grows and changes while they're waiting for something to happen. There are a few who go out of the gate and never return. Where do they go? France? Or do they stay in Germany?

Anna can hear the tannoy, that's why they're all outside, because of the tannoy, and she told them, You go, I'm just going to have a little rest.

What now? Is it curiosity, is it the desire to be there when it happens, *if* it happens? Maybe it's just boredom again. Yes. No. She wants finally to be part of life again, she wants to drag the sorrow of her body into the snow and cool off, she wants to freeze and wait and listen to the voice from the tannoy, she wants to be like all the others.

Anna supports herself on the bunk bed, she can feel the weakness in her arms as if they were empty tubes, despite this she takes her coat from the nail, puts it on, buttons it up, sets off, step by step, slowly, along the central gangway towards the door. She starts to sweat, she stops, catches her breath, continues on her way. The doctors have said she has turned the corner, You need to mix with people again, move back into the corrugated-iron hut. They were Germans, settled in Lübeck, one an expellee fortunate to have a brother in the city. They were friendly to her, said, You were terribly lucky, they asked, Who did that? But a woman from the camp – they were not happy about that, You're not a doctor? they asked Frau Kramer, and their eyes said, How could you do that?

Reaching the door, Anna opens it and an icy wind blusters in, snow swirls around, another winter in Germany, it is cold, the end of November, the voyage by ship, the warmth, the bright sun, the arrival in the heat of Palestine, everything now seems like a fugitive dream, unreal, it never happened. She closes the door behind her, the people are a little further on, lots of them, the entire camp has assembled on the central square by the gate, Anna looks to the left, to the forest, bare trees, silence, but here where there are people, there is talking, a crackling comes from the tannoy, the voice speaks, it is muffled, you have to strain to understand what it is saying, it says, "Afghanistan?"

The voice waits, the people wait, Anna approaches the crowd, someone turns around, it is Sarah, she gives a start and runs over to Anna, behind her Anna can see Shimon looking at his sister uncomprehendingly. Now his eyes find his mother, who has not been on her feet for ages, he nudges the little girl standing next to him, the little girl turns to him then looks over at Anna, she opens her eyes wide and calls her name, a number of heads turn, one of them belongs to Frau Kramer, who comes over at once, Frau Kramer, the woman from the camp who, if the doctors had had it their way, ought never to have been allowed to save Anna.

Only seconds have passed, the voice speaks again, it says but a single word: "No." Nothing more, the people hear it, some react, they talk, a murmur begins that falls silent again at a stroke because now the voice says, "Argentina? Argentina? Abstain."

Ruth and Aaron, Mr and Mrs Abramowicz, Marja and Dana the doll, Ariel and old François, all of them heard. It is not cold, there is no snow on the ground, it is warm, very warm, they are sweating, the people have assembled in the camp, there is no forest around the camp, only rocky land, around the rocky land is sea, the island is called Cyprus, the camp is much bigger, thousands stand together, they are bored too, they too have gramophones, books, chess, they too plant things that will grow and change, they too stand here and wait because the crackling is once more interrupted by the voice that says, "Australia: Yes."

A cheer, short and sparing, for there is more to come, country after country, Yes, No, Abstain, the crackling comes from the tannoy, but it also hangs in the shimmering air, many are standing in the shade, shade is scarce, others have put up umbrellas, but most do not mind, they have been through so much, escaping with their lives by a whisker, that the sun is the least of all dangers. Quite other questions hang in the air, What if the majority say No? Where will we go then? A supreme effort has gone into preventing this, Catholic South America wants an international Jerusalem, not a Jewish one, the city must form a Corpus Separatum, so David Ben-Gurion said, Yes, a whole city in return for your votes, not any old city, the city of cities, the South Americans will abstain or vote Yes, that will balance out the Arabs, who are voting No, and the British, who will abstain because of the Arabs on one side and the Americans on the other. The U.S.A. will vote Yes, no doubt about that, it is a question of votes back home, a No would be dangerous for the president, there are too many Jews in America, luckily the Americans have ensured that it will not be four hundred thousand more, the Americans are in favour of the state of Israel, Mr Abramowicz says, his heart is full of pride about having such a powerful ally, Yes, yes, Aaron replies, one lot because they're Jews and the others because they're not. Aaron is sticking with the Soviet Union, which will not hesitate to say Yes, That's an ally, he does not care that the Soviets might only be doing it to drive the British out of the Middle East finally. Mr Abramowicz brushes aside this sophistry, at this historic moment he has no desire to debate with Aaron, he wants to savour the feeling. The women say nothing. The children say nothing. Since Emil's death Dana the doll has not spoken again, Ariel has not read another book since the voyage, Marja stands there, listening to the adults talk, she feels like a fountain into which stones fall and sink immediately, Ariel listens to nobody, for him only the future exists, only the tannoy, Ariel is an arrow that must fly through fifty eyelets to Eretz Yisrael, What do you mean eyelets, they're axes, No, they're votes: Yes, No and Abstain.

Ruth looks around, Where is François? Standing over there with other old people, she misses him, he has found new companions, We're too young for him. Since Pöppendorf, since the separation from Anna, Shimon, Sarah, no, earlier, since Peretz secretly jumped ship to plan the new escape with Ephraim Frank, Ruth has felt that her community is breaking up, How short this path has been since she became pregnant, she misses Anna's silence at her side even more. She thinks, Where will I go with my child if Israel comes to nothing? She is yet to say anything to anybody, Now I understand you, she says silently to Anna.

At that moment the voice resounds over the tannoy. "Belgium? Yes. El Salvador? Abstain. Ethiopia? Abstain."

"So far everything's going to plan," Gershom Sarfati says, acting calm. The colonel and his wife are sitting side by side on the wide sofa, in armchairs to the left and right their sons are leaning forwards to hear better what the voice is announcing from the large wireless set against the wall opposite, directly below the set of antlers the colonel inherited from his father, who shot the stag in Greece, but maybe he just bought it there, nobody knows for sure, there are too many voices in this large family, Gershom Sarfati sticks to his father's version, The truth, he once told his sons, is manufactured, it doesn't come about by itself. Peretz eyes his father, who looks geriatric beside his wife. I never noticed that before, Peretz thinks, But you couldn't see it before either. Twenty years only take effect over time, now they have reached the point where their joint path forks – one of them heading to death, the other to old age, this is painful, it seems as if the war did this too, even though Peretz just went away and now has come back. He and Anna are closer to one another, We can grow old together, Peretz thinks, but the thought leaves behind a strange feeling, all of a sudden Peretz feels like a naïve little boy who knows nothing of the world, and this time it is not because of Avner, his elder brother, who has come in his Palmach uniform and now sits here behaving as if he has already stepped into his father's shoes, and this feeling is so old that Peretz long ago gave up trying to express it in words. You can't choose your family, is what his mother once told him after a terrible argument with Avner, from which he emerged, as usual, the loser, she was trying to console him but Peretz heard her talking about herself, I didn't choose you, I could have had other sons, sons who get on better, that is how it had sounded, Peretz recalled it now, How long was I away? he asks himself, Almost three years, but nothing has changed.

At that moment the voice over the tannoy announces, "France: Yes."

Sarah has reached Anna, now she beams at her mother and says, "It's so lovely you came out!" She links arms with Anna to give her support, Anna lets it happen, the realisation that she has real maternal feelings towards Sarah surprises her, How did I manage that? she wonders, With persistence, if you have no mother you need to be utterly loyal to acquire one, biological children have to do the opposite, to gain their freedom, but for Sarah attachment is more important, Anna thinks all of this in a single moment, she knows it is true, they have become mother and daughter so that Sarah can begin to seek her freedom, Anna submits to this truth, which just happens to be there, it changes nothing immediately, only in the long term, now Frau Kramer arrives, concern on her face, she wants to talk of the cold but opts to keep quiet, she supports Anna on her other side and together the three women go over to Shimon and Lisa, who are watching them, standing there holding hands, and the other people look so big that tears come to Anna's eyes, she herself does not even know why, it is this image of two children who think they belong together, but the world is so big and wild, and from there, from the midst of the world, the voice now comes over the tannoy, it belongs to a man called Trygve Halvdan Lie, the first secretary general of the United Nations and the only Norwegian Colonel Sarfati has heard of, he cannot pronounce the name properly, but for him that is unimportant, he says, I'm happy we've got him on our side, but secretly he is surprised each time goyim throw their weight behind the Jewish cause, What's in it for them? he wonders, without being able to find an answer.

Fifty-six U.N. diplomats have assembled in Flushing Meadows, New York is cold at this time of year, but in U.N. headquarters nobody notices, Trygve Halvdan Lie has a large, oval face with a massive lower jaw, which gives the impression that he could crunch through bones if he had to, but he restricts himself to calling out each country in turn.

Avner says to his father, You know what it means if the majority say Yes, and the colonel gives the slightest of nods, he does not wish to discuss the matter to avoid unsettling his wife, but Lydia Sarfati has her own channels, she says to Peretz, "I'd like you to stay with me."

Peretz nods, he is the younger, he will stay with his mother, he is not best pleased, but it means he has her all to himself for a while, that has not changed either. His mother smiles at him, she is nervous, from the wireless comes the stoical voice of the secretary general.

Old François says to one of his new acquaintances, a man with thick white hair and an equally white beard, Truth, justice and freedom are the pillars of human society, but can you imagine it will happen like that? The other man thinks for a while, and from the tannoy Trygve Lie says, "I am determined that nobody should be allowed to exert influence over this vote."

François and his companions have not understood what this is about, but it is not particularly important to them, the U.S.A. has voted Yes, there is huge rejoicing, Mr Abramowicz embraces his wife, Mrs Abramowicz laughs so heartily her straw hat almost falls off her head, she is wearing it because of the sun, Marja and Ariel are delighted because their parents are happy, François's acquaintance says, No, in fact I can't imagine it will happen like that. François nods, he looks worried, he longs to be back in France, back on the train when they were all in good spirits, when the sun shone but did not burn, when they passed through an aromatic forest, when they were free for the first time in ages, free from the memory. He turns to his people, they stand there, Aaron has put his arm around Ruth, Mr Abramowicz has lifted Marja onto his shoulders, he radiates confidence, François recalls the scrawny figure carrying his children through the house at Rykestrasse 57. Now he has turned into a large, almost massive man, with a strong neck and a beard like the Chassidim wear. François misses Anna and Shimon and Sarah, he has lost so many people, there were so many he failed to help stay alive. He sighs, They're still on this earth, he thinks, That's good enough.

The vote is coming to an end, someone cries out, Twenty-five Yes votes already and only seven Nos. But now comes the turn of the Arabs. The tannoy announces, "Egypt? No. Iraq? No. Iran? No. Lebanon? No."

*

In cold Germany, where the people are standing in D.P. camps looking up at the tannoys, these are four Nos, then comes another Yes, an Abstain.

In Tel Aviv, at the corner of Boulevard Rothschild-Allenby, where the Sarfatis are sitting at home, there are four enemy neighbours, one hundred kilometres to Rafah on the Egyptian border, one hundred and thirty to Lebanon. Syria votes No, We're encircled, Avner says, the colonel nods.

"That was to be expected. Probems only occur where people seek to expand."

"Are we expanding then?" Peretz asks. The colonel does not look at his younger son, he juts his chin towards the wireless and says, "Well, that's what the Arabs think."

Lydia Sarfati sighs, she is troubled, she says, "There's going to be war." The colonel puts his arm around her, plants a kiss on her cheek, she looks small and slender beside his corpulent body, Like father and daughter, Peretz cannot help thinking. What about Anna and me? No answer comes.

"Soviet Union? Yes."

The vote at the end of the first extraordinary General Assembly of the United Nations on 29 November, 1947, lasted no more than a quarter of an hour. It was 16 Kislev, 5708, that was how long the Jews had been counting their years. The Sarfatis stood up and embraced each other, the colonel sang "The Hope", the national anthem of the future country, Lydia Sarfati fetched champagne from the fridge, they toasted each other, drank a few sips, then Avner and his father went on their way. Outside in Boulevard Rothschild they were met by the joyful delirium of the city, laughing faces, dancing, singing. The colonel was in a hurry, the driver standing beside the dark limousine outside the house greeted him with a smile and a salute, then they embraced briefly, the love of one's homeland can even disrupt military hierarchy for an instant. The colonel and his son got in, and they set off, the car hooting loudly as it nudged its way through the crowds at walking pace, then crossed Allenby and headed south to Levinski, where it took a left turn eastwards.

Anna celebrated by forgetting the sorrow of her body for a while. She celebrated by freezing like everyone else, by singing like everyone else. She tried smiling like everyone else. She leaned on Frau Kramer, Sarah hugged her excitedly, now she had a mother, a father, a brother *and* a homeland, almost as it was before. Shimon trotted over, grabbed her legs and beamed, before running back to Lisa, a few young people started a snowball fight, it had been a long time since there was so much joy in Pöppendorf, in Berlin-Schlachtensee, in the Bavarian camps that were some of the largest in Germany, in the Austrian camps, on the secret routes from Czechoslovakia to Germany, in Szczecin, where even now there were Jews still hoping to make it to the West, although since the division between the victorious powers this had become increasingly difficult.

Nobody was celebrating in the house where Shimon was born, the Sweden Pavilion had been cleared out, one day luxury apartments would be for sale here, and on the estate agent's website people would one day read the history of the house from the Vienna International Exposition of 1873 to the present day, but there would be no reference to its short period as a shelter to homeless Jews, as if this interlude had never occurred.

Nobody was celebrating in Rykestrasse 57, Germans lived there now, refugees from the East. In the synagogue a few houses down, Rabbi Martin Riesenburger *was* celebrating. Celebrating with him was the chairman of the Jewish Community of Berlin, Erich Nehlhans, unaware that in a few months' time he would be taken prisoner by the Russians. The charge? It read:

Anti-Soviet agitation
and supporting the desertion
of Soviet soldiers
of the Jewish faith.
The sentence?
Twenty-
five
years
hard labour.

Erich Nehlhans celebrated, unaware that he would die in Siberia.

The French Jews celebrated, who had decided already when in the Résistance that they would be Jewish-French citizens.

The American Jews, who were always both in equal measure, celebrated, the British Jews, who did not have such an easy time of it, celebrated.

The Jews in Ethiopia celebrated, the Jews in Yemen, in Morocco, in Iran, in Iraq, the entire global diaspora celebrated, maybe even the Jews of the twelve lost tribes in India, who knows?

Ruth and Aaron celebrated with a little dance, Mr Abramowicz lifted his shrieking, laughing wife into the air and exclaimed:

"Praised are you,

Eternal our God,

Sovereign of the Universe,

Who is good and beneficent."

And those standing around, Ruth and Aaron, Mrs Abramowicz in the air, the children, strangers said, Amen! Old François said, Amen, and celebrated with one eye laughing and one eye weeping. The earth was round, it turned impassively, the destiny of the world had neither improved nor deteriorated, Karl Treitz and Margarita Ejzenstain were still dead, Emil would never open his eyes again, Dana was still a doll, Ariel would never read another book, Shimon was not yet talking, Lisa still held his hand in the snow and saw her grandmother and Anna

Sarfati side by side, as if they belonged together in this huge world.

Otto Kruse was still called Otto Deckert. On 29 November, 1947, he smoked makhorka to combat the hunger and the freezing cold of Siberia, wondering whether Anna was still alive and, if so, whether she had gone to Palestine.

In the immediate aftermath of the vote Haganah confronts an Arab militia on the continuation of Levinsky in Hatikva, a district of Tel Aviv. Jaffa, the ancient port virtually surrounded by Jewish Tel Aviv, is home mostly to Arabs. After the vote window panes are smashed, people gather up their possessions and flee the newly created state on donkey carts, on motorbikes, in minibuses.

Some will say later that the Arabs were just frightened.

Others will say that they were driven out.

People die on the day that Israel is reborn. Houses suddenly stand empty, fields are no longer cultivated, shops remain closed.

Nobody knows which laws have come into force. They are followed blindly.

EIGHTY-EIGHT

Gudrun had dyed her hair black. You look like a gypsy, her grand-mother said when she came to visit. The words were not accompanied by a smile. Gudrun just gave a shrug and left the apartment to go and see her best friend. The two women were on their own in the kitchen.

"That one is completely out of control," Emma Kruse's mother said, giving her daughter an angry look.

Emma tried to change the subject. "Otto's finally changed depart-ment," she said. "He's moved to customer care, which is much more suited to him than deputy managing director."

There was no reaction from Emma's mother, unspoken accusations were reflected in her face.

"Would you like another coffee?" Emma asked in an attempt to mollify her mother, who nodded grudgingly. Emma hurried to the cooker and put on some water to boil, she wanted to escape her mother's glare, she made a mental note to ask about Gudrun the next time she visited the fortune teller, Out of control, her mother's words resounded in her head like an echo, they evoked serious danger, great urgency, imminent catastrophe and made her so nervous that she was unable to open up the paper filter for the coffee funnel.

"What does Otto say?" her mother asked sternly to her back.

Emma paused. "Otto?" she said, playing for time.

"He's still called Otto, isn't he?" Her words were infused with poison.

"Yes, of course," Emma said nervously. "Otto isn't exactly thrilled either."

She did not know what else to say, there was no way she could tell the truth, the two of them appeared in her mind, father and daughter, Gudrun was now as tall as Emma, a proper woman if you just glanced at her, and Otto did not set any boundaries, he let her do as she pleased, Emma could not find words for what she saw, she heard phrases from Otto's mouth, It'll be alright, she'll settle down again. What would her mother say if she knew that? Finally the filter opened, she placed it inside the funnel, opened the jar of coffee, four cups, her mother drank a lot of coffee. As she counted the spoonfuls she heard herself speak. "Otto told her in no uncertain terms that this was the very limit and I think she understood."

But rather than swallowing the bait, her mother examined it carefully, she said, "I'm sorry? He *let* her do it? I'd never have believed it." By now she was both furious and disappointed. Emma closed her eyes and put the funnel on top of the pot.

"Young people experiment with all sorts of things these days," she said weakly, but she was interrupted by her mother, who snapped, "They have no upbringing." To Emma's ears it sounded like a death sentence. "No manners at all, where on earth will that lead us?"

Emma opened the cupboard and took out a fresh cup, for her mother disliked drinking her coffee from a used one. The water was taking an age to heat up, she stood there pretending to wait, but in actual fact she was seeking refuge.

"Where's Heinrich?" her mother said.

"In his room," Emma replied quickly. "He must be doing his homework."

Frau Huber got up from her chair without a word and left the kitchen. Emma stayed behind, the water finally came to the boil, she poured it over the coffee and felt both liberated and abandoned.

EIGHTY-NINE

Heinrich almost missed the sentence. He had already started the next one when he paused and went back. Confused, he read the whole paragraph again. It was one of those entries in which Father talked about himself, he wrote about the new department he was working in, he joked about it being called "customer care", he wrote of a "long-haired, scruffy subject I'd loved to have hauled over the coals like I used to those partisans." Whenever a customer came in he and his colleagues would talk of "an 'insurance case' and slap our thighs with laughter."

Heinrich understood little of this, he thought that Father and his colleagues had fun discussing their customers in such a way. Father had described "customer meetings" as a succession of insults, but Heinrich could not imagine it was like that. After threatening "serious consequences, which I found ludicrous after all my experiences on the front line, the subject cracked, revealing to me just what sissies he and his like truly are.

"My colleagues behind the glass partition greeted me with a round of applause that in all honesty I had deserved. And Goldgruber said of me . . ."

Then came the sentence containing a name Heinrich had never heard before. But it was still there after the third reading. Heinrich closed the book, his gaze lost itself in the window pane. In the distance he could see the bare wall of a house, in front of this an empty site, beyond lay back-yards, tall trees, the backs of houses, roofs, the sky was overcast, what did this name mean?

NINETY

Lisa sat high in the sky and looked down. The voice over the public address system said they were just to the south of Cyprus, If you look out of the window to your left you'll have a fine view. Lisa peered out, in the middle of the blue lay the island, an animal hide with a long neck, nestling in the white foam of the sea, traversed by tall mountain ridges, the heart of the island dark green, all still perfectly visible in the late sun.

The aeroplane began its descent, Please fasten your seatbelts. Lisa had imagined flying to be quite different, she had thought it would make you feel free. But she felt anything but free, she was wedged between seats, between people, the window was tiny, Freedom, she thought as the pressure in her ears increased, is not a physical condition. Freedom, she thought as in the far distance she made out a coastline in the evening light, is not a feeling, it must be something else, halfway between body and soul.

Lisa swallowed to relieve the pain in her ears until the woman in the adjacent seat nudged her and held out a tin of sweets, saying, It'll help. Lisa smiled and took one, it did indeed help, she looked out of the window again. They crossed the coastline, a narrow white strip of surf dividing the sea from the land. Beyond stretched an expanse of reddish-brown earth, the first lights had been turned on, Lisa saw tiny houses, lines that must be asphalt, she could not help imagining the people that belonged to all this.

Lower and lower the plane sank, closer and closer came the reddish-brown earth, it disintegrated before Lisa's eyes into forms and colours, cars, city streets, rectangular fields, green groves, lower, but still no people, How small we are, Lisa thought. The landing was imminent, the light vanished rapidly, buildings rose to the left and right, some now reached higher than the plane, and suddenly a wide, grey runway appeared beneath them, they skimmed across it, there was a jolt, a short bump onto the ground, and the flight was over, Lisa was still wedged in, but now she had arrived in Israel. The sun had set. The woman beside her smiled. She was aware that now she was a Jew amongst Jews.

NINETY-ONE

He was dreaming, but the dream was strangely familiar. Someone was wrenching open his eyes, beyond which sat a blonde girl he could see through the narrow gap between his lids. The girl let go of his eyelids and then opened them again. Now she was no longer a girl but a young woman with short hair. She smiled the smile of the past and opened her mouth, but a man's voice came out, saying, Reporting, Sir! I'm back! Then the voice smiled Gudrun's smile. He closed his eyes to see properly this time, and behind his lids was the dream of a dead man whose arm was twitching, the dream was a Jewish woman cleaning in the background, the dream was himself, bending over his daughter and listening to whether any words were issuing from the dead mouth, whether any sounds were coming from the silent throat, something that could negate his own death, but the twitch was just a twitch, the dead man was dead, the Jew was his slave, outside was a country that did not belong to him, and all of a sudden Karl Treitz was standing beside the dead Gudrun, pointing to her and saying, That's me.

NINETY-TWO

Here is the Voice of Israel! It is Shabbat, 15 May, 1948. You will now hear a live broadcast from our studio in Jerusalem, where David Ben-Gurion will address our young nation at this difficult hour.

"Something unique occurred yesterday in Israel,
and only future generations
will be able to evaluate
the full historical significance of
the event.
It is now up to all of us,
acting out of
a sense of
Jewish fraternity,
to devote every ounce of our strength
to building up
and defending
the State of Israel,
which still faces
a titanic
political
and military struggle.

"Now is not the time
for boasting.
Whatever we have achieved
is the result of the efforts of earlier generations
no less than our own.
It is also the result of an unwavering fidelity
to our precious heritage,
the heritage of a small nation
that has suffered much,
but at the same time
has won for itself
a special place in the history of mankind
because of its spirit,
faith and vision.

"At this moment
let us remember
with love and appreciation
the three generations
of pioneers and defenders
who paved the way
for later achievements,
the men who created
Mikve Israel,
Petah Tikva,
Rishon LeZion,
Zikhron Yacov,
and Rosh Pina,
as well as those
who recently established settlements in the Negev Desert
and the Galilee Hills;
the founders of Hashomer

and the Jewish Legion,
as well as the men
who are now locked in fierce battle
from Dan to Beersheba.

"Many of these about whom I have spoken
are no longer amongst the living,
but their memory remains for ever in our heart
and in the heart
of the Jewish people.

"I will mention only one great person of those
who are still among us.
Whether or not he holds an official position,
and whether or not we agree with his ideas,
he remains our leading figure;
there is no other single person
who has contributed so much
to the political and settlement achievements
of the Zionist movement.
I refer, of course,
to Dr Chaim Weizmann.

"The State of Israel was established yesterday
and its Provisional Government
has already turned to the nations of the world,
great and small,
in the East and in the West,
announcing its existence
and its desire to
cooperate
with the United Nations

in the interests of international peace and progress.
We have received unofficial reports
that several countries
have recognised
the State of Israel.
The first official recognition
came
from the government of the United States of America.
We hope
that other nations
in the East and in the West
will soon follow suit.
We are in contact
in this matter
with all members of the United Nations
and with the United Nations itself.

"But we should not deceive ourselves
by thinking
that formal diplomatic recognition
will solve all our problems.
We have
a long thorny path ahead of us.
The day after the State of Israel
was established,
Tel Aviv
was bombed by Egyptian planes.
Our gunners
brought down one of the planes.
Its pilot
was taken prisoner,
and the plane added

to our fledgling Air Force.
We have also received reports
that our country
is being invaded
from the north,
east,
and south
by the armies
of the neighbouring Arab States.
We face a troubled and dangerous time.

"The Provisional Government
has already complained
to the Security Council
about the aggression committed by members
of the United Nations,
and by Britain's ally, Trans-Jordan.
It is inconceivable
that the Security Council
will ignore these wanton acts,
which violate the peace,
international law,
and U.N. decisions.

"But we must never forget
that our security
ultimately depends
on our own might.
It is the responsibility
of each one of us,
and of every municipal body,
to take appropriate defensive measures,

such as

constructing

air raid shelters,

digging

trenches etc.

We must concentrate in particular

on building up a military striking force

capable of repulsing

and destroying

enemy forces

wherever they may be found.

"Finally, we must prepare

to receive our brethren

from the far-flung corners of the Diaspora;

from the camps

of Cyprus,

Germany,

and Austria,

as well as

from all

the other

lands

where the message of liberation has arrived.

We will receive them with open arms

and help them

to strike roots

here in the soil

of the Homeland.

The State of Israel

calls on everyone

to faithfully fulfil his duty

in defence,

construction,

and immigrant absorbtion.

Only in this way

can we prove

ourselves worthy

of the hour."

NINETY-THREE

Frau Kramer stood on the other side of the road and looked at the house. A late nineteenth-century building, two storeys with a raised ground floor, dark-blue tiles to chest height, above these pink plaster, tall box windows. Through the windows she could see heavy chandeliers with electric candles, shadows danced across the walls. The entrance was set deep into the façade, a small flight of steps led up, above this hung a red sign with orange writing:

Hot Martha

Men went in, came out, stood outside, chatted, smoked cigarettes, nobody paid any attention to the old woman standing in a dark entryway diagonally opposite.

A jumble of many voices strayed from the pub. People talking, overlaid with music, popular German songs. Songs Frau Kramer knew from the radio. Here is a man, Beautiful maid. I'm in love with love. Stranger. Oh, when will you come? From time to time a woman's laugh would rise above the hubbub, from time to time one of the men would bellow something.

Frau Kramer gave a start when a well-dressed man of her age came out and sauntered down the street. The idea that a man who could have been Maria's father was one of her customers made Frau Kramer clap her hand over her mouth.

Having stood there indecisively for half an hour, she summoned up courage, crossed the road and entered Hot Martha.

Inside she was met by air thick with smoke, heat, noise, glances. Frau Kramer felt numbed, she regretted having come, she made for a free seat at the long bar, which promised support and protection. Someone jabbed her roughly on the shoulder, she turned, an elderly lady, older than she was, thrust her wrinkled, raddled face right into hers and yelled, "Piss off! This is *my* place!"

Frau Kramer looked at the woman blankly, her face was thickly powdered, her withered mouth painted over the edges of her lips, her hunched body in a pink tulle dress, her thin legs in black fishnet stockings, her feet in high-heeled shoes, she wore a gold chain around her delicate neck.

"Didn't you hear me?" the woman screeched. A slim man in a dark-grey suit appeared from somewhere and shouted. "It's O.K., Rosi, she's with me."

Frau Kramer turned to the man, bewildered. His clean-shaven face looked young, his nose was long and narrow, his mouth wide, a grey hat was perched on his head. Was this Fritz Kleinert? A cigarette bobbed up and down in the corner of his mouth, he gave Rosi a friendly smile. Rosi shot him a sceptical look in return, then shrugged and said, "I don't mind just so long as she doesn't start poaching around here."

"Don't worry, Rosi, she's not on the game."

"I see! Sorry, my lady, you never can tell."

Before Frau Kramer could react, Rosi turned away and returned to her seat, where two young men greeted her with smiles.

"Come with me, Frau Kramer!" the man said loudly.

She woke from her daze and followed him through the crowd. Frau Kramer saw women of Maria's age, young girls barely older than Lisa, she saw a chunky, matronly waitress wandering between the tables, laden with beer glasses, her arms were as thick as a man's. She saw men sitting on their own at the bar, ignoring everybody else.

The man turned left into the back, where the light was dim, tables were set in small niches where people sat, looking like lovers. In the wall to the rear was a small wooden door, he opened it, turned on the light, a bulb dangled from the ceiling, he waited for Frau Kramer to come in, shut the door, the sounds from outside the room became quieter, more muffled. Frau Kramer looked around. A desk with a red telephone, papers, a tall window above, to the right a cheap veneer cupboard, to the left a shabby bookshelf housing files. A wooden chair in front of the desk, a brown-leather high-backed armchair behind it. Dirty white walls, the paint peeling off in places. Finger-width gaps yawned between the worn floorboards.

"Please sit down, Frau Kramer," the man said. He walked around the desk, sat in the armchair opposite her and gave a fleeting smile. "I'm Fritz Kleinert," he said. "I've been waiting a long time for you to come."

Frau Kramer was about to say something in reply, but Fritz Kleinert shook his head gently and said, "You're not here because of Maria, are you? Otherwise you would have come long ago."

Frau Kramer composed herself, she said, "How did you know I was Maria's mother?"

Fritz Kleinert smiled. "Maria looks just like you, Frau Kramer, has that never occurred to you?"

Frau Kramer said nothing. After a pause, Kleinert said, "I don't have much time."

Frau Kramer nodded, she cleared her throat, she hunted for the words she had set aside, she wanted to give an explanation for her visit, but that was irrelevant now.

"How did my husband die?" she asked.

Kleinert looked at her, he looked at the desk, put his cigarette in the ashtray, placed his hands beneath the desk, leaned forward against the desktop. In silence he watched the cigarette smoke rise in a thin column before being blown away at mouth level. Frau Kramer saw tears glistening in his eyes, she thought she must be mistaken.

"Your husband saved my life, Frau Kramer," Kleinert said softly. "He treated me like his son. He . . . he even told me."

"What did he tell you?"

"That I was his son."

He looked at Frau Kramer, in his eyes was a plea, as if he were trying to say, Don't take this away from me. Frau Kramer thought of her husband's letters, she had not read them since that time. Now they were all in her handbag. But she knew she would not take them out, what use would that be? She stared at Fritz Kleinert. He did not look anything like her Karl, and yet she could understand her husband. There was something they had in common. She could see it but was unable to put it into words.

"Tell me more," she said.

Kleinert looked at her hesitantly. He had a vague fear that the old lady could cause him trouble. But he also knew that he had to grant her request. Taking a deep breath, he sank back into his armchair and pondered briefly how to begin.

"When the pencil had worn down," he said, "your husband asked the foremen for a new one. But they didn't give him one. This was around New Year. Afterwards it turned terribly cold, in our rags we almost froze to death. I was very young back then, I really could have been his son."

He paused and looked at Frau Kramer as if gauging the effect of these words, as if wondering, Will she cope with this? He took another deep breath.

"The new foremen were brutal, they looked for people to do away with. We lived in fear." He interrupted himself, made an uncertain gesture, then said at the top of his voice, as if standing in a pulpit, "You can say what you like about the Russians, but they never did things like that. Our own people! It was devastating. Like losing the war all over again!" Pausing again, he gave Frau Kramer a searching look. He blew air through his cheeks like someone lifting a heavy object. He eyed the cigarette thoughtfully, its ash was getting longer and longer, and said, "He wasn't the first to get it. But he was one of the oldest. They made him work longer hours, beat him when he tried to pause for breath, withdrew his rations. All purely arbitrary. The rest of us wanted to complain, but the Russians rarely showed their faces and the foremen knew how to intimidate us." He shook his head, again there were tears in his eyes, but still he tried to assess the effect his words were having on the woman opposite him. Without any success.

"To this very day I don't understand why they treated him like that. He was a good man!" He paused, wiped away the tears, looked at her. "They wanted to kill him," he said. "God knows why. He lost weight, he looked like a Jew in a concentration camp." He fell silent again, his eyes were dry but his lips quivered as if he were struggling to retain his composure. And still his observant eyes scanned the old woman, who could not understand why he was doing this.

"When the new foremen came," he said, "it was too late. He was so emaciated that his body was no longer able to keep food down. They took him to the infirmary. That was the last time I saw him."

He said no more, his gaze turned inwards as if observing Wilhelm Kramer lying on the stretcher again, beneath a large woollen blanket, eyes wide open like someone desperate to stay awake until the end, like someone who refuses to admit defeat even though on the verge of death. When the stretcher bearers lifted him up, Fritz Kleinert's eyes followed them, exactly twenty years ago now, there, behind the thin wisp of smoke, right beside the bookshelf was the cell door through which they carried Wilhelm Kramer. Kleinert knew he would never forget how Kramer turned his head back in his direction, the first stretcher bearer was already out in the corridor, Kramer's feet were already out in the corridor, and of all the men who were standing there in silence, Kramer looked at him and said out loud, as loud as he was able, so loud that everybody could hear, Look after Fritz for me!

We will Willi!

We'll look after him, Kramer!

Don't you worry!

Until you're back, comrade!

Then the second stretcher bearer was outside too, a guard closed the heavy door, Kleinert heard the key turn in the lock. He swallowed, his eyes wandered over to the woman who had come in through the other door. Croakily, he told her, "At some point, around the end of February, we heard that your husband had died."

He fell silent, saw himself working below ground, he felt the heat, the humidity, the room went dark, as dark as in the dim niches of the phoney couples behind the door, he heard the words, who had uttered them first? He could not remember.

"There was no funeral. He just disappeared. Just like that . . ."

Kleinert cried. He cried for Wilhelm Kramer and for himself, for the burden of this and other memories that he could not rid himself of.

Frau Kramer sat opposite him, not knowing what she should be thinking or feeling.

"What about Maria?"

He lifted his head. So she *had* come because of her daughter! Pulling himself together, he wiped away the tears and tried to speak clearly.

"Maria came to me, Frau Kramer. She was afraid."

"Afraid?" Frau Kramer exclaimed in surprise and disbelief. "Afraid of what?"

"She said to me, Give me something I can hold on to."

"But she had me!"

Kleinert paused, then said, "Look, Frau Kramer, I'm no saint, I'm sure you've worked that one out. But I'm not heartless. Before your daughter came to me she'd been in the area for a week. Poaching custom. The girls were mad at her, especially as she wouldn't even take any money. She . . ." He hesitated, scrutinised Frau Kramer, but the old lady looked composed as if trying to say, Go on.

"She was just screwing around, do you understand me? Without rubbers, with blokes I wouldn't even let near my horses. Trying to fuck herself to death or something."

He stopped talking and shrugged, as if by way of an apology for his choice of words.

Frau Kramer stared right through him, Why? Why? Why? Why? She withstood the pain, she was used to this, she felt strong and helpless, at the mercy of the world and imperturbable. It was an intoxication that sharpened her perception, she could hear the noise at her back, she could feel her daughter somewhere above her on the first floor, she understood the man opposite her, she grieved once more and still for Wilhelm Kramer and for her own arduous life, but she stood firm, nothing would knock her down save for death itself.

As if he had heard her thoughts, Kleinert said quietly, "Maybe it's something to do with a past life, who knows?"

"A past life?" Frau Kramer repeated without having understood.

He raised his shoulders and let them fall again, exhausted.

"I don't know, Frau Kramer. These eyes of mine have seen a lot, believe you me, in the war, in prison camp and since I've been back. Don't get the idea that my sort don't ask any questions. Why can't I lead a normal life? Why can't I just be happy? Wife and kids, a home of my own, an honest job, why can't *I* have these things?" As he nodded slowly he fixed his gaze on Frau Kramer. He meant every word he had said.

"You keep searching for a reason. The war, the Nazis, the Russians, hunger, suffering. Parents. But others went through exactly the same or even worse, and when you meet these people you see they haven't landed up in the same place as you. Why?" He was raising his voice as if enraged by an invisible foe.

"I don't know, Frau Kramer! I've no idea! So then you try to work things out and say, It's from a past life. A Chinaman once told me this. You cocked something up, did something dreadful and that's why you find yourself in the mess you're in. But it's just gibberish, Frau Kramer, don't take it seriously. Just gibberish about a failed life!" Throwing his head in his hands he burst into tears and sobbed loudly.

It took Frau Kramer a while to get her head straight. Everything had been said, this visit had changed nothing, she had come to close a gap and now she realised that it was impossible, the gap was not memory but death itself, this was what all the talk had been about, everything ended with death.

She wanted to go home, away from this underworld she had entered, but Fritz Kleinert would not stop wailing.

She slapped the desk with her palm, a loud whacking noise. Kleinert flinched and stared at her.

"I'll be off now, Herr Kleinert," she said. "Thank you for your time. Please look after my daughter as well as you can in this profession."

She paused as if to say something else, but then refrained, Enough is enough, she thought.

She stood and smoothed her skirt, then left the room, the pub, the red-light district of Lübeck. She went back the same way she had come, Maria's route to work, she felt cheerful, she strolled along easily, so different from the walk there when she had scurried from one building to the next like a thief, so her daughter would not see she was being followed.

A past life. The words ran through her head, over and over again, without her wondering why.

NINETY-FOUR

Heinrich lay on his bed. He stared at the ceiling and said, The first of September, 1974. His eyes wandered to the alarm clock, which stood beside him on the bedside table. Time to get up. In a few minutes he would go into the kitchen, where Father and Mother would sing.

Gudrun had failed to come home again, Mother would beam at him, acting as if she had not developed worry lines on account of her daughter, Father would hug him, acting as if he had conceived his boy out of love, Heinrich swallowed but his mouth was dry. He would have loved to leap out of the window to his freedom, he would have loved to disappear for ever from the lives of these people who, for inexplicable reasons, had become his parents. He would have loved to spare himself what he had decided to do. But there was no way out.

He got up, dressed, grabbed the bag he had prepared, left his room, crossed the hallway and entered the kitchen. Sitting there was Mother, beaming at him just as he had expected. Next to her sat Father, serious, stern, dignified, with striking features, a life-long liar, looking at him with that exaggerated attentiveness, which he had long since decrypted as one of the tiny details in this great camouflage suit he wore.

His parents sang Happy Birthday, Heinrich listened to the end, he stared at the marble cake with its eighteen candles, the two wrapped presents, the table set for breakfast, on his boiled egg the blue cosy his mother had knitted. Gudrun's absence was a well-worn question mark, too often and too long, his parents had their suspicions and had no deisre to know, only Heinrich knew for sure, I'm the secret service in this family, he thought, feeling a great surge of contempt.

The song was over, Mother looked at him expectantly, Father looked at the cake with his eyebrows raised, Heinrich sighed, bent over, took a deep breath and blew out the candles, MotherMama clapped as if he were still nine years old, she too worked permanently on her camouflage, but it was a camouflage against herself, Heinrich swayed between fury and pity as he looked at her. Father said, Come on, open your presents, but Heinrich sat up straight again, he swallowed, he cleared his throat, his voice quivered as he spoke.

"I've got presents for you too." He paused, he watched the anticipation on his mother's face turn to confusion, saw his father trying to read his expression. Heinrich composed himself, he put his hand in the bag, took out a package wrapped in red paper, gave it to his father. Then he put his hand back in the bag, another package, the same wrapping paper, but smaller. He gave it to his mother.

His father hesitated, raised his eyebrows at his son, tore open the paper slowly, his mother did the same. Heinrich turned and left the kitchen. He went to his bedroom, fetched his case, his bag, cast a final glance at his room, then closed the door and went back into the kitchen. He stood in the doorway. Father was holding his diary, Mother her tarot cards, two people who knew nothing about each other, Heinrich could have howled if his gaze had not met his father's. He turned around and left the apartment.

NINETY-FIVE

The second coming. 15 May, 1948. Peretz on the quayside. Sarah was the first to see him, she shouted, There he is, there he is, there he is! She stretched her slender arm over the railing, her index finger picked out a tiny figure in the waiting crowd, she hopped up and down with excitement and now Anna saw him too. Shimon did not see him, Peretz was too far away, the circle of his face too small, too many strangers were down there, Peretz merely one of them.

The ship hove to, pitching awkwardly like a stranded whale. Anna did not know what she should be feeling, she was afraid of seeing Peretz again, afraid of the reality of war. She saw military everywhere around the port, she knew the uniforms, she remembered Emil, If only he could see this, she thought, Jews fighting for their rights, and for a moment she was deeply moved. But the soldiers, the armoured vehicles, the artillery positions in place to defend the port of Tel Aviv stirred other memories in her and soon she felt fear again.

The ship came alongside the quay, slowing all the time, until finally the fenders hanging there on ropes were squeezed against the harbour wall. Men leaped off the ship carrying thick ropes that they immediately secured to iron bollards. Then the gangway was lowered, it was narrow and steep, the last stretch of the path separating the passengers from Israel.

The second coming. 6 Iyar, 5708. Shabbat. Peretz stood on the quayside, looking up at the ship, he saw two slim masts, he saw the crowd of people on board, he knew it was no more than two hundred and fifty, he thought of the *President Warfield* with her many thousand pioneers, compared to which the *Orchidea* looked like a fishing boat. He sighed, that was the past, the present was more modest, but the ship had arrived, there were no more British out there on the high seas, they were busy with their withdrawal but had commandeered Haifa in return. The old enemy was leaving, the new one was in the country already.

Peretz watched the gangway being lowered, the ship's first physical contact with Israel. The sun shone because it almost always did, it was in the west and blinded him, the people on board amassed beside the railing, Peretz's eyes scanned the crowd, but he could not see Anna, Anna, who would immigrate without his daughter because she lay in a grave in Germany, perhaps he would never see it.

Peretz banished the thought, the first few people descended the gangway, watching their step, the way down to Israel was steep, these were no pioneers, it was a legal arrival in this country that was but a day old, a new-born baby, and already all the neighbours had risen up to kill it, to cast them all into the sea from which they had come, to destroy this new homeland at once, Will we have to fight for ever to survive?

Peretz banished the thought, the people disembarking looked exhausted and happy, there was movement amongst those waiting, all of them surged towards the arrivals, people flung their arms around each other's necks, some cried for joy, some wept, some were silent or calm. Peretz's eyes searched but could not find. What if they had not gone aboard, what if the information had been false, if they had decided otherwise?

Peretz banished the thought. More and more people came ashore, they carried cases and bags, small children and babies, people Peretz did not know, but Jews, new citizens for Israel, there was nothing more important than this, Keep hold of this, Peretz thought, Everything else is secondary. He almost smiled, had he ever managed to feel this rather than just think it? Where did the conflict come from? he had given everything for the Zionist cause, he had fought, he had killed, he had smuggled Jews halfway across Europe to bring them to this land. And yet it had given him no sense of fulfilment. He thought of the German soldier he had killed for the loudhailer, he remembered exactly which day it had been.

He banished the thought.

He saw a woman coming down the gangway. She looked older than he remembered, older and more frail, she held the railing on both sides, she moved uncertainly, an image flashed in his mind, Anna, coming towards him out of the forest, he holding the loudhailer, how much time had passed since then? Three years, three eternally long years. He saw Sarah following her, holding hands with Shimon, Shimon with clumsy steps, his eyes fixed on the steep surface below, he had grown. My son, Peretz thought bitterly. He banished the thought, he thrust out his chest and pushed his way forward through the crowd.

NINETY-SIX

It said "Kramer" in the dark-green passport that Lisa offered the Israeli border official. The woman was strikingly young, barely older than herself. She was wearing a green army uniform, a rolled-up beret lay beside her on the desk. Long brown hair fell over her shoulders, Lisa felt as if she were standing next to a girl guide.

The woman leafed through Lisa's passport which was so new and unused that it kept shutting again.

"It says 'Jewish' here," she suddenly said in English.

Lisa nodded. She was proud that she had managed to achieve that at least.

But then she saw the disbelief on the Israeli woman's face.

"Are they still doing that?" the woman said, now looking angry.

Lisa was puzzled, she said, "I asked them to."

"*You* did?" the woman said, confused.

Lisa nodded.

The woman looked from the passport to Lisa, from Lisa to the passport. Then she shrugged. "What is your reason for coming to Israel?"

"I might stay here."

Now the woman smiled at her openly. "You're going to love Israel!" she said.

NINETY-SEVEN

The embrace. The kiss. Shimon, who does not want his father to lift him up. Sarah, who clings on to Peretz. All around them the city, the sea, and somewhere further in the distance, where they cannot see: war. If we're unlucky, Peretz said, they'll divide the south from the centre. In the north too, Peretz said, enemy troops were everywhere. I've got to go away today, Peretz said, Back to my unit. I'll bring you to my parents, Peretz said.

Anna let everything happen. She embraced when it was time to embrace, she kissed when it was time to kiss, but her head, just her head, remained a high-security wing which nobody had permission to enter, which she never left. She smiled, she said, We've finally arrived, she thought of her mother's poem, it was far away, far from love a star shone in the sky, it was the nameless sun releasing its light onto everything, allowing nothing to remain hidden, not the tiniest crease on a face and in the mountains, nor the faintest regret in a heart and at the front.

Shimon! Come here and say hello to your father!

Leave him, he'll get used to me again in good time.

Peretz smiled, he held fast onto Sarah's categorical decision, which was written on her face like an exclamation mark, You are my father, she is my mother, I belong to you both!

Peretz had never thought that one day this would comfort him, he never thought that Sarah's naïve obstinacy would be fruitful. And now she leaped in to replace the dead child that lay between Anna and him like a wall of guilt and accusation, Why didn't you take better care? Why do you only give me another man's son? Why did it have to turn out this way?

NINETY-EIGHT

They drove through the city. Military everywhere, the people in uproar, in fear, in uniform, in arms. Vehicles, infantry, some signs on the vehicles had been painted over in makeshift fashion, Anna got the impression that the weapons too had made their way to Palestine via secret routes, as if they too had a life of their own, as if they too were homeless and forever in search of a place where they could be themselves, deadly, bringing death, the antithesis to life, its dark shadow, as if people were only complete with their own negation.

"Look," Peretz cried as they drove through the city in his open jeep. "Look! The Jews are arming themselves for their battle for survival!"

This filled him with pride, but a few seconds later his face was filled with worry. They did not have enough people and too few weapons.

"It may well be our final battle," he said softly. Then all of them would be homeless again, and perhaps the Jewish people would be exterminated after all. He fell silent, now was not the time for faintheartedness and fear. Now was the time to give it one's all, even one's own life.

Anna watched the city go past from the passenger seat with Shimon on her lap. My new home town, she thought, everything turned on its head, she thought, what is foreign is now mine, while what is mine is lost.

Dusty streets, Bauhaus architecture, art nouveau villas, concrete boxes with small windows, magnificent chalets as in central Europe, proud synagogues, orthodox Jews acting as if there had been no mobilisation. Little green, a lot of beige and brown, a lot of white and grey. A large vault of blue over everything. Is this country so beautiful that people have to fight over it? Anna sighed, perhaps I have to keep looking until I have all the forms and colours imprinted on my mind. Maybe it's a question of will, maybe it needs to be contradictory to unleash all energies. And the war? Nobody knew what was going to happen.

The jeep bumped up and down over the uneven road surface, doubledecker buses came towards them, motorcycles, donkey carts, armoured vehicles. Anna saw signs in Hebrew she could not read, she saw people with exotic faces and Israeli uniforms, she saw children playing football in the street, she smelled aniseed, dust, diesel, sewage. The streets were littered with the detritus from the independence celebrations of the previous day, blue-and-white garlands festooning the fronts of buildings, small flags bearing the colours of the new state, fallen to the ground, Anna had still been on the ship and the captain had put the radio through the tannoy system, they had heard the voice of a man, The State of Israel will be open for Jewish immigration and for the

Ingathering of the Exiles; it will foster the development of the country for the benefit of all its inhabitants; it will be based on freedom, justice and peace as envisaged by the prophets of Israel; it will ensure complete equality of social and political rights to all its inhabitants irrespective of religion, race or sex; it will guarantee freedom of religion, conscience, language, education and culture; it will safeguard the Holy Places of all religions; and it will be faithful to the principles of the Charter of the United Nations.

They turned into a street which looked different from the others. Black façades, windows without glass, a burned-out double-decker bus in the middle of the street, it reeked of rust and charred rubber. Soldiers with wheelbarrows, pickaxes and shovels were busy clearing away the debris.

Peretz steered the jeep slowly around the bus. Close up it looked like a large dead animal.

"That was the Egyptian air force," Peretz said. "Yesterday," he added. He pointed to a man in an officer's uniform, who was standing behind the bus surrounded by soldiers.

"Wait here a moment!" he said to the women. He stopped the car, leaped out and went over to the men.

Shimon wanted to get down from his mother's lap, she held him tight, he said, "Want to get out!" In shock at the fact that he had spoken, Anna let him go. Before she knew what was happening he had climbed out of the car.

"I'll go," Sarah said. She jumped down from the jeep and followed him. Anna watched them.

Shimon went over to the bus. He stood beside the vehicle and gave it a thorough inspection. Above the driver's cab was a white sign whose red letters were still visible, on the left it read EGGED, then a 13 and then three Hebrew characters.

"Horrible, isn't it?" Sarah said to Shimon, who glanced up at her, turned back to the bus, stared at the burned-out seats, the broken windows, the scorched paint that lent the bus a rather sombre air, the steering wheel warped by the heat. Shimon shook his head.

"Just broken," he said in his child's voice, before looking Sarah in the eye again, and she had the uneasy feeling that he meant it.

"Hey, you two! Get away! No children here!" They turned around. The voice belonged to the officer who, along with Peretz and the soldiers, was looking in their direction and gesturing with his hands that they should move well away from the bus.

"Do they belong to you, Peretz? Just make sure they don't get up to any mischief." Peretz left the group and came over to them. He was furious.

"I told you to stay in the car!" he yelled at Sarah.

The girl gave a terrified smile. "Shimon said something."

Peretz did not react.

"Take him and get back in the car!" He went back to the men.

They drove on. Anna stroked Shimon's head. Shimon gazed out at the city. He did not say anything, but now Anna knew that he was keeping quiet.

NINETY-NINE

Heinrich got to know Lena at Ronnie's. Ronnie's real name was Ronald, but he played banjo in a Hillbilly band. Lena's real name was Lena, and yet she came across to Heinrich as so unreal and ethereal that he could not take his eyes off her the whole evening, and got drunk for the first time in his life. He had no idea what he was drinking, it was a transparent liquid that looked like water and tasted like bitter medicine. The bottle he had taken from the cabinet and not let go of since was now two-thirds empty.

"That's white rum!" someone shouted in Heinrich's ear over the din of the music. Nothing could shock Heinrich anymore, he just looked around in the dim light of the large hallway, which was so jammed with dancing people that from where he was sitting he could make out nothing but feet and legs.

With an effort he turned his head to the left and came across Lena's face, up close to his glassy eyes. He grinned stupidly and said, "Too good to be true."

Lena frowned. "The rum?"

Heinrich was still grinning, but he shook his head and cried, "You!"

Lena got to her feet and looked down at Heinrich. Then she waved a friend over and together they managed to move him to a quiet room.

That night Heinrich vomited countless times, even when all that remained in his stomach was bile. Lena and her friend cleaned him, the sofa he was lying on and the carpet beside it, they emptied the bucket, washed the cloths, brought fresh water and listened to Heinrich, whose torrent of words was interrupted only by his retching.

The following day Heinrich awoke in a bed. He turned over. Lena was sleeping next to him. To his surprise he realised he was completely naked. Outside the sun was high in the sky, a fresh breeze wafted in through the open window. Heinrich felt good.

Lena woke up. She turned and gave him a dozy smile.

"Well, you fake Kruse, you kept us on our toes last night!"

"I can't remember a thing."

"Nothing at all?"

"No."

Lena looked at him doubtfully, then shook her head. "Nutcase." It sounded both reproachful and gentle, which confused Heinrich.

All of a sudden he remembered what Lena had called him.

"Did I talk?"

Lena nodded.

"What did I say?"

Lena shook her head. Before Heinrich could say anything else she gave him a kiss.

ONE HUNDRED

Gudrun dreamed that she was not dreaming, but maybe she had been having a non-dream about dreaming ever since she inhaled the smoke from the water pipe. Perhaps she was lying down, she was not sure, she tried to remember what she had been doing before she stopped knowing whether she was lying down or not. She looked down a long corridor that narrowed the further it went, and right at the end was a tiny square opening, it was like looking the wrong way through a telescope, beyond the end of which was what she had done before she stopped knowing whether she was lying down or not. Screwing up her eyes, she tried to fathom in greater detail what was happening over there. Aha, she said quietly when she realised that over there asphalt was sliding beneath her shoes. Right, she mused, either I walked or ran. If she managed to get to the end of the corridor she might see more. But as she had no clue whether she was lying down or not, she could make no decision about whether to get up or not, in order to try to get to the end of the corridor. It was tricky. Gudrun attempted to close her eyes, but as she did not know whether she was dreaming and *had* closed her eyes, or awake and looking, she could not decide whether to open or close her eyes. A movement in the distance diverted her attention. A face had emerged, Gudrun could see bad teeth, a scruffy beard, she saw a cigarette wandering up to the mouth and away from it again. The face seemed familiar and it almost looked as if the mouth was moving to speak. But how was someone going to speak to her if it was unclear whether she was awake or not? The movements must have another meaning, perhaps Bernd was eating something. Oh yes, Gudrun muttered when she heard the name. Who had uttered it? Gudrun debated turning around and looking behind her to see whether someone was standing there talking. But it was not clear that behind her existed at all. Why would she want to turn around? It would be like wanting to crochet a blanket out of time, she mused. Absurd. Suddenly she felt her body carrying out a movement, or was it the earth that had turned? She was just about to start contemplating it again when a new face popped up, this time very close. She smiled when she recognised her brother, What a strange dream, she mumbled, for she had never dreamed of him before or had a non-dream in which he featured. But now he was here and his face was so close to hers that she was surprised by all the details. The long hair, for example, she muttered, He never had long hair. She grinned because she suddenly felt like her mother and even sensed her mother's words in her mouth like mutterings her tongue was playing with, Heinrich, what *do* you look like? Things moved around Heinrich's head and even she herself seemed to be moving, but his face always remained in the same place, always right in front of her, and Heinrich's mouth moved as continually as Bernd's had just done. What's going on? Gudrum mumbled, without being able to find an answer, but suddenly Heinrich's face vanished and she was staring at a house, where on earth had this house come from? it looked so familiar to her, as if she had gone through that door once before. The houses began to move, they flashed past Gudrun's eyes, nothing but houses inside which she may have been, or maybe not. Gudrun had the feeling that her head was being held tight, if she could have turned it she would have checked to see whether it was her hands holding it. Where are my hands? she muttered, but her hands were silent, her feet were silent, her entire body was silent, and this could only mean that Gudrun's body did not exist, there was just Gudrun and these house fronts and the pane of glass between them. Gudrun became sad, for she realised that if this were the case then her life would be very lonely. At least I've got eyes, she thought, that I can see with, and thought that maybe nothing existed except for faces and house fronts and the car in which she was driving through the city with Heinrich beside her and someone at the wheel in front. Gudrun raised a hand, to indicate her surprise, but then her mouth moved and said, Where are you taking me? Heinrich said, You can stay with us to begin with and then we'll see, O.K.? She was about to consider this, but her mouth was already saying, Who's the woman driving? That's Lena, Heinrich said, You'll like her. Gudrun grimaced, What a prophecy, she thought, Lena doesn't even have a face, just the back of a head with long hair and slim arms holding on to a steering wheel. But then the back of · the head turned around, revealing a face, Gudrun tore her mouth open wide in astonishment and looked behind too, where there was another world.

"Tomorrow I'm going to crochet a blanket from time," she told Heinrich. But she no longer believed her words, for the universe had put itself together again before her eyes, without hope and without illusion. Turning her head to the house fronts on the other side of the window, she muttered, "My non-dream is over."

ONE HUNDRED AND ONE

Tel Aviv, 26 May, 1966

Dear Grandma

It's been a week now since I arrived. It's unseasonably cold; Nili Burg, who I'm staying with, even had to borrow a jumper from me. She's very nice but quite old, definitely over eighty. She still does everything herself though: shopping, washing, cooking, mending her clothes. And her eyes are bright, they shine when she looks at me. Nili is a Yekke, which is what they call German

Jews here. So I'm a Yekke too, not merely a Jew amongst Jews. She told me a joke: what's the difference between a Yekke and a virgin? Answer: a Yekke will always be a Yekke. Not particularly flattering, is it? But Nili thinks it's funny. She says it's all very inconsequential compared to what Israel means. Even now, so many years after the state was founded, her eyes twinkle when she talks about it. Everybody pulled together, worked together, shared everything. It sounds so wonderful that I wish I'd been a part of it.

I've spent the last few days wandering though Tel Aviv. The city's name means "spring hill", isn't that beautiful? I love Tel Aviv, I like the bright colours and the houses. But the people most of all! They're not quiet and inhibited like at home; they talk loudly and wave their arms around, not in the least concerned if other people can hear them – quite the opposite, in fact. The moment you stop anywhere they'll immediately look at you and you'll be in the middle of a conversation! Hebrew is such a beautiful language to listen to; it's a shame I can't understand it.

This morning I took the first step towards accomplishing my mission. With Nili's help I went through the Tel Aviv telephone book. But either they don't live in the city or it's like at home and they're ex-directory. Nili told me there's a national archive in Jerusalem with personal data going back to Ottoman times and the British mandate. It's got all the data relating to immigrants since the foundation of Israel. Unless something surprising happens I expect I'll have to go there. But I want to visit Jerusalem anyway.

Dear Grandma, I hope you're well and don't feel too lonely. Sometimes I worry about that. I hope you understand how important this trip is for me. I feel as if my whole life has been a preparation for it.

You'll always be in the very core of my heart, in the same place as my parents.

Love, Lisa

ONE HUNDRED AND TWO

Peretz only understood when his mother opened the door, only when he started speaking and pointing with his hands, My mother, My wife, only when he hesitated, barely noticeable to the uninitiated, before adding, My son.

Lydia Sarfati stood there, smiling, gazing at the faces of the strangers, she came down the three steps and embraced her daughter-in-law. She had decided to smile, no matter what impression the wife of her youngest son made on her, A good start is everything, as her father always used to say, and this was one such moment, which is why she was only vaguely aware of who she was embracing, it could have just as easily been Avner's wife, Lana, and she had ever so slightly made use of this thought to help her through the encounter. But when she hugged Anna Sarfati's skinny body, a body offering barely any resistance and which seemed barely physical, Lydia Sarfati got a shock, for it felt as if she had just put her arms around nothing at all. She let the moment pass and turned to the girl. Poor child, she thought, she knew all about Sarah's history and made sure she treated her exactly the same, for it was part of her plan to do right by Sarah.

But then she squatted next to Shimon and beamed at him and said something in Hebrew that Shimon did not understand. She laughed at his bemusement, took his head in her hands, planted a firm kiss on both cheeks and then hugged him so hard that his feet lost their grip.

Looking down at his mother, Lydia Sarfati's son felt sympathy and regret, which stabbed into his chest like a physical pain.

Lydia let go of Shimon, she stood up, Come in, she told them, motioning with her hand, she was still smiling the good start, and Anna followed her mother-in-law into the house, taking Shimon and Sarah by the hand.

ONE HUNDRED AND THREE

Lisa travelled through this foreign country, she saw the barren landscape, the small train stations, the villages. The harsh light of the Mediterranean fell on everything, casting sharp contrasts. Lisa felt lost, she was home-sick, she thought of her grandmother, Tobias Weiss, David, who she might be in love with. She hoped the Israeli national archive would be of help. After Ramla, the train turned to the east, the countryside became mountainous, the train followed the winding course of a river, open woodland looking like thinning hair grew on the mountainsides, the air changed, it became fresher, the train slowly began its ascent.

Lisa knew she was heading towards the narrow end of a corridor, that the train was travelling to Jerusalem between two dotted lines which a war had drawn through Judea, the lines meeting at almost exactly the point where Lisa was going to get off, at the old Ottoman station. Lisa knew that this line made Jerusalem a divided city. And now it came into view, a sand-coloured collection of houses and hills, from a distance it was almost impossible to see where underground Jerusalem finished and the houses began. Lisa did not understand the city when she looked at it for the first time, but Oz Almog was already waiting in the small Ottoman station. He had driven to Khan from the south in his saffron-yellow humpback Saab. Oz Almog was a handsome man with bushy eyebrows, beneath which alert eyes peered out at the world. He would explain to Lisa why Jerusalem and not Berlin was the fiercely contested navel of the world, forget the superpowers. He would drive her to the top of a hill in the south and show her Jordanian-occupied East Jerusalem, he would stretch out his arm, point here and there, name the four great districts of the old town, he would recount anecdotes such as the one about the German Kaiser Wilhelm, who came to Jerusalem in 1898 to consecrate a church, he would say, The Kaiser wanted to drive into the old town and so the Ottoman authorities blasted a hole in the ancient city walls, and Oz Almog would smile as if he knew that All things must pass apart from human stupidity. This hole still exists, he would say, and talk of the British General Allenby, When he captured Jerusalem from the Ottomans in the First World War he arrived at the same part of the wall through which the Kaiser had driven in his car. But Allenby got out and entered Jerusalem on foot. And then he would smile at Lisa and say, That's Jerusalem: a stage for things that play a role in a totally different part of the world. He would talk about the many Christian churches battling for a place on Calvary, often by highly dubious means, he would talk about the valley between East and West Jerusalem, which once was considered to be the gateway to the underworld, and about the city's name, whose pagan origins he would relish revealing, and he would repeatedly give a mischievous smile, voicing his opinion noisily like someone who knows that nobody shares it, Because, he would tell Lisa more than once, the people here don't want to hear that Jerusalem is just a city and that you can give up a city. Instead they prefer to wage war for a heap of stones. And then he would pause and look at Lisa as if wondering, Can I share these thoughts with her? He would apologise and say, Let me tell you something: Jerusalem is the Golden Calf. Lisa would soak up his words, his gestures, his movements and his many faces, all connected by the same friendliness, and wish she could have had a father like that.

Now the train pulled into the station. The journey to Jerusalem was at an end, Lisa stood up, took her luggage, alighted and met Oz Almog's sharp eye on the platform.

ONE HUNDRED AND FOUR

Her eyes could see the road beyond the window, one storey lower people going about their business, all concealed in similar bodies with similar movements, similar faces with similar expressions, similar clothing. Her ears could hear the sounds of everyday life. Her lungs breathed in and out, in and out. Her heart ached in a similar way to all hearts, she knew this, she had discovered it in her numerous sessions with those who were cast out, those who loitered, those waiting in vain for any opportunity, always meeting them in the same places, always engaging in conversations that took a similar course, clichés of everyday life, intolerably conventional, as if they were old Frau Huber outside her optician's and old Herr Sedlmaier from the greengrocer's next door, as if they had failed to pull out all the stops to do something radically different. They had failed, and when Gudrun, in the middle of a deep chasm between a couple of sober hours, was assailed by this realisation like a downpour of excrement and she felt putridly normal, putridly and nauseatingly conventional in her self-destruction, it dawned on her, That's what all of us do. That and nothing else! This self-delusion, this padding of thought processes with nothing but soft feelings, soft convictions, soft certainties, soft habits, everything soft. And yet they had believed themselves to be much tougher than anyone else, had slapped their chests proudly when the intoxication of sheer madness flaunted itself as in a peep show, a controlled loss of control! Letting the world go off the rails under laboratory conditions! Gaining power over impotence! We'll drive out the bad with something worse! No! With that something worse we'll find out what the bad really consists of and by that alone is it exorcised! We'll destroy it and find a true feeling within! Intoxication as a medicine for the soul!

Everything was fake.

Even her most deadly convictions, her coldest shoulders, her greatest sorrow, her extreme anger were nothing but padding for her head. It had been her belief that if you destroyed, if you tipped poison into the water, drank it and watched the body perish, then something unknown would happen, something surprising. How naïve! How absurd! How all too human! How understandable! How desperate! How watchfully blind! Gudrun had lain in the sitting room of her dealer, Bernd, unable to move, incessantly thinking, Thanks! How terrible, but thanks! She did not know who she was thanking, she was just very happy finally to have found out that this path was a hoax she had played on herself.

But this did not stop the path from moving beneath her feet. She had waited too long, the realisation had come too late, her head was already stuffed with soft things, there was barely space for the truth to slip in, she remained stuck in the middle of pleasantly lethal rituals, the Huber routines and certainties, and fell asleep, still unable to get a foothold, so it was little short a miracle that her brother turned up out of the blue and took her away.

In the end he *was* good for something, Gudrun thought as her eyes continued to follow the activity in the street. She breathed in and out. In and out.

In

and

out.

She focused on the pause, the moment of tranquillity that existed when the air had been expelled from her body and before it was inhaled again. She found it difficult to stay there, her body wanted air, her soul took flight, What is there? she wondered.

Suddenly she knew and at that instant Heinrich entered the room. She peered at him. He looked as if he had been turned inside out. How fruitlessly he tried stretching himself away from the dead centre instead of realising that this is where he needed to return! How neatly he folded his worries between his eyebrows! She could practically see the headache that must have afflicted him from the back of the neck upwards ever since he had taken on the burden of his sister. Gudrun interrupted every attempt Heinrich made to begin the conversation.

"I won't stay long," she said. "I just need to make a few phone calls, then you'll be rid of me." Heinrich stared at his sister, he knew her manner of presenting faits accomplis and she caught him on the wrong foot each time.

Gudrun interpreted his silence as an inability to say, That's exactly what I was going to talk to you about, she wanted to get away fast, pack her things and clear off, she thought, There's still that woman, she thought, I'm not going back to my folk, he can forget that, she thought, Why did he bother bringing me here if I'm such a nuisance?

"Please stay," Heinrich said.

"Please stay?"

"Yes."

"What about your girlfriend?"

"Don't worry about her."

"I'm not worried."

"O.K. She said it's O.K."

"Why should I stay, are you going to look after me?"

"No, I'm just giving you the option."

"What would I do here? I'd just get in the way." She pointed at the mattress.

"That's no bother."

They fell silent, Gudrun breathed in and out, she felt her own lack of self, she could think of no other way to describe it, selflessness would have sounded too positive, she would have loved to talk to him differently, but their conversation ran through the room as if on Huber rails, she was laced in a corset of fear, Heinrich wore something similar, she thought, The little brother and sister, both magicked into animals, you into a deer, me into a cow, she thought, We've nothing to say to each other, we never did have.

"I've got something to tell you," Heinrich said. Here it comes, she thought, here comes the next platitude. Almost uncertainly, almost timidly, Heinrich said, "I found out that Father's a Nazi. He did terrible things in the war. His real name is Josef Ranzner." He did not say, I've been reading his secret diary for years, I've always kept my eye on Dad because I never knew how I could make sure that he really looked at me. He would have loved to say this, but he tried to keep it brief to prevent Gudrun from losing patience and stopping listening or interrupting him, he dreaded those moments.

Gudrun stared at her brother in astonishment, his words stood in the room like surreal sculptures, completely logical, completely out of place, completely as if in the middle of a conversation somebody had said, And now the weather.

All of a sudden she burst out laughing without knowing why, she could not make head or tail of it, the whole situation, this room, she and Heinrich, and now the old man, her laughter grew louder, she noticed the dumbfounded expression on Heinrich's face, which looked so similar to Heinrich's dumbfounded expressions from before, and laughed and kept laughing until her belly ached.

A door opened behind Heinrich, the woman driving the car appeared in the crack, Gudrun's eyes took this in, but she could not concentrate on it, she was busy with the joylessness of her laughter, she heard her laughter turn into a strange barking, into a coughing, it became voiceless, just a hyperventilation, a muscular reflex which refused to stop, like hiccoughs. Her face was wet from all the laughter, she shed tears without joy and without sorrow, peculiar tears as if there were a third sort of crying.

ONE HUNDRED AND FIVE

Lydia Sarfati sat in the kitchen, missing her two domestics. Outside the sun was shining, it was late morning, she was alone.

Lydia realised that they could not have stayed, We're at war now, Latifa, the younger one, had said, Nobody would understand if we kept on working for you. Lydia had given her and her cousin, Sana, money to leave the country and still she felt guilty. She hoped that they would make it to Transjordan. There to give birth to sons who will fight against us. Those were Gershom's words when she asked him for money for the cousins, when he gave her the money nonetheless, as if he were conscious of the guilt too, ugly words she had tried hard not to hear, but not hard enough.

She missed her men, I might not be coming back, Gershom had said to her softly before he left. Avner had already arrived at the Syrian border. And Peretz, where was Peretz? She had no idea.

Five days of war. I ought to listen to the radio. But she did not want to know anything, she desired her peace, she already had her hands full with the new Sarfatis now laying siege to her house.

There was a knock at the door. Lydia got to her feet, I must have the key copied, she thought as she went to the front door. Outside were Anna, Sarah and Shimon, looking at her. For a moment Lydia had the impression that these people before her were strangers, even the boy seemed unfamiliar. She dismissed this vision and smiled. She would have loved to say, Come in, we've a huge amount of work to do, but all she could do was motion them in with her hand, We don't even speak the same language. She sighed. Beginnings are always hard.

ONE HUNDRED AND SIX

Peretz lay on his back, staring up at the night sky. He had never seen so many stars. Maybe I'm just imagining it, he thought. He felt the uneven, rocky ground, jabbing into him uncomfortably in several places. The Czech rifle across his chest. He could sense the breathing of the other men lying beside him and at his feet. The night was virtually silent, how could this be possible with so many people lying together in such a small space? here the soldiers of the Israeli army, down there, barely fifty metres away, the Egyptians, north of them, to the left, the inhabitants of Yad Mordechai in their houses, behind their barricades and defensive walls. So many people, none of them asleep, surely their breathing must create a wind that would rustle the leaves of the olive trees on the plain, their countless thoughts, Hebrew, Arabic, their feelings, surely the sky must light up in iridescent colours. So many hearts, all beating faster than normal, surely they must be audible.

A slim, waxing moon rose in the east, climbing slowly higher, the air turned a little cooler, a gentle breeze wafted in from the coast, brushing Peretz's face on its way to the Dead Sea. Crickets chirruped as if not a soul were there. Some flower gave off its tangy scent to attract night-time insects. Shooting stars drew their short trails of light in the darkness before dying out. Peretz had never seen so many before, he was certain of this, for he had never lain out on the earth for a whole night waiting for an order.

After a long time, during which Peretz asked himself what he was fighting for, knowing the answer, then not knowing it, depending on whether he thought of Israel or Anna, Shimon and his mother, the darkness was first blunted, then became milky. The stars faded, the crickets fell silent, the breeze abated, Peretz froze in his thin uniform. The first light was yet to reveal any colours, only grey silhouettes, the houses of Yad Mordechai, the gentle plain before it, the olive trees beneath which the Egyptians were hiding. Peretz was no longer lying on his back but on his stomach, others lay beside him, together they peered down.

The order was not a word. It was given when the inhabitants of Yad Mordechai suddenly appeared from behind their barricades and walls and started shooting. Peretz leaped to his feet and raced with the others down the hill, making a direct line for the olive trees, because of the munitions shortage the commandant had impressed on them that they should not shoot until they actually caught sight of the enemy, so they did not shoot, but ran as fast as they could, Don't run too far, the commandant had said, Otherwise you'll end up in the firing line of the kibbutzniks, but run far enough or you won't be of any use. They ran until they could see beneath the tops of the olive trees and then they saw the khaki-coloured backs of the Egyptians, and then they raised their rifles, cocked them and then they shot, and Peretz shot at an Egyptian back, but in the middle of his shot the Egyptian vanished, and Peretz saw the German fall, saw the German lose grip of his loudhailer, saw the loudhailer clatter on the rocks, and then the German was gone again and the Egyptian lay before him, no longer moving. Peretz ran on further and shot, now the Egyptians turned to them, tried to react, but it was too late, from the left the kibbutniks stormed, the Egyptians did not know where to flee, they scampered wildly in all directions, Peretz watched one of them smash into an olive tree as if he had not seen it.

The German did not appear again, but later Peretz would think, Wasn't it just as rocky as that in Italy, wasn't the air just as dry back then, wasn't it May too, the 8th rather than the 22nd? but it's not such a big difference.

Then Peretz would put these thoughts to one side. The German was history, fallen in battle. Over and done with. Only his bloody loudhailer was still there, sometimes Peretz got the impression that it made sounds all by itself.

ONE HUNDRED AND SEVEN

Another step. And another step. The pavement was slippery, it was raining. It was cold. The houses stood so close together, there was no gap between them into which she could have disappeared. She dragged herself on, bent over. Her belly burned with both fire and ice. The night was so dark, she could scarcely see a thing, only lights without any source, they were all around, blinding her, reflecting on the black pavement. Her legs could barely go any further, so violently did the pain rage in her belly. She slipped, knocking into a house, sliding to the ground. She lay totally crooked, leaning partially against the wall. The rain fell endlessly, without her being able to formulate a single thought, she just lay there, feeling the cold, the wet, the burning. Her final customer, she had always known that he would come one day. Now he had been, all her fears had been realised, now at last she had felt that one sensation that encompassed everything, sorrow, pain, fear, excitement, hope, love. She vomited on the pavement, she began to cry, she was astonished that love could be so dreadful, so impersonal, such a dark force. The burning became unbearable, she saw her mother, her father, her brother, from what time did these images come? She knew, now she could see when it was that the glass had shattered, when the fissure had torn through them all, through herself most deeply. She could no longer feel her legs. She realised that it had been just a misunderstanding, nothing more, she had misconstrued something, she had failed to understand that it was love that had unleashed her into the world, not scorn. She saw her mother. She toppled forwards, the left side of her face lay on the pavement, she saw the lustre of the wet close up, she felt the cold of the stone. Her legs were gone. Her belly was ablaze, she could hardly breathe, she was panting. Rather than appreciating that life was a gift, she had believed it to be a curse, rather than understanding that the body was a home, she had despised it in every conceivable way. She saw her mother at the door, the door was closing slowly, she was afraid it would shut tight, she stuck a foot in the way, the fire reached her chest, ice-cold, blazing, her breathing was intermittent, she put a foot in the door, she pushed her body against the door that was trying to close, she was shivering from head to toe, she could not breathe, she gasped for air, she pushed against the door.

Suddenly the door gave way, she fell into a bright room, she kneeled on the floor, her mother was standing in front of her, looking down, smiling, she put her arms around her and pressed her head into her belly and said, Stay.

ONE HUNDRED AND EIGHT

Why should he stay any longer? Josef Ranzner stood in his office, looking out at the River Isar that rushed past no more than a couple of hundred metres away. He looked across the meadows, glimpsed the buildings on the other side of the river, towering above tall trees. This city had always remained alien to him. And yet everything had begun with such promise. But the work for Gehlen's organisation had failed to bring him any fulfilment and even the new post felt like a substitute drug. His cover was no longer secure, Heinrich could have spilled the beans to anybody, the idea of being taken away by the police from his ordinary daily life, from his ordinary marriage, the prospect of being abducted by Jews and tried in Israel, the thought of Emma, who had not dared to ask about the diary, the sight of her tarot cards, the thought of Gudrun, the thought of Karl Treitz, the thought of Anna – Ranzner turned away. All for what? The only sensible course of action would be to look for Anna, but how could he get into Israel without being discovered? Josef Ranzner felt like a caged animal. He could not escape, he could not simply disappear and start again from scratch somewhere else, he could not do anything. But I have paid, Ranzner thought bitterly, pressing his narrow lips together until they almost vanished from his face, I have paid with hunger, cold and hard labour! Others had been put into some sort of job straightaway, without having to endure so much as a single day's imprisonment. He thought of Rauff and Brunner, Gehlen had helped both of them, put his protective hand over them, given them employment. And so many more who had escaped far more lightly than he. What have I done except serve my country? a loud voice inside him wondered. What else have I done except serve my country all my life long to the present day? Ranzner felt a sense of emotion stir inside, which he had thought long gone. Here I stand, he thought, tall and alone and I can say, I have nothing to reproach myself for! I have always fulfilled my duty, always acted with the utmost conscientiousness, not once was I ever sloppy, not once did I put personal issues above the national interest . . . Anna appeared before his eyes, slim and distinct and unfading. He pressed the heels of his hands against his temples. You, every time! a shrill voice screamed inside his head, Go away, disappear, leave me in peace! You Jewish whore! Why didn't I kill you? Why didn't I make a clean break, why didn't I draw a clear distinction, why, why, why,

"Why!"

He flinched. The walls were thin, his colleagues were at their desks to the left and right, I must be careful, Ranzner thought. But he no longer wanted to be careful, he wanted to be free from the past, wanted only to look forwards, just live his own life from now on. He wanted . . . Well, what do I want? he wondered. He looked out of the window of his office, he saw the Isar, the meadows, the tall houses behind the trees, and did not know what else he wanted apart from to see Anna again and to find

Karl Treitz. Absurd wishes of an absurd life, he thought, A mad love for a prisoner, a crazed belief in salvation from death. I have nothing, I never had anything, I never will have anything.

Ranzner turned away from the window. He packed up his things and left the office. Ignoring his work car, he took a tram to the station. He sauntered along Goethestrasse where he went into a bar. He drank wine, then whisky. When he began to feel their effect he left the bar and went to another establishment. He paid the entry fee and once inside chose a tall, slim, young woman and accompanied her to the second floor. He stayed all night. The following morning he took the bus from there to the office. From the office he returned there.

ONE HUNDRED AND NINE

"You rang yesterday, didn't you?"

"Yes."

"The ambassador would like to speak to you personally. I'll put you through."

"Fräulein Kramer?"

"Speaking."

"Hello, Fräulein Kramer. My name is Rolf Friedemann Pauls, I'm the ambassador of the Federal Republic of Germany in Israel, which means I'm your ambassador. And I have to say, when I heard of your case I thought, 'What a brave young woman!' So I'd just like to let you know that we at the embassy and I personally hope very much that your search is fruitful."

"Well, that's very nice of you, Herr Pauls, but I need a little more than that."

"Just say! We'll do whatever we can to support you!"

"I'm looking for a way to find Anna Sarfati, which was my reason for coming to Israel. But it turned out to be a mistake. The Israeli national archive has no list of names or current addresses. Do you have any means of finding the information? Peretz Sarfati is in the army, I suspect he's a high-ranking officer by now."

"I'm afraid my hands are tied, Fräulein Kramer. When I came here a year ago people were hostile to me, you see. Because of my past, a lot of people in this part of the world regarded my appointment as incomprehensible, thoughtless even."

"They told me you were with the Wehrmacht."

"Yes, that's true, I can't deny it, nor will I. But I was a soldier serving my Fatherland, which doesn't automatically make me a criminal."

"I can't judge that, Herr Pauls. All I know is that the war made me a German by sending my parents to their deaths. And people like you were part of it all."

"I am so very sorry, Fräulein Kramer, please believe me. I am in no way implying that I'm innocent. On the contrary, I'm fully aware of the historical responsibility that now weighs down on the German people, and on me too, and it will continue to do so for generations."

"That's not going to help me in my search for Anna Sarfati, unfortunately."

"May I ask why you're looking for this woman?"

"My reasons are private. From what you're saying I infer that you have no influence over the Israeli authorities."

"That is the case, regrettably. They tolerate me here and I'm grateful for that. But I'm afraid I can't achieve much more than this apart from my contribution to the reparations negotiations."

"Reparations?"

"That's what we call it. It's a terribly unfortunate word, a dreadful euphemism. Of course we can't repair anything. But we must try to move on from the historical and moral burden and the only way we can do this is by strengthening the friendship between Germany and Israel."

"After everything that's happened? Do you really believe it's possible?"

"Yes, Fräulein Kramer, I'll tell you honestly and frankly that I do believe it's possible. I understand your reservations. But neither the Germans nor the Jews can focus exclusively on the past, where there's nothing that can help us make a better future. We must look forwards and hope that time will heal the wounds. And I'm prepared to make my modest contribution to this."

"If that is your mission then I wish you best of luck, Herr Pauls. But mine is a very different one. Thank you for your time."

"No, Fräulein Kramer, I should be thanking you."

"Goodbye."

"Goodbye, Frau Kramer, and I wish you all the best."

ONE HUNDRED AND TEN

"Anna, is that you?"

"Yes. Ruth? Where are you?"

"We're in Haifa!"

"You're here?"

"Hurrah!"

"How did you get this number?"

"Peretz send it to me in Cyprus via the Red Cross. Didn't you know?"

"No. So what now?"

"We're going to be in Atlit for a while, that's directly south of Haifa. The British used the place to intern Jews, and that's what it feels like too. But the gates are open. We've got to stay here a while because there are so many people arriving, it's unbelievable! There's just no space anymore, they've got to build and build so that we can get somewhere to live as soon as possible."

"And are you well?"

"Fantastic! Aaron's already got a job in the camp administration. We learned to speak fluent Hebrew in Cyprus, which is coming in handy for him now. And I'm sewing uniforms for Israeli soldiers. Oh Anna, I'm so happy!"

"What about your baby?"

"I expect it'll be born here. But that doesn't matter anymore. Everything is fine, we're just so happy!"

"We must see each other."

"You ought to come here. How are you, Anna? Is everything alright? I heard about your baby. I'm so sorry, Anna! We were all very sad to hear about it."

"Thank you, Ruth."

"How about Peretz, how did he cope?"

"It's alright, he . . . he was really looking forward to this child."

"François sends his greetings as do the Abramowiczes, and of course Aaron too. Is Sarah well?"

"Yes, she's fine. She's doing an apprenticeship with a Yiddish newspaper. Peretz doesn't like it, he thinks they're communists, but she's learning quite a bit and she's meeting people. I think she's fallen in love."

"Anna, I've got to hang up now, there's a queue behind me and my time is up. I'll call again as soon as I can. My love to everyone! See you soon, Anna, very soon!"

"See you soon, Ruth, I'm really happy for you, for all of you, send my love to everyone, will you?"

ONE HUNDRED AND ELEVEN

Oz Almog had an idea. He did not go into much detail, he had two telephone conversations, one with Anat, his wife, the other with the man whose name she gave him.

The following morning he took Lisa in his saffron-yellow Saab. They drove through West Jerusalem, from south to north. Ramat Rachel. Arnona. Talpiyot. Buildings were going up everywhere as if striving to meet a deadline. Oz Almog pointed to the right, The Armistice Line, he said, the shooting there's becoming more frequent, that's why we're driving this way.

The sun sat in a cloudless sky. It was still cool, a faint dampness still hung in the corners of the buildings, in the shadows of the hedges, a fine dew still held the dust on the ground. Lisa looked out of the window.

"Does that work sometimes?" she said.

"Sometimes. But I can't promise you anything."

ONE HUNDRED AND TWELVE

The new house was in Tel Aviv's old town, which is what Peretz called Jaffa Port and the surrounding hillsides, on which houses stood closely bunched together. These buildings appeared ancient, as if they could tell of times long forgotten.

"Who lived here?" Anna asked as she wandered slowly through the rooms that looked as if the owners had gone shopping, and crossed the internal courtyard crowded with pot plants, some withered, some still alive. In the centre was a circular fountain, she leaned over its brick wall, the water was crystal clear. The surface of the courtyard was set out like a mosaic. She looked up, above her the expanse of blue sky.

"How old is this house?" she asked.

Peretz smiled. "Do you like it?"

Anna wanted to say Yes, but she hesitated, She walked on through the rooms.

"What sort of patterns are these? And these decorations?"

"They're Arabic."

"Does the house belong to Arabs?"

"Not anymore."

"Where are they?"

"They emigrated."

"Emigrated or expelled?"

"Emigrated."

Anna turned round and looked Peretz in the eye.

"Are you telling me the truth?"

Peretz nodded. "They didn't want to live in a Jewish state, so they left."

"And you bought the house off them?"

"They just left, Anna, just like that, from one day to the next. Many here did the same. The Arabs hate us, they'll never come back, or if they do only as soldiers to destroy Israel. The house is the property of the state now."

Anna said nothing. She looked around, a beautiful, old house. If you looked out of the kitchen window you could see the sea. If you looked out and ignored the pots and pans hanging on the wall beside the window, the plates and cups on the shelves, if you ignored the rusty metal teapot on the old gas cooker. If you ignored the sink still full of dirty glasses.

Peretz watched her and said, "The sun sets in the water, over there." He pointed past her at the horizon. Anna said nothing, she clasped her arms around her body, it was warm but all of a sudden she felt chilly. Growing impatient, Peretz said, "They won't be coming back, many more Arabs have left the country since the war. And it's better that way, believe me, Jews and Arabs can't live together in the same country, we're far too different." He paused, then continued, "You wanted to move out of my parents' house as quickly as you could. And you didn't want to live on a kibbutz, even though that might have been the best solution."

"I don't want Shimon spending all his week in a communal children's house, separated from his . . . parents. And from Sarah. That's all."

Peretz was quiet. The two of them stared out of the window.

"If you don't decide quickly someone else will move in here, all the other houses have gone."

Anna looked at him. "Did only Arabs live here before the war?"

Peretz nodded reluctantly.

"And they've all gone?"

Peretz shook his head.

"Those who didn't want to go stayed."

"Show me one of their houses."

"Why, Anna?"

"I want to see one of those houses."

Peretz clenched his jaw and shot his wife a furious look. Then he pulled himself together and said, "Come here!"

He left the house, marched down the steep alley, Anna following at the double, Peretz strode so quickly, the sun was high in the sky, the people had withdrawn behind protective walls and under shady roofs, an old man with a donkey came up the hill, he had pulled his hat down over his head, his emaciated body was bent, Anna saw the sea below and as far as the horizon, where the sun would set, Peretz charged along narrow alleyways, the houses with Arabic decorations, the patterns in the walls, Anna saw them everywhere. Suddenly Peretz stopped and pointed at a house.

"Here live some Arabs who stayed."

Anna was out of breath, she was sweating, the sun was stinging her eyes. The house looked sealed up, the shutters were closed, a wrought-iron gate prevented access to the front garden. Anna looked at Peretz.

"Do you want to ring the bell and talk to them? Go on!"

Anna looked from Peretz to the house and from the house to Peretz. Suddenly she turned away and went up the hill, Peretz looked at her, confused, then followed.

"What's wrong? Don't you believe me?"

"Yes, Peretz, I do believe you. Let's take the house." She wanted everything to be legal, she wanted the Arabs to have left because they had the choice, she wanted to escape Lydia Sarfati's mistrustful, clueless gaze, she did not want to work in the fields on a kibbutz, she wanted to live in the city, she wanted to show Peretz that she appreciated his efforts, that he had done everything right, she intended to sleep with him soon. She envisaged a new child. A child in Jaffa. Everything's going to be fine, she thought. She would not heed anything else. She took his hand. Together they went up the hill.

ONE HUNDRED AND THIRTEEN

It crackled. A gong sounded. A man with a sonorous voice said, "It is twelve o'clock. This is the Voice of Israel. My name is Mordechai Primann. Here are today's missing persons announcements sent by the Jewish Agency for Israel.

"Sara Rosenbaum from New York, born in Korov, Galicia, Poland, is looking for her younger brother, Jaakov Rosenbaum, thirty-six years old. The last time they saw each other was in the ghetto of Bielsko-Biała in June 1942, before the last transport to Auschwitz. There the family was separated, the men from the women, and Sara Rosenbaum survived. Other survivors have told her that her younger brother also survived, but they have not seen each other since.

"Abraham Gerschenson from Miami, born in Białystok, Byelorussia, is looking for any surviving siblings. At the end of the war he left the Red Army and returned to Białystok. There he was told that the younger members of his family had escaped into the woods where they joined the partisans, but none of them returned to Białystok.

"Lisa Kramer, née Ejzenstain, originally from Poland, grew up after the war in Lübeck, Germany. As a baby she lost her mother, Margarita Ejzenstain; her father, Thomasz Ejzenstain had earlier been killed by the S.S. Lisa Kramer is looking for Anna Sarfati, who she met in Pöppendorf transit camp, where she was with her grandmother, Marta Kramer.

"Those were the announcements for today. The people being sought can contact us or the Jewish Agency for Israel directly, and if requested we will immediately put you in touch with those looking for you. It is now five minutes past twelve. This is the Voice of Israel. My name is Mordechai Primann."

Anat Almog switched off the radio. She ran her hand through her thick, brown hair and reached for the pot of coffee sitting in the middle of the round table. She looked at the faces of her two small children in turn – Binah, slender and pale like herself, Erez, tall and strong like his father. Children who were no longer children. Children who had grown up with their father and mother, who thought they knew everything about their parents.

Between them, Lisa. She looked at Lisa, she smiled at her.

"Now we have to sit tight and wait, my dear."

ONE HUNDRED AND FOURTEEN

The truth about the randomness of human encounters, the truth that it made no difference whether you met in the street, in the same family, or in bed. The truth of the meaninglessness of the search for meaning, not because there was no meaning, but because the mind led you to believe everything, even the believable lie that meaninglessness is really meaningless and not one of countless havens to which people flee to avoid seeing the randomness, to avoid seeing that randomness allows for no conclusions, none at all. The truth that coincidence and meaning were not contradictions, but complements in a dreadful cosmic harmony. The truth that . . .

Gudrun broke off, for now came the Yeses and then the rings would be exchanged, Heinrich and Lena Scholz, For God's sake, why do you want to take her name? Because our name is a lie, because really we're called Ranzner. Really? Do you know what's really going on? Really you're only interested in painting over it with another lie, really you're doing the same as Dad, you're changing your name to make it clean. But it won't be clean, it'll stay as dirty as it was. Children of a murderer!

Gudrun broke off again, for now they were coming down the aisle, man and wife. For some time now there had been three of them, but you could not tell by looking at Lena, they were still able to deceive the outside world, such as the two in the front row, Herr and Frau Scholz, he a bank employee, she a housewife. They had no clue. Nice, harmless, naïve, random people. Gudrun shook her head indiscernibly.

Movement in the rows of pews, people standing to follow the newly-weds to the entrance. A wedding march from the noisy band. What do you think about us getting married? You're asking me, your younger sister? Shouldn't you ask Mum at least? I don't want anything more to do with our parents. So now I'm supposed to give my blessing? I just want to know what you think about it, Gudrun. Not a lot. Are you trying to prove that family can be a nice thing after all? Don't give me that embarrassed look, you wanted my opinion, now you've got it.

That's enough, Gudrun thought. She stood up, she was wearing a dark-blue satin dress that she had borrowed from Lena, Yes, I'm going to take over the vacant post of head of the family, Yes, I'll come to your wedding, Yes, I'll celebrate with you and hope that you'll be happy, even though that won't help.

Rain was waiting for them outside the church, relentless, fine rain, as if God had said, Let's see how tenacious you are. The unmarried women took their umbrellas and went down the steps, all of them students from Lena's Romance Studies course, they turned and waited. When the bridal bouquet flew in their direction they forgot the rain and umbrellas and did their best to catch it, randomness, there it was again, Gudrun saw it in everything, this gesture, that look, Heinrich and Lena's house-mate, who now smiled at her, everything random, What was his name again? No idea, Gudrun had watched the other tenants from Heinrich and Lena's apartment as if they were extras in a film, an inconspicuous lot, only this one here, he at least had not slipped her mind, he was approaching her, Hello, would you like a lift to the restaurant? Say yes, smile, down the steps, a 2C.V., what next? My dealer had a Citroën like this, Your *dealer*? The way you look that wasn't even a joke. Gudrun laughed and was surprised to find herself laughing, then asked, What do I look like? Like someone who means exactly what they say. I see. Come on, get in.

And this wedding, what should she say about it? A celebration like any other, she sat next to . . . What's your name again? Don't tell me you can't remember, Gudrun! I'm Ben, and if the two of them move out next week we'll have neighbouring rooms, so please remember my name. Aye-aye, Herr Ben Thingummybob, what's in a surname? Look at my brother, he's no longer called what was never his name in fact, but something different again. What do you mean? Exactly what I've just said. But your surname's Kruse, isn't it? I know you from way back, you lived two doors down and Heinrich was in my class. Oh, he never told me, what a small world! There's really quite a lot your brother hasn't talked about. That's true, he prefers watching, my little big brother.

The wedding, what should she say about it? The couple were at the centre of the festivities, they danced the first waltz, Gudrun shrugged, If it's got to be Catholic, then there's got to be a bouquet, if a bouquet then a waltz too, she was already quite drunk as the wine was delicious, Isn't it, Benni Flatmate? What's your prized surname, if I may ask, but please only tell me if it's true. Schwimmer? *What?* Schwimmer? You're not serious! You've got to change that.

ONE HUNDRED AND FIFTEEN

Emma was proud of her achievement. She had managed to get by on her housekeeping money for four months. Obviously she no longer needed to go shopping for her husband and children, just herself. The electricity and gas bills had fallen too. But four months – that was a long time.

Emma sat in the kitchen, counting the last of her money.

"Thirty-two marks and seventy cents," she muttered when she had finished. Not even enough for another tarot session with Madame Claire. She looked out of the window. All day a layer of fog had lain over the city, it was so gloomy the sun might have set at any minute. But now, in the evening, a cold wind swept through the sweets, tearing the last leaves from the trees and allowing the sun to flare up far in the west, just before it set. The sight was so beautiful that it brought tears to Emma's eyes. It was so beautiful it looked like a tarot card and this tarot card looked like a metaphor for her entire life. And this life felt as if it were coming to an end. Emma got up and left the kitchen, she crossed the hallway and entered the living room, which had never seemed so big before, in fact she had even secretly hoped that Otto would sell the house one day. Now, however, she saw just how much space there had been for all these years. She left the living room, crossed the hallway and went into Otto's study. Alien and abandoned, what on earth had he done here to make it impossible for him to stay, did it have something to do with the little book that Heinrich had given him? She had not dared ask him, he had been so furious and yet so silent that she thought, He'll tell me when he's ready. But the time had never come, he just grew ever more silent, scarcely ate at home, arrived increasingly late from work, ignored her, shut himself away in his study with his supper, she had sometimes felt like a maid.

One day he simply failed to come home, and that was four months ago now. What had happened in this room without her noticing?

She moved to the other side of the hallway and entered first Heinrich's room, then Gudrun's. Museums. Empty and full of questions. I never expected anything from you, Emma muttered. But just to go like that . . . She closed up the pain and closed the door and took a deep breath.

The bedroom was like a half-dead body, she inhabited the living half, the dead half was occupied by Otto's absence, after Otto's be-back-soon had vanished without saying goodbye, like Otto himself.

She felt that all these rooms and their stories were somehow connected, but she had no idea how. She sat on her half of the bed and turned off the light. After sitting there for a while she slipped under the duvet and went to sleep.

The following morning, after a small breakfast of rolls and filter coffee, Emma packed a suitcase with the essentials, a few changes of clothes, her washbag, a second pair of shoes. Then she put on her best winter coat, Otto had given it to her one Christmas when the children were small, Emma could not even remember the year. It was a lambskin coat that must have cost a lot of money. She took a matching fur hat, and got into her black winter boots and warm gloves. Picking up the case, she went to the front door, opened it, turned around once more, looked at the apartment, saw in her mind Heinrich and Gudrun as small children romping around the wide hallway, their father behind them, I am the monster, he cried, putting on a voice, the children laughed and hid. The vision faded, Emma left the apartment, pulling the door to behind her.

It was a cold morning, the coat provided welcome warmth as she waited for the tram. She went to Marienplatz, got out and continued on foot. Well-trodden, familiar paths. She wandered down Kaufinger-strasse, heading for Stachus. The shops were opening, frozen people rubbed their hands together, rolled up metal grilles, unlocked doors, folded back window shutters. Cars drove past.

With her case Emma walked to the spot where Otto had approached her many years ago, what was it he had said? She could not recall the words, only the feelings they had unleashed. She turned around and there, a few doors down, was Huber Optician's, the shop was already open, Emma saw her mother appear in the back room and then vanish again, she knew what her mother was doing, she knew every hand movement, she had come to bid farewell, she had worked out what to say, Mother, she would say, I'm going away, not for long, I'm visiting a schoolfriend, can you believe that Evi got in touch after all these years, and now I'm going to see her, she lives in Augsburg, that's not far. The children are fine, Otto is terribly busy, you might not bump into him. She ran through her speech several times, on each occasion the script was different, what she said got longer and more detailed every time, an entire story that she would never be able to remember.

Emma Kruse switched her case to the other hand. She peered a while longer through the display window of her mother's optician's and watched Frau Huber appear, disappear, appear, disappear.

When the while had passed, Emma turned away and kept going towards Stachus. There she took the tram to Munich central station.

ONE HUNDRED AND SIXTEEN

Who came to Maria Kramer's funeral? A few prostitutes who saw their own bodies lying there; her pimp, Fritz Kleinert, who did not look up; a few punters who thought they had loved the dead woman; an old lady. And two plain-clothes police officers trying to solve a murder. They watched the mourners, they wondered, This one? That one? They had already interrogated Fritz Kleinert and would do so a number of times again. They intercepted the punters at the cemetery exit and summoned them to come to the police station. The old lady recognised the officers, she looked at them, she let her eyes wander amongst the group, she saw the faces, one of the prostitutes was old Rosi, Rosi had tears in her eyes, she shot a glance at the mother that said, It was our turn, yours and mine, not hers. But that was not right.

Now Frau Kramer realised why she had sat tight in Lübeck after Lisa had left. For this day beneath this cold winter sun, by this earth frozen solid. Now she realised that she had always loved her daughter, that love was not the reason for her daughter's difficult path in life, but something else, over which she could wield no influence. She realised that her despair had sometimes made her harsh and unfair, no, not the despair but her attempt to evade the despair, her fear of being guilty for her daughter's life because she was the one who had given it to her.

All this was now gone, lying buried at her feet, her last tie to this city in which there were two graves and one apartment, what now? Where can someone like me go? She turned and left the cemetery.

ONE HUNDRED AND SEVENTEEN

Josef Ranzner woke up. He turned on his side and opened his eyes. Next to him lay Anna, snoring with her mouth open. Her breath smelled sour. His gaze alighted on the alarm clock, which sat on the bedside table next to Anna. Time to get up. Time to go outside, get into the car, drive to the office, time to work, time to behave as if nothing in his life had changed.

Anna awoke. She looked at him. She did not smile, her eyes wandered to the clock then back to him. Her voice was hoarse, the voice of a smoker.

"You've got to go," she said.

Ranzner nodded. "I'm on my way, Anna."

"Enough of this Anna! You owe me for two nights, from now on it's just Frieda, is that clear? And if you don't pay, soon I'll be Frau Schneider to you."

Ranzner nodded again, stood up, got dressed.

"Don't worry, Anna, I get paid today, then I'll give you your house-keeping."

"Enough of your craziness! You can forget showing up here again unless I get the dough, do you hear me? I'll tell my pimp otherwise and he doesn't waste too much time talking, if you know what I mean."

Ranzner nodded, he smiled at Frieda Schneider, he put on his suit trousers, his jacket, coat, hat, leather gloves. He thought about giving Frieda a goodbye kiss, but decided against it. When he opened the door to the hall he said, "See you later, Anna."

Before Frieda could reply he closed the door behind him and went down the old wooden staircase with its creaking boards, then out into the street. It had snowed so much that his feet were wet after just a few metres. His car was completely snowed in, he tried to manoeuvre it out of the parking space, but the tyres just spun. Ranzner froze. The prospect of having to travel on the tram without a ticket did not appeal to him. The prospect of turning up to work late again and being challenged by his boss. The prospect of turning up to work in these clothes, unwashed, unshaven, soaked through, freezing. The prospect of the same prospect from his office window as the day before, the day before that and all the days before.

Ranzner got out of his car. He stood indecisively on the street. He could not take a taxi, he could not buy a coffee. He got moving. Across Goethestrasse towards Munich central station, a right turn into Schwanthalerstrasse. As he crossed Sonnenstrasse he could no longer feel his feet. But he kept going, he had experienced worse things than this pain. When, shortly after he crossed Kaufingerstrasse where it meets

Augustinerstrasse, he stopped for a moment. He looked in the direction of his mother-in-law's optician's, he considered the possibility of asking her for money, but decided against it. The prospect of an encounter with the old bag was not an appealing one. He went on through Munich's old town, paying no attention to the people tramping through the snow around him, his entire body was shivering.

When finally he reached his destination he was barely able to move. It took minutes for him to remove his leather gloves. His fingers could hardly hold the keys, he needed both hands and all his force to open the door. Stiff with cold he climbed the stairs to the apartment.

The apartment was unheated. Ranzner went into the bathroom and ran a bath. But the water did not warm up. He flicked the switch but the light did not go on. He looked around. Everything was covered with a fine layer of dust. He entered the bedroom. He went into the other rooms. When he was back in the hall he stopped.

"She's gone back to her mother," he shouted. "And that's where she belongs." He was annoyed all the same. Without thinking about it he had always assumed that Emma would wait for him. He took offence that she had not.

"It's her duty!" he said. But perhaps the tarot cards had told her, Go back to your mother! Josef Ranzner laughed out loud. "Tarot cards! How ludicrously superstitious! I've no time for all that now!" he said sternly, before returning to the bathroom. He got undressed, stood in the bath and took a cold shower. Afterwards he shaved. In the bedroom he put on clean underwear.

When he was dressed he went into the kitchen. He was hungry but there was nothing to eat, nothing at all. He was livid. He wanted to make some filter coffee, but remembered that the electricity was switched off. For how long had he not paid the rent, electricity or heating bills?

"Nothing but lather!" he cried, going to the rack and putting on a warm coat, scarf, thick gloves and a winter hat. He went to the front door, opened it, turned once more, glanced back at the apartment.

He spat on the parquet floor then stepped out and slammed the door shut.

He walked through the city. He had time.

"I've taken the day off," he said. "I'll go in again tomorrow." By evening he had still not eaten anything. He was so hungry that his stomach was hurting. Just one or two more days, then he would be able to withdraw money again. He went to the station, prowled amongst the crowds, watched the trains arrive, stared at the people, especially the women.

Late that evening he went to his car. Unlocking it, he got in, started the engine and turned the heating up high. He listened to German songs on the radio. Whenever there was one he particularly liked he sang along. At some point he fell asleep.

He woke in the middle of the night. The engine had died, the radio fallen silent. He was freezing. He opened his eyes but could see nothing. For an instant he thought he was still underground, still captive, but then he realised that it had snowed again. He got out of the car.

The night was crystal clear and so cold that everything looked as if it had set stiff, even the houses appeared stiller and more silent than usual. There was not a soul on the street. Josef Ranzner looked around. He could not go home, he could not go back to Frieda. He did not want to go to his office anymore. He did not know where Emma was, he had lost contact with his children.

He rearranged his clothes, he pulled the scarf more tightly around his neck and his hat further over his ears, he closed the gap between his gloves and the sleeves of his coat.

Then he started walking.

ONE HUNDRED AND EIGHTEEN

Lübeck, 29th June, 1966

My dearest child

I'm very happy to hear you're well in Jerusalem. I'm keeping my fingers crossed that Anna has somehow heard about the radio broadcast. Here life goes on as normal. Don't worry about me, I'm fine. Actually there's nothing really to tell. Except perhaps for the fact that I'm considering going on a long trip. I've always wanted to see a little more of the world than just Lübeck. And there's no real reason for staying here, is there? I'd love to cross the sea on a ship some time, or see the pyramids in Egypt, or maybe even fly in an aeroplane to some distant country. The world is so large and full of wonderful places that I don't know! I'll write to you as soon as I've made a decision.

Look after yourself, darling, you're all I've got left in this world.

Love, Grandma

ONE HUNDRED AND NINETEEN

Michael Scholz was born on 5 November, 1976, in Rechts der Isar Hospital. It was a complicated birth, the mother's contractions were not strong enough, it took sixteen hours for the baby to come out. Michael was too weak to suckle from Lena's breast, she was too exhausted to keep encouraging him. After three days the doctors advised regular bottle feeding. They also offered the mother an injection to dry up the milk flow straightaway, thereby preventing further complications. Lena agreed.

At the time Heinrich was doing an apprenticeship at B.M.W. The family moved out of their shared apartment and into social housing in south-east Munich. Gudrun took over their old bedroom.

The day they left would remain long in Gudrun's memory. When Lena had already gone downstairs with Michael on her arm, Heinrich said goodbye to his sister. They embraced.

"It's your turn now, little brother," Gudrun said. "Look after yourself!" Heinrich had no idea what she meant by that, he did not dare ask, he just nodded and followed his wife down the stairs. Gudrun could tell everything about him just by looking, she gave him a tender, concerned smile, Little big brother. Then she heard the door close on the ground floor and went back into her new-old apartment, where Ben Schwimmer was waiting for her.

ONE HUNDRED AND TWENTY

"Please stop talking German to each other! I forbid you! Only Hebrew is to be spoken in my house, do you hear me?"

Anna and Sarah went quiet. Shimon stared at Peretz. He did not say what he was thinking: Why are you saying that in German then? But Peretz could tell he was thinking this and it annoyed him. He suppressed the desire to justify himself.

They were sitting at breakfast in the inner courtyard of their new house, it was early morning, the sky shone bright blue above their heads. The noises from the street did travel as far as them, children struggling up the hill to the school, ox and donkey carts and small panel vans making deliveries to the local shops, neighbours chatting before going on their way. Soon Anna and Sarah would bring Shimon to nursery. Then, in the same school building, they would attend the Hebrew lessons that were offered to immigrants.

"It's for Shimon's sake too," said Peretz, who had to add something to his outburst. "If he only ever hears German he'll find it much more difficult." Now there was a tone of bitterness in his voice.

The women did not react, they drank their coffee in silence. After a pause Peretz said even more softly, as if speaking to himself, "The children's house in the kibbutz would have been much better for him."

ONE HUNDRED AND TWENTY-ONE

One morning the Almogs' telephone rang. Erez picked up and spoke for a while before calling Lisa, putting the receiver in her hand without a word and shrugging as if to say, No idea what they want.

"Fräulein Kramer?" a voice said on the other end of the line.

"Yes . . . speaking."

"Good morning, Fräulein Kramer, I'm sorry to disturb you. It's Rolf Friedemann Pauls here, the German ambassador in Tel Aviv, do you remember?"

"Good morning, Herr Pauls. How did you find me?"

"We have our channels."

"And I thought your hands were tied."

"It wasn't a problem in your case, Fräulein Kramer, because you're German."

"So why are you calling?"

"Fräulein Kramer, I'm terribly sorry to have to tell you that your mother died a month ago. The news reached us via a circuitous route, and then I remembered our telephone conversation. Well, now I'm 'phoning you. Please accept my heartfelt condolences, Fräulein Kramer."

It was a while before Lisa understood. She took a deep breath and said, "Do you mean Maria Kramer from Lübeck?"

"Yes, exactly, Maria Kramer. She is your mother, isn't she? At least, you do have the same address in Lübeck."

Lisa paused. What should she say? All of a sudden it made sense.

"Have you heard anything of Marta Kramer?" she asked.

"No, as far as I know there was no mention of a Marta Kramer. Who is that?"

"Herr Pauls, thank you very much for calling, but I have to go now. Goodbye."

"Goodbye, Fräulein . . ." There was a crackling when Lisa hung up.

She sat on the chair, she had turned pale. Erez and Binah came to her. They caught Lisa as she fainted.

It was only seconds before she came round. Erez carried her to her room and laid her on the bed. Binah brought her a glass of water. She smiled at both of them gratefully. When she had drunk the water she said, "I have to go back to Germany."

ONE HUNDRED AND TWENTY-TWO

On the evening of 14 March, 1950, Peretz felt a sense of relief. His father telephoned to say that the Knesset had passed the Absentees' Property Law, to be applied retrospectively to 14 May, 1948. I know the custodian very well, Gershom Sarfati told his son, Let me sort it out. You'll pay a symbolic sum to the state, then the house is officially yours and nobody can take it away from you. What if they haven't fled abroad? Peretz asked. Then, his father said reassuringly, they are resident absentees, it doesn't change a thing, they don't have a claim on it anymore. Peretz thanked his father and hung up. He was sitting on a sofa in the living room, looking about him – the stone floor with its ornamental hollows, the round arches to the courtyard, the slender, turned columns, the old brick fireplace in the corner which they had not yet used. All this now belonged to him and his family. Peretz leaned back. Return if you like, Abdulha Al Sayyed. But you won't be able to do a thing.

That night Peretz dreamed that it had snowed. The snow was several metres high, but when they tried to use the fire they discovered that it was bricked up at the top. They froze, Anna froze, Sarah froze, Shimon froze, and Peretz froze most of all, but no matter how much he begged the others to warm him up, they would not.

Peretz woke with a start. His entire body was trembling. Then he relaxed. What a notion, he thought, snow in Tel Aviv. He fell asleep again. But the following morning he recalled his odd dream. He said nothing to Anna about it.

ONE HUNDRED AND TWENTY-THREE

When he got to his car, two dark figures approached, one punched him in the pit of the stomach, the other caught him as he collapsed. They opened the car door, shoved him onto the back seat, one of the two men sat beside him, the other climbed in the front. Ranzner wanted to say, The tank's empty, but to his surprise the engine sprang into life, They've thought of everything, it occurred to him, and suddenly he was gripped by fear, he looked at the men, dark winter coats, hats pulled down over their heads, black leather gloves, one word darted into his mind: Mossad! He wanted to fight, he tried to escape from the car, but the man sitting beside him elbowed him in the temple. He passed out.

*

When Ranzner came to he was sitting on a chair, peering into a room he vaguely recognised, through the window he saw that the trees had grown, then noticed a man on the other side of the familiar desk, who he only knew from photographs. This man had a large, angular head with short, dyed-black hair, his eyes were jovial and inscrutable. He smiled.

"Welcome, Herr Kruse, my name is Wessel. How are you feeling?"

Ranzner was going to say, Fine, but remained silent and rocked his head from side to side. Wessel smiled at him engagingly, rested his elbows on the desk and touched the tips of his fingers together. He looked deep in thought, then snapped out of it.

"I have to admit I was a little surprised when I found out we had a former S.S. Obersturmbannführer in the service. But look, I have almost six thousand employees, so it's perfectly conceivable something like that could happen." He glanced briefly at Ranzner as if to check he was paying attention, then continued, "You see, Herr Kruse, the world out there has changed. Even my predecessor grasped that at some stage. And that's why a decade ago he began to pension off all employees who were compromised by their past." He sighed, moved his hands wide apart and gave Ranzner a laconic smile. "But you seem to have been forgotten, even though you're very much compromised, as I've since discovered."

Not knowing what to say, Ranzner remained silent. His head was aching from the blow he had sustained, his stomach was so empty that he had cramps. His relief that he had been abducted not by Mossad but by his own secret service faded with every word that fell from Wessel's lips. Wessel seemed to have misconstrued Ranzner's silence.

"Look, Kruse," he said, leaning back. "My predecessor was a brilliant man, but terribly backward-looking. Instead of training new people he made use of the old ones. He needed know-how, as the British say, and that was all around him in spades. So he seized the opportunity and didn't ask too many questions." Wessel leaned forward. "The former Gestapo chief in Lyon, Klaus Barbie. Eichmann's former assistant, Alois Brunner. The former head of the Jewish desk in the foreign office,

Franz Rademacher. The inventor of the mobile gas chamber, Walther Rauff. The former officer in detachment 9 of Einsatzgruppe B, Konrad Fiebig. The former chief of the Moscow advance detachment of Einsatzgruppe B, Franz Alfred Six. The former S.S. Obersturmbannführer Heinz Felfe." He paused and looked at Ranzner as if expecting a reaction.

"At the beginning of the 1950s around a third of his employees were former Nazi members, a small percentage of whom were former S.S., S.D. or S.A. people. Top-class individuals, if you want to put it that way." He paused, giving Ranzner a friendly and inscrutable look. He leaned back.

"Now consider this. At the time the German parliament had the same cross-section of individuals. Don't you think that's interesting? The politicians covered for Gehlen and his organisation – we scratched their back and they scratched ours." He leaned forward again.

"That's all history. Apart from the fact that it's getting increasingly difficult to justify my predecessor's staffing policy, these people distinguished themselves more by their problems than their brilliance." He raised his hands in conciliation.

"This may not be true of you, Herr Kruse, I'm not going to make any judgements. But these days the enemy is fighting quite differently, giving no quarter. If a federal chancellor has to resign because a spy from the East has made his way into the highest political echelons, then we have to try new approaches. Otherwise we risk turning into another Finland." He raised his eyebrows and gazed at Ranzner's emaciated face.

"Moreover, since the Social Democrats took power the balance in parliament has changed." He raised his shoulders as if begging forgiveness.

"So all that's left for me to do is to thank you for your many commendable years with us, and to give you a piece of advice. If you still wish to avoid being called to account by the Israelis or an overzealous German court, I suggest you lead a discreet existence for the rest of your life, starting from now." He smiled at Ranzner as if he had just revealed to him a delicious recipe. Then he pushed a button on his telephone, a door opened behind Ranzner and a young woman appeared.

"Herr Direktor?" she said. Wessel gave her a friendly smile, then turned to Ranzner and gestured briefly past him at his secretary.

"Fräulein Kupfer will give you the necessary papers to sign. Then you'll move into a small apartment in the south-east of the city, they're just building an attractive housing complex there. Someone will drive you. We've wound up your apartment in Lehel, we're going to auction off your artworks and pay off your debts with the proceeds. If you're careful with your money, your pension will suffice. You will retain your current identity, we're assuming that it isn't compromised. Please don't go back to your workplace, not even to say goodbye. It's safer that way." He smiled contentedly, then something else occurred to him.

"By the way, your wife has left the country, so we've stopped the surveillance." He smiled again, then something else occurred to him.

"Oh yes! This," he said, taking something out of his desk drawer. Ranzner recognised his diary. "I'm going to keep so it doesn't fall into the wrong hands. It's only for your protection. It would be better if you didn't write anything personal in the future." He gave Ranzner a jovial smile.

"All the best, Herr Kruse," he said kindly. "Farewell." He stood up. Realising that he had to play along, Ranzner copied him, they shook hands, then Wessel gestured towards his secretary again, but this time his arm was showing the way. Ranzner obeyed.

ONE HUNDRED AND TWENTY-FOUR

It's beautiful here, Anna thought on the way home from taking Shimon to school. It was 13 March, 1951. A fresh morning, the scent of almond blossom filled the air, there were large bougainvilleas in some front gardens, their lilac-coloured flowers glowed in the early light. From the houses came the sounds of people busily occupied, the sun was not yet scorching, the air was a pleasant temperature. Far below, the glittering sea across which she had come. At the second attempt. I'm free, aren't I? she thought. I survived, didn't I? Everything turned out fine, didn't it? Now I'm an Israeli citizen, my Hebrew is improving. Shimon has made friends, I'm pregnant again, Peretz is happy.

She continued walking, aware that nothing was fine, because "fine" was a term from her childhood, and her childhood had perished inside her. She had to plan in advance all the joy she felt, she had to gather up the meaning of life like someone who has dropped their breakfast tray. Now she was crawling around on the floor, eating scraps while thinking nourishing thoughts.

When her house came into view, surrounded by other houses in which Arabs had once lived, she stopped. You'll never be free, a bold voice said inside her, no matter where you are. She thought of the nights with Peretz, she could offer no more resistance, she was caught in the web she had spun for herself, nothing had changed even though years had passed, Peretz was still not Peretz, she was still searching for Shimon's father, while still trying to lock everything away so she could keep rehearsing her act, in the hope that one day she might be so perfect that she could believe it herself, because it would have become true, even though she had long known that hope was the biggest trap of them all, even though she had long known that the prospect of a life in hope was the prospect of a life locked away. She almost wished another war would come to sweep away everything she had only just built up for herself, she almost hoped that Peretz would die a hero so she might finally be free.

But she dismissed these thoughts, got moving again and went home.

ONE HUNDRED AND TWENTY-FIVE

Oz Almog put Lisa's case into his car, Don't be silly! he said, I'll drive you. Anat gave her a farewell hug, What a shame you have to leave. Binah and Erez came along for the ride, the four of them sat in the small car, the men in front, the women behind. A couple of hours then we'll be there, Oz said.

The sun was shining, When doesn't the sun shine here? Lisa asked, essaying a smile. Oh, Erez said in his deep voice, It does happen, the last time was two years ago. He laughed as people do when trying to lighten the mood.

They drove northwards along the southern Armistice Line, the city awoke, work had already begun on the construction sites, It'll be too hot later on, Binah said. Lisa saw the streets of a city she had barely got to know, Will I ever return? The rush-hour traffic grew slowly heavier, The British with their roundabouts, Oz grumbled. They went on, broad streets, cars, motorcycles, in the distance always hills densely populated with houses, lots of sandy, dusty earth, very little greenery. It was all very different in my homeland, Oz said, It took me a long time to get used to this landscape. I come from Bulgaria. My surname used to be Bisanti, sounds like Byzantium, don't you think? But we spoke Ladino. In the sixteenth century lots of Jews moved to Bulgaria, they'd been expelled from Spain by the Catholic Monarchs, so for a long time we thought we were from there too. But the name doesn't fit. It's a beautiful name, Bisanti, Lisa said, Much nicer than Almog, Binah said, either feigning or concealing resentment, Lisa could not tell which.

They drove out of the city, Lisa turned around, a last glimpse of Jerusalem, how different everything seemed to her, now she saw where the rocks ended and houses began. Can you see the hill over to your left? Oz said. He thrust his arm out of the window, Lisa looked across a valley to a wooded hill, on the summit of which stood an angular building. That's Yad Vashem. One day, when you know more, you must come back and tell your story to the people there. Lisa's mind was preoccupied with other thoughts, Why did you change your name? she said. Oh, Oz said, that was silly, really. After the founding of the state Ben-Gurion wanted every Israeli to have a Hebrew surname, in the army we were told this on a daily basis. That's why I did it, Almog means coral, I used to like it. Today I regret it though. Many people are in the same boat. What about you, Binah asked, Why are you still called Kramer? Lisa thought of her grandmother, who now needed her support, she looked out of the window, they were driving along one of the river valleys that led through the corridor to the west, on one of the road signs it said "Highway 1" beneath "Tel Aviv–Yafo".

"My parents are both dead," she said. "I belong to my grandmother."

Oz nodded his approval, nobody commented on this. Then he said, In a while we'll have get off this road and take the Burma Road to Tel Aviv. It was built in only eight weeks because we weren't able to take Latrun in the War of Independence, today it's still occupied by Jordan.

They fell silent and drove through barren, mountainous country-side, the road gradually winding in broad arcs down to the coast. It became hot and sticky, stopping slightly away from the road they sat on the ground and from Anat's picnic basket ate dates, oranges, sand-wiches, biscuits, they drank water, then packed everything up again and continued on their journey.

The landscape changed, they drove through small villages, through orange plantations, past olive groves, the traffic became heavier.

The airport was surrounded by small villages, construction was in full swing here too. Oz Almog navigated the car unerringly through a tangle of streets, Lisa saw large advertising hoardings with European faces, one of the hoardings was in German, publicising *Neueste Nachrichten*, It's the biggest daily paper, Binah said, the Yekkes have terrible trouble learning Hebrew. She gave Lisa an affectionate smile, as if she were one already.

When they stopped beside the international departures terminal at Lydda airport, Erez leaped out of the car and hauled Lisa's luggage from the boot. I'll carry it, he said to his father. The four of them went to the check-in desk, the terminal was busy, people were scurrying in all directions, everything was so modern, it was as if they were in a Western country.

Lisa checked in her suitcase, the lady behind the desk handed over her boarding card. They headed for passport control. Together they stood in the queue and tried to engage in small talk. Orthodox Jews had gathered in one corner, men in black coats and hats, they were singing together loudly, Americans, Oz said, who've been here on a pilgrimage and are now going home. Lisa caught snippets of Yiddish conversation, I thought that had died out. Weeds never go away, Erez joked, but his father shot him a stern look.

They were not allowed to accompany her to the gate, Sorry, said the customs officer, a man in military uniform, Security regulations. They embraced, Come back, I will, thanks so much for everything, Any time, I really mean that. Bye! Lisa went, she waved at the people waving, then their farewell was over, she continued down the corridor, she clutched her handbag, all at once she realised how at ease she had felt, a Jew amongst Jews, Now I know what it's like.

There were many people at the gate, including Germans, Lisa could not tell if they were Jews, I expect that's true of me too, she thought. The time ticked away, Lisa wondered whether she should write in her diary. But then the boarding announcement came, people rapidly formed a queue, each of them was wished a good flight, Lisa too. She stepped onto the tarmac, behind her was the aeroplane that would take her back to Germany, Lisa felt the urge simply to stay, not to fly back, she thought,

I could ring Grandma. But then she pictured her grandmother in her mind and kept walking. Slowly she ascended the aircraft steps. She was welcomed on board by the stewardess, she looked for her seat, Row 13, Seat D, she sat down and looked out of the small window. Outside the sun of Israel was shining, the sun of the Mediterranean, light like this did not exist in Germany, I'll miss it, she thought, but she meant much more than that.

Over the public address system a quiet voice said, Boarding completed, it was addressed to the crew. The stewardesses began to close the heavy door, but soon stopped, there was a pause, Maybe they're still waiting for someone, speculated Lisa's neighbour, a German travelling with his wife. A stewardess came down the aisle, wearing a professional smile, and bent to her.

"Are you Lisa Kramer?"

Lisa nodded, surprised.

"There's an important message for you," the woman said. "Would you follow me please?" Lisa stood up, all of a sudden worried, What if something had happened to her grandmother? What if she arrived too late? She was gripped by anxiety, her heart pounded faster, she followed the woman to the front. There she was met by a man who introduced himself as a security officer.

"The message is from Anat Almog in Jerualsem. Do you know this person?"

Lisa nodded. An accident! Thoughts and images jostled for position in her mind, the yellow Saab, Oz, Binah, Erez.

"It reads: 'Anna Sarfati has got in touch. She would like to see you.' It gives an address in Tel Aviv. Will you accept the message?"

Lisa nodded silently, she took the piece of paper the officer held out to her. She looked around helplessly.

"It refers to a request broadcast on Kol Yisrael," the officer said to the stewardesses standing next to them.

"Aha," the women murmured, their expressions towards Lisa changed.

"If you'd like to stay in Israel we'll fetch your case from the hold," the officer said.

Lisa nodded without thinking.

"Please, come with me."

The stewardesses wished Lisa the best of luck, she thanked them in a daze, then went down the steps and followed the man who walked ahead with rapid steps, back to Israel.

ONE HUNDRED AND TWENTY-SIX

They cycled through the city with spring all around them, sprouting trees, young greenery, people coming back to life after a long, cold winter, shining wet asphalt after the last rainfall, the sun was shining as if it too had become youthful again.

They cycled through the city, Ben in front, Gudrun behind, she knew the way but did not want to remember it, for a while at least she wished to act as if she had no idea where they were going. Ben had insisted on this outing, Although my parents pretend to be very progressive I know they're not. Gudrun had shrugged, If needs must, since she had been together with Ben she had learned that such things were not inevitably unpleasant, You'll like them, he had said, Even if I don't, was her reply. He had laughed and taken her in his arms, she loved the fact that he took every opportunity to do this, she could say what she wanted, he found it all funny or charming or sexy, his love for her seemed to be so immense she sometimes found herself doubting it was genuine. You're my sanatorium, she had said, Come on, sanatorium, show me who built you.

As they got closer, and when Gudrun saw the street, her ease dissipated, she got off her bike, What's wrong? Ben called out, I need to do this very slowly, she explained, I can only go step by step, not on wheels, who cycles back into childhood? She put out her arm, A beggar always use to sit there, with a goatee and hat, not just a tramp but a real beggar, like in a book. Ben got off, they walked together, he shook his head, I don't remember him. You didn't go and share your break-time snack with him every afternoon, did you? Did you do that? Gudrun nodded, Don't imagine I had a strong social conscience. Why did you do it, then? She shrugged and drew down the corners of her mouth. Ben smiled, he liked the faces she made, they were all so expressive, what appeared normal in other people made her look as though she were a character actress on stage, with him sitting in the front row of the stalls. She was now walking very slowly, I think, she said, I felt he was the only person who was genuine. Ben nodded, I think I feel that I understand what you mean. Gudrun smiled, over there stood the house, she had avoided it until today, just as she had avoided Kaufingerstrasse, it appeared unchanged, she knew from Heinrich that her parents no longer lived there, not anymore. I'm an orphan, she thought, I expect I always was. Ben grabbed her arm, Here it is, he said, pointing to the house she had almost walked straight past, Gudrun collected herself, Right then! Ben did not move, he took several deep breaths.

"There's something you need to know before we go up." Gudrun's eyes widened, That would have been my line, she thought, if these were my parents.

"We're Jews," Ben said, "but nobody knows." Gudrun stared at him. A laughter was triggered inside her, a laughter she knew well, that third laughter for which there was no explanation, a terrible laughter whose violence frightened her, she had learned to control it, but she could not hold back the tears it produced. Ben stared back in horror, What's wrong? She shook her head, she must not speak if she wanted to confine the laughter, the violence, the terror to her mind.

After a while she was able to breathe again. Noticing Ben's confusion, she hugged him, Sorry. Ben wanted to see her face, he took her by the shoulders, she smiled at him, her eyes were still gleaming wet,

What's up, he asked emphatically, Is it because I'm a Jew? She shook her head.

"No," she said. "It's because our father murdered Jews."

ONE HUNDRED AND TWENTY-SEVEN

Peretz stood in the doorway of his house. The woman before him unbuttoned her headscarf, her serious face was wet below the eyes, she took off the headscarf, thick black hair flowed out, she shook it and stood there and said, Shit! Peretz opened his mouth, he wanted to say something, he noticed the man on the street in the background and gazed at him, but the young woman before him was too strong, her power did not release him from its grasp, her voice was dark and melodious, without any accent she said, I grew up here, this house will never be yours, yours and your family's, you will never be happy in this house, the fact that you stole it from me and my family will make you ill. She spoke softly and intensely, as if in a trance, as if she really could see into the future, as if the future stood written in Peretz's eyes and all she had to do was read it and convey it to him out of cool compassion, as if she were trying to say, You'd better leave here before you're destroyed by bad luck. Peretz tried to wriggle free, he forced out words, he said, We bought it from the state. The woman did not react, she looked at him with her dark eyes whose beauty Peretz felt like a pain. Her full lips quivered faintly, Peretz saw the gentle arch they formed, in its perfection this face was an epiphany, unchallengeable in every respect, and Peretz felt that if she kept standing here any longer he would snap like a piece of wood, all he wanted was for her to go and never come back, yet at the same time her force attracted him, a force in which there was no doubt, no hesitation. Coward, she said, spitting the word at his feet and grimacing, which would have made him recoil had he not been so paralysed. Turning away, she replaced her headscarf and left, and Peretz stood in the doorway, he watched her go, he watched her walk down the street beside Abdulha Al Sayyed towards the sea, wondering whether she was his daughter or his wife, he felt a vague relief because Anna and Sarah were not at home, closed the door, and leaned against it from the inside, trying to calm down. But no matter how deeply he breathed, the anxiety in his chest remained.

Later he would think, Little Arab bitch! Later he would become furious because she had dared confront him in this way. Later he would think of words he could have said to her, he would have said, No! would have bellowed, No! Go away! Or I'll give you and your father a good hiding! The force of his voice would have swept the little Arab bitch away from his door and out of his front garden like a strong gust of wind. Later he would try to laugh about them, Let them curse us, he would think, These Muslims, he would think, trying to believe the feelings he wished to generate with his words.

ONE HUNDRED AND TWENTY-EIGHT

"Anna?"

"Ruth! Shalom! How lovely of you to call!"

"Anna, you've got to come to Haifa."

"What's wrong?"

"The old man's dying. He wants to see you."

"What? So sudden? I . . . I don't know what to say."

"Say that you'll come, obviously. Please! It's important to him."

"What about Peretz?"

"He didn't mention Peretz, just you."

"Alright, I'll come."

"Tomorrow."

"So soon?"

"If you want to see him alive you've got to come tomorrow."

"Fine, I'll come tomorrow." She hung up. She looked around the sitting room. She checked the time, it was late, Peretz was not yet home, Shimon already asleep. She went into the bedroom and packed a small bag with the essentials. Then she went to bed.

ONE HUNDRED AND TWENTY-NINE

"Anna Sarfati?"

"Speaking. And you're Lisa Kramer?"

"Yes."

"Where are you now?"

"At Tel Aviv airport. I was already on the plane when I got your message."

"We were lucky then, weren't we?"

"You bet. I would have stayed longer, but Frau Kramer's daughter died and my grandmother is now all alone in Lübeck."

"I understand. It'll only be a brief delay, one or two days, maybe, then you'll fly back to Germany."

"Yes. Should I come round?"

"That would be lovely. You've got the address, haven't you?"

"Yes I have."

"How will you get here?"

"I can take a taxi."

"Great. It won't take you more than an hour. I'll get the guest room ready for you and make you something to eat. See you soon!"

"Bye!"

ONE HUNDRED AND THIRTY

We'll work it out!

I don't care!

You're not your father!

I'm not interested in what my parents think!

I love *you*, Gudrun Kruse, not your Nazi father.

Gudrun was lying in bed, hearing Ben's words over and over again. She had requested some time out and had moved back into the room next door. And now, for the first time, she was frightened.

No, it's got nothing to do with the fact that you're a Jew!

I'm not my father!

I love you, I couldn't care less what your religion is or which people you belong to!

I just need some time to digest it all!

"What is there to digest? We love each other and that's that!"

Oh, really quite a lot, my love. Have you ever asked yourself why a covert Jew should fall in love with the daughter of a covert mass murderer? Why the daughter of the covert mass murderer should return the love of the covert Jew?

She did not say this. She did not dare, and yet this was precisely what was nagging at her. What is love? Why does love do such things? Is it coincidence? It can't be coincidence? And now they were lying in separate beds again, because she, Gudrun Kruse alias Ranzner, wished it thus. Why should it be the daughter of the mass murderer rather than the Jew?

She tried to sleep, but could not. She turned herself and her thoughts and her feelings from one side to another. A shot of something now! Of what? Heroin or lead? To dive, to dive down again and feel nothing, to slip back into the ocean again, to swap her legs for fins and go under, far away from everything, from everyone, especially herself. To marvel at her own death like a miracle.

Late that night she went next door to where Ben lay in his bed, writing in his diary. They looked at each other. A smile darted across Gudrun's face and vanished.

"I can only do it with you," she said. "Not on my own."

"What luck! Come here!"

She climbed in and lay beside Ben in bed. He switched off the light and took her in his arms. They lay awake for a while before falling asleep.

ONE HUNDRED AND THIRTY-ONE

Jaffa, 11th June, 1966

What a day! I must try to describe it as precisely as I can, and not leave out any details.

I took a taxi from the airport to Tel Aviv, my heart was thumping and my mind spinning, what would I find out, what would Anna be like, who would Anna be?

Tel Aviv was jammed with people and vehicles, as if in the short time I'd spent in Jerusalem another hundred thousand people had immigrated and were now buzzing around all over the place in search of the things one needs to live. Perhaps that was just my impression, because I was in such a hurry that the traffic made me impatient and nervous.

When we finally got to the narrow streets of Jaffa I was astonished. I'd never expected to find a place like this in Tel Aviv, so old, so different from the part I'd got to know after my arrival in Israel.

The taxi stopped outside the house, the driver pointed and said, Here it is. I thanked him and was just about to pay when the front door opened and a middle-aged woman came out, her shoulders hunched forward, slim, tall. She quickly wiped her hands on a white apron, then opened the gate to the front garden. Her eyes, I thought as she came closer and smiled. Her voice, as she said something in Hebrew and paid the taxi driver. Then she switched languages, gave me a friendly look and said, Come in! I had only a hazy memory of her, back then I thought she was a giant, but now she was standing in front of me and I was as tall as she was. She hugged me, held me tight, while the taxi driver took out my case and put it down beside us.

"Welcome, Lisa!"

"Thank you."

"Please, do call me Anna, it's what you used to do."

I nodded silently, behind me the taxi drove off. Suddenly the two of us were standing alone in the street, the sun was shining, it was hot.

The house was beautiful, the decorations in the floor. The inner courtyard with a cistern in the middle. It was cool, that was the most astonishing thing.

"This house used to belong to Arabs, and sometimes I wonder if that isn't still the case."

This is what Anna said, with an air of resignation. She showed me the guest room to the rear of the house, it was small with a window looking out onto a vegetable garden belonging to the neighbouring house.

"Shimon's bedroom is right next door," Anna said with a smile. "If he hadn't heard your announcement on the radio you wouldn't be here now." She shook her head and said softly, as if to herself, "It's a miracle that it hadn't completely disappeared from his memory."

We went into the kitchen where there was a small, square wooden table with three chairs. I saw modern appliances, a mixer, a fridge, an electric cooker. The dresser looked old, the walls around it even older – judging by the window alcove at the front they must be thick.

"This is where we eat when we're in a hurry, or when I'm alone with Shimon."

"Where is Shimon?"

She sighed. "Either he'll come or he won't."

I looked at her, an image flashed into my mind, her on a pallet bed with sunken cheeks, deathly pale after losing all that blood, my grandmother on a stool beside her. That must have been after the stillbirth. Shimon and I in the snow, but I can only feel his hand, I can't actually see him. I can picture Anna coming out of the corrugated-iron hut, tall and well wrapped up, offering a weak smile.

We sat down. Anna Sarfati. We looked each other and smiled as if trying to gauge how we felt about this.

"Funny, isn't it?"

Those were her words. I nodded. Yes, it was funny, but the funny thing was not that it had happened. The funny thing was that to me it seemed the most natural thing in the world, a result of this result of that result, endless, and our meeting, too, seemed nothing more than a knot in a long thread. But at that moment we were sitting in the absolute here and now, with no idea about the future.

Anna got up, she opened a cupboard and took out two plates.

"The cupboard and the plates belonged to the Arabs too."

"How can that be?" I asked, surprised. Anna put the dishes on the table, she looked at me with her eyes that I'll never forget, eyes like an abyss, green and shining, far apart, large eyes, sad eyes. Resting her hands on the table, she let her shoulders slump forward.

"The worst thing," she said, "is that things repeat themselves and there's nothing I can do about it, Lisa. Nothing at all." She turned around, drawer, cutlery. She put a pot on the table, took a ladle.

"It's just a soup, but it's delicious."

A hotpot like my grandmother might have made. With beans, carrots and potatoes. She served me. When she noticed me watching her she smiled.

"Although you've grown big," she said, "I recognised you straight-away." She nodded. "That's good, you remained true to yourself."

"Have you changed so much since you were a child, then?"

"I don't have photos anymore." Of course, this was something I was familiar with. Who in my family had any photos of their family? She took off the apron and hung it over the back of the third chair. Then she sat down.

We sat there, two lost souls, eating our hotpot. Eating really was the best thing I could do, for although I'd had all these questions in my head before, now that I was with her I couldn't think of a single one. I felt trapped by her aura, she seemed to be the only person in the world with her own unique pace. This hypnotised me, and it would take some getting used to.

After a while she said, "I had another child five years later."

I was confused briefly, but then understood. Five years later.

"How wonderful!" I said.

She nodded, then slowly shook her head, but said nothing. She looked into her soup, then at me, and said, "For Lana it's wonderful. For me it was more like a necessity."

I didn't dare ask direct questions, and she must have been able to tell by looking at me. She gave me a friendly smile.

"I like you, Lisa. You are how you are. You don't hide anything and you don't pretend. That's lovely." She was embarrassing me.

"When I look at you," she continued, "I see myself as I may once have been. But perhaps I'm mistaken and I was never like you, perhaps I was always . . ." she was searching for words, she looked at her dish and said, "like this hotpot."

I couldn't help laughing, she laughed too, and so the two of us sat in her kitchen laughing at Anna Sarfati's comparison of herself to a soup. Without thinking I said, "I reckon you're the most beautiful woman I've ever seen."

She laughed and waved her hand dismissively. Then she said something I'll never forget.

"Beauty is like candlelight. It attracts the moths too."

"But surely only when it's dark?"

She gazed at me intensely with her shining green eyes, I could not interpret her look. All of a sudden I thought my words had been naïve and silly, as if I'd offended her with my thoughtlessness. I wanted to say something, apologise, but she beat me to it.

"You're quite right," she said. Then she continued to eat her soup, and I did the same, to avoid making any other mistakes.

After a while I could not bear the tension anymore and said, "Anna, I came looking for you for a completely different reason."

She nodded slowly, she looked at me, she waited. Then I talked about Piotr, whose name we only know through Anna and who doesn't have a surname, but perhaps she knows it because she saw him that time with Karl Treitz, didn't she? At the same time I felt like someone having to feel their way through a dark room. She didn't help me, she sat there, waiting, giving me such an intense stare that I became increasingly uncertain as I spoke. When I was finished she took a deep breath.

"Finished with your soup?" she said. I nodded, she took my plate and hers, got up and put both of them in the sink. Then she turned and put her hands on the dresser to support herself, looking all of a sudden like a young girl, barely older than me, rather than a middle-aged woman. She was not smiling, she had an expression I'd never seen on anyone's face before.

"So this is how I have to repay my debt," she said softly, so softly I could hardly hear her. It was as if she'd been talking to herself, and when I asked her what she meant she snapped out of it and looked at me as if she were the one who'd come from far away. I didn't understand the situation and felt uncomfortable.

"We can talk another time," I said.

She shook her head vigorously, her hair swirled briefly.

"No, we won't be able to when Shimon comes back and I've got to pick Lana up from school soon. It has to be now."

"What debt?"

"Isn't that obvious, Lisa? Your grandmother saved my life, and she did it so skilfully that I didn't become infertile. But I left and never got back in touch with her. All these years I thought about you time and again. But I was so tied up with my own life that I did nothing. I could have come to Germany, at any time! I could have tended my daughter's grave."

I was about to say something, but she put up her hand.

"I know your grandmother promised to look after it. But it's my child lying there. I just ran away, like a little girl."

Her face changed, she now looked like a stooped old woman, gazing full of bitterness back at the past.

"And now you've come." She paused, pushed herself away from the dresser, held out a hand to me and said, "Come on, let's go for a walk! It's easier to talk about these things in the open air."

It was even hotter now, but perhaps it just felt hotter because the old house was so cool. We walked down a street with low houses on either side, some with new façades, others looked ancient. A little further on was a new house, box-like and twice as tall as the others. Anna told me that old houses were increasingly being torn down because people wanted more space and didn't always appreciate the old ones.

"Particularly those Jews who come from Arab countries, they don't see the point in keeping these houses." She shrugged as we continued on our way, still heading towards the sea.

Now I was able to savour the view for the first time. Anna Sarfati had journeyed across this sea twice to get here. I'd just jumped on a plane and then landed in Israel a few hours later. Mind you, I'd done that twice too.

ONE HUNDRED AND THIRTY-TWO

Out of the blue Anna said, "Shimon is Josef Ranzner's son."

Lisa stared at her. Anna returned her gaze, now with entirely expressionless eyes, as if what she had said had nothing to do with her, as if she were an oracle speaking the truth. Then something cracked in her face, in her entire body, she bowed her head and closed her eyes.

"Or he's the son of one of the four adjutants who took their turn after Ranzner," she said quietly.

She felt a sudden pain in her belly, she bent double, leaning so far forward that she toppled over, Lisa just managed to catch her before she hit her head on the pavement. Anna felt pain, as if about to give birth, as if five men were penetrating her at once. She was amazed that for all these years she had been able to walk upright at all, a clear voice said, I never imagined it would be like this, where are the tears of release, have they dried up, did I wait too long, has all my sorrow fermented into this searing pain?

After a while the pain subsided, Lisa helped Anna to her feet, Anna held her belly, a door opened and a woman came out with a chair and a glass of water, she helped Lisa sit Anna down on the chair, she tipped the water into her mouth. She was wearing a headscarf, Anna turned and recognised the Arab house that Peretz had once showed her. She smiled at the woman, middle-aged like herself.

When Anna had finished the water, the woman said, "Just leave the chair over there when you've finished with it." She pointed to the wrought-iron gate. Anna thanked her, the woman nodded and went back into her house.

All of a sudden Anna grabbed Lisa's shoulders and pulled her down so that the tips of their noses were almost touching.

"Nobody knows, Lisa, nobody! Promise it'll stay that way, promise me!"

"What about Shimon?"

She shook her head forcefully. "Nobody, do you understand? Nobody!"

"But why not? Surely the truth is better than . . ."

Anna shook her head again, so violently this time it was as if she were trying to efface Lisa's words.

"Shimon thinks that Peretz is his father. What else can I tell him? That his father is one of five men who raped me and left me lying on the ground? Should I tell him that?"

"But isn't it the truth?"

"No! It's madness! And Shimon's got enough problems as it is. He . . ." She broke off, she searched for words, then she said, "He's complicated, he and Peretz don't get on particularly well, and he's been quite distant from me for ages."

"But maybe it would help him if he knew . . ."

"No! Absolutely not. It would destroy him. Promise me, Lisa, here and now! Promise me!"

She held Lisa so tightly that it hurt, staring at her with such intensity that Lisa began to get anxious.

She wrenched herself free and stood up straight, Anna stared at her uncomprehendingly and slowly she let her arms drop.

"I'm the wrong person, Anna. I'm really sorry. You should have told your son, he needs the truth to understand where he comes from. It's the same reason I came to see you. I didn't want to find out about Shimon's father, it's none of my business."

She paused, she looked around. The sun burned down on her, the sea below, the old and new houses of Jaffa, nothing was important anymore. She felt as if she were standing on a stage, the broiling heat, a cobbled street, in the middle of which sat a madwoman on a chair belonging to a Palestinian, and she herself, what role was she playing? The role of the character who appears in the wrong play and gives the wrong answer? Lisa shook her head.

"I'll go back now, I'll pack my things and fly to Germany. My grandmother needs me."

She turned away. Anna watched her, a faint pain still tugging at her belly. But she hauled herself out of the chair and followed Lisa with slow steps. She did not see the Palestinian woman come out of the house and remove the chair from the street.

ONE HUNDRED AND THIRTY-THREE

By the time Anna got home Lisa was standing outside with her case, waiting for her. Anna felt like a routed army, What have I been defeated by? This young woman? She knew the answer. Exhausted, she moved to the metal fence that separated the front garden from the street and leaned on it for support. There was so much she wanted to say to modify the tone their conversation had taken, but realised that with all the things she could say there would have been one sole aim: Lisa's silence. She looked at Lisa, Lisa with her youthful clarity stood before her like a magic mirror, she would always answer truthfully. And me, she asked herself, have I become so lost in my own labyrinth that I cannot even tell the truth when I want to? She sighed.

"I'm sorry, Lisa. You're right, I shouldn't have told you."

She hesitated, the truth was what she wanted to keep hidden, but she could use it as a compass.

"I used you," she said.

Lisa nodded. "Yes, you did."

"I wanted to unburden myself, without having to fear the consequences. I'm so very sorry. Please forgive me."

Lisa relaxed slightly. Not a madwoman after all. She nodded again, faintly at first then more firmly.

"Of course I forgive you, Anna. What happened to you must have been horrible."

Anna paused. She was struggling to retain her composure.

"The worst thing is that as it was happening I felt something. I'm sorry, Lisa, I shouldn't be telling you any more. But I can't say it to anybody else."

Lisa said nothing.

Anna bent forwards, the pain in her belly was still there.

"It was as if that meant they couldn't destroy me. Because I fought back with something, because I didn't just let them have their way with me."

She broke off. Lisa put her case on the ground, she went to Anna and gently took her in her arms. Anna held her tight as if she were a little girl. Lisa pressed her cheek to Anna's head, she gently stroked her hair.

"I will never tell a soul, Anna. Nobody, I promise," she said softly. Anna raised her head, she smiled through the tears.

"Thank you, Lisa," she whispered.

They stood there for a while, then Anna said, "Don't go yet. I'd like you to see Shimon and Lana." Lisa hesitated, Anna looked at her in supplication and said, "You can say what you like, anything, I don't care."

"Alright, I'll stay. But only until tomorrow."

Anna smiled, now looking like a young girl again. She nodded bravely.

"Only until tomorrow," she said. Lisa picked up her case and they went inside.

ONE HUNDRED AND THIRTY-FOUR

The name had not yet been uttered. They continued from where they had left off. But this time they had not gone home. They rang at the door, Ben said, It's me, then it buzzed, Ben pushed the heavy door, took Gudrun's hand and the two of them went up the broad wooden staircase together, as far as the open door and the slim man with inquisitive eyes standing beside it, This is my father, Dad, this is Gudrun.

They had sat with the parents, Esther had come from Rosenheim to be there too, now they were in the kitchen and there was no cholent, but Wiener schnitzel with fried potatoes and cranberries. As they ate Ben started talking.

"Mum, Dad, Esther, what I'm about to say won't be easy, not for you nor for Gudrun and me. But I've got to say it all the same because it's important."

Esther was about to crack a joke but a gesture from her mother kept her silent. Ben took Gudrun's hand, now their hands were firmly clasped on the table, a sign for everybody.

"Gudrun's brother, Heinrich – do you remember?" he continued. "He was my classmate, and when he got together with Lena he moved into our apartment and then Gudrun moved in too." He smiled at Gudrun, then turned back to his family.

"Some time ago Heinrich found out that his father had taken part in the murder of Jews in the Third Reich." Ben took a deep breath, he shot a glance at Gudrun, who was sitting there, holding on to him tightly with her hand, her eyes, her heart.

A pause.

"I'm so sorry for you," David Schwimmer said, looking sympathetically at Gudrun.

Judith Schwimmer stood up, walked around the table, bent over to Gudrun and put an arm around her.

Esther Schwimmer said nothing and did nothing. She looked from Gudrun to Ben, and back to Gudrun.

Later on Gudrun talked, and as she was talking she regretted not having talked in greater detail with her brother, she had no idea where her father had been stationed, where he had murdered. The only thing she knew were her father's lies.

"What are we going to do now?" Esther asked all of a sudden.

"What are you talking about?" Ben said, confused.

Looking Gudrun in the eye, Esther said, "Your father murdered Jews and evidently he lives here in Munich. Are we – Jews – going to keep our mouths shut and make sure he's not brought to justice just because he's the father of Ben's new girlfriend?" There was a silence. Everyone looked at Gudrun. Gudrun searched inside herself, she knew the only acceptable answer, Take him, he's yours, there was no way around it, but still she searched inside herself for a No. A No would now be like love itself.

All she found was pity. For him, for the Schwimmers, for herself, for everybody. She shook her head, No, Jews must not cover up for a Jew murderer, this poison must not continue to flow, she declared open season on her father from now.

"What's your father's real name? Do you know?" Esther said.

Gudrun told her.

When the name was uttered there was a multiple echo, as if she had called out in a ravine.

ONE HUNDRED AND THIRTY-FIVE

The two women sat on a stone bench in the front garden beside the wall of the house. They drank tea. The bougainvilleas shielded them from the street, occasionally they heard people go past. It was late, countless stars studded the sky above them, like a thick white snake the Milky Way ran from one end to the other. The heat of the day had given way to a pleasant warmth.

"Well, what do you think of Lana?"

"Very sweet, she looks just like you."

"Yes, that's what everyone says. Peretz doesn't like it. But he would have preferred a son anyway."

"Did he say that?"

"Not in so many words, but I know him well enough."

"I was at the grave of your eldest daughter in Lübeck, the same name was written there. Why did you do that?"

"Oh, when she was born I felt it was the same person, but this time she was alive."

"The same person?"

"Yes. As if she'd been born a second time. Maybe I was just kidding myself to make everything better again. But as far as I'm concerned there's only one Lana with two bodies. One's buried in Lübeck, the other's sleeping in the nursery. Do you think that's crazy?"

"No, I completely understand, but I find it hard to believe that it's true."

"Josef Ranzner believed in reincarnation. He tried to make me believe that Nazis keep coming back."

"He talked to you about that?"

"Once. At the time I thought he was a coward – and that he most certainly was. But now I sometimes think there was a grain of truth in what he said, a very tiny one."

"I'm definitely not coming back."

"How can you be so sure?"

"I don't know. I wouldn't even like to live a second time."

"You've got the whole of your life ahead of you."

Lisa nodded and said nothing. Secretly Anna understood her.

There was no chance of seeing Peretz, he was on a military exercise in the Negev. And Anna had no idea where Shimon was. Lisa noticed that whenever Anna spoke about her son a deep furrow appeared above the bridge of her nose.

At around twelve the two women said goodnight and went to bed. Lisa wrote in her diary. She tried to capture everything, but she was too tired and could not finish. She lay on her back, staring at the dark ceiling, with the feeling that already she knew too much about these people. She began to think about things psychologically, it felt claustrophobic inside her head.

Before she fell asleep she thought what a pity it was that Shimon had not come.

ONE HUNDRED AND THIRTY-SIX

It was not the early light the sun cast across the sky from the east, even before it rose, that woke Lisa the following morning. Someone opened the door and entered her room with heavy footsteps. She opened her eyes and saw a large shadow draw near. She just managed to shift to the side before the shadow dropped onto her bed and lay still.

Shimon stank of alcohol and tobacco. He promptly began to sleep off his inebriation. His breathing was deep and regular.

Lisa gradually recovered from her fright and realised that he must have stumbled through the wrong door. She got up and took off his shoes. Then she dragged him by the arm as close to the edge of the bed as she could, to leave enough room for herself. She tentatively lay down beside him. His face was turned towards her, in the growing light she could see it in sharp contrast.

And so they lay, side by side.

How handsome you've become, Lisa whispered. She gave him a kiss on his sweaty brow, she took his hand and thought of the past, of snow, of corrugated iron huts and the games they had played without talking to each other. Diverse images that had been forgotten and now sailed through the space inside her, weightless and everlasting. She closed her eyes and went to sleep.

ONE HUNDRED AND THIRTY-SEVEN

When Lisa awoke the following morning Shimon was gone. He had left behind a note, she could see that he was not used to writing in Latin script. In wonky, scrawly letters it read: *Medusa, HaMasger Street, this evening, please come!*

Anna had given her the note, a deep furrow above the bridge of her nose. They had breakfast and engaged in small talk. All of a sudden Anna looked at her intensely.

"Lisa, I'd rather you didn't go to Medusa."

"What is Medusa?"

"It's a club. I presume there's a concert taking place tonight."

"Why do you want to dissuade me from going?"

"It's . . . not a safe place."

"You don't want me to see Shimon, do you?"

"It's not what you think. You can tell him what you like, although I think would be better for everybody if he learned the truth from me."

"I won't tell him a thing. But I do want to see him."

Anna gave her a look she could not read. Then she nodded and changed the subject.

ONE HUNDRED AND THIRTY-EIGHT

Medusa was a gloomy bar set between two low-rise box-like buildings on the six-lane HaMasger Street to the north of the inner city. A plain, iron door was the entrance into a basement, the name Medusa was written in charcoal on the wall above.

Shimon Sarfati and four other young men were singing on a small stage, *"When I was younger, so much younger than today"*. The band's name was written in English on the bass drum: The Desperates. They wore white shirts and grey waistcoats. They all had the same haircut as The Beatles.

The small, square space was packed, people of Lisa's age or a few years older, the noise was deafening, the smoke from countless cigarettes hung in the air like fog.

Lisa fought her way through to a long bar to the side of the stage, she began to sweat, people were shouting at each other to make themselves heard. She ordered a glass of water and watched Shimon. He was standing at the very front of the stage, sometimes he closed his eyes, sometimes they were open, focusing purely on the music. As he sang his movements were completely natural, as if oblivious to the hundreds of people watching him.

After a while Lisa noticed that a lot of women were clustered near the stage watching Shimon. She realised that he was perhaps not quite as immersed in himself as she had thought. He exchanged glances with the audience, gave a smile here and there, waved at somebody, pointed to someone else. The women seemed to know this.

Not a safe place, she remembered Anna saying. She felt stupid and naïve, but she did not move from her spot. I've only come here to see him again, no other reason. She knew that this was not the truth, but it dissuaded her from leaving Medusa straightaway.

There was a thunderous applause, which Shimon savoured with a smile. He lit a cigarette as he announced the next song, and it was the first time that Lisa had heard him speak. Before the music started he reached for a broad round glass on a speaker behind him and took a big gulp. Then he sang a rock number in Hebrew. The rhythm was fast, the guitarist threw in some quick solos and Shimon moved as if he were standing not in front of a few hundred people, but thousands. Lisa realised that she knew all of his gestures, she had seen them time and again on television, they seemed to belong to the fixed repertoire of a pop singer. And yet there was something about Shimon that made everything he did appear unique, as if he were the original and not a copy. Lisa was so taken by this notion that she forgot everything else.

When the concert was over The Desperates' fans stormed the stage, almost all of them heading for Shimon. The other musicians seemed used to this, they ignored it, packed away their instruments and left the stage.

Lisa made to leave the club, she had no desire to rush at him like one of his worshippers, and she did not want to spend any longer in this foul air. Maybe he'll come home at some point, she thought.

When she was close to the exit a voice boomed from the speakers. "Lisa, wait!" it said in German. There was a brief silence, not a real silence, more like a dip in the noise level, but this dip was so deep that the place changed in an instant. Lisa turned and looked into Shimon's eyes, he was watching at her from the stage. Many other pairs of eyes were fixed on her too, and for a brief moment Lisa felt as if she were looking at a photograph. Then the image moved again, the noise level rose once more, wiping the moment away. Lisa watched Shimon make his way through the crowd. When he reached her he said, "Come on, let's go." He simply put his arm around her shoulders, nodded to the bouncers and took her out into the street. It was dark and considerably cooler than in the club. Lisa shivered until she became accustomed to the temperature.

They walked along HaMasger Street, cars, lorries, motorbikes drove past, all seemingly in a hurry, and this hurry generated a noise that sounded like anger to Lisa's ears. She noticed how tall Shimon was, a head taller than her. She felt secure and tried to resist this feeling.

They came to a large building site protected by a picket fence. Behind it soared skeletons of columns, walls and floors, poured-concrete steps led upwards. Shimon looked for a particular spot, finding it he wrenched a broad slat from the fence.

"Come on!"

Lisa hesitated. Without any lighting the building site beyond was indistinct, scattered all over the place were objects she could only grasp the outlines of.

"I come here often," Shimon said. "I'll guide you."

Overcoming her reluctance, Lisa slipped through the hole in the fence. Shimon followed her and replaced the slat. He took Lisa's hand and led her to the stone steps.

They climbed to the seventh floor and stood on the roof. Shimon drew Lisa almost to the edge. Letting go, he pointed at the city far below, an unevenly illuminated expanse of land that seemed to extend in all directions. Only in the west did the lights end abruptly, that was where the sea began. Distant sounds floated up to them, engines, car horns, sometimes a human voice. A night bird flitted past noiselessly. The sky above was full of stars. The city appeared like an enormous spaceship, making its way through the universe alone. Shimon was spell-bound by the view of night-time Tel Aviv. After a while he turned to Lisa.

"Welcome to my home! I hope you like it."

Lisa did not know what to say. Shimon smiled.

"When I woke up this morning I was holding your hand."

Lisa nodded. "I know."

"But you were asleep, weren't you?"

"Yes, I was asleep."

He turned away and then back to her. "Why did you come to Israel? Why did you look for my mother?"

Lisa stared at him. She wanted to say, Because an S.S. commander had a subordinate who was lured to his death by a Pole, and the commander was your father and the subordinate was called Karl Treitz and the Pole was called Piotr and death was my mother. Instead she swallowed; then said, "I wanted to see you all again."

He nodded as if the answer was adequate. Coming closer, he said, "When I woke up this morning the first thing I saw was your face. I thought I'd died and beside me lay a sleeping angel." He was not smiling, he was staring straight into her eyes, she could not look away, his eyes were soft and warm and completely open, like the eyes of a child. He came even closer, he put his arm around her, she did not resist.

ONE HUNDRED AND THIRTY-NINE

Heinrich had not been expecting a letter like this. He waited two days before showing it to Lena. They were sitting in their cramped kitchen having dinner, little Michael asleep on her arm. She read the letter through twice. Then she let her hand drop and looked at her husband.

"So are you going to accept?" she said.

474

"Not a chance!" Heinrich said. "You do understand that, don't you?"

Lena gave him a thoughtful look.

"Of course I do. But times have changed. There aren't people like your father there anymore. And the pay is almost double – from day one." Her eyes were now imploring him.

"Think of your family!" she went on. "We want Michael to have a little brother or sister. The past is history, leave it be! Now it's all about the future."

Heinrich reported for work one week later. When he showed the letter at reception a young man, four or five years older than himself at most, took him down long corridors to the head of personnel.

Herr Strobl sat in a small office behind a narrow metal desk with a grey protective coating, surrounded by shelves brimming with folders. He was smoking a cigarette, the round spinning ashtray in front of him was full of butts. He had a thick handlebar moustache, his dark, straight hair was neatly combed. Side parting. Herr Strobl gave a brief smile and pointed to a chair, Heinrich sat down.

"You can start straightaway, if you like."

Heinrich gave him a baffled look.

"Don't you want to . . . assess me or test me or something like that?"

"Already done, long ago. That's why we wrote to you."

"But you know nothing of my abilities as . . . well, as an intelligence officer."

Herr Strobl smiled indulgently, he took such a big drag on his cigarette that it glowed brightly.

"Now don't go getting the wrong idea! You're not the only relative we employ. At the moment we're doing this to keep as many posts as possible in our budget. If the people at the chancellor's office get the impression that the B.N.D. has more than enough staff, they'll get rid of jobs, and the president doesn't like that."

Heinrich stared at Herr Strobl. Tentatively he said, "This is a joke."

Herr Strobl puffed on his cigarette and shook his head.

"It's no joke. You wouldn't believe the kinds of people we have here. Hairdressers, sales assistants, taxi drivers – all relatives of those who are or were employees. Most of them from Bavaria."

"But why don't you look for qualified staff?"

"Too time-consuming. We'd have to run checks on them all, and on all their relatives too. We've already done that on people such as you." He shrugged. "It wasn't my idea."

"So what do I have to do?"

"You'll stay with me in the personnel department, we've got a position that needs to be filled by the end of the year. It's all red tape, You won't even realise you're working for the B.N.D. And the salary – well, that's why you came, isn't it?" He grinned and took another puff of his cigarette, the ash now so long that it fell on Heinrich's personal file, Herr Strobl brushed it away with a flick of his hand. Then something else occurred to him.

"Just one question, Herr Scholz. Here it says your sister, Gudrun Kruse, had, well, a complicated childhood. He looked up and raised his eyebrows."

Heinrich hesitated before saying, "She suffered terribly as a result of our father's past."

Herr Strobl raised his eyebrows. "Jog my memory, would you? The records relating to V-9245 are missing. I assume his file was removed before I took over this job last year."

"Are you a relative too?"

Herr Strobl gave a broad grin. "A nephew. I'm a graduate, which means I'm the boss here."

Heinrich nodded. "Our father was a . . . fellow traveller in the Third Reich."

"Fellow traveller?" Herr Strobl snorted and pulled a scornful face. "Then I'd expect the entire country to be plagued by psychological problems."

Heinrich shrugged.

"Right. Let's draw a line under this, shall we? She seems to have got back on the right foot ever since she's been with that Jew."

"Jew?"

"You mean you didn't know? They keep it a secret, but of course we know things like that."

When Heinrich came home that evening he felt weird.

ONE HUNDRED AND FORTY

He stood at the window, there was a chink in the curtains. He was holding a pair of binoculars. In the tower block opposite, seventh floor, third window from the right, the light went on at 7.00 p.m. precisely. A bathroom. Josef Ranzner peered excitedly through the binoculars. A girl, maybe fifteen, appeared at the window and got undressed. When she was naked Ranzner began to masturbate, trying to keep the binoculars steady with the other hand. All the while he addressed the young girl in a whisper, now she was tying up her long hair and getting into the bath. At the precise moment that she drew the shower curtain and vanished from Ranzner's view he ejaculated into his underpants, immediately feeling that old sensation of regret that had been a constant companion ever since he had been able to think, and whose significance even now seemed to be an unbroken seal. Ranzner was momentarily seized by the fear of dying alone. He thought back to the only woman he had ever loved, he did it every day. But her features had changed, it was as if his memory could not decide between two possibilities and so it showed them both in one face.

Suddenly the doorbell rang. Ranzner jumped. For a second he was worried that Mossad or the B.N.D., or some overzealous German court had been watching him and now they had come to arrest him, expose him in front of the entire world, just as . . . He paused. Father? An image flickered in his mind: the Reichsführer S.S. Now Ranzner was confused, something was wrong, but he could not work out what.

The image flew away. Ranzner forgot the incident. He carefully placed the binoculars on the sitting-room table and tiptoed into the hall. He was glad that the lights in his apartment were switched off for his observation session because they were visible through the spyhole from outside, he had checked this himself.

It was pitch-black in the hall. Silently, Ranzner felt his way forward. The spyhole was his guiding star, it shone brightly in the darkness, right in front of him. Ranzner approached it slowly.

When he squinted through it he saw in the brightly lit corridor a young man in three-quarters profile. The man looked immediately familiar, but at first he did not know why. He withdrew his head from the spyhole, only to put it straight back for another view. He could scarcely believe what he was seeing, but there was no doubt about it. Karl Treitz had found him! Karl Treitz had embarked on a search for him and was now standing on the other side of the door. How on earth could that be possible?

The young man in the corridor rang a second time. To Ranzner's surprise, he opened his mouth and called out, "Father! It's me. Heinrich, your son! Please open up. I want to talk to you! Father?"

Josef Ranzner did not know what to think. There was something not quite right about this man, it was better to exercise caution. Ranzner decided to observe him first to gather more data. He stayed at the door, spying through the hole, until Heinrich Scholz gave up and left.

Relieved, Ranzner went into the bathroom.

ONE HUNDRED AND FORTY-ONE

"Grandma?"

"Lisa! What a wonderful surprise! How are you?"

"Aren't you angry that I haven't been in touch for so long?"

"No, my child, of course not! You've got all your own things to be getting on with. Tell me, how's life in Israel? How long have you been there now? Almost half a year, isn't it? Are you going to stay over there?"

"Oh, Grandma, it's not how you think it is."

"How is it then? Is something wrong?"

"Grandma, I'm pregnant – by Shimon."

"Lisa! My, my, that is some news. So what are you going to do?"

"I want to come home!"

"Of course! Come home! Do you have any money?"

"No."

"I'll send you some via the embassy, I've already enquired and you can do that."

"You already enquired?"

"Just in case your money ran out. But my God, Lisa, how did that happen?"

"I love him, Grandma. And he loves me too. But he just can't . . . There's something that's stronger than his love for me. I . . . I'm so unhappy!"

"Lisa, darling, you've got to use your clever head. I'll telephone the embassy first thing in the morning and you go and collect the money. Then you can book your ticket home. Where are you staying?"

"Oh, with Shimon's bassist still, he's got a large apartment. I think his parents have money. Shimon and I were living here together. He moved out last week. He says he can't commit! But I know that he loves me, Grandma! How can both of those things be true? I never knew that was possible!"

"Lisa, you poor thing! Go and get yourself a hankerchief. You do have things like that there, don't you?"

"Loo paper."

"Loo paper will do. And then stop crying. Listen, perhaps one day Shimon might realise that he loves you and wants to be with you too, you don't know that yet."

"Grandma, he's so . . . he's so lost! He's like a drug addict, he consumes everything, emotions, alcohol, cigarettes, hard drugs too, he's got no boundaries. The same thing has happened to so many women with him. And I'm so stupid I rushed into it with open eyes!"

"It's got nothing to do with stupidity, Lisa. You can't control the course of love."

"No, evidently not."

"Have you at least found out anything helpful from Anna?"

"Anna told me that Shimon is the son of one of five S.S. men who raped her one after the other. The first was Josef Ranzner."

"My God! Does Shimon know?"

"No. Shimon thinks Peretz is his father. She told *me*, a stranger! And then she begged me not to say anything because she wanted to tell him herself. But since then she hasn't done a thing. She's so scared that Shimon will throw himself off the nearest building if he finds out the truth."

"Oh Lisa, what have you got yourself into?"

"Grandma, I want to get away from Israel. I can't stand it here anymore."

"You'll come home to start with, won't you?"

"Yes."

"Will you give me another call tomorrow? When you've booked your flight?"

"Yes."

"Alright. Stop crying now and go to bed."

"Yes, Grandma. Good night. Love you, Grandma."

"I love you too, very much."

"Grandma?"

"Yes?"

"Maria is dead, isn't she?"

"How did you know?"

"I'm really so sorry, Grandma! I ought to have replied to your letter. But my head was just full of Shimon."

"It's not so bad, Lisa! You've got to live your own life. That's the most important thing there is, do you hear me? The most important thing of all."

"Are you very sad?"

"I was. Now I'm feeling a little better. And I'm happy that I've still got you. And a great-grandchild too, soon!"

"But I'm far too young to have a child, Grandma! I wanted to be free, I wanted to travel and have new experiences!"

"And you will, Lisa. Life is a journey, but you never know what's coming next."

"Goodnight, Grandma."

"Goodnight, Lisa. Sleep well."

ONE HUNDRED AND FORTY-TWO

Shimon was floating in the darkness. The darkness was lit up. Shimon fell without ever hitting the ground. Shimon flew without any wind. Shimon could not see, hear or feel anything. I'm dead, Shimon thought. The thought stood clearly in the room, Shimon remembered the needle he had pushed into the crook of his arm, he remembered the hand holding it, the arm that led up to a left shoulder, the shoulder had a counterpart on the other side, a neck had grown between them, on the neck sat a head, Shimon reconstructed his body from the memory, he placed a mirror in his soul and used it to inspect himself. I was a young man, he thought, he saw the face of a young woman, he stretched his thoughts out to her, but all they touched was a memory. He had no senses any longer, he was dead, and yet the memory of Lisa was painful. Suddenly a voice pierced his soul, not his voice, whose voice? He did not know the voice, it said, Quick! Resuscitation! Shimon heard a bang, the voice said, Again! Another bang and now Shimon heard a high-pitched sound, the high-pitched sound had been there all the time, he had not been paying attention to it, but all of a sudden the sound changed, it was no longer consistent, but jumpy. The voice said, Phew! That was really close. He heard other sounds, he heard the voice of a young woman, she said, He's a handsome chap, he heard metal on metal, he heard footsteps, he heard doors opening, he heard wheels rolling along a floor, the rolling stopped, a door closed, he heard nothing for a while, then he heard a regular sound like water dripping. I want to sleep, he thought, but he could not sleep, he lacked a body to feel tired, I'm a soul inside a bottle, he thought, he became sad and cried without eyes, without sobs. As he cried he heard the dripping sound, it was like a tap, I'm living in my dead body, he thought. He strayed though the lit-up darkness, he found a place that was completely white, white and refreshing, there he lay down and stopped waiting.

ONE HUNDRED AND FORTY-THREE

Lana knew the military base in Tel HaShomer, to the east of Tel Aviv, where her father was stationed. That is why she imagined her big brother lying there on a sofa when, at the end of March 1967, she went with her mother in a taxi to Chaim Sheba Hospital. It's right beside Papa's work, she had told Lana. But what's wrong with Shimon? she had asked. Wiping the tears from her eyes, her mother had smiled and said, It's nothing serious, darling, he just needs to rest!

To Lana's surprise her brother was not lying on the sofa in her father's office, but in a prefab which stood in a large complex of buildings, some low, some taller, all connected by a labyrinth of small roads and paths. The roads were lined with grass verges, lilac-blue jacarandas blossomed there, people in white clothing hurried hither and thither.

When Anna found out the state her son was in she would have gladly relinquished control over her body. She would have dropped to the floor and lain there, the doctors would have picked her up and placed her next to Shimon, attached her to the same tubes, inserted the same needles. Anna would have realised none of this and yet she would have been connected to her son.

She pulled herself together for Lana's sake. Squatting beside her daughter in the ward corridor, she said, "We can't see Shimon today, darling, the ward doctor said he's got to rest a little longer."

"But surely we can have a look at him, that won't wake him up, will it?"

"Look, darling, I'd prefer it if we came back when we can talk to him. You know what your brother looks like when he's asleep."

Lana looked her mother in the eye, then said, "Why are you lying, Mama?"

"I'm not lying, Lana."

"Yes, you are. Shimon's not resting, no-one goes to hospital for that. I'm not a baby anymore. I know that Shimon smoked and drank too much. That's why he's here, isn't it?"

Anna bowed her head, tears filled her eyes and ran slowly down her face. She nodded weakly and said, "Yes, my darling, that's why he's here."

"And it's also to do with Lisa going away, isn't it?"

Anna nodded once more. "Yes."

Lana put an arm around her mother and hugged her tightly. "Don't cry, Mama. Lisa's bound to come back."

ONE HUNDRED AND FORTY-FOUR

Tel Aviv-Jaffa, 30th March 1967

Dear Ruth

How are you? I hope you, Aaron and your three children are well and happy.

I bet you're surprised that I've sent you this letter. I wouldn't blame you; after all, I haven't managed it these last few years. You must feel as if I've lost all interest in keeping in touch with you, your family and our other friends from our time as refugees. After the old man died – in my mind he'll always be the old man – we became even more estranged. That's fifteen years ago now. How many times have we seen each other or spoken since? Three, four? Not more than that, and every time it was you coming to Tel Aviv either alone or with your family. I've never visited you in Haifa.

Please believe me when I say I didn't want it to be that way. I've never stopped missing you and the others. I shared your excitement when you had your children. I worried about Marja, especially when they took away her doll. When Ariel began his studies in Tel Aviv I visited him and shared his delight at having finally got away from his orthodox parents, but that hasn't reduced my affection for the Abramowiczes in any way.

Sarah sometimes pops by with Schmuel Seligmann, they seem very happy together in spite of the large age gap – Schmuel is almost twenty years older than she is. Now she's got a permanent job at Haaretz she has enough money to get by without our help, and it's good for her. I'm pleased that's she's finally becoming independent of us.

But that's not what I wanted to say. I want to tell you something that you ought to know. In fact you ought to have been the first to know, considering you looked after him to the very end. But I can also understand why it was me he revealed the truth to.

When I went to see the old man on his deathbed, we were alone in his room while the rest of you were waiting in the corridor, wondering what he might be confiding to me. Well, he didn't only tell me his real name. He also told me why he had dispensed with this name. He begged me to keep it to myself, but I think he knew perfectly well that I would anyway. You would never have done, because you've never had anything to hide. But he recognised that he and I were birds of a feather, or at least that's how it seems now.

He told me that he . . .

Anna sat up. She had never expected it to feel like a denunciation to write, Isaak Hirsch was a Kapo, a foreman in Auschwitz, Isaak Hirsch collaborated, Isaak Hirsch was only able to say it to me, because at the moment of my greatest humiliation I collaborated too, and although he couldn't know this he seemed to sense it. We were accomplices, and now I'm going to betray him.

Anna sat in the kitchen, looking out into the front garden. Peretz had put bars on all the windows of the house because of the unrest at the border. There are enough Arabs *in* Israel, he had said. Now she felt as if she were in a cage. She shook her head. Peretz and the Arabs, what did he have against them?

She knew what to do. She would have to ring Ruth to arrange a visit. She would have to go to Haifa. And she would have to tell her everything, the old man's secret as well as her own, for the two were linked, she herself had forged this link with her silence, and now it could no longer be broken.

She would tell her everything, for she wanted to talk about Shimon, she had to talk about Shimon, Shimon dominated her life, it had been like that from the beginning, from the moment of his conception, and now Shimon might never regain consciousness, he would lie there absolutely still, as she had seen him, but she could not talk to anyone about this, she felt as if she had been silenced along with him.

Peretz could only react angrily, it had always been this way, he had reacted to Shimon like that from the beginning, over any little thing, Not all fathers are the same, she had told herself, But he looks after him, she had told herself, He can't show his feelings in the way he'd like, and in her head a voice had answered, Don't kid yourself. She had maintained her balance with lies and the truth, and this was the result.

She scrunched up the letter and threw it into the bin under the sink. She went into the sitting room, where the telephone sat on a small side table next to the sofa. She sat down and picked up the receiver. Then with one finger she began to dial Ruth's number.

ONE HUNDRED AND FORTY-FIVE

Shimon's eyes saw the two doctors standing on either side of his bed, one older, shorter, greyer, the other younger, taller, balder, both of them had glasses with metal frames, ballpoint pens stuck out of the breast pockets of their coats. The younger doctor was studying a clipboard that he held in his hand. Shimon's ears heard what they were saying to each other, This one came to us from intensive care a month ago, the younger man said, Heart failure, in a coma for three weeks, a miracle he came out of it. The older man looked at Shimon briefly over the top of his glasses,

What was it? The younger man gave a terse laugh, Heroin overdose, but they missed that completely! The older man raised his eyebrows, he gave his colleague a probing look, I see, he said, So, opiate withdrawal, cold turkey? The younger man nodded, In a coma! And now? the older man asked, the younger man shrugged, They shunted him over to us because he flew into a rage when he woke up. What's he getting? the older man asked, the younger man looked at his clipboard and said, Diazepam. The older man lowered his head for a closer look at Shimon over his glasses, he said, How's he reacting to it? The younger man shrugged, He's peaceful, he said. Everything alright physically? The younger man nodded, Physically he's in good health. The older man stood up straight, turned to go and said, Good, discharge him around the middle of the month, give him a packet of this new substitute, you know he'll have withdrawal symptoms when he's off the sedatives. The younger man nodded, he plucked a ballpoint pen from the breast pocket of his coat, as he wrote he muttered, Fifteenth of May, sixty-seven, methadone, pack of thirty.

Shimon's eyes saw the two men leave the room, Shimon's ears heard the older man tell the younger man, My hands are tied, the instructions come from the Ministry of Defence, they want to show the Egyptians that we're prepared for any emergency. Before the younger man closed the door from outside he said, Throughout the whole country? Shimon was not able to see the older man nod, he did not hear the younger man lower his voice and say, That, by the way, was Colonel Sarfati's son, he did not see the older man briefly raise his eyebrows without saying anything in reply, as his hand reached for the next door handle.

When Shimon was alone, he turned his head. The white walls of the room slipped past his eyes, the bedside table with a glass of water, the picture of the three horses, the ceiling with its neon light, the chair on the other side and finally the window came into his line of vision, Shimon's eyes saw the white bars fixed on the outside, beyond these the trees with their lilac-blue blossoms. He stayed there like that in his bed. The sun wandered across his pupils, the door opened and closed, two hands fiddled with his right forearm, they pulled out the cannula, stuck on a plaster, the door opened and closed. The sun wandered over Shimon's retinas, the sun wandered through Shimon's soul, the sun set, Shimon closed his eyes.

It was night when Shimon opened them again. He felt different, it was as if someone had pulled a plug out of his ears, as if he had been watching a long film without any sound and all of a sudden someone had turned up the volume, and the wind was back, the trees had a rustling, the corridor outside had footsteps, his own body had a breathing, a beating heart. Thoughts poured into his consciousness like a gawping crowd locked out for far too long and now finally rushing in with senses sharpened to absorb everything, comment on everything, label everything, a sympathy, an aversion. Shimon lay in his bed, unable to move. The more that happened, the louder his heart pounded, the more he struggled for breath, he lay in bed, feeling as if he were running as fast as he could, he lay in bed, feeling as if he must collapse to the floor at any moment because all his strength would vanish, he tried with his eyes to hold on to something external, but it was dark, he could not see well enough, he tried to grasp the mattress with his hands, but the mattress had a consistency, it had a resistance, the wind whistled right through Shimon's ears, swirling up the thoughts like leaves, the thoughts were all crying out at once, Shimon tried to understand them, but his heart was pounding, Shimon tried to steady his breathing, but his breathing whistled like the wind in his ears, the wind in his ears had footsteps in the corridor, Shimon was worried that everyone was leaving, everyone was going past his door with their footsteps, which were carrying them through his ears, now he lay in his bed, unable to move, he could only run as fast as he could, could only fall for as long as he could, could only fear for as long as he could that, far below, the hard floor was racing towards him through the darkness in his eyes, and when they collided, he and the floor . . .

*

When Shimon came to it was light, the sun was shining in through the window, he lay in his bed, his limbs ached as if he had stiff muscles. Supporting himself on his elbows, he looked around. I'm still here, he said. He broke off. An impalpable pain shot through him. Lisa had been with him the whole time like his own back, invisible yet close. Now he had turned to face the world again and she was gone. He sank onto the bed, he stared at the ceiling. Nothing had changed. Everything had changed.

On 15 May, at 7.30 a.m., the ward doctor came in, Shimon recognised him as one might recognise someone from a dream. He was the younger of the two, his ballpoint pen was in his breast pocket, the clipboard in his hands had vanished.

"The country is mobilising, Mr Sarfati," he said. "With the exception of the Arab population and people like you, almost all young men and women are busy protecting the country from destruction by our enemies. You should be ashamed of yourself. Go home." He left Shimon's room without shutting the door.

ONE HUNDRED AND FORTY-SIX

The difference was so obvious! Anna was sitting in an E.G.G.E.D. bus going north, thinking about how Lydia Sarfati had treated her grand-daughter. I didn't want to see it before, even though it was plainly visible. The landscape drifted past, reddish-brown earth, orange groves, the sky so blue, the people on the bus chatted, dozed, ate their sandwiches, fruit, drank water or Coca-Cola, looked out of the window like Anna. Beside her sat an elderly man, at least sixty, who kept darting sideways glances at her, Anna sensed he was waiting for an opportunity to start a conversation, but she would not grant him one, she was sweating, the air conditioning was not working, she was wearing a dark-red, knee-length skirt, a white blouse, her suitcase was almost exactly beneath her in the bus's luggage hold, music clanged from the defective speakers. Arik Einstein's soft, warm voice sounded tinny as it sang, Come, chocolate soldier

come to me,

come to the trenches,

be calm, have no fear

of returning to dust.

The butcher gives the executioner flesh,

the executioner feeds the rifles

and all men are equal as they lie

beneath flowers in the earth, Turn it off! someone shouted. Other voices chimed in. The bus driver shouted something back. A loud babble of voices struck up, the bus driver made an angry gesture with his arm and lowered the volume. Peace was gradually restored and the drone of the engine, the rushing of the airstream regained the upper hand. The man beside Anna smiled ironically, he said, They prefer war. Anna nodded tersely before focusing again on the countryside.

Lydia Sarfati invaded her head again, Anna saw her smile, her warmth, She was never like that towards Shimon, she thought, able to accept this for the first time and even surprised that she had secretly borne a grudge against her mother-in-law because of the woman's keen instinct, now she could understand this as she saw the countryside drift past, fertile earth, open water, but now they drove for a short while close to the Armistice Line. The road was narrow and bendy, the bus made slow progress, the occasional jeep at the side of the road, an artillery piece between the pines, men in uniform. Peretz had warned her, It's not safe, he said, making a face that seemed to say, I can't tell you any more. Anna had shrugged, When has it ever been safe in Israel? there's been war from the day I arrived. But it's going to be different this time, Peretz had replied. She had gone nonetheless and was now looking forward to the moment when the truth would be told and she would have nothing more to hide, for the first time in so many years.

At eleven o'clock they arrived at the Givat Haviva kibbutz, tall trees, green grass, houses with gable roofs, Anna thought of southern France, it was a good feeling, I'm not so far away, she thought, surprising herself that after all these years she still viewed the world from the perspective of Europe.

The bus stopped at a crossroads at the far end of the village, she had to get out. The elderly man said goodbye with a hint of regret in his voice, Anna nodded again silently, then she was off. The driver got out, short, stooped, peaked cap, strong arms, a doer, he wrenched open the luggage hold, lugged out Anna's suitcase, placed it at her feet, doffed his cap, said goodbye without looking at her, and jumped back onto the bus. The heavy vehicle jolted down the road, the engine roared, the driver showed no consideration for the comfort of his passengers, he just wanted to crack on, Anna watched the bus drive off, leaving a trail of dust behind it. The bus got smaller, its noise diminished to nothing and suddenly she was standing all alone in the silent countryside.

Why don't you want me to come and see you in Haifa? she had asked Ruth on the telephone, and Ruth had said, Aaron and I aren't getting on at the moment, he'll stay at home with the children. We can have a walk, you and I, and afterwards we'll have lunch with the Abramowiczes. Anna had agreed. She stood at the side of the road, beside the stop sign, the occasional car came past, it was hot, but there was a pleasant breeze, the sun was almost directly overhead, the shadows were small, the land bathed in light, the kibbutz houses peeked out between the trees and bushes as if hiding, there was not a soul to be seen. Somewhere beyond the kibbutz a tractor was crossing a field, but it was not visible. The sea must be in the distance to the west. Anna missed it, all of a sudden the sea felt like a great security, she would escape to it whenever things got on top of her. But here she was in the centre of Israel, the entire country stretched out around her, encircling her, offering no way out, just a crossroads in the void. She wished she could be as proud of Israel as Peretz, she wished she had come here on her own and been forced by circumstances to fit in with the masses, had become one of many, an Israeli woman rather than a Yekke unable to forget her origins. The phrase "aren't getting on" passed through her head, it rolled from one side to the other like a heavy ball. Ruth and her clarity, she knew precisely when something began and when it stopped again. Me, on the other hand . . .

From the west a noisy vehicle drew closer, trundled towards the crossroads, an E.G.G.E.D. bus, it said "Beit She'an" above the windscreen, That's it.

ONE HUNDRED AND FORTY-SEVEN

When Anna and Ruth found each other amongst all those people arriving and waiting they were both secretly shocked, What has time done to us, we were young, that's past. They embraced, still comrades thrown together by fate, more than once they had escaped death, but death was a hedgehog, always waiting at the end of the path, And we ran like hares, do you remember?

The bus station was on the edge of the old town.

"Let's go for a walk across the fields, there's a left-luggage office here," Ruth said.

No sooner had they crossed the road than Beit She'an was behind them. They strolled in silence across a ploughed field, the earth was rust red, a farm track ran in a straight line towards a low mountain range, a hot wind was blowing, the air was dusty.

After a while the noises from the city receded, eventually becoming engulfed by the shimmering air.

"I was going to write you a letter," Anna said.

"But you didn't," Ruth said with a smile.

Anna shook her head. "No, it wouldn't have been the truth."

"The truth? What's that?" Ruth said. She sighed and burst into tears. Anna flinched, all the phrases she had prepared were washed away, she went to Ruth, Ruth pulled herself together, she looked her friend in the eye.

"I was never as pretty as you," she said.

Anna wanted to say something, but Ruth shook her head. "Aaron had an affair," she said, sobbing. "There was a time when I'd given up on you, Anna. I thought, what can I expect from her? But when you rang it was exactly what I needed." She smiled fleetingly, then the pain returned and she sobbed again. Anna put an arm around her, she was still in shock, she had not imagined their meeting was going to turn out like this.

Wiping away tears with the back of her hand, Ruth said, "He owned up, he says he loves me and the children and doesn't want to lose us. But I saw her and I could understand." She howled, Anna held her tight, but it was too hot for long embraces, she linked arms with Ruth and gently urged her to go on. Ruth was oblivious, she allowed herself to be led.

"I've tried to go on as if everything were normal again, I was about to call off our meeting. I thought, if I concentrate on the children and day-to-day stuff then the wound will heal. But it doesn't."

They continued walking. When Ruth, her eyes puffy, asked what Anna had wanted to say, she waved a hand dismissively and replied, "It's not important. It can wait for another time." Ruth nodded gratefully and Anna felt the truth inside her like a tear-proof material from which everything was made, all of life, the whole world. She was happy beside her unhappy friend, and tried to comfort her as best she could.

ONE HUNDRED AND FORTY-EIGHT

The Abramowiczes lived in an Arabic house with a courtyard. Anna was able to tolerate the analogy. Mr Abramowicz sat on a chair, wearing a white shirt and black trousers, his portly stature was astonishing, effacing the memory of the scrawny man who had carried his children up to his wife through the house at Rykestrasse 57. Mrs Abramowicz had become a powerful-looking woman with an ample bosom, beside these people Anna felt emaciated, Why have they done that? she wondered, there had to be a reason for it, but she could not fathom what it was.

All of a sudden Marja was in the room, slim and pale and serious. She embraced Ruth and Anna, she smiled, her face looked sickly, her skin waxen, How lovely to see you! You've got so big! Nothing but empty phrases to make her feel good, nobody could tell if she sensed this.

They had lunch in the courtyard, Mr Abramowicz talked about politics, he said, We'll show them, Mrs Abramowicz laughed at him and said, You especially. Mr Abramowicz laughed too, but then he said, I fight in my own way, I do my bit to reinforce the Jewish character of our state. Ruth thought of Aaron, who read Yeshayahu Leibowitz and demanded the strict separation of state and Judaism, she wondered whether the views of a man who had cheated on his wife were still valid, she decided against putting this to Mr Abramowicz.

Anna watched Marja. Noticing this, Marja smiled at her, it looked false, Anna was even more horrified, What on earth is wrong with you?

Later she left the courtyard and Mrs Abramowicz talked in a grim tone of the many therapy sessions, anti-depressants, attachment disorder, sleeplessness, all words she and her husband had been served up as an explanation for their daughter's behaviour, God's testing us, God will expel the Arabs, he will also remove the shadow from Marja's soul. But Anna could think only of Dana the doll, she stopped herself from saying, You ought never to have taken it away from her.

ONE HUNDRED AND FORTY-NINE

Daniel Katz, the bassist, did not return home from the war. He was on the northern front and had been pleased by the armistice which his government had agreed with the Syrians for 9 June. On the morning of 10 June, the new defence minister, Moshe Dayan, in consultation with several other ministers in Levi Eshkol's government, broke the armistice and seized the Golan Heights. Daniel Katz did not live to see this last great victory of his country over its Arab enemies. He was hit by a mortar shell and blown apart. His corpse consisted of bloody chunks of flesh and splintered bones.

Shimon found this out two days later, when all of a sudden Mr and Mrs Katz were in Daniel's apartment. They told him about their son's death and informed him that he would have to leave that same day. Shimon could sense Mrs Katz's bitter glances, which said, You, of all people, are still alive. He knew that they were not favourably disposed towards him, they had let their son do as he liked, that was all. There was no reason to fight back. Shimon had not been happy in the apartment alone. Lisa had grown far too close to him, here they had been happy, here their happiness had been shattered, it was from here that his escape had begun. Escape from what? This was the question that had been bugging him ever since his discharge from the psychiatric ward, and to which he was unable to find an answer.

Now he was out on the street again. Slowly he headed for Jaffa, he did not take the bus or a taxi, he walked, he gave himself time, he went slowly, gazing at the city he loved, which overwhelmed him with its people, its noise, its uncertainties cast in stone, he went slowly, as if searching en route for an opportunity to change direction, to aim for another destination. He stopped several times, drank a coffee in Dizengoff Street, had lunch on Yehezekel Kauffmann Street. He sat for hours in a small park by the French hospital and looked at the sky, the trees, inside himself.

But in vain. There was no escape, no exile, no better way.

By the time he arrived at his parents' house it was evening, the sun stood red above the sea, casting a streak of light, the streak glided over the surface of the water to Shimon, who clutched onto this view like a drunkard.

Peretz opened the door. When he saw Shimon he turned away without a word and went back into the house. Shimon followed him. Lana came running from the courtyard, her face beaming, she rushed to see her brother.

"Shimon!" she said.

But before she reached him Peretz grabbed onto her and said, "He's not fit company for you."

Anna came in from the courtyard, she saw her son and her daughter, she hurried over to Shimon and hugged him, but Shimon had eyes only for Lana, who did not understand what was going on, she tried to wrest herself free from her father but he held her so tightly that it hurt.

"Let her go, Papa!" Shimon cried.

Peretz turned, he came to Shimon with Lana and planted himself beside him.

"You're not my son," he said. "Lana's my daughter. But you . . ." He spat out the words, his mouth was a cannon that struck everybody. Shimon stared at his father, what he saw was not the anger he knew. He looked for his mother's eyes, his mother was staring at Peretz, Shimon saw the rebuke of the betrayed accomplice in her face.

"I don't care!" Lana cried. "Let me go!"

The last word became a scream. Peretz let go of his daughter without looking at her. Lana threw herself at Shimon, she clung to him, Shimon hugged his sister.

"I don't want to see you here anymore," Peretz said.

"Then you won't see me anymore, either," Anna said.

Peretz pressed his lips together.

"Nor Lana," Anna added.

"We'll see about that," Peretz said. He turned away, crossed the courtyard and vanished into his study.

Shimon let go of Lana and stood up straight. He looked at his mother.

"I've been meaning to tell you for ages." She looked at him with eyes that begged for forgiveness, indulgence, a proper hearing.

"Who is my father?" Shimon said.

"A German."

"Who?"

"A German." Anna looked her son in the eye. She was unfazed, the tears had no meaning, she opened herself up like a book, a voice inside her spoke to Shimon, it said, Read!

Shimon was unable to read. He stared at his mother. Lana had gone quiet, her eyes shifted from Anna to Shimon, from Shimon to Anna. Shimon was digesting the truth, Peretz was not his father.

"I've always known," he said abruptly.

ONE HUNDRED AND FIFTY

Frau Kramer intervened only when the doctor approached her granddaughter's splayed legs with a scalpel. Until that point she had sat at the head of the bed, holding Lisa's hand. She had realised even before the doctors that the child was not making the final turn. Closing her eyes she had seen Margarita Ejzenstain, who had died so long ago that she could barely retrieve the woman's features from her memory. She tried to calculate to the day the length of time between the early morning of 21 October, 1944, and the afternoon of 14 July, 1967, but she was distracted.

Lisa lay beside her, the girl's skin gleaming with sweat, her face showing a fear of the unknown, she missed Shimon, time and again she thought, If he were here, none of it would be so bad, but the force of nature inside her body did not worry about such thoughts.

Lisa tried to follow her grandmother's advice to use her breathing and voice to manage the contractions, which were occurring at ever decreasing intervals and becoming stronger, longer and ever more like waves of force and pain. Sometimes it did not work, her voice cracked and then her grandmother held her hand more tightly, offering words of encouragement, Don't be passive, my child! Join in! Don't just suffer it! You *want* to bring this child into the world!

But the baby seemed to be stuck with its nose to its mother's pubic bone. And so the whole process took longer.

When the head doctor, a man so young he could have been Frau Kramer's grandson, approached with the scalpel to cut through Lisa's perineum, the old lady let go of her hand and stood in his way, right by her granddaughter's splayed legs. Before the doctor could react, she said, "It's a moon-gazer. You'll just do damage with that." Then she turned, felt Lisa's belly and began to press and massage in various places, ignoring the five people – two doctors and three nurses in the white uniform of Lübeck's Marien Hospital – who stood around watching in astonishment as she delivered Tom Kramer from his mother.

ONE HUNDRED AND FIFTY-ONE

The lawyer received her at home. She lived in the north of the city and her name was Mrs Vakar, her voice had sounded young on the telephone, but this was all Anna knew. She had taken the local train across the Yarkon River, which wound its way north of the centre of Tel Aviv to the sea. She had got out at the university. Not familiar with the area, she had to ask for directions. A wide street led in the direction of the sea, Anna walked until she met a pedestrian who told her the way. She turned northwards into a narrow street that led up, detached houses on the hillside, small and squat, flat roofs, white-painted concrete, open garages beneath, windows above, narrow paths and steps leading between the houses, further up she glimpsed gardens which had only just been laid out, young trees, ordered flower beds. She looked for the house number and squeezed her way between two cars to an unremarkable-looking door. She rang, and shortly afterwards the door was opened by a woman with a narrow, dark face. Smiling at Anna, she said, "Mrs Sarfati, I presume? Please come in."

Anna followed the woman, she had never encountered such a slender person before. Mrs Vakar took her into a windowless room.

"The house is under siege, so I have to work here," she said.

Anna gave her a look of amazement.

Mrs Vakar laughed. "My husband and our three children. If I don't hole up here they won't leave me in peace."

Anna understood, she sat before a wide desk whose dark-red veneer and brass fittings did not match the sober compactness of the room. Mrs Vakar opened a notebook and picked up a pen. As she jotted down some notes she said to Anna, "I should tell you now that it can get nasty."

"What do you mean?"

Mrs Vakar stopped writing and looked at Anna. "I'll be perfectly honest with you," she said. "What you told me on the telephone doesn't sound good. If your husband makes good his threat and claims in a divorce petition that he never knew Shimon was not his son, you will be considered the cheating party. And then the rabbinate will award custody of your daughter to him rather than you. Do you understand?"

Anna nodded.

"What's more," Mrs Vakar continued in a business-like tone, "your husband is a well-respected officer in the army, one of the many war heroes this country is so richly blessed with. It's got even worse since the Six-Day War. And you're a housewife. Do you understand?"

Anna nodded once more.

"Getting married in Israel is so wonderful. The ceremony, the rabbi, the traditional clothes, the music." She smiled briefly, then continued, "But divorce is war. If you can't prove that your husband has behaved inappropriately according to the Jewish moral code the rabbinate will not agree to a divorce. Unfortunately, back in the day David Ben-Gurion gave the religious leaders responsibility for some important issues to encourage them to support a coalition. Jurisdiction over family matters was one of these. Do you know the joke about the couple that go to see the rabbi for a divorce?"

Anna shook her head. Mrs Vakar laughed wickedly and said, "Well, the rabbi first asks the man then the woman whether this is really what they want, and because they both say Yes, in the end the rabbi says, Well then, the two of you are in agreement! So continue to live together happily and at peace. Do you understand?"

Anna nodded uncertainly, the joke sounded familiar somehow, but she could not remember where she had heard it before.

"Are you prepared to fight?" Mrs Vakar asked her.

Anna blew air through her cheeks, looked at Mrs Vakar and thought about this.

Returning her gaze, Mrs Vakar waited attentively.

Anna liked her, she was pleased to have found a woman, the only one in the telephone book. She thought of Peretz. Have I ever loved him? She could not say, was that enough of an answer? She nodded and said, "Yes."

ONE HUNDRED AND FIFTY-TWO

Shimon sat by the telephone, procrastinating. He procrastinated for so long that Lana, who had been watching him from the inner courtyard, came in and said, "Just call her!"

Shimon turned his head in surprise and smiled at his little sister. Lana went back out to the courtyard, lay down on the cool stones, looked up at the sky and threw him the occasional searching glance. She had no idea about Shimon's options, she was unaware that he had already been in touch with his old guitarist to arrange a fix, she did not know about the methadone that had run out.

Shimon picked up the receiver, Now! But before he dialled the number he paused, What am I going to say to her? That I'm sorry I want to see her? *Do* I want to see her? He thought of how they had learned of the birth, a short letter addressed to his mother. Tears of emotion had filled her eyes when she showed him the letter. Shimon could not help but smile, mothers were so predictable, no matter what happened you could rely on their instincts. He dropped the receiver into his lap, What do I expect from life? He wanted something special, something extraordinary. Now he had become a father and he did not know his son, while he was a son who did not know his father, Nice tradition, that. But this was not what he had envisaged for himself. Singing? His head was full of music, full of lyrics, full of doubt. A real musician doesn't let the situation get him down, a real musician is still a musician even when he's not making music. He thought of his guitarist. All he had to do was call and say his name, nothing more. Then he would hang up and tell Lana there was something he had to do. He would take the bus to Medusa, because that was where the guitarist was playing with his new band. He would have something to drink, surely he would still get a discount there, and after the gig . . . Shimon put the receiver to his ear again and dialled the number. He waited. On the other end of the line a voice spoke, it passed through Shimon's soul like a wind, he had not been expecting that.

"It's me," he said, then listened. "Fine. How about you?" he said. The voice at the other end spoke, then went quiet.

"What about your studies?" he said. The voice spoke again.

"I want to see you," he said, "both of you." He had not planned to say this, it was the voice, her voice, he was powerless against it, he wanted to hang up and crawl down the line to her, his hands felt her magic skin and he wanted to tear himself away before he grafted himself onto her. He heard what the voice had to say, the voice kept talking, he forgot his hands, he forgot her voice, he heard what the voice was saying, he did not like it.

"Not in Germany," he said. "No way." He listened, he shook his head, he lost patience, he raised his voice. "If you love me then come to the place *I* can come to." He regretted raising his voice but could not take back his words, the voice at the other end did not grow louder, but softer, sadder, it spoke, he listened, he felt that he was shutting himself away inside, becoming inaccessible, he knew it, he could see the mechanism but was unable to resist.

"No, in that case," he said. He hung up without saying goodbye, he was still sitting in the living room, he refused to believe that she could not leave Berlin, she had come to Israel, after all, had hung around with him for months, she had people behind her with money, he knew all about her, she could not pull the wool over his eyes, he did not believe her. Picking up the telephone, he dialled a number.

"It's me," he said, then listened.

A voice said something, he hung up.

"I have to go and do something!" he called out to Lana.

"When will you be home?" she called back.

She's watching over me, he thought. He felt harassed.

"I don't know!" he said, before leaving and walking to the bus stop.

As he waited in the balmy evening air he thought of Germany, What had his mother been doing hanging around with a German? A German! She had told him he was dead. Could he believe that, at least?

A V.W. bus came round the corner and stopped beside Shimon, the driver opened the door by hand and with the help of a fragile-looking lever system of metal rods, Shimon gave him a coin and sat in the narrow passenger compartment, in the darkness he saw only pairs of eyes, it reeked too strongly of people. With a rattle, the bus pulled away.

ONE HUNDRED AND FIFTY-THREE

"The whole of life is the eye of a needle and you are an arrow shot through by a god who doesn't care how you feel, who only wants to win back what is his, what others challenge him for, and because of it he will annihilate them all. You are a means to an end, you have no target, you must simply fly through the air as he has determined. At the end waits death, the great release, the vast domain that no-one will take away from you, where you can settle. There you will suffer neither hunger nor thirst. Beyond hope and fear, and beyond good and evil you will find the peace you have been seeking for so long.

"And now imagine this: you are adjusting the eye of the needle yourself. The god drawing the bow is you. The arrow you are shooting is your passage through life. What you wish to win back is the heart inside your own breast. You must annihilate the enemies besieging your soul. Death is your victory over yourself.

"Which seems to make more sense, the first version or the second one?"

Lisa put down the book, Tom was lying asleep beside her. From outside the brief light of the December sun shone in. She could have gone ice-skating, it was that cold. She could have gone present-shopping or to buy a new dress that was only one size bigger than those she used to wear. Before Tom.

Instead she had stayed in Tobias Weiss's old apartment, looking out of the window across the red roofs of the city they had wanted to leave for ever. Sitting in her old place of exile, she felt like a snail in its house, safe and secure from the outside world.

There was only one person whose presence she longed for, but in a telephone conversation this person had told her that he would never come to Germany, anywhere but Germany. Lisa could have said, You're German too, your father's German, your mother's German, your son's German. But it would have been a lie because he would not have acknowledged it as the truth. And could she blame him? A Jew amongst Germans, she knew better than he did what that meant. She thought of the Schwimmers, they were like jugglers, forever tossing their two identities into the air and trying to catch them again, forever running the risk that one might crash to the ground. She thought, I couldn't live like that. She thought, No wonder they talk so much, all the time they must be trying to hide the secret from themselves. She thought, Nonsense, Lisa, everyone must live their life the way they see fit. She thought of the phrases she had read in the book. She thought, If death is victory over myself, what happens if I achieve this victory before I die? She thought, Could there possibly be an existence that encompasses both life and death? She turned her head and looked at Tom's tiny face which had grown since the first time she had set eyes on it five months ago. She thought of Mosche and Selma and Tobias, who had met in the hospital waiting room while she was having contractions next door. A former Wehrmacht soldier and two Holocaust survivors. They had got on well, indeed they had a lot in common, an entire war, Perhaps, Lisa thought, after a reasonable period of time it will be irrelevant which side people were on, because it was the war which created these sides in the first instance, they belong to it and they end with it too. Then she thought, Wars end slowly, this war is still in the process of ending. When will it be over? She smiled at Tom, unaware of all this, and wondered whether her son would outlive the war. Or would that only be for her grandchild?

ONE HUNDRED AND FIFTY-FOUR

Peretz was unable to concentrate on the old man's speech. He was sitting in the fourth of twenty rows at Beit Berl College, half an hour north-east of Tel Aviv, and David Ben-Gurion, the college's founder, was standing at a slim lectern in front of him. Around Peretz in the large auditorium sat two hundred officers of the Israeli armed forces, it was an important speech, but Peretz was trying in vain not to allow other thoughts to distract him.

Ben-Gurion's nose had grown bigger with age, by contrast the rest of his face seemed to have shrunk, the two tufts of snow-white hair, which grew above his ears from an otherwise totally bald head, looked like small angel's wings, Peretz imagined them growing and growing until one day they carried him away, it could not be that much longer. Ben-Gurion was the image of a prophet, despite his advanced years his gaze was sharp and clear, he uttered phrases that made the soldiers shift uneasily in their seats, phrases saying that the captured areas must be handed back as quickly as possible, saying that an occupation of the Palestinian areas put at risk the support of the Western democracies, without whose help Israel's existence was threatened, phrases making it perfectly clear that it had been a mistake to break the armistice with Syria, a mistake to seize the Golan Heights, he, Ben-Gurion, wondered whether this war would not bring other wars in its wake.

Peretz felt exactly the same as the other officers who themselves wondered what the old man was going on about, some suspected he was trying to manoeuvre back to the heart of power, while some saw him as yesterday's man, and others listened to him as one might listen to a seer speaking in poetic analogies that do not have to be tested by facts. They all kept quiet, because they were being addressed by the father of their country, the man who for decades had stood as solid as a rock and without whom there might not even have been an Eretz Yisrael. The past was mythical, it had the face of the old man, the voice of the old man, all of them had grown up with him, to them he was more of a father than their own fathers, a stern, wise patriarch, who would look out for them until his death and who now was saying, We must keep East Jerusalem, I propose that the Arabs should be moved to new parts of the city and Jews settled in the old town, I propose that the old Jewish quarter should be torn down and habitable houses built there in its place. At last, phrases that everyone could agree with, there was applause, Peretz clapped too, but he felt like an extra placed there to occupy a chair that otherwise would have been empty. His thoughts strayed to other phrases, Anna's phrases saying that she definitely wanted a divorce, phrases that made it clear to him she would fight for custody of Lana. Peretz was afraid of a legal battle, his family would find out, his father and – worse – his brother. His poor mother would hear the whole wretched truth, he would stand there like a weakling, he did not even have his own son, he had brought up someone else's brat instead, Anna had laid a cuckoo's egg in his nest. If he lied before court, saying he had known nothing, he would be shooting himself in the foot, if the truth came to light that he had even voluntarily allowed her to use him. If he consented to a divorce what should he say to his parents? We didn't love each other anymore? He already knew what his father would think, he would think that he,

Peretz, had made life too easy for himself, had lacked staying power to pull through the bad times together, he might suspect his son of having an affair. Again it would be pointed out that his brother had taken the better wife, had the more successful marriage. And what if he refused to divorce? Then he would be the fool who failed to understand that his wife no longer loved him, then all would suspect *her* of having the affair. And again he would be the weakling, the idiot.

He refused to believe it, he felt like the king on a chessboard who, having lost all his pieces, was now reduced to fleeing from one square to another. But he was too much of a soldier not to realise that he would lose this battle with Anna too.

Worst of all was that his feelings for Anna had not changed since that distant day when she had walked towards him out of the forest near Tulce. The pain of having failed to conquer her in all the years that had passed since burrowed its way deeper and deeper inside him, causing him to doubt whether what he felt really was love.

ONE HUNDRED AND FIFTY-FIVE

Berlin, 21st October, 1970

How time flies! Twenty-six years ago today the world was at war and still I wanted to enter this world. Seventeen years ago today I saw Maria Kramer at the door of our apartment. Four years ago today I celebrated my birthday with Shimon in his bassist's apartment. A year ago today Grandma moved to Berlin to be with me. Today . . . what is today? I try not to think of Shimon, I go to work and dream of studying again. Every day Tom fills me with joy and every day I'm sad because he doesn't know his father. It's not the sort of weather I would have wished for on my birthday. I'm celebrating the day by writing in my diary again. Tobi came this morning, it was lovely to see him again. He's got grey hair now and he still talks with endless filler words. But he's well, he's found a Hamburg woman who likes him, next time he's going to bring her with him. Tom and he are best friends already, they sat for hours on the floor looking at picture books, well, maybe not for hours, but a long time anyway. Then he left and I was happy that there are a few people in my life who don't simply disappear.

This evening I went to the cinema with Esther Schwimmer. Esther came to visit because she's got another friend living in Berlin. She had tickets for *Five Easy Pieces*. The film was so sad, Jack Nicholson was Shimon, I cried the whole time. Esther wanted to leave, she said, It's your birthday, you can't spend it howling in the cinema! I had to laugh as the tears ran down my face and I missed Shimon so much.

Where's my life going from here?

ONE HUNDRED AND FIFTY-SIX

Tel Aviv-Jaffa, 14th July, 1971

Dear Tom,

Happy Birthday! You're four years old now! That's really quite big. I'm so happy for you and delighted to be your grandmother.

I hope you like the toy car I sent. It's got a steering wheel on the top so you can really drive it!

I hope you have a wonderful day and a great party! Your father sends you birthday greetings too. He told me he'll call you later if has a chance.

A big hug and kisses from Israel

Love, Grandma

Dear Lisa,

I hope you're all well. I'm feeling better now. I finally moved out of the house in Jaffa. I never felt like the legal owner there in any case. After much dithering, which was partly down to Peretz's endless deployments in Sinai, he decided not to go to court. Clearly it was too much for him to fight two wars of attrition at the same time. The issue of custody of Lana, thank goodness, will soon resolve itself as she comes of age.

I'd love to be able to say that Shimon's in good shape, but I'm afraid he's not. He keeps trying to get off the drugs and go on with his music, but he hasn't managed it yet. He talks a lot about you, Lisa, and about his son. He always carries around with him the picture you sent me last winter, of the two of you. But he battles with you too, he doesn't understand why you insist that he comes to West Berlin. Couldn't you meet in a neutral place? Maybe you could think about it some time.

I'll write to you again as soon as I can. I do have the time now, after all. According to Jewish tradition Peretz was obliged to surrender part of his assets to me, and he kept to this. I have put some money in an envelope, I'm sure you could use it.

Please regard me as your mother-in-law, who is most grateful that one day you entered her life.

Love, Anna

ONE HUNDRED AND FIFTY-SEVEN

Peretz found the loudhailer in his parents' garage. He had no idea how it had ended up there. Now he was sitting in their garden, his mother and her two Yemeni housemaids were making lunch. It was cool, the old jacaranda tree he used to climb as a child with Avner had already lost its leaves. The large mimosa growing beside it, whose leaves Peretz loved to tickle then watch as they folded up, was now entirely woody.

Peretz twirled the loudhailer in his hands, the area where he had scratched out the swastika beneath the imperial eagle was still clearly visible. Putting the loudhailer to his lips he recalled all the transports it had accompanied him on. Doing good things had been his greatest desire. But the greatness of this desire was matched by the greatness he desired to achieve himself, something he now realised with painful clarity. And the loudhailer had sat in his memory like a bogus message.

Lydia Sarfati came out of the terrace door. When she saw the tears in her son's eyes she was shocked. She sat next to him on the small bench, she put her hands in her lap to prevent herself from giving him a hug, from experience she knew that this impulse could meet with resistance.

"Is it still because of Anna?" she said softly.

Peretz shook his head. He looked into his mother's eyes and said, "Mama, what was I like when I was younger, before I went to Germany, to war? I can't remember."

Lydia Sarfati was relieved, she smiled at her son and said, "You were a little dreamy, you were fun-loving." She sighed. "You and Avner, sometimes you were the best of friends, at other times you argued horribly, but that was only because you were so different. He was pragmatic and you were . . . well, different. I always thought you might become an artist, a musician perhaps, you used to really enjoy singing."

A film of moisture covered her eyes. She said, "You would rack your brains about everything, you always wanted to know exactly what something was like, not just how it worked. It made me so proud of you, but at the same time I'd be worried that you were asking too much of your head." She wiped her eyes and looked at her son. Peretz took a deep breath. He spun the loudhailer in his hands.

"This used to belong to a German," he said.

Lydia did not reply, the house was full of objects like this, she had lost track ever since the Six-Day War.

"I . . ." Peretz said. He paused, pulled himself together, swallowed. Placing the loudhailer between his legs he looked at the mouthpiece pointing towards him. "I shot him," he said, "to get the loudhailer." He hid his head in his hands and wept. Lydia Sarfati was confused, she sat next to her son unable to comprehend what was happening.

"But Peretz," she said, "it was wartime."

Peretz shook his head. Through his fingers he said, "It was the eighth of May, Germany had surrendered. The British had never let us off the leash before. It was the eighth of May, he knew it and I knew it. But I shot him." He went quiet, only his body which tightened spasmodically betrayed that he was still crying. One of the Yemeni housemaids, a short, slim woman with large eyes, opened the terrace door behind them very slightly and asked something, Lydia Sarfati turned to the woman and hesitated before standing up and following her into the house.

ONE HUNDRED AND FIFTY-EIGHT

Berlin, 10th September 1971

Dear Anna,

Thanks very much for the package! Tom was thrilled with the car; it's been his favourite toy for weeks. I told him his father sent it, I hope you understand.

Thank you also for the money, which is incredibly handy. I bought some winter clothes for Tom. It can get bitterly cold here in Berlin, but of course you know that better than anyone.

Please tell Shimon that I haven't changed my position. If he wants to see Tom he'll have to be off drugs, absolutely clean. I'd prefer the boy not to see his father high as a kite or in withdrawal. For me it's never been about Germany or not Germany.

Either there's been a persistent misunderstanding or he's fabricated this as an excuse to avoid having to change anything in his life.

I love him and I miss him every day. But so long as he's unable to look after our son, I have to do it for the both of us – all my life if it must be. It's not how I imagined my life would pan out, but sometimes I think that applies to us all. For now, I cherish the hope that everything will work out in the end.

I'm so pleased to hear that you're better and <u>of course</u> you're my mother-in-law. There will always be a place for you in my heart, no matter what happens between Shimon and me.

Love, Lisa

ONE HUNDRED AND FIFTY-NINE

In spring 1973 Anna went for a walk. The air was fresh and she was enjoying wearing a warm coat. She looked at her watch – five o'clock – she still had time. The traffic was dense and noisy. How colourful this city is, she thought as she passed the shops, whose goods – suits, shirts, dresses – hung beneath the awnings, obliging her to sidestep onto the road. Orthodox Jews in their traditional black attire, girls in miniskirts, businesswomen and men, just as you might meet in New York or London. It was rush hour, people were trying to get home or doing a quick bit of shopping, everyone was heading somewhere with purpose, all in a hurry, Anna was jostled, people were not particularly polite, but she did not mind. She saw white faces, brown faces, she saw Russian faces, North African faces, she saw faces she could not place at all. But they were all Jews, all of them probably spoke a different language at home. She felt as if Israel were a very thin piece of paper on which was written a long text in Hebrew, and this piece of paper lay on top of a reality that was Yiddish, Russian, Polish, Yemeni, Moroccan, Algerian, Arabic, Ladino, Palestinian.

And German.

She loved this diversity, she looked forward to the evening. The junction of Dizengoff and King George. Buses, cars, people walking in the middle of the road, the pavements spilling over with pedestrians, Bauhaus-style buildings framing the picture, shops, a large cinema, building sites. Anna walked on. Southwards on King George to the next junction, Ben Tsiyon Boulevard to the left with its palm trees and lawn, Anna turned right into Bograshov Street, a residential quarter, four-storey houses with sharp lines and large windows, all the same, Anna had memorised the house number, she crossed the road diagonally, all of a sudden she was in a hurry too, it had nothing to do with the time, or perhaps it did.

Then she was standing outside a small bookshop, which looked weighed down by the tall building that rose above it. It was brightly lit, the walls full of shelves, the shelves full of books. Between these books sat people on rows of chairs, some were still wearing their hats, they must have only just arrived, I'm not too late, Anna thought. The glass door tinkled as she entered. People turned to her, then continued their conversations in hushed tones, the air smelled of paper and breath, a peculiar combination. Anna found a free chair on the far right of the second row and sat down. She unbuttoned her coat, she looked around, the people were savouring the atmosphere, the door tinkled, Anna turned to look. A short, slender man entered the shop, Anna recognised his bent nose, his thin neck, his observant eyes took in everybody in the room with a quick glance, had he recognised her or not? Anna could not tell. He went over to a man who said, Good Evening, helped him out of his coat, smiled and talked to him. At the very last moment, just before the coat disappeared, the man thrust his hand into the side pocket and pulled out a book, then went over to the table waiting for him at the front, facing the rows of chairs. A chair, a small lamp, a glass of water. He sat down, adjusted the chair, the lamp, the glass exactly as he wanted them. Without greeting the people who had come here because of him, he opened the book, the room fell silent. He cleared his throat, took a sip of water.

Then Abba Kovner, the Lithuanian Jew, who had once wanted to poison a town in Germany out of revenge, read a poem in Hebrew:

At a Hotel

Mother and Father begin to die within me.
Thirty years after their violent death
They steal away quietly from my rooms
And my blissful hours.

I know for certain the voices are silent
And things are free. Without any resentment,
They will no longer visit my home. After all
A living man needs to stand here alone. Somewhere

Father wakes up now, slips on his sandals
And pretends not to see
Mother wiping away her tears
As she knits a warm sweater
For her son on his way, at the stopover.

ONE HUNDRED AND SIXTY

When the reading was over, the audience clapped. Anna was barely conscious of the applause, Abba's voice had drawn her into a funnel that came out of him and went back into him. Now he was silent, there was no smile, he gave a faint bow, still focused as if about to read another poem.

The audience rose from their seats, Anna stayed put, many people bought books, paying for them at the till, where the man who had greeted the poet was standing and smiling. They formed a queue, the head of which was beside the author, books were opened, placed in front of him, Thanks for the wonderful reading! I really enjoyed it! Could you write: For Rebecca? Sign right here please!

Everything obeyed a choreography, from her chair sometimes Anna could not see Abba, sometimes she caught a brief glimpse of him between bodies, sometimes their eyes met as if by chance.

The crowd in the bookshop gradually thinned. When the last customer had gone, Abba put his fountain pen in the inside pocket of his jacket, drank the rest of the water and looked at Anna. "Fancy seeing you again," he said with a smile. "Are you free now?"

"I was going to ask you the same question."

"I know a good Italian in Arlozorov Street. It's owned by a Lithuanian, another dinosaur from the old days."

Anna accepted, Abba said goodbye to the bookseller, who expressed his satisfaction and ogled Anna as he helped Abba into his coat.

Outside they were met by a light drizzle. In front of the bookshop was a light-blue V.W. Beetle, Abba sauntered towards it, key in hand.

"A German car?" Anna said.

"It's a good antidote to the hatred."

They got in, Abba started the engine, which made its typical trundling rattle, turned two knobs to switch on the headlights and windscreen wiper. Then they drove off. Anna watched him furtively.

"I was worried about you all those years ago," she said after a while.

"I can understand that – *today* I can understand it. Back then I would have laughed in your face, insulted or ignored you, or forced you to feel a different emotion."

He gave her a fleeting smile, then looked ahead again, the traffic had improved slightly, but the roads were still busy.

"I never thanked you for driving me to Tulce."

"Please don't! I didn't deserve any thanks. In those days I only used to think in terms of quantities, I was so preoccupied with scraping together what was left of us that I never really paid attention to individual people and their stories."

"I think you're mistaken."

Abba looked at Anna in astonishment. "Are you telling me I'm mistaken about myself? This is something new," he said.

Anna smiled. "At the time you suspected me of being a collaborator, didn't you?"

Abba shot her a wary glance, for a brief moment Anna saw the predator living inside this slight body, it had grown old, it had deep lines around its mouth and eyes, it was more stooped than before, but it was still here, still dangerous. The moment passed, Abba put on an innocent face and said, "I don't remember."

Anna could not help laughing. "You see, you paid careful attention to individuals."

"Were you a collaborator, then?" Abba said.

Anna shrugged. "Is a slave a collaborator?" She meant the question seriously, she had not been able to find an answer.

Abba looked at her, she saw the momentary shock in his eyes. "Not at all," he said.

They drove on in silence. Abba concentrated on the traffic, Anna tried to relax. The impression he gave was still the same, his mixture of violence and tenderness, his eyes that sparkled with intelligence and were able to camouflage themselves so skilfully. His voice.

"Did you enjoy the reading?"

"Yes, especially the first poem."

He gave an indulgent smile and sighed. He said, "Good poems are like beautiful women. You never get over the first one." He darted her a glance. Anna felt like a blushing young girl, she failed to disassociate this comment from herself.

Silence again. The city was lit up, Anna looked straight ahead, the drizzle grew slightly heavier, the wiper left streaks on the windscreen. The city beyond painted a diffuse picture of lights blurring into each other, red, green, white, yellow. Anna abandoned herself to her feelings, which had no name and no orientation, which were just feelings, nothing more.

"Here we are," Abba said after a while. He parked the car at a large junction, Arlozorov and Ibn Gabirol. The same four-storey buildings with sharp lines stood here too, the same large windows had been used, some were now dark, others lit up.

The restaurant took up the entire ground floor of a corner house, taller than the others and detached. People sat at tables behind a large glass frontage, eating and drinking and talking to each other.

Abba was welcomed like a state visitor, a waiter in a dinner jacket took their coats, another in a black-and-white uniform led them to a private room, rustic furniture, dark-red velvet, copies of Italian Renaissance paintings on the walls, in the centre of the room an Adonis statue, diffuse lighting, a slim candle on the table. The waiter brought a menu and wine list, then left them alone. They looked at the menu, Abba recommended a dish and a wine, Anna said yes to both. The waiter came, took the order, collected the menus, left the room.

Italian pop music played softly from invisible speakers, Anna smiled at Abba.

"Ad Lo-Or – do you remember giving me that password for the house in Tulce?" Anna said.

Abba nodded. "I often used it, it seemed highly appropriate for the times we were living in."

"I spent years wondering what it meant."

"Now you know."

Anna nodded. Then she shook her head. "No, actually, I don't."

Abba smiled. "I drafted an explanation for it when I was sitting in a British prison in Egypt."

"An explanation?"

"A poem. A long poem. Would you like to hear the beginning?"

"Of course!"

Abba concentrated, all of a sudden he looked exactly as he had in the bookshop, serious and aloof. The waiter interrupted this ritual, he arrived with the red wine, poured a little for Abba, Abba brought the glass to his nose, gave it a sniff, then nodded and put the glass back down, the waiter half filled both glasses, put the bottle down, left.

Abba took a sip of wine, prepared himself again and said, "In my parents' house – on a little table in a corner of my room, I left a small clay figure. The first work by my own hands. In the evening I had brought it home from school. In the morning Vilnius was in flames. I left my room – and never returned. Should I go on?"

"Yes please!" said Anna, surprised that the poem had already begun.

Abba breathed in and out and said, "The form of the figure was imperfect, but there was so much love in it and a hint of budding life. And a young girl bent over a floral garland at the end of the harvest. More?"

Anna nodded and smiled, Abba seemed like a little boy.

"In the sewers – where we destroyed a camp of the last soldiers, to get out – from the fallen ghetto to high in the forest. The river of scum carried my notebook of bones, the hands of a beloved friend were a reminder to take it. To the other side of the curtain."

He shook his head. "No more, please. It's too long ago. I was so different, so . . . charged up with everything that had happened. I was glad to be able to leave some of it behind." He stopped. His hands were on the table. Anna put hers beside them, their fingers touched, held each other.

With a smile she said, "You're still the same man I've thought about so often."

ONE HUNDRED AND SIXTY-ONE

It was hard work convincing Tom that going to the cinema with friends was not the best way to celebrate his fifth birthday. Lisa was sitting with her son at the breakfast table in their small apartment in Berlin-Neukölln, the view from the window took in a wide open space on the other side of the road, the space was green, allotments, which is why Lisa had chosen the apartment, If I'm not free, she had told herself, then at least my view is. The day was going to turn gloomy, the sky was grey, it was too cold for the time of year.

Tom sat there restlessly, his legs were jiggling, she saw dissatisfaction and incomprehension in his eyes. She waited.

"Can't Papa come to see us?" he said.

"No, my darling, Papa's afraid of coming here."

"But why?"

"Well, the fact is, your papa was once here as a young boy, and at the time he and his mama and lots of other people were locked up and had to wait for ages before being allowed to move on."

"But why did they want to move on?"

"They wanted to move on because they didn't like it here."

"But it's lovely here!"

"Yes, my darling, it's very lovely here, but it wasn't so lovely all those years ago."

"Why not?"

"There was a big war, which destroyed lots and lots of houses in the city, and when your papa was a little boy, even younger than you, he had to live amongst all these destroyed houses and couldn't go away."

"Why not?"

"Because there were people who didn't want him to go."

"What sort of people, Mama?"

"The same people who made the war and whose fault it was that all the houses were destroyed – wicked people."

"Are they still around, the wicked people?"

"No, not anymore, they're all gone."

"So Papa can come then!"

"You know what? Papa doesn't believe that all the wicked people have gone."

"Let's tell him then."

"I have already, but he's so scared that he doesn't really listen."

"Is Papa that frightened?"

"Yes, my darling, Papa is *really* frightened."

"Mama?"

"What, darling?"

"Is Papa a coward?"

"No! What makes you say that?"

"Because he's so frightened."

"I'd be frightened of such wicked people too, anybody would be frightened."

"Even though they're gone?"

"Do you remember that dog that barked at you?"

"Oh yes! I got such a fright."

"Since then you've been more careful around dogs, even though this one has gone."

Tom thought about it. He chewed on his bread and Nutella, his gaze slid over the small breakfast table, he shuffled on the wooden chair.

"O.K. then," he said.

"What?"

"We'll go and see Papa."

"He'll be so pleased!" Lisa hugged her son, gave him a kiss on the cheek and sighed. "Right, let's get ready so you're not too late for kindergarten, Mama has to go to work now, you see? And afterwards Grandma will pick you up and bring you home."

ONE HUNDRED AND SIXTY-TWO

The thin line between too much and too little, Shimon walked it for the length of a flight. He did not fall, he kept things under control, he clung to his armrest, to the hand of his little sister who was no longer little. He was dying for a fix, Just one, just for the flight, just one very last fix. He drank wine until Lana said, No, he wanted to argue with her just as a distraction, she would not allow that either. He wanted to bawl at her, You're just like your father, but it was so quiet on the aeroplane, people were so calm that he kept his mouth shut. He smoked one cigarette after another until Lana threatened to move to the non-smoking area unless he stopped.

When they landed in Brussels he felt a sudden exhilaration, as if he had only just become airborne, as if he had administered himself a fix, as if he could fly without a plane and without wings.

On the train to Antwerp he fell asleep. Why Antwerp? he had asked his mother when the suggestion was made. Lisa's got friends who've got friends there, they won't be around and you can use their apartment, was her answer, It's big, there's room for everybody. She had wanted to come with them, but Shimon had threatened not to go, so she abandoned the plan.

Lana read a book. From time to time she looked out of the train window, So close to Germany, she was sad that they could not go there, to the land of criminals, the land of their ancestors, What's it like, she had once asked her mother, when you're the only survivor? Her mother had stared at Lana, searching for words that would be appropriate and not sound too harsh, then she had said, There's a lot of responsibility, too much sometimes. At the time Lana did not understand, but now, by her brother's side, someone still preoccupied by survival, she got an inkling of it.

"What are you reading?"

She was jolted from her thoughts. Shimon had woken up and was blinking at her. She showed him. A red cover. *The Avengers*. Written in large, black letters. Between the definite article and the noun sat a small swastika, clamped like a nut in a nutcracker.

"Mama gave it to me," Lana said.

"What's it about?"

"The Jewish Brigade in the British Army. After the war some of them hunted down Nazis and killed them."

"Peretz talked about them."

"Exactly, he was part of the brigade, but he didn't want to have anything to do with the killing."

"That's what he says today."

"I believe him. He's not a liar."

"No."

Lana put an end to the conversation by continuing to read. Shimon looked out of the window, it was already nine in the evening, but the sun was still in the sky. The countryside awakened vague memories, so much green, wherever you looked something was growing. Half-timbered houses, small villages that looked as if they had risen from the earth. Somewhere inside him a string had been touched, and all of a sudden he could remember a feeling on which a picture hung, through the picture flowed a wide river, above the river was a pontoon bridge and he, he had wanted to leap into it and be dragged out to the wide open sea.

ONE HUNDRED AND SIXTY-THREE

Tom's eyes were out on stalks when he stepped onto platform 3 of Zoologischer Gartenstation, holding his great-grandmother's hand. Before him stood a black steam locomotive of the German Reichsbahn. Thick, grey smoke billowed from its mighty funnel. The driver of the locomotive, standing up in the cabin, laughed when he saw Tom, who had stopped agape by the monster. He pulled at a cord by his head and the engine gave a loud, high-pitched too-oo-oo-oot. Then, by way of a greeting to Tom, he put two fingers on his peaked cap and snapped his wrist forward.

Frau Kramer pulled her great-grandson to one of the carriages where Lisa was waiting with the luggage. They climbed on and looked for a free compartment. Tom sat by the window and peered out, Frau Kramer sat beside him, with Lisa in the window seat opposite.

The train started up with a jerk and slowly pulled out of the station. After a quarter of an hour they were passing barbed-wire fences and watchtowers, then the train stopped again. The station sign read, "Berlin-Staaken". It was only a brief stop, doors were opened and crunched closed again. The train moved on. After a few minutes two men in the pale-green uniform of the G.D.R. border police opened the door to the compartment and said, Good Morning, passports please! The women gave them three passports, the men inspected these thoroughly, then returned the documents and closed the door.

Lisa looked at her son sitting excitedly opposite her, commenting on everything he saw outside. The women gave each other the occasional smile, like accomplices. Tom was unaware that he was the reason for this. He had never undertaken such a long journey before. And at the end of it his father was waiting for him with lots of presents.

When, an hour later, the train passed through a village, Tom asked his mother to read the station sign. Lisa had to concentrate very hard to catch the sign as it rushed past, but she managed it.

"Nauen," she said, smiling to her son. Tom repeated the word thoughtfully, then quickly forgot it again. The village itself, old houses, a small pretty station, flew past, remaining where it was amongst fields and trees.

When the train stopped in Schwanheide, Tobias was waiting on the platform. They embraced, Herr Weiss tried to carry all their luggage for them, but had to leave one suitcase to Lisa. Holding Tom's hand, Frau Kramer followed the two of them to the car park. She glanced behind her. She recalled this station very well, and for an instant a feeling crashed through her like a heavy weight, a sorrow, faces, names. Then she drew herself up, left the moment behind her and walked with Tom out of the small station.

"Over there!" the boy cried, thrusting out his arm. He had spied his mother and Herr Weiss amongst the row of parked cars. They were standing by the open boot of a white Volvo, waving at them.

Tom was allowed to sit in the front. Herr Weiss put a thick, square piece of hard foam under his bottom so he was high enough and plugged in his belt.

They set off. As he drove, Herr Weiss explained to Tom that they would drive across the Hansa line and onto the Flemish Road, that this road got its name because it went to Flanders, and that nobody could remember when it was actually built.

Lisa and Frau Kramer sat in the back. Placing her hand on her grand-mother's forearm, Lisa said, "Are you alright?"

The old woman sighed and said, "Don't worry about me. I'm just old, I'll be dead soon, that's all."

"Grandma! What are you talking about?"

Frau Kramer shrugged and looked out of the window. Lisa watched her for a while, and then said, "When?"

Frau Kramer turned to her and smiled. "Oh, it'll be a while yet, my love, don't you worry."

"You shouldn't have come with us."

"But of course I should! I've got to see Shimon again. And I want to meet his sister. And I want to see father and son together. And I've got to know if you're alright."

"Oh, Grandma." Lisa rested her head on Frau Kramer's shoulder, but only briefly, because she was worried that the weight of it would be too much of a strain for her. It was perfect weather for a car journey, not too warm, a choppy wind swept white clouds across the sky from the west, Lisa felt as if they were heading to where the clouds were coming from, as if the clouds themselves were passengers and they would meet and rush past each other, without saying a word and without either party understanding what was driving the other, what was pulling them.

After three hours they reached the Netherlands. The German border guards waved the cars through, but a queue had formed on the Dutch side, the officers were checking every vehicle.

On the other side of the border they turned off the highway and stopped in Emmen. Tom feted everything he had never seen before as a major discovery, number plates, streetlamps, makes of car. They parked in the town centre, which seemed to consist of nothing but new houses and building sites. The houses were built from the same red bricks as in Lübeck, but here they were flat and cube-like rather than tall and narrow.

They found a restaurant and sat at a table on the terrace beneath a large umbrella. A waiter came over, a young man in civvies, checked shirt, blue jeans, shoulder-length hair, and without a word gave them three menus.

It was nine o'clock in the evening by the time they arrived in Antwerp. The sun stood low in the west, it would soon set. Tom had fallen asleep,

Lisa had brought him into the back so he could lie down, Frau Kramer dozed in the front. Herr Weiss fought off tiredness. Lisa was wide awake.

Antwerp old town was full of winding streets, but the directions Lisa had been given by Mosche and Selma took them unerringly to their destination. It was still a while before they parked in a narrow street between palatial houses from times past, and a tall man stepped out of the darkness and opened the rear door of the Volvo because he had seen Lisa.

ONE HUNDRED AND SIXTY-FOUR

Shimon opened the door. Lisa's face met him from the dim light of the car. Lisa's eyes. Lisa's mouth. Without thinking he bent and kissed her, there was no barrier, no unfamiliarity, no resentment, the present flushed all that away. Both knew that everything would come back, but for the moment that did not matter.

When Shimon saw Tom, his head in his mother's lap, he said, "I'll do it."

He walked around the car, opened the other door and carefully lifted up his son, feeling for the very first time the weight of his child, carried him into the house and up a narrow, steep staircase to the bed that had been prepared for him. He laid him down, took the shoes off his little feet, the socks, took off his trousers, covered him up. He sat on the edge of the bed and gazed at him. After a while he said, "Hello, Tom, I'm your father."

He sobbed and his own tears took him by surprise. He got up, left the room, closed the door quietly and a feeling surged in him that he had never felt before. He wanted to be there for this child always, protect him from any dangers, he was struck by the question of how he could have left him alone for so long, in the land of criminals, and he resolved to talk this through with Lisa as soon as possible. He needed a cigarette. Lisa had got out of the car to help her grandmother. Tobias saw to the luggage in the boot. Lana Sarfati came out of the house to greet them. When Frau Kramer saw her she cried out in astonishment, "My God! You look just like your mother!"

Lana laughed brightly and embraced the old woman.

ONE HUNDRED AND SIXTY-FIVE

"What went wrong back then?"

"It wasn't your fault."

"You say that lightly, but I'm not so sure."

"I was a drug addict, it couldn't end well."

"But I knew that and got involved with you all the same."

"You just thought I was great."

"Do you think the two things are completely separate?"

"Yes. You don't, then?"

"No, I think everything is linked to everything else. Look at us. Both on the run since we were small, both orphaned, both looking for something to give us security."

"But I'm the addict."

"It's been a long time since I've been lied to. You're still being lied to."

"What do you mean by that?"

Silence

"Oh, nothing."

"I want to know what you meant by that."

"Let your mother tell you, please don't force me to!"

"My mother told you and not me?"

"She was worried about you."

"Worried about me, and that's why she's still lying to me? I want you to tell me right now, right now, or I'm going back."

"What about Tom? Didn't you come because of him, too?"

"Don't change the subject! You know something about me that I don't know."

"It's not about you, Shimon, it's . . . just something about your parents, and I'm very sorry I know, I didn't ask to know, your mother told me on the day I saw her again in Tel Aviv. I'd actually come for a very different reason, but then . . .'"

Silence.

"Tell me."

"But please don't be angry, you've got to understand her. She was just frightened."

"Tell me."

Silence.

"O.K., then."

Silence.

"Your mother told you that your father was a German and that he's dead, right?"

"Yes. Isn't that the truth?"

"It is. But she didn't love him. He raped her. Him and four other S.S. men. She doesn't know which of them is your father."

Silence.

*

Shimon does not move. All of a sudden he is lying as if paralysed in bed, Lisa's entire body is wrapped around him, skin on skin, he has taken it in, he knows what it ought to mean, but he cannot feel it. He cannot feel anything. He thinks he now needs something stronger than a cigarette.

"I'm sorry, my love," Lisa whispers into his ear, "I . . . I couldn't go on pretending that I didn't know. Forgive me." Lisa cries the tears that Shimon cannot shed, Shimon has taken it in, he knows what it means, he knows what he should be feeling, but it does not happen. Nothing happens. Tranquility infuses him.

Lisa says, "It's got nothing to do with you, Shimon, please listen to what I'm saying! You are you, you're not what happened between your parents."

Shimon says, "But you said everything's linked to everything else."

"But not in that way. Shimon, please!" She turns his head towards her. In the dim light of the streetlamp he looks exactly as he did six years earlier in her bed in Anna's house. This time he is not asleep and not drunk, but with a pain in her chest Lisa feels as if he is not there. She holds his head in her hands, he looks at her, he recognises her, he knows that he loves her. But he cannot feel it.

She says, "You have a son. If you can't fight for me and you can't fight for yourself, then at least fight for him."

Shimon looks past Lisa to where Tom is lying asleep in his little bed, with no idea how close his stranger-father is. If he leaves now, Lisa can tell the boy that there was a problem, the aeroplane broke down, he fell ill, something. Shimon Sarfati. His initials in the Latin alphabet. They appear to him as a hidden clue, always visible, there, right before his eyes his whole life long. All of a sudden being a father seems like a prison, How can someone in freefall hold on to a child? She should have taken care, she really ought to have taken care! Slowly he frees himself from Lisa's grasp, he has forgotten what she means, now she is merely shackling him, he ignores her pleas, her tears fail to move him. Deep within himself he hears an appalled voice insisting that he is about to do something dreadful, unforgivable. But to him it sounds like the voice of an anxious little boy.

Lisa has no intention of making a scene, she does not want to wake Tom, she stays in bed, crying as silently as she can. Shimon puts on his clothes slowly, methodically. When he is dressed he leaves the room without a word. He takes nothing but his wallet and passport, Lana will have to deal with the luggage. He just wants to go, to get out.

ONE HUNDRED AND SIXTY-SIX

When Tom woke the following morning, Lisa pulled herself together. She had barely slept a wink, but she said Happy Birthday to her son, she sang him a song, disguising the tears she was shedding with a smile. She gave him the presents she had brought from Berlin, she unwrapped the cake she had baked in Berlin and stuck into it five colourful candles she had bought in Berlin. She lit them and Tom blew them out. He showed no interest in the unfamiliar suitcase in the corner. When he asked about his father, Lisa lied to him. She said he was unable to come because he was very sick.

"But Auntie Lana has come, do you want to meet her?"

Tom did not want to, he thought of his friends at kindergarten that he had swapped for his father, and now his father was not here.

"Couldn't he have told us earlier?"

Shaking her head, Lisa said, "Sometimes these things come on very suddenly." She took several deep breaths until she felt sufficiently composed, then said, "Look, Uncle Tobi's here, Great-Grandma's here, Auntie Lana's here and I'm here – so many people and they've all brought you something!"

"But no children, no friends."

It took Tom a while to accept the situation. Then he played with his present, a small wooden fort with cowboys, Indians and horses, the gate could be opened and closed, there were lookout towers and even a cannon.

Lisa left the room to alert the others, she lied, she talked of an argument, she begged them to back up her story of an illness. Lana was confounded and worried. She had been prepared for everything apart from the possibility that Shimon might vanish in the middle of the night. Frau Kramer could see that Lisa had not told them everything, she felt her granddaughter's pain as if it were her own, but she brushed it aside and said, "Maybe he'll come back."

"Yes," Lisa said meekly, "maybe."

Everyone knew what to do. They went to Lisa's bedroom with the presents they had brought. They sang for Tom, who watched them, they smiled as joyfully as they could, this day was going to be hard work.

For Tom it turned out to be an acceptable birthday. He got to make all the decisions, he was allowed to eat as many sweets as he wanted. When, over breakfast, he announced he wanted to go swimming, they drove another hundred kilometres to the west, to the beach at Blankenberge. Tom was the centre of the world and the four adults orbited around him tirelessly like satellites. Secretly there were other orbits, other centres and other feelings. When they returned to the house in Antwerp, for a moment Lisa was as alert as she had been the evening before, for a moment just the repetition seemed to offer her a second chance, for a moment she expected Shimon to open the door again and kiss her.

But no. The apartment was deserted, Shimon's case was exactly where it had been that morning. The place where he had been lying in bed next to her was empty.

Before Tom went to sleep he asked his mother, "Will Papa get better?"

"He certainly will," Lisa said softly.

Tom smiled blearily. "Great, then he can come and visit us at home next time." He fell asleep.

Without undressing Lisa fell onto the bed. She tried to give up hope, but she was too tired. Sleep overcame her even before she could get under the covers.

ONE HUNDRED AND SIXTY-SEVEN

He had wandered around Antwerp without success. Someone had told him, You need to go to the Netherlands for that. He had made his way to the station and taken the first train to Amsterdam. He slept during the journey, but ate nothing. He chain-smoked. His stomach was empty and it ached. It was nippy, he was only wearing a thin jacket over his shirt and he froze. Lisa's words, her pleas, her despair, her body. Tom, lying unsuspectingly beside them, asleep in his little bed. Shimon wanted it all to disappear from his mind and was looking for something that might help with that. He wandered along the canals, the shops were not yet open, the city with its narrow streets, its little old brick houses stood there damp and sedate. He went back to the station, bought himself a snack, which he ate without tasting, just to keep his body alive, like filling up a car to get you to your destination. He loitered around the station in the hope of finding someone who could sell him something, but police were patrolling the empty concourse. Later he found a pale-looking boy hanging around the Dam, who told him he should go to Zeedijk. Shimon asked the way and walked to a narrow, winding street lined with low houses. There were shops here, bars, nightclubs, but he had to wait for dusk before the dealers emerged.

He spoke to an athletic, bearded man with blond dreadlocks and an Alsatian on a lead. Together they slunk into a small alleyway between two run-down houses. Goods in exchange for money, Shimon also bought some kit off him, a small syringe, a spoon, a sachet of vinegar. The man left him alone, Shimon sat in the darkest spot he could find and took off his jacket. Because he had no water he kept spitting on the spoon until there was enough liquid. He added the white powder and the vinegar, then held his lighter beneath it until the powder dissolved. He drew the brown liquid up into the needle, tossed away the spoon, took his belt off, wrapped it around his forearm and pulled tight. He pushed up his sleeve, clenched his fist several times and looked in the dark for the right place to insert the needle. When he thought he had found it, he pushed the needle beneath his skin. He felt the pain, he knew that he could die, he thought of the danger of unknown dealers. But he would not be dissuaded, he drew up the plunger slightly and looked for blood. Glimpsing something dark in the tube, he untied the belt with his teeth and pushed the heroin into his arm.

Within seconds everything changed. He stood up and enjoyed the movement of his body. He left the jacket containing his money and passport. He walked down the dark alley, out into Zeedijk, where cars and people and lights and sounds were waiting for him. Everything joined into a harmony, the world was one great work of art in which everything had its place, its colour, its oscillation and its feeling. Everything was linked to everything else, including him and Lisa and Tom, they formed a perfect triangle that nothing could destroy. Finally he had found the happiness he was seeking, the happiness of forgetting. The happiness of unconsciousness.

The following morning he woke up in a confined space. He was lying on a camp bed, there was a small, barred window. The door would not open. The memory came back, Lisa's words, Lisa's despair, her body, the little boy. Shimon was no longer able to defend himself against the emotions lurking behind the images. He cried uncontrollably until a Dutch police officer opened the door and invited Shimon to follow him. Still weeping he was taken to a desk, on the other side of which sat an officer at a typewriter. Surname: Sarfati. First name: Shimon. Date of Birth: 9/11/1945. Place of birth: Berlin. Nationality: Israeli. Mother's name: Anna Sarfati. Father's name: All I know is that he was in the S.S. The perplexed officer glanced up at Shimon, then snapped out of it, typed "Unknown" and asked questions about the night before, which Shimon answered truthfully.

It took a week for the Israeli consulate-general to confirm Shimon's identity and make arrangements for his deportation. Over the course of that week he became convinced that he had made a big mistake. But it was too late. The door had closed, he had lost for ever the only people who had ever meant anything to him. He had no heroin and not enough cigarettes. His body was in pain. At the top of his voice he sang, Papa was a rolling stone, and wept for himself, as if he were standing with Lisa and Tom at an open grave and seeing himself lying in it, All he left us was alone.

ONE HUNDRED AND SIXTY-EIGHT

He had been brought new clothes by the consulate, a white shirt, blue jeans and trainers. Someone from the defence ministry had made a tele-phone call to ensure that there would be no link between Shimon Sarfati and the illegal possession of drugs. He was in an aisle seat of an EL AL D.C.-8, holding on for dear life. He sweated and smoked cigarettes and ordered wine until he was drunk. When he felt unable to drink any more without throwing up or losing control of his senses, all of a sudden his head became perfectly clear. The aeroplane stopped moving, Shimon was sitting in the middle of a limitless space, looking around in astonishment.

This lasted only a few seconds before fading away. Sobered, Shimon sensed the plane's movements and heard its noise. He grabbed onto his armrests and the memory of a brief moment free of anxiety.

ONE HUNDRED AND SIXTY-NINE

When Shimon looked up at the façade he felt a reluctance to enter the confines of the buiding. He was standing outside 7 Hibner Street in Petah Tikva, a stout box with four storeys, made from bare concrete. The windows were large. Shimon knew these houses, they had been built everywhere in the 1960s to accommodate refugees from the Arab states and immigrants from all over the world. Usually he felt comfortable amongst such buildings, they seemed far more honest than Jaffa with its beautified antiquity. But on the third floor of this house his mother was waiting for him. He had called her from the airport, he said, I've got to talk to you, and he said it in such a way that she could imagine what was awaiting her. His intention had been to confront her, How could you keep that from me? But now he wanted to leave again, go anywhere, down the street, just keep going straight until he reached the end. What he wanted most of all was to lose himself in the world.

He smoked one more cigarette, then pressed the doorbell above the name Anna Stirnweiss. The buzzer sounded almost instantly, as if his mother had been waiting at the door to her apartment ever since his call. Shimon went up the stairs. His mother was standing by the banisters, watching him. In her eyes was a mixture of joy and concern and questions and a hidden accusation, Shimon had known this expression ever since he had been able to think. He ignored it, he gave his mother the obligatory embrace, he noticed that she was not quite so stooped, did not let her shoulders hunch as far forward as she used to. She looked younger, The separation's done you good.

She went ahead of him into the apartment. She had not been waiting at the door but cooking, his favourite meal, tzimmes with honey and nutmeg, shining chunks of carrot on a large white dish, dried plums, as well as hummus, chopped peppers, sliced cucumber and tomatoes. A cheese platter. Red wine. Bread. Two plates, four glasses, a carafe of water, cutlery.

Shimon saw the table laid for dinner, he stood on a thin line between a feeling of being bribed and another of being loved, he could not decide between the two. He sat and poured himself some wine. His mother sat opposite him. She smiled and said, "I'm so glad you've made it back, safe and sound." She looked timid, as if the allusion to Amsterdam might send him into a rage. Shimon noticed this, he ignored it and downed his glass in one.

"I can't eat first and then talk, Mama."

"O.K., let's talk straightaway." She gave him a brave smile.

"Tell me how the S.S. men fucked you," he said, looking at her brutally, mercilessly, expectantly. Anna was more shocked by the expression on his face than by what he had said. She poured herself a glass of wine, her hands were shaking, she noticed it, she ignored it, she drank the wine.

"Your self-pity disgusts me, Shimon." She looked him straight in the eye, he had not been banking on an answer like that. He stared at his mother, he could not find a distinct emotion, his anger had dissipated, he felt sore, suddenly the love had vanished and he was naked.

"What you did to Lisa and Tom is simply unacceptable. I don't care how difficult your life is, or what accusations you hurl at me and the rest of the world." She stared at him, with his anger now gone he was disarmed. She thought for a moment and said, "Shimon, I'm sorry I kept the truth from you for so long; maybe this is why you're so lost. But at some point people grow up and take their lives in their own hands, at some point they say, So what? I can still make the best of this."

She paused for breath, she searched for the right words, she said, "Are you really surprised that I didn't tell you the truth? Do you see where we're living? Would you have liked to grow up in Israel with the knowledge that you were the result of a rape? Carried out by two or three or four or five S.S. men? Would you have preferred that, Shimon?" She poured herself more wine and drank.

"So long as you think others are responsible for your misfortune, you'll never be anything but an egoist, do you hear me? An egoist with a small heart who's chucking his life away." She took another sip.

Shimon had recovered from his mother's onslaught, now he sat there listening to her. Everything is linked to everything else, Lisa's words came into his head.

"You really took the easy way out, didn't you? You couldn't say anything and I had to see how I got by? Is that all you've got to offer, Mama?" He shook his head as he looked at her. He said, "You're asking me to look after my son and Lisa, but you did nothing, you were only ever interested in yourself and your secret, you foisted me on Peretz in the hope that the truth would simply disappear. And you're the one calling me an egoist?"

Anna began to cry. She shouted, "Don't you understand? I was raped! By five men! My life was finished, but I wasn't dead! I wasn't dead! And to make matters worse, I was pregnant!"

"To make matters worse, that's nicely put, Mama."

"For God's sake, Shimon, do you really not understand? I love you! As far as I'm concerned you've got nothing to do with those men. You're my son, no matter how it happened. But I was a broken woman." Putting her hand on her chest, she said, "Inside here everything was broken. But I couldn't just lie down, take drugs or drink myself stupid! I had to make sure that I escaped with my life, Shimon. And Peretz was my saviour, and he was your saviour too. Suddenly there was the prospect of more to life than just wanting to forget but not being able to."

She sobbed. "I thought I couldn't love Peretz properly because of what had happened to me. I thought, as time passes and the memories fade I *will* be able to love Peretz. I was so young, Shimon, far younger than you are now."

She stopped talking and lowered her head. She wiped the tears from her eyes with the back of her hand, she sniffed, she said, "Please believe me, Shimon, if I'd known any better I would have done things differently. But I couldn't. And when you were born . . ." She broke off and looked at Shimon as tears ran down her face.

"You were so pure and innocent, so beautiful. It was like a miracle. How could something like you have come from such a horrific experience? Although I couldn't understand, it gave me the strength to carry on, *you* gave me the strengh to carry on, Shimon. Without you, perhaps I . . . I'm sorry Shimon, I'm so sorry." Her voice failed. Shimon said nothing. He was searching inside himself, there was nothing he could say. He poured wine for himself and his mother.

"Let's eat, Mama," he said after a while.

Anna nodded courageously, she pulled herself together, smiled at her son, dried her face with the napkin.

They ate.

ONE HUNDRED AND SEVENTY

"Is that all, Grandma? Bring up a child, no husband, go to work, don't get any further with your studies? Is that all?" Lisa sighed and continued knitting the scarf she was going to give Tom for Christmas.

Frau Kramer, who was busy making gloves for her great-grandson, dropped her knitting into her lap and looked out of the tall window, across the deserted allotments to the high tower of Sankt Christophorus. An icy draught drifted through the window frame. Outside it was already dark, the beginning of December 1974. An eventful year lay behind them. Tom's leaving kindergarten, the holidays at the North Sea in Tobias's summer house, Tom's first day at primary school.

And at the same time it was a year when nothing had happened, a lost year for Lisa. Without looking at her granddaughter, Frau Kramer said, "Do you remember the pastor I told you about?"

"Yes, of course."

"His name was Karl Bergmann. The name came back to me last week, quite out of the blue."

"Are you sure?"

Frau Kramer nodded, she was absolutely sure, and she was amazed by how memories sometimes vanished from the mind, only to pop up again unscathed. She did not tell her granddaughter that she had remembered the pastor's name some time ago, and she withheld the misgivings she harboured concerning Lisa's hopeless search for clues about her parents. She decided it was pointless to discuss with her the question of whether this life was not enough. Who could possibly answer that one? She thought, When I look at Tom I know why I'm still alive. She knew that this did not work for Lisa. The following day Lisa embarked on her search for Karl Bergmann. She telephoned various dioceses in West Germany, telling all of them what she knew. But nobody was able to help. She cycled to the central post office in Donaustrasse and pored over the telephone books of West German towns, but so many people were called Karl Bergmann that she abandoned her plan to ring them all.

One morning two months later, in early 1975, the telephone rang as Lisa was getting her son ready for school. Frau Kramer picked up then called her granddaughter. On the other end of the line was a secretary from the archbishopric of Cologne.

"Frau Kramer," she said, "do you remember me? You called before Christmas. I think I've found your Karl Bergmann. He's running a mission in Brazil. He left Germany only a few years after the war, which is why it was hard to track him down. But I was lucky, he's from Cologne and this is where he came back to initially. I don't have an address or telephone number, unfortunately. If you ask me, I think he's living a very basic life."

"Don't you even have a lead?"

"The only thing I've got is this name here." She said something that Lisa could not understand. Only when the woman spelled it out did a word appear on the notepad: Codajás.

"I can't tell you any more, I'm afraid. If you ask me, he's living with savages."

Lisa thanked the woman and hung up. She had to focus on Tom, make him a roll for break time, put a bottle of water in his satchel and make sure that he did not go out into the cold without a scarf and hat.

When Tom and Frau Kramer had left, she sat down on a chair in the kitchen with the slip of paper in her hand and read the word again. Then she sighed and wondered how far she was prepared to go to find out information.

ONE HUNDRED AND SEVENTY-ONE

Kibbutz Givat Chaim, 21 March, 1974

Dearest Lisa,

I find it hard to write this without dropping to my knees and begging you for forgiveness. I'm sorry, I'm sorry, I'm sorry!

Well, I'm still alive. And I'm feeling better. Recently I've been telling myself that what happened had to happen exactly as it did so I could write you this letter.

Peretz found me a job in this kibbutz. It's an hour north of Tel Aviv. A few houses surrounded by fields, nothing else. I've been here since September.

I live in a house with the Franks. My bedroom used to be the storeroom. Then they made a hole in the wall and now it's got a window. Every Thursday I work with Ephraim Frank in the orange groves, he uses the bow rake and I use the leaf rake.

We aerate the soil, do the weeding, check the trees for pests. Sometimes he tells me about Germany, about his childhood in Dortmund, about the beautiful cities, the concert halls. About his negotiations with Eichmann when he was arranging for boats full of Jews to go down the Danube to the Black Sea and from there to Palestine. He could have bailed out any time – once he went to the Zionist Congress in Switzerland but then returned to Germany to save even more Jews! He never talks about these things unless I ask him. If Peretz hadn't told me beforehand who Ephraim Frank was, I probably wouldn't know to this day.

He also talked about Bricha, Peretz's work, the large number of Jews who came to Berlin, fleeing the pogroms in Poland. About the *President Warfield*. Pöppendorf. My story – our story.

I like Ephraim, he's a very special guy. When I asked him if he was thinking of writing a book about his life, he said, "I live in the present, not in the past." And then he just went on working.

I work hard here, it does me the world of good. I'm trying to knock my ruined body back into shape. I've stopped smoking, I don't drink alcohol anymore. And I'm clean.

I love you, Lisa. I want to learn how to be a proper father. If you still want me to I'll come to Germany.

Please send Tom a kiss from me and tell him that I'm with him even though he can't see me.

Love, Shimon

ONE HUNDRED AND SEVENTY-TWO

In the autumn Sarah turned up at the door unexpectedly. She looked as if she had not slept a wink all night. Anna invited her in and gave her something to eat. She suspected that Schmuel had left her, but Sarah shook her head without saying a word. Anna gave her Shimon's room, Sarah got into bed and slept until the following morning. When Anna woke her she wanted to go straight back to sleep. But Anna forced her to get up and take a shower.

Later they had breakfast. They sat at the table, Sarah in the place where Shimon had sat months earlier to confront his mother. Children, Anna thought. She said, "What's wrong?"

Sarah stared at the empty plate in front of her. Impassively she said, "I've left him."

"Why? Wasn't he treating you well?"

Sarah looked up in surprise.

"Yes, he was. He was . . . very good to me." She took a deep breath. "He didn't want to have any more children, he said, I'll be geriatric by the time they're grown up." She shrugged. "So I didn't have any." She paused, then said, "And now I'm forty-one." She was gasping, as if lacking oxygen, she said, "And it's too late." She closed her eyes.

Anna tried to think of something to cheer her up. She said, "You've already been a mother, Sarah. Think of Shimon. You helped me get through with him. For years you were the only person he trusted apart from me." In that very moment she asked herself whether this was the truth. Two women with grand delusions: one, because she had to conceal the fact that she had become a mother so violently; the other, because she needed to be adopted by a stranger to survive the death of her family. How lonely Shimon must have been!

Sarah waved a hand dismissively. "Oh, that's a long time ago now. I fulfilled my purpose, he doesn't even think about me now."

"He will, Sarah. Maybe not tomorrow. He's got to get a grip on his own life first."

After a pause, Sarah said, "I ought never to have become your daughter." She closed her eyes, tears seeped between her lids and rolled down her cheeks, silent tears, her face remained rigid, the jaw muscles tightened beneath her skin.

Anna wanted to comfort Sarah, she wanted to go and put an arm around her. But she could not.

Eventually Sarah stood up, the chair made a muffled sound as she scraped it across the floor with the backs of her legs, wood on stone. Anna heard her front door open and close. She felt the impulse to call Shimon and make him visit Sarah. But she stayed seated and did nothing. All in good time, she thought.

ONE HUNDRED AND SEVENTY-THREE

Shimon took the train from Frankfurt to Berlin. He could have flown, but decided against it. He sat in a compartment with Germans, it was cold and wet outside, November rain smacked against the window. Shimon felt under scrutiny until he noticed that everyone was eyeing everyone else, as if looking for an opportunity to break the silence. But they failed to find one.

The ticket inspector, a man of around fifty, tall, stocky, handlebar moustache, short grey hair beneath a blue peaked cap, slid open the door and asked to see their tickets. For the second time Shimon was being checked by a German uniform, for the second time he shuddered internally.

When the ticket inspector had left, the little girl sitting opposite Shimon wanted to go out into the corridor. Her mother was not happy about this, a whispered argument struck up between the two. Shimon understood the girl only too well. He stood up abruptly and left the compartment, to discover that other passengers had had the same idea. Arrival at Berlin Zoologischer Garten. People were already in the corridor, suitcases in hand, all keen to get out after the long journey, or perhaps after spending so much time in fear of one another. Shimon felt this fear almost viscerally, it gripped him, it prevented him from moving freely, he thought, If only they wouldn't keep staring at each other. Sensing he was only too willing to draw connections with the past, he forced himself not to. He wanted to give this country a chance, he had to, if only to make his stay here bearable.

When the train stopped the throng set in motion, dissipating once on the platform. Shimon was one of the last to alight, he had one large case and one small one, the small one contained presents.

In no time at all the platform had emptied, Shimon saw only one or two people, and a few more on other platforms. Slowly he approached the stairs, went down into the ticket hall and to the exit. He was back. In the city of his birth, which was still boxed in, still divided.

He stepped into the night. It had stopped raining, the streets glistened black in the glow of the streetlamps. Lisa had written that he should take a taxi. He got into the back of a black Mercedes and gave the address. Righto, the driver said, and off they went.

As the taxi made its way through the city Shimon looked out of the window. Old houses, new houses, entire streets from different eras, gaps between buildings, occasional ruins, parks, wasteland, constant change, a patchwork rug, a ghost train of the past and present. Shimon could not take his eyes off it, he had never seen a city like this, a city like an open wound, a city like an allegory of demise and resurrection. He felt a profound and totally unexpected affinity with this place.

The taxi came to a stop twenty minutes later. It had begun to rain again. Shimon stood with his suitcases in front of a tall apartment block from the late nineteenth century, with a broad entrance of solid wood. Set in the entrance was a door, beside it bells and nameplates.

He searched his feelings for the urge to flee. But he found nothing save for the fear that she might have stopped loving him, and the fear that his son might be disappointed in him. He went to the door, found "Kramer" and pushed the button.

"Shimon?" Lisa's voice.

"It's me," he said.

The door buzzed, Shimon pushed it open, it was astonishingly heavy.

He found himself in a wide hallway, stairs branched off to the left and right, straight ahead he saw another entrance with a double door, the door was open and he could see a courtyard, beyond that another building and more doors. The door behind him banged shut.

He was unsure what to do. Turning back, he heaved open the door to the street and looked for directions beside the bell. Through the intercom, Lisa's voice said, "Shimon, it's the left-hand stairs in the building at the front!"

He climbed the stairs. On the third floor a door stood ajar, bright light streamed from the apartment into the dimly lit stairwell.

As Shimon drew closer he heard footsteps, then the door was opened fully and there stood Lisa, holding hands with Tom in pyjamas.

Blinking blearily at his father, he said, "Hello, Papa."

Shimon put down his luggage and knelt beside his son.

"Hello Tom. I'm so glad to meet you at last," he said, giving his son as big a smile as he could.

Tom was embarrassed, he half turned and said, "Come on, Papa". He went past his mother to the other end of the hallway. Shimon picked up his cases and was about to follow Tom.

But Lisa stood in his way. They were face to face, eye to eye. Tom watched them.

Shimon saw Lisa's lips quivering faintly, he saw her nostrils flare imperceptibly, all of a sudden his heart began to beat faster, all the way up to his neck. He had never been so sober, so exposed when face to face with a woman. He could not move, more than anything he wanted to drop the suitcases and hug her, but he could not, one of the presents was fragile. He had to put his luggage down slowly, he had to take his time, he had to manage the transition, he had to stand up again, he had to take a step towards her.

He did it all very slowly, his temples throbbed, in his head there was a heat, as if he had blushed. He felt like a little boy standing before a tall woman.

When he was upright again Lisa suddenly embraced him, she was not slow or careful, Shimon forgot his fear, he pulled her towards him, all he could feel was her lips on his, all he could smell was her skin, all he could see was her beauty.

Then out of the corner of his eye he saw Tom, still watching them.

Tom had never seen his mother like this. So many feelings assailed him at once that no single thought could settle in his head. He could not know that this first image of his parents would stay with him his whole life.

Shimon freed himself from Lisa, took hold of the small case, squatted down and said, "Look what I've brought you, Tom."

Lisa closed the front door behind him. Tom came closer, cautiously and full of curiosity.

Frau Kramer lay on her bed in the dark room, listening to every sound coming from the hallway. She had feigned tiredness to avoid disturbing the young ones with her presence, and she had intended to go to sleep when Shimon arrived. But without success.

ONE HUNDRED AND SEVENTY-FOUR

Berlin, 16th July, 1975

He's still here because of me. But I can sense that he doesn't feel comfortable. He makes no bones about the fact that he's a Jew. It's his form of ethnology. He says it to people casually and then watches them try not to react. He lives in a state of permanent provocation. The only breaks he has are when he's working in the consulate and when he's at home. He's even tried to provoke Grandma. He told her about Abba Kovner and said how he wishes he'd succeeded in poisoning Hamburg.

Grandma looked at him and said, Then the Legend of the Well Poisoner would finally have come true. He didn't know what to say to that. I think he respects her now. But he can't find peace. He doesn't take any drugs, he's not smoking or drinking, and he's trying his best to be a good father. I can't expect any more from him for the time being. If only he'd stop believing he'd already achieved his goal. I love him so much, I just wish desperately that he could manage to be himself.

He says he hates the Germans' do-goodiness, all of them spend their whole time trying to show that they're doing the right thing, he calls it please-and-thank-you. The Germans have a please-and-thank-you morality, a please-and-thank-you culture, a please-and-thank-you consciousness. Please-and-thank-you sex. He's so radical! I understand what he means, but I wish he could stop generalising all the time. Doesn't he see that this is exactly what the Nazis thrived on? In spite of this he's been meeting up with a few musicians, three goyim and a Jew. They want to start a band. This might be a way forward.

Tom has changed quite a bit in the last few months. He's become truculent, he tries to defy me whenever he can. He listens to every word his father says. For his seventh birthday Shimon gave him a remote-control seaplane. Those things are expensive; I wish he'd used the money more sensibly. They're like little boys, the two of them. They went to Wannsee with Tom's friends and spent the whole day playing with the plane. When they got home Tom was happier than I'd ever seen him. I just hope Shimon realises how much responsibility he has.

What about me? How am I? Am I happier now? Yes and no. Yes, I'm happier with him, he's the man I want to spend my life with. I've managed to swap my office job for a part-time post at the university. It doesn't make a huge difference financially and it's getting me closer to studying.

But still my mind is churning with thoughts of Karl Bergmann and Codajás. I went to the Portuguese studies department at the university. I was lucky as they specialise in Brazil. One of the professors was just holding his office hour, so I paid him a visit. He said it sounded like a place name. He advised me to consult an atlas. I found Codajás on the Solimões River, in the middle of the Amazon. And I'm still asking myself if I really want to do this. I'd have to leave Tom with Grandma and Shimon, and fly to São Paulo, from there to Manaus, and then go 300 km. by boat upstream to Codajás. Shimon knows nothing about Karl Bergmann, I ought to tell him soon so he can get used to the idea. I should start saving for the trip, but what have I got to save? I'd have to work even longer hours and study less. If I managed to get myself there I'd have to reckon with the possibility of contracting malaria, dengue or some other tropical disease. I'd have to survive the hot climate for weeks. And all this to find a man who might know something that could ease my inner turmoil.

Poor Tom. What a pair of parents! One searching, one fleeing. It's a miracle we've been able to live together for eight months. Thank God he's still got his great-grandmother. She's a support for us all, even for Shimon, though he might not admit it. Since Maria's death she's seemed more and more like a seer. At times I wonder whether she's even interested in the difference between life and death . She'd like to be around for us as long as she can. I worry about a time when she won't be here anymore.

ONE HUNDRED AND SEVENTY-FIVE

The call came on 14 June, 1977, one month before Tom's ninth birthday. They were at home. Lisa, Shimon, Frau Kramer, Tom, having supper. Tom ran to the telephone because he thought it might be one of his friends. He said a few words then called for his mother. Esther Schwimmer was on the line. Lisa spoke to her for a while, then came back into the living room and sat on her chair.

"What's up? You look like you've just seen a ghost!" Shimon said.

Lisa stared at him. "Josef Ranzner's living in Munich."

ONE HUNDRED AND SEVENTY-SIX

"Absolutely no way!"

"Why not? I don't understand, please explain."

"She's over it. She doesn't have to see that arsehole again."

"But you're doing to her exactly what she did to you back then."

"That's different."

"No, Shimon, it's exactly the same."

Shimon knew that she was right, but he was unable to admit it.

"It's not about your mother, is it?" Lisa said. "It's about you."

Shimon sensed that she had spoken the truth. He said nothing. The two of them were sitting alone in the kitchen, Tom and Frau Kramer were already asleep, it was late, the sky was still dimly lit by the sun, which had dragged its ancient day across the surface of the earth and was now making a morning, a noon and an evening elsewhere. The longest day of the year was a mayfly like all the others, and now it was coming to an end. The air was balmy, the kitchen window wide open, people were barbecuing in the allotments opposite, they could smell it, they could hear a guitar and someone singing softly, people were out in the streets, their voices drifted upwards. Lisa drank red wine, Shimon water.

In spite of their tiredness they had stayed up to make time for each other, and to come to a decision at last.

"I *have* to go to Munich," Lisa said. "I must try to find something out, Shimon, I must."

Simon looked at her and nodded slowly. She had to. Everything in her face, her demeanour showed him that this was the case.

"Alright. I'll stay here with Tom," he said.

"You don't have to do that; you could come too. Tom's in good hands with his great grandma."

"I know. But I need time, I'm not as quick as you."

She looked at him, she thought, I need *you*, but she did not say it, she would have to get through this without him.

ONE HUNDRED AND SEVENTY-SEVEN

This time it was Esther rather than David Schwimmer at the station. She was manifestly older, but this had only enhanced her beauty. They hugged, then Esther took Lisa to her parents. There was a summer warmth in the city, In Berlin the lime trees are still in blossom, Lisa said. They spoke little, Esther drove the car, a pale-green Renault 4, carefully through the streets, I haven't had my licence for long, she said.

They arrived in Lehel. Esther drove past her parents' house. She stopped two doors further down and pointed to a house, a row of windows, and said, That's where he lived. His son was in Ben's class. Lisa nodded, Aha. Esther turned the car round, parked, switched off the engine, she looked at Lisa. Lisa took a deep breath.

"What's Gudrun like?" she said.

Esther shrugged. "Perfectly nice. Ben's head over heels in love."

"What about the thing with her father?"

Esther rocked her head from side to side. "Well, I don't think it's easy. But she's a tough one. She's been through quite a lot."

"What?"

"I only know this from Ben. Apparently she got into drugs when she was young. Lived on the streets for a while, things like that." She looked at Lisa. "But you know all that."

Lisa nodded, she did know, but in spite of this, and perhaps because of it, she was amazed.

They took her suitcase from the back seat and crossed the road, Esther opened the door, she said, "Even if the occasion's not a particularly nice one, I'm delighted to see you."

They went up to where David and Judith were waiting. David was virtually unchanged, Judith had some strands of grey. Ben and Gudrun were sitting in the dining room, they stood up when Lisa came in, instinctively Lisa looked for similarities between Shimon and Gudrun. But Gudrun was quite different, an open book, you could read her every emotion, now she was nervous and anxious and gutsy and she offered Lisa her hand.

"Hello, I'm Gudrun."

Lisa took her hand. Shimon's half sister. Perhaps. Lisa greeted Ben, who had been watching her closely and now looked satisfied. For dinner there was cholent again, as it was almost exactly ten years to the day since Lisa had spent the night with them for the first time, You've got the same room, Judith said. Ben celebrated the coincidence, Esther denied it, the siblings argued half in jest, half out of habit. Gudrun said little, Lisa watched her secretly, but Gudrun sensed it and cast her timid looks, to Lisa she came across as a person without a skin, each touch seemed to terrify her, but she was strong too, and there was something symbiotic between Ben and her, they seemed to understand each other blindly, So different from Shimon and me, Lisa thought, unable to pin a clear feeling to this thought.

David Schwimmer was unusually quiet. Later, when everyone had gone to bed and Esther was sitting in Lisa's room, looking at photos of Shimon, Tom and Frau Kramer, she explained why.

"He's troubled because Gudrun can't give birth to Jews."

Lisa was surprised, she had not imagined Esther's father to be like this, but Esther just shrugged and said, "He's a Zionist, even though he prefers living in Germany. And that means the children of every Jewish man who takes a non-Jewish wife are lost."

"Lost?"

"Well, lost to the Jewish people, lost to Israel. The two of us are off the hook." She grinned. "But Ben should have found himself a Jewish girl."

"Did he talk to Ben about it?"

"Of course, but you know my brother. He said, I know all that, Dad, I mean I'm a Jew, aren't I? And that was that."

Lisa could not suppress a laugh. "And the fact that Gudrun's the daughter of a mass murderer, who got Israel" – she searched for words – "into this population shortage in the first place, don't you think that's got something to do with it?"

Assuming an expression of naivety, Esther said, "Who knows?"

On Saturday morning the atmosphere was different. David and Judith had got up early, David had left the house, Judith was busy cleaning and doing the washing, making only the occasional appearance in the dining room, where her children were having breakfast with their guests.

They spent a while chatting about nothing in particular, and then Gudrun abruptly said, "I was at my brother's place a couple of days ago. He lives very close to our father, in Neuperlach." She paused, as if concentrating on an inner voice.

"Heinrich wouldn't give me the address. Somehow he found out that Ben's Jewish. And now he's worried that he wants to take our father to court."

"Is that what you want?" Lisa asked Ben.

"It's what *I* want," Esther said. "But only after you've spoken to him."

"I lied to him," Gudrun said. "He didn't believe me." She raised her shoulders and let them fall again.

"We need to go and see him first."

"Isn't your father in the telephone book, under his false name?"

Gudrun shook her head. "Either he has no phone or he's gone ex-directory."

Three of them set off.

ONE HUNDRED AND SEVENTY-EIGHT

Neuperlach was still under construction. Ben did not know the area. He was at the wheel of Esther's Renault 4, beside him sat Gudrun, with Lisa in the back. When Ben saw the densely planted, box-like tower blocks and the wide streets that cut through them like swathes, he shuddered.

"Ghastly!" he said. Lisa did not comment, she was reminded of Gropiusstadt in the south of Neukölln, the same tower blocks, the same concrete, the same cranes towering all over the place, the same combination of construction sites and buildings that were already inhabited.

"Is this where your brother lives?" Ben said in disbelief.

"Yup – it's cheap," Gudrun said, looking out of the window. She did not say what was going through her mind, If he wants to punish himself, then let him. If he thinks that things can be cleansed through ugliness, then he has to live in an ugly place.

They found the street, the house number and parked the car. They approached a building with at least fifteen floors, Gudrun said, He lives on the ninth. A hundred bells in rank and file, Gudrun found Scholz, she rang. There was a buzzing, Gudrun said, He knows we're coming, I phoned him. Four lifts, one waiting on the ground floor, ninth floor, Lisa felt the acceleration. Then they were upstairs, two corridors, from each of which another two corridors branched off, Gudrun knew the way.

Finally they stood outside a white door with a spyhole about two-thirds up. Gudrun rang again.

When Heinrich Scholz saw his former classmate and housemate, he was unsure how to react. He looked as if he wanted simply to close the door again. But this was not an option.

With a winning smile, Ben said, "My God, Heinrich, why didn't you stay in our apartment, it was much nicer!"

Heinrich smiled bitterly, he did not know how to respond, he had always avoided long conversations with Ben, who was far too quick, far too verbose. Far too ironic. He and Gudrun were well suited to each other.

Lena appeared carrying little Michael, Gudrun took her nephew from her and gave him a kiss, Heinrich watched this scene and now stood uncertainly in the hall.

"This is Lisa Kramer, by the way," Ben said. "I presume Gudrun's told you about her?"

Heinrich nodded stiffly, Lisa found no opportunity to shake his hand. Eventually he brought himself to invite them into the sitting room. Lena offered them tea or coffee, Ben wanted coffee, Gudrun tea, Lisa nothing, Lena disappeared into the kitchen.

The Scholz family had a brown-leather sofa suite, two pieces, one long and one short, set at a right angle to each other around a brass and glass coffee table, as well as a matching armchair on the other side. A large television set faced them, its back to the window. On the wall was a copy of an Arcimboldo painting.

Heinrich sat on the sofa with his legs apart, his elbows resting on his thighs, his fingertips touching, looking tense and expectant, his head bowed, his eyes fixed on the glass top of the coffee table or the flokati rug beneath it.

Gudrun sat beside him with Michael, the small boy watched Ben and Lisa.

Ben cleared his throat, it was his job to break the ice. He grinned at Heinrich and said, "Do you remember when we used to play football in the Englischer Garten?"

Heinrich looked up without lifting his head, he said, "Yes, I do."

"Do you fancy joining us some time? We still play on Wednesday evenings."

Heinrich shook his head. "Too far."

"But surely you've got a car. You could park at our place and we could cycle there together."

Heinrich shook his head, he said, "No, Ben, I haven't been in that street since my eighteenth birthday. And you know why."

Ben nodded, "Yes, yes, I know, your father was an Obersturmbann-führer and murdered people."

"Jews," Heinrich said, casting him a furtive glance.

Ben nodded. "I know, Jews, like me. But that's not why we're here today, Heinrich. Lisa's come from Berlin because she's hoping your father might be able to help her trace her parents."

"Jews?" He gave Lisa a searching look.

Lisa nodded, she said, "They were Polish Jews. My mother was called Margarita and my father Tomasz Ejzenstain. My mother shot . . ."

". . . Sturmbannführer Karl Treitz, I know."

"But there was a Pole who lured the Sturmbannführer to her. His name was Piotr and that's all I know, unfortunately."

Heinrich stared at the flokati through the glass, That rug needs cleaning, he thought, he looked up at Lisa, whose eyes were still fixed on him.

"Maybe your father could help me, maybe he knew him," she said.

Heinrich nodded. Gudrun was now looking at him, little Michael was having fun with Ben, who was pulling faces and grinning at him.

"What will you do if you get the information you need?"

"I'll try to find Piotr."

"What about him?" Heinrich said, gesturing towards Ben with his head.

Interrupting his game, Ben said, "If you want, Heinrich, I won't do anything."

"You say that."

"If you don't believe me obviously I *can't* do anything."

Heinrich thought carefully, he did not want to insult Ben openly. "It's not that I don't believe you, but you're not on your own."

"There's me too, Heinrich," Gudrun said all of a sudden. "I swear to you that I'll see our father taken to court, whether it means having to go to the police or Simon Wiesenthal. Either you help this woman now, so she finds out something about her parents before any investigation, or you don't." She put Michael on his lap.

"Have a good think about how you want your son to see you when he's grown up. One thing's for sure: I'll tell him. I'll say, Your father was too cowardly, he was more concerned to see your butcher of a grandfather get off than to help an orphan find out a little more about her murdered parents. Think about it, Heinrich, you know I'm talking sense."

She paused and stared at him. At no point had she become angry or upset. Now she was sitting beside her brother, as if she had just said how sweet his son was. Lisa was surprised, she would never have thought that this shy woman could deploy such strength. She looked at Ben, but he did not notice her, his eyes were fixed on Gudrun.

Heinrich sat in silence, holding Michael. Lena came with tea and coffee on a tray. Like a waitress she set the drinks down in front of their visitors, then straightened up. Michael stretched his arms towards her, she went around the table and lifted him from her husband's lap.

"Give them the address, Heinrich!" she said. It sounded as if she finally wanted to be rid of the subject, or the people, or the feelings hanging in the room, or of everything at once. Heinrich did not move or meet anyone's eye as he told them the address.

"Thank you," Lisa said, but she was looking at Gudrun.

ONE HUNDRED AND SEVENTY-NINE

"Hello?"

Lisa recognised Anna's voice.

"Good morning Anna, I hope I'm not calling too early."

"Lisa! What a lovely surprise! No, it's an hour later here. Are you alright? Is everything O.K.?"

"Yes, don't worry, Shimon and I are fine, we're as happy as we could be."

"That's a relief. I thought . . ."

"No, no. He's trying very hard. He and Tom are getting on fantastically. I'm calling because of something else. I don't know quite how to tell you." She broke off and looked at Esther, who was sitting opposite her at the dining table, watching anxiously.

"Anna," Lisa said slowly, "we've found someone you . . . you thought was dead. We . . . it's . . ." She heard a terrified sound on the other end of the line. She paused, at a loss as to what to say next. What am I doing? she thought, and felt a sudden pain in her chest. "Anna, I'm really sorry, I ought to have kept my mouth shut, I'm so stupid, I . . ."

Lisa could hear her crying. After a while Anna said softly, "Please forgive me, Lisa, I just needed to digest that."

"Of course, but . . ." Lisa stopped, sensing that every word she uttered was digging into a wound. "There's something else." Anna was silent. Taking a deep breath, Lisa said. "We went to see him, rang at his door, but he didn't open. I think he's scared. Esther, a friend of mine here in Munich, suggested we lie in wait and then overpower him. Maybe it's no less than he deserves. But I don't want to go that far, I don't want to use violence. It would make me feel like . . . like a Nazi.

That's why I thought . . ." Lisa broke off. She did not dare articulate her request. She could hear Anna's breathing and suspected that she had read her thoughts. Esther raised her eyebrows. Lisa shrugged. She was waiting.

"O.K." Anna said, pausing as if to be sure of her decision. "I'll come to Munich."

ONE HUNDRED AND EIGHTY

Anna sat by the telephone, staring into space. Not a single thought passed through her head. She saw. Josef Ranzner's face above her. She lay. Naked on her back, her legs apart. Josef Ranzner's sweat, dripping from his face onto hers, Josef Ranzner's gaze, exploring her body, Josef Ranzner's hands, holding her arms, Josef Ranzner's stomach, lying on her stomach, Josef Ranzner's sex, thrusting into her sex, Josef Ranzner's rhythm, fast and clipped like a barrage, as if trying to penetrate right through her and out the other side, Josef Ranzner's jaw muscles, grinding and grinding, as his eyes observe every movement of her face, because every movement heightens Josef Ranzner's excitement. Josef Ranzner's orgasm. Josef Ranzner's exhaustion. Josef Ranzner's withdrawal, his cold shoulder. No relief, only sorrow because Josef Ranzner has simply abandoned her like that, the rape reaches its climax after the climax, when Josef Ranzner leaves without a goodbye, when the door closes and Josef Ranzner turns his attention to more important things, while she lies there, a woman torn open, worthless, abused, discarded, used again and again and again and again by the lower ranks like a poor family's only handkerchief, everyone has blown their nose now, at last we can chuck it away, nobody can use it anymore, not even us.

Anna got up. She shook off the images. She thought of Abba. Abba the avenger, Abba the wise one, Abba the hero, Abba the criminal, Abba the poet. Abba had everything. All she had was forgetting and remembering, lies and the truth.

Now she was in a hurry. She wrote her daughter a letter and left it on the kitchen table. She packed a small case, she called a taxi. She sat in the kitchen with her case and waited. When the bell rang she took her suitcase and left the apartment.

She went straight to the airport. She bought a Lufthansa ticket. She had a coffee, she ate something.

She had to wait three hours, but the time passed without her noticing. She sat at the gate, watching the people come and go, she heard their voices, she felt the presence of even more people moving above and below her, she sensed the vibration of the huge building she was in. The space inside her merged with the space in which she sat. When her flight was called she boarded the plane. She sat at her place by the window. When the plane took off she felt its entire weight heaving itself into the air, climbing higher and higher until it left the land behind and Anna Stirnweiss flew across the sea to where she came from.

ONE HUNDRED AND EIGHTY-ONE

The doorbell rang. As ever he went in the dark to the spyhole. He expected to see the three women standing there again, one of whom was without a shadow of doubt the reincarnation of Emma. Once more he would enjoy observing them through the spyhole, but of course he would not open the door, the whole thing seemed too suspicious. Behind it all, ultimately, was that young man who had called out Father, the one with the Karl Treitz mask.

When he squinted into the corridor he saw a woman standing there looking at him, as if she could see through the spyhole directly into his eyes. He stepped back. But he had to peer through again, for this woman had unleashed something which could not be stopped.

Although he told himself, She can't see you, he was convinced the second time too, that she actually could. Her gaze bored so deeply into his soul, deeper than any other gaze had been able to, deeper even than he could see himself. Without his realising it, his lips formed a silent word.

Anna.

He took off the chain, he turned the knob of the security lock, the bolt slid out, he pressed down the handle and slowly opened the door.

The door opened slowly. Anna looked into Josef Ranzner's eyes. His face was mapped with lines. Gudrun, who stood to one side of the door, slapped her hand over her mouth when she saw the state her father was in. He was stooped and had become small and emaciated, Anna towered above him, almost a head taller. They stared into each other's eyes, Josef Ranzner stood there, looking expectant and trusting like a child. No fear, no guilt, no bad conscience, no defiance.

"Please come in, Anna," Ranzner said. His voice sounded thin and brittle. Turning sideways, awkwardly and with tiny steps, he opened the door wider and invited her in with a wave of his hand. Fear flashed inside Anna like a dazzling light that is immediately extinguished. What can he do to me? She nodded and went inside. Gudrun, Lisa and Esther followed, Ranzner ignored them.

The apartment was clean and tidy, furnished simply but neatly. On the table in the sitting room was a pair of binoculars, there was a gap between the curtains, beyond that a patch of wasteland and more tower blocks.

"Sit down, Anna," Ranzner said. He pointed to a small, blue corduroy chair without armrests. Anna sat. Ranzner remained on his feet, he gazed at her, his face was peaceful. "Everything will be fine," he said. "Would you like something to drink?" Anna nodded, Ranzner walked past the other women to the kitchen and returned with a glass of orange juice, he put it down in front of Anna and sat on a chair opposite. The table stood between them, Ranzner was sitting higher up than she was. When it dawned on Anna that all those years ago she had sat before him exactly like this, an icy shudder ran down her spine.

"What's wrong? Don't you want to drink anything?" Anna picked up the glass and pretended to take a sip.

Ranzner smiled at her and said, "So, where have you been?"

"Cleaning up the blood stains," Anna said. Ranzner did not understand. "From Sturmbannführer Treitz." Now Ranzner understood. He nodded his approval.

"Poor Treitz. I never found him."

Anna understood what he meant. "We must look for Piotr," she said. "Piotr?"

"The Pole who lured the Sturmbannführer into the trap."

"Oh, him, yes, yes, we have to look for him. But why, Anna?"

"He knows where the Sturmbannführer is."

"How would he know that? He's only a Pole. Poles don't know anything, they're stupid."

"Yes, they're stupid, I know."

"Are you only saying that to please me, Anna?"

"No, I know they're stupid."

"How?"

"Piotr told me where the Sturmbannführer is."

"That can't be right or you'd know where he is."

"I've forgotten."

"You're the stupid one, then."

"Yes."

"You're trying to deceive me, aren't you, Anna? I can see right through you, you can't fool me."

"No."

"No, Obersturmbannführer."

"No, Obersturmbannführer."

"That's better, Anna." He smiled at her. "Drink," he said. Anna took hesitant sips from the glass. She had no idea where this was going, she felt that at any moment she might leap up and run away. She collected herself.

"Maybe you've just forgotten Piotr's surname, that's why you don't want to look for him."

Ranzner raised his eyebrows and smiled again. "Of course I've forgotten. After all, he was just a Polack, a Kaminski." He was still smiling.

Anna stared at him. She said, "I've got to go now, Herr Ranzner." She stood up. Ranzner got out of his chair, he came to her.

"What a shame," he said. "Maybe you'll come back soon and we can talk more. It was wonderful to see you."

He offered her his hand, which was so soft and wrinkled, his handshake weak. Anna made for the door, Ranzner followed, they walked past the three women standing there like a silent Greek chorus, who had witnessed everything and were now following Ranzner to the door, Gudrun in tears, Lisa in shock, Esther shaking her head. Ranzner seemed not to notice they were there.

When the women were out in the corridor, Anna turned and said, "Do you remember raping me in Konin, Herr Ranzner?"

Ranzner nodded and said with a smile, "Oh yes, that was our favourite game, wasn't it, Anna, it was always very nice. These days I can't do it properly anymore. I can only look through the field glasses." For a brief moment he seemed slightly melancholic, but then he pulled himself together and said, "If you see our children will you send them my regards?"

Gudrun could not control herself any longer. She said, "*I'm* your daughter, Father!" Ranzner glanced in her direction, as if he had heard a noise, then his gaze returned to Anna.

"I'll be waiting for you every day," he said. "See you soon, Anna." He closed the door, leaving the four women in the corridor.

ONE HUNDRED AND EIGHTY-TWO

Five days later Josef Ranzner died in his bed. No-one was present. The body was only discovered when the police forced their way into his apartment to arrest him after Simon Wiesenthal had contacted them to press charges. It looked as if he had passed away peacefully.

ONE HUNDRED AND EIGHTY-THREE

Two days before her grandson's ninth birthday, Anna Stirnweiss went back to Berlin.

ONE HNDRED AND EIGHTY-FOUR

Set in a lawn at Hüttenweg 46 in Berlin-Dahlem, and surrounded by fir trees and beeches, stood a U.S. army church-cum-synagogue, a white building that could have been mistaken for a gymnasium had it not been for the tall, slim bell tower.

On 2 September, 1977, an unseasonably warm Friday morning, Lisa Kramer married Shimon Sarfati. To begin with they had been unable to agree on a joint surname. Lisa wanted to be called Sarfati. Shimon wanted finally to be rid of Peretz's name, but he recoiled from the German "Kramer". Just before their civil marriage at the town hall in

Neukölln they decided that the father should have the same name as his son.

From Neukölln the wedding party – Anna Stirnweiss, Marta Kramer, Peretz Sarfati, Lana Sarfati, Tobias Weiss and his companion, Mosche and Selma Teichmann, the entire Schwimmer family with Gudrun Kruse, the four musicians from Shimon's band with their instruments, some of his friends and acquaintances from the Israeli consulate-general in West Berlin, some of Lisa's student friends from the history seminar at Berlin's Free University, Tom's best friends and their parents and the newly established Kramer family – went to Dahlem for a Jewish wedding ceremony in the church-cum-synagogue at Hüttenweg 46.

Lisa was not wearing a remodelled curtain, she did not sit outside surrounded by rubble, it was not cold and wet, no military vehicles patrolled the streets, no refugees were in sight waiting for something to happen with their salvaged lives. And yet, as the rabbi spoke his text in Hebrew and German, Anna could not help looking over at Peretz, their eyes met, silently she asked for forgiveness and then reached for Lana's hand, who was sitting beside her mother, and told herself it was for the sake of love, which had been triumphant after all.

From Dahlem they went to Schlachtensee, this had been Lisa's idea, to swim and have some fun after all the formalities.

ONE HUNDRED AND EIGHTY-FIVE

While they were still at the lake, sitting on blankets under shade-giving trees and eating the picnic they had brought with them, a discussion began as to whether Josef Ranzner had said "Kaminski" in the same way he would say "Polack", or whether it might indeed be Piotr's surname. Maybe the answer was both.

The only person who was convinced that she had something to work with at last was Lisa. Of course you've got to believe it, Esther said, after all, it's what you've been wanting to find. Anna said nothing, she had her doubts. The thought of Josef Ranzner made her shudder. She could not rid herself of the idea that by appearing at his apartment she had fulfilled his greatest desire.

Gudrun was watching Tom play with his friends in the water. Into the middle of the conversation between Esther and Lisa, and without taking her eyes off the boys, she said, Anything's possible . . .

Lisa nodded, if anything was possible she had to try it. Shimon had not heard any of the conversation, he had swum out into the lake with his musicians, Lisa saw them far in the distance, tiny black dots in the middle of the glittering blue lake. She decided to do some investigating before broaching it with him. She glanced at her grandmother. The old woman was sitting on a folding chair beside Anna, smiling at her grand-daughter, not giving away what she was thinking, My child you have everything now, what else do you want?

ONE HUNDRED AND EIGHTY-SIX

"There's a chance, Shimon. Why shouldn't I seize it? Why shouldn't I go on looking?"

"What do you want to find? An old man at most, or a grave. Kaminski! There are millions of Kaminskis!"

Lisa did not respond straightaway. In the dim light of the bedroom she could barely make out her husband. Sinking back into her pillow she stared at the ceiling.

"What have you got against it, Shimon? Tell me the truth!"

After a while, Shimon said, "You're starting to come across as addicted as I was. You might not be taking drugs, but you just can't stop. I *did* stop, I did it for us. But you . . ." He broke off.

Lisa was shocked. It was some time before she was able to assemble a clear thought. Then she said, deliberately, "That's not fair, Shimon. I'm not abandoning anybody. I'm not unpredictable. And I don't love you any less just because I'm on the hunt for this man." She turned to him, propping herself on her elbows, and tried to look him in the eye.

"In any case, you didn't do it for us," she said, "you did it for yourself. There isn't a pact between us, Shimon. Isn't it enough that we love each other?"

Shimon said nothing, he had closed his eyes. Lisa gave up. She turned onto her other side, she wanted to sleep.

As she was drifting off she felt Shimon press up close and put his arm around her. Bringing his lips to her ear, he whispered, "I'm sorry. Can I help with your search?"

GLOSSARY OF HISTORICAL CHARACTERS

AVIGUR, SHAUL, né Saul Mayeroff, later Saul Meirov (b. 1899, Dvinsk, now Latvia; d. 1978, Israel), was a Jewish secret intelligence agent and politician. In 1939 he became commander of the Mossad LeAliya Bet's operations (Institution for Immigration B, "B" standing for "illegal"), organising from Tel Aviv and Paris the flight of European Jews to Palestine.

BEN-GURION, DAVID, né David Grün (b. 16 October, 1886, Płonsk, Congress Poland; d. 1 December, 1973, Tel HaShomer, Israel), was one of the founders of the Social Democratic Party of Israel, party chairman from 1948 to 1963, and the country's first prime minister.

BEN-NATAN, ASHER, né Artur Piernikarz (b. 15 February, 1921, Vienna; d. 17 June, 2014, Israel) was the first Israeli ambassador to West Germany. As a Jew he was forced to flee Vienna in 1938, but he returned to Austria immediately after the war. As leader of Bricha in Austria he facilitated the emigration of large numbers of Jews.

BEVIN, ERNEST (b. 9 March, 1881, Winsford, Somerset; d. 14 April, 1951, London) was a British trade union leader, Labour Party politician and secretary of state for foreign affairs from 1945 to 1951.

BIDAULT, GEORGES-AUGUSTIN (b. 5 October, 1899, Moulins, Auvergne; d. 27 January, 1983, Cambo-les-Bains) was a French politician. In the Second World War he was an active member of the Résistance. After the war he served as foreign minister in Félix Gouin's provisional government until the Constituent National Assembly elected him president of the provisional government on 19 June 1946. He again took over the foreign ministry.

BORSODY, EDUARD VON (b. 13 June, 1898, Vienna; 1 January, 1970, Vienna) was an Austrian cameraman, editor, film director and screenplay writer of Hungarian origin.

CHECKER, CHUBBY, né Ernest Evans (b. 3 October, 1941, Spring Valley, South Carolina) is an American rock and roll singer.

DANTZIGER, SAMUEL, 37 years old, survivor of Auschwitz concentration camp, was shot dead on 29 March, 1946 by a German policeman in a displaced persons camp in Stuttgart during a raid, after he had identified the man as a former Auschwitz guard. As a result of this incident the American Military Government forbade German authorities from entering Jewish D.P. camps.

DEKEL, EPHRAIM, né Ephraim Kresner (b. 1903, Litin, Ukraine; d. 22 August, 1982) came to Israel in 1921. In 1923 he joined the military secret intelligence service of the Jewish underground army, Haganah, in Tel Aviv, later becoming its head. From 1928 to 1948 Dekel was also head of the fire service in the British Mandate of Palestine, which in reality was a front for Haganah. In 1946 he became the European commander of Bricha, based in Prague.

ELEAZAR BEN JUDA BEN KALONYMOS, known as Eleazar of Worms (b. ca. 1176, probably Mainz; d. 1238, Worms) was a German rabbi, author and cabbalist. One of his books was *Ha-Rokeah* (*The Perfumer*), a work on ethics and Jewish law. On the night of 22 Kislev 1196 he was busy writing a commentary on Genesis when two crusaders forced their way into his house and killed his wife, Dulcina, his two daughters, Belat and Hannah, and his son, Jacob. His wife ran a shop selling parchment rolls to support the family, allowing him to dedicate himself to his studies. A large proportion of his liturgical writing is a protest against Israel's suffering and expresses hope for redemption and revenge against the tormentors.

FRANK, ERICH, later Ephraim, code names Ernst Caro and Aroch (b. 4 March, 1909, Gelsenkirchen, son of Emma and Herman Frank; d. 17 March, 1996, Israel). Until the Wannsee Conference in 1942, Frank organised the emigration of German Jews in personal negotiations with Adolf Eichmann. He escaped in the last ship down the Danube, making it to Palestine via the Black Sea and Mediterranean. After the war he returned to Europe at the request of David Ben-Gurion, to take command in Munich of German Bricha, the organisation that arranged the transit of surviving European Jews to Palestine.

GEHLEN, REINHARD (b. 3 April, 1902, Erfurt; d. 8 June, 1979, Berg am Starnberger See) was a major general in the Wehrmacht, head of the Foreign Armies East (F.H.O.) department of the German general staff, head of the Gehlen Organistion and first president of the Federal Intelligence Service (B.N.D.).

HAARER, JOHANNA, née Barsch (b. 3 October, 1900, Tetschen, now Czech Republic; d. 30 April, 1988, Munich) was an Austrian-German doctor and author of best-selling educational guides (before and after 1945), which were strongly in accordance with National Socialist ideology.

HARRISON, EARL GRANT (b. 27 April, 1899; d. 28 July, 1955) was an American lawyer, academic and civil servant. In summer 1945 he was sent by U.S. President Harry S. Truman to visit a large number of the displaced persons camps in the American zone of occupation, and compiled the so-called Harrison Report about the unacceptable conditions he witnessed there, thus alerting the U.S. government to the particularly difficult situation of the displaced Jews. This led to the Americans, as the only one of the four occupying powers, setting up D.P. camps that were exclusively for Jews and also run by them.

HÖNOW, GÜNTER, (b. 21 October, 1923, Stahnsdorf near Berlin; d. 25 January, 2001, Berlin-Zehlendorf) was a German architect of the post-war modernist school.

JAKUBOWITZ, ZWI (b. ?; d. 18 July, 1947) was a fifteen-year-old refugee on the *President Warfield* (Exodus) who was shot dead when the Royal Navy boarded the ship. Three other people died during the hours-long battle to take the ship: a British soldier, boatswain William Bernstein and Mordechai Boimsteing, a passenger. More than one hundred people were seriously injured.

KLEPPER, JOCHEN (b. 22 March, 1903, Beuthen an der Oder, now Poland; d. 11 December, 1942, Berlin) was one of the twentieth century's most important composers of liturgical songs. On 28 March, 1931 he married Johanna Stein, the Jewish widow of a lawyer and thirteen years his senior. She had two daughters, Brigitte and Renate. As Johanna and her daughters were Jewish the family came under increasing pressure after Hitler's takeover of power. On 18 December, 1938 Johanna Klepper was baptised in the Martin Luther Memorial Chuch in Berlin-Mariendorf. Afterwards the couple were given a Christian blessing. Klepper's elder stepdaughter, Brigitte, managed to emigrate to Britain via Sweden shortly before the war broke out. At the end of 1942 the younger daughter's attempt to leave Germany for sanctuary abroad failed and she was on the verge of being deported. From a personal communication he received from Reich Minister of the Interior Wilhelm Frick, Klepper also realised that mixed marriages would be compulsorily dissolved and that his wife was under threat of deportation too. In the night of 10–11 December, 1942 the family committed suicide with sleeping tablets and gas.

KÖPCKE, KARL-HEINZ (b. 29 September, 1922, Hamburg; d. 27 September, 1991, Hamburg) was a German newsreader.

KOVNER, ABBA, (b. 14 March, 1918, Sevastopol; d. 25 September, 1987, kibbutz Ein HaHoresh, Israel) was an Israeli writer, resistance fighter and partisan leader.

LEIBOWITZ, JOSEF (b. ?, Lithuania; d. ?). Holocaust survivor. Ephraim Frank's right-hand man in the Munich years.

LEIBOWITZ, YESHAYAHU (b. 29 January, 1903, Riga; d. 18 August, 1994, Jerusalem) was an Israeli scientist and philosopher of religion.

LEVI, PRIMO (b. 31 July, 1919, Turin; d. 11 April, 1987, Turin) was a Jewish Italian writer and chemist. He is best known for his work as a witness and survivor of the Holocaust. In his autobiographical report *If This is a Man*, he recorded his experiences at Auschwitz.

MCNARNEY, JOSEPH TAGGART (b. 28 August, 1893, Emporium, Pennsylvania; d. 1 February, 1972, La Jolla, California) was a high-ranking U.S. Air Force officer. Between November 1945 and January 1947 he was commanding general of U.S. forces in Europe and military governor of the American occupation zone in Germany.

MÜHSAM, ERICH KURT (b. 6 April, 1878, Berlin; d. 10 July, 1934, Oranienburg concentration camp) was a German anarchist writer, publicist and antimilitarist. As a political activist he played a key role in establishing the short-lived Bavarian Soviet Republic, for which he was sentenced to fifteen years' imprisonment, although under an amnesty he was freed after five. In the Weimar Republic, as a member of the Red Aid, he fought for the release of political prisoners. On the night of the Reichstag Fire he was arrested by the Nazis and murdered by S.S. guards in Oranienburg concentration camp on 10 July, 1934.

NEHLHANS, ERICH (b. 12 February, 1899, Berlin; d. 15 February, 1950, Soviet Union) was, alongside Hans Münzner, Leo Hirsch, Leo Löwenstein, Fritz Katten and Hans Erich Fabain, a founder member the Jewish Community in Berlin, of which he was also chairman for a time.

PRIMANN, MORDECHAI, né Friedman (b. 2 May, 1932, Jerusalem) was, from the 1950s, a broadcaster on the radio station "Kol Israel" (The Voice of Israel). He became very popular on account of his charming voice. Later he taught at Lifshitz College in Jerusalem. He has two daughters, one son, sixteen grandchildren and five great-grandchildren.

RIESENBURGER, MARTIN (b. 14 May, 1896, Berlin; d. 14 April, 1965, Berlin) was a German rabbi.

RUDOLPH, WILMA (b. 23 June, 1940, Saint Bethlehem, Tennessee; d. 12 November, 1994, Brentwood, Tennessee) was a U.S. athlete and Olympic champion. Her achievements earned her the nickname "The Black Gazelle".

TRUMAN, HARRY S. (b. 8 May, 1884, Lamar, Missouri; d. 26 December, 1972, Kansas City, Missouri) was an American Democratic Party politician and, from 1945 to 1953, the thirty-third president of the United States.

WESSEL, GERHARD (b. 24 December, 1913, Neumünster; d. 28 July, 2002, Pullach) was, from 1 May, 1968, to 31 December, 1978, president of the Federal Intelligence Service and a former lieutenant general.

ZAMARET, SHMARIA (b. 17 October, 1910, Babruysk, Russian Empire, now Belarus; d. 26 August, 1964, kibbutz Beit HaShita, Israel) had the codename Rudi Siegelbaum. From the start of the Second World War, he worked for the Mossad LeAliya Bet in France, Greece, Switzerland, Belgium and other countries, later becoming Ephraim Frank's contact in France.

ZEVE, SALLY (b. 1910, Kaunas, now Lithuania; d. ?) Holocaust survivor. Between December 1945 and his sentencing by an American military court in July 1948, he was the joint owner of the Bavarian Truck Company in Munich, Barer Strasse 27 (the barracks at the Alte Pinakothek). According to Shlomo Kless, who himself worked for Bricha as an envoy from Palestine, the real purpose of the Bavarian Truck Company was to organise lorries for secretly transporting Jews out of Germany.

STEVEN UHLY is a writer and journalist born in 1964 in Cologne and is of German-Bengali descent, with roots also in Spanish culture. He has studied literature, served as the head of an institute in Brazil, and translated poetry and prose from Spanish, Portuguese, and English. He lives in Munich with his family. His book *Adams Fuge* was awarded the "Tukan Preis" of the city of Munich in 2011. His novel *Glückskind* (2012) was filmed as a prime-time production by director Michael Verhoeven for ARTE and the 1st German Channel ARD.

JAMIE BULLOCH is the translator of Timur Vermes' *Look Who's Back*, longlisted for the IMPAC award and the *Independent* Foreign Fiction Prize, Birgit Vanderbeke's *The Mussel Feast*, which won him the Schlegel-Tieck Prize and was runner-up in the IFFP, and novels by F. C. Delius, Jörg Fauser, Martin Suter, Katharina Hagena and Daniel Glattauer.